DELIVERANCE
OF
DRAGONS

DELIVERANCE OF DRAGONS

BOOK THREE

of The Dragon Prophecy

MERCEDES LACKEY
and JAMES MALLORY

 Tor Publishing Group   NEW YORK

DELIVERANCE OF DRAGONS

Copyright © 2025 by Mercedes Lackey and James Mallory

A Tor Book
Published by Tom Doherty Associates / Tor Publishing Group
120 Broadway
New York, NY 10271

www.torpublishinggroup.com

Tor® is a registered trademark of Macmillan Publishing Group, LLC.

The Library of Congress Cataloging-in-Publication Data is available upon request.

ISBN 978-1-250-39477-4 (trade paperback)
ISBN 978-1-250-37573-5 (hardcover)
ISBN 978-1-429-94978-1 (ebook)

Our books may be purchased in bulk for promotional, educational, or business use. Please contact your local bookseller or the Macmillan Corporate and Premium Sales Department at 1-800-221-7945, extension 5442, or by email at MacmillanSpecialMarkets@macmillan.com.

First Edition: 2025

Printed in the United States of America

0 9 8 7 6 5 4 3 2 1

To The Wyrd Sisters: Rosemary, Bonnie, and India Edghill
To my extremely patient agent, Russ Galen
To my coauthor, Mercedes Lackey
To Sanaa Ali-Virani, EDITOR
And most of all to Terry Ann:
She kept the dead from walking, and
without her this would have been
a very different book containing far more errors.
To her, my humble and heartfelt thanks.

—JAMES P. MALLORY

Elvenkind had given up their magic long ago, in the childhood of the world. They had done so in order to save the world, and the Light—but that was something that was not spoken of outside of the Sanctuary of the Star. Humans and other races were not to know of this . . . [Jermayan] was not certain that even a Dragon should be told.

Then again, he was not certain that a Dragon didn't already know.

MERCEDES LACKEY AND JAMES MALLORY,
THE OBSIDIAN MOUNTAIN TRILOGY

Contents

PROLOGUE: Darkness Visible   1

CHAPTER ONE: Sword Moon to Fire Moon in the Tenth Year of the High King's Reign: The Smoke of That Great Burning   9

CHAPTER TWO: Thunder Moon in the Tenth Year of the High King's Reign: Shadows Linger   25

CHAPTER THREE: Thunder Moon to Fire Moon in the Tenth Year of the High King's Reign: Everything That Rises Must Converge   35

CHAPTER FOUR: Thunder Moon to Fire Moon in the Tenth Year of the High King's Reign: A Valley of Dry Bones   54

CHAPTER FIVE: Thunder Moon to Harvest Moon in the Tenth Year of the High King's Reign: The Cold Equations   67

CHAPTER SIX: Harvest Moon in the Tenth Year of the High King's Reign: All Heads Turn When the Hunt Goes By   80

CHAPTER SEVEN: Harvest Moon in the Tenth Year of the High King's Reign: The Wind That Shakes the Stars   96

CHAPTER EIGHT: Harvest Moon to Rade Moon in the Tenth Year of the High King's Reign: We Were to Wed in Harvest Time   110

CHAPTER NINE: Harvest Moon in the Tenth Year of the High King's Reign: Where Late the Sweet Birds Sang   133

CHAPTER TEN: Harvest Moon in the Tenth Year of the High King's Reign: To Harvest Fire and Flame   145

CHAPTER ELEVEN: Harvest Moon in the Tenth Year of the High King's Reign: Shadowplay   162

CHAPTER TWELVE: Harvest Moon in the Tenth Year of the High King's Reign: The Road of Swords and Tears   180

CHAPTER THIRTEEN: Harvest Moon in the Tenth Year of the
    High King's Reign: Dark of the Moon   195
CHAPTER FOURTEEN: Harvest Moon in the Tenth Year of the
    High King's Reign: The Real and the True   215
CHAPTER FIFTEEN: Harvest Moon in the Tenth Year of the
    High King's Reign: Change Is Only the Beginning   231
CHAPTER SIXTEEN: Harvest Moon in the Tenth Year of the
    High King's Reign: The House Divided   250
CHAPTER SEVENTEEN: Rade Moon in the Tenth Year of the
    High King's Reign: Wisdom, Mourning, and Fate   266
CHAPTER EIGHTEEN: Rade Moon in the Tenth Year of the
    High King's Reign: On The Track of the Setting Sun   293
CHAPTER NINETEEN: Rade Moon in the Tenth Year of the
    High King's Reign: Patterns of Force   308
CHAPTER TWENTY: Harvest Moon and Rade Moon in the
    Tenth Year of the High King's Reign: A Kind of Wild Justice   324
CHAPTER TWENTY-ONE: Rade Moon in the Tenth Year of the
    High King's Reign: Memory, Tradition, and Dreams   342
CHAPTER TWENTY-TWO: Rade Moon in the Tenth Year of the
    High King's Reign: In Winter's Shadow   354
CHAPTER TWENTY-THREE: Rade Moon in the Tenth Year of
    the High King's Reign: Transit of Lies   365
CHAPTER TWENTY-FOUR: Woods Moon in the Tenth Year
    of the High King's Reign: Like a Bright and Terrible Machine   391
CHAPTER TWENTY-FIVE: Woods Moon in the Tenth Year of
    the High King's Reign: A Past with No Future   409
CHAPTER TWENTY-SIX: Woods Moon in the Tenth Year of
    the High King's Reign: Death Is the Hunter   425
CHAPTER TWENTY-SEVEN: Woods Moon in the Tenth Year
    of the High King's Reign: The Unicorn Riders   435
CHAPTER TWENTY-EIGHT: Woods Moon in the Tenth Year of
    the High King's Reign: A Cold and Logical Slaughter   452
CHAPTER TWENTY-NINE: Woods Moon in the Tenth Year of
    the High King's Reign: A Home upon the Pyre   472

CHAPTER THIRTY: Woods Moon in the Tenth Year of the High King's Reign: Running after Dreams   483

CHAPTER THIRTY-ONE: Woods Moon in the Tenth Year of the High King's Reign: Dance of Equals   515

CHAPTER THIRTY-TWO: Woods Moon in the Tenth Year of the High King's Reign: The Long Walk   534

CHAPTER THIRTY-THREE: Woods Moon in the Tenth Year of the High King's Reign: Perplexed in Darkness and Entangled in Ruin   552

CHAPTER THIRTY-FOUR: Woods Moon in the Tenth Year of the High King's Reign: The Lord of the Four Quarters   558

CHAPTER THIRTY-FIVE: Woods Moon in the Tenth Year of the High King's Reign: A Sword of Lightning   562

CHAPTER THIRTY-SIX: Woods Moon in the Tenth Year of the High King's Reign: A Shield of Broken Glass   570

CHAPTER THIRTY-SEVEN: Woods Moon in the Tenth Year of the High King's Reign: Of Ribbons and Razors   585

CHAPTER THIRTY-EIGHT: Woods Moon to Cold Moon in the Tenth Year of the High King's Reign: To Surrender Is Not the Same As a Beautiful Retreat   600

CHAPTER THIRTY-NINE: Sword Moon in the Eleventh Year of the High King's Reign: The Anvil of Necessity   643

CHAPTER FORTY: Sword Moon to Fire Moon in the Eleventh Year of the High King's Reign: The Shadow of the Beginning   653

CHAPTER FORTY-ONE: Thunder Moon in the Eleventh Year of the High King's Reign: Blood Sings Deep   661

CHAPTER FORTY-TWO: Thunder Moon in the Eleventh Year of the High King's Reign: The Forest Wide Will Be Your Bride   667

EPILOGUE: Thunder Moon in the Eleventh Year of the High King's Reign: Like a Device of Frost and Silver   673

PROLOGUE

DARKNESS VISIBLE

*Though there are many songs of the High King's reign,
there are none of her journey westward through the lands she
had once conquered.*

No one who was a part of that journey will ever speak of those days.
— Thurion Pathfinder, Private Journal

Before Time itself came to be, *He Who Is* had been: changeless, eternal, perfect. And all was Darkness, and *He Who Is* ruled over all there was.

Then the Light came, dancing through the Dark and making it into Dark and not-Dark. Making it a finite, a bounded thing. Where there had been silence, and Void, and infinity, there came music, and not-Void, and Time . . .

And a world.

He Who Is lashed out against this debasement of *His* perfect Nothingness, and the Light realized *He Who Is* meant to take from it the beautiful world of shape and form and time and boundary it had created. Light could not destroy the Darkness without destroying itself, but Light could bring life to flourish where destruction had walked.

The new life was as changeable as *He Who Is* was changeless, and to this life, Light gave weapons. Light Itself coursed through the new life's veins, and Light fell in love with silver life. Light left the high vault of heaven and scattered itself across the land, and silver life traveled to the places of the Light to rejoice in it.

But *He Who Is* vowed *He* would win in the end. This time, *He* bound *His* war into time, to let *His* tools learn from the enemy *He* would ultimately destroy. To all the things of the Light, *He Who Is* held up a dark mirror. For the Bright World, a World Without Sun. For life and love, death and pain. For trust, treachery. For kindness, power.

For skill . . . magic.

For Life . . . the Endarkened. *He Who Is* created thirteen intermediaries to scour the Bright World of life: the Dark Guard and their King. *He Who Is* sent *His* Endarkened forth from their lair beneath Obsidian Mountain and *His* creations glutted themselves upon blood and pain. The land around Obsidian Mountain became a wasteland where nothing lived, and each night the Endarkened ranged farther to spread their desolation. But they were few and Life reproduced quickly. So King Virulan worked a great magic to change his twelve vassals so that their bodies could bring forth more soldiers for this great war. Only Prince Uralesse had foreseen Virulan's intention, and hid himself from the casting of that great spell. Once it had been cast, there was no power left to do it again—no matter how much Virulan wished to do so—and thus Uralesse remained as *He Who Is* had made him.

The eleven who were then the Created-and-Changed brought forth life from their bodies, and soon, where the Endarkened had been one interchangeable and unchanging people, they were three: the Created, the Created-and-Changed, and the Born.

The children of *He Who Is* were bound by the laws of time and matter, and in that realm even *His* vast power could not create a sorcery that did not require payment. *His* creatures of magic did not possess infinite power, for the power of the Endarkened came from the pain and fear of their victims and from the anguish and despair of their victims' deaths. Each spell they cast was paid for in the blood and suffering of others.

Of slaves.

The first Elflings the Endarkened took cried out to Aradhwain the Mare and wept for the vast openness of the Goldengrass. Time passed in the Bright World, and the Elfling victims cried out to the Sword-Giver and the Bride of Battles, to Amretheon and Pelashia, to the Starry Hunt. None of their Brightworld Powers saved them.

Then one day a captive struck back with the Light itself. With magic. The Light had hidden the only weapon which could slay the eternal beautiful children of *He Who Is* in the changeable world of form and

time. Only the audacity of the Light had led it to disclose its great secret, for if it had not shared that secret with Elvenkind, the Endarkened
and *He Who Is* would have remained ignorant of it . . .

Until it was too late.

And so *He Who Is* gave new orders to *His* Endarkened. The time of
slaughter was over. The time of war had come.

The Endarkened threw themselves into preparations for the coming
war. It was to be a harvest of blood and pain as the world had never seen.
The King of the Endarkened rallied his troops and prepared his twisted
weapons of Darkness. When this war was over, no living thing would
remain in the Bright World—no blade of grass, no flower, no tree. No
fish in the water, no bird in the air, no beast on the earth would remain.

And Elvenkind would die first.

But as the King of the Endarkened began to discover, Elves were extremely hard to kill.

⊰⊱

For the first twelve turns of the Wheel of the Year, the girl born to
be High King lived within the walls of Caerthalien Great Keep.
The War Prince of Caerthalien and Caerthalien's Ladyholder had raised
her in ignorance of her heritage and her House, for she was the last War
Prince of Farcarinon. As she took her first breath, Farcarinon was destroyed, leaving her, a child barely a candlemark old, as the War Prince
of an erased High House. Farcarinon's only crime had been to seek the
High Kingship for its prince, and Bolecthindial Caerthalien had sworn
that there would never again be a Farcarinon to reach so high.

To kill the child would have been a simple matter had not the mad
Astromancer of the Sanctuary of the Star placed Peacebond upon the
infant. The Sanctuary of the Star—where the child had been born and
where the Lightborn trained to become the great Mages who served
the War Princes—was no place for a baby, but Celelioniel Astromancer,
ruler of the Sanctuary of the Star, was determined that Vieliessar Farcarinon would live. Just as she decreed that Caerthalien must foster the
child, she also decreed that Caerthalien must return the child to the
Sanctuary when Vieliessar reached the age of twelve.

And so Vieliessar was raised in ignorance of her history and even her name.

Then, at the very moment Vieliessar was to leave Caerthalien Great Keep for the last time, Ladyholder Glorthiachiel of Caerthalien could not resist telling Vieliessar the truth: she was a prince of the Hundred Houses, and Caerthalien had slain her parents and ravaged her lands. Under a spell of silence and obedience, Vieliessar was forced to accompany the Candidates' caravan to the Sanctuary of the Star—a place where she was meant to spend the rest of her life toiling as a common drudge. Even though she was hailed upon her arrival as "The Child of the Prophecy" by one of Celelioniel's confidants, it did not change her fate.

Her fury, even banked, might have cost Vieliessar her life, save for one thing no one had foreseen. Vieliessar had Light within her, and as the years passed, she became one of the greatest Adepts ever trained by the Sanctuary of the Star.

In the ancient repository of history and knowledge where she and all the other Lightborn studied, Vieliessar discovered a prophecy and a foreshadowing: *In the time of the Darkness to come, the Hundred Houses will be erased as if they had never been. The world will run black with blood, and all living things will die.*

Only the Child of the Prophecy could save Elvenkind.

Vieliessar took a long time to understand what the Prophecy meant and what her place in it was, for *The Song of Amretheon*—which contained the text of the Prophecy—was very old, and its verses had become tangled with time. She might never have acted, save for the actions of Hamphuliadiel Astromancer. Privy to the same knowledge that had driven Celelioniel mad, Hamphuliadiel sought to destroy the power of Amretheon's Prophecy by destroying its instrument.

Intent upon fulfilling the Prophecy, Vieliessar left the Sanctuary to seek training from the last Swordmaster of Farcarinon. But without an army, even the Child of the Prophecy would be helpless against the coming Darkness. There was nothing she could do but attempt to unite the Hundred Houses under her leadership—and the only way she could do that was war.

In battle after battle Vieliessar took domains from their War Princes. As her legend grew, the commonfolk flocked to her banner—and their princes followed them. Pursued by the Grand Army of her enemies at every step, Vieliessar fought the nine great battles that broke their power. Every person who survived the last great battle pledged fealty to High King Vieliessar Farcarinon.

All but one.

Prince-Heir Runacarendalur of Caerthalien had once led his father's army into battle against Lord Vieliessar with delight, for he had spent his entire life in service to the Way of the Sword. But the first time he faced Vieliessar upon a battlefield, he discovered a terrible secret that could doom both of them: he, the pampered scion of Caerthalien, and Vieliessar, the rebellious outcast prince of an erased House, were Soul-bonded.

Where the Soulbond touched, two souls were irrevocably linked, twined so closely together that the death of one Bonded meant the death of the other. For moonturns, as his army pursued hers, Runacarendalur struggled with the question of whether to end Vieliessar's life and her war by killing himself, or to keep the Soulbond a secret for as long as he could—for if it was known, House Caerthalien's allies would all turn against them, believing Caerthalien and Vieliessar were conspiring to trap them.

As the probability of Vieliessar's victory continued to mount, Runacarendalur suddenly found himself unable to choose one way or the other, for his brother Ivrulion Lightbrother bespelled Runacarendalur so that he could do nothing—not even give warning of Ivrulion's twisted ambitions. Ivrulion had been barred from succeeding his father to the Caerthalien throne first by Runacarendalur's unexpected birth and next by becoming—against his will—Lightborn. In Vieliessar's string of victories and her growing power, he saw a way to gain what he wanted most: Caerthalien.

But when Ivrulion faced Vieliessar on the final battlefield, he died when his magic turned against him. Vieliessar claimed victory, but Runacarendalur refused to swear fealty to her, and fled back into the West.

Having won, Vieliessar now had to rule. From the day her dying mother gave birth, Vieliessar had been known to be the Child of the Prophecy, though she herself had heard that title for the first time more than a decade later. At first she did not understand what it meant. Later, she despised it, and later still, tried to reject it. At last she had bent her neck to the yoke of the inevitable and accepted it in all its frightful weight and glory: when Darkness came to sweep Elvenkind from the land, only the Child of the Prophecy could stop them.

But the Prophecy did not tell her *how*.

She began with one truth: the Darkness would come. And when the Darkness came, Elvenkind must fight.

To fight required an army, and so Vieliessar would make an army from the tailles and meisnes of the quarreling Elven domains. To unify them, she must become High King: take the Unicorn Throne, unite the Princely Houses, turn a hundred quarreling armies into one undivided force.

It should have been impossible. But the Prophecy was no mere foretelling. It was a spell that had waited uncountable centuries to find its target. It shaped Vieliessar into what it required, and by the visions it sent her and the demands it made upon her, she received all the proof she needed to believe in the Prophecy's truth and the reality of the threat.

And so she seated herself upon the Unicorn Throne.

The peace of her reign lasted perhaps a quartermark, if that long.

There was no moment to rejoice in the attainment of her goal, no time to prepare for the war to come. When the Darkness—the *Endarkened*—came, her people were caught off guard. They had believed that Vieliessar's Enthroning set the seal upon the beginning of an era of peace. Even Vieliessar had believed that. The Prophecy said that the Child of the Prophecy would save Elvenkind from the Darkness—but when the Darkness came, she had been helpless against it.

They had all been helpless.

Even when they had seen that their enemy would not fall to sword or pike or arrow, Landbond and prince, mercenary and knight, each had stood their ground to give those whom they protected the chance to flee to safety.

And those heroes had died to the last soul.

Only by sheerest chance did her people discover that the Flower Forests were places the Endarkened could not enter. It was all that saved them.

It had taken Vieliessar two full turns of the Wheel of the Year to gather up and organize—to *find*—her scattered people in the aftermath of that terrible Enthroning Day. To gather up the remains of the herd beasts and the precious irreplaceable warhorses. To fight for leadership of her people once again, this time with words instead of swords. And every step had been paid for in blood and magic.

So far as anyone could determine, the Endarkened treated this war as a game whose outcome was never in doubt. Time after time Vieliessar had seen the Endarkened forces draw back at the moment of victory, sparing their foes for no other reason than so they could torture them another day. And the enemy was as clever as it was mad. If the Endarkened could not enter the Flower Forests, they could send others in their stead: Lesser Endarkened, goblins, serpentmarae, stonedrakes and icedrakes and firedrakes; snow lions and ice tigers and packs of wolves . . .

Monsters and predators and creatures of magic. Her people learned to kill them all. She had called the people of the Hundred Houses to her with the promise that the day she gained the Unicorn Throne her people would no longer be divided. Noble and Landbond would answer to one judgment and to one rule, and there would be no more of highborn and low.

Of all the promises she had made, that one had been made true. All her people were komen now. All were equal.

And together they had learned to run for their lives.

Two Wheelturns after Enthroning Day, the Lightborn discovered that Celenthodiel was dying. The Flower Forest had given all she had to give. To continue to draw upon her would kill her—and destroy their only protection against the Endarkened.

And so Vieliessar had gathered her folk together and said:

"We will go west to the Dragon's Gate, cross the Mystrals, gather up those of our people who remain there, and make our stand against the Endarkened on the Western Shore, with Amrolion and Daroldan at our side."

She did not know then that this was an empty promise, for Amrolion and Daroldan had both fallen to an army led by Runacar Caerthalien.

CHAPTER ONE

SWORD MOON TO FIRE MOON IN THE TENTH YEAR OF THE HIGH KING'S REIGN: THE SMOKE OF THAT GREAT BURNING

Any plan, no matter how abysmally stupid, is better than no plan.
Without one, no one will follow you, and without followers you can
do nothing. You can always change your mind after you begin, but
to begin at all, you have to have a plan.

—The Lost Book of Gunedwaen Swordmaster

The Western Shore had once been a land of forests. Delfieraratha-dan was the largest, extending down into Amrolion, but to Delfierarathadan's east lay the Forest Gandimak, and to its north ran the Forest of Izalbama.

Beyond these borders lay Maridi-al-Nak, and uncertainty.

Maridi-al-Nak was a dense and ancient forest with trunks as enormous as border towers. In fact, many of its trees had been used for that purpose by the domains of the Western Shore.

When there *had* been domains of the Western Shore.

The climactic Beastling attack on the domains of the Western Shore had erased—in all possible senses of the word—Amrolion and Dar-oldan. The spells cast had destroyed the Sanctuary Road and the river Angarussa, which had been Delfierarathadan Flower Forest's eastern border. Before the earth-shaking, all of Delfierarathadan had burned, and the Western Road had been buried in clouds of ash. The rain that accompanied the final battle had washed the ash into pools and furrows of black sticky mud. In another span of moonturns, even the ash would be gone.

But the battle had not quite erased everything.

Along the southern edge of the Medhartha Hills, ran the optimistically named Northern Road. To call it a road was vainglory, for it was barely more than a goat track. Its primary use had been to reach the Angarussa River without going through Delfierarathadan Flower Forest. Where the Maridi-al-Nak ended—or at least ceased to border the Northern Road—the Forest Izalbama replaced it. There had been other work than husbanding these forests for the Foresters of the Western Shore to do, and so both Maridi-al-Nak and the Forest Izalbama presented an impenetrable and neglected density of brambles, nettles, and fell-timber. Izalbama ended on the banks of the Angarussa, for before the High King's War, Cirandeiron's foresters had been vigilant in keeping the eastern bank of the Angarussa clear of anything that could hide a Beastling ambush.

The fact that the Beastlings no longer felt any need to hide made the road no safer.

Of the hundreds and thousands of komen, Warhunt Mages, and Rangers who had fought in that doomed campaign, there were less than five tailles of souls left. Among them was Lady Aglahir, who, even though she was the greatchild of one of Damulothir Daroldan's elder siblings and barely old enough to have flown her kite a few moonturns before, was now War Prince of Daroldan. Most of the survivors were Warhunt Mages from the party sent by the High King a decade ago to aid her vassals. There were a handful of Daroldan Rangers, and the rest were Sword Pages and Craftworkers, anyone who had been lucky enough to be on the edges of the battleground when the Beastlings struck it with their spell. Their progress along the road was slow, for they had to forage for every necessity, and they had begun their journey exhausted and injured.

If the Wheelturns-old rumors were true, there was only one place of refuge left west of the Mystrals—the Sanctuary of the Star.

⚎⚏

As always, Kathan Lightsister had Called a wellspring when they stopped at midday, and Tangisen Lightbrother had Called fire. There was a limitless supply of kindling all around them, and the young Lightless under Kathan's direction filled cookpots with wild-gathered

herbs and jointed the carcasses of rabbits and pigeons. Nindir Lightbrother's Keystone Gift was animal communication, so he had been able
to lure enough of the skittish wildlife into the cookpot to keep them all
from starvation.

But not very far from it, Isilla thought. Angweth Ranger had resumed
work on a small project he had begun with wood from the wreckage of
the Flower Forest. *A bowl this time. Maybe a tea canister.* Angweth had
already made hair clasps and combs; simple objects that raised morale
disproportionately. He carried a bundle of ahata branches culled from
the wreckage of Delfierarathadan, and Isilla knew he hoped to make
arrow shafts from them once he had the time.

The gaggle of refugees had slowly coalesced into smaller groups on
this journey, and Isilla, Tangisen, and Dinias had formed one of the
groups-within-the-group, for they had been friends together since before the False Parley. Isilla sipped from her makeshift cup of hot water
flavored with roadside herbs. She missed true tea even more than she
missed bread.

"I'm worried about Rondithiel," she said.

"If he survived the last battle, he can survive anything," Tangisen
answered.

"No," Dinias said quietly, shaking his head. "*We* can, because we're
young and stupid. But Rondithiel was old before he left the Sanctuary to
join Lord Vieliessar's cause. They say he has seen the reigns of a dozen
Astromancers."

"Well, he won't see another one after Hamphuliadiel. Raise your
hand everyone who thinks—" Tangisen began.

"Stop it!" Isilla hissed. "I don't care who is Astromancer, whether it is
Hamphuliadiel or Vieliessar or even Pelashia Flower Queen. Rondithiel
is *dying.* Can neither of you see it?"

Dinias looked in Rondithiel's direction. "I talk to rocks," Dinias finally said with a helpless shrug. "We're all tired. Tangisen?"

"We're all tired." Tangisen echoed Dinias's words, staring down at
his hands and not looking at either of them. He'd exhausted himself
keeping the conflagration away from the battlefield during the last battle, and hadn't spoken much since. The ebullient young Lightborn with

the Keystone Gift of Fire who considered the battlefield merely an extension of the xaique board was long buried.

Isilla folded her mouth into a tight line. It wasn't that they couldn't see, she thought, but that they wouldn't. Rondithiel had been a fortress and refuge for as long as they'd known him. No one wanted to think he was merely mortal. "Rondithiel shoulders everyone's problems and fears with no thought for himself," she said quietly. "But who can lead us if he doesn't? Aglahir Daroldan is little more than a child."

"And somehow I doubt Hamphuliadiel is going to be eager to welcome her with the honors due a War Prince," Dinias said, lowering his own voice even more. "Would Caerthalien have succored Aramenthiali if this had happened before the High King's War?"

"He's only the Astromancer," Isilla protested. "While she—"

"Is not," Dinias finished. "And the Astromancer now rules as a prince. You saw. I am not sure he will take *any* of us in. And I am not sure I want to be taken in, come to that. We haven't heard from Harwing after he left us."

Harwing had left the Warhunt Mages sent to the Western Shore to scout the transformed Sanctuary of the Star. No one had heard from him again, even before the Great Silence that had destroyed their ability to Farspeak.

"Do you think we're doing the right thing by going to the Sanctuary?" Dinias asked. They had all agreed at the beginning that the Sanctuary of the Star was the only place left to go, but since they were Lightborn they would continue to discuss it until the Hunt came for them all. "I mean, should we go there at all? It will be all right—probably—for Thorodos and Serchalion and most of the Lightless, and—"

"No," Isilla said, succinctly cutting off what promised to be a lengthy catalog of people who would probably be all right at the Sanctuary of the Star. "And there's nothing else we can do."

"The High King—" Dinias began.

"Is dead. Or in chains. And it does not matter which, since she—or whatever War Prince has erased her—isn't here. Nor can we cross the Western Reach as easily as we did ten years ago, so it's not as if we can go find out."

"Go ahead, Dinias. Tell us our other choices," Tangisen urged bitterly.

"That's the trouble," Isilla began. "There's—"

She broke off. Thorodos Ranger had returned, and gone to whisper in Rondithiel's ear. The elderly Lightbrother got stiffly to his feet, and he and Thorodos stepped away from the fire to confer. Isilla was about to join them when Rondithiel walked back toward the fire and spread his hands for attention.

"My brethren, my companions, lords and ladies, there is unexpected news. While it is of advantage to us, it is also troubling, and so we will cut our rest short so that—"

The sudden uprush of questions made it impossible for Rondithiel to continue.

"Come on," said Tangisen, getting to his feet. "I want to see what kind of disguised-Gift-of-the-Light it is *this* time."

⊰≣≣⊱

I was not expecting this," Pendray Lightsister said blankly.

At midafternoon the party stood at the edge of what ought to be the banks of the Angarussa River. Instead of a river there was a lake, its surface choked with the same ash that mounded itself on the lake's shores. There was no way to tell how deep the new lake was.

"It will make crossing easier, at least," Tangisen Lightbrother said, after a long silence. "It's a lake, now, not a river. We can just go around it instead."

"How could this happen?" Aglahir Daroldan asked. She knelt at the edge of the lake and swept the water in front of her clear of ash.

Rondithiel knelt down beside her and cupped up some water in his hand. When he let it flow through his fingers, it left behind a coating of ash and cinders on his skin. "This lake is yet more consequence of the spell that caused Daroldan Great Keep to collapse into the sea," he said, wiping his hand dry on the skirts of his robes. His voice, honed by centuries of striving to be heard over the noise of rowdy Postulants, carried easily. Most of the refugees were standing on the lake's edge by now, gazing down at it as if doing so would make the water give them a reason for the lake's existence. "As many of you will remember from my lectures"—there was scattered laughter—"a non-magical consequence can arise from the physical effects of a spell. Cold will freeze water, Thunderbolt will kindle a fire—"

"And if you shake the land hard enough, things will break," Isilla said under her breath.

As if something had only been waiting to hear her words, the surface of the new lake began to boil.

"Get back!" Thorodos shouted. His hands flew as he echoed his own command in Sign for the other Rangers. Isilla grabbed Tangisen and Dinias and pulled them back up the path.

Isilla's skin crawled with the touch of magic. Alien magic. Western Shore magic. *Beastling* magic. The Sea-Beastlings could enchant and shape water into any form they chose. The spell didn't usually last long, but it didn't have to. "Beastlings!" she yelled.

Automatically Isilla began to time her heartbeats, so she would have some idea of how long the spell had been running. It was habit, taught to her in the Sanctuary and instilled deeply into her subconscious by now.

The surface of the water exploded upward, forming a tentacle. There was a crackle and a violet flash as several Lightborn cast Shield around the border of the lake. The tentacle rose up higher, and then toppled sideways like a tree. The Shield-spell failed under the overload, and the column of water crashed down upon the grass and into a cluster of Lightborn and Pages, then swept back like a wave at the shore.

Where it retreated, the ground was empty.

Isilla realized she was waiting for an order from Rondithiel that would not come. "Move the water!" she shouted. "Only the water! Send it to the ocean!"

Send and Fetch were two of the earliest spells a Lightborn learned, and Candidates always got up to mischief once they had mastered them. Fetch allowed one to Call an object to themselves—even if there were barriers in its way—providing the caster knew what the object looked like and where it was. Send allowed one to do the same thing in reverse.

Everyone here knew what Great Sea Ocean looked like by now. In moments, the lake was empty. The refugees who had been in the path of the water-tentacle were nowhere to be seen. Eleven people were gone.

Including Rondithiel Lightbrother.

❈

No matter what spells they tried, they could not retrieve any of those who were missing, or even discover where they had gone. Candlemarks passed, and the day turned to twilight.

The sun is setting, and I do not think any of us wishes to remain in this place, Isilla thought. *We must move on now to find a safe place to spend the night.* "Hear me!" she said. "We must number our dead and move on. We can cross the riverbed and find a place to camp. We will be in Cirandeiron, and—"

"We don't have to do what you say!" Carath shouted. She was one of the few surviving Daroldan Sword Pages, so she was of noble blood. She might even be War Prince by now, who knew? "You aren't our masters—you aren't even *komen*! Why should we take your orders?"

"Because you want our spells." Tangisen walked forward until he stood between the two groups. "Light at night? Fire when you want it? Food for your cookpot? That's all us. We'd like to keep the Rangers, but as for the rest of you: good luck getting to the Sanctuary alive. Do you think this is the last time the Beastlings will attack?"

Isilla looked around and realized sinkingly that the Lightless had all gathered in one group, and the Warhunt in another. The Western Shore Lightborn stood uneasily beside them. The High King had declared the Lightborn to be free, but these Lightborn would go where their Lightless masters told them to go—even if that master was a child not yet old enough to fly her kite. It hadn't mattered when Rondithiel was alive, for he had been the acknowledged leader of all of them. But Rondithiel was gone now, and Tangisen wasn't helping matters.

"Any party needs a leader," Isilla said, quietly but firmly, as she took her place beside Tangisen. "That much we all know to be true. Do you think we mean to rule you forever? Of course not. Once we reach the Sanctuary of the Star there will be no leaders and followers—only Hamphuliadiel and his rule."

Several of the Western Shore Lightborn shot Isilla startled glances.

"Didn't you think of that?" Tangisen asked them mockingly. "Or did you forget the part about how the Astromancer has set himself up as a War Prince in all but name—and that your domains gave their fealty to the High King?"

"Tangisen, *shut up*," Isilla hissed. She wanted to kick him, but settled for gripping his forearm as hard as she could.

Carath's face settled into a mask of anger. "Daroldan will follow its own," she said. "Rangers and Lightborn both."

If she were Vieliessar, Isilla thought in helpless frustration, she could find the right words to change Lady Carath's mind. Or some way to make the rebellion not matter. But Isilla was not Vieliessar. "Fine," she said. "Everyone who wishes to follow Carath Daroldan, do. Everyone else, follow me."

Carath looked horrified at the title Isilla had just given her and opened her mouth to speak.

Isilla strode off without looking back to see who followed her.

She stalked along the dry streambed for a candlemark before she was willing to slow down and look behind her. Her heart lifted to see that the other Warhunt Mages had elected to follow her—not as if she, in any sense, was their leader, but rather as individuals who had all made the same choice she had.

But Rondithiel wasn't among them, and her heart ached with his absence. *Lord Vieliessar sent the Warhunt into the West and only two and a half tailles survive.*

Behind them, the riverbed was empty as far as she could see.

"Well that showed them," Tangisen said blandly, when he caught up to her. Isilla tried very hard not to laugh. It seemed wrong somehow.

"We should stop here for the night," Dinias said. "We'll have enough daylight left to prepare Rondithiel's leave-taking. And Annandil Lightsister's."

We don't have bodies—how can we burn them? Isilla thought in anguish. But their brethren deserved a proper funeral. *Rituals are for the living.* "You're right," she said. "Let's gather the wood we'll need."

⋈

A funeral pyre might be made of anything that would burn, but before the time of the High King, great lords had surrounded themselves in death as in life with rare perfumes and costly essences, and if a Lightborn was considered "worthy" they might receive as fragrant and expensive a pyre as their lord and master. (Isilla could not remember the last time she'd seen a proper pyre lit; their deaths were so many and their resources so few.) The refugees found little they could use to send their beloved dead to the Vale of Celenthodiel with honor, but they did their best with what they had.

There are no Tablets of Memory upon which to inscribe their names, no Line to remember them—for Rondithiel was of Farcarinon, and who survives of Farcarinon save the High King? Perhaps Hamphuliadiel will let their names survive upon the rolls of the Sanctuary—but I doubt it, Isilla thought.

By the time they had gathered wood for the two pyres and prepared their makeshift camp, it was fully dark. No body lay on either pyre, but each one was covered in a pall of Lightborn green. Atop that, the Lightborn had placed green branches and meadow flowers, attending as scrupulously to Annandil's pyre as to Rondithiel's. Normally the eldest Lightborn conducted the leave-taking, but by unspoken consent, Isilla spoke the words to the Lightborn gathered around the two pyres.

"We come to celebrate the leave-taking of two of Pelashia's Children. Rondithiel of Farcarinon, Annandil of Laeldor, you have served long in the Cold World. Go now to the Warm World, where it is always summer, and go with joy."

The going-forth of one of the Lightborn was as swift as the fire that consumed them. Isilla closed her eyes, and in that moment felt herself drawn up into a linkage with the others. There was a brief flash of light and heat, and when she opened her eyes again there was nothing left of the two pyres save a few tiny flecks of ash eddied by the wind. The ground wasn't even scorched.

I have walked in the Vale of Celenthodiel, and it is as real as bread. I have never seen my long-passed Lightbrethren there. I do not think Celenthodiel is the Warm World we speak of so easily, and I can only hope there is some place for us to go in the end. The komen ride with the

Hunt forever. The Landbond go into the earth to be reborn as next year's harvest. What is there for Lightborn?

Dinias and Tangisen came to stand beside her, offering silent comfort.

"It hardly matters who leads when we are all going to the same place and there is only one road to get there," Isilla said. True for the dead, and true for the living as well.

"Are we?" Dinias asked. "Really? Seriously?" He took the step that allowed him to turn and face her, looking searchingly into her eyes. "We're the Warhunt. We don't hide. We don't run away. We *fight*. The Astromancer isn't going to welcome us with open arms—*we* know that if the Daroldanders don't. We all know what happened to Harwing—or rather, we *don't* know, and that's good enough for me. Let those others betray their oaths—*I'm* going to find Lord Vieliessar and help her fix whatever has gone wrong. You all know she would have come west if she could. You *know* it. So let's go find her!"

Soft murmurs of agreement from the others followed his words.

"I say we do what Dinias says," Isilla said, putting her hand on his shoulder. "But I *also* say we do it in the morning. Are you with us, Warhunt?"

This time there was cheering.

❦

A long time ago, when he first went to the Sanctuary of the Star, Harwing of Oronviel learned that the Sanctuary ran on gossip. Candidates gossiped among themselves, Postulants gossiped among themselves, and probably the servants and the Lightborn did too.

That was then.

In Hamphuliadiel's reborn Sanctuary, discussions were brief, factual, and always to the point. News of Areve and Arevethmonion that was deemed to be of importance to the Lightborn was conveyed by Momioniarch or Galathornthadan before the evening meal. Time between the end of the evening meal and bed was spent in listening to lectures on their place in the world and on the sacrifices of the Astromancer who kept them, the Light, and the Lightless safe. News of the world beyond the Sanctuary's woods and fields was . . .

Nonexistent.

Even the vast fire in the west that clotted the sky with smoke did not bring forth an official explanation, let alone an inspiring lecture, but for the first time in Harwing's recent memory the prohibition against gossip was flouted. The mystery and strangeness of the western conflagration was simply too visible to pretend it out of existence.

Hamphuliadiel started his own whisper campaign of course—the fire in the west was merely Amrolion and Daroldan at war with either the Beastlings or one another. Nothing important. Nothing to warrant the Sanctuary's attention.

No one believed that.

On the seventh day after the smoke in the west had first been spotted, Hamphuliadiel summoned Harwing.

⌗

Momioniarch Lightsister came to Harwing's table at the end of the meal to order him to attend upon the Astromancer. He carefully showed Momioniarch only what she expected to see: delight at his summons to Hamphuliadiel's presence mixed with slight apprehension about what he might have done to merit such personal attention. He concealed both hope—that he was to be admitted into the Astromancer's inner circle—and fear—that the Astromancer or his minions had somehow read Harwing's true thoughts. He kept his mind blank as he followed Momioniarch to the public Audience Chamber. On the list of named chambers, it was called Penyamo-chamber, for each room in the Sanctuary except the sleeping chambers was named for some fruit or flower. No spell could breach its wards, and the use of physical force against the Sanctuary of the Star was—or at least had once been—unthinkable.

Harwing had been inside Penyamo-chamber only once before, on the day he had been bespelled to obedience and loyalty to Hamphuliadiel Astromancer. Then, the doors had been of plain serviceable bronze—but that had been ten Wheelturns ago. Now the doors had been reshaped into something even more ornate than the doors of the Shrine.

The central figure was a Vilya tree in flower and fruit, its blossoms picked out in elvensilver and its fruits in gold. The tree was flanked by two figures with their hands raised in praise: one in the robes of a Light-born (and surely the figure's resemblance to Hamphuliadiel was merely a coincidence), and the other a Farmholder in ragged homespun, who for some incomprehensible reason had brought a hoe and a hayfork with him.

On the ground around the Vilya were scattered swords and pieces of armor, and in the background of the image, depicted in low relief and picked out in copper that had been allowed to go green, was a vista of endless fields and placid herds. The iconography was clear: the Astro-mancer and his Lightborn now ruled over everything, the Lords Komen included. This was not as satisfactory a state of affairs as Harwing had once thought it would be.

The doors swung open silently as he and Momioniarch approached them, and Orchalianiel stood waiting to conduct the two of them to the foot of the throne.

Hamphuliadiel's suite of rooms had expanded since he became Astromancer Eternal—the Astromancer could now boast of a private dining chamber, a personal library, and a private reception chamber in addition to his sleeping room and the public Audience Chamber. It might have been more appropriate for Hamphuliadiel to summon one of his Lightborn to his private reception chamber rather than to the place he used to overawe petitioners and the Lightless, but Harwing never argued with anything that Hamphuliadiel or his minions said.

He will love me, then trust me, then rely upon me utterly. And when he finally does that, and admits me to all his secrets, I will rip his heart out with my own hands. He will pay for what he has done to the Lightborn and to the world.

The chamber was as long as the hall in a Great Keep, though nar-rower. The floor was visible only in narrow bands between expensive—and now irreplaceable—carpets of price, and the walls were lined with ornate and beautiful shelves and cabinets containing gems, furs, in-gots, spices—anything costly and rare—and draped with tapestries for which there was no other place. The effect of the room's shape was to focus the eye upon the raised platform and the ornate ivory chair at the far end. Its seat was wide enough for any two men, and its back extended several hand spans above Hamphuliadiel's head. The ivory was so thickly encrusted with gems and gold that the material beneath was nearly concealed. Upon its seat Hamphuliadiel had made for himself a vast and luxurious cushion of silk pillows the same shade of Lightborn green as his robes.

Such a chair was appropriate for a War Prince, or the High King, not the Astromancer of the Shrine of the Star. But the *hradan* of the Fortunate Lands had moved in a direction no one could have predicted. The Astromancer Eternal had become more powerful than any War Prince. (Whether the Astromancer Eternal was more powerful than the High King, Harwing did not know and would not speculate on, for in the Sanctuary of the Star, thoughts were seldom private things.)

As Harwing reached the foot of the steps, he dropped to his knees and reached out for Hamphuliadiel's hand, laying his cheek against it in reverence. "My lord Astromancer calls for me and I am here," he said. He doubted that Hamphuliadiel's inner circle accorded him the degree of worship Harwing had just demonstrated, and he strongly suspected the Astromancer liked it a great deal. "How may I serve the Light?"

"Rise, my brother," Hamphuliadiel said. "I have a task for you—but first, I wish to know what you think of the fires in the west."

"My lord?" Harwing did not have to feign confusion. "You have said what it is, so I have paid it no further attention." He kept his eyes deferentially downcast as he got to his feet.

"Battle between Amrolion and Daroldan, yes," Hamphuliadiel said, sounding faintly disgruntled. "And you were right to dismiss thoughts of it once you had heard my wise counsel. But the Astromancer must shoulder burdens that ordinary souls never imagine, and so I was forced to wonder: What of the Lightborn who are being compelled to take part in their petty wars?"

Harwing knew Amrolion and Daroldan weren't at war with each other, so the Lightborn could hardly have been coerced into either fighting or Healing. But if Hamphuliadiel said that was what was happening, Harwing firmly intended to believe it.

"I don't understand, my lord Astromancer." This much Harwing could say in perfect honesty. "The Western Shore is far from us—and its

War Princes still walk in darkness and think the Light only a petty tool that their Lightborn wield at their command."

"And yet I have been Called by the Light to serve and protect all those who likewise serve the Light, no matter how much they rebel against my authority and wise counsel. Thus I must send word to our brothers and sisters of the Light that they have not been forsaken. I must tell them that there will always be a safe haven for them here at the Sanctuary of the Star."

Harwing waited in attentive silence. The Astromancer frowned, ever so slightly.

"I am sending *you* to the Western Shore, Harwing Lightbrother."

"No!" The refusal was swift, automatic, and entirely honest. How was he supposed to murder the Astromancer if he was a hundred leagues away? "I mean—"

"I know what you mean, my brother." Hamphuliadiel looked more pleased than irritated by Harwing's panicky refusal. "But we Lightborn must serve where we are called by the Light. None of us is exempt from this duty—not even I. Do you not think I would give anything I possessed to go in your place? To see what great disaster has befallen the Shore? To comfort my brothers and sisters of the Light and welcome them home from exile? But I may not do so—and so I send you."

"Astromancer—my lord—you—you do me too much honor," Harwing said, nearly babbling. "Tell me what I must do to serve you in this, I beg you."

"Tomorrow you and Ulvearth Lightsister will set out for Daroldan at first light. The Lightsister is from Amrolion and will know the way to cross the Angarussa. Tell me all that you see and hear along your way—I will send spellbirds for your use. Rescue any Lightborn in need of your aid, and carry my message to as many as you can. If there is danger, return to the Sanctuary at once, for you are dear to me, Brother Harwing, and I would grieve at the loss of you."

Until Hamphuliadiel spoke that last sentence, Harwing had held out hope that this mission he had been ordered to go on was actually a mission. But Hamphuliadiel would never have given Harwing the freedom to determine when he would return if he meant Harwing to return at all.

"I will do all you ask, Lord Hamphuliadiel. I serve your will gladly and in all things," Harwing said resolutely.

There must be some way to turn this to his advantage. But he would not think of that. Not here.

⚜

On the morning he and Ulvearth were to depart, Harwing rose long before dawn. He dressed in his traveling garments. It felt odd to wear trousers again after so long, but they were part of the traveling costume of a Lightborn: the trousers, plus a copy of the traditional robe crafted in sturdy wool instead of samite and slit up the front and back so that he could ride astride. Trews, boots, gloves, and an entirely unnecessary (at this time of year) cloak completed the costume, and every thread and skein of it was colored Lightborn green. He picked up a green leather carry bag containing an assortment of incenses, tea blends, and cordials, and prepared to leave. *I only hope I don't have to skulk somewhere in this garb. It would be difficult.*

He still had no answers to his questions.

Why had Hamphuliadiel ordained Harwing's death? (If he had.) And why shroud it in such an elaborate (and costly) masquerade? It wasn't as if it was necessary: when people under Hamphuliadiel's rule died, dying never involved actual death—just people who vanished between one day and the next, and people required to pretend the dead had never existed at all.

Means, motive, and performance: every act stands upon three legs, and so far Harwing could only see one of the three.

I suspect we are to be killed somehow as soon as we have sent Hamphuliadiel our report. I think that it is not so much that I have become a problem, and more that I won't be missed. But the loss of two Lightborn and three horses is still a high cost to pay for the information we can provide, meaning Hamphuliadiel thinks it's that valuable. Or it's that important: the two things are not always the same. . . .

At the last moment before leaving the chamber, Harwing hesitated. His hand went to the dagger on his belt. He knew where the Astromancer's sleeping chamber was. He could kill Hamphuliadiel where he slept. Gunedwaen would be avenged.

He thought carefully, then he took his hand from his dagger. If his attempt failed, he would be caught and killed, would have died for nothing, and possibly would even have killed an innocent victim, for it was a simple thing to disguise one person in the seeming of another. Perhaps this mission was a test after all.

And if someone does try to kill me during our lovely summer stroll, I can always come back here and kill Hamphuliadiel after I have killed them.

He slid the door shut behind him and walked off down the hall.

CHAPTER TWO

THUNDER MOON IN THE TENTH YEAR OF THE HIGH KING'S REIGN: SHADOWS LINGER

What you seek determines who you must be to go searching for it.
Who you are determines how you will go. The tale of that seeker
begins years before the first step.

—Gunedwaen Swordmaster, The Art of War

The air was soft with night as Harwing walked across the garden to the gate. It was two moonturns before Harvest, and he could smell the rich scent of growing things, as the vast fields surrounding Areve filled with future treasure. Though he could not see them, he knew that the orchard fruits were changing from green to a spectrum of golds, the grain and barley fields were a dark succulent green, and the grape vines were beginning to show their promises. Surrounded by so much bounty, it was hard to remember that the whole of the West—and possibly the whole of the Fortunate Lands by now—was a ghostlands where nothing remained but marauding bands of looters.

"Hail the Light," came the soft challenge.

"I see you, Irchel," Harwing responded. He took a step forward.

Irchel turned to unbar the gate for him, then paused, looking over his shoulder. Ulvearth Lightsister was coming up the path to join them. Her outfit and accessories mirrored his, though the cloak she carried was heavily embroidered and of a brighter shade of green.

"Hail the Light," Irchel said again.

"I See the Light," Ulvearth answered quietly. It was the countersign Harwing had been supposed to give, but as he thought it unlikely he would ever see the Sanctuary again, he hadn't bothered.

"Safe journey, Lightborn. Harwing, Ulvearth," Irchel said, opening the gate.

"If we aren't back before Harvest, save us a pie," Harwing answered. Irchel just laughed.

⊰⊱

Harwing and Ulvearth walked in silence toward Rosemoss Farm. It was still too early for even the faintest breath of dawn to be discernable, and Harwing spun out a globe of Silverlight to light their way. The sleepy complaints of birds in the trees above made him smile a little, but Ulvearth took no notice as she trudged on stolidly beside him.

When they reached the stable yard, he was suddenly, bitingly, homesick for the stables of Oronviel, with Lord Thoromarth in and out a dozen times each sunturn to see how his latest darlings were shaping for the races in Harvest Fair. But the world Harwing had been born to was as lost as Celephriandullias-Tildorangelor had once been.

Better we had never found that place. Better Vieliessar had not won the war. Can the world as it now is be worse than the "darkness" of Amretheon's Prophecy?

A young boy, clearly set in the doorway to watch for them, staggered sleepily to his feet and went inside, to emerge with a brace of mules—the result of a lengthy series of Calling spells, for Areve lacked the wherewithal to breed them. There was a cart in the corner of the stable yard, which Harwing had ignored; now he stared in bewilderment as the mules were hitched to it.

Apparently the Astromancer Eternal's implication that the (clandestine) mission would consist of Harwing and Ulvearth and perhaps at most a pack horse to carry supplies, had not been . . . entirely accurate.

A moment later two komen wearing chain mail shirts came out of the barn, leading their mounts, and were followed by Sword Pages leading warhorses.

There were not many komen at Areve—two or three tailles at most—and they were billeted at what had once been Rosemoss Farm. The *komentai'a* guarded the village and the herds from the Beastlings and occasionally acted as Hamphuliadiel's personal guard. What they did with the rest of their time, Harwing did not know, but he was certain they were not allowed to stand idle. Hamphuliadiel demanded labor from everyone.

That Hamphuliadiel even *had* komen to demand labor of in the first place was little short of astonishing.

The Hundred Houses had stripped their domains bare of combatants after the debacle of the False Parley, for no one had expected the war to last more than a few moonturns. They had taken the usual levy of servants and ostlers with them, but that didn't mean they'd taken every soul on their lands to war. The Landbonds had been left behind, and some of the Farmholders, and of course the Great Keeps were not left wholly uninhabited.

But the Winter War had gone on far longer than anyone thought it would, and when the War Princes did not return, the farms and manor houses had been assaulted by bandits and raiders. Their former inhabitants fled to the nearest keep for protection. Then, one by one, the keeps fell and the only place in the West offering safety and a full belly was Areve.

As the Sword Pages led the elderly destriers out into the stable yard, the magic of the docility and obedience charms embedded in the animals' forelocks gleamed faintly, and Harwing winced inwardly at the sight. Unlike the beautiful animals Thoromarth Oronviel had once bred—swift silken warhorses, graceful as dancers; palfreys as bright and gentle as hearth-dogs; racers that would outpace the wind and run from sunup to sundown without stopping—the destriers kept at what was once Rosemoss Farm were not worthy of the name. If these were destriers, they were the dregs of the lines bred by the dregs of the domains. *If they were ever to see a proper battle, they would surely be uncontrollable. But they do very well to intimidate farmers and Craftworkers and Landbonds.*

He glanced over at Ulvearth. She looked sleepy and resigned in equal measure. Of course, Harwing didn't know what she'd been told. Maybe she'd expected this all along.

Well, I suppose Hamphuliadiel has to send komen if the two of us are to be murdered, Harwing went on mentally. *You can't ask just anybody to do something like this. People would talk.*

Harwing studied his escort. Their hair was intricately braided and ribboned and clubbed, but it was too dark for Harwing to read the battles and victories—if any—woven into those braids. *Hedge knights,* Harwing decided critically. *If that.*

"May I say 'good morning,' my good komen, or is it too early for that?" Harwing asked lightly. It wouldn't hurt to try to ingratiate himself with them. A helpful and amiable Lightborn might be underestimated when the critical moment came. "I am called Harwing, and this is Ulvearth Lightsister. How shall I name you?"

"I am Garmund and this is Alleth," one of the komen answered grudgingly. On his overtunic, Harwing could see the place where his House badge had been carefully picked loose, to be replaced with that of Areve: a silver tower on a field of Lightborn green. Garmund mounted his horse and flicked his fingers at his Sword Page. The boy quickly mounted up behind Alleth, shaking out the leading rope he held.

"Much too early," Komen Garmund agreed, not unkindly. "But Lord Hamphuliadiel would have it that we were well away before morning bells, so that this journey is not gossiped about."

So that you can come back and say you were only away for a day's hunting. Say anything you like; no one will question you. In Areve—in the Sanctuary—no one asks questions, Harwing thought. "Then I suppose we must hurry," Harwing said, still smiling, still cheerful. "Come, Lightsister. Our mounts are ready."

Ulvearth turned to the cart, and climbed up beside the driver instead, ignoring the waiting animal. She'd said nothing since she'd greeted Irchel, and Harwing wondered why.

Once everyone was mounted, the party headed out into the uncultivated meadows and pastures claimed by Areve. The larks began to sing, and the stars began, one by one, to vanish. In the east the sky began to turn the very darkest shade of blue.

Ry dawn they had crossed into Rolumienion lands. The air still smelled of smoke from whatever had burned in the west, but they were too far away to see anything. Harwing had assumed that once they'd detoured around all the fields and orchards that made up Areve's lands they would turn westward to strike the Sanctuary Road. He'd paid very little attention to the conditions in the Western Reach when the Warhunt traveled west. Now it was ten Wheelturns later, and this time Harwing paid very close attention.

Item: We aren't turning west.

Item: There are boundary stones that enclose, at minimum, the whole of the lands. Arevethmonion isn't available anymore, though there's some Light to draw upon from other Flower Forests.

Item: If we keep going in this direction, we'll cross Rolumienion and fetch up against the foothills of the Medhatara Range. No one knows what's on the other side of them.

Item: Even if we aren't taking the Sanctuary Road for some mad reason, we're supposed to be investigating what's happened on the Western Shore. Which implies that at some point we should turn . . . west.

Item: There were no watchtowers at the border, though that may be an artifact of bordering Sanctuary lands. But no border steadings, or Farmholds, or manor houses—not even in ruins. They're not standing empty. They're simply gone.

How and why?

This is all very interesting, but it doesn't explain what Hamphuliadiel is getting out of this. And there has to be something.

At midday, they stopped to rest and to eat. The driver unyoked the mules and hobbled them to graze, while the Sword Pages did the same for the destriers and the riding horses. Harwing set a simple boundary around the area with Shield—he could reinforce it if they were actually attacked. From the mule cart the Sword Pages extracted a canopy and some carpets, and (using the cart itself for two of the anchor points) had soon erected a pastoral shelter complete with a basket of spell-preserved provisions. The two komen took little interest in the hot food, but the contents of a wooden cask among the provisions seemed more than welcome.

Ulvearth had not moved from her seat on the cart during all this time.

"Come on," Harwing said gently, holding his hand up to her. "You should eat. And rest."

She regarded him with an expression of unsettling blankness, and he wondered again what Hamphuliadiel had done to her—and why she was here. Then she put her hand in his and allowed him to help her down and settle her at the edge of one of the carpets.

Harwing had the oddest sensation that they were being watched.

⊹⊱⊰⊹

He'd asked Belfarna to brew tea—since a Lightborn was of higher rank than a Sword Page—and moments later all but snatched a tea canister from her hands as she attempted to dump its entire contents into the kettle on the brazier.

"No. That's for hot water, not brewing, and that's too much tea anyway. Is there another teapot packed? Bring it."

Belfarna trudged grudgingly back toward the rear of the cart.

This was another point of evidence—not that Harwing needed it—for the Sword Pages, like their knightly masters, being upstarts from some Farmhold. Those of noble rank learned to properly brew tea as well as drink it: Belfarna had probably thought the small cylindrical box held a single pot's-worth of leaves.

He opened the canister and sniffed it to discover the blend. *"Rest after Sorrow."* How fitting.

"Here's your pot," Belfarna said grudgingly, returning with a large wicker basket. "Shall I make tea now?"

Harwing glanced over his shoulder. The two komen were still engrossed in their drinking, though Alleth had opened the hamper by his side and was rummaging desultorily through it. Araminon, the other Sword Page, was waiting beside the two komen for orders—though what they might want that wasn't within arm's reach was a mystery to Harwing. The muleteer was nowhere to be seen. *"Every act of kindness, even to an enemy, may be a blade in the dark against their overlord."* He forced himself to smile engagingly at Belfarna.

"Rather than that, I would be grateful if you were to allow me to make the tea and serve you with it, so you will see how it is done." Harwing took the wicker basket from Belfarna's hands. "Proper tea is one of the ornaments of a noble household. Thoromarth Oronviel was heard to say this many times."

Belfarna knelt down beside Harwing, though she still looked suspicious. Harwing opened the lid of the hamper. It contained a simple earthenware teapot such as anyone might pack for a journey, several plain earthenware cups, and several more of the small cherrywood canisters—including one filled with honey-disks.

"Do you think Araminon will wish a cup of tea as well?" Harwing asked. It was well to know how many would drink before filling the pot.

"Him?" Belfarna said in derision. "He's Komen Garmund's son."

That seemed to settle the question in Belfarna's mind, and the rude noise Araminon made hearing his name mentioned seemed to confirm the matter. Harwing removed the red clay brewing pot from its nest and closed the hamper carefully. He rinsed the pot with water from the teabrazier to warm it, measured in enough Rest after Sorrow for three, and closed the hamper again.

"It seems like a lot of work for a hot drink," Belfarna said. Her voice now held more curiosity than resentment.

"I suppose," Harwing said. "But sometimes it's nice to be able to focus on something other than your problems. Besides, there are many far more complicated rituals to perform if one serves in the Great Keep of a High House."

"Did you? What was it like?" Belfarna asked eagerly.

I was a stableboy before I was Called. But that truth wouldn't serve him here, and another one would.

"I served Thoromarth Oronviel, as I have said. I was many times in the hall of his Great Keep, for he gave wondrous feasts and entertainments. If you have never seen one, you cannot imagine how enormous a Great Keep is—take a hundred Sanctuaries of the Star and pile them all together, and you will barely begin to sketch its outline. Why, the kitchens alone were large enough that Lord Thoromarth could feast all the castel and all the village at once, and even such a humble and necessary place was made beautiful, though only the servants would ever see it."

Belfarna's eyes were wide with wonder, and Harwing went on spinning tales about Harvest Courts, and battlefields, and the glory of seeing the whole meisne of Oronviel ride forth to war. When the tea was brewed, he mentally ran down the tables of rank and precedence that he had memorized in his Service Year at the Sanctuary, and served Ulvearth first, then Belfarna.

The Sword Page accepted her tea bowl a little doubtfully, making a face, and Harwing showed her how to drink it with a honey-disk clamped between her teeth. In the Sanctuary, their seniors had never let the Candidates put as much honey in their tea as they wanted, and so this custom had developed and been passed down to each new generation.

The taste of Rest after Sorrow brought back so many memories— good, bad, and bittersweet—that Harwing had to take several deep breaths to maintain his composure. *What would Gunedwaen say if he could see you weeping over a cup of tea? He would say: Do not waste your tears on the truth. Save them to ornament your lies, so they will be believed.*

"Did you ever go to war?" Belfarna blurted out. While Harwing had been distracted by the beautiful mechanics of tea, Belfarna had extracted from the hamper a loaf of bread that had been split open and filled with meat, cheese, and tart quince jam. Harwing cut modest slices of the loaf for himself and Ulvearth, and gave the rest to Belfarna, for the child's eyes had followed it hungrily and Harwing remembered always being hungry at that age. Seeing the way Belfarna wolfed down the meal—her shoulders hunched, her back to Araminon and the komen—only served to further convince Harwing that she was not being properly fed.

They were on their third cups of tea when the two komen finally bestirred themselves, shouting for Lendrod. The muleteer appeared shortly thereafter. Harwing quickly collected the cups and rinsed them before packing them away, and then emptied the pot, rinsed it, and packed everything back into the hamper.

"Shouldn't I be doing that?" Belfarna asked.

"In time," Harwing assured her. "I have much to teach, if you would learn."

Before Belfarna could answer, Araminon thumped her—hard—between the shoulders. "Come on, you lazy narrat—I'm not doing all the work by myself!" He looked toward the hamper curiously. "What's in there? Let me see."

He grabbed for the hamper. Harwing picked it up and stepped back. "No," he said succinctly.

Araminon's face darkened with anger. "We aren't in Areve now, Lightborn! You have to do what I say!"

The idiocy of the statement actually startled Harwing into laughter. Without Lightborn, there'd be no Healing, or pest-free harvest, nor a hundred dozen other things. *I have gotten so used to being free that I find a child's rudeness discomfiting.* Before he could respond, Garmund came toward them. "What's going on?" he asked Araminon.

"The Lightborn has a box and he won't let me see it."

"That's right," Harwing said blandly. "You're a miserable rude un-schooled child and you would not be allowed to live in a Farmholder's pigsty, let alone in a Great House. To call yourself a Sword Page is an insult to your betters—of whom, one presumes, there are many."

Araminon looked confused and irritated. Garmund reasoned his way through Harwing's sentence and then slapped his son hard enough to make him stagger. "Leave the witches alone, boy. Now go pack up."

Araminon picked up the beer barrel and slouched resentfully in the direction of the cart. Belfarna glanced from Harwing to Garmund and then went to secure the hamper of provisions and follow Araminon.

"Witches." No highborn ever called us that—Lightborn, and Mages, and Green Robes, and sometimes even sorcerers, yes, but not witches. More evidence that friend Garmund was never komen until he told Ham-phuliadiel he was. Harwing didn't know what use the information would be to him, but Gunedwaen had taught him that all facts were useful.

"So what's in the box, Green Robe?" Garmund said. He had an easy smile on his face, and Harwing was instantly mistrustful. *He has lost face, and will try to reassert himself by violence. Shall I let him—or shall I escalate the conflict?*

"Tea. A teapot to brew it in. Some cups. Nothing more."

"You Lightborn and your tea," Garmund said, shaking his head as if in amusement. "Keep it if you want. There's just one thing."

Harwing braced himself. "And what's that?"

The blow came as expected. Harwing set only the faintest touch of Shield against it—enough to cushion the blow, but not enough to keep him upright. He obligingly fell sprawling, dropping the box gently to the grass while making it look as if it had been thrown from his arms. For good measure, he let the Shield around the encampment fall, as if his concentration had been broken.

"I don't want to hear 'no' from you again," Garmund said.

CHAPTER THREE

THVNDER MOON TO FIRE MOON IN THE TENTH YEAR OF THE HIGH KING'S REIGN: EVERYTHING THAT RISES MVST CONVERGE

Every act of kindness, even to an enemy, may be a blade in the dark against their overlord.

—Harwing Lightbrother, *The Blade with Three Edges*

The sun was westering. There had been no sign of castel, manor, farm, or the Domain Emellas border, which was west of them, and which they must cross sometime if they were to go toward the Shore. Rolumienion seemed to not be just uninhabited, but erased: there were no marker stones along the road (which was overgrown), no sign of manor house or farmstead or marketplace. Not even a border tower.

Nothing.

Clearly Garmund was looking for some place with walls and a roof to spend the night, and—equally clearly—he was not going to find one.

Harwing put out a hand and touched Lendrod on the arm. The muleteer regarded him with dull indifference.

"We need to make camp for the night while there's still enough light to see by," Harwing said. "Stop here and unharness the mules. I see no difference between this place and any other place in Rolumienion, and I will conjure a spring to water them as soon as I may."

"They'll be safe here?" Lendrod asked. "My ladies?"

He must mean the mules. "Yes. I will cast a Shield around this place," Harwing said. "And wards to watch over us while we sleep." Shield would keep out everything—but Harwing could only maintain Shield while he was awake. The wards would be of limited effectiveness at keeping out things like spears or arrows. And he now doubted Ulvearth was able, let alone willing, to help.

If it had not been for Ulvearth, Harwing would have left the party almost at once. But Ulvearth, as Lightborn, was as dear to him as any blood-kin. He could not have taken her away without people noticing, since she rode on the cart. He'd wait for tonight to make his move. The two of them could be far away by morning.

Lendrod brought the mules to a halt. Harwing dismounted and tied his mount's reins to the back of the cart. The komen still rode serenely northward, apparently oblivious to the mutiny in their ranks.

Harwing dug in his bag for a handful of uncharged spellstones and paced the bounds of the area he'd chosen, dropping a spellstone at each of the eight compass points (when you didn't have a boundary, you made one). That finished, he returned to the cart. The mules had been unhitched and were grazing placidly. Harwing untacked his horse, rubbed her down with a tuft of grass, then hobbled her and turned her out as well. He was just feeling around for some underground water he could coax to the surface when his concentration was rudely shattered.

"Hey, you! Green Robe! What do you think you're doing?" Garmund bellowed. Apparently he'd finally noticed there was no one following him.

"Making camp!" Harwing shouted back cheerily.

Alleth turned his mount and trotted back. Belfarna followed him on foot. She had both destriers in tow, and the animals were following reluctantly, ears flat. *I know they are wearing Quieting charms. Maybe they're defective ones?*

"Well, Lightborn, you seem to know your business," Alleth said, swinging down off his horse's back. At the same moment, one of the destriers decided it had been patient for long enough. It shook its head and danced, then turned to bite its companion.

Harwing reacted without thought, snapping Shield into place to protect the destriers from each other as he shouted at Belfarna to drop both leads. At the same moment he cast Sleep over the two horses and expanded Shield over the whole campground. The horses both stopped and stood quietly, heads down. "They should be easier to handle now," Harwing said mildly.

The only sound was the scream of a pair of hunting hawks overhead. Shield turned the afternoon sky an intense lapis color. Alleth was staring at him as if he'd grown a second head. Within the bounds of Shield the grass held eerily still, making the sunlight seem even warmer.

I know you are no komen, for even a hedge-knight would know what Lightborn magic can do. The question is, do I tell you so? Or wait until you admit it? "I'd like to check the Quieting charms on your warhorses, if you permit," Harwing said, as if nothing had happened. "They seem rather skittish."

"Oh, Garmund took those off when we started up again," Alleth said. "He says it makes them too logy to work."

"Well, removing them makes them want to kill each other, and probably everything else in sight. If you want to improve their tempers, gallop them before you hobble them for the night. And I'll find their Quieting charms and make sure they're fully charged."

"Do I answer to you now?" Alleth asked. He didn't sound irate, just curious.

"Would you really rather answer to Garmund?" Harwing asked. "I am a Lightborn acting as envoy to the Western Shore. That gives me a higher rank than my escort. Which is you." If nobody had mentioned that before, Harwing would repair the lapse. A troop must have a leader, and he didn't trust Garmund at all.

Shield rippled in waves of purple light as it was struck repeatedly from without. Harwing did not need to look to know that Garmund was hammering at it with the pommel of his dagger.

Alleth's look of amiability didn't change. "Then I'd best see to saddling Dewdrop," he said, nodding toward the destrier.

Harwing dropped Shield. Garmund came on at a quick trot, only reining in his mount when the alternative would have been to trample Harwing.

Ulvearth still sat on the mule cart's seat, gazing placidly and silently at nothing.

"What do you think you're doing, Green Robe?" Garmund bawled. "*I* say when we stop—and where!"

"If you like," Harwing said indifferently, raising Shield around the campsite once again. "But the rest of us are stopping here."

He watched as Garmund hesitated over his sword and reached for his whip instead. Harwing raised his hand and cast Fetch. The whip flew from Garmund's hand to Harwing's.

"I am a Lightborn, trained in the Sanctuary of the Star, member of the Warhunt, and disinclined to deal with your posturing. I am Hamphuliadiel Astromancer's envoy to the Western Shore, and without me you do not have heat, light, water, or defense from the Beastlings, who—may I remind you?—have overrun the West. If you can tell me there's a better place to make camp within a halfmark's ride, I am willing to go there, but I doubt you can. Further, I need time to see to your destriers, so if you will be so good as to tell me what you did with their Quieting charms, I can begin."

"I will kill you in your sleep," Garmund rumbled, his face turning dark with rage.

"Did I mention I rode with the Warhunt?" Harwing said. "What do you imagine that is? If you were a true and real komen I would ask where I faced you in battle, but I know the answer to that already. Now. The charms, please. Or I bespell you and send you back to the Sanctuary stripped naked and tied backwards on your horse."

Garmund dismounted and took a step toward Harwing. Harwing did not move. He cast a complex series of spells—the Postulants had crafted such spell-series for their entertainment during Sanctuary training and oh how long ago that all seemed now—and Garmund's dagger slipped gracefully from its sheath to hover above Harwing's outstretched palm, spinning slowly end over end. "*Lightborn,*" Harwing repeated. "I call no one my master. Not even Hamphuliadiel."

There was a long tense moment, which Garmund's son Araminon broke with laughter. "If you think I am doing all your chores, witch-boy, you're wrong!"

"Give the Green Robe his charms," Garmund said to Araminon in a deadly voice. He stalked off.

"Annoying Lord Garmund is a really bad idea," Araminon said gleefully.

"You know very little about Lightborn. Now give me the charms."

Araminon hesitated, and it was clear he intended to play games. Harwing cast the strongest instance of Fetch he could wield. One of the pouches at Araminon's belt jerked loose and flew into Harwing's hand. Harwing opened it and pulled out the two charms before tossing the empty pouch to the ground.

Araminon backed away, looking sick.

Did they really not know what Lightborn could do? They who live at Rosemoss and do the Astromancer's bidding? Where in all of Leaf and Star did Hamphuliadiel find these people? "Take the riding horses, untack them, rub them down, hobble them, and turn them out. If you mistreat any living thing here, you will not enjoy the consequences," Harwing said.

Ignoring Araminon, he walked toward the destriers. Dewdrop was saddled and ready. His stablemate was ground-tied a short distance away. Alleth regarded Harwing curiously.

"Everything's fine," Harwing said. A Quieting charm required some of the subject's hair, herb lavender, a small twist of silver wire, and an amber bead. The charm was woven or knotted into its target's hair and removed when the effect was to be mitigated. He stroked the destrier's forehead, identified Dewdrop's charm, and braided it back into the gelding's forelock. Dewdrop shook his head, throwing off the last of the Sleep spell, and then nosed at Harwing's chest.

"I have nothing for you, greedy one," Harwing said fondly. "After your gallop, we shall see." They might not have been trained destriers—if they had been, Alleth, Garmund, and both Sword Pages would be dead by now—but they hardly deserved the treatment they were being subjected to.

Alleth vaulted into the saddle and collected the reins. Harwing dropped Shield again, and horse and rider galloped forth. Dewdrop seemed happy for the chance to run.

"What's this one's name, do you know?" Harwing asked Belfarna as he combed through the remaining warhorse's mane and then began to braid the charm into place.

"Sunbeam," Belfarna said, shrugging.

They cannot have been given such names at birth. So they were stolen, or lost, and their new owners name them as if they were barnyard creatures. No wonder the heart goes out of them. "Well," Harwing said, "let us call up a wellspring so that Sunbeam may drink, and then we can attend to the other beasts."

⊰⧈⊱

That evening the atmosphere was cool in a way that had nothing to do with the long summer twilight. Garmund snarled and grumbled and raged—quite audibly—about impertinent witches and jumped-up Landbonds, and Alleth remained miraculously deaf to everything he said. Under the pretext of unpacking, Araminon ransacked the wagon. He was obviously looking for the wicker hamper Harwing had forbidden him to touch, but was willing to destroy anything he found—such as the cage with the spellbirds, which he immediately opened.

The freed spellbirds battered themselves against the walls of Shield until they dissipated. Once he figured out what had happened, Garmund beat Araminon with his horsewhip, and Araminon squalled like a boiled cat, but it was clear no particular damage had been done to him, and that this was a fairly regular occurrence.

And now there is no way to send word to the Sanctuary of the Star; spellbirds return to the location where they were made.

As Harwing finished unpacking the cart he made a quick inventory; there were two more casks of wine and a second huge hamper of spell-preserved food.

Item: Either we are actually going somewhere and will arrive at our destination in the next four to five sunturns, or . . .

Item: Someone or multiple someones will die within the next two sunturns, after which the survivors will return to the Sanctuary.

Item: The food and the wine will run out long before the fodder. There's enough of it here for a fortnight. Why?

That was the real question. Why?

Alleth was harmless and agreeable. Belfarna was young enough to be turned into whatever Hamphuliadiel wanted. Garmund and Araminon were troublemakers, but troublemakers were easy to "disappear" in Hamphuliadiel's little fief. Harwing was fairly sure he'd gotten away with his own impersonation of a loyal and subservient minion. Ulvearth moved like a creature bespelled—like Harwing, she was one of the abducted Lightborn; her home domain was Amrolion.

Could Hamphuliadiel possibly just be sending her home? Unlikely. But . . .

At this point in his repeated musings, Harwing's thoughts always hit a wheel-rut on the road of knowledge and halted. There was no need to go to all this trouble and expense to kill any of them, and Hamphuliadiel was notoriously cheap, so he must have some other goal in mind.

It was a pity Harwing couldn't figure out what it was.

Doesn't matter. Once everyone's asleep, I'll bespell them so they stay asleep. I'll free the destriers, and take Ulvearth and all three riding horses, and go . . .

Where?

Doesn't matter. Decision's made.

After he was sure the komen were occupied and Araminon wasn't looking for more trouble, Harwing unrolled his and Ulvearth's bedrolls under the wagon and set up the tea-brazier. (He suspected Belfarna would be joining them: Alleth was not a brutal master, but neither was he a protective one.) It was full dark when all these small tasks had been completed, and Harwing brewed tea. Outside the perimeter of Shield, the sparks of watching eyes could be seen in the long grass.

They could not all be foxes.

Eventually Garmund drank himself unconscious, Alleth rolled himself up in a blanket, and Araminon stopped sniveling. Ulvearth went where she was led and stayed where she was left. There were spiced meat pies in the hamper, and Harwing appropriated six of them for the evening's meal. (Another thing to wonder about: Why were they being fed so luxuriously if they were going to be killed?) He ate two, Belfarna ate three, and Ulvearth picked one to pieces and mechanically ate the crumbs.

Harwing drank tea. Belfarna and Lendrod made their beds in the wagon. Ulvearth lay down in her bedroll. Lendrod soon began to snore.

Harwing continued to drink tea. After another half-mark, he set Sleep on all of the Lightless. In another candlemark or so, he'd make his preparations to leave, and hope Ulvearth would come with him.

⊰🙰⊱

It was deep night when Harwing awoke. Someone was singing. *(What?)* Shield was down. He restored it automatically and it flared a bright purple.

How in the name of Pelashia Flower Queen did I fall asleep?
And who's singing?

No, not singing. Not quite. It was a wordless humming that seemed at any moment to be about to resolve itself into a tune, but that moment never came.

He looked under the wagon. Both bedrolls were empty. Where was Ulvearth? Harwing got to his feet. He cast Silversight, turning in a slow circle as he searched for what had awakened him. Out of the corner of his eye he saw movement. Ulvearth was kneeling on the rug where Araminon and the two komen slept. Harwing saw her hands move, but even with Silversight he could not be sure of what she was doing, for her cloak concealed her upper body and the sleeping komen blocked the rest of her.

But when she stood up, the blood on her knife and her robes was very clear.

It was a carving knife, Harwing's mind told him, with an unbreakable grip on inessentials. Komen who made no other preparation for a long journey almost always carried tools to dress out deer or other game they hunted along the way. Harwing did not think, somehow, that these komen would be doing any more hunting.

He ran toward Ulvearth. She turned to meet him, walking slowly, an eerie and frightening smile on her face.

"Sister, what are you doing?" he asked quietly. He reached out for her wrist and took the knife away. She surrendered it easily, her smile unshakable.

"They must die, for they are Lightless. This is what must be." Her voice was soft and reasonable, as if she were a teacher explaining matters to a pupil who was inclined to be difficult.

"No. No, I—"

He never knew afterward how the sentence he was about to utter would have gone. There was a sudden thunderous hammering coming from every direction at once.

He wasn't sure what happened next, only that the dark was very deep.

⊰⊱

For a long time, Harwing Lightbrother simply assumed he was dead. It was dark, he was warm, nothing hurt, and he couldn't remember how these things had happened.

It was the screaming that roused him from his happy delusion. Someone was being tortured. *Ulvearth?* He sat up quickly, hit his head—*hard!*—and rebounded, barely managing to avoid banging his head against the floor.

"Sword and Star—I thought you were dead!" Belfarna's voice untangled the rest of Harwing's memories. The weirdly implausible mission. Ulvearth's madness. The attack.

"What happened?" Harwing asked. *And where are the others?*

"The Beastlings overran us. They killed Alleth, Garmund, and Araminon, then brought us here. The two of us, I mean. They took the Lightsister and Old Lendrod somewhere else."

If he was to have help—and answering questions was help of a sort—Harwing would need to tell Belfarna the truth, though that went against every tenet of his training. "No. Ulvearth did that. I saw her do it, just before the attack. And I wish I knew why." Harwing wasn't sure he wanted to put the idea into Belfarna's mind that Lightborn could spontaneously go mad, but on the other hand, concealing the truth could have dire consequences.

"She killed them? How? I thought you witches weren't allowed to kill things."

"With the *Light*," Harwing said. "We aren't allowed to kill using *the Light*. She stabbed them to death."

"But why?" Belfarna asked. She sounded curious, not grief-stricken.

"Bespelled to do it, I think," Harwing said. "I'm sorry," he added awkwardly. "I know how hard it is to lose someone."

Belfarna laughed a little, the sound forlorn and sad. "They weren't my friends. I didn't even know Komen Alleth that well, and he was my master. He owed some debt to my father, so that when Da died, Alleth promised to train me. I don't think he really knew how, but I like horses and becoming a knight sounded a lot better than spending a lifetime digging ditches for a jumped-up witchborn. It wasn't a hard choice."

Harwing was about to say something when the scream came again. "What's that sound?" It sounded very human, but that could be a trick.

"The Lightsister, I think. All the way here the Beastlings kept asking me what was wrong with her. I didn't know—and I wouldn't have said if I did." There was no particular emotion in Belfarna's voice.

"Don't be afraid," Harwing said. "I'll get us out of here."

Belfarna laughed again, and this time the sound held more mockery than melancholy. "My mam was from Cirandeiron. I mean, when anyone was still there, you know? When I was growing up, she told me stories about fighting the Beastlings, and I guess she even fought them a couple of times before we went to the Sanctuary. They aren't as scary as the Astromancer is. I think I'd rather be here than there."

"We'll escape," Harwing said again. *Somehow.*

This time Belfarna didn't bother to answer.

⚏

Spellmother Frause gazed down at her subject. The witch-woman lay on the bed in the gathering house—was tied to the bed, actually, since she was a danger to herself and others. Whatever had injured the witch's mind was a type of sorcery Frause had never seen before—and she had been healing the injuries of the Folk and crafting spells against their enemies since she was little more than a cub.

It had been purest luck that their paths had crossed. Frause, and the other survivors of the battle for the Western Shore, had been heading eastward. They had expected to rest and reprovision when they reached Centaur Newtown.

When Frause and the others had arrived at Centaur Newtown, the village had been abuzz with the news that a scouting party had left the Witch King's Tower. The group had been overrun and destroyed, but there were four survivors.

Although one of them probably wouldn't survive for very long.

Frause longed for her forest's cool green shadows. Her hidel in Forest Northendegryn now seemed further away than ever, but in case this was some new threat that the Folk would have to deal with, Frause had asked to take possession of the witch-woman, so that she could study the spell.

She'd had little luck so far. The Bearward Spellmother sighed and turned back to her table of herbs and potions.

Just as well I was here. If the witchborn have learned new spells, we need to know about them before our Rune runs into them in the war, Frause thought. She ran her fingers over the witchborn's green cloak, which lay neatly folded at the edge of Frause's worktable, along with the rest of the clothing the Elf had been wearing. Most of the spell that clouded the witchborn's mind was in the cloak's embroidery—that was how it had passed undetected at first—but Frause's attempts to unpick the threads and undo the spell caused the Elven witch agonizing pain.

You are growing too soft for this work if something like that moves your heart, Spellmother. You saw what these butchers did upon the Shore. Why should this one not suffer as we have?

"Because dead Elvenkind can't talk," she told herself aloud.

"Does she yet live?" Healer Helda asked, entering the chamber. Keloit, Frause's last cub, was Helda's mate, and Spellmother Frause gave all praise to the Tribal that Keloit had survived the battle in the West relatively unscathed.

"She does," Frause said. "I don't know why I bother with all this. *Burhealdor* Vithimir will just kill her along with the others. And if he does not, Deornoth will."

"Why not ask why Vithimir brought back prisoners at all?" Helda said. "Oh, not the old one—the Woodwose will make the rest of his life sweet and easy. And the child may be young enough to reclaim. But the *witchborn*—!"

"Will die," Frause said firmly. "But not before I have discovered how this spell works." Frause picked up a tiny knife from her worktable and began heating it in the flame of a lamp. When she looked down at her subject, the witchborn's eyes were open. Watching her.

The witchborn's face was pale, her eyes feverish. Her body was gaunt with privation and marred with the scars of many beatings. Those scars had been given to her by another, and Frause wondered who could have dared to harm a witchborn, for she had always thought they were great powers in their stolen lands.

"Do you thirst, Elf?" Helda asked gently. The Elf-woman nodded fractionally. Her mouth worked as she tried to speak, but it was too dry. Helda poured a spouted cup full of sweet water and held it to the woman's lips, raising her head with her other paw.

"Burn . . . Burn my robes," the witchborn whispered once she had drunk. She began to choke. Only the leather straps binding her to the bed kept her body from thrashing as she convulsed again.

Frause stared at the Elf for barely a heartbeat before seizing one of the bottles on her worktable. She motioned to Helda to hold the Elf's head still, and pried open her jaws with one long claw. She poured the tincture of Night's Daughter into her subject's mouth. It took only a few breaths to do its work, and her captive fell unconscious.

"If I burn her garments, I may never trace the spell to its roots," Frause complained.

Her marriage-daughter looked at her with loving exasperation. "You wanted to know how to break the spell. Burn her clothing as she says. Question her when she wakes."

"Hah," Frause said derisively. "As if she will survive the spell-breaking."

"Maybe the other witch knows how it was worked," Helda offered.

"Perhaps," Frause said musingly.

⊰⊱

Sometime after dark, their prison was opened. Harwing blinked at the sudden brightness of lit torches. All he could see was legs and hooves (vaguely equine and twelve in number). Centaurs, then. That didn't bode well for the future. He tried to get to his feet, but the sharp end of a pike was pointed at him and Harwing was told to stay where he was.

"I am not talking to a chicken coop, Spellmother," a deep male voice said. "If you want me to hear what the witchborn has to say, bring him out."

"If you insist." The voice sounded feminine, but not quite Elven.

"Doesn't matter either way," a new—also female—voice said. "We have to get the other one out anyway."

"Hey! What? *No!*" Belfarna said, scuttling as far back from the door as she could.

"Oh come on," the female voice said in exasperation. Someone got down on their hands and knees and crawled into the coop, ignoring Harwing.

It was an Elf.

It took Harwing a moment to realize that, for she was outlandishly garbed and disguised. She wore a short tunic with feathers and ribbons sewn to it, and where her skin showed, it was painted in the way some komen painted their destriers. The effect was . . . exotic. And unsettling. What were *Elvenkind* doing here with Beastlings?

"Hello, boy," the woman said to Belfarna. "My name is Khimle. You're going to come and live with me now, and you'll never be cold or hungry again."

"She is not a boy. And she's a Sword Page," Harwing said, spurred by some perverse imp of negative helpfulness. "She probably hasn't been that cold or hungry."

"Shut up, witchborn," Khimle said matter-of-factly. She leaned in to whisper something in Belfarna's ear. The girl made a faintly alarmed sound, and Khimle laughed. "Like that," Khimle said, and when she backed out of the coop, Belfarna followed her.

Harwing wasn't sure what he was supposed to feel about Belfarna having been taken away to a fate unknown, but he decided he didn't care. He wasn't even certain what he felt about the sight of Elvenkind living with Beastlings the way Khimle obviously was.

He was so *tired*.

"Now come out, witchborn," the other female voice said firmly. "And mind your manners."

Meekly, Harwing crawled out of the chicken coop and got to his feet.

The speaker was a Bearward.

Harwing had heard of Bearwards, and studied them during his time at the Sanctuary, but they were creatures of deep forest and he'd never expected to see one. The female was covered in fur the color of dark honey, and wore necklets and armlets and a long vest over a wide sash of printed blue fabric that was wrapped around her torso in such a way as to provide an assortment of available pockets. Her head was rounder than that of a bear, with a shorter muzzle and higher forehead. She looked as much like an actual bear as Centaurs looked like horses (there were three of them here, all looking as if they wanted to kill him). Harwing regarded her long claws. (Her *very* long claws.) He wondered giddily if they made things harder to grasp, or easier.

Then he noticed the Minotaur.

Bearwards were not small creatures. Even the females towered over the average Elf by a cubit or more. But Minotaurs made Bearwards look . . . dainty. The Minotaur standing beside the Bearward was very tall. He was black as a raven's feathers from head to tail, against which the pale amber of his eyes was a startling contrast. His enormous curving horns had been painted and gilded in an elaborate pattern, and the tips looked sharp. His face and head were perceptibly bovine, but no beast's eyes had ever held such a look of intelligence. The hair on his skull and torso was thick and curly, and seemed to grow down his spine as well. He had a tufted tail, which at the moment was switching irritably. He wore boots, a kilt, leather bracers, and a short vest. Every article of his clothing was finely made and ornamented—if it had been one of the Elvenborn dressed so, Harwing would have assumed him to be one of the Lords Komen at the very least.

I wonder if he gets down on his hands and knees to eat grass?

"This is Deornoth, who is King-Emperor Leutric's eyes and ears here

in the West," the Bearward said, indicating the Minotaur. "I am Spellmother Frause, Bearward of Forest Thendegryn, foster mother to the
Elvenborn called Rune who is blood brother to my lastling Keloit. Deornoth would know what you know of the Witch-King and his evil, and
I am to ensure your answers are true. I would have sent my apprentice
instead, save that I must do at least as much for you as I would do for a
dog, and I would make known to a dog that his master or his mate was
gone, never to come again." Her muzzle wrinkled in an expression Harwing couldn't interpret, and her teeth looked very sharp.

"Ulvearth Lightsister is dead," Harwing guessed.

"Yes. Will you tell me what you knew of her? I am afraid it will make
no difference: you will be executed regardless." Frause sounded almost
apologetic.

"Yes, of course. Thank you. I was planning to die soon anyway," Harwing answered politely. He felt giddy and lightheaded, cut off from the
emotions he probably ought to be feeling right now.

(Like panic.)

"You could not have been planning to die before you came here,"
Spellmother Frause said reprovingly.

"I could so have," Harwing protested irritably. "I was sent west by
the Astromancer because Delfierarathadan had burned. I planned to go
back to the Sanctuary and kill him. After which the other Lightborn
there would certainly kill me."

The Minotaur stopped fidgeting and stared at him. "This Astromancer of yours sounds interesting," he said noncommittally.

"And evil. Don't forget that part," Harwing answered.

"Hm," the Minotaur said. "Come with us, witchling. I think we have
much to say to each other. And you may not necessarily die."

⫸⫷

The next campaign Runacar had meant to mount after the Battle of
the Western Shore had been the capture of the Sanctuary of the Star
and the destruction of its village. Now that would have to wait.

*"The High King comes west. The High King comes at the head of all
her army."*

When Runacar brought Melisha's warning to Leutric, King-Emperor of the Folk, Leutric immediately threw himself into preparations for the battle and did so with a desperate fervor, for the Folk believed that if the High King crossed into the West, disaster would follow. Runacar believed that if Vieliessar managed to pass through the Dragon's Gate and gain the Western Reach, Runacar's army could never force her east again.

And so Runacar's entire plan of battle came down to one single stratagem: get there first. Runacar had no intelligence about the state and number of the High King's forces, and no way of getting any. For that matter, he had no idea of the state of his *own* forces, for after the apocalyptic end of the Battle for the Western Shore, the survivors of his army had scattered to the nine winds. Even so, he did not wait to construct a plan of campaign, or even wait for supplies to be gathered. What he needed must join him along the way, or he must do without: reaching the pass before Lord Vieliessar was vital. And to win, the Otherfolk not only had to reach the Western Pass of the Dragon's Gate before King Vieliessar's army did, but—if they could—reach the central Ceoprentrei Valley and prepare the battleground in advance.

Runacar refused even to imagine defeat, even though to win, the Otherfolk would need not just a general, but a miracle. He was no longer War Prince Runacarendalur Caerthalien, first among the Hundred Houses. He was Runacar Houseborn, the King-Emperor's Battlemaster and General. And if a miracle was what was needed, Runacar intended to find one. He had spent a decade of Wheelturns fighting to give the Otherfolk the West and their freedom, and he was not about to let what he had won with cunning and sword fall once more to the land-hunger of the *alfaljodthi*.

⊹⊟⊢⊹

As they marched (a fine and inaccurate word for what Runacar's force actually did) they crossed the track of Elves who had survived the fall of Daroldan, but not even Runacar's aerial scouts could find them. Possibly they'd already reached the Sanctuary of the Star—it was the only way for them to vanish in so short a time.

For a few days after that Runacar worried about attack, but either the Sanctuary and its Mad Astromancer hadn't noticed his army (difficult to imagine) or it didn't have the resources to engage them.

And as the sunturns passed, determination became leavened by hope.

Each day's march ended the same way: with three candlemarks of drilling his foot soldiers (he could never decide whether the Centaurs should count as cavalry or not), and another lecture on strategy and tactics, all accompanied by more politeness, tact, and actual fawning than a Less House would have used to woo a High House bride for its Prince-Heir. Runacar wasn't sure whether or not he missed the days when he'd given orders, not explanations, but there was no use wishing for them; they were gone forever.

Runacar's days did not end at sunset, nor begin at dawn. There were a thousand things an army must do to be prepared to march, and this army must do them *on* the march. Runacar set his students, his apprentices, and as many of the veterans of the Eastern Shore as he could, to implementing evening and morning battle drills to teach the newcomers to the army the basics of how to fight against a large group when you were a member of another large group.

The battle drills were complicated things, and as often as not ended in a complete tangled mess, but Runacar persevered. More of the Woodwose rode on horseback now than he'd ever seen do so before, but they viewed horses as a means of transportation and not as an extra weapon, and he did not have enough time to convince them—or their ponies—otherwise. They rode their horses to likely hunting grounds and then hunted on foot; Runacar wished they hunted from horseback, so he could take those skills and shape them for war, but it was unlikely the Woodwose would spontaneously become cavalry in a handful of sunturns just because it would be convenient. He would adapt to what he had.

The Centaurs, the Minotaurs, the Woodwose, and even the Bearwards he could drill in tactics, because those tactics had been defined and refined for use by people who were shaped and sized roughly like him, but they wouldn't work nearly as well for those who were not. So those others—the Fauns, the Brownies, the Wulvers, the Palugh, the Hippogriffs, and more—Runacar lectured. He taught anyone who would listen (at least the Gryphons would listen) the principles of warfare.

Objectives, strategy, tactics—what you wanted and what you would give up to get it.

What you had to have to fight before you even started.

How to tell when your side was losing and what to do about it.

At first, only Andhel, Tanet, and the Gryphons came to listen with the others, but soon all the Woodwose came, and with them Centaurs, Minotaurs, even Brownies. After a few sennights, Radafa could recite the text of Arilcarion's *The Way of the Sword* flawlessly from beginning to end, and occasionally Runacar heard the Gryphons arguing among themselves about the meanings of some of the verses. It made his head hurt if he listened, so he tried not to.

In his bleakest moments, he knew he was riding to his own death. Winning meant killing his Soulmate. (*Vieliessar Farcarinon. High King.*) Winning meant *dying*.

To the Otherfolk, he would die a hero.

And after that the Otherfolk would join him in death, because not one of them—even Andhel—was capable of waging war on the scale that would follow the High King's death.

That was the crux of the matter, right there. Elvenkind were specialists in war. And despite the helpful attempts of the Hundred Houses to teach the Otherfolk how to fight (by slaughtering every one of them they could catch), the Otherfolk were still hopeless at it.

Oh, the Centaurs and the Minotaurs were good fighters. So were the Bearwards and the Woodwose. But that was in battles that were hardly more than skirmishes—small groups, strike-and-flee tactics barely distinguishable from those of a particularly inept band of outlaws. The Western Shore Campaign had taken ten Wheelturns and staggering amounts of diplomacy to put together, and at that Runacar's army had nearly fallen apart a hundred different times.

What Runacar's army *hadn't* done was work together. Not in the way an Elven army (like the one they were about to face) did. The Otherfolk were as factionalized as the Hundred Houses had been; the only difference was they hadn't spent thousands of turns of the Wheel fighting each other because of it.

There was one bright spot to the march east, and it hardly counted, since it couldn't affect the battle, but the Centaurs (Sword and Star knew how) had managed to scavenge a few trained destriers from somewhere, and brought them to him. They'd probably been young warhorses who had gotten lost during a battle, but the last battle in the West had been many Wheelturns ago and the beasts were woefully out of practice. Two were geldings, one was a mare, and the last was a stallion who was so grateful to be under saddle again that when he wasn't he tried to follow Runacar around like a dog. Runacar had no way of knowing their names, so he named them: Jiskadar, Folwin, Chanista, and Atishinan (which meant "Black Horse"—well, at least it was true). Runacar worked them gently in the morning drills, conditioning them and getting them to know and trust him. He still mourned Hialgo, the grey destrier he'd trained up from foal-hood, killed at the Battle of Daroldan.

But concentrating on what one did not have was an impulse Runacar had been trained out of early, so he focused instead on what he could improve with a recitation of *The Way of the Sword* and a few candle-marks of combat practice stolen from each day's march.

The army navigated by sun and stars, and each day Runacar's army grew larger. Ascensions of Gryphons, Wilds of Wulvers, Dances of Minotaurs, Droves of Centaurs. Flights of Hippogriffs, Tumbles of Fauns, Pounces of Palughs, Workings of Brownies—even the entire Mystery of Aesalions . . . all of them came.

To fight for their freedom. To fight for their lives. To fight for *him*. For Runacar Houseborn. For the High House Prince who fought for *them*.

By the time the army reached the far northern edge of what had once been Domain Ullilion, the Otherfolk army had acquired not only supplies, but a baggage train to carry them. The carts and horses came from the Centaurs, who had come out in force, but the supplies those carts carried came from the Brownies: tiny plump dark-skinned Elvish-appearing folk no taller than Runacar's forearm was long. Like many of the Otherfolk, the Brownies possessed magic, and were mysteriously able to clean and mend, gather and supply, and even cook large and delicious meals despite their diminutive size. Beyond that undeniable usefulness, Runacar privately suspected that no enemy wounded would long survive once Brownies took the field with their long sharp knives.

Each day the spark of hope Runacar nourished kindled more hotly. If the High King's army was larger, let it be so.

She had never faced such an army as his.

CHAPTER FOUR

THUNDER MOON TO FIRE MOON IN THE TENTH YEAR OF THE HIGH KING'S REIGN: A VALLEY OF DRY BONES

In war, it is often as important to know who knows a thing as it is
to know what they know. Ignorance, no matter who suffers from it,
is always a potent weapon.

—Gunedwaen Swordmaster, The Art of War

O nce upon a time the High King's enemies had gathered in a magical pavilion of shining gold to discuss how they would arrange her doom. Instead, she had defeated them in the Nine Battles, and for a time she and her councillors met beneath the same golden canopy to speak of bringing peace and justice to all the world.

Now the golden pavilion was gone, as were the councillors who had occupied it: Telthorelandor, Cirandeiron, Aramenthiali, Nantirworiel, Oronviel, and Vondaimieriel. Vieliessar hardly knew which of the abeyant Hundred Houses could claim even one surviving descendant now. Farcarinon—for example—numbered her and Rithdeliel, and that was all. Both gallantry and knighthood had been early casualties of the war, and the lineages of the Hundred Houses had become a fiction for heralds. Every House of the Grand Windsward had been erased; the Silver Swords of Penenjil were their only surviving relict. Every House of the Arzhana was gone, except for Thadan. Most of the nobility of the Uradabhur had been slaughtered in the Winter War and the civil wars and the insurrections and rebellions it had brought in its wake; the rest had died fighting the Endarkened.

Half her subjects died on the day of her Enthroning. More died after reaching sanctuary in Tildorangelor: of grief, or broken hearts, or carelessness in the face of their new enemy and its tools. More yet had died in the battles they waged between themselves.

Most of the two Wheelturns Vieliessar spent in Tildorangelor had been spent fighting against those who thought *they* should be High King. Or that there should be *no* High King. She had struck down every form of anarchy and imperium that rose up. Her people could not survive as a thousand quarreling households, and if she did not give them something to replace serfdom and privilege they would fall back into the old traps of slavery and exploitation.

She had sworn to replace the rule of might and privilege with law and justice—and to keep that vow, Vieliessar had turned to Guilds and Societies, social systems that at the time of the fall of the Hundred Houses had been used only by the Craftworkers. To abolish the traditional forms of governance her people had come to rely upon without setting something in their place would bring chaos. In addition, Guild memberships would cross the ancient lines of House fealty, further undermining the power of the War Princes angered by the loss of their traditional rights.

The Guild of the Lawspeakers had been formed almost simultaneously with the Lightborn Guild, and once there were three Guilds (Lawspeakers, Craftworkers, and Lightborn), it was inevitable that there would be more. The Guild of Knights (Mounted, Afoot, and Archers). The Farming Guild. The Horsemasters' Guild. None of what Vieliessar provided was glorious. But it was efficient. It worked.

And despite every change to their society and their lives, there was one constant: Vieliessar was High King, and the High King had a council. In these dark days Vieliessar's councillors and their offices were a mix of desperate pragmatism and ancient noble offices turned to new purposes.

Tuonil, titled Royal Huntmaster, was in charge of providing food, not entertainment; Lady Helecanth was Commander of a High King's Guard that did not exist. Shanilya Arshana was styled Mistress Cellarer—a title she had chosen herself, as (she said) rats lived in cellars—and performed some of the functions of Swordmaster in gathering and consolidating information. Nadalforo—a farmworker's daughter who had once led a Free Company—was present as Cadet Warlord. Lawspeaker

Commander Gelduin reported for the Law Lords—those who were the High King's eyes and ears and voice—and who were the people's eyes and ears and voice as well. Gatriadde Mangiralas, whose tireless work had not merely saved their surviving horses, but created the new breed suited to their new kind of war, had been Horsemaster. When Gatriadde was slain, Fierdind, who had been Cadet Horsemaster, became Horsemaster in his place. Aradreleg, as chief of the Healer's Society (Societies being subsets of Guilds, as Orders were subsets of Societies) was in charge of both Lightborn and Lightless Healers and reported to the High King, while Iardalaith, leader of the Society of Warhunt Mages, reported to the Warlord. The lines of report for the Council Lightborn—Thurion, Aradreleg, Iardalaith—showed the abrupt nature of Vieliessar's reforms all too clearly: Thurion was on the council not only because Vieliessar sometimes thought she would go mad if he was not, but as one of the two officers of the nascent (and by the mercy of the Light never to be invoked) Regency Council.

At the rustle of her councillors' arrival, she turned to greet them. There was no ceremony as each of them seated themselves on the cushions and low stools that were the chamber's only furnishing. But as the others seated themselves without fanfare, Rithdeliel stepped forward and knelt at Vieliessar's feet.

Nearly all of Vieliessar's people now dressed in the manner of Elven Foresters, in leathers and concealing cloaks of tattered and painted homespun. Lord Rithdeliel still wore sword and baldric and spurred boots; surcoat bearing the High King's device, and—when on the field— full armor. It did not matter to him that he must live in a tiny wooden house high in a tree and brew his own tea. Rithdeliel of Farcarinon was Warlord to the High King, and he would uphold that dignity with his dying breath. Vieliessar did sometimes wonder if Lord Rithdeliel had gone mad. But if he had, surely it was madness of a gentle and forgivable sort.

"My lord King, Rithdeliel Warlord answers your summons," he said, just as if this were some castel's great hall and she a War Prince holding court in the full glory and majesty of her rank.

"Rise, Lord Rithdeliel, for I have need of your wise counsel," Vieliessar answered, just as formally.

Rithdeliel rose fluidly to his feet, and followed her back to the center of the room. She lowered herself to a floor cushion and Rithdeliel took the last of the rude wooden seats.

Vieliessar regarded her council. All these disparate personalities—each intelligent, gifted, and loyal—were here not merely to advise, but to ensure that the High King's decisions were made openly and intelligently, without threat or favoritism. Of everything that had made up the world as it had been, only loyalty and trust remained.

And Vieliessar was about to betray it.

From the very beginning, she had lied to her people, and built her story lie upon lie, as delicately crafted as any work of diplomacy. Word that the Shore Domains were desperately embattled had come only a few moonturns before Vieliessar's Enthroning: at that time she had sent most of the Lightborn to aid them, announcing that she would soon send an even larger force.

But then the Endarkened came. By the time her folk headed west more than two Wheelturns later, they left Tildorangelor not only because they had exhausted her Light and her protection, but in the belief they journeyed to save the Western Shore.

But they did not march to succor the domains of Daroldan and Amrolion, though that remained the center of her lie. The true reason Vieliessar risked so much with this westward march was to reach the Great Library at the Sanctuary of the Star. If there was a defense against the Endarkened, knowledge of it would be there.

Nothing of this showed on her face as Vieliessar regarded her councillors.

"What do you have to say to me?" she asked.

"The harvest has been full," Tuonil said. "Much can be preserved. The folk will not starve, even with the losing of the winter planting and spring harvest."

"It is as Huntmaster Tuonil has said. There has been neither hoarding nor deliberate waste. The Law is satisfied," Lawspeaker Gelduin said.

Each member of her council spoke in turn; questioned, if necessary, by their fellow councillors or the High King herself. Their reports were a litany of challenges accepted and met, and that would have been both soothing and reassuring, if all present did not know what they were a prelude to.

"And now to the next matter that concerns us," Vieliessar said. "We must move, and soon. Thurion Lightbrother, how much longer can Saganath Flower Forest shelter us?"

"And provide a defense against the Endarkened as well?" Thurion answered wryly. "Not long. We depleted all of the Uradabhur Flower Forests far too deeply in the Winter War—and when we removed the boundary markers between domains we drew upon every copse and thicket with even a shard of Light. The smallest may never recover."

"Every Lightborn must make a speech to answer a question," Rithdeliel said. The mockery was not particularly barbed; Rithdeliel Warlord had long since given up making complaints about the presence of the Lightborn in council.

Thurion gave him a small ironic bow. "Never would I presume to tax the attention of one of the great Lords Komen, for their patience and intellect are a byword among the Lightborn. Thus: already Saganath Flower Forest begins to sicken. Within the moonturn, she will begin to die."

"So we must go soon," Rithdeliel said, nodding in acknowledgment of the riposte. "And while it is still summer. Even if the Dragon's Gate cannot be closed by weather—at least not any longer—" He paused as Nadalforo made a rude noise. "—our people will suffer if we must travel in the cold, nor will winter magically vanish once we reach the West."

"Vondaimieriel's nothing but hills and trees, and that's hard going now, summer or winter," Nadalforo (Cadet Warlord) said. The former First Sword of Stonehorse Free Company had fought many battles there before Caerthalien had wiped out the mercenary companies.

"And none of those trees is part of a Flower Forest," Thurion said. "The closest one on the western side is Enerwirchereth in Mangiralas, and that's a long distance to cover without shelter."

"What about Nomaitemil?" Vieliessar asked. "That's between Saganath and Enerwirchereth."

"In the Mystrals," Master Dandamir said with a shrug. "Somewhere."

"South through the Ceoprentrei valleys," Thurion said instantly. "It isn't really part of anyone's domain—Jaeglenhend and Vondaimieriel both claimed it, but it's outside the lawfully agreed-upon boundary markers of both domains."

"So Vondaimieriel didn't drain it," Aradreleg Lightsister said. "And neither did we. Even when we took down the boundary stones, I don't think anyone thought to shift the ones at the foot of the pass."

"Does Nomaitemil hold a Shrine?" Vieliessar asked Thurion. She knew the answer perfectly well, but the purpose of council was to share information with those who did not have it. Her people already tried to make her into a Greater Power; best that she refrain from making oracular speeches in council.

"No; the closest one is Shrine Manostar, on Vondaimieriel's western border. It's farther than Enerwirchereth by a sunturn or two. And Enerwirchereth is four sunturns' ride from the Vondaimieriel side of the pass."

"But a Shrine in a Flower Forest offers more protection than a Flower Forest alone," Nadalforo said. "If we can make Enerwirchereth, we can make Manostar."

"Agreed," Thurion said. "They're both small compared to Tildorangelor or even Arevethmonion, but on the other hand, they've had ten Wheelturns to recover from being tapped."

("We hope," Aradreleg Lightsister muttered under her breath.)

"To spend even four sunturns without refuge will be a difficult matter," Rithdeliel said with a magnificent understatement. "And—as you say—Manostar is two sunturns farther than Enerwirchereth."

It will be impossible, Vieliessar thought. *But we can't stay here and we can't retreat, and I must reach the Sanctuary of the Star!* "What of Vondaimieriel Great Keep?" Vieliessar asked. "It is nearer than either. Can we rest there before going on?"

"The Great Keep should be intact, both stones and wards," Iardalaith Lightbrother said slowly. "As it lies in the foothills of the Mystrals and hard upon the Northern Pass Road, it was the last place to be vacated in the war. That works in our favor. We expect that the whole of the Western Reach will be a ghostlands from the Mystrals to the Angarussa, but the worst of the damage should be west of the Sanctuary of the Star. Both we and our former enemy"—here Helecanth inclined her head in acknowledgment and Iardalaith flashed her a brief smile—"moved too fast after the False Parley—so called—to properly lay waste to the countryside east of Farcarinon."

"So Vondaimieriel Great Keep should be intact," Nadalforo said, nodding. "A skeleton garrison at best. And surely eager to open the castel gates to their overlord and King." She smiled wolfishly.

Vondaimieriel's War Prince had died in the civil wars following Vieliessar's Enthroning. Vieliessar had no idea who remained of Vondaimieriel's ruling house among her people; perhaps Lawspeaker Gollor or one of the knights-herald did. She might not be able to present Vondaimieriel with anyone it would recognize as a legitimate authority.

"Unlikely," Rithdeliel said briefly. "We shall have to fight for it."

"We have taken keeps before," Iardalaith said. "Once we have invested Vondaimieriel, we may be able to hold it even against the Endarkened. What we cannot do is feed ourselves while we do so."

"And either it still has stores—which means we will have to fight even harder to take it from whoever is guarding them—or it does not, in which case it stands empty and so shall we," Nadalforo said.

"That is a matter we can set aside for a while yet," Vieliessar said. "We must reach Vondaimieriel before we can cook supper in its kitchens."

"If we are to cook in their kitchens, at least that means we are not the kitchen rats," Thurion said with feigned lightness.

Aradreleg laughed sharply. "Rather would I be a kitchen rat than Lightborn did it mean I had a kitchen to skulk in."

"And rather would I be sitting in Caerthalien Great Keep with my every whim gratified," Helecanth responded briskly. "Of course, had our lord and liege not gained the Unicorn Throne, I should certainly have been dead long since."

The Endarkened would have come whether I was enthroned or not, Vieliessar reminded herself, even as Gelduin gently rebuked the others for wandering from the point.

"My lords, nobles, and gentles," Vieliessar said, and the cross-talk in the room was instantly silenced. "We cannot retreat and we cannot stay

here. To move forward requires not only destination, but method." She
smiled coaxingly at them all, for with the gaining of the High Kingship,
Vieliessar had returned to her earliest training: Kings and War Princes
might command and rage, but Lightborn asked and persuaded. "And so
I have an idea that I wish to set before you. . . ."

⊣⊨⊢

The trouble with a bad idea, Shanilya Thadan thought to herself as
the council meeting came to a close, *is that if you don't have a good
idea, you have to use the bad one anyway.*

Shanilya had been familiar with that concept even before the Endarkened had come. The Domains of the Arzhana lay between the Feinolons
and the Bazhrahils on a high and barren plateau, level and inhospita-
ble and cold, and those who chose to make their place there were few.
That the Arzhana was a place that not even the Beastlings would go had
been a taunt from their enemies and a source of pride to them. Across
all the leagues of high cold desert that separated the Uradabhur from
the Windsward, only six Houses had staked a claim: Sigoric, Adovech,
Mallereuf, Gucerich, Rodiachar . . .

And Thadan.

Thadan was the richest, Thadan was the foremost, Thadan held the
western side of the pass called Oblivion Gate through the Feinolons
and into the Grand Windsward. Before the world had fallen it had been
said, perhaps in jest, that the Less Houses of the Arzhana bred up komen
because nothing else would grow there. What was truth was that the
Houses of the Arzhana had sent their knights into the West to fight,
and the Houses for which they rode sent grain and silk and steel to the
War Princes of the high cold desert, and no one had spoken of buying or
trading or a traffic in hired swords.

It was Shanilya Thadan who first heard of Thoromarth Oronviel's
unseating at Harvest Court, and of Vieliessar Farcarinon's accession to
Oronviel's throne. Shanilya had conferred quietly with her fellow Arzhana Houses, and watched, and waited, and told the tally of Vieliessar's
victories one after the other. And after the Battle of the Shieldwall Plain,

War Prince Shanilya Thadan had gone to her fellow War Princes with a plan: Thadan and its meisne would ride to the new High King to present her with the fealty of the whole Arzhana—which would mean that the other five War Princes of the Arzhana need not make the long and difficult journey themselves.

They would only need to swear fealty to Thadan first.

It had not taken as much persuasion as would have been needed in another place, for the Houses of the Arzhana did not war with one another. And so they had all found it good, and War Prince Shanilya Arzhana had gathered up the whole of her meisne, and added to it enough komen from the other Houses to assure her safe passage through the Uradabhur as it was then, and rode out.

And now, Shanilya Arzhana and that meisne was all that was left of the six Houses of the Arzhana. Her children, her Consort Prince, her kin, her vassals . . . any she left behind her had been slain by the Endarkened.

But every child of the Arzhana knew survival was more important than pride. And if the Arzhana taught one thing to its children, that thing was how to survive. That was wisdom many others had needed to be taught in the moonturns after the terrible bloody day of the High King's Enthroning.

There had been some who wished to say that the Endarkened were the judgment of the Starry Hunt upon Lord Vieliessar for daring to place herself upon Amretheon's throne, and that her death would lift that curse from them. There were others who said the Endarkened could be bargained with, appeased, bought off with tribute. That it was better for some to die than all. There were many foolish things said in those first sennights, as the survivors of the Endarkened's first onslaught cowered in the Flower Forest and waited to die.

Shanilya had known that it didn't matter which tale, or if any of them, was true. Truth was that the people would not survive if they fought among themselves. They would not survive if all the War Princes began once more to quarrel over who was to be High King.

Thus, for moonturn upon moonturn, Shanilya kept herself far from the High King's court and from its many factions. And if those who plotted rebellion died . . . well, that was a time when many died. And when the High King decided that the folk must leave Tildorangelor and travel westward, there were few left who would rise up and call Lord Vieliessar—or Lord Rithdeliel, or Lady Helecanth—to the Challenge Circle.

Yet even so, the High King delayed acting until all—down to the least of those who had been Landbonds—had been given their say and agreed to her plan. If nothing else could have persuaded Shanilya to give Vieliessar her loyalty as well as her fealty, that would have done so, and so it did.

Afterward, Shanilya allowed herself to become a councillor to the High King. But still she watched. And waited. Following today's council meeting, she wondered even harder. She had never believed the tale that the High King rode to the relief of the Shore. No ruler would turn their back upon a greater threat—such as the Endarkened—to face a lesser, and if Daroldan and Amrolion had not saved themselves by now, they were surely beyond all rescue.

It was not the distance they would have to cover which caused Shanilya unease—they had journeyed much farther in the unprotected open when they had left Tildorangelor. It was not the danger—for there was danger whether they stayed or went, and if the High King died, she had given two children to the succession and named strong Regents to guide them.

What is this journey really for? What lies on the far side of the Mystrals that is worth the risks and the deaths?

It was in Shanilya's mind to seek audience with the High King once they were all safely lodged in Nomaitemil. It was the High King's pride that she turned away none who wished to speak with her, and was not Shanilya Arzhana as great a prince as any who yet remained in the world, she who held all of the Arzhana-as-was in fealty? Shanilya would go, and together she and the High King would drink tea, and she would satisfy herself as to the thoughts in the High King's mind. And having heard the High King's words, Shanilya Arzhana would decide what she would do.

But first they must win through to Nomaitemil.

⊰⊱

So the High King means us to return to Ceoprentrei. It will be a bitter homecoming.

Rithdeliel well remembered how—a seeming lifetime ago—the High King had gathered her armies and her folk in the mountain valleys while she led the Twelve and their vassal Houses on a merry dance. While she stole from them all the things they needed to vanquish her. He remembered the meisnes of more than a score of the Hundred Houses united beneath her banner in the belief she could win.

To know that all the High King's folk would now fill a war camp barely the size of Farcarinon's-as-was was to drink deep of the cup of shame and failure.

He knew the High King saw this as her failure, and she was wrong. It was he—Rithdeliel of Farcarinon—who had failed her. In his pride as High King's Warlord, he had let himself forget that the whole purpose of his office was not to wage war, but to gain victory. He should have found some way to prevent that disastrous Winter War, and if he had failed there he should have forced her to leave Celephriandullias-Tildorangelor—that haunted place of ghosts and witches—and return to the West at once.

It could have been done. Not easily, but it could have. And if it had been . . .

He wanted to believe the Endarkened would not have come for them if Vieliessar had been enthroned in the West. He wanted to believe anything but that the might of the Hundred Houses had dwindled Wheelturn after Wheelturn until its people had become this ragged mob of commonborn.

But Rithdeliel could not doubt the evidence of his senses. If the Endarkened were all to vanish tomorrow, never to return, could Elvenkind regain its previous glory? Did Arilcarion and his sacred truths still rule their actions? Could the clash of swords in holy combat once again sweeten the air with its glorious music?

Did anyone even care?

Those of the princes and the Lords Komen who had survived,

Rithdeliel knew well, were those who had been able to forget who and what they had once been. But Rithdeliel would not forget. Someone must remember. And someone must pray that Pelashia Flower Queen, that Aradhwain Bride of Battles, that the Starry Hunt—that some Great Power would aid them before their name was no more than a memory borne upon the night wind.

CHAPTER FIVE

Thunder Moon to Harvest Moon in the Tenth Year of the High King's Reign: The Cold Equations

It is not enough to destroy an enemy if you cannot hold what you have taken from him.

—Arilcarion War-Maker, *Of the Sword Road*

In Sword Moon, Delfierarathadan had begun to burn. Nothing else, Hamphuliadiel told himself, *nothing else at all* had happened in Sword—but a few sunturns later, in Thunder Moon, he had gone to the doors of the Shrine of the Star and sealed them so that they could never be opened again.

In Thunder Moon, he had also begun taking a special cordial brewed from his own recipe: it provided deep and reliably dreamless sleep. Hamphuliadiel had no interest in anything his dreams might want to tell him. *He* was the Astromancer Eternal: *he* would decide how the future unfolded.

But Delfierarathadan was still burning.

Hamphuliadiel Astromancer considered the matter long and carefully, and dispatched a small party to investigate. Harwing Lightbrother and Ulvearth Lightsister were sent: Hamphuliadiel presented Ulvearth with a lovely cloak when he gave her the mission. Most of her instructions were in the embroidery, but after all, that was safer for everyone. And he was certain the defenders of the Western Shore would welcome the aid of two more Lightborn.

With them, he sent two of his more troublesome komen—Alleth and Garmund. Garmund was lazy, and a liar; Alleth was far too intelligent for Hamphuliadiel's peace of mind. The Sword Pages and the muleteer

would be collateral damage; Hamphuliadiel didn't care. It was important for him—and of course, for the Lightborn and Lightless he served
so tirelessly and unstintingly—to be surrounded by nothing but loyalty.
Loyal minds filled with loyal thoughts strengthened everyone. It was
Hamphuliadiel's responsibility to keep it that way.

So all was quiet for the rest of Thunder Moon, and for all of Fire
Moon. No one from Harwing's party returned. No spellbird arrived.
Areve was not attacked by Beastlings.

Then came Harvest Court—and Hamphuliadiel's peace was decisively shattered once and for all.

⊰⊱

Before the destruction of the Hundred Houses, the Leaping Fires had
been built in the courtyards of every castel, manor, farm, and keep,
when all male children of an age to become Arming Pages (or Apprentices), leapt the fire. Three sunturns of celebrations were held wherever
the fires had been lit, and after those celebrations, the sennight of Harvest Court began.

No more.

In the village of Areve, in the Moonturn of Harvest, in the reign
of the all-wise Astromancer Eternal, no one wondered any longer how
there could be a Harvest Festival without a Harvest Court, let alone
without a War Prince. At Harvest, there were feasts and games. Betroth-
als were plighted and marriages solemnized—and, of course, the boys
dared the fire. The new form of the Festival had become a part of the life
of the city Hamphuliadiel had created with his tireless and unappreci-
ated labor—a city that far surpassed any of the works of the bygone and
vanished War Princes.

(Not to mention surpassing any deeds that criminal Lightsister and
apostate War Prince, the so-called High King, Vieliessar Farcarinon,
had ever done in her brief and regrettable lifetime.)

For Harvest, the Sanctuary opened its larders, and beer, bread, and
sweet cakes graced the tables of Areve's inhabitants. There were contests
for the best livestock, and even dogs and chickens were entered. There
were many prizes to be had, for the Astromancer must certainly be seen

to exceed the generosity of the War Princes. His rule was more just, his lands richer, his folk happier, their livestock finer—in every way, Hamphuliadiel Astromancer was more than the War Princes' equal. He was their superior.

And so Hamphuliadiel awarded prizes with a lavish hand—spices and tinctures from the Sanctuary's stillrooms, wine and cordials from its cellars, lengths of thick soft warm woolen fabric, cloak clasps and boot leather—even daggers, their hilts chased in elvensilver and enchanted so that their blades would never dull, rust, or shatter.

Give my city of peasants their toys and games at Harvest and Snow and they will labor dutifully the rest of the Wheel. I can shape their festivals just as I have shaped their labor. Three fewer days of festival is a small price to pay for all the benefits my subjects gain.

Let there be one fire for all and one feast for all—let all be as equals before the Eternal Light. Or so I shall tell them, and their children, and their greatchildren. And so they will have no choice but to believe.

For am I not as humble as I am merciful? I, Hamphuliadiel of Haldil—No! Hamphuliadiel Haldil. War Prince.

And Astromancer Eternal.

⊰⊱

In a field north of Areve, the stubble had been plowed under, and a low fire had been built in a long trench, even as trestle tables were set up in the field and laden with roast meat, fresh breads, butter, and candied fruit and little cakes dressed with spun sugar and ribbons. Every family of Areve was here, and there was music, and dancing, and games of chase and catch to occupy the time before moonrise. Even kites were flown, by those girl-children who had gained that privilege in Flower Moon.

Tonight was the beginning of Harvest Festival.

Raneril stood to one side of a group of boys his age who were playing an elaborate game with a wooden ball. He'd used to like the game, but that was before everyone started throwing the ball *at* him instead of *to* him. It was nothing he could complain about to his lady mother; she had so many worries he didn't want to add to them. And so he'd begun to avoid the other boys and their games.

Things hadn't always been this way. A long *long* time ago Raneril had lived in a great castel keep. His mother had been a famous knight, and a member of the Ladyholder's personal guard.

But then most of the people left—except for the children and the babies—and the Lightborn were gone, so the food was always cold and sometimes stale, and his mother, who had been left to guard the keep, worried constantly.

And then one day there was no more food, and no more wood, and they had to leave. Just the two of them. They had been the very last to go, for Mama said it was a great wickedness to cast away something the War Prince had put into your hands, but no one had come back from the war, and she had no choice. Then they walked for a very long time, because there were no horses to ride anymore, and finally they came to Areve.

Mama had warned him never to tell anyone he had noble blood. If someone asked, Raneril must say he was the son of a Craftworker, and Mama would say she was a Craftworker, and everything would be peaceful and quiet. Mama said she was quite content to sew tunics and trews and cloaks so everyone could have warm clothes.

That had been several Wheelturns ago, and now Raneril had eleven Wheelturns. He was almost grown. He could have leapt the fire last Harvest, but Mama had said he was too young, and she hadn't let him see if he could be Called by the Light either, although Raneril really didn't want to be a Lightborn.

Everyone here always talked about who they'd be apprenticed to if they didn't become Lightborn. Nobody talked about being komen because commonborn couldn't become komen. Raneril didn't like it here in Areve, and he didn't want to be a Craftworker. He was nobly born. He wanted to fight. So Raneril made up his mind. He would leap the fire at Harvest Court—*this* Harvest Court—and then he would be old enough to be a komen, and he and Mama could go home, and Mama could train him and give him his sword and spurs. Some of the other komen here would probably want to come with them, and maybe some of the Lightborn too, if he asked them.

Raneril told only one other person about his plans—his friend Lorsan, who had actually been born in Areve—and he'd sworn Lorsan to secrecy. Raneril said Lorsan couldn't become a knight because he wasn't noble, but he could be Raneril's trusted personal servant when Raneril got back to his castel.

And now Harvest Moon—and the Festival—was here.

There was a glow of light in the sky, and then the moon rose up like a big golden bowl. The musicians stopped playing, and the drummers began to lay down a pounding rhythm. The boys made a long line in front of the fire. Raneril took a place next to Lorsan, though he had to shove his way in among the others to do it, and nobody made a place for him. He hoped his lady mother wasn't looking for him—or at least, that she didn't recognize him before it was over.

The drums got louder, and a flute began to play, and everyone was chanting: "Jump! Jump! Jump! Jump!"

Raneril didn't see who jumped first—he'd meant to be first, but up close, the fire looked very wide and very hot—but the knowledge that the fire leap had begun rippled down the line. Half the watchers were cheering for each leap now, making the chanting ragged.

And still Raneril hesitated. He looked at Lorsan, wondering if he was scared too.

Lorsan was looking back at him, but he wasn't smiling. "Go on, jump, you filthy komen," Lorsan said. And then he shoved Raneril as hard as he could.

Raneril windmilled his arms frantically, trying to regain his balance, or jump, or *something*. Just as he decisively lost his balance, he saw Lorsan spring across the fire trench, and heard the cheering that followed a successful leap.

And then Raneril fell.

There was a roaring in his ears, and he was wondering how much the fire would hurt. He closed his eyes tightly, because that might make it hurt less. Then there was a bright flash of purple light, and Raneril opened his eyes in surprise. He was confused for a moment when he saw a Lightborn walking toward him, but then he understood.

He'd fallen. Lorsan had pushed him. And the Lightborn had cast a spell so Raneril wouldn't get burned.

"Up you come, now, youngling," the Lightborn said, reaching down a hand. "No harm done, but you've had your chance. You can try again next Harvest. Plenty of boys need two or three chances at the leap; it's nothing to be ashamed of. Now come along; I'll take you back to your family."

Raneril discovered he was somehow standing beside the Lightborn. He was the only one left—the others had all Leaped. Even Lorsan. The Lightborn had a hand on his arm, and everyone was laughing and cheering because no one had been hurt.

I could have done it if Lorsan hadn't pushed me! But nobody will believe that—not even enough to set Truthspell on me!

Raneril thrust the Lightborn's hand away and began to run.

⚜

Carath Daroldan had never even imagined becoming War Prince of Daroldan. She knew her genealogy as well as she knew how to read and write and dance and fight, and though she was descended from the Direct Line, there were nearly a great-taille of lives between her and the throne.

Not anymore.

When the survivors of the fall of Daroldan Great Keep left the Shore, they had been more than five tailles strong. They lost eleven souls at the False Lake—including Aglahir Daroldan who had been War Prince for a full sennight—and after that the party broke apart over whether to continue toward the Sanctuary of the Star or to go in search of the High King. Carath knew they must go on to the Sanctuary of the Star. The Lightborn had always served the War Princes, and once they got to the Sanctuary of the Star, there would be hot food and clean clothes and soft warm beds, and—most of all—safety.

Carath had hoped to stop at Cirandeiron Great Keep for rest and supplies, but it was gone. So, as Lord Morenthiel said (he was from Amrolion, which was why she didn't know him), they might as well push straight on. At least it was still summer, and the upcoming harvest meant there was fruit on the trees and grain in abandoned fields.

Six sennights later they were in territory her Lightborn remembered from their days at the Sanctuary. Once the Lightborn told them they were close enough to reach the Sanctuary that night, everyone agreed to continue their journey even after sunset.

"And look," Thorodos Ranger said. "Here comes the Harvest Moon. It is a good omen, I think." He pointed eastward, where the great glowing golden orb of the moon was rising into the twilit sky.

"And my lord of Daroldan will sleep in a soft warm bed tonight—as will we all," Lord Morenthiel said.

Carath didn't bother to reply. They'd been walking since dawn and she was exhausted. She was weary of meat without salt, of fruit that was either bitter and half-ripe or rotting and bird-pecked, of having to sleep in her clothes, and of all this endless *walking*. But she was War Prince of Daroldan, and so she did her best to set an example for the others. Even when she was cold, and tired, and her feet hurt.

"Hist! Someone comes!" Angweth Ranger said.

Carath Daroldan squeaked indignantly when Lord Morenthiel picked her up and sprinted to the edge of the road. The twigs crackled and caught as he forced through them.

"You are too important to risk, my lady," Morenthiel said, clutching her tightly.

She heard someone scream.

⊰⊱

Raneril's humiliation and betrayal began to fade to a numb sense of injustice as he ran. Just as he was becoming resentful that nobody was coming after him, he saw the strangers.

All his life Raneril had known that strangers meant trouble, but even though he'd spent many afternoons dreaming of how he would vanquish the brigands and lead them to the Astromancer who would award him spurs and armor for his bravery, when trouble was actually here, he was shocked and tired and out of breath and not fast enough to escape it.

As he tried to dodge, one of the strangers grabbed him. He screamed as a hand was clapped over his mouth and a voice hissed in his ear:

"Shut your mouth, you grubby little savage! Where do you come from? The Sanctuary?"

"Anything else in the West is Beastling territory, Meneroth; where else could he have come from?" a second voice said. "And stop shaking him. It isn't healthy."

"That depends on for whom, Thoro," the one called Meneroth said. But the shaking stopped.

The one called Thoro squatted down until he and Raneril were eye to eye. "I am Thorodos Ranger of Daroldan," he said. "I travel with the War Prince of Daroldan and her embassy to the Astromancer of the Sanctuary of the Star. What's your name?"

"Ruh—Ruh—Ruh—*Raneril. Ilietiel. Ranerilietiel.* I live in Areve. It's Harvest. I fell into the fire." Raneril thought, horrifyingly, that he might cry. But he took a very deep breath and the moment passed.

"You know, that happened to me, too," Thorodos said seriously. "I made it across the next time—as you will—and I spent the moon-turns in between deciding what I wanted to be. That meant I knew my choice while others were still deciding. So I got what I wanted—to be a Ranger—and the others, well, some of them had to wait."

He smiled, and Raneril smiled back. "Have you come to visit the As-tromancer?" Raneril asked. "Most of the time he's very busy—but this is Harvest."

"Then we have come in a good hour," Thorodos Ranger said easily. "Will you take us to him?"

Munariel saw Raneriliet flee after his disastrous attempt at the fire-leaping. She told herself she would wait a little before going after him—no need to draw more attention to him than he had already done by his foolishness, and she needed time to compose her thoughts, lest she spoil his temper further.

From the moment she had arrived at the Sanctuary of the Star, Mu-nariel had known it would be a bad place to insist upon her noble rank, especially since no one knew where House Inglethendragir's War Prince was. (Or any of the War Princes, in fact.)

Fortunately it was easy enough for Munariel to dissemble to the Lightborn of Areve and the Sanctuary. The Wheelturns she had spent waiting in Inglethendragir's Great Keep with the others who had been left behind had given Munariel the rudiments of skills beyond account books and inventories and the Way of the Sword. If she was not happy to spend her days making garments in exchange for poor food and indifferent shelter, she was able to, and at least she and Ranerilietiel were safe.

Only they weren't safe after all. And the danger came from the most unlikely source.

Ranerilietiel himself.

She had given the diminutive—Raneril—as his true name to hide his rank, and that part of her weavings had been a success. He'd been six when they left Inglethendragir; too young to be called by his adult name, but (unfortunately) old enough to know his place in the world, and to expect to become a knight.

But there was no place in Areve for children who wanted to grow up to be komen.

There were a few komen at the Astromancer's village of refugees. They lived at the nearby manor house, and everyone said that it was purely charity that they had been given any place at all, for in this new world, the Lightborn would protect the people from all dangers, there would be no wars ever again, and no more need for komen.

Munariel had no real objection to this. The Western Reach was nothing but ash and ghostlands, and if Hamphuliadiel Astromancer wanted to defend her and the other refugees with magic instead of komen, he could do so with Munariel's blessing.

Over and over Munariel warned her son that nobody in Areve could know Ranerilietiel was of noble rank, for jealousy bred danger. But Raneril only thought of the bright armor, the blooded destrier, the be-gemmed sword: all the attributes of storysong komen that he expected would miraculously appear once he was of age. She'd held him back from the fire-leaping the previous Harvest because after that came apprenticing, and she knew he would not go meekly to a life as a farmer or herder or apprentice craftsman. She'd kept him back from being Called to the Light because who knew what the Lightborn might learn from him while they were Calling the Light?

She'd meant him to forgo the fire this Harvest, for then she could have spent a whole Wheelturn explaining to him why he could never become a komen and must set his mind to a different path. He would be twelve Wheelturns next Harvest; old enough to consider dangers.

But tonight everything had gone wrong. He tried to leap the fire—and failed. Munariel sighed, getting to her feet. Raneril couldn't get lost in the fields, and the lands near Areve were safe enough, but . . .

"Ariel? A word?" Tanila was one of the weavers. Her son Lorsan played with Ranerilietiel. (At least the boy had one friend.)

"Peaceful Harvest, Tana." The salutation came reflexively. "Of course. How may I aid you?"

"It is *I* aiding *you*," Tanila said, and Munariel's heart sank. Tanila was known to be clutch-fisted with favors and always expected a return on them. Tanila never forgot a favor she bestowed, nor did she ever forget to remind the recipient of her generosity. Munariel held herself ready for any shock as Tanila put a hand on Munariel's arm and led her away from the fire.

"My boy Lorsan came to me after his fire-leap," Tanila said. "And now that he's a man—oh, don't laugh, they all do think it, don't they, just as you and I thought ourselves women grown with an afternoon of kite-flying—he decided I should know about some wild talk your boy's been spreading."

"Not about the Lightborn?" Munariel said in horror she did not have to feign. To criticize the Lightborn—or to fraudulently claim to be one—was the only thing in Areve more deadly than claiming noble rank.

Tanila looked momentarily surprised. "No! Nothing like that! Lorsan said that your boy had been saying that once he jumped the fire you'd make him a komen and then lead an army back to . . . some castel; I disremember the name of it."

"Inglethendragir," Munariel said automatically.

"Yes, that's the one," Tanila said, nodding in satisfaction. "But it doesn't matter, since he ended up *in* the fire tonight rather than over it, didn't he, and Light bless Uldreyn Lightbrother for being there when he was needed. So I don't suppose you'll be leading any armies before Snow Moon, will you?"

"Nor after," Munariel said, forcing a laugh. "It's good of you to let me know, Tana. Gossip is such an ugly thing, isn't it? And you know yourself what sorts of fantasies children spin. I will speak to him, never fear. As soon as I find him," she added, not quite under her breath.

"Headed off down the Sanctuary Road, I imagine," Tanila said. "Best go fetch him—don't want to miss the feast! Good eating all Harvest, you know."

"It is," Munariel said, automatically, numbly. "Thank you again. I will go find him."

"The Astromancer's love go with you," Tanila said, turning back toward the firelight.

The Astromancer will see us dead by the springtide, if he finds out there's any truth in my boy's wild tales. Munariel sighed deeply and began to walk west along the Sanctuary Road. As she often did, Munariel thought of just taking Raneril and leaving the Sanctuary. But where would they go? *Straight into some Centaur's cookpot, that's where,* she reminded herself. Only Areve was safe.

When she saw Raneril, she began to run, because he was leading a group of strangers.

"Mama!" Raneril cried, running toward her. "They are from Daroldan! The Beastlings killed everybody there!"

⊷⊟⊱

Momioniarch was the first to reach Hamphuliadiel with word of the newcomers, barging in to the Astromancer's retiring chamber with the certainty that her trespass would be forgiven in the face of her astonishing news.

"Refugees from Daroldan," she said tersely, as Hamphuliadiel regarded her with puzzlement beginning to turn to irritation. "All that survive. Amrolion and Daroldan are lost. The Beastlings rule the Shore—and Caerthalien leads them."

Hamphuliadiel got slowly to his feet. "Are you certain?" he asked tersely.

"Merith, Arbane, Cyran, and Inchel are among the refugees," Momioniarch said. "I trained those children myself; they went back to Daroldan the year before Vieliessar came. They cannot lie to me—nor would they even think to. The Sanctuary is neutral, after all—this is what everyone knows." Momioniarch allowed herself a tiny smile. The Sanctuary had not been neutral since Celelioniel Astromancer stepped down.

"How many refugees are there? Are they the whole? Are they certain it was Caerthalien? Which Prince?" Hamphuliadiel was thinking furiously. His keystone to fuel the second stage of Areve's growth had been to annex Amrolion and Daroldan to the Sanctuary. The two Shore Domains had the skilled Craftworkers and the trained komen he needed to make his city of refugees a true domain, capable of holding the lands he meant to claim against both Beastlings and War Princes. He'd even prepared a touching ceremony of reconciliation for the apostate princes to enact (should they have survived), since Leopheine and Damulothir had inconveniently pledged fealty to that eternal thorn Vieliessar.

All those plans were useless now.

"Perhaps three tailles of them," Momioniarch answered. "There was no organized retreat. Everyone who could flee, fled, once Daroldan Great Keep was pulled into the sea by Beastlings. The Caerthalien prince is Runacarendalur, Bolecthindial's heir; the refugees report a parley truce was staged by Leopheine and Damulothir because they knew Runacarendalur Caerthalien would honor it. He did. Many saw him. He led the Beastlings; there were *alfaljodthi* in their ranks as well."

The loss of the Western Shore—so crucial to his plans!—was so great that the "why" of it was almost irrelevant—but if a Beastling army had destroyed two domains in the flower of their strength, it meant the Beastlings could no longer be considered a minor annoyance.

It also meant they would be coming for him next, now that the Sanctuary and Areve were all that was left of the Hundred Houses.

"Who have they spoken to of this? Don't tell me you've left them alone?" Hamphuliadiel could not keep the accusatory whine from his voice.

"Of course not, Astromancer. Galathorn is with them. They're all so busy stuffing their gullets with pies and meat that they haven't had time to say what they shouldn't."

"And the War Prince? Damulothir? Is he with them?" That would be a disaster.

"The current War Prince of Daroldan is a girl too young to fly her kite," Momioniarch said, dry as bone. "Her name is Carath, and I wager she has eight Wheelturns, if that. An upper chamber groom styling himself *Lord* Morenthiel of Amrolion intends to tell everyone she's his betrothed. You must give him credit for quick thinking, Lord Astromancer. He might be of use to us."

"I will oversee their wedding myself before tonight's moon sets," Hamphuliadiel vowed. "Tell Lightbrother-Steward to prepare lavish accommodations for all of them—baths, fresh clothing, sweetmeats and wine; he'll know what to do. And tell Galathorn to bring them here as soon as he can pry them away from the table. I will receive them appropriately."

"Here? Not your Audience Chamber?" Momioniarch looked faintly indignant on Hamphuliadiel's behalf.

"Here," Hamphuliadiel confirmed. "We will show them the world not as it has become, but as they believe it still is."

And that meant Lightborn living frugally and abstemiously, Lightborn who toiled at their Magery without thought for any worldly rank. Lightborn who were meek and biddable—and above all, humble.

Humble and obedient.

HARVEST MOON IN THE TENTH YEAR OF THE HIGH KING'S REIGN: ALL HEADS TURN WHEN THE HUNT GOES BY

All life is battle, yet not all opponents are enemies who may be met upon the field. One's battleground may be the bedchamber, the Great Hall, or some other common place. One who opposes you in good heart must also be conquered. Even if they be kin or ally, they still oppose your will. To prevail, you must control their thoughts just as you control the battlefield. A foe who thinks the cost of winning too high will surrender instead.

—Author Unknown, Notes Toward a Unified Theory of War

The generosity of the folk at the Harvest feast was sweet after so many sennights of meager feeding. And it was heady indeed to have not one, but two Lightborn to attend to them and to see that all their needs were filled. But, at least so Thorodos Ranger thought, it was a little odd, as well. Few of the folk asked them for their fresh news—and those who did were quickly discouraged by Galathorn Lightbrother, who each time would feign to have just thought of some innocuous question he must ask first. Of course, these folk were lowly Craftworkers and Farmholders, by their look, and such would find any Lightborn a bit intimidating. But still . . .

You've been on edge since that Beastling magic killed so many of our folk, Thorodos told himself sternly. But he wished Isilla Lightsister was still with them. She'd tried to warn them about the Sanctuary of the Star, but the Daroldanders had rejected her counsel, and Thorodos was starting to fear that had been a mistake. They had all been terrified and grieving after the attack at the False Lake, and Daroldan had fallen less than a moonturn before. Prince Carath, War Prince or no, was a child. It had been no time to make decisions, good or bad.

And now it is far too late to change them, Thorodos thought.

"Good feeding, at least." Meneroth Ranger spoke softly, for Thorodos's ear alone. "But never did I look to see the Sanctuary have so many hectares under tillage that it would need a dozen silos to store it all. And a vast city here, with no castel save the Sanctuary of the Star."

"It does not seem to me to be a good thing," Thorodos answered, equally softly. "Nor did Isilla Lightsister make it seem so, in her tellings. Yet we have chosen to follow the prince of the Line Daroldan, and it is for her and her advisors to determine our fates."

"Let us hope she finds better ones than that—" Meneroth Ranger broke off and got to his feet.

Thorodos turned, and saw that six Lightborn were approaching the table. The bonfire—and the Silverlight lanterns hovering in the air—made their green robes gleam with an eldritch radiance. Neither Ranger was used to seeing robed Lightborn save at the High Table; in Daroldan, most of the time they had worn what anyone else did: if you tried to land a fishing net dressed in a long robe, you deserved whatever happened to you.

The Lightsister who had originally welcomed them was leading the party. "My dear friends," she said, smiling warmly, holding out her hands to take in everyone there with her words and gestures, "the Astromancer thanks you—as do I—for taking such good care of our guests. Work keeps him from your sides on this day of rejoicing, but he says you shall not be stinted in his absence." Here she dug into the pockets of her robe and came out with both hands full of something that gleamed. "A peaceful Harvest to all!" she said, and flung both hands wide.

The items she threw were silver disks and tiny figurines. Most were scattered to the ground; a few bounced along the table and one even fell into the cider pitcher. Thorodos and the others from Daroldan watched in mingled astonishment and disgust as the people of Areve leapt to their feet and went scurrying after the tokens, squabbling and fighting among themselves. It reminded him of birds after corn.

"The Astromancer asks that you follow me," the Lightsister said over the noise of their bickering.

⇥⇤

Even though most of the furnishings had been removed, and the Daroldan Lightborn taken elsewhere, the remaining refugees filled the Astromancer's retiring room like penned sheep at shearing time. Moren knew that the High King's Lightborn—the ones who'd run off back at the Angarussa—had no good words to say about Hamphuliadiel, but Moren saw nothing particularly out of place with Hamphuliadiel Astromancer's behavior. The room he welcomed them to was simple and plain, and the Astromancer sat on a low cushion, wearing the same robe all the other Lightborn wore.

"I greet you all in the name of the Light, and welcome you to the Sanctuary of the Star and the town Areve," Hamphuliadiel said. "I will offer sacrifices in praise of the good fortune that led you here to me in safety, for with the sorrowful news you bear, Areve and the Sanctuary of the Star are truly the last bastion of Elvenkind in all the land."

"We had heard as much." Moren stepped forward, putting an arm around Carath to bring her with him. "I am Morenthiel of Amrolion, of the Line Direct, betrothed to the War Prince Carath Daroldan. By our troth, these are my people."

Moren—Moren*thiel*—of Amrolion waited expectantly. His claim of nobility was an abrupt and audacious gamble on his part, but he knew it would be backed by the other "lords and komen" who had come to the same conclusion he had: a sudden elevation in rank was poor enough repayment for the loss of their homes. As for the commons, even the Rangers—what did they care who ruled over them, so long as they were ruled?

Moren—Moren*thiel*—knew this wild masquerade would not survive even the night without the truth coming out—but once the Marks had been set on him and his bride, not even the truth could dissolve their union. He'd been careful to ensure that little Lord Carath Daroldan drank deeply from the pitcher of strong cider at the feasting table, and now she was nearly asleep on her feet.

"I realize that the Shore Domains declared fealty to Lord Vieliessar," Moren continued as the silence lengthened. "Yet she abandoned us to the Beastlings, and so I declare our oath as void. We have come to sue for pardon, my lord Astromancer."

Hamphuliadiel got to his feet slowly, as one heavy burdened with troubles and responsibilities. "My children, what need is there to sue for pardon when I offer all of you unstinted welcome? I have prepared a place where you may bathe and refresh yourselves before you rejoin our festivities. And I shall solemnize your wedding at once, Lord Moren-thiel, for I am certain Lady Carath will take great comfort in the knowledge that she is under your protection."

"Naturally Amrolion and Daroldan expect to provide all possible aid to both the Sanctuary of the Star and Areve," Moren said importantly. Having claimed to be a War Prince, he knew he must behave like one. And it was a promise he knew he'd never have to keep: there was nothing left for the Shore *to* provide.

"And so you shall," the Astromancer said, giving him a measuring glance that made Moren slightly nervous. "Know that in the coming sunturns I shall speak personally with each of you, for such a dire attack upon our people must not go unavenged. For now . . . you have come home to us and we rejoice. Rangers, your help is welcomed in this very dark hour." The Astromancer clapped his hands to summon another Lightborn. "Orchalianiel, bring the wine, the fruit, and the flowers. Out of disaster must always come new beginnings."

Momioniarch Lightsister led the Rangers and commons from the chamber, though the rest of the "nobility" remained as witnesses. Orchalianiel Lightbrother and two others prepared the table—the wine, the Vilya (fruit and flower). The Astromancer even provided, from among the gifts dedicated to the shrine, a dagger made of elvensilver, its hilt inlaid with Bearward teeth, for Morenthiel to present to his bride as a morning gift. (It was a decade, at least, before Carath would come to their marriage bed, but that did not affect the nature of this ceremony.)

Moren worried that little Carath would rouse enough during the ceremony to bring it all crashing down on him, but—praise the Light!—she did not. Momioniarch Lightsister held the girl to her side to keep her upright, and gave Carath's responses for her. The Astromancer himself set the Marks on them—just as if this really were a wedding between two princes—and then the matter was done beyond all undoing. Moren was—legally, legitimately, unimpeachably—the Consort Prince of Daroldan and the War Prince of Amrolion, just as Carath was War Prince of Daroldan and Ladyholder of Amrolion.

"And now I must bid you farewell," the Astromancer said, rinsing his hands in a basin held for him by another of his Lightborn servants. (Moren thought that "Lightborn servants" had a very good ring to it, and decided he would look into getting some of his own.) "Rest well, my dear ones, till I see you again."

⇥⊟⊞⇤

We might need to place a geasa on dear little Carath until she accepts her new place in things, but that is hardly something we haven't done before. The Lightborn will come to me willingly, and I have a use for the Rangers. The rest of the so-called "nobility" will be forced to renounce their stolen privileges of rank soon enough—if they have no other useful skills they can work the fields. Moren will be something of a problem, but when all see that he, War Prince of Daroldan and Amrolion, yields to my authority, he can certainly be allowed a bit of playacting before— sadly!—he sacrifices his life in defense of his bride and his city. Or perhaps I will make him the governor of Areve. If he is properly humble.

Such thoughts ran idly through Hamphuliadiel's mind as he made his way belatedly toward the Harvest festivities. To go among the Lightless, to receive their praise and worship, was a wearing and tedious duty for Hamphuliadiel at any time. With the refugees awaiting interrogation, he was filled with more impatience than usual, but it was a custom he dared not neglect.

Hamphuliadiel crossed the village green, with its communal well and fountain. His village had grown far beyond its humble beginnings. Now Areve's lands—which were in truth the Sanctuary's lands— covered more than forty hectares of cropland, and there were many stone houses, and many purpose-built districts, much as if a War Prince's Great Keep had been turned inside out, and all the workshops and foundries and storehouses it contained scattered across the land-scape. Of course, because of Beastlings—and, Wheelturns ago, Elven bandits—the city had its own strong stone walls to guard it, but on Festival nights, all the gates were traditionally left open.

The houses became smaller and closer together as Hamphuliadiel neared the outer wall. There were only a few hundred villagers in the city—only the crippled and the elderly would have forgone the first night of Festival. The north gate was, as usual, ornamented with small twists of ribbon and straw, its lintels smudged dark with libations of wine and cider and blood (the witless peasants still sacrificed to the Flower Queen no matter how many times Hamphuliadiel told them it was a foolish and wasteful superstition).

Outside the gate was the field where the fire-leaping had been held, and the whole of Areve had gathered to see it. Hamphuliadiel was soon recognized, of course, and the smallest children came running to him, crying out for treats. He smiled indulgently, patting their heads, and delighted them by using Fetch to bring sweetmeats from the Sanctuary kitchens and bestow them one by one.

Every table must be visited, of course. Every villager must be able to say that the Astromancer looked them in the eye, or touched their shoulder, or laid the personal blessing of the Light on their mewling brats. Trinkets must be tossed or presented: the largesse Hamphuliadiel and his Lightborn bestowed this first night of Harvest was the price of keeping this rabble happy and pacified.

But apparently, not everyone was. A Hippogriff swooped down out of the sky to perch upon the wall. The smarter villagers had already abandoned the north gate, running toward others. It would have saved them if there had only been one Hippogriff, but just as the panic reached its peak, two—six—perhaps even a dozen more of the winged monsters dove out of the sky to perch upon the wall, braying with laughter at the sight of their victims.

"Death to the False Astromancer!" cried an unknown voice.

"Get that gate open!" Hamphuliadiel shouted, dropping Shield.

The Lightbrother nearest him stared mutely, wild-eyed with terror. It occurred to Hamphuliadiel at that moment—a great insight, he must

certainly save it for the autobiography he meant to write—that sending the junior Lightborn to watch over the commonborn Festival while
most of their seniors stayed within the Sanctuary of the Star to enjoy a
considerably nicer evening was probably a bad strategic move.

"Pay attention."

The soft voice—*so close!*—was nearly enough to make Hamphuliadiel
raise Shield again. He turned in the direction of the voice, just as the
water underfoot—*how?*—crested over his boot-toes. Wherever it had
come from, it was as cold as liquid ice. The cold—as well as the wet—
quickly seeped through the leather of his boots. He stepped backward,
then sideways, as inconspicuously as possible. Nothing helped.

"Gunedwaen always told me that gloating was best done over one's
enemy's lifeless body. But I think you should be alive to hear me do
it, don't you?" In defiance of all reason, the voice belonged to Harwing
Lightbrother.

"I've done nothing to you." Now, fleetingly, Hamphuliadiel cursed
the ambition that had returned him to the Sanctuary so quickly after he
had gained the Green Robe. He had never served on a battlefield, never
been on a Beastling hunt, and knew very few spells that would be useful
for killing someone.

"Nothing but steal my will and my *self* for a decade. Nothing but
set yourself up as Astromancer *Eternal*. Oh, and let us not forget the
cloud-hunt you sent me on, whose purpose I still do not know, with
poor Ulvearth going along to execute everyone. She's dead, by the way,
and for this—and for so many additional reasons that to list them all
would unacceptably prolong your existence—I will have your life tonight. In short: I hope you enjoyed the sunset, because it was the last
you will ever see."

Hamphuliadiel looked around wildly, but there were no Lightborn
to be seen anywhere. They'd abandoned him! He turned toward the village. The fighting there was over. The gate had been torn from its hinges,
and bodies were scattered everywhere. The pale stone of the wall was
spattered in blood.

"I will give you anything you wish," Hamphuliadiel said urgently.
"Your powers are greatly needed. This is the Sanctuary's darkest hour."

"Yes. Yes, it is," Harwing agreed amiably.

The clouds boiled away, exposing the moon once more. The ground trembled; a dozen Bearwards, followed by an uncountable number of Centaurs, charged through the darkness beyond the fields, heading for the undefended village. The ground beneath him trembled with the force of galloping hooves.

It was only as the Beastlings passed him without a single sidewise glance that Hamphuliadiel realized why he stood alone here, abandoned. Harwing had Cloaked both of them.

Hamphuliadiel summoned Dispell. When he cast it, he realized that Harwing had combined Cloak with Hush: now Hamphuliadiel could hear screams of terror and of rage coming from Areve.

All the sounds blended into one great din that seemed to have a weight and pressure of its own. The chaos was brutal—a weapon in itself—and the noise made it nearly impossible to think. Hamphuliadiel wondered if that was Harwing's intention. Irresistibly, he glanced back toward Areve once more. He could no longer see the Beastlings. Flashes of light told him his Lightborn were doing their best to save the townspeople.

The screams and the shouts of the young Lightborn melded with the howls of the Beastlings and the shrieks of the villagers. Their meaning was all too clear: *Hamphuliadiel Astromancer—save us all!*

"Listen to me, Harwing! Listen to me!" Hamphuliadiel demanded urgently.

"Oh, I can hear you." Harwing's voice was soft and merry, and for the first time Hamphuliadiel felt true fear rather than mere irritation.

"I am the only force for order these people have!" Hamphuliadiel cried.

"If that is true, then they are already lost, *Lord* Astromancer. But come. Dry your foolish tears. They're not who I want. I want *you*."

"You have allied yourself to those monsters!"

"They saved my life. I thought I'd do them a favor in return. They want your little village gone, and in ten Wheelturns of captivity here, I learned one thing of use to them. I learned that on the first night of Harvest, Areve is absolutely unprotected."

"How dare you?" For the first time in his many Wheelturns of rule, Hamphuliadiel was truly outraged. *An* alfaljodthi—*a Lightborn—one of us—making common cause with Darkspawn monsters? It is a betrayal of the Light itself!*

"Besides, someone ate my horse, and I had to get back here somehow," Harwing continued reasonably. "Have you ever ridden a Hippogriff? I don't recommend the experience."

"Harwing. Dear child. Please. *Listen to me.* All you have done tonight can be erased. We can rule here together," Hamphuliadiel said urgently. "The Lightborn are your brothers and sisters—save *them* if you save no one else."

"As you saved Ulvearth? All she wanted was Ciadorre, and you killed Ciadorre." Harwing held out his hand, pale violet lightnings coruscated from his fingertips. "Come. Take my hand. We will discuss it."

Hamphuliadiel cast Shield instantly, driving a curtain of violet energy between him and Harwing. He was safe now, but somehow it hardly mattered. His feet were still wet. His boots were ruined. He was standing in sucking treacherous mud.

It is impossible to think!

And Harwing had disappeared.

⚬⧉⚬

In heartbeats the clouds returned to obscure the moon, this time bringing the torrential autumn rain that wasn't due for a moonturn or more. The droplets spattered off Shield, making it flash and sizzle. Hamphuliadiel had never before realized how *annoying* Shield was, for it flared bright every time something struck it, no matter how small and harmless. The raindrops caused it to glitter like a sunlit river, while the rising winds were tossing sticks and pebbles at it without cease, causing an arrhythmic series of brighter flashes.

It was giving him a headache.

I cannot see from within this thing! Hamphuliadiel thought pettishly.

He looked around as carefully as he could through Shield's maddening scintillation. The fire trench was to his tuathal hand, its remaining coals flaring as they were blown upon by the storm, and smoking where the raindrops struck. If not for the rain, the fields would be aflame, for the wind had lifted everything it could from the trench, and scattered that far and wide.

To the deosil, Hamphuliadiel could see the long blank stretch of the north wall, darkened in places with smears of blood, and bodies—some moving feebly—scattered across the ground before it.

But more important than that, the Hippogriffs were gone. Hamphuliadiel knew the location of everything within the Sanctuary: a simple Fetch would arm him with sword and dagger in case Harwing or some of the Beastlings came back. But nothing—not spell, not solid object, not sound—could pass through Shield. He would have to render himself momentarily defenseless to cast Fetch. Still, nobody was in sight just now. Surely it would be safe to drop Shield for a moment. Harwing wasn't here. Harwing had probably run away.

Yes, that's it. Harwing lashed out in anger, or was forced to this by the Beastlings. But the boy would never consider killing me. He was terrified by what he'd done. He ran away.

Hamphuliadiel dropped Shield.

But before he could cast Fetch, he felt the warmth of a body pressing against his back, and saw the flare of a Shield he had not cast surround him—*them*. One strong arm was wrapped around his torso, and the other held a blade against the pulse-point of his throat. "Shield is only effective when maintained," Harwing murmured in his ear. "Now—don't move, please; this blade is extremely sharp and you don't wish to die before you've heard my victory oration—I will end your life tonight. You must have expected that, and really, I'd have thought Vieliessar would have gotten around to killing you a long time ago. But I will do far more than that. Once you are dead, I shall utterly profane your legacy—and erase it as well. Your name will be unknown to every age that follows this. If any. You know, I don't really care about that part anymore. That's odd."

"The Beastlings— They will overrun us. We must defend—" Hamphuliadiel whimpered. Terror made his voice breathy and high.

"Weren't you paying attention?" Harwing asked lightly. "They're already here."

"No!" In any other situation, Hamphuliadiel could have made a lengthy speech, but in this uttermost extremity, the single syllable of negation was all his terrified mind could muster.

"*Yes.*" Harwing lifted the dagger from Hamphuliadiel's throat and relaxed his grip on Hamphuliadiel's torso.

Hamphuliadiel felt himself begin to sink into the ground.

It was only when the slurry of mud and water rose up over his knees that Hamphuliadiel understood what was happening. He began to kick furiously, scrabbling for purchase, for some way to escape the sinkhole.

Just as he thought of throwing himself to the ground and crawling free, Harwing grabbed him by the elbows and pulled his arms back behind him. Hamphuliadiel kicked out. He tried to haul himself from the sinkhole by leveraging Harwing's grip. Nothing worked. There was only the pain.

"There's just one more thing." Harwing was kneeling behind Hamphuliadiel now, his grip on Hamphuliadiel's wrists relentless. "The Lightborn—as you well know—walk in the Vale of Celenthodiel for as long as the Hunt shall ride. And as you might imagine, I don't really want to see you there when I go."

Harwing abruptly released him, and Hamphuliadiel sank rapidly. He struggled madly, but his sodden robes clung to him like a shroud, trapping his legs. At the last instant, he was able to halt his descent by spreading his arms wide and digging his fingers into the slippery mud on either side of the sinkhole.

But that was all.

If the field had not been harvested— If only the field had not been harvested—!

There were no stalks to cling to, no roots to hold him secure. He was in a deep narrow hole, up to his chest in chill slurry, gasping for air as if he was already submerged. Gripped by terror bordering on hysteria, Hamphuliadiel could not think of one spell that could save him.

Not one.

Harwing stepped around Hamphuliadiel to face him and squatted down in the mud, leaning forward so his face was near the Astro-mancer's. "You are going to die. You are going to be sucked down into the center of the earth to smother and die and rot, and no one will re-member your name or find your body. And it is still less than you de-serve."

Harwing feinted at Hamphuliadiel's eyes with his dagger, and, de-spite himself, Hamphuliadiel raised one hand to protect himself before he realized the fatal error of the act. His elbow slipped over the edge of the pit. His fingers dug into its wall and found only endless mud in which he could find no purchase. All that was now keeping him above ground was the fingers of his left hand dug into the furrowed earth, and they were not enough. He felt himself sliding downward. He felt the filthy mud settle against his skin.

Harwing continued to watch, an expression of mild interest on his face.

Hamphuliadiel remembered the night he had taken the colts to the Shrine. He remembered the vision he'd had then, of being buried alive.

But this time there would be no waking.

The Astromancer of the Sanctuary of the Star—of Shrine Areveth-monion—the Astromancer Eternal—screamed, over and over, begging and howling as he clawed desperately at the sodden earth, as his body was dragged deeper into the sinkhole, as the thin mud rose up over his chin, his lips, his face.

Mother—! he thought, as the mud closed over him, as even his out-stretched hands could no longer touch the air, as he continued to slip downward.

And then Hamphuliadiel of Haldil, Hamphuliadiel Anyfather, the kitchen boy born of Bethros's Line Direct, son of the Sword Page Einar-tha of Bethros, knew nothing more.

"Don't worry," Harwing said to the mud. "I will be their Astro-mancer now." He got to his feet and kicked a few clods of earth over the grave.

By morning the mud would be dry.

⋈

The Otherfolk army reached Caerthalien—or what once had been Caerthalien—and their line of march (so called, Runacar always mentally appended) now followed the Northern Pass Road. (In practice the Wulvers raced ahead, slept until the column reached them, and then did it again, and the Palughs probably slept in the trees for the entire day.) No matter how much distance they covered in a day, Runacar wanted them to move faster. After Caerthalien came Ivrithir, and after Ivrithir, Vondaimieriel. In southern Vondaimieriel, almost to the Mangiralas border, lay the debouchments of the Dragon's Gate. It would be the matter of a sunturn, two at most, to reach the top of the pass. And then . . .

Runacar didn't know. He'd long since given up asking either the Gryphons or the Hippogriffs to overfly the Mystrals and tell him what was on the other side. They simply refused. Drotha was happy to do it, but the Aesalion either gave no reports, or gave reports neither Runacar—nor any of his commanders—could decipher. Runacar didn't press the issue. As little as he liked to head blindly toward an unknown battlefield, Runacar liked the thought of the High King knowing there was an army marching to meet her even less.

But no matter how hard the road each day, at the end of it he demanded they train. Over and over, he told them the same thing:

"The Elves begin to train for war from the moment they can walk. The Hundred Houses made war all their lives: it was their sport, their worship, their reason for being. Vieliessar was skilled enough to destroy the combined forces of the Hundred Houses with an army of rabble, and she has had ten turns of the Wheel to make that army even better."

He could only hope *his* army believed him. The Otherfolk had clashed with Elvenkind all their lives, but they'd clashed with Elven *hunting parties,* not Elven armies. Even the Battle for the Western Shore had not involved the tactics Runacar expected he would see from the High King, for Amrolion and Daroldan had been unique in their enemies and their strategies.

Until Runacar had destroyed them.

He did not think he could expect such luck a second time.

You won't know how the battle will go until it's over, he told himself.

For this battle, no prediction can hold true. There's no point in trying to write the praise-songs yet.

Or the laments.

⛤

Not a single beast with fur or feathers from here to the Dragon's Gate!" Andhel flung down her bundle of javelins in exasperation. "How can I hunt what isn't there?"

At the beginning of the march, game had been abundant in the West, flourishing in the absence of hunters and foresters. There'd been good hunting in Caerthalien: deer, rabbit, partridge, and enormous herds of feral goats. But by the time the Otherfolk army reached Vondaimieriel, there was nothing to hunt at all. Runacar began to suspect that Vondaimieriel was a ghostlands. The grass grew, the trees were in leaf, the summer fruits hung lushly on bush and branch. And that was all. Runacar didn't want to let anyone know how worried he was. (He certainly didn't want to suggest that the Darkness had anything to do with matters—and Melisha wasn't around to ask whether it did or not.)

The Woodwose did most of the pot-hunting for the army—or those parts of it that ate meat, anyway—ranging far from the line of march to do so. It was the second day they had come back empty-handed, and Andhel took it personally.

"You can't," Runacar said reasonably. He was sitting in the doorway to his tent, making notes for the evening's drill. *And to think I thought making an early camp would be restful.* They'd stopped a candlemark before sunset once they reached the foothills: Runacar could train troops in the dark, but he couldn't train troops in the dark *on a hillside.*

"We're going to starve," Andhel said with gloomy relish.

"Not if you sweet-talk the Gryphons into bringing us back some deer from the West," Runacar said lightly. The Gryphons, Aesalions, and Hippogriffs all hunted for themselves and had not reported any lack of game, but of course they could cover hundreds of leagues in search of prey.

Andhel glared.

"At least *they're* having good hunting," she grumbled.

"Fine," Runacar said briskly. "Problem solved. They'll hunt. You practice."

Andhel made a face and stooped to pick up her weapons. Runacar wasn't sure what they were made of, but despite their lack of metal points, the javelins were deadly sharp.

"Rune," she asked hesitantly. "Will we win?"

Runacar tried not to sigh, though he'd expected this question. He hadn't wanted to cover it until the eve of battle, and he could have deflected the question now, but he needed something to distract Andhel from the lack of game and the possible reasons for its absence.

"I don't know. I don't know what she'll bring with her. But I do know this: if the day starts to go against us—and if you can't tell when that happens, you haven't been listening to my lectures—I need you and the rest of the Woodwose to do one thing."

"What's that?" Andhel asked suspiciously.

"Run. Run behind their lines. Strip their dead, dress yourselves, try to blend in."

"But—" Andhel said, clearly outraged.

"*Do it*," Runacar said firmly. "As many of you that can. Then find the High King—if she lives, which, if we lose, I have no doubt she does—and *kill her.*"

Andhel stared at him for a long moment, eyes wide. "You'll die too," she said in a small voice.

"I will," Runacar said evenly. "But you won't. And I promise you with all I am, Andhel—her generals will turn on one another the moment her pyre is lit. Anyone who survives the civil war that follows will be easy prey for your people—if you remember what I taught you."

"And we'll win," Andhel said dubiously. "In a war."

"I've taught you what the Hundred Houses never knew. The purpose of war is to win," Runacar answered. *And Vieliessar taught it to me first.*

⟢⟣

Each night Runacar stumbled into his "Warlord's Pavilion" (a tiny thing; he vaguely remembered the Lightborn had used such tents as personal quarters), and fell into bed almost before he removed his boots, to sleep a few short candlemarks before the army must pack up and move again. Though a proper Warlord's pavilion would have been in the center of the encampment, each night Runacar made sure his was set at the very edge of camp, as far from the others as was safe. He did it so that Melisha could come to him—if she wanted. She'd left while he was still on the hospital island, and if he hadn't seen her in the distance a few times while they were still in Cirandeiron, Runacar might have given up hope of seeing her again. But he knew Melisha was following them—or *leading* them—for some purpose of her own.

And one night his hope—and his patience—was rewarded.

CHAPTER SEVEN

Harvest Moon in the Tenth Year of the High King's Reign: The Wind That Shakes the Stars

When a thing is so, do not waste time debating the matter, or whether it can be so or not. It is. Move on.

—Gunedwaen Swordmaster, *The Art of War*

It was a night like any other for Runacar: drills and lectures and mediating spats between groups of Otherfolk who had never found a reason to be in each other's company before and did not like it now. Only after every task was done and quarrel settled could Runacar stagger off to his tent to catch a few candlemarks of sleep.

Tonight, when he finally reached it, Melisha was there.

The Unicorn was lying on his bedroll, and the light from the lantern he held seemed to make her glow. He closed the lantern's gate and then let the tent flap fall closed. Melisha still glowed, her spiral horn giving off a pale silvery radiance like moonlight.

"Hello," Runacar said, as he sat down on his campaign chest to pull off his boots. He'd composed a hundred speeches in his head for when he saw her again, and forgot every one of them the moment he saw her.

"Is that all the welcome I get?" Melisha teased, as she got to her feet.

"It's as much as you deserve," Runacar said, trying and failing to be cross with her. "Where have you been? I've missed you."

"Here and there," Melisha answered vaguely. "Congratulations on your work, by the way. It won't even slow the Darkness down, but it's good work nonetheless."

"It only has to stop the High King," Runacar answered, after a long moment to process what she'd said. Discouraging news, but at least it was honest. Assuming she knew what she was talking about and—oh, yes—not flat-out *lying*.

"And then you win and she tamely retreats and leaves you the Western Reach," Melisha suggested.

"No," Runacar said. "And then I slaughter every last soul in her king-domain above the age of eight, and Leutric delivers his mysterious Darkness-killing weapon to the Woodwose."

For a long moment Melisha looked as if she couldn't decide whether to weep or laugh. She lowered her head, turning half away from him. "At least you plan to spare the children," she said quietly.

"Tanet and Andhel have promised the Woodwose will care for them, and Bralros has pledged that the Centaurs will as well," he answered. "They won't be held accountable for anything their elders have done." He wanted to be defensive, but he only felt tired. "These are your rules and Leutric's, not mine. He won't give up his Darkness-killing weapon until he knows it won't be used against the Otherfolk. The High King is mad, so she might agree to his terms. But her army won't."

"But you led such an army once, did you not?" Melisha asked softly. "And you agreed."

"I'm the Banebringer's brother. What did I have to lose?" Runacar said sourly. "And . . . I've lived with your people for a long time. I was helpless, and they didn't kill me. They fed me, clothed me . . . They—you—you were *kind*. All of you. Kinder than any of *us* would ever think of being. I know your people now, at least a little. Thousands of armed knights and foot knights won't . . ." He broke off, seeing the scene too vividly. "You saw what happened on the Shore. They'd rather kill us and die themselves than leave us alive while they run for their lives."

"That is a problem," Melisha agreed neutrally. "But come. You were on your way to bed. I'll tell you a bedtime story."

Runacar laughed sharply. "Am I still in the nursery, to hear wonder-tales? You are a wondertale all by yourself."

"A compliment," she answered, coiling her tail over her back. "We should call you Runacar Honeytongue for your sweet words."

"Truth," Runacar countered. "Nothing more. So tell your tale."

"You aren't in bed," she pointed out.

He snorted in amusement and undressed, laying boots and sword near to hand and settling himself in his bedroll. The pallet beneath him was hard and thin, but the ground was blessedly free of small sharp rocks. Brownie magic, he suspected.

"Now I am," he said.

"So you are," Melisha answered. She settled herself beside him, her forelegs stretched out in front of her as if she were a cat. This close, Runacar could smell her scent, like cinnamon and flowers. And sunshine—if sunshine had a smell.

"It is a long tale," she said. "But we shall have time to finish it, I think, before you are called to battle. And now I begin: Once and once and once, in lands beyond Greythunder Glairyrill, and beyond the Peaks of Leunechemar, and even beyond the Sea of Storms, which is the Great Sea Ocean of the East, there lived a race—your own race, my darling—whose hearts were forged for war. In endless battle, they vied against their own, until at last all their people were united under one King, one Master, one General."

"That's not long ago," Runacar objected mildly. "And it's here. You're talking about Vieliessar."

"Hush," Melisha said. "I am not. Do you think the world tells each tale only once?"

"But—"

"Don't interrupt. As I was saying, the Elven Kingdoms were all united, and then their ruler turned his eyes to the kingdoms surrounding his own. In that day, long ago, all the Nine Races ruled over vast kingdoms of their own, and over great armies as well."

"I should like to see a Palugh Warlord," Runacar said sleepily. It had been a long and wearying day, and Melisha radiated heat and comfort that was irresistibly lulling. Apparently this was to be a bedtime story after all.

"Brazen boy," she said fondly, leaning down to rub her cheek against his. "I cannot tell you the tale of all those battles, for they happened in a time and in a way beyond even a Unicorn's memories. But they were wars not of a season, or of a Wheelturn, but of century upon century of

Wheelturns. Endless. And they set such a wound upon that land as is not even now repaired."

She sounded sad, and Runacar wanted to comfort her, to say it was a long time ago and all those folk were long dead. But before he could find the right words, she went on.

"As you would expect, the Elven King gained many early victories against the rest of the Nine Races, and it took long and long for the others to set aside their ancient quarrels and unify against them. But at last they did, and against that enemy Elvenkind could not prevail."

"And then they all died, and we aren't here at all," Runacar said muzzily.

"No," Melisha said, and her voice seemed to come from far away. "And then Elvenkind, knowing what their fate would surely be at the hands of those they had so long oppressed, retreated to their own kingdom, and built a thousand thousand ships, and filled them with all they possessed, and set sail into the unknown west . . ."

If there was more to her tale, Runacar did not hear it.

Not that night.

⛬

Runacar was still dream-muddled when Stormchaser poked him awake.

"Good morning good morning good morning!" the Wulver caroled, pouncing on the still-groggy Runacar. "It's a beautiful day!"

Stormchaser wasn't the only one to come to Runacar's pavilion in the mornings. Sometimes it was Tilwik or one of the other Fauns. Sometimes it was one of the Palugh—Sundapple or Cloudfoot or Shadowdance. He had no idea how all of them arranged things among themselves. Maybe they diced for the privilege of waking him. It was possible.

"You'd say that if it was raining," Runacar responded, dislodging Stormchaser with a mighty shove. "Or blizzarding."

"Those are good days too," Stormchaser agreed, sitting back to regard Runacar with bright-eyed interest. "All days are good and beautiful, and no two are alike. Isn't it wonderful?"

Runacar muttered something indecipherable. Seeing his expression, Stormchaser laughed, and bounded out of the tent.

The Wulvers had been one of the major surprises the Otherfolk held for Runacar, for they were not mentioned, even obliquely, in *Lannarien's Book of Living Things,* and he wasn't sure that any of the Elvenkind who might have—*must* have—seen Wulvers knew what they were seeing.

Wulvers were furry all over, like the dogs and wolves they most closely resembled. Their coats were mostly of an eminently camouflageable dun-grey shade, long and impeccably groomed, darkest along the back and over the face. Their throats and bellies were reddish-tan, their ears were large and upstanding, their teeth were long and sharp, their tails sickle-shaped—and there ended the resemblance to any canid ever whelped. Their muzzles were blunt compared to that of a wolf, and their dark amber eyes were knowing and merry. Wulvers did not have paws: their forelimbs ended in hands that were nearly Elven. With open hands, Stormchaser could hold a dagger or a cup and do all the things that required hands. With those hands closed into fists, he could outrun a deer.

It was still dark outside and the sun would not rise for a candlemark or more. While it was still dark, Runacar would grab his breakfast, eat it as he fed and saddled his horse, and ride off to conduct a short practice session with his cavalry (the Centaurs) while the camp was dismantled and packed.

And then, once again, they would march. At least Runacar was spared one worry: his aerial scouts might still not be prepared to cross the Mystrals, but now that his army had reached Vondaimieriel they could fly high enough to see both passes of the Dragon's Gate. Vieliessar had not yet reached it.

Only give me another sennight, and I can be there before her. And if she has the same infantry she had at First and Second Mangiralas, her archers will cut my vanguard to pieces. And what will I do then? Three-quarters of my army has never been on a battlefield in their lives, and no Storysinger's tale can take the place of having been there. . . .

He forced himself not to think of that, but that only meant his thoughts turned to Melisha instead. No wonder the Hundred Houses had thought Unicorns to be a myth. They could never have slaughtered the Otherfolk with such abandon if there had been Unicorns among them. But that wasn't the point, really—if there even was a point. The point was her story.

The first time they met, Melisha had said that she was going to tell him a story. Runacar had thought then that it would be something about the Darkness—something *useful* about the Darkness, like an explanation of why the Darkness hadn't killed everybody centuries before Runacar had been born. But instead it was a history lesson—if not an outright wondertale—about something else entirely.

The tale really didn't make his people—by whom he meant both Woodwose and *alfaljodthi*—look particularly good. Or particularly clever, given that they lost the war they'd been fighting so completely that they ran off to . . .

Here.

Runacar tried to imagine the distance they'd traveled, but though he'd traveled farther than most komen—all the way to the Grand Windsward during the Little Rebellion—he'd never been east as far as the shore of Greythunder Glairyrill. No one had. He tried to imagine as much land beyond that river as stretched from the Western Shore to the Grand Windsward, and then a whole ocean beyond that, and more land at the other side.

He couldn't.

How many had sailed west? How big had their ships been? Had they known Jer-a-kalaliel was here when they sailed? If they had not, they must have been truly desperate.

As desperate as he was now.

Runacar didn't want to think about that either.

⚬

The Endarkened did not reckon the passage of time as their victims did. They paid scant attention to the seasons of the Bright World: in the World Without Sun, they counted the passage of time by the Risings of their King. The Endarkened were immortal and unchanging, and even those who had been born of rut and flesh believed themselves as one with the cold darkness wherein the stars burned. All other life was evanescent and mutable, and once the Bright World was scoured of all life, the sun and the rain would beat down only upon lifeless rock.

And then would come a war such as the stones and the stars had never witnessed.

Among the Endarkened themselves.

⊰⊱

Zicalyx spread her great scarlet wings wide, landing soundlessly beside her brother on the hilltop overlooking the place called Saganath. The Flower Forest was discernable to them as only an absence so profound that one could not even say of it: *it is dark,* or: *it is bright.* Both Endarkened knew that the prey sheltered unreachably inside the hateful Absence, but to enter it meant sickness, infirmity, injury—even death. Death was a thing no Endarkened had ever experienced, ugly and terrifying, for it held the hint of an eternal living, an eternal awareness, instead of eternal darkness, eternal joy, eternal—perfect—utter—nothingness.

And at that, death was preferable to injury, for the Endarkened would gleefully attack any of their brethren who could not fight back.

"How fares your watch, brother?" Zicalyx asked, and was rewarded with a disgusted grimace.

"How do you think?" Narghail growled. "The Elflings are safe within, and they have far outstripped the children of the Cold Nursery who follow them. It will be a thousand Risings before those arrive."

"How, when the whole of the land is not a thousand Risings wide?" Zicalyx said, scoffingly. "Surely you exaggerate."

"I don't care! They won't come out and *play!*" Narghail shouted. "I want to play with them!"

Zicalyx struck Narghail so hard he sprawled onto his back. In an instant she sprang upon him, the talons on her hands and feet digging bloodily into his shoulders and thighs, her mouth nearly touching his own.

"And so do we all, but more than that, we wish to see our glorious King in action," she hissed. "Ours to find them, his to lead us in battle."

"It isn't fa—" Narghail whined, cutting himself off when he saw the anger blazing in his sister's yellow eyes. "He and the Created-and-Changed leave little behind them," he finished simply. "When they strike at the Elflings at all."

"And that is their right, for they are the Created of *He Who Is*. We are merely Born," Zicalyx reminded him. She could not remember a time when she had not known the ultimate goal of her people—to scour all life from this world and then to return to the blessed Void, the formless uncreated nothingness of their master, *He Who Is*. She had always thought that ending to be absolute and as utter as pain and darkness themselves.

But lately—she could not say just when—Zicalyx had begun to wonder. Of course *He Who Is* would take back the Unchanged. *He Who Is* might even take back the Created-and-Changed.

But what of the Born?

King Virulan said the Born were equal to the others. That they were all one, united in their appetites, their fealty, and their goal. But was it true? Or was it just possible that once the Great Task was done, the Born would be erased just as the Children of the Cold Nursery were to be erased?

It was impossible to be too careful. And so Zicalyx made sure that those Endarkened who looked to her—while unshakably loyal to their dark and terrible liege—were careful to give the Created every opportunity to die.

If Virulan was the only Created alive at the moment of their utter victory, surely he would realize he must speak for the Born—or never speak again.

"To think such thoughts is not treason or rebellion. It is only truth." Zicalyx could not remember where she'd heard that, either. "The daystar comes," she said to her brother. "Let us go where it is always night. The Elflings will cower in the Absence until we drive them forth."

She lifted herself from his body, and Narghail rolled over and got slowly to his feet. He was grumbling beneath his breath, but so softly Zicalyx could pretend not to hear it.

Besides, she knew she was right. The Elflings never wanted to leave the Absence. They knew that outside that shelter there was nothing for them. Nothing but death—slow, merciless—at the hands of the Endarkened.

⁂

"I t is not forbidden," Zicalyx said stubbornly to Shatub. It was some time since her conversation with her brother, and she was trying out her arguments upon a new audience. Shatub was Born, as Zicalyx was, but his mother Shurzul knew who he was and Shurzul was one of the Twelve. "I would never go against the will of King Virulan."

Shatub glared at her. He attempted to find a flaw in her argument and could not. Zicalyx was as clever as Shurzul, and Shurzul was clever enough to have held King Virulan's attention for nearly a hundred Risings.

Endarkened did not normally care about kinship ties, a concept they understood in only the vaguest possible way. Neither the Created-and-Changed nor the Born saw their Endarkened children: those unfortunate necessities King Virulan had ordained were raised out of their sight by the Lesser Endarkened. But just as each female Endarkened knew the father of her child, so the Lesser Endarkened knew the entire lineages of the children they tended, and were careful to teach it to their charges. The Endarkened had no desire to protect their offspring, but to torment another's child could easily be seen as an insult to the one who had borne or sired them.

The World Without Sun was filled with such petty vendettas.

Newly adult Endarkened might join the Court if they chose, but they were ignorant and vulnerable, and the games their elders played with them were very *very* rough. Most of them chose to hide until they were certain they could survive among their own kind. Even though encouraged by his mother's acknowledgment, Shatub had only recently begun to go among the adult Endarkened.

Still, Zicalyx was clever.

"If you did, he would punish you with his own hands," Shatub said.

Zicalyx laughed. "I would beg him to give me to you instead—for I am certain that thus my death would be quick."

It took Shatub several heartbeats to work out the insult in her words, but when he did, he roared and charged at her. His lunge was fruitless, for Zicalyx leapt above him with a single beat of her ribbed scarlet wings, and clung to the rough stone of the ceiling with her claws, still laughing.

Shatub tried to decide whether it would be fun to catch her and harm her, or whether the chase was beneath his newly adult dignity. Zicalyx was fast and lithe: here, in the deep levels of the World Without Sun, there was an endless maze of tunnels in which she could elude any pursuer. He finally settled back on his haunches, growling faintly. When she saw that, Zicalyx sprang to the floor once more.

"The King has said we may go to the World Above just as we choose, so long as we do not wake the Bones of the Earth from their sleep," Zicalyx said coaxingly. "The King has said we may only go against the Elflings at his word, but it is not against his will to seek. It is not against his will to find. It is not against his will to watch what we have found."

Shatub thought hard, but could still see no flaw in her logic. "Just to find?" he asked. "Just to watch?" It had been many Risings since any Endarkened had flown against the Elflings. Obedient to Virulan's word, Endarkened had watched as Elfling lives trickled through their grasp like drops of fresh blood.

"Only that," Zicalyx promised.

"It is tedious. Let the Lesser Endarkened do it." Shatub was still certain there was some trap in Zicalyx's words, but he couldn't quite find it.

"They are slow and cannot fly," Zicalyx scoffed. "Do you wish to carry them around as if you were a pack animal? That would be much more tedious!"

Shatub bared his fangs in reluctant agreement. In this matter, he was certain Zicalyx was right. The Lesser Endarkened were useful for tasks the Endarkened felt were beneath them, but when King Virulan had created them, he had taken care to make them inferior to the Endarkened in every way. They were short, ugly, stupid . . . and they did not have wings.

Shatub spread his wings irritably. He was becoming bored with this conversation.

"I've made Narghail do it," Zicalyx said in a rush. "My brother."

Now *that* was interesting.

"I went to find him among the young," Zicalyx said to Shatub. "I told him I would protect him—" She broke off, frowning impatiently, as Shatub howled with laughter. "I *did* protect him!" she protested. "And he does everything I tell him, so I will continue to do so. If anything happens that displeases King Virulan, it is Narghail who will be blamed!"

Now Shatub gazed at her in admiration, his anger forgotten. "Very well," he said. "Let us gather our boon companions and go and look upon these Elflings."

⊰⊱

Melisha wasn't waiting for Runacar when he returned to his pavilion that night. He was trying not to care when he looked back and saw a silvery spark in the distance. He knew it was she, and went instantly to meet her, using his Silverlight stone sparingly to see him over the unfamiliar ground.

It was still before midnight, though that was late enough for an army that rose before dawn. Runacar had gotten used to the quiet and dark of a world without the torchlight and Silverlight of keep and castel and farm to illuminate it, but the hushed darkness of Vondaimieriel wasn't like that. It was unnatural.

⊰⊱

Melisha stood at the edge of a stand of old trees, radiating silvery light as if she were the moon brought to ground. Deer had browsed away the lower branches of the trees when those were young and tender; there was no risk Runacar would hit his head on a branch he couldn't see. The branches that survived formed a canopy above his head.

"No bedtime story tonight?" he asked when he reached her.

"That depends on where you're going to sleep," the Unicorn replied. Melisha's face wasn't built to display emotions, but Runacar heard them in her voice. He knew she was smiling.

"Wherever you wish," he answered grandly, swirling his cape in a low courtly bow.

Melisha snorted. "My wishes aren't being consulted here," she said. "If they were, we wouldn't be fighting a two-front war." She knelt gracefully, settling with her legs tucked neatly beneath her, her tail curved over her flanks. How someone who looked so much like a deer could remind Runacar so much of a cat was clearly another Unicorn mystery.

"Against the Darkness as well as the High King," Runacar suggested, seating himself beside her, his back to the trunk of one of the trees. "Speaking of whom, how do you know she's marching west? The Gryphons haven't seen a thing."

"They don't cross the Mystrals."

"They don't need to, if they fly high enough—as you well know."

"Unicorns can't fly," Melisha pointed out.

"But they evade questions very well," Runacar answered promptly. "What do you think I'm going to do, go tattling to Leutric?"

"That's the least of my worries," Melisha said. She stretched out until her head was resting on Runacar's knee. He reached out cautiously to rest a hand on the silky silvery fur of her neck. He had been the Prince-Heir of the wealthiest domain in all the land, raised amidst luxury, and Melisha's fur was still the softest, warmest thing he'd ever touched.

"A little higher," she said. "My ears itch."

"You should have arranged to be born with hands," Runacar said mildly. He discovered that the ears of Unicorns itched in much the same way the ears of horses itched, and there was silence for a time.

"So what are you worried about most?" Runacar said at last.

"Everyone and everything dying," Melisha said. "Out of all the possibilities there are, only one leads through to our survival. And that possibility is . . . improbable."

"The Otherfolk and the High King's people making common cause," Runacar said, and Melisha made a wordless sound of agreement. "I'm sorry," he said. "I don't think that's even possible. If it was just Vieliessar, then yes, I'd say our folk had a good chance: the High King is utterly mad, and if she enlisted Landbonds and bandits in her army, why not Otherfolk? But her princes won't allow it."

"And she can't compel them?" Melisha asked.

"Not in this," Runacar said. "I'm sorry. You didn't see the Western Shore Campaign, but you must have heard tell of what happened there."

"Which leaves your solution: slaughter every one of her people."

"Except the children," Runacar said. "And the hope that Leutric will give up this great weapon to one of the Woodwose. And then hope one of them can wield it."

"That's a great deal of hope," Melisha said, sighing.

Runacar said nothing.

Do you think I want to kill these thousands upon thousands of folk? Folk who are not komen? Folk who have done nothing wrong except follow their mad King? To slay the whole of her army will be horror enough, but then I have to seek out every soul who was not on the field that day and end them in cold blood, for all that they've never offered me harm. And let me miss just one—warrior or stripling or, or dairymaid, it matters not in the least—and all of you will die, for if my people excel at anything, it is in how to hate and how to avenge.

The silence stretched.

"So Elvenkind sailed into the unknown west," Melisha said, and it took Runacar a moment to realize she was taking up her story where she had left off. "And when they came to the shore of the Sea of Storms, their King ordered that every ship be dragged ashore. And when they had been unloaded of their horses and their precious cargo, every ship was set afire."

"Why?" Runacar asked, startled. He'd been lulled by the sound of her voice until this turn in the story.

"So that no one could turn about and sail back to where they had come from, my darling," Melisha said sadly. "The King well knew the anger he had roused in the folk over whose lands he had ridden in conquest, and thought it more than possible that they would follow him and his people even to the edge of the world, did they only know where they had gone. And it was for just that reason that—when the ships had burned to ashes, and the ashes had been scattered—he marched west with all his folk. And they marched for a very long time."

"They'd fall into the Glairyrill eventually," Runacar pointed out.

Melisha snorted. "They would, if they had known where they were going, and had gone in a straight line, but they did neither of these things. Perhaps, if they'd had magic—"

"Where were their Lightborn?" Runacar asked.

"If you go on interrupting, you will never know the end of the tale," Melisha said, tilting her head so that the end of her horn brushed against his shoulder. "They had no Lightborn, nor any other kind of sorcerer. They had no magic at all. Some say it was for the lust of what others had that they began the great faraway wars. And that may be so, but I do not know."

Runacar drew breath to ask another question, and then changed his mind. Wondertales didn't have to make sense, after all.

"Ah, the beginning of wisdom," Melisha said into the silence, and Runacar chuckled. "And so they went on for many years, following their great herd of horses, and the good grass, and the turn of the seasons. And at last, after a very long time, they came to the shores of a wide and rolling river. And what do you suppose they saw there?"

"Water?" Runacar guessed. *"Ow!"* he added, as Melisha poked him.

"People," Melisha continued serenely. "People such as those their greatfathers had fought against—though Elvenkind knew as little of that as did these new people they met."

"Did they fight?" Runacar asked warily, when Melisha did not seem inclined to continue.

"No," she said at last, and he could not tell whether it was joy or sorrow or just weariness in her voice. "They did not fight. Not then."

"So—" Runacar began, but Melisha was getting to her feet.

"That's quite enough for tonight," she said. "Come along. It's late, and you should sleep. I'll tell you the next part another time."

She walked beside him until he was within sight of his tent, then turned away and began to run, vanishing into the night so quickly that she might never have been there at all.

And Runacar did not see her for the next four days.

CHAPTER EIGHT

HARVEST MOON TO RADE MOON IN THE TENTH YEAR OF THE HIGH KING'S REIGN: WE WERE TO WED IN HARVEST TIME

A true knight must not only be able to wage war, but ornament it; they must be able to forge every element of their gear, from quilted leather aketon to the standard they carry into battle, and train every destrier they ride. And when battle is won, they must be able to memorialize it in poetry and in song.

—Arilcarion War-Maker, *Of the Sword Road*

I f Vieliessar means to come through the Dragon's Gate—and she must; there is no other way to bring a large force through the Mystrals quickly—the place we must stop her is the Gate itself," Runacar said.

The army's march was over. When the sun rose, his army would begin its ascent into the Dragon's Gate pass. There would be no combat drill tonight, nor any lecture. The discussion of the battle they must fight—and the infinite ways it could go—would take their place.

It still felt odd to Runacar to prepare for battle without having made the sacrifices to the Starry Hunt, without the pledging feast and the victory cup. They hadn't had them during the Western Shore Campaign, either, but that campaign had been different—a long series of feints and rushes. This battle was closer to the type of wars Runacar had been taught to fight.

He wished he didn't want so desperately to run away.

"No coward nor oathbreaker may ride with the Starry Hunt. No horse will bear them, no rider will call them comrade. They will wander as hungry ghosts until the very stars grow cold." Neither Elrinonion Swordmaster nor Lengiathion Warlord had told him this—for them it had not

needed to be said. It had been Runacar's tutor who had put that idea into words, his tutor who had taught young Prince Runacar to read and write from *The Way of the Sword*, and *Of the Sword Road*, and so many other scrolls like them. All those writings by long-dead Warlords and Sword-masters had all proceeded from one essential truth: there would always be war, and Elvenkind would always fight.

(He thought about the story Melisha had told him. Perhaps war was bred in their bones, just as they bred horses for speed and hounds for scent. Perhaps his people had no choice.)

Runacar didn't find the location of the camp a comfortable one for reasons beyond the fact that this might be the last sunset many in this meisne would ever see. The Dragon's Gate had been made over into the symbol of Elven power and Elven madness. To camp in its shadow was as if, in a way, to already be in combat.

Runacar had known intellectually that the pass through the Mystrals had been hugely enlarged—he'd been here at the time it had been done, after all. But memory had made the pass something other than what it was, and seeing it now was a shock.

What they made here is an insult to the land itself, Runacar thought, as much bemused as disgusted. *Half a blight, and half a brand of ownership of something no person can own. I shall not be sorry to see it gone.*

Smooth, flat, level—stone had been pulled through the earth to create an erection on a cyclopean scale, one that a Great Keep could only envy. The road rose, brutal and defiant, in switchbacks that did not so much ignore the terrain as torture it into submission. The road even gouged a great gobbet of stone out of the shoulder of Stardock, the highest point in the Mystrals. He supposed they were all lucky that the Grand Alliance hadn't ordered its Lightborn to remove the mountain entirely.

"It floods here every spring now," Keloit said sadly, looking up at the pass. The Bearward's nose wrinkled, as if he smelled something bad.

When they'd met, Keloit was a child. Ten Wheelturns had made him a husband and a father. Ten more would see him on the threshold of old age. Few of the Otherfolk lived long lives by Elven standards. Of Runacar's friends, only Radafa and the Woodwose would be alive a few decades from now.

"We'll fix it," Runacar told Keloit. *Though the Flower Queen alone knows how. Perhaps the Aesalions can come and drop rocks on it from now until the stars grow cold.*

"It isn't spring now, cub," Bralros said, not unkindly. The grizzled Centaur veteran switched his tail absently. "And we have a war to win." He looked at Runacar. "Never been this far east. What's up there?"

"Ceoprentrei. A chain of mountain valleys behind the ridge, mostly south of the pass," Runacar said. "Water, pasturage, defense—and the main pass to the Uradabhur. There's a Flower Forest too, I think. Elven-kind made the Dragon's Gate out of the pass a long time ago—"

"And have been improving matters ever since," Riann said. The Gryphon tilted her head to one side, as if to inspect the mountain road more closely. "Why there, Runacar? If it is so important to keep the army from reaching the West, why not meet them on the other side?"

"They can run away there," Runacar said grimly. "And she knows the territory too well. She nearly won the whole war there in the Tam-abeths."

Runacar, his apprentices, and his commanders—and, of course, any-one who cared to be here—were gathered around the makeshift sand-table in front of his tent. It was nothing more than a square of ground denuded of grass and soaked with water. The representation of the bat-tlefield he'd sculpted from the mud wasn't entirely representational, but it was accurate enough for the discussion of tactics.

A cluster of Brownies—flanked by two Wulvers and a Palugh—sat across the mud-map from Runacar, and gazed at it intently. Now Runacar glanced up at Keloit, Pelere, and Andhel, who stood just behind them. Of his three apprentices—the greatest of his students—Andhel had the passion and the diligence to become his successor.

Audalo, the last of Runacar's apprentices, was apprentice no more: he was the Heir-in-Waiting to Leutric, King of the Minotaurs. Though Leutric had also gained—at the cost of enormous work and decades of toil—the title "Emperor of the Folk," no one believed Audalo would sim-ply succeed him as Emperor. Audalo must spend his time now learning all that Leutric could teach, in the hope he could acquire those alliances in his own right, if he chose to. If not, the Imperial rule would begin and end with Leutric.

"We don't want the army to get away, and we don't want it to break through," Runacar said. "Here's the terrain. What do we do?"

"We let them reach the top of the pass—those valleys—and we don't let them march through," Pelere said instantly. "Only . . . if we don't want them to escape, we have to hold both approaches to the pass, and how do we do that without them seeing us?" She frowned at the map as if it were a personal enemy and tapped a forehoof impatiently.

"We hide?" Keloit said uncertainly. "In . . . Maybe in the Flower Forest?"

"Then how do we hold both passes?" Andhel asked. "That Flower Forest is at the far end of the valleys." The Woodwose pointed southward. "More than a day's walk."

"*Some* of us can fly," Riann said smugly.

"Exactly," Runacar said. "We can move faster than she can, individually at least. She won't be expecting to fight in Ceoprentrei, so her entire army will be on horseback, and—" He was interrupted by the harsh rasping caw of Gryphon laughter.

"And her horses will run to any place we Gryphons are not!" Riann said merrily. The Gryphons might be staunch pacifists, but they relished a good joke as much as anyone.

The Gryphons won't fight, but they're big and frightening-looking, and that's a help—especially since the High King's army thinks of them only as ravenous animals and has no idea what they're really like. The Centaurs and the Woodwose will do their best, the Minotaurs are good fighters and good sorcerers both, and nobody in their right mind wants to face Bearward Berserkers, but Sword and Star help us all if we have to face her Warhunt. . . .

"Exactly. So if things go in the best way they can, she'll turn the army south—away from you—to regroup," Runacar said.

Slowly and carefully, Runacar led his captains—and his audience— through the possibilities they would face. In the worst possible case, they would reach the top of the pass after Vieliessar did and have to fight to gain control of the terrain. In the best case, his army would have time to reach the top, secure both passes, and hide itself before the High King's forces arrived. In either event, his army would chase Elvenkind south through the linked valleys, bottle them up far from the Dragon's Gates, and . . . do what they must.

Kill them all. Trap her army, and kill it, and then go looking for the survivors, and that will be such a stain on my soul as even the Hunt Lord himself cannot erase.

Reflexively, Runacar glanced skyward. One of the Aesalions was circling, his wings iridescent black like those of an enormous carrion crow. He thought it might be Drotha, but he wasn't sure from this distance. Runacar was not completely sure how much of the Mystery of Aesalions had come to fight. The Aesalions loathed one another—that more than Drotha had come was little short of miraculous. And if—*when!*—the Otherfolk won, the Aesalions would have to do the bulk of the slaughter, little though Runacar relished the thought of being the one to unleash them that way. The Aesalions were utterly uncontrollable and nearly unkillable—not only were they utterly impervious to magical attacks, they couldn't even sense magic's presence. Though an ordinary weapon—if you could manage to strike them with it—worked very well.

Runacar thought of Juniche's death atop Daroldan Great Keep: its Lightborn defenders had Fetched a poisoned net to fall over the Aesalion and trap him atop the watchtower, then killed him with spears and hammers. Runacar told himself that preparation of such an ambush required foreknowledge of an attack, something Vieliessar's army wouldn't have. But her army *did* possess everything they needed save the advance knowledge that Aesalions would be in the battle: a few Lightborn, some raw material . . .

Stop it. Are you some witless child, puling and yowling because your pony might take harm upon the field? People will die. That is the nature of war. But we have no choice.

In his heart, Runacar was certain that if the High King was coming west, she wasn't coming to visit. She was coming to retake the West, and the first thing she'd do when she got here was push his people—push the Otherfolk—out of it. And kill all of them she could.

"My people." Runacar caught the wording of his thoughts and grimaced. *For good or ill, I have chosen my side and my folk, and with them I shall keep faith until my death.*

He finished his council of war, telling his people that he was certain they were ready to face any eventuality. (Even as he knew that they weren't, even as he knew too many of them would die.) Hoping they believed the lie and didn't see the truth; it was all the protection he could give them. When at last his students had dispersed to their own places, and the camp had settled itself for sleep, Runacar realized that sleep—at least for him—would be long in coming.

But the night was soft, and uninhabited by anything that wished to do him harm, and so he went for a walk. At the very least, no one would see him fretting over what was to come, and that alone was worth a thousand komen on the field. (Or so Lengiathion Warlord had always sworn.)

As soon as Runacar left the encampment, silence descended like a heavy velvet cloak. There were no night sounds to be heard—no owls calling, no bats whistling, no distant howls of farm dogs nor the melancholy chorus of wolves singing to the moon. He hoped the silence didn't worry anyone else as much as it did him.

Inevitably, his walk led him to the foot of the road they would take tomorrow.

The passage of Wheelturns had given the grass time to begin its reclamation of the Sanctuary Road, had given winter snow and spring rains time to soften the imprint of hooves and wagons that had scarred the white clay. But where the turf ended and the stone began, the road was as new and unmarred as it had been the day it was created. Even with no more light than the Hunt Road in the sky—for the moon was dark—the stone surface gleamed as bright as still water. He saw what Keloit had meant: the soil below each switchback was barren, the topsoil washed away by Wheelturns of springtide flooding. He took a cautious step forward, and set his foot upon the Mage-made road. His boot grated on windblown grit, scuffed over the slight roughness of the granite.

"They certainly built things to last."

His sword was half-drawn at the first word, for the games the War

Princes and their children had played among themselves were rough
and never ending, all bent to one end: the perfect knight. The perfect
warrior. There was a part of Runacar that would always expect ambush
anywhere he went.

Then he recognized Melisha's voice and let the sword slide back into
its sheath as he turned to face her.

As always, the Unicorn was perfect, as radiantly immaculate as if she
had only a moment before stepped from some unimaginable stables and
the attention of its grooms. But even to think of her that way brought a
pang of mental dissonance, half composed of the thought that Melisha
could ever be a possession, and half from the thought that she did not
belong in created places.

"Where have you been?" he asked, pleased that he could keep his
voice low and even.

"Here and there," Melisha said vaguely. "Last-minute preparations.
I'm sure you understand."

"You aren't coming to the war, are you?" Runacar asked in horror.

"You make it sound like Midwinter Masque," Melisha said chidingly.

"Well, no, but—" He stopped. Melisha certainly knew her limitations, and had not been shy of enforcing obedience to them before now.
"If you want to tell me any more stories, you're running out of time," he
said instead.

"It's only the one story," Melisha said, and: "That's why I came back.
But not here." She turned and walked away, her hooves making soft dull
sounds in the dry summery grass. Runacar followed.

"Why does it matter?" he asked as they walked. "This story? Telling
it? What happens in Ceoprentrei isn't going to be changed by some improving homily, you know—even if the story's true."

"And if it isn't?" Melisha asked, not sounding particularly insulted.

"Then it matters even less," Runacar said simply. "Who cares what a
bunch of Elvenkind who aren't us and who didn't even have Lightborn
did or didn't do before Amretheon Aradruiniel was enthroned?"

"At least you've been listening," Melisha commented.

Runacar waved a vague hand to signify his complete indifference,
and they walked on in silence.

"Well," Melisha said at last, "this looks like a nice spot. You can pick grapes while we talk."

Runacar could faintly discern the low brushy shapes of what had once been a vineyard, now overgrown with brambles and long grass, its grapes lush and ripe and untouched by birds or beasts (even the scavengers had fled Vondaimieriel). "Are we talking?" Runacar asked idly. "If we are, I have some questions, such as where all the animals are. They aren't here."

"West," Melisha said simply. "They're running away from the Darkness, and what comes with it. Animals have much more sense than people, sometimes."

"They do," Runacar agreed. "Animals wouldn't try to harvest grapes in the dark," he added. (He had his Silverlight stone with him, of course, but it was visible for furlongs once it was exposed.)

"Hmph." A moment later, Melisha began to glow—her horn brightest of all—until there was more than enough light to pick grapes by.

"They'll turn you purple," Runacar pointed out, as he spread his cloak on the ground and knelt upon it. He didn't have anything to carry the grapes away in, but he didn't think that was going to be a problem.

"I'll risk it," Melisha said dryly, lying down beside him.

He soon had a mound of grape bunches piled in front of him, and began plucking them from the stems to feed Melisha (and occasionally himself).

"Delicious," she said, nuzzling his palm. "And so much more civilized than having to stick your whole head into the vines. You're right, of course. They do stain."

"It's nice to be right occasionally," Runacar muttered.

"Don't play the tragic hero with me, my darling. It cuts a bit too close to bone. But as I said when I left off this story, one day Manafaeren led his people to the edge of the Glairyrill, and discovered that there were other people living in the Goldengrass."

She paused expectantly. Perhaps he was meant to recognize the name, but he didn't. At least he understood the rest of it. "Manafaeren met the Otherfolk," Runacar said.

"Yes," Melisha answered neutrally. "It had been a very long time since his folk had beached and burned their ships, and perhaps Time ran faster then, or perhaps they had been cursed, but the folk of Manafaeren lived brief and joyful lives, and had forgotten not only their past, but their past wars."

"Lucky them," Runacar muttered. Melisha pretended she hadn't heard.

"They greeted these strangers warily—just as the Otherfolk greeted them, of course—but the Goldengrass was vast and its grazing lush, and each people had much to share with the other. And so the folk of Manafaeren lived peacefully with all the folk of the Goldengrass for a very long time."

"Melisha, what is the *point* of this?" Runacar asked, a little desperately. This story had become too improbable for even a wondertale, and, at the same time, somehow more sinister. If Melisha meant to teach him about Elvenkind and Otherfolk living in peace, surely this was a lesson he'd already learned?

"There is no point," Melisha answered. "Only truth. Because one day, the Darkness came. And of every ten creatures that walked beneath the sky, nine died."

And this is the foe Vieliessar High King wishes to go to war against? Runacar kept himself from speaking aloud with an effort, though less of an effort than he made to keep himself from picturing the reality behind Melisha's words. Nine out of ten. Eleven tailles of a great-taille; twelve komen alive out of every hundred and a half.

A wondertale. That is all this is. A wondertale. Not history. Not fact.

"And then what happened?" he asked, keeping his voice light with an effort.

"And then Runacar ran out of grapes and never heard the end of the tale," Melisha said tartly. Runacar turned back to the vines to pick more. When more had been gathered, and Melisha had eaten a mouthful or two, she continued her story. "And when the Darkness was gone, the folk of Manafaeren knew one thing only: that the Darkness was not of their own familiar form and shape, and so it must be some part of the Otherfolk, who had many forms and shapes. And so they cried betrayal, and fled away to the Teeth of the Moon, where they built a great stone city, and shut themselves away from all they had once known.

"But as their wounds healed, so did their hatred and fear increase, for the Darkness changes everything it touches. Their logic strayed from truth, and they concluded that to destroy all folk wearing a shape not their own would be to destroy the Darkness, and so they would make themselves safe."

"And nothing has ever changed," Runacar interrupted bitterly. "The High King died, the *alfaljodthi* have fought among themselves ever since, and even so, they have *never* stopped hunting the Otherfolk!" He pushed himself to his feet, scattering loose grapes everywhere. "Why tell me this now? It doesn't change anything! All it does is tell me nothing is ever going to change! *Nothing!*" He turned away, fists clenched at his sides, fighting to control his breathing, though against laughter or tears, he didn't know. "We might as well turn back now, and go back to what's left of the Western Shore, and wait to die," he finished softly.

"No." Melisha had gotten to her feet. She delicately threaded her gleaming horn beneath his arm, and then her head and neck, until she was standing beside him and he had his arm draped over her withers. "This is a story of hope, I promise you. There's not much more to tell. The story isn't finished yet, though the part I have to tell ends soon. But you must craft the next verses of this song by yourselves. Will you hear the rest, my darling?"

Runacar closed his eyes, blinking back not tears so much as desolation. He didn't know when he had started hoping for peace, believing it could be gained with only one more battle. But after each battle there had always been another battle to fight, and now Melisha was telling him that there would never be an end. That Elvenkind would always fight, and slaughter, and hate. . . .

"Yes," he said roughly, when he realized she would not continue without his assent. "Tell me the rest."

"The Otherfolk knew many things, and had watched and learned for many years. They knew the Darkness would return, and when it did it would not be to winnow, but to harvest. A Red Harvest. When it came, the Darkness would slaughter all and everything, so that all things living—even grass, even trees—would be gone forever. The Otherfolk knew that if the peoples of the land did not all stand together, death was certain. But Elvenkind had become their enemy, and would not listen.

"And so the Otherfolk and the Brightfolk went to the Great Powers of the land, and they begged those Powers for hope. And perhaps it was the Great Powers that answered, or perhaps it was only the need of those who petitioned them, but one of the Powers put on flesh and form, and stepped from the Flower Forest clad in fur and hoof and horn. . . ."

There was a long silence, as if Melisha was nerving herself to go on.

"This Power had little in the way of magic, but that did not matter, because *she* was magic. Magic incarnate. She was the greatest of us all, and her name was Pelashia Celenthodiel."

Runacar realized he was waiting for the story to go on, and then realized it wasn't going to. *Where is the rest of the story? What happened then?* "But Pelashia Celenthodiel was Amretheon Aradruiniel's *Queen*," he said, sounding indignant even to himself.

"Yes, my love," Melisha said quietly. "I am very much afraid she was."

"They had no Lightborn. They had no magic at all."

"One of the Powers put on flesh and form"

"Her name was Pelashia Celenthodiel"

It's not possible. It's not possible. Amretheon's Queen: the common ancestor every one of the Hundred Houses can claim. Every prince, every Line, every House traces back to her.

"Pelashia Celenthodiel was Amretheon's Queen," Runacar repeated raggedly. "That means the *alfaljodthi* are her children."

"Yes," Melisha said quietly.

Runacar did not know how long it was before Melisha spoke again, or whether she had been speaking for some time and he simply hadn't noticed. He wished he weren't listening now, but Melisha's voice was sweet, and kind, and filled with love, and Runacar needed that love as a starving creature needed food.

"She gave your ancestors the magic they lacked, in hope they would come to see the Brightfolk and the Otherfolk as their true kin—or at least as not kin to the Darkness. She meant to bring warning of the Red Harvest, though that was millennia away, for surely Amretheon's folk adored her and surely they would heed the warning given by their Queen. As the seasons passed, and her youth and beauty remained unmarred by time and age, the people called her Flower Queen, for she was as changeless as the Flower Forest they named for her. Her children grew to adulthood and took husbands and wives, and the husbands sired children, and the wives bore children, and the children grew strong and tall and married in their turn.

"No one can know what words Pelashia Celenthodiel said to Amretheon Aradruiniel. Perhaps she was at the verge of winning her lonely and silent war against fear and blind hatred. Perhaps all that Amretheon's people needed was a little more time. If that is true, they did not get it. One day, urged on by what malicious counsel no one knows, Amretheon, then old and full of years, chose to go hunting, as he had not done since the days of his youth. In the forest, he loosed his bow at a quarry only half seen, and when he rode forward, he saw that he had slain his Queen."

"He saw more than that, didn't he?" Runacar said roughly.

"He did. He saw she was not Elven. And that knowledge drove him mad," Melisha said calmly.

"He died. And none of Pelashia's children succeeded him," Runacar said flatly.

"Amretheon died as all but the most ethereal of the Brightfolk must die. But before he did, the tale of Pelashia's death plunged his kingdom into war. His children—*Pelashia's* children—fled Tildorangelor, and Celenthodiel, and Kalalielahwyr with all those who loved them, and all who did not love them followed them to slay them. And after that there was no High King—until now."

⧫

The walls of his tent were yellow with morning light. Runacar stared at them. He had no memory of leaving Melisha. Of coming back here. He wasn't even sure what had awakened him, for this morning no one had come to disturb him. It was as if a single sentence Melisha had uttered had supplanted every thought, every sensation.

"Her name was Pelashia Celenthodiel"

"One of the Powers put on flesh and form"

"Her name was Pelashia Celenthodiel"

"Pelashia Celenthodiel"

"Pelashia Celenthodiel"

Runacar did not want to believe it. He did not want to *understand* it. Melisha's tale made the whole history of the Hundred Houses a lie, a farce, a terrible joke. Runacar tried to convince himself that this was some incomprehensible Unicorn trick. He couldn't.

And that meant . . .

That meant that if Leutric's strategy of appeasement was based on giving Elvenkind to the Darkness in exchange for the lives of the Otherfolk, it was fatally flawed: the Elves were Otherfolk too. If the Darkness was after the *alfaljodthi,* it was also after the Woodwose. With both Woodwose and *alfaljodthi* gone, there would be no one left who could use Leutric's weapon, whatever it was.

And even if that weren't true, even if all of Elvenkind was dead and the Woodwose had won, Leutric's mysterious "weapon" would be useless without a dedicated pan-Otherfolk army to deploy it, support it, and capitalize on the victories it brought.

Runacar could form such an alliance and keep it together. He knew this without either pride or vanity; by now he had very little of either left to him. But the problem with that was that he was going to be dead sometime in the next few days. Vieliessar could do the same as he could or better—of that Runacar was certain—but she was going to be as dead as he was.

Because until she was dead, his side hadn't won, and the moment either he or Vieliessar died, the other would too. *Melisha never wanted you to kill them. She wanted you to form an alliance with them. But she never told you* how.

As if bespelled, he went to catch and saddle his mount. The details of their army's deployment had been settled sunturns before, and all seemed to be going just as Runacar had arranged: the non-combatants

and the supplies not immediately necessary remained in the Vondaimieriel camp, and those who would fight (or in the case of the Gryphons,
spread their wings and look alarming) ascended the mountain. As the
scouts set forth and the army prepared to march, no one approached
him for orders, for the time for training was over.

Soon—very soon—they would fight.

Nothing had changed—aside from his new realization that even
winning the battle at Ceoprentrei wouldn't be enough to save the Otherfolk. Trapped. They were all trapped, and there was no way out.

The camp kitchen was still set up, but today Runacar had no appetite.
He mounted his mare and turned her head toward the Dragon's Gate.

⊰⊱

As the path rose, Runacar looked out across the autumn-gold hills
of Vondaimieriel. So beautiful. So haunted. And soon to be swept
away by the Darkness—whatever it was. All of what he, what they, had
done—the organizing, the training, the moonturns of campaigns—had
been futile. In the end, the Darkness would have them. Unless an intricate chain of events he could only dimly grasp occurred in precise order.
They would have a chance then. If—

His chain of thought was abruptly broken when Andhel rode up beside him, then turned her pony to bring his mare to a stop.

"The scouts are back," she announced. "There's nobody at the top of
the pass."

"Are they sure?" Runacar asked automatically. Inside, he was filled
with hope and fury: there was a path to victory! But he couldn't see it
yet . . .

"*I'm* sure, Elfling." The Palugh's voice came from just behind him. In-
ured by now to their sense of humor, Runacar barely twitched—though
he did turn to confront the speaker. Sundapple—who was curled up,
perfectly at ease, on the horse's rump—bristled his whiskers in the Palugh version of a smirk.

"I went," Sundapple said. "Those smelly idiot Wulvers went. And
even Andhel went, just in case I was too bored to talk to you later. There's
nothing up there but grass, and water, and lovely stones for basking on,

and fat tamias and escurials. And birds, of course, though really they're usually not worth the effort."

"Did you cross the valley to the eastern side?" Runacar asked instantly. Even if Vieliessar was not yet on the march, her war camp would be visible, he thought.

Sundapple looked annoyed. "Of course not," he said. "Because—"

"Crossing the Mystrals is forbidden," Runacar, Andhel, and Sundapple said in chorus.

"All right," Runacar said, sighing. "We'll have to— Wait. You said there were mice?"

"You can't have them," Sundapple said instantly. "They're mine."

"But they're *there*," Runacar repeated. That made no sense. Everything larger than an earthworm had been fleeing westward for the last ten Wheelturns. There shouldn't be anything larger than a honeybee in Ceoprentrei—if that.

"Yes. They're there," Sundapple agreed. He closed his eyes in utter boredom and began, slowly, to vanish—in the sense of rendering himself invisible, not of leaving. The *departure* of a Palugh was considerably more abrupt.

"What does it mean, Rune?" Andhel asked.

"I don't know," he said simply. "But even the birds and the hares have fled—you're the one who said how bad the hunting's been since we came east of Caerthalien—so I don't know why there's anything alive in Ceoprentrei."

"And anything you don't understand is likely to be a trap," Andhel said cheerfully.

"It is," Runacar said with a sigh. She was quoting him, he realized. "So here's what we're going to do. Sundapple, I want an entire Pounce of your people back up there and invisible, just in case someone's using some kind of spell none of us knows about. And a Wild of Wulvers. I'll send them down to the Flower Forest; I want to know if there are any Brightfolk in Nomaitemil, and if there are, why. Andhel, find one of the message runners. Send them to Leutric with the report on what you found in Ceoprentrei. At least he'll have something to work with if we all just vanish. Tell Tanet I want Woodwose scouts to watch the valley constantly and report back in relays. If Vieliessar's scouts see them, they won't think 'Otherfolk,' they'll think 'Elvenkind,' so we'll still have the advantage. I don't know what's going on, but this is *not* going to be a replay of the Siege of Daroldan," he said fiercely.

Andhel nodded, her eyes sparkling with excitement, and chivvied her pony up the outside of the moving column.

"I hope you don't expect me to talk to the Wulvers." Sundapple's voice came, seemingly, from empty air.

Runacar laughed, a little surprised that he still could. "Of course not," he said easily. "I have minions for that sort of thing. Just remember: the sooner you're back up there, the sooner you can go after those mice."

"You almost sound intelligent," Sundapple said archly.

Runacar looked around. His army filled the road to the Dragon's Gate. When both armies stood on the grass of Ceoprentrei, there would be battle, and only one army could win. He realized that on one level Melisha's story didn't matter. It didn't change who he had become. And it didn't change what he would fight for.

He touched his heels to his mare's sides and sent her trotting up the road.

⊶⊷

The air was filled with the delicious scent of burning flesh. "See?" Narghail whispered. "It is just as I have said!"

Shatub aimed a negligent cuff at his head, and Zicalyx snickered.

"Silence, maggots!" Marbuglor hissed. Since Marbuglor was one of the Created-and-Changed (and far more powerful than any of them), the younger Endarkened quieted at once and watched the scene before them.

The viewing party's membership had increased remarkably since Zicalyx had spoken of her plan to Shatub: there were over a dozen of them now. This made Zicalyx slightly uneasy, but she wasn't quite sure why. *It is probably because so many Created-and-Changed have come,* she told herself. *Everyone knows they are always ready to attack the Born. When Born are young, they are helpless. Just as Narghail was helpless when I took him under my protection.*

"What is the meat *doing*?" Gholak asked incredulously. Behind her, the other Endarkened jostled and shoved for a better view.

In the meadow to the north of the Absence were perhaps twenty of the loathsome Elflings, along with the beasts they ate and the beasts that helped them control those beasts. The carcass of one of the eating beasts, flensed and spitted, turned slowly over a banked fire.

"The same thing they do every time the sky grows light," Narghail said importantly. "They bring their beasts forth to eat grass."

"If they just ate the grass themselves it would make more sense," grumbled Narghail.

"*You* will eat grass first," Zicalyx answered. "Great Mistresses, I was the one who tracked these Elflings here, and I was the one who set my brother to watch—silently! unknown!—to see what they would do. And when I found that they had lost their fear of us—"

"Naturally, you did not act alone," Marbuglor interrupted smoothly, "but brought your word to those who are wiser and more powerful than you will ever be."

"Naturally I relied upon the vast knowledge of those far more powerful than I," Zicalyx answered immediately. *And thus I escape all blame— especially if something goes wrong. And I would wager a caskworth of Elfling eyes that no whisper of this has reached King Virulan even now.*

Of course Lord Virulan, King of the Endarkened, did not wait passively on the Throne of Night to be told things. He didn't trust any of his subjects nearly that far. He had magics greater than any Zicalyx could dream of, and naturally he was known to use them to spy on his subjects. (If he had not, he would have ceased to be King very quickly.)

"What are we waiting for?" Gholak demanded. "The meat is there! Let us carry it off to be *our* meat!"

Zicalyx stared at Gholak in amazement and horror. She had meant this outing to raise her status in the World Without Sun—not to go directly against the will of King Virulan. Out of the corner of her eye, she saw that Marbuglor's face held a similar expression.

If the King were to find out— But he will not find out! Which of us will tell him when the punishment for disobedience is so great? Zicalyx thought hopefully.

There was a long moment in which the decision teetered like a knife about to fall. Obedience and safety? Or transgression and blissful slaughter? Then Shatub shrieked and flung himself in the direction of the Elflings and their beasts, and Marbuglor and Gholak followed close behind.

⊰⊱

"They're coming," young Niviel whispered. Methestel supposed he should name her "Niviel Lightsister" even in his thoughts, even though the child was barely old enough to fly her kite. In these dark times, children took up weapons the moment they were old enough to lift them. Niviel had seen twelve Wheelturns. Niviel was one of the Warhunt.

"Then get you gone," Methestel said, and watched as Niviel turned and ran for the safety of Saganath.

Elvenkind had quickly learned that its enemies were like evil children; they must constantly be distracted, for when the Endarkened attacked, the only hope of survival was to somehow *not be there*. The only victories Elvenkind could claim came when the Endarkened were made to waste their energy on trivial targets while ignoring lives and resources Elvenkind could not afford to lose.

But even a decoy target must be living. Must be *Elven*.

Those who chose themselves for this great task called themselves the Company of the Hare—*Asharnab* in the old tongue—in honor of the small wily creature whose tactics they adopted. One could leave their ranks—alive—at any time just as simply as one joined. All those who remained knew that their lives were to be short, but memory of their deeds a thing that would live forever.

Methestel gave a low whistle of warning. Immediately the flock-guards and herd-dogs began to drive the sheep back toward the forest. Perhaps some of the beasts would survive. If not, their lives would have been given for all. Just as his was about to be.

Methestel ran toward the first of the weapons caches which the Company of the Hare had buried during the bright noonday hours.

⊰⊱

The Elflings ran in circles among their beasts, clearly too terrified by the sight of the Endarkened to seek shelter in the Absence. Narghail pulled ahead, and Shatub let him. If there was to be any trouble, better that Narghail reached it first. Behind Shatub the rest of the Endarkened followed in a rustle and thunder of great scarlet wings. There was no thought of taking captives back to the World Without Sun; not this time. They would slaughter everything within their reach.

"See them squeal in terror!" Gholak cried ecstatically.

Now Narghail soared over the muddle of Elflings and beasts, to land between them and the Absence. He lunged at the nearest Elfling. The Elfling flung a flask at him in predictable and useless defiance. The delicate glass shattered against Narghail's shoulder and began to release billows of smoke into the air.

And as he became enveloped in thick white smoke, Narghail began to scream.

❈

Only Zicalyx saw what was happening to Narghail. The others—even Marbuglor—were engrossed in picking targets of their own. The Elfling who had thrown the flask ran, but Narghail did not seem to notice. He writhed and howled, clawing at his own flesh, attempting to fly and unable to. The stench of burning Endarkened flesh joined the oily acrid scent of the white smoke.

Zicalyx hesitated, considered seizing the bottle-thrower, then quickly wrapped herself in a spell of invisibility and bounded into the sky—her own safety was far more important than revenge. An instant later, a flight of arrows struck the place where she had stood. The grass around the arrows caught fire and began to burn.

❈

Shatub circled back to land at the north side of the grassland, counting on his speed and reflexes to gain him sufficient prey before it could get to shelter. Preoccupied with his choice of targets, Shatub did not see what had happened to Narghail, nor that Zicalyx was absent from the slaughter. Shatub grabbed the nearest meat, disemboweled it with a swipe of his talons, then flourished a whip-like skein of magic that skinned a dozen of the herd beasts alive. Their screams of agony and terror joined the music-sweet clamor all around him. Astonishingly, more Elflings had appeared from the forest verge to join the battle, clearly mounting a hopeless attempt to drive off Shatub and his fellow Endarkened. There were at least two Elflings here for every Endarkened.

As Shatub glanced around himself to see where his brethren were, a body blundered into him, nearly knocking him from his feet. The body was wreathed in white smoke, and Shatub struck at it reflexively before seeing wings hanging from its back in smoking tatters.

Narghail! One of us!

Narghail ran away, still screaming, still burning. When he looked around, Shatub could see that more of his brethren lay writhing in anguish upon the smoldering grassland. Many of the wounded were so studded with arrows that the shafts looked like some strange spiky coat. They struggled, but only succeeded in driving the arrows deeper into their flesh. Others ripped arrows from their bodies in handfuls, blind to all but the pain. Some Endarkened fled on foot, as Narghail had, too crazed by pain to cast the spell allowing them wingless flight.

The Elflings were clustered around the most helpless of the Endarkened, hacking at the thrashing bodies.

"Fools! *They have set a trap!*" Zicalyx shouted. She hovered above the melee, becoming visible again to shout her warning. Flights of arrows were launched at her and she leaped out of the way. The arrows fell to the ground, where the grass began to burn.

Shatub bounded into the sky, abandoning the attack. At the moment, his thoughts were of two things. Escaping—and being first to tell this tale to King Virulan. The uninjured survivors were scattered across the sky, all with the same thought Shatub had: get to King Virulan first. The first to arrive would be able to make sure that Virulan knew that all they had done was to loyally spy on the others to report them to his King.

When he heard the hiss of another flight of arrows, Shatub reflexively dodged. Only one of the arrows struck him, passing through the meat of his thigh before the feathers on the shaft stopped it. Reflexively, he grasped the head to break it off.

His hand began to burn. Oil dripped from the arrow onto his flesh. First came blisters, then came smoke and blood. He scrubbed his hand frantically against his skin, but only succeeded in spreading the burning substance. At the same time, the wound in his thigh became alive with pain. It burned and stank and emitted billows of pale smoke, and the flesh around it dissolved, making the wound grow larger each moment.

The desire to be first to gain Virulan's ear warred with the urgent desire for the pain to stop. Pain won. (The Endarkened cherished others' pain, not their own.) Shatub dove down and flung himself into a stream far distant from both Elflings and Absence, and splashed water over his body in anticipation of sweet relief.

It did not come.

His hands burned. His ornaments burned. His leg burned, its wound filled with tongues of flame even underwater, the glowing white poison it contained making the water bubble. He screamed in utter frustration and began clawing at his own flesh, desperate to excise the strange poison at any cost.

He failed.

⊰⊱

A lifetime ago, Ragriel had been First Axe among the foresters and woodsmen of Oronviel. It was a familiar thing to heave the great heavy axe with its long haft of ahata-wood back over his shoulder, to mark the target point by eye and to send the blade whistling down to that very spot.

But never had he struck a tree with as much glee as he struck this.

The head of the burning Endarkened rolled away from its body. The jaws snapped futilely at air, the yellow eyes blazed—for it yet lived—with hatred. Ragriel used the side of his axe to swat the head toward the fire pit. The body it had been separated from flailed, blind now and deaf; life's blood ran thickly from the stump of the mindless living-dead thing's neck and bubbled as the decapitated body panted for air. Ragriel struck again and again, to cleave the body at every joint. He kicked the carcass into position so he could more easily strike at his targets. In moments the body had been reduced to a pile of parts: wings, hands, arms, legs, split and quartered torso.

But still alive. Oh yes, still alive.

The fire was large and the fire pit was deep. Ragriel kicked the pieces into the flames.

The monsters were strong and fast, immune to nearly all the spells the Lightborn knew, and able to shrug off any wound they received. Even beheading didn't kill them—all it did was keep the monsters from casting whatever form of Shield they used.

Sometimes, that was enough.

⊰⊱

So it worked?" Thurion asked, as the survivors of the Endarkened attack returned to shelter and safety.

Ragriel answered Thurion with a laugh of pure triumph. "Better than anyone might hope! My heart is sad that the *ikhlad*-fire is so difficult to make, or we might claim victory over the Endarkened over the course of a single War Season!"

Elvenkind had sought to find something that would work against the Endarkened since the day of the High King's Enthroning, and all the people, from Lightborn to Lightless illusionist, from huntsman to scholar, Craftworker to komen, had pooled their knowledge together, for knowledge now was too precious to be left to only one mind. It was a Lightless illusionist who had remembered reading of a burning substance distilled from rock that was as sticky as greenneedle sap in the spring and unquenchable besides. The Houses of the Arzhana had traded it to the Grand Windsward for use against the Beastlings, but it had never been used in war.

Until now.

"When we reach the Western Shore, we will have it in abundance," Thurion said to Ragriel. It had been the work of five Wheelturns to amass even an *arthal's*-worth. *And we have used more than half of our store today. Let us hope we have aggravated the Darkspawn sufficiently, or Vielle's plan will not work.*

"I will undertake to pour it down each one of their ugly throats with my own hand," Ragriel said. "Let them choke on fire instead of on our blood!"

"Leaf and Star grant your words are heard," Thurion murmured. Then, after a pause: "You know that even what has been done today will not kill them."

Ragriel smiled wolfishly. "Their heads are buried beneath flaming coals to roast, and the limbs of their bodies are burned, buried, or scattered to the Nine Quarters. *These* Endarkened will never return to plague us."

Or at least, not for a very long time, Thurion thought.

HARVEST MOON IN THE TENTH YEAR OF THE HIGH KING'S REIGN: WHERE LATE THE SWEET BIRDS SANG

There are few difficulties in holding a Domain or even the King-Domain taken by force or treachery so long as one is seen to be one of the Line Direct—or if not, is seen to give that line more reverence than one's own. The nobles will have self-interest for their whip and curb, and the commons only ask that nothing is seen to change.

This is true no matter what manner of creature gathers together: even cats and ravens prefer their Princes to their liberty.

—Author Unknown, Notes Toward a Unified Theory of War

Shurzul admired her reflection in the Brightworld mirror. It gave an odd sort of reflection, imperfect and garishly bright—not beautiful, but truly exotic. She had ordered it brought from one of the Elfling places she and her sisters had destroyed. There were several such items scattered about her chambers—after all, she did so want dear little Hazaniel to feel at home here.

The Elfling child sat quietly in the corner, playing some elaborate game with scraps of fabric and some adornments Shurzul had grown tired of. On either side of him a lantern burned with clear yellow flame, for his eyes could not adapt to the lightlessness of the World Without Sun.

It had been several Risings since Shurzul had plucked him from the slave-pits on an impulse she herself did not fully understand. If the novelty had not outweighed the inconvenience of the Brightworld brat, she would have slaughtered him long since: much of the food he was offered made him sick, and he collapsed into unconsciousness several times each Cycle. But her slaves had learned how to tend him, and he trusted Shurzul now, as only the innocent could trust.

I must make something of him—something unique and terrible enough to retain Virulan's interest—and favor. The King of the Endarkened had not yet tired of her, and the rewards of his favor were sweet. Yet Virulan's interest could wane as quickly as it had waxed, and he saw conspiracies everywhere. *Even when no conspiracy exists, he suspects one. And his word is both law and truth.* It was amusing to contemplate the fact that King Virulan had killed far more of the Endarkened than the Elflings had—only somehow Shurzul did not think Virulan would share the joke, and she was certain the Elflings would not. The Elflings had no sense of humor at all.

She glanced over at Hazaniel, still enwrapped in his game, and shuddered. *Imagine speaking to one of them as an equal! It is bad enough that they exist at all!* She must discover a use for Hazaniel soon—one that would gain her power and status, of course. She closed her eyes and began to turn possibilities over in her mind. . . .

"Mama!" Shatub flung open the door, vaulted over the Lesser Endarkened who tried to bar his way, and flung himself at her feet. "Terrible news!"

Shurzul shrieked at the sudden interruption and struck Shatub across the face, the heavy rings on her hand cutting several gouges in his skin. He did not recoil, but simply clutched harder at her legs and tried to bury his face in her lap.

"What is it? What is it?" Hazaniel's voice was high and frightened.

Shurzul kicked Shatub away from her with a warning hiss, and went to kneel before the child. "Why, nothing is wrong, my darling. It is merely a child of my own, come to pay his respects to his mama."

"Would he like to play with me?" Hazaniel looked hopeful.

Yes. Very much. "Perhaps soon, but not today," she said, forcing her voice to the sugar-sweet purr she used when talking to the Elfling child. "Now come. Let your servant take you away. You may come back in a while."

The Lesser Endarkened Shurzul had tasked with Hazaniel's safety shuffled forward. It was the one the child itself had chosen, for Hazaniel liked its dense fur and did not seem to be bothered by its mandibles and clusters of eyes.

"Mistress says come," it said in its croaking voice, and Hazaniel pulled himself to his feet, hand clutching its fur, and shuffled off obediently, looking back over his shoulder at Shurzul.

When the door to the inner chamber had closed, she turned back to Shatub. *"Speak!"* she demanded.

"We went only to look—I swear this to you! Only to look!"

This did not sound good at all. *"What did you do?"* Shurzul demanded.

And Shatub told her everything.

⚔

This can still be salvaged, Shurzul told herself once again. Fortunately, Gholak and Marbuglor were already destroyed, and who could say when they and the others who had gone on that unlucky expedition would be brought back among the living by *He Who Is*? All of this could be blamed on them. *King Virulan will always expect treachery from any of the Twelve-Who-Were.*

And the thing that mattered most was being the first to bring Virulan the news.

None of the others will dare approach him as he walks in the Garden of Tears. But I dare!

She paused on the threshold, steeled herself, and stepped inside.

If she had not been one of the Created-and-Changed, if this errand was not as much about saving her own position as about saving her playing pieces, Shurzul would certainly have been overwhelmed by the raw potential that swirled through the Garden's air. Not magic, but the fuel of magic, so thick and rich it seemed as if she could bathe in it, or drink it down like a fine wine. She inhaled deeply, her nostrils flaring at the scents of rot and blood and piss. Faint moans and sobs—the sounds of broken minds deep in madness and despair—rose and fell like gusts of wind.

"My lord?" she whispered. "It is I, Shurzul." She made herself small and humble, furling her wings and tail tightly against her body, and bowing her head.

A moment later she heard an anguished shriek from one of the living artifacts, and then Virulan stood before her. Shurzul risked a quick peek upward; Virulan's expression was dark and brooding. But not angry—not yet. "Are you so anxious for my company, my firebrand?" he asked. "Or have you come to tell me my realm is fallen?"

The second guess was too close for comfort, but Shurzul would not still be alive if she could not lie with face and body and voice as well as tongue. "I bring you news, great King. News that no other will bring you, for they fear you—just as I fear you, of course, Lord Virulan, but my love and my loyalty are stronger." She bowed her head further, and waited.

"Then rise, my love, and tell me this news." Virulan set a talon beneath her chin and raised her head until Shurzul was forced to stare directly at him. He searched her gaze with his own, and she could feel his mind pressing at her mental shields, even while the rich suffering of the Garden of Tears intoxicated her so deeply she could barely remember why she was here.

When he released her, she began to speak, quick and soft.

"As my lord knows, the Elflings lie in the Great Absence that is near the foot of the Dragon's Bones, and we await your word to hunt them again. One Narghail frequently watched them, hoping to be the first to bring you news of their movement, and one Zicalyx watched over him, for Narghail is young and prone to error." She went on speaking, telling a version of the story that no one could dispute: that others had wished to see what Narghail saw, that a party led by Marbuglor had gone, that when Gholak saw Elflings out in the open, away from the shelter of the Flower Forest, she had attacked them, even knowing that it was against the King's own express command. "And the Elflings are possessed of some new weapon, a weapon without magic, an oil that burns through the skin and cannot be stopped. Five were taken, my lord. Five of the glorious children of *He Who Is*. And Gholak and Marbuglor were among them. They are no more."

"No more?" Virulan repeated the words as if he'd never heard them before. "Gholak no more? Marbuglor no more? Endarkened gone?"

"Yes." Shurzul hung her head and did her best to look miserable. "But more escaped. Shatub, child of my body and your creation, brought this news to me, for he fears your wrath, as all do."

"They don't fear it enough if they do things like this," Virulan muttered, so low that Shurzul was certain she was not meant to hear it. Then he gazed deeply into her eyes once more. "Well done, Thirdmost among the Endarkened."

Thirdmost! After Virulan and Uralesse, of course, but . . . Thirdmost! "This is an honor I dared not even imagine," Shurzul murmured tremblingly, showing Virulan an expression of awe and adoration leavened with a touch of disbelief. The prize she had long sought had dropped into her waiting talons, but it was a dangerous prize, for her sisters and their spawn would seek to topple her from that pinnacle.

"Are we not superior to the Brightworlders in every possible way?" Virulan asked. "If they shall have their High King, shall I not have a High Queen? But come. Walk with me as I ponder these matters."

They wandered through the Garden of Tears. Shurzul did her best not to gawk, for while she had known of this place, as all the Endarkened did, she had never before been invited to enter it.

"What of your Brightworld pet? The Elfling?" Virulan asked as the two of them paused to admire a particularly beautiful display. The Dryad had been seized with her tree, and then her tree had been infested with wood-eating parasites. As the insects ate the wood, so they ate at her body. She was skeletal and starved, her long bony fingers clawing fruitlessly at the ever-dripping taps sunk into her tree. Virulan picked up the bowl of nectar that was lying beneath one of the taps and offered it to Shurzul. When the two of them had emptied it, Shurzul replaced the bowl. The soft plink of the Dryad's heart blood echoed through the chamber as the bowl began to fill again, drop by drop.

"Hazaniel? Oh, very promising indeed," she said. "I have not entirely decided what I shall do with him; for the moment I am content to convince him that I am good, and kind, and that I love him." She laughed, an icy silvery sound. "Every moment of his delusion makes his eventual discovery of the truth even more delightful."

"My Shurzul," Virulan said huskily. "Your cruelty puts even Khambaug's to shame."

"I think, truly, that I could never exceed her mastery of the body, but perhaps one day I shall be able to equal her mastery of the mind," Shurzul said humbly. It would not do for word to get back to Khambaug that Shurzul placed herself above her—not in the area of Khambaug's great expertise. "But tell me—if it is your will, my lord—how will you repay the Elflings for their impertinence?"

"They will come into the open again. They always have," Virulan said.

"But must we await that?" Shurzul asked eagerly. "We can drive them from their sanctuary with fire, so quickly they will know they must never dare to use their burning oil weapon against us again. Oh, what glory it will be for me to see you first in battle, your magnificence striking down as many as your fangs and talons do! Say I may accompany you, my lord! Say all of us created by *He Who Is* may fly with you on this great mission!"

It was not particularly difficult to feign intoxication and delight at the mental image she had conjured, for the atmosphere of the Garden of Tears was heady enough to beguile any of her kind into unwary speech. Like all that Virulan did, his permission for her to walk here was both punishment and prize.

"Delay in pleasure makes it all the sweeter," Virulan said archly, running his fingers through her hair.

"No pleasure is sweeter than that of seeing our King and Lord foremost in butchery," Shurzul insisted. "To see him kill is sweeter than any kill by mine own hand." She rubbed her cheek against his shoulder. "Oh, my precious glory, I beg you, deny yourself these pleasures no longer! The burden of kingship is heavy—surely you are entitled to its sweets as well?"

"Would it truly please you to watch?" Virulan said at last.

"To watch *you*," Shurzul answered, greatly daring. "That is the greatest pleasure I can imagine." She stroked his wings gently, and he raised them higher to furl them about them both.

"Then you shall have what you wish, for I will deny you nothing. Come. I will summon the people to give them this word."

"And afterward . . . there will be sweets for us both," Shurzul purred, her eyes glowing with promise.

⁂

The Gryphon courier returned swiftly. Leutric had given Runacar no new orders, or even any advice: well, Runacar had expected as much. But there was little to do on the trek up to the Dragon's Gate but think, and so Runacar did.

There didn't seem to be any way out of slaughtering all the followers of the High King—not and have any hope of survival. Nor did Runacar think an alliance between the Otherfolk and Elvenkind was even remotely possible.

But there might be a way to avert the need for a massacre. There was no point, however, in giving such orders (or, to be perfectly accurate, in starting the rounds of discussion with his commanders that were necessary to get everyone to agree to do as he asked) if they had to go into battle the moment they arrived.

⁂

In the middle of the afternoon, one of the Woodwose scouts returned to tell Runacar that Nomaitemil was empty of Brightfolk—or any folk—but far larger than it ought to be.

"And ringing with magic!" Alras said, who sounded both triumphant and puzzled. "Anyone could see it."

"But did *you* see it?" Runacar asked patiently. The Woodwose spoke as if they could see the Brightfolk as clearly as Runacar could see the majority of the Otherfolk. Perhaps they could—at least some of them—but it was never good to make assumptions about a scout's report. And especially not when that scout had not been trained by an exacting High House Swordmaster.

"Well . . . no," Alras admitted. "But Stormchaser and his Wild and Sundapple and his Pounce looked all over it and said so. And they're still up there."

"Good work," Runacar said, and Alras beamed at the praise. "Now report to Tanet and do what he tells you."

Alras executed a ducking motion that Runacar supposed was meant for either a bow or a salute, and trotted off. Once he was alone, Runacar allowed himself to frown. If the Flower Forest had expanded that much, the scouts couldn't have searched all of it. On the other hand, the Brightfolk would have no reason to hide from them. And while Dryads weren't known for wandering, they could leave their groves if they had to. He thought briefly of sending another courier to Leutric to ask how fast a Flower Forest grew, and dismissed the idea: none of the Otherfolk who had seen Alpine Nomaitemil had thought its growth was cause for alarm.

Very well. The Flower Forest was uninhabited. Runacar could do nothing about its unexpected growth—and for all he knew, it might be normal behavior for a Flower Forest. For a moment he almost wished he knew more about Magery, then quickly dismissed the thought. *Look what the Light made of Ivrulion.*

⊰⊱

When Runacar's army reached the top of the pass, they found Ceoprentrei utterly deserted.

We've won. Runacar did his best to suppress the thought—to number your victories before you'd won them was notoriously unlucky, and even though he hadn't sacrificed to the Starry Hunt since the Battle of Shieldwall Plain, Runacar still feared Their power.

To have reached Ceoprentrei first was a very good thing. His army was already moving down the valley toward the Flower Forest. The grass was knee-high, and the Wulvers and Palughs were only shadows as they moved through it. He glanced reflexively skyward. The Gryphons, Hippogriffs, and Aesalions were no more than faint specks in the high sky, circling and waiting. If the enemy army was on the march, they would have already seen it by now and reported.

(Assuming, of course, any of them deigned to report something like that.)

They'd beaten the High King to the battlefield, and now all they had to do was hide themselves in Nomaitemil and wait until they could trap her in Ceoprentrei.

Keloit and Pelere joined him almost immediately. To Runacar's mild surprise, Pelere brought Bralros with her. The grizzled old Centaur wore a padded leather breastplate with flat iron rings riveted all across the front. His war hammer was belted at his side.

"Wanted to see what you were up to," Bralros said.

"I want to see what I can of the High King's camp," Runacar answered. "It should give us some idea of what we'll be facing, and even a guess about when, if we're lucky."

"Now, how is a look at a bunch of tents going to tell you something like that?" Bralros asked skeptically.

"Pelere?" Runacar asked. This had been one of her earliest lessons as a member of his original strike force.

"Well, nobody wants to do all of their packing at the last minute," the Centauress said reasonably. "So their wagons and carts and suchlike will be all lined up ready to go—and half-full, too. Their beasts will all be gathered up close, and watched, so they don't have to go chasing them in the morning." As Pelere continued to enumerate the signs by which one could tell an enemy's camp was about to move, Runacar heard the drumming of hoofbeats on the turf behind him. He wasn't particularly surprised to see Andhel arrive. She flung herself from the back of her mount even before it stopped; the pony wheeled wide, took a few meditative steps, shook itself, and began to graze.

"Where are you running off to?" Andhel demanded. "Nobody's supposed to go into the east."

"I am going to *look* into the east," Runacar said. "Not go there. You can probably see all the way to the Bazhrahils from the top of the pass."

"And see a lot of other things, too, so I hear," Bralros said derisively. "Like what the High King's having for dinner."

Andhel darted a glance at Runacar that was probably a lot less circumspect than she hoped. He knew she didn't think he was going to run off to join the High King's army, but alone of everyone here, she knew that his death in the battle to come wasn't just a possibility, but a certainty.

"And how long before she comes?" Andhel asked. "That, too?"

"Rune will know everything!" Keloit announced grandly. In his cub-days he would have meant it truthfully; maturity had added a layer of gentle mockery to his words.

"Or so he hopes," Andhel answered, with a flash of her old spirit.

But when the small party reached the Eastern Gate and looked down across the Tamabeth Hills, they saw . . .

Nothing.

No war camp. No pavilions. No herds of oxen and horses and sheep. And not a glimmer of firelight. A war camp would have cooking fires and forge fires alit no matter what candlemark of the sunturn it was. And there was nothing. The hills and valleys were already in deep shadow by now—the ascent to the top of the pass had taken most of the daylight—so it was too dark to look for the other obvious signs of an army on the move: felled trees, wagon ruts, a well-trampled trail.

Runacar stared down into the valley. "She's supposed to be here," he said, bewildered.

"If Melisha said it, it's true," Bralros said firmly. "Maybe they're just hiding."

"Maybe," Runacar said dubiously. The Lightborn could certainly make cookfires invisible—or unnecessary—and ordinary light disci-pline would do the rest. "We can take another look in the morning," Runacar said at last. "And anyway I—"

"You'll want scouts to watch the pass tonight," Andhel said. "And that's us, Rune, not you. *You* are going to go get a good night's sleep. You look worse than you did after Drotha pulled you out of the mud."

"Dear lady, my gracious thanks," Runacar teased, sketching a mounted bow.

"And we'll wake you if we see anything at all," Andhel said, as he opened his mouth to continue. She turned away to look out over the valley. "Doesn't look like there's anyone even there," she said, as if to herself.

--- ⊰⊱ ---

Andhel said she'd stay where she was, and that Runacar could send Tanet, the scouts picked for night watch, and their supplies out to her. Keloit gallantly announced he would stay to keep her company until they did, so Runacar and the two Centaurs headed back in the direction of the Flower Forest. He was so proud of his apprentices. For what they were, and what they had yet to become.

"I've been thinking," he said, as they went.

"I'd be surprised if you hadn't been," Bralros said mildly.

"I know my idea was to bottle them up in Ceoprentrei and kill them," Runacar said. "And we all know why. It isn't that . . . Well, I've never really . . . I hadn't been able to see a way around it." *Especially not after Daroldan.*

"But now you have," Pelere said encouragingly.

"Maybe," Runacar answered. "You know the plan already—lure them or herd them south, catch them between the Gryphons and your forces, and once they're all here, have the Earthdancers close the eastern side of the pass." *And hopefully keep the Warhunt occupied while the Minotaur Mages do their work.*

"Then we find out if they've left any behind, kill the ones we have, and send Drotha and his little friends to wipe out the others. If there are others," Bralros said dourly.

"Except the children," Pelere said.

And good luck with convincing the Aesalion Mystery to distinguish between an adult and a child, Runacar thought, not for the first time.

"But what if we can just seal them up here in the Mystrals?" Runacar asked. "Stop them without killing them, get our own people back to Vondaimieriel, and seal the western side of the pass as well as the east?"

"How?" Bralros asked bluntly.

"Have the Gryphons grab any of the commanders they can find. Carry them off to some nice glacier or something and leave them there. I don't think the High King's army would even consider surrender—not against us—but I bet we can make them run. Retreat, you see, is fully sanctioned by Arilcarion's doctrine, providing you intend to come back and win later," he added dryly.

There was a long silence. Finally, Bralros spoke.

"Do you think it would work?"

Runacar let out a breath he hadn't even known he was holding.

"Maybe. Partly it depends on the size of the force the High King is bringing and its composition. The Gryphons—and the Hippogriffs, too, if they can—would probably have to pull at least a thousand commanders from the field. It will be dangerous. If they can get their talons on the High King, that would be ideal, but remember, she's Lightborn as well as komen. And she'll fight."

"Not if someone just drops her once they get high enough," Bralros said sourly. "Even witchborn can't fly."

Runacar was startled into a laugh. "If you can talk Riann and the others into doing that, you can do so with my very good wishes," he said. "I'm not saying this will work—or even that it should be tried. But it's an idea."

"And after they run off, and we have the High King—or someone—or a lot of Houseborn someones—what then?" Pelere asked.

"We'll need to know where her keeps are anyway, so we can rescue the children," Runacar said. "The Woodwose should be the ones to question them. I don't think anyone else is going to get any answers. But if we're lucky, the Woodwose might be able to get the High King—or her successor—to sue for parole."

"And that means . . . ?" Bralros asked.

"They promise very *very* sincerely to stay right here in Ceoprentrei if we let them live," Runacar said dryly. "I'm not sure how long they'll honor their parole, and I am positive they'll violate it. But not immediately. So we seal them up here in the valley, and . . . go tell Leutric."

"We still get to kill at least some of them, don't we?" Bralros said, sounding faintly exasperated.

"Inevitably," Runacar answered lightly.

And Vieliessar will probably be one of them.

HARVEST MOON IN THE TENTH YEAR OF THE HIGH KING'S REIGN: TO HARVEST FIRE AND FLAME

When you go into battle, always be sure you want to win the war.
—Author Unknown, *Notes Toward a Unified Theory of War*

Thinking back on the first war camps the Otherfolk had made under his tutelage, Runacar wondered how they'd all managed not to starve to death. He'd had to learn so much, once he no longer had the servants and vassals that he'd always taken for granted to do things for him. And once he knew how to support a war as well as wage it, he'd had to learn how to teach what he knew: what was necessary, what was important, what couldn't be duplicated, what *shouldn't* be duplicated, and what they didn't need at all.

He had succeeded. And so the chain of camps the Otherfolk built within Nomaitemil was tidy, comfortable, and welcoming. *It will be a good legacy to leave behind me,* he thought. *Assuming anyone is left alive a Wheelturn from now.*

⁂

Runacar didn't get much sleep that night. His desperate last-ditch idea had to be passed through his army and discussed with its commanders. That was accomplished with what amounted to (at least among the Otherfolk) unseemly haste, but it still meant candlemarks of discussion, of information passed to other groups, and of additional listeners with new questions.

And all this discussion would be for nothing if Riann and the other Ascensions weren't willing to commit to it. To come in low enough to snatch commanders from their saddles meant flying low enough to be shot, and Runacar knew Vieliessar had excellent archers. He couldn't consult the Gryphons until morning: he wasn't willing to risk a signal fire when the High King's army might have advance scouts in the Tamabeth Hills or even somewhere on the heights above Ceoprentrei.

The decision of the ground forces came long after midnight: they wouldn't change their plans, but they wouldn't pursue if Elvenkind ran south.

It was the best compromise Runacar could hope for. Trying not to kill an enemy on the battlefield was a good way to die yourself. And the whole plan hinged on making Elvenkind run. Even without their commanders, they weren't likely to do that if they didn't take losses.

"We planned to herd them to the middle of the valley anyway," Vorlof said, as he handed Runacar a mug of hot mulled beer. Centaurs believed that there was nothing worth doing if it had to be done without beer, and Runacar had come to agree with them. "So we break to the left and right and leave the south open."

"We've been planning to get them into the forest," Ganfrin agreed, with a glance toward Runacar. "Under the trees, the advantage is ours," the Bearward added, baring a mouthful of sharp white teeth.

"And they can't sneak out the back," Pelere said, making it half a question.

"No." Runacar was happy to be able to state something with certainty. "Nomaitemil runs right up to the rock wall at the three valleys' end, and if there was another way into either Jaeglenhend or Vondaimieriel through this part of the Mystrals, someone would have found it and used it. The only other pass is a long way south of here, and it's narrow."

"Well, that's good," Pelere said, with a sigh.

Keloit joined them. He met Ganfrin's eyes for a moment and then looked away: Ganfrin was the leader of the Bearsarks. Shock troops. Few of Ganfrin's folk would be alive at the end of the battle.

"Rune?" Keloit said apologetically. "It's almost dawn."

Runacar got up with a sigh. "Well, let's go see what the Gryphons have to say."

⊰⊱

It was still dark when Runacar walked out of the Flower Forest, the sack of signal equipment over his shoulder and his apprentices behind him. The stars filled the sky overhead, bright jewels gleaming against the darkest velvet. This high, the air was chill, and he was glad of his cloak. A little distance away the herd of horses drowsed peacefully, some with Brownies asleep on their backs.

It was difficult not to think that each sight, each sound, each moment, was something unique, something to see this one last time and never again. But if the Bond had been chosen for him (for both of them), it was Runacar who had chosen how and why his life would end.

His hands moved automatically, unpacking the bag, filling the shallow tin pan with tinder, pouring the coals from the clay firepot over them, adding oil from a flask. When the fire flared bright, he took up the disk of polished silver and angled it so the firelight caught in it and flared toward the open sky.

And then he waited.

Just as Runacar was certain no one had seen his signal, a winged shadow crossed the bright night sky, and a few moments later, Radafa settled lightly to the ground. Some of the horses raised their heads for a moment to regard him curiously, then went back to whatever they'd been doing. They'd been raised with Gryphons since foalhood, and didn't fear them.

"You don't look happy, Runacar," Radafa said, in his harsh whispering tones.

"He's decided to change the plan," Pelere said.

"Ah," Radafa said in feigned delight. "Elvenkind isn't going to come west after all? Good. We can all go home." He fluffed out his neck feathers in a Gryphon smile.

"Not exactly," Runacar said. "But I have an idea. At least I think I do. And with no sign of the High King's army, we should have a few sunturns to discuss it."

"No sign?" Radafa said, puzzled. "But . . . they're down in the valley, in the Flower Forest. Didn't you see them?"

"No," Runacar said levelly, after a long pause during which he damned all kings and thrones to the Cold Dark, "I can't see through trees."

"Oh," Radafa said, sounding embarrassed. "Well."

You sneaked over the Mystrals to take a look, didn't you? Runacar thought. He didn't bother to say it aloud. "So they're there," he said, taking a deep breath. "Good to know. It will take them most of a sunturn to get to us if they start from Saganath, so we still have time. Let me tell you what I propose, and you can tell me if you think it will work. I know it's not up to you," he added quickly, forestalling the inevitable protest-and-explanation, "but if it won't work at all, there's no point in discussing it."

Runacar outlined his plan in much the same way he had to his ground forces. When he'd finished, Radafa cocked his head, thinking. "People will still die, won't they?" he said at last. "Even if we do this?"

"Yes," Runacar said. "People will die, I'm afraid. And Elvenkind too. But it's all I can think of to try."

"And you know more about war than any of us," Radafa said simply. "At least it's a chance. I will bring it to Riann. We will try to decide as quickly as possible," he added, with a faint air of apology. "But . . . it's still night."

And while Gryphons could be awake and active during the hours of darkness, the precision flying needed for a Gryphon discussion was something better done in the light of day.

"I know," Runacar said. "And if the High King happens to attack while you're trying to come to an agreement . . . well, it's up to you. It always has been."

Radafa lowered his head to give Runacar a quick Gryphon caress, rubbing his cheek along Runacar's face. "I know. And no matter what happens, you're trying not to kill. That's the important thing. I know you understand us as little as we understand you," Radafa added. "You try. And so do we. That's important too."

"I know," Runacar answered quietly. "I know it is." *I just wish I'd had more time to try.*

"Hunt well, my friend," Radafa said. "I will see you after the battle."

"Fare you well, Radafa," Runacar answered, as the Gryphon turned away and bounded into the air.

⊰⊱

"My lord, you should not be here. It is not safe," Helecanth said quietly.

The two women crouched in the bushes of the scrub land that edged Saganath Flower Forest. Vieliessar had never been able to take the comfort the other Lightborn could in the fact that the Flower Forests would exist when Elvenkind were gone. It seemed so much more likely to her that the Endarkened would simply burn them all down.

"You know I will sense it should they come in numbers," Vieliessar answered, just as softly. At the far edge of her perception—so distant it was only a faint sickly headache—she could sense Endarkened. Following them. Watching. *Only a few,* she told herself. *Only a few.*

"Even so," Helecanth said implacably. "No risk to you is acceptable. The people fear your loss even more than they fear death."

"Death is something many will find today," Vieliessar responded. "And you guard my heirs against the day when I shall find it myself." Helecanth made a noise that might mean anything at all. The children she had secretly borne for her King thought Helecanth no more than their mother's chief komen. One of them would follow Vieliessar as High King. And if the day of the High King's death came too soon, it would be Helecanth who held Vieliessar's great king-domain for that child until they were old enough to hold it for themselves.

It was still at least a candlemark before sunrise. The foothills and the lower slopes of the Mystrals were still wreathed in shadow, but Stardock's crown, and the lesser peaks to either side, were already pink and gold with morning light. Today would be a late-summer day as sharp and bright as a new sword, but here at the edge of the Flower Forest it was still dark and cool, and Vieliessar could almost believe that the world was a safe and peaceful place.

The road through the pass was visible as a wide flat notch on Stardock's deosil flank. Vieliessar had come to take a last look at the Dragon's Gate—and to see every obstacle that stood in the way of reaching it.

"Come away," Helecanth repeated, and Vieliessar gestured her irritably to silence. The crossing of the Mystrals to reach the West—to reach the Shrine of the Star—was the most desperate of desperate gambles. And the purely physical obstacles that stood between Vieliessar and her goal were as deadly as the Endarkened. The distance they must cross to gain any sort of shelter was brutal: the nearest Flower Forest—Alpine Nomaitemil—was as far from the Pass Gate as the bottom of the pass was from Ceoprentrei, and the flat meadow at the top offered no concealment.

Even if her folk reached Nomaitemil's safety, they could not remain there for long. The Flower Forest might—praise to Sword and Star—have escaped the wars unbroached, but the Lightborn would drain it quickly with their Calls upon its Light. And to gain the Western Reach, she and all her folk would have the whole to do over again: descending from the Dragon's Gate Pass and reaching Vondaimieriel Great Keep, or Enerwirchereth Flower Forest, or Shrine Manostar.

After Nomaitemil, after Vondaimieriel, the Sanctuary of the Star. The secret to destroying the Endarkened must lay within the Great Library in the Sanctuary of the Star. It must!

"Come away," Helecanth urged for the third time. Vieliessar turned toward her, eyes flashing with anger, but Helecanth was undaunted by the High King's temper. "Everyone knows what they must do, down to the children too young to fight," Helecanth said. "All have given their consent that your plan shall be their action."

Vieliessar turned away again. "Then it is as good as done." She took a deep breath, and mastered her temper with an effort. "Know that my love and gratitude goes forth to all who will die this sunturn, and to all who have died to bring us this far. May they rejoice forever in the Vale of Celenthodiel."

Helecanth inclined her head. "May the Hunt ride forever." After a moment she put her hand on Vieliessar's arm once more, and this time, Vieliessar allowed herself to be led back into the depths of Saganath.

⊰⊱

Only five left now! Only five!

Zicalyx huddled in the smallest fissure she could squeeze her body into. It was high in the World Without Sun, only a little below the surface of the Bright World, but that was good. No one would stumble upon her here. And there was no one looking for her (she assured herself). She'd done nothing wrong (not that this mattered if one's enemy was powerful enough), but she still felt the need to hide. To keep apart from everyone until she could think through the events of the day.

Endarkened slain! Endarkened tricked!

By *meat*.

Meat cowered and died. That was its function. It did not devise new weapons with the power to harm and kill the beautiful children of *He Who Is*.

The word of the terrible new weapon the meat had deployed had spread through the World Without Sun like blood through water. The success of the meat was intolerable, and more, it was disturbing.

Of course King Virulan planned immediate vengeance. He was already choosing the Born he would send to do his work, and if any thought such choosing was an honor, they were as stupid as her brother Narghail. That was one of the reasons why Zicalyx was here: if he could not find her, he could not order her to go. If those who went on this mission were successful, they were clearly angling to supplant King Virulan. If, on the other hand, they slew few Elflings and brought home no prizes, they were disobeying the King's orders, which would be punished as rebellion. And worst of all, Virulan or one of his Born courtiers would be sure all of this was her fault, as she was the one who had found the meat and watched over it. She did not intend to be found until something else had occurred to seize Virulan's attention.

Because the one spark of joy to be found in all of this was that so many more of the Created-and-Changed were dead.

Only five remain of those He Who Is *has made with* His *own Will! Only five! When they are all gone,* He Who Is *cannot love them best. He will love us, because we will be all that is left.*

She dared not let Virulan—or anyone—see that joy in her heart.

The center of the Flower Forest was crowded almost beyond capacity. The Elves talked together of what was to come, the sound of their voices no louder than the wind that ruffled the summer leaves. Some drew their families together for the task ahead. Others bid farewell to partners or children with the knowledge that this was probably the last time they would see those beloved faces. Healers—both Lightborn and Lightless—moved among them, doling out small vials of poison. No one knew what happened to the captives the Endarkened took, but all agreed it was better not to know.

Beyond the gathering the horses waited, each two or three with a groom to soothe and calm them. Over the last sennight Vieliessar's people had painstakingly gathered the precious livestock from the far reaches of the forest, and the Lightborn wove spells over them so that when the time came to run, they would run where they were bidden.

That was enough for goats and sheep and chickens, and dogs needed no encouragement to stay with their charges, but the horses would be asked to do more, and were cosseted accordingly. Elvenkind no longer possessed destriers or palfreys or any other of the hundred breeds of horse that had once been their treasure and joy. Now Elvenkind bred horses for speed and stamina, and the Arzhana battleponies they bred could fight as well as they could run.

Vieliessar stood to watch the leave-taking preparations, so that the blessing of the High King could be given to those who might ride with the Starry Hunt by sunset. The other enclaves of Elvenkind who would flee today had known the sunturn and the candlemark of this rade for sennights. Communication by magic was lost to them, and to send a message by bespelled animal risked drawing the Endarkened's attention, but the sun-alphabet once used by the border towers was still known, and it had become the only long-range form of communication Elvenkind had left.

"Mama!"

Vieliessar knelt quickly as her daughter called to her. Princess Adalie-riel, eldest born, flung herself into Vieliessar's arms, followed quickly by her younger brother Calanoriel. Calan was less than a Wheelturn younger than Liri, and acknowledged heir to the High Kingship.

If he lived.

Vieliessar hugged them both fiercely; it did not matter to her heart that she had not given birth to them: they were her children and her heirs. "My young *alakomentai'a*—are you ready to conquer?" she asked.

Liri had nine summers—old enough to fly her kite next Flower Moon. *If she lives,* the eternal voice whispered in the back of Vieliessar's mind. Both royal children were already expert with sling, with dart, and in hunting and hiding. Next Midwinter—if Vieliessar lived, if the children lived, if *anyone* survived this day—Vieliessar would Call the Light in Liri for the first time. She did not know whether she hoped or feared to find it.

Her father has it in full measure, yet never were we taught at the Sanctuary that the Light would follow this bloodline or that. . . .

"I don't want to have to hide, Mama!" Calan said. "I'm not a child anymore! I have seen eight summers! I can fight!"

Vieliessar ruffled her son's hair as she rose to her feet. "But you must follow Lord Rithdeliel's orders as he gives them, my heart, or you will not learn all you must learn to grow up to be King."

"Calan will be High King and I will be his Chief Warlord," Liri responded instantly. "And our army will be the largest there ever was!"

"But not yet," Helecanth said, stepping from behind Vieliessar and swooping Calan up in her arms. "Today is a day for riding very fast," she said as she took Liri's hand. "Come. Let us find horses as swift and daring as each of you, so you may bring each other honor."

Helecanth walked away, Liri skipping along beside her and Calan looking over Helecanth's shoulder to wave.

"The Endarkened—if they come—will seek other targets first," Thurion said quietly.

"Do you seek to comfort me, when I know so many will grieve for their lost children before the sun rises again?" Vieliessar asked. She tried desperately to keep the bitterness out of her voice, but knew she failed.

"To give you hope," Thurion said. "Your plan is a good one—even Nadalforo First Sword said so. And she always finds fault."

"Only so she can goad my lord Rithdeliel into lecturing her about knowing her place," Vieliessar said, grudgingly amused.

"And to be so lectured is her greatest joy," Thurion answered instantly. "She would not deprive herself unless she must."

"It will work," Vieliessar said, under her breath. "It must," she added. *But always before we have taken moonturns to move to new places of safety. Small groups, creeping from haven to haven, while elsewhere we lured the Endarkened to us so they would not see . . .*

"It must, so it will," Thurion said, turning both her words and their meaning inside out. "They will not expect such audacity from us."

"If only I could know *what* they expect," Vieliessar said, and now she could not keep the anguish from her voice. "Or what they want—other than our deaths. They hunt us as if we were Beastlings—but where are their cities? Their homes? Why do they scour us from a land they do not even choose to claim?"

"These things I do not know," Thurion told her gently. "But there is one thing I do: you shall prevail."

This was not empty flattery—Vieliessar had never received that from Thurion and knew she never would—but rather an acknowledgment of what they both knew: as Child of the Prophecy, the whole weight of Amretheon's Prophecy cloaked her in its imperative to be fulfilled. The Child of the Prophecy would stand against the Darkness, unite the people, and . . .

And what then? Thurion knows as well as I that The Song of Amretheon *tells not of an ending to this war, only its beginning.*

There remained to her one faint spark of hope, known only to Vieliessar, Thurion, and Helecanth: Because Vieliessar yet lived, somewhere westward of the Mystrals, War Prince Runacarendalur Caerthalien did too. And since he did, there must be some haven there.

If only her people could reach it.

"Come," Thurion said. "The Silver Swords prepare to ride."

The Silver Swords of Penenjil numbered eight tailles and four captains, never more nor less. Their weapons were two longswords, wielded one in each hand, and each of the Silver Swords was an expert in that unique—and lethal—style of combat.

Once it had been said that they had never been defeated in war or battle; now it could only be said that they were not all dead yet. In this

new world of darkness and blood, that survival was the greater miracle, for the Silver Swords were always in the vanguard of any rade. No
longer did they ride the legendary grey stallions of Penenjil's breeding;
instead they rode the battleponies that had been Gatriadde Mangiralas's
last gift to his people. The stubborn, bloodthirsty, and nimble animals
were painted in a pattern of light and shadow that combined luck-tokens
and names of Power with a camouflage that would confuse the eye at
any distance.

Now each rider stood beside their painted steed and awaited the
command to mount. "Master Dandamir, how goes the day?" Vieliessar
asked.

Dandamir, Master of the Silver Swords, bowed his head in salute before he spoke. "Any day when we may ride to battle is a glorious day
indeed, my King. And sweet the victory at its end, even at the cost of our
lives, for to die is to ride forever."

"May our dead ride forever," Vieliessar answered quietly. Last night,
after the Company of the Hare had repulsed the Endarkened, Vieliessar
had made the sacrifices and said the prayers, but she did not know any
longer if—in her heart—she believed. She had begged the Starry Hunt
for aid so many times, and aid had never come.

Dandamir saluted her once more, then gave the order to mount. The
order to ride followed a heartbeat later. Moving as one, the Silver Swords
vanished silently into the shadowy forest. They would be the first to
break forth into the open, flourishing their swords and chanting their
war songs.

Once the Silver Swords were clear of Saganath, the rest of her folk
would follow, riding out from a hundred different places, upright and
armed in the midst of riderless horses. So many of them, and so scattered, that—or so Vieliessar hoped—the Endarkened could not kill
them all.

*Until we reach the road to the pass itself. And then we will be easy prey.
Unless our plan works and the Endarkened do not come at all.*

Today's strategy was based upon one scrap of hard-won knowledge:
the Endarkened had never followed an attack in force with another attack less than a sennight later. Endarkened attacks were brief and sav-

age, yet sennights or even moonturns might pass between assaults, and there had never yet been a siege. They could only hope that last night's trick provoked such a delay.

Helecanth returned to Vieliessar's side. "I have seen them made ready," she said. "They ride separately. One goes soon, the other nearly last."

"That is well done of you," Vieliessar said steadily. She would not give voice to what all of them were thinking: *Perhaps one of them will survive.*

I must have a living heir of the body. I must! My people will not follow me if only one life stands between them and another civil war. They deserve as much certainty as I can give them. Even though it is built upon a lie.

"My lord King," Helecanth began. "One last time, I—"

"No," Vieliessar said, raising a hand to silence her. "This is what must be. I was Lightborn before I was King. Today, for all our sakes, I must be Lightborn once more."

"Then the Silver Hooves defend you, and grant that this night I may ride beside you once more, whether it is over the land or among the stars," Helecanth said. She took Vieliessar's raised hand to her lips and kissed it, then turned and strode away.

"Come," Thurion said gently. "All the people know that we Lightborn are to guard you this sunturn. Do not let them wonder why you dally here."

"Cloudwit," Vieliessar mocked gently. "As if anyone could have eyes for me at such a time." But she followed Thurion when he led her away. The two of them passed through the last horselines. Beyond them her other army waited.

The gathered Lightborn seemed like a great array, though there were barely twelve great-tailles of them now. Among their numbers were some who had never seen the Sanctuary of the Star—those in whom the Light had been Called in the Midwinter before Vieliessar had become High King, or in those Midwinters soon after. They had performed their vigils and pledged their oaths in other Shrines than Arevethmonion, and were as much Lightborn as those who had worn the Green Robe for hundreds of Wheelturns.

But today those who were Lightborn-to-be were added to that number. These had been babes in arms, or yet unborn, when the battle of the Shieldwall Plain was fought. But the Light had been Called in them, and the Light had answered, and in this war, everyone who could fight must fight.

Vieliessar moved among her people as Lightsister among Lightborn. Some of those here she had trained with in her Sanctuary days. Some she had taught. All of them were the closest kin she had left, for the Light that ran in their blood linked them to her more closely than any shared parentage could do.

"It is time," Thurion said quietly.

Talk ceased, and the Lightborn quickly organized themselves hand to hand in a long spiraling coil, that would let them combine their power and allow all to see what one saw. Vieliessar felt it the moment the chain was complete. The shock of power when the last hands closed on each other was a palpable thing, emphatic as a blow. Thurion held her right hand. No one held her left, for Vieliessar was last in the chain.

Now to see if the monsters have been taken in by our deceit.

Carefully, so carefully, sheltered by the magic of the Flower Forest, Vieliessar cast a spell of Overshadow as a fisherman might cast a net. She caught a mind and forced her will upon it, and suddenly she could see the landscape from the vantage point of a hawk on the wing.

The rising sun kindled the sharp snow-capped peaks that framed the Dragon's Gate, and touched them with gold and fire. The Dragon's Gate Road was a ribbon of beaten gold. The Tamabeth Hills lay below, its hills gilded with golden grass and morning sun, its valleys still lost in morning shadow and fog.

The hawk's eyes watched as, from all across the Tamabeths, horses emerged, ridden and riderless mixed together, the pattern of their flight seemingly random. They spread out among the goat-tracks and deer paths until they moved in a long irregular line heading westward by a thousand tangents. It would not be enough to fool the Endarkened.

If they came.

Please let them come. This once, I beg you, Riders, let them come!

Time passed. The hawk saw the long shadows shorten, then, suddenly, dawn light struck sparks from naked steel as the Silver Swords clashed and brandished their weapons. The Silver Swords had reached the road to the Dragon's Gate and begun their ascent.

Half a day to reach the Eastern Gate.

Half a day more to reach Nomaitemil.

Perhaps They *will not come at all.* But even as Vieliessar thought those words, nauseating cold swept through her body and broke Overshadow. The world dwindled to the trees of Saganath, dappled with morning light, their promised safety revealed to be a lie.

"They come," Vieliessar gasped, closing her eyes tightly. "Send forth the Company of the Hare." In answer, she heard the call of a war-horn nearby, then a distant answer to that call.

She took another deep breath to steady herself, then searched anew for eyes with which to see the fate of her brave comrades. Her body ached with the stiffness of long stillness, but the first thing a Postulant learned in the Sanctuary of the Star was to ignore the body's demands. This time there was no need for her to use subtlety—the Endarkened would fly neither faster nor slower for the taste of magic on the wind.

She had more luck than she had hoped for. A Silver Eagle was hunting above the pass itself. Once the great birds had been sacrosanct, unlawful to hunt or to tame. Now it was merely a tool to her need. It was as they had hoped: the Endarkened came in numbers far greater than the group that had attacked last night. Vieliessar felt joy ripple through the Light-born, joy quickly stifled so as not to interrupt the spell of Overshadow.

From the Silver Eagle's vantage point she saw—*all* of them saw—the Endarkened fall upon the diversionary force. Everything was happening in accordance with the most optimistic possible hope, and that worried Vieliessar deeply. The Endarkened could see the horses and riders on the road to the pass. It made no sense for them to attack the smaller force when the larger was plainly visible. No Elven commander—even one new-made—would have fallen for such a transparent ruse.

And yet the Endarkened did.

The outcome of that battle was never in doubt, though it was a thing of feints and tricks and traps on one side—poisons, nets, catapults; Light-less illusions; every weapon and diversion her people could devise—and no more than brute strength and the power of flight on the other. The Endarkened were creatures of magic, but they saw little need to use their spells against so helpless a foe. This was not war to them, but sport.

Vieliessar would have wept at the slaughter if her tears had not all been shed long and long ago. "Now," she whispered, as the last of the Company fell.

With one will and intent, the Lightborn gathered up all the remaining power Saganath could possibly spare. They drew upon the Flower Forest as its flowers withered and the leaves browned and fell from the trees. They shaped that power as an artificial autumn fell upon the mosses of the forest floor into the one force they had found that could halt the Endarkened, even temporarily.

In the blink of an eye, the cool morning sunlight became a fire a thousand times greater than the blazing beacon of summer noon; a fire no creature between Leaf and Star could stand against for even a moment. Iardalaith had named the spell Sunstroke; it was light and heat and the force of the Lightborn's conjoined wills, and all these things had only one target:

The Endarkened.

Sunstroke crisped their great wings to ash, charred and cracked their skin to leave it oozing ichor. They fell from the sky, and the air was filled with the discordant music of their screaming. Two tailles of her Lightbrethren gave their all to this casting, making it their Final Spell, the one that burned away both Light and life, its casting a last desperate act.

And Endarkened died. But not of Sunstroke.

Through her borrowed eyes, Vieliessar saw the Endarkened turn on one another, the stronger killing the weaker to drain their lifeforce. The survivors fled. Not one of them stopped to help another. The Endarkened were cowards. Hurt them, surprise them, and they turned and fled. The drained Endarkened were already dissolving, their bodies killing the grass beneath them, until the bodies—five, five out of *twelve*—lay in the center of widening circles of bare and poisoned soil.

The only thing the Lightborn could do for Saganath now was leave her.

They moved to the horselines, mounting in the same order they always had. There was no rushing, no jostling, and certainly no fare-wells. The presence of even one Lightborn drew the Endarkened as honey drew the wasp. A few moments, and the first group was away, scattering through the wounded Flower Forest the moment they were in the saddle.

They would stay apart from each other and from the rest of Elven-kind until they had no other choice.

⊰⊱

The survivors of the dawn attack limped back to the World Without Sun. They told of an Elvish weapon—murderous, mysterious—that had been as if the sun itself had descended among them. Few of them had escaped uninjured. Many—too many!—had been reduced entirely to ash. Dead beyond sorcerous reincarnation.

This has been unnatural, Virulan thought to himself. *Never again will I send my people where I do not go. From this moment forward, King Virulan's place is in the forefront of every attack!*

He summoned the remains of the Twelve. Only four of them yet lived—Uralesse, Khambaug, Lashagan, and his own darling Shurzul—but of their bodies had come hundreds of new Endarkened, and from those in turn more hundreds, until Virulan could number his Endark-ened in the thousands.

"What is your will, my King?" Uralesse bowed low as he knelt be-fore the Throne of Night. Virulan gestured irritably for him to rise, and beckoned Shurzul to his side. He thought Uralesse seemed somewhat startled by that gesture. *Good! Let him fret and fear. No one in the World Without Sun is safe unless I, Virulan, say they are safe.*

"You know already that five of your brethren have been unmade. In return, we shall unmake all that is left of Elfling kind." His outrage at the new weapon of Elvenkind had driven all thought of caution from Virulan's mind.

It would have been more prudent—so Uralesse said—for the King to go first to his Rest, and destroy the Elflings upon his Rising. The Endarkened did not sleep, precisely—not as the Brightworld races un-derstood the term—but at regular intervals, adult Endarkened retreated for a period of deep contemplation that might—were a non-Endarkened to observe it—be likened more closely to death than to sleep.

Their young had no need of this sort of rest, of course, and even the oldest Endarkened could set the need for rest aside, for a time, without ill effects. But to forgo it altogether was to court first madness, then the loss of power. And Virulan did not intend to dispense with either. But when Uralesse made that utterly appropriate suggestion, Virulan cast it instantly aside.

"Never! We shall take wing now, at once, every one of us, before their memory of their blasphemy fades! We will strike like a great hammer, and this time we will spare none! Today, Elvenkind will die!"

Under his arm, Shurzul writhed in ecstasy, and Uralesse seemed stunned by the boldness of his King. "Go!" Virulan shouted. "Summon *all* my people! We fly! We slay!"

⫫

Flight after flight of the Endarkened left the World Without Sun for the Bright World. The sun was already westering, the attack for which the Endarkened were retaliating was more than a half a sunturn in the past. Virulan's people were a flock, a swarm, a legion, as numerous as the birds of the air—when there had been birds of the air here. Just as he had ordered, all that remained behind in the World Without Sun were children, slaves, and the Lesser Endarkened.

"First come, first served," was not an Endarkened watchword, but it could easily have been. Virulan had gone up with the first wave of Endarkened, and he had not waited for more to join him. High in the high sky, they flew west. Behind them, Obsidian Mountain seemed to boil as flight upon flight of Endarkened followed their King.

CHAPTER ELEVEN

HARVEST MOON IN THE TENTH YEAR OF THE HIGH KING'S REIGN: SHADOWPLAY

If you would sacrifice your life in battle, from heroism or other cause, first ask: Will your death do more harm to your people than the battle? You are a component of all your decisions balancing profit and loss.

—Runacar Warlord, A History of the Scouring of the West

Runacar had hoped to spend at least a few more candlemarks catching up on lost sleep, but it seemed he'd barely settled himself into his bedroll again when Andhel arrived.

"They're coming," she said, dropping to her knees beside him. "Something's coming, anyway. Elvenkind. Horses. It doesn't look like the armies that attacked on the Shore. But it's coming this way."

"What's coming?" Runacar asked sharply, sitting up. "Numbers. Dispositions." *You're going to have to do this without me very soon, Andhel. Remember your lessons!*

"Mixed groups of riders and free-running horses. Some horses carry packs but no rider. Small groups. Thirty to fifty in each. Roughly five grand-tailles so far, leaving out of the Flower Forest all along the western side. And just . . . running toward the pass. Or toward the hills, anyway; they're not heading for the Sanctuary Road. Nobody in armor. No banners."

As Andhel made her report, Runacar found his boots, shook out his cloak, picked up his sword belt and buckled it on. His armor awaited, carefully packed against this day, but it would make him too conspicuous now.

"That makes no sense," he said. Every Elven army traveled with a *khom*—a herd of remounts—in addition to the komens' destriers and their regular riding palfreys, but they, along with everything else in the baggage train, followed the army—they didn't precede it. Had there been a rebellion among her forces? If an enemy had attacked her baggage train and driven off the horses, it would cripple her army.

He didn't have enough information.

"Tell Bralros and Pendor to get the army ready to fight," he said, picking up his saddle and hefting it to his shoulder. "No later than noon. And we need to get our horses under cover as soon as possible."

"Where are you going?" Andhel demanded.

"To look for myself!" Runacar called over his shoulder.

⊰⊱

The sky had lightened by now enough to extinguish all but the brightest stars. Dawn would break first over Jaeglenhend, then in Ceoprentrei, and at last in Vondaimieriel. Runacar tried not to wonder which of his friends would see the sunset. From now until the battle began, the only Otherfolk who would move in the clear would be Woodwose and Wulvers: from a distance, the Wulvers looked like dogs, and the Woodwose . . . well, they were Elvenkind, after all. The High King's army had to believe itself safe and alone so that it would come ahead in force. If Elvenkind saw the Otherfolk before they were fully committed to Ceoprentrei, it would destroy the Otherfolk's only real advantage: the High King had no idea their army existed.

"What do you think it means?" Andhel asked. She'd followed him as soon as she'd relayed her messages, and now she and Runacar rode side by side. "The riderless horses?" Andhel's battlepony was painted grey and green and dun, with grasses braided into mane and tail, and artfully tattered ribbons around its neck. Very much like its rider.

In his earliest encounters with the Woodwose, Runacar had believed the Woodwose didn't know how to ride horses and didn't want to learn. He'd eventually discovered that while the Woodwose preferred to eat horses rather than ride them, they were perfectly capable of riding when a horse was available and convenient. They simply didn't think of horses as either partners or tools, and they were wholly unwilling to use either saddle or bridle.

"I don't know what it means," Runacar answered patiently. "What you're reporting isn't how an army moves. It isn't even how *our* army moves, let alone the army of the High King. All I can think of is that there's been a rebellion of some kind."

"If they didn't want her to be their king, why not just leave?" Andhel said.

Runacar laughed sharply. "This is what Elvenkind leaving looks like," he said. "Drive off her horses, split up into a number of groups so she'll have to split her own forces to chase them. It would have been nice if we'd known this was going to happen ahead of time," he added.

"Wouldn't Melisha have told you if that's what's going on?" Andhel asked doubtfully.

Wouldn't she? Yes—if she knew. Of that Runacar was certain. He wished Melisha had picked another story to tell, and another time to tell it. Or that she had come up with the idea to make Elvenkind sue for parole herself.

"That's what worries me most," Runacar answered briefly.

⁂

The Woodwose scouts had organized themselves in much the same way the fire-starters had been organized in Delfierarathadan: a chain of relays strung all the way across the meadow that lay between the two passes. Runacar didn't see them until a pair stood up out of the long grass: their skins were daubed with mud and paint, and their heads were covered with cowls of woven grass.

"Any change, Nindir?" Andhel asked.

"None," the Woodwose said. "More riders come out of the trees, and more horses. Some of the horses have packs, but no riders." He looked toward Runacar expectantly.

"I'm going to go take a look for myself," he said. "This might be anything. Until they're actually on the Pass Road, we can't be sure. They might be intending to fight each other first."

"If they are, can we go down and help?" Nindir asked hopefully.

"You'll see all the fighting you could possibly want when they get here," Runacar said. *Dear stars above, when did I begin to sound like Elrinonion Swordmaster?*

Andhel blew Nindir a mocking kiss, and she and Runacar rode on.

⇥⇤

By the time they reached the Western Gate, it was full day. The sky was a bright cloudless blue, the brisk alpine wind was scented with the last of the summer flowers, and birdsong could be heard on the air. The day was almost too ordinary—beautifully ordinary, in a way Runacar had never learned to cherish before the fall of the Hundred Houses.

"There's fighting," Tanet said, the moment Runacar arrived.

"Where?" Runacar asked. He vaulted from his palfrey's back and ran toward the observation point, crouched low.

It was as if the whole population of some Great Keep had decided to flee for its life. The hilltops of the Tamabeths were deserted, but horses ran through their folds and valleys—hundreds of them. Some stragglers were still leaving the forest. All were mounted, all rode hard for the first cover they could find, but the Dragon's Gate was clearly their eventual destination; the Dragon's Gate was the only route over the mountains—it was that, or simply climb until your mount would take you no further. No one Runacar could see was properly (as the Hundred Houses thought of propriety) garbed for battle, or even for a day's hunting. All wore hoods and cowls and tunics and trews in mottled duns and greys and greens, many with light cloaks, or scarves, or long tails to their hoods. They weren't staying together, but fanning out in ones and twos, keeping themselves widely spaced even if that meant riding over the rough ground parallel to the road.

Wait. Those aren't horses. Where are their destriers?

The first of the riderless beasts had already reached the road, and Runacar could see them clearly now. Their legs were thick, and their heads would barely come up to a destrier's cheek. His thought of cart-ponies (incredible as such an idea was) was instantly discarded. No pony bred of Mangiralas had ever looked like this. They were all varying

shades of dun—save for one that was black with a white star on its forehead. Any Horsemaster who brought them to Mangiralas Fair would
have been laughed out of the domain.

In that moment, Runacar wished sharply and despairingly for a
Lightborn to cast a spell of Long Sight, for he knew he was missing vital
information that he *just couldn't see.*

"Those animals down there aren't destriers—or palfreys—or pack-
horses," Runacar said to the others. "And so I know less than I did when
I got here. What I don't see is any fighting."

Nindir smirked, and Andhel swatted him.

"There," Tanet said. "At the far edge of the forest. You can't see them
now—they're too close to its edge."

Runacar adjusted his gaze away from the pony vanguard. Now he
could see what Tanet was indicating, but he still wasn't sure what he was
seeing. Winged red things darted and swooped. They vanished below
the tree line for so long they must be landing, then soared into the sky
once more. *Not carrion birds. They're too big. . . .*

"The red fliers. Not Otherfolk?" he asked.

"No," Tanet said briefly.

One of the not-Otherfolk soared high enough to catch the rays of
the rising sun. The light illuminated its wings in a flash of scarlet. Not
feathered. Ribbed. Like a bat's.

Later, Runacar would look back on this moment and wonder why he
hadn't known what they were at once. But no one had said the Darkness
would look like . . . people.

"*They* aren't fighting," he started to say, nodding toward the horses
and riders headed for the pass. "They're—" *They're running for their
lives,* he meant to say. But before Runacar could finish his sentence, the
whole world was filled with blinding light. It was as if the sun had come
to earth.

He roared with pain and surprise and flung himself to the ground.
Runacar could hear the cries of the other Woodwose; he reached out
blindly, flailing, and caught a wrist. Andhel's. "Who can see?" he demanded. "Anyone?"

He was worried, angry, and very close to fear. No matter how he tried,

Runacar couldn't force his eyes open. Tears trickled down his cheeks, and even with his eyes closed, flares of color drifted across his sight. *Silver Hooves, I beg you: do not force me to go into the battle blind....*

"I can." A familiar voice. Drotha. Not Runacar's best choice for an observer, but at the moment, he had no other options. "What do you want me to look at?" Drotha asked.

"Look down where the flash came from," Runacar said tightly. "The forest everybody's running away from," he corrected himself. Drotha wouldn't have seen the flash—at least, not if it was of magical origin. Aesalions could not sense magic, let alone be affected by it.

"Nothing," Drotha said, sounding disappointed. "Just people running this way, and winged people flying away. Red ones," he added conscientiously. "I've never seen people who looked like that before. Do you want me to go look closer?"

"No!" Several voices were raised in protest.

"Well, if Drotha didn't see it, that flash of light must have been magic," Tanet said hoarsely.

Runacar was finally able to keep his eyes open. They itched and burned, and it took effort not to rub them. "It wasn't Lightborn magic," he said. "At least, not any I've ever seen. But it makes no difference. If anything, it helps us. I didn't see any scouts. If they're running from giant red bat people, they won't be as cautious."

"No," Tanet agreed. "We watched all night, very carefully. Nothing came from the forest before the running horses."

"I didn't see anything either," Drotha said innocently. "Of course I didn't cross the mountains. Leutric forbade that. But you can see a lot if you fly high enough."

As soon as he could see again, Runacar took another cautious look out over the east. All who had wished to leave the forest had, apparently, left.

No. There was one last group leaving now. This scattered fantail trailed far behind the other riders, but they didn't seem to be servants or vassals. As he gazed thoughtfully down at the migration and waited for inspiration to strike, Runacar's eyes were drawn to a pair of riders riding directly for the trailhead. He watched them absently for several heartbeats before he understood why his eyes were compelled to follow the two unknown riders.

Or . . . one of them.

That's her. That's Vieliessar.

For a moment all Runacar wanted to do was spur his mount forward and ride to her side. *This is why all the War Princes of the Alliance would have killed you if they'd known about the Soulbond,* his mind said with inane pedantry.

He forced himself to look away.

The first riders out of Saganath had arrived at the base of the pass. They were garbed in motley like the others, and rode the same seeming breed of animal. But unlike everyone else, this band rode in disciplined formation and—also unlike everyone else—this group had remained together, even though they were of a sizable number.

Every one of the riders carried two swords sheathed across their backs.

One of Runacar's first lessons as a child—long before he was even allowed to hold a wooden sword—had been in the heraldry of the Hundred Houses: their colors and devices, the secondary banners that meant "heir," or "warlord," or "cadet branch," or "no quarter"—those, and a dozen more. He had learned to recognize every device from a great distance and under the most unfavorable conditions, for inability to identify who was entering—or leaving—the field could (in the old days) have cost lives—or, worse, victory.

Among those symbols had been, naturally, the heraldry of those irregular meisnes he might never be expected to meet on the field, such as Glasswall Free Company (a lightning bolt striking a hand-mirror), Foxhaven Free Company (a running fox above a left-facing sword), and that of the Silver Swords of Penenjil: a Vilya above two crossed swords on a field grisonnant.

The riders below him wore cloak brooches, the first jewels Runacar had seen on any of the pony-riders. The brooches were of elvensilver, which made them jewels of great price. Of course, a cloak brooch was far smaller than a banner, but such personal devices were also designed to be recognized from a distance.

The ponies moved into full gallop as if they were one beast, and suddenly every rider drew both swords and struck them together so they rang. Then each of them tossed both swords into the sky, and—incredibly—caught them as they came down again.

Blessed Flower Queen—those are *the Silver Swords of Penenjil!*

"I recognize the riders in the vanguard," he said aloud. "They're the Silver Swords of Penenjil. They declared for Lord Vieliessar even before their domain did; her enemies faced them on the field at Ifjalasairaet. Before that day, they'd never left their own domain, not even to fight beside their War Prince. If they're here, that is, without any question, the High King's army." He could not keep the puzzlement from his voice.

"Them?" Drotha said, disappointed. "I thought she'd have more people for me to kill."

"So did I," Runacar said, very quietly. Melisha had said the High King was crossing into the West with her entire army. But down below he saw barely enough riders to make up the array of Caerthalien-as-was.

"This changes nothing," Andhel said. Runacar nodded fractionally, and she went on, more confident now. "We know they're Houseborn, and we know they're good at killing—a match for any of you lazy louts, Tanet. But you aren't going to be fighting them. The Minotaurs and the Centaurs are. And because they're Houseborn killers, they'll be arrogant, and they'll miss things. And we'll win."

Tanet smiled a crooked smile. "You've been listening to Rune too long, Andhel. You sound just like him."

Andhel didn't dignify the comment with a response.

"She's right, though," Runacar said. "And more to the point, if the High King's army is running from something, it has to be close behind them, or they wouldn't push their horses so hard—assuming you could call those things horses. So as soon as the Silver Swords are halfway up the pass, I want you to pull back. Take the other watch posts with you when you do. I want all of you well-hidden before they get here."

"And then we'll give them the surprise of their lives," Andhel said with bloodthirsty glee.

"Not that it will take very long," Drotha said sulkily.

Drotha padded along beside Runacar and Andhel when they left the lookout point, his wings mantled and his poison-barbed tail curved up over his back. The poison had a bitter scent of its own, a pervasive rankness distinct from the Aesalion's own scent. If anyone was lunatic enough to want to hunt Aesalions, they'd clearly be easy to track.

Not that anyone would be *that* lunatic.

While none of the Otherfolk took particularly well to the sort of discipline Runacar had been trained to, he had long since learned that if you had Aesalions in your meisne, all you could do was indicate the general direction of the enemy and your displeasure. And right now there were . . . a very large number of Aesalions with his army.

He'd thought, when they mustered, that his army wouldn't be large enough to beat the High King's army. Instead, they would be meeting them with nearly equal numbers. Runacar wished that made him more confident about the outcome, but he had faced Vieliessar on the field before. Anything was possible. *"—but far fewer of them are likely,"* as Lengiathion Warlord had been fond of saying.

If they aren't coming west in battle array I want to know why, and there's precious little hope of that. No matter why they're coming up the pass, there's only one thing we can do.

We fight and we win.

Runacar and Andhel stopped along the way back to the Flower Forest, to tell the other sentries what they'd seen at the pass and to reaffirm their orders.

"You know," Runacar said mildly to Drotha, "if any of their herd animals get wind of you, we won't need to fight. They'll trample everything underfoot when they flee."

Drotha smirked at him, the expression disconcertingly Elven on the Aesalion's flat face. "If you wanted me to leave so you could have some privacy, you should have said so," he said. "There's more to see from the sky anyway."

He turned away to spring across the meadow in great leaping bounds, like a giant cat chasing invisible butterflies, until suddenly his great wings spread and he soared skyward like a battle-kite.

Runacar sighed. "And to think I *wanted* to be Leutric's Warlord," he said.

"Even if you didn't, he would have wanted that. Eventually," Andhel said. "You Houseborn are good at war."

"Apparently we always have been," Runacar said, thinking of the story Melisha had told him. He looked around. The only thing in sight was a group of Centaurs wrangling the horses into concealment. "Melisha . . ."

"Never listen to Unicorns," Andhel said firmly. "They'll only upset you."

"She— Wait. *Unicorns?* There's more than one?" That was an astonishing notion.

"Where do you think more Unicorns come from?" Andhel asked inarguably. "I don't know how many there are, but there's a lot more than one. They come and help sometimes, if you really need help. But they don't—didn't—live in the Western Lands. What did she tell you?"

"That Elvenkind came from a land beyond the Sea of Storms. That they came here because they lost a war—a war they'd started, which argues poor judgment on the part of our ancestors. And once they were here, they . . . kept on fighting."

"Maybe it's what you do. *We* do. Like Gryphons make stories, and Minotaurs dance. But it would be nice if you could stop."

"Wouldn't it?" Runacar said with a sigh. "Right now I just wonder where the rest of Vieliessar's army is. If she's bringing them through the Southern Pass, she's going to have to do some extensive stone-shaping."

Andhel snorted. "Melisha would have mentioned, if she meant you to be in two places at once."

"I don't mind being a pawn, but it's nice to be asked," Runacar said. "Right now I wonder what that array down there is running from. Tanet said those red bat things we saw earlier weren't Otherfolk. How certain was he?"

"You think we don't know our own?" Andhel asked.

"I think I was Leutric's Warlord for nearly ten years before I saw either a Palugh or a Wulver," Runacar said. "Not to mention the Sea Folk."

"Yes," Andhel said, "but that's different. Ocean and forest hide a great many things. None of us knows the full number and kind of the Sea Folk, except maybe the Gryphons, and *you* can't see half the Folk of the Land, oh great and mighty Houseborn warrior." The words she had once flung at him in anger and hatred were now no more than gentle teasing. "But you can't hide anything in the sky, you know."

So all that flies is visible. And known. Runacar restrained himself from glancing skyward to check. "No red bats?" he asked.

"The only red things in the sky are the Aesalions, and they aren't all red."

⊰⊱

Runacar and Andhel returned to the forest camp. Riann did not come to bring the decision of the Ascension, and Runacar supposed he would go into battle without knowing. But he'd trained his captains and his apprentices well, and they were used to commanding a battlefield of chaotic changeability.

The Woodwose sentries joined them as they waited, with fresh reports on the composition of the attackers. Runacar converted their tallies into figures he understood. They were facing a force of about ninety great-tailles. With them were about twice that number of free-running horses, and no end of sheep, goats, and dogs.

But nowhere in that tally was there any mention of supply wagons or pack mules, and there were no outriders, no foot knights, and no servants—or, to be scrupulously exact, everyone was dressed the same and mounted the same, so there was no way to tell which rider belonged to what element of her army.

Runacar composed a report of everything he currently knew about the enemy force, and told it to one of the Wulver messengers. Windrunner repeated it back to him word-perfect after only three tries. Runacar's words would go down the mountain to one of the Gryphons, who would also memorize it. Leutric should have the report before the sun set.

By then, everything would have been decided, one way or the other. He donned his armor, and saddled his horse, and waited.

And then the waiting ended.

❧❧

The Silver Swords reached the top of the pass. Immediately on their heels came the first wave of riderless horses. The Silver Swords dismounted, moving among the milling animals to separate those with blue handprints on neck and rump from the others. They quickly relieved them of their living burdens, and sent the beasts moving down the valley to Nomaitemil. By the time the Silver Swords had finished that task, the second wave of riders had arrived, followed quickly by more riderless horses, and a third mounted wave. Soon Ceoprentrei became a roiling mob of wranglers afoot and on horseback, whimpering infants, barking herding-dogs, and complaining horses. More were arriving—horses, Elvenkind, livestock—in a constant flow.

In such a confusion, to seek out one individual was nearly impossible, and Dandamir, Master of the Silver Swords, did not try. Instead, he looked westward. The High King would want a report of how the Western Lands lay as soon as she arrived.

Framed in the now-vast opening of the Western Gate, the hills of Vondaimieriel were the color of autumn, the gold of ripeness not yet turned to winter's dun. In the far distance, he could see the walls of Vondaimieriel's Great Keep.

But I see no manor houses, nor beasts of the field turned out to graze, nor the fences and furrows of cropland. I do not smell even a wisp of smoke on the wind. This might mean anything or nothing. We will not know truly until we go.

"The Heir! The Heir!" Githachi rode toward Master Dandamir, Calanoriel before her on her saddle.

"The Hunt be praised," Dandamir said quietly. "Are you well, my prince?"

"I am, my lord," Calan answered stoutly. "My mother? My sister?" he asked hopefully.

"Still to come," Dandamir said, hoping he spoke truth. "Now get you gone to safety." He locked eyes with Githachi. "See him safe to Nomai-temil," he said.

"I obey," she answered. "Come, little lord. We shall race the herd and make it run."

The boy yelped with innocent delight as she spurred her destrier on-ward.

Dandamir rode around the edge of the herd, marshaling his komen. He scanned the eastern sky. There was no sign of the winged monsters there.

Perhaps they will leave us in peace until we are settled in the West. A moonturn, even a sennight, would be enough. I pray to our brothers of the Hunt for this grace.

It would be nightfall before everyone reached the top of the pass, and the Lightborn—and the High King—would be among the last to reach it. But Ceoprentrei itself was not safety. Only Nomaitemil could promise safety.

Dandamir put that thought from his mind. Since the fall of Celephriandullias-Tildorangelor ten thousand Wheelturns ago, the Silver Swords had been tasked with one commission and one only: Protect the High King. Through all the long years that spanned that day until the day she had come, they had trained, and watched, and waited for the appearance of the one who was their charge. Dying, Master Kemmiaret had passed to Dandamir the great secret that only the Master of the Silver Swords could know, and Dandamir husbanded it now against the day and hour of his own death.

"Come!" he shouted to his companions. "Saddle fresh mounts! We return to the High King's side!"

Within the candlemark, Dandamir and his troop rode down into the Tamabeth Hills alongside the upward-moving refugees.

⊰⊱

The sun rose to midheaven and began its slow descent without the Endarkened's return. Vieliessar hoped that luck would hold. *I pray we may be settled within Lady Arevethmonion herself by the time those monsters fly forth again.*

The Lightless stragglers were nearly a league ahead; the Lightborn were still scattered among the thousand shepherd's tracks of the Tamabeth Hills. Vieliessar, with Thurion beside her, rode between the two groups, leading one and following the other. Again and again Vieliessar drew breath to speak to Thurion, only to close her mouth again. Her thoughts were nothing she wanted to share.

When Thurion spoke at last, she flinched as from an unexpected blow.

"You might as well say aloud what you are thinking," he said mildly. "Or have you forgotten what my Keystone Gift is?"

"True Speech," Vieliessar answered. "And yet I know my shields are proof against it."

"If we did not know one another so well, and were we not alone, yes, they would be," Thurion answered gently. "You think it was the war you waged that brought us to this day. You fear that you have doomed us all—or that your acts are meaningless, and we are all doomed anyway."

The accuracy with which he spoke her thoughts surprised Vieliessar into jagged laughter. "Perhaps I shall prevail by such methods as will make the Banebringer but a portent of sorrows to come," she said bitterly. "And . . . perhaps it would have been kinder to all to let everyone go on as they had been," she added softly.

"And die?" Thurion said. "You cannot say you summoned the Endarkened, and we know the fate of those Houses that stood alone against them. Bethros . . . Haldil . . . of the twenty houses of the Grand Windsward, the six of the Arzhana, how many yet survive? You know the answer as well as I. And if we are to join them . . ." He paused for a moment, while he gazed silently at the road ahead. "If we are to join them in death, whatever that death may be, then you have freed all your people to meet it standing each beside the other as equals. If the Landbond were free only a handful of Wheelturns, if the Farmholders and hedge knights had only that length of time to go without fear of their overlords, then you have done a thing that will be honored forever."

"You speak as if there will be anyone left to make such songs," Vieliessar answered irritably. *From the moment I declared my claim to the Unicorn Throne, all I have done is watch them die.*

"Why else did Amretheon make his Prophecy, if not to warn us of a thing we could survive?" Thurion answered promptly.

"Our ancestors were mad," Vieliessar responded, and Thurion chuckled.

"Then you may accuse them of madness, when you see them again," he answered, and fell silent.

But Thurion had started her thinking, as he so often did, and about something other than all the ways this day could go wrong. What *were* the Endarkened? Why did they persecute her people? Nothing that they did made any sense. Not by the Code of War. Not by a mercenary's pragmatism—or a king's. They might come in force, or by ones and twos. Sometimes they stayed away for moonturns, at others, small groups of them would attack daily for a sennight.

Without understanding the enemy, there was no way to win. Yet Amretheon had thought it worthwhile to compose his Prophecy. Why do that if the battle he foresaw so clearly was unwinnable? Why not tell her how to win it when he had told her so much else? Over and over Vieliessar had asked herself that question, had sacrificed at the Shrines for her answers, had begged the Silver Hooves to send her true dreams . . . and had received nothing.

The Great Library at the Sanctuary of the Star was her last hope.

⊰⊱

Perhaps they cannot cross the mountains," Thurion said when they stopped to water their horses.

It was late afternoon, and the Endarkened had still not returned, and Vieliessar began, cautiously, to hope. Many of her people had already reached Ceoprentrei and the upper half of the road to the pass was filled with horses and riders.

"You know as well as I that Lord Runacarendalur lives," Thurion went on, when Vieliessar said nothing. "I cannot imagine him hiding in the depths of a Flower Forest, can you?"

"I cannot imagine him knowing it would work," Vieliessar responded instantly. "I would think him at Amrolion, or Daroldan, but he would not go, nor would they have him. Perhaps he shelters at the Sanctuary of the Star."

"Perhaps," Thurion agreed. "But that is not why you wish to go there."

She turned in her saddle to stare at him, knowing shock and betrayal was written on her face.

"I need no Keystone Gift to guess your plan," Thurion said gently. "You say—you have always said—that you ride to the relief of the Shore, and no one will doubt that, even though their cry for aid was a decade ago—even Farmholders know that much of *The Way of the Sword*. Moreover, I believe you will ride to their aid as soon as you may—but that is not why you go west. You go to seek a weapon. Nothing we have tried has gained us the victory. Even the *ikhlad*-fire, even Sunstroke, are weapons that take more from us than they give. Celelioniel discovered the Prophecy in the Sanctuary libraries—who is to say there is not more to find?"

Vieliessar stared at him mutely. Thurion, unfazed, continued.

"Let me help. To reach even Arevethmonion will take until Rade if not longer—unless a Lightborn goes. I know as well as you that your council will forbid you such rash action, but will you not trust me to go in your place? From Nomaitemil I can reach Arevethmonion by Door, and in the Sanctuary I will either find what you seek, or—"

"Or be imprisoned by Hamphuliadiel, should he still reign there," Vieliessar said bleakly.

"But if he does, is that not one more proof the West is safe from the Endarkened? Besides," Thurion added impishly. "Hamphuliadiel likes me."

Vieliessar snorted derisively. "Undoubtedly he will decide to make you Astromancer in his stead."

"But promise me you will—" Thurion began.

—⧗⧢—

I will see you flayed alive and your still-living body set out in the field as food for *crows!*" Vieliessar snarled.

Master Dandamir stood beside his mount. Behind him stood a demi-taille of the Silver Swords. Helecanth stood to his tuathal side, regarding her liege-lord imperturbably.

"Then you must find a field and a tanner to do the work," Lady Helecanth said, "and that must wait upon your safety."

"You were not to come back. Not for *any* cause!"

"And yet the Silver Swords can do more good here than elsewhere," Master Dandamir said steadfastly. "That we met the commander of your guard on our way to you is good fortune indeed."

Vieliessar drew breath to speak again, but Helecanth forestalled her. "I bring you glad tidings, my lord. Your heir and your daughter both live, and are even now being brought to safety."

"Then we must join them as soon as we can," Vieliessar said tightly, and turned away.

The High King's party rode on in a silence born of weariness. For so much of her life Vieliessar had taken the simplest things for granted: a dry bed and a warm fire, and soup to drink by the fireside. The reality of these things had been taken from her one by one, and when they were gone, even the possibility of them was taken, until such homely comforts seemed like legends out of the most distant past, miraculous and inaccessible.

⧉

As the road climbed she could look back across the long shadows of the hills and forest below. The setting sun had painted the Tamabeth Hills with blue and violet: even though the mountains were still a blazing vault of gold, night was falling. The mist had already begun to rise, lending the landscape behind her a truly ghostly appearance.

The last of the day's warmth had departed with the light. The chill wind was soft with moisture, and Vieliessar shivered at its touch.

"They're coming," Thurion said softly.

At his words, Vieliessar abruptly realized it was not cold and exhaustion, but nausea that made her shiver. She looked toward the sky, but there was nothing to see save the first pale stars of evening.

Never before have they followed an attack in force so quickly with another. I have gambled all my people upon one throw, and I have lost.

"Master Dandamir," Vieliessar said quietly. "The Endarkened come. It is for you to say how we will go."

"Ride ahead, my lord King," Dandamir answered without hesitation. "Lady Helecanth with you, the Lightbrother with us. If we do not follow, discover Githachi, who has charge of the Prince-Heir, and say to her that she is the last of the Silver Swords. She will know what must be done."

"May the Starry Hunt take you into its care, and defend you while you live," she answered softly. "Make ready," she said to Helecanth, and cast the spell upon their mounts that would make the animals run until they died.

CHAPTER TWELVE

HARVEST MOON IN THE TENTH YEAR OF THE HIGH KING'S REIGN: THE ROAD OF SWORDS AND TEARS

I have heard folk speak of the High King's campaign as if it was a thing certain in victory from the moment it was announced. We who were there in that time knew it would be a road of swords and tears: it would destroy all that was loved and familiar, and even so, victory would not be certain.

—Thurion Pathfinder, A History of the High King's Reign

The wind whipped past her face, chill and cold, and Vieliessar pressed her face into her pony's neck to give him what aid she could. The battleponies were not capable of the ravall, but their endurance was greater. They would make it to the top of the pass before they died.

At each switchback Vieliessar could look back and see the Silver Swords, their horses moving at a walk to spare them for the battle to come. And it was a battle Vieliessar must hope would come, for the Endarkened could so easily ignore the Silver Swords, even with such tender bait, and fly onward to attack Vieliessar—or even the folk gathered in Ceoprentrei.

As they climbed the mountainside, Vieliessar and Helecanth passed out of twilight and back into full sun. Abruptly the air was warm once again, the rocks around them radiating the day's heat. The horses were gasping for every breath now, their sides heaving like a blacksmith's bellows, but still they ran. Closer and closer they came to the pass itself, and just as Vieliessar thought they would make it, a sound came from Ceoprentrei that meant utter disaster.

It was the sound of war-horns, calling her army to . . .

Hunt?

❧

Dusk had fallen over Ceoprentrei. Painted ponies ran everywhere, chased by riders intent on relieving them of their living burdens. Folk shouted orders and commands, as the people slowly re-formed into their customary groups. Rithdeliel of Caerthalien, Warlord to the High King, could look back over a day that had been tedious, nerve-wracking, and overfull of sheep. The only thing rendering it remotely bearable was that he had Gallatin with him. The destrier was the last one left to them; the High King had ordered their few remaining truehorses (most of them elderly) left behind in Saganath Flower Forest, but no power in all of Jer-a-kalaliel could have induced Rithdeliel to mount one of the scrubby Arzhana ponies and treat it as if it were a destrier.

For the hundred thousandth time, Rithdeliel cursed the prank of fate that made the Lightborn both the army's only effective weapon and the people's weakest link: they must always presume that the Endarkened would attack the Lightborn first, and so the safety of the many required the Green Robes to hold themselves apart.

Even when one of them was the High King herself.

At least the Silver Swords had gone back for her. It would have been unbearable if they had not: no matter how much Lord Vieliessar attempted to style herself as nothing more than the Child of the Prophecy, she was noble by birth and by right of conquest, and it was no kindness to those she ruled to pretend otherwise.

Rithdeliel would gladly have changed places with her if that were possible. She would know how to weigh the fact that Nomaitemil Flower Forest was enlarged a hundredfold from its previous self. To see it so was more grace than Rithdeliel could have dared to hope for, since it meant that shelter was only a quartermark away, but . . .

But for the fact that the trees were not mere saplings of a decade's growth, but trees whose girth spoke of centuries of growing.

He did not know how it had come to be, and what Rithdeliel did not know, he did not like. Even after one of the Rangers had ridden down to Nomaitemil and brought back a branch of Vilya as proof that the forest was neither trap nor illusion, Rithdeliel did not wish to send the flocks and herds down the valley. Nor to enter the Flower Forest himself.

But it was madness to tarry in the open this way, and once Prince Calanoriel was recovered, Rithdeliel had no choice but to give the order to move south. No matter what the Endarkened had done on every other occasion, it was a hopeful dream to assume they would all be safe before the monsters noticed. There was no place in Rithdeliel's life—in any competent Warlord's life—for dreams. All Rithdeliel could bring himself to feel was a weary relief that the work would soon be over.

Then the Gryphons came.

One moment there was nothing. The next, monsters came on silent wings, flying so low a mounted knight might have reached up to touch them. Gryphons. Not Endarkened. At least the Silver Hooves had granted them that much.

Rithdeliel drove his spurs into Gallatin's sides, and felt the hot-blooded stallion surge forward. Gallatin was terrified. He wanted to run—well, let him, so long as he ran where Rithdeliel wished him to.

Rithdeliel raised his war-horn without conscious thought, and the calls rang out mellow and low.

The quarry is in sight. Hunt at will. (Hunting calls, not the signals of war. Arilcarion had never meant the Code to apply to Beastlings.) The notes rang from the granite slopes, answered and echoed by the horns of other commanders.

The archers (on foot, praise the Silver Hooves, for it was nigh-impossible to control a horse that had scented Gryphon) nocked and loosed instantly, but to no avail. Two—three—five—of the abominable patchwork grotesques swept across the whole breadth of Ceoprentrei and then turned to follow Elvenkind heading for Nomaitemil, with chaos and terror as their vanguard. But even in all that clamor, Rithdeliel heard the roars of beasts and the clash of swords from the direction of the forest.

A trap: the Gryphons mean to herd us!

The Beastlings had used the unnaturally overgrown forest as cover. And the princess and the Heir-Prince were riding right toward them.

Even if Rithdeliel had been leading trained cavalry bespelled to indifference, it would have been impossible to organize and mount a charge. He cursed vehemently and long at the sheep scattering everywhere; Gallatin jinked and shied, and once even leapt over one of the woolly obstacles.

And then the field cleared and Rithdeliel could see the enemy's line. Minotaurs, Bearwards, and Centaurs—an impossible, and deadly, alliance. It took a taille of armored knights working with master huntsmen to slay a single Minotaur bull safely, and there were a dozen or more here.

And Rithdeliel was the only one on the field in proper armor.

He cursed the desperate need that had led the High King's komen to abandon their armor on a hundred battlefields, and the paucity of resources that meant they had not replaced it. To wear armor properly took training and practice—and even many who still possessed their armor chose not to wear it.

In the name of expediency.

In the name of camouflage.

To survive in a world that had trampled Arilcarion's wisdom beneath taloned jeweled feet, and drowned knightly honor in a sea of blood.

Rithdeliel drew his sword and howled a war cry that had not been heard in more than a century.

"Farcarinon! Farcarinon and victory!"

※

Cattle bawled and dogs barked and chickens and ducks and geese demanded to be set free of their cages. The sky was as filled with light as the air was with sound, but the sun was setting to the west of the great peaks, and the sound, Githachi thought, would go on forever. Yet every other thing happening in Ceoprentrei barely ruffled the surface of her mind, for Master Dandamir had entrusted her with the most precious treasure they had, and bid her hide it well.

Githachi glanced nervously skyward as she rode south; any child of the Grand Windsward would always fear the open sky. On her saddle-bow, Calanoriel sat up very straight. No child born since the final battle fretted or fidgeted, but beyond that, Calanoriel was very conscious of being Prince-Heir, and gazed around himself calmly, letting the people see his fearlessness.

"Good fortune will follow good fortune, my prince," Githachi said to him. "And that you are here with me now is surely the first of many good things to come."

"When my sister and my King are safe, then we will rejoice," Cala-noriel said gravely. "And when we have won."

Githachi did not know whether to agree with him, or to gently re-mind him that the ways of the Silver Hooves were often hard to com-prehend, when the choice was taken from her. A shadow—long known, long feared—passed above her, flying low.

"Gryphons!" she cried, not needing to look, as the first of the great blue-and-gold monsters glided low through the Western Pass and across the valley. The wind from the forest carried the scent of the monsters to all the beasts in the valley and suddenly there was chaos, as every horse, sheep, goat, chicken, cow, and dog tried to stop dead, change di-rection, or both at once. She ducked her head against her pony's neck and clutched Calanoriel tightly to her chest. Githachi was not in the vanguard of the folk making their way to safety, and took a moment to give thanks, for though no one was safe when the Winged Ones were hungry, outliers were more vulnerable to being snatched into the sky.

I survived the High King's Enthroning: I can survive this, Githachi told herself grimly. She could already see Nomaitemil's welcoming trees and smell its unmistakable perfume upon the wind.

And then, just as the vanguard ahead reached Nomaitemil's shelter, sanctuary became horror.

Centaurs erupted from the Flower Forest swinging their war ham-mers and howling like wolves. Behind them ran a Clamber of Bearwards, roaring their own challenge, their muzzles flecked with foam. Githachi sobbed in pure rage. *Is it not enough that we are prey to the Endarkened, but now to their children as well?*

There was no time for her despair. *Think!* she told herself. *You must save the prince!*

The Bearwards reached the Elven refugees and began to kill. Horses and riders fell before their blows, and Gryphons dove from the sky, stampeding animals in all directions.

All Githachi's pony wanted to do was go somewhere the Gryphons were not: he would run in any direction his senses told him meant "away." Githachi prayed that safety lay back in the way they had come, but that hope was dashed before it had truly formed when she heard the sound of war-horns behind her. Her folk were besieged upon all sides, but she vowed by the swords she wore that her charge would not die.

She had reached the eastern wall of the valley, where rough stone had been shed from the mountain flanks to make a treacherous sloping field of boulders and gravel. Her mount did not like the uncertain footing there and ran along the bottom of the rocky slope instead; he was lathered with sweat and his sides heaved, but he was nowhere near blown enough to stop. Githachi watched the terrain carefully, whispering orders in Calanoriel's ear, her arms wrapped tight around him.

And when she saw what she sought, Githachi stood high in her stirrups, bracing herself one-handed against the saddle, clutched Calanoriel tightly to her chest, and leaped.

Her swords were on her back; she dared not fall upon them. The Prince-Heir was in her charge; she must keep him from harm. And so she flung her body up and back, as a juggler might push off from a practice mat, somersaulting over the running pony's rump and landing in a crouch, her charge and her swords both safe. She did not spend even an instant to give thanks for the good fortune that saw all their bones unbroken, but took Calanoriel by the hand, running up the slope to the place she had spotted.

It was a crack in the valley wall, where the stone had given way before the persuasion of Winter High Queen. And it was wide enough to hold a child.

"Here," she said, gasping with exertion as she thrust him forward. "Into this space, and lie quiet until you know it is safe."

Calanoriel stared at her, his eyes wide with a fear verging on panic, his hand clutching his dagger. Then he nodded and turned away, scrambling over the stones and wedging himself into the narrow space.

Githachi drew her swords, and ran toward the battle.

⊰⊱

It had always been a doctrine of war, first set down by Arilcarion and enlarged upon by those who had studied him, that the most elegant strategy was also the most efficient. To crush an enemy army's will to fight—and even its *ability* to fight—with one adroit maneuver was the most praiseworthy victory of all. A battle that was quickly over was a battle that would provide ransoms, reparations, and indemnities to the victor. Humble an enemy sufficiently, and they would have no choice but to sue for clientage, and thereby enrich the victor to an even greater extent.

The refinement of this philosophy had led Elvenkind to organize its meisnes in tailles, the tailles into demi-tailles, the demi-tailles into lesser tailles, so that every element of the army would have a commander able to fight on and attempt to achieve the objective no matter how much of the higher command had been incapacitated.

All these things Rithdeliel knew just as he knew water was wet and fire was hot. And none of it was of any tactical use when he faced a horde of Beastlings. Who was their leader? What did the others care if that leader fell in battle?

In other circumstances, it would have been impossible for Rithdeliel to move Gallatin in the direction of not just one Bearward, but a clamber of them. But Gallatin was in the midst of hundreds of other horses, and there were Gryphons in the air above him. His every instinct told him to run. It only remained for his rider to give him the direction.

And Rithdeliel did. He could see only one possible course of action. Kill one of the monsters, and the others might lose heart and flee. At the very least, the people would see it could be done. The army would rally, and fight with renewed heart.

Or it would not, and they would all die.

Rithdeliel spurred Gallatin forward, willing the gallant beast to stand just long enough for him to strike one blow. It must be enough. He doubted he would get a second chance.

He was nearly within reach of his target when he felt something seize him from behind. In another moment he was dragged from the saddle and carried into the sky.

⊰⊱

This battle began so promisingly. Runacar thought he should have realized at that moment that it was going to become a disaster, but as Lengiathion Warlord had always said: *"The greatest weapon in a commander's arsenal is hope."*

The Gryphons had decided to remove the enemy commanders. (Runacar wasn't sure how they decided who those were, since the entire enemy army seemed to be dressed for hunting and nobody was carrying a banner.) He'd ordered the Woodwose to encircle the enemy army from the rear to halt any mooted retreat, since their effectiveness would be greatest there. In the swiftly failing light, it was impossible to tell them from the enemy.

He had then taken command of the center. It placed him in the forefront of the fighting. Runacar knew Vieliessar would be looking for him—as he for her—and she would expect him to be leading the enemy army's center. If the High King's army did not believe they had broken his army's center, they would not pursue his forces into the forest—and into the trap.

And so it was that Runacar, riding out of the forest at the head of his center, was the first to see that the enemy army was using its children as its forward wing.

In a thousand sleepless nights, plotting out every possible contingency for this inevitable battle, it was one he'd never imagined. Children! The whole of the enemy column riding for the shelter of Nomaitemil was too young to fly their kites or leap the fires, and most of them were clutching children younger still.

None of them was holding a weapon.

In an instant, the field was chaos. Runacar would happily have let the children flee into the forest, only he'd lost control of his army in those first precious moments and they were reverting to instinct, tradition, and wild guesses.

That doesn't matter, he told himself. *I planned for this.*

All I need to do now is find Vieliessar . . . and kill her.

⊰⊱

Shanilya Arzhana had reached Ceoprentrei in one of the first groups of riders, and thus was able to turn her attention to the orders the Warlord gave. At his word, she separated combatants from children, pack horses, and sheep. As the potter sets the shaped clay aside, she dismissed each battle group as it was formed and turned to prepare another.

When the Gryphons appeared, Shanilya did not hesitate. She sounded the call to battle and rode hard for the Western Pass. Securing a line of retreat was vital. The battleponies were hardy and brave, but no horse would stand against a Gryphon.

But as soon as the hope of retreat was formed, it died, for four Gryphons stood on the rocks above the Western Gate, great wings mantled and gleaming eyes alert for prey. More Gryphons flew low through the pass; Shanilya vaulted from the saddle before she could be thrown from it, and did not need to order her meisne to do the same. The now-riderless horses fled down the valley, mad with fear, and Shanilya and her bodyguard prepared to fight.

There was no safety to be had in the open, but the valley walls were a thing of cracks and fissures and pocket canyons, and that was where Shanilya led her komen.

In fleeting glances she saw flashing wings in the high sky—Gryphons, circling—and other Winged Ones darting into the great mob of people and animals penned between the valley walls. Again and again the Gryphons swooped down upon them, flying off with living prey struggling in their claws. She caught a glimpse of Rithdeliel's scarlet armor as a Gryphon soared away, and her heart sank. This day would cost them dear.

Her bodyguard had barely reached the valley wall when she realized the Gryphons had not come alone. A troop of Centaurs trotted toward them, grim-faced and armed for war.

Retreat was possible, but useless. Shanilya raised her sword above her head and ran forward, screaming the war cry of the Arzhana.

"Come and die!"

❦

Bespelled to a dead run, Helecanth's and Vieliessar's Arzhana horses had far outrun the Silver Swords. They had just reached the switchback below the last leg of the pass road when the sound of war-horns came from ahead. Helecanth knew the sounds of battle, its rhythms, its ebb and flow. She had already been a belted knight, her spurs given by Bolecthindial's own hands, when he made her the head of his heir's Twelve. *(All dead, they're all dead now.)* Her new master had all of twelve Wheelturns on the day she knelt before him to pledge him her fealty.

In all the time Helecanth had served Prince Runacarendalur, there had been battle. The wars of War Season. The Beastling plagues of autumn and springtide. The harrying of outlaws that knew no season. Her trade—insomuch as a komen could be said to have a trade—was warfare, and Helecanth was very good at what she did. She could read a battlefield from its sounds, from its movement, and say: *This is but the beginning,* or: *The fighting has been long, and both sides grow reckless,* or: *The battle is over, though the losers do not yet know it.*

The battle in Ceoprentrei was still in its first moments, Helecanth judged, not long enough to make predictions of victory. But despite that, Helecanth could already say who the winner would be.

The Endarkened.

"My lord—my lord prince—wait." Helecanth reached out to grab the bridle of Vieliessar's mount and drag it to a halt. "There is no purpose to running blindly to our deaths."

"Shall we stay here, rather, and meet death standing instead of running?" Vieliessar asked furiously, striking Helecanth's hand away. Both battleponies fought to run until Vieliessar lifted the running-spell from them. They immediately halted, foam dripping from their mouths, sides heaving.

"I thought, rather, a spell of concealment might serve us as we ride on," Helecanth said quietly. "Those are not war calls. They are hunting calls."

Vieliessar stared at her for a long moment, and Helecanth thought she must prepare herself to meet a harder blow with calm indifference. However, once more, reason overruled passion.

"I'm sorry, dear friend," Vieliessar said quietly. "You are right. Give me but a moment. Nomaitemil is within my reach, and she is strong and willing." The High King's face was tightly drawn with pain and weariness and rage, but when she spoke, her voice was light. "Now let us see what game my army courses," Vieliessar said.

⊰⊱

In the spectral twilight, Gryphons soared between the valley walls, stooping down into the melee to pluck riders from their saddles and carry them off. More of the enormous winged monsters were perched on the rocks above the Western Gate, waiting and watching like carrion crows. Riderless horses trotted in frantic circles, seeking escape from a vast army of Beastlings. If the High King had not bespelled both their mounts, they would have bolted.

This is the end for all of us. Pelashia grant safe haven to Thurion and all of our folk who do not go to ride with the Silver Hooves tonight, Helecanth thought. *I grieve that I shall never see him again.* As if in a dream, she raised her own war-horn to her lips, only distantly aware that the High King had commanded it. The new call was neither of hunting nor of war, but a grim warning that their people were no longer the hunters.

The Endarkened come. The Endarkened are on the wing. Fly—fly—flee.

Distantly, Helecanth heard her horn's call echoed. *The Endarkened come. The Endarkened are on the wing.* But what should have been the sound of many was the sound of few. Leaders lost in battle, unhorsed, slain. Her warning was useless.

As she looked to her lord for orders, she saw a troop of Centaurs trot down the field. Their armor—boiled and studded leather corselet, chain coif—was spattered with blood. The Beastlings circled the battleground like herd-dogs driving sheep. It was clear they were here to keep the High King's people from fleeing back into the Uradabhur.

Then Vieliessar dropped Cloak. The Centaurs checked and stared, and above them, above the pass, Helecanth heard the squall of a Gryphon.

"Let us die as wolves, not as prey!" Vieliessar shouted, spurring her mount forward.

So be it.

The Centaurs paused for an instant, clearly expecting them to dismount—or to be flung from their horses' backs when the beasts panicked. The sight of their dismay made Helecanth laugh—if she must die today, it would be with fresh blood upon her sword.

Her pony ran beside Vieliessar's as they reached the Centaurs. Helecanth had hunted the creatures only rarely, for the infestation was primarily in the domains south and west of Caerthalien. While they had been a contentious nuisance to those domains afflicted with them, they had always been disorganized enough to be little threat.

That, like so much in the world, seemed to have changed.

Engage.

Feint.

Turn.

Block.

Horse and rider against a hideous amalgamation of both.

The Centaurs knew to surround them, to stay clear of each other's lines of attack, to attack horses before riders. Someone had trained them. Eight against two. The world narrowed to this battle only, this small and private war. The mathematics of combat made the outcome seem inevitable, but there was more to battle than sums and logic and the balance of resources against needs.

The first exchange of blows was inconclusive. Both sides were committed. There was nowhere to run. Helecanth's sword struck a glancing blow across one hairy unarmored flank. The Centaur spun on its forehand—a move so oddly resonant of a destrier's trained response that it startled her—and kicked her battlepony in the shoulder with both back hooves. The exhausted animal staggered, stumbled, tried to retreat . . .

And sank to its knees. Finished.

The Beastlings have the advantage, striking from below.

Helecanth realized that the same moment the High King did: Hele-canth saw Vieliessar vault from her saddle, sword in one hand, dagger in the other, to land upon a Centaur's back as if she intended to ride it.

Helecanth kicked free of her stirrups and parried the horizontal strike of a mace with her forearm, catching it low upon its shaft. Even through the padded metal bracers she wore beneath her rough home-spun tunic, the blow was enough to numb her arm to uselessness, and she dropped her dagger—but her sword was in her other hand. Her an-swering blow struck the beast on the side of his neck; the armored coif it wore barely blunted the force of her blow, and the monster went to its knees. Behind her, she sensed her horse attempting to lunge to its feet.

Another Centaur attacked on her off side. She jumped back, and her mount took the blow instead. Wild with pain, it flung off its spell-induced meekness and went for the nearest tormentor. For a brief in-stant, the Centaurs were distracted enough that Helecanth could make her way to Vieliessar's side. But there was only time to fit herself to her liege-lord, back to back, before they faced their enemies again.

The eight were now five. Elven swords had greater reach. Hammers and maces could do more damage; possibly even shatter a blade. The Centaurs wore bracers, but their upper arms and their lower bodies were bare.

Find the weakness and exploit it. Her own sister, Lady Heledor, who had become Cadet to Lengiathion Warlord, had been Helecanth's first teacher. She narrowed her thoughts to those undefended places, her blade singing in her hand like a living thing.

A Centaur reared, its naked belly just out of her reach. She lunged forward quickly, risking a strike from those heavy punishing hooves, and cut, springing backward quickly as the Centaur crashed down onto all four feet.

Not a killing blow. Not all at once. But the beast will bleed and bleed . . .

The sound of the larger battle had become background noise as she fought, but suddenly a sound broke through. The high agonized shriek of a Gryphon. Helecanth did not look away from her foe, but abruptly the sky above her was filled with gold and azure feathers.

"Run!" Vieliessar screamed. But there was nowhere to run to.

The Endarkened had reached Ceoprentrei.

⛬

This would be the last flight, the last slaughter, the end of the Red Harvest. It deserved a special celebration to mark its beginning. There were great banquets held to mark the occasion, displays of exotic finery, exquisite slaughter to empty the slave pens for their witchling victims.

And then, the Endarkened launched themselves from Ugolthma.

In flight upon flight the beautiful children of *He Who Is* left their citadel, soaring wingtip to wingtip until the whole of the brightening sky turned blood-red with their bodies.

If the others all die in battle, it will not matter. Only let Virulan die somehow—and Uralesse too—and I will rule the World Without Sun. There will be glorious war as we, the last of the Created-and-Changed, slaughter every one of the Born. And He Who Is *will have to love us, for we will be all that's left.*

As the dark legion flew south and west, grass and bushes replaced the beautiful sterility of rock and sand on the ground below. Dying Flower Forests dotted the land, stubbornly clinging to life.

The Endarkened lit the torches they carried and tossed them down at the trees as they flew.

Soon the sky was filled with the smoke of burning.

⛬

Endarkened vision was keen, their magical senses keener: west of the hateful Absence where the Elflings had hidden, east of the range of mountains their race knew as the Dragon's Bones, King Virulan could see clots of Elfling stragglers galloping along the road that led across the mountains.

Elfling Mages! All of them. Oh, the feasting and the sport . . .

He was tempted until he heard the high wild scream of a Gryphon. He saw several of the creatures circling the mountain valley, and the valley itself was teeming with life—Elflings, Centaurs, Minotaurs, every fecund unclean thing that the Light had made.

A feast.

The little Mages will keep.

Virulan selected his first target, and dived.

He should have been paying better attention.

HARVEST MOON IN THE TENTH YEAR OF THE HIGH KING'S REIGN: DARK OF THE MOON

All know her father was Serenthon Farcarinon, yet too easily we forget that her mother, Nataranweiya, was of Caerthalien, and close kin to both its rulers. Yet none who saw her in her great rages would doubt, for Glorthiachiel's temper was a match for Bolecthindial's, and she was the image of them both . . .

—Thurion Pathfinder, A History of the High King's Reign

As Child of the Prophecy, Vieliessar had asked for miracles and had even created miracles, but no miracle she might devise could save her people now. The Beastlings had trapped them here in Ceoprentrei, the Endarkened had followed, and it was small comfort to know that the Beastlings were also to become the Endarkened's victims.

Her breath choked upon a sob of rage. The first of the Endarkened had been joined by two, by four, by six, until they were too many to count. Their first targets were the winged things: Gryphons and Hippogriffs. They sprang onto their backs, tearing their wings from their shoulders and riding them down to the ground as the creatures screamed in agony.

"Not even a beast should die so," Vieliessar whispered to herself.

Then a new Beastling entered the fray. It took her a moment to identify it: black wings with red and yellow bars, the body of an ice tiger, a glittering black barbed tail.

Aesalion.

It laughed as it dove on the Endarkened. That was—somehow—more terrible than its appearance. It laughed. Suddenly Vieliessar wished she was anywhere but here.

"My lord, we are succored," Helecanth said softly.

Vieliessar felt the whisper of a Lightborn spell over her skin; saw movement from the corner of her eye as Thurion dropped the Cloak spell that had concealed the arrival of the Silver Swords. Their presence created a surreal bubble of calm in the midst of the chaos. Vieliessar realized that the Centaurs were staring at the Aesalion just as she was, frozen motionless by the sight. In another instant, they would shake off the terrible fascination and resume their attack. But now they were far outnumbered.

"Go," she told them, raising her voice to be heard over the din of the battle. "I give you your lives." As she spoke, she stepped backward toward the Silver Swords. There was a silent frozen moment until the Beastling leader nodded in simple acknowledgment, and the five remaining Centaurs turned and trotted away.

The single Aesalion had been joined by a dozen more, filling the sky like ravens come to feast. The Endarkened had abandoned all other targets to deal with them; the air crackled and roiled with magic, and blood from the battle above sprayed those engaged in the battle below.

"My lord, we must get you to safety," Master Dandamir said.

Despite their island of calm, Vieliessar felt a vast rage rising up to choke her. "Do you see any safety anywhere?" Vieliessar demanded, her voice harsh. "What I need is—"

"Here they come," Thurion said. A sidewise glance showed her two riderless horses trotting toward them as calmly as if madness did not rage about them. Vieliessar ran toward the nearer, vaulting into its saddle. An irrelevant thought struck her: *At least they will not see me fall to the ground as if I have lost my senses. . . .*

"The Western Pass is clear," Dandamir said as he rode to join her.

"No," Vieliessar said. "I will not abandon my folk."

"You will do—" Dandamir said angrily.

"Vielle!" Thurion said urgently. "Think! The Aesalions have the power to—"

Vieliessar ignored him. She turned her mount and spurred it into the battle. Her fury and despair were so intense that she welcomed the chance to kill with blade and dagger and fist before she died.

⊰⧓⊱

Songsmiths and Loremasters and Storysingers all told of battle as if it were a single thing. Like a loaf of bread or a stoup of ale: seamless from one end to the other.

It was not.

A battle was not one thing: it was many. This komen fought that komen. A line of archers fired at a swiftly changing target. Infantry formed against a charge, or scattered to protect themselves from one. A battle was a thousand tiny brawls.

And so Vieliessar rode through the myriad gaps that opened and closed all around her as if the fight was some dance at a Festival Fair, and not a great mill that ground out death between its stones.

The sun was gone from all but the highest peaks of the Mystrals, and only the false light of twilight remained. It was enough to show movement, but not detail—unless one was Lightborn, and dared to cast Silversight in the presence of the Endarkened. When she did, Vieliessar saw that the eyes of the Beastlings glowed as if they were dogs, cats, foxes.

If we fought our own kind, we could not fight on with so little light to see by, for who would know the enemy?

Vieliessar did not stop to ask herself what she was so desperate to find, nor where the overmastering need to find it—to *kill* it—had come from. Rage drove out fear and despair, drove out weariness and shame. All that was left was the sword in her hands and the imperative to kill. Even so, she could mark the battle's rhythms and its histories as if she watched ripples spread upon a once-quiet lake. Here the combatants had not yet noticed the Endarkened. There, they had seen them but chose to fight on. Or tried to flee, and couldn't. Or stood, frozen in horror.

Most of the winged Beastlings were dead now—except a few Aesalions—and some of the Endarkened had alighted atop mounds of corpses to butcher targets on the ground. Some fought with stolen swords in mocking parody of Elvenkind. Others fought with teeth and claws. Some merely harvested the battlefield as Elvenkind and Beastlings both tried to flee, carrying captives alive into the sky.

There was no hope of using Sunstroke against the Endarkened here. In Saganath, the Lightborn had all been gathered together to merge their strength in the depth of a Flower Forest, and even so, the spell had cost them a score of Lightborn lives and nearly killed the Flower Forest. In the madness of this battle, Vieliessar only knew the Lightborn were here because some of them had preceded her through the pass and so *must* be here.

She could not escape the fantasy that this battle was some nightmare reenactment of her Enthroning; it was as if all the moonturns that stretched between that day and this were a mistake now to be rectified. When the Endarkened left this battlefield, they would leave behind them no survivors.

No survivors. No survivors. The phrase beat through Vieliessar's mind as if it was the beat of her heart, as if it was borne upon the furious blood that pounded through her veins. She did not know if it was judgment, prayer, or prophecy—or even truth. Bodies pressed against her horse's flanks. Hands clutched at her bridle, her saddle, her legs. Vieliessar fended them off with sword and fist. The sound the Beastlings made in dying sounded very like the death-screams of people.

And as she forced her way through the combatants, Vieliessar saw Ceoprentrei turn from the site of a battle to the scene of a riot. She could almost taste the panic bubbling to the surface. Soon, the only thought in every mind would be escape, no matter what the cost. And there was nowhere to run to.

Not anymore.

And still Vieliessar drove her mount onward, forcing her way through the living tide that kept her from her goal. She had failed too many times. This one task she would—she *must!*—succeed at. She did not realize what—*who*—she searched for until she saw him.

He was in full armor of radiant gold, his destrier brilliantly caparisoned, as if he had ridden from some glorious past war into this terrible present. His visor covered his face, but that did not matter. Vieliessar did not need to see his face to know him. To know who had trained the Centaurs to fight as if they were komen.

Her world narrowed to one thing in that timeless instant: to reach Runacarendalur Caerthalien and *end him.*

⟞⟡⟝

Runacar heard one of the Gryphons scream in ultimate agony. He gazed skyward (hearing the ghosts of his former teachers say that to look skyward in the midst of a battle was a good way to die much sooner than you might wish to), trying to find the source of the sound. When he did, his first thought was indignant disbelief, a child's protest: *That's not fair!*

Barely had Runacar registered the creatures' presence when outrage turned to horror. Blood fell like rain upon the combatants below. The same scarlet bat-winged things he'd briefly seen this morning had followed Vieliessar's army here. They were nearly as large as a Minotaur, and their leathery ribbed wings—spanning as much distance as a Gryphon's—glowed redly in the last rays of the sun. They soared and dove above the battle like ravens—anything in the sky was their target, and they tore Gryphons and Hippogriffs to pieces with their bare hands.

And there was nothing Runacar could do to help the Folk of the Air.

He shouted for archers, but they were already loosing arrows uselessly into the sky. As each dying Gryphon and Hippogriff crashed to the ground, the flying red things launched themselves toward new prey.

—dead, Radafa must be dead; it's Riann's Ascension over the battlefield and those monsters, the red-winged things, they—

But suddenly, their prey became a match for them.

Aesalions stooped from the sky, striking the red invaders midflight as a hunting hawk takes a pigeon. When their scarlet quarry fought back, the Aesalions writhed and twisted in the air with felinoid grace, ripping at them with claws and striking them with barbed and venomous tails.

For an instant every creature on the field below stood shoulder to shoulder and cheered in bloodlust, before turning to their own combats with renewed vigor. Runacar's hackles stood up and his hand went to his armored breastplate, where the talisman Spellmother Frause had given him lay. Only her magic had saved Runacar from being caught up in the emotions the Aesalions were broadcasting, and he hoped desperately that he was not the only person wearing one.

"The thing that makes the Aesalions truly terrifying is their ability to evoke whatever emotion they choose in those around them." He could not remember who had written that. It wasn't in Lannarien.

Now the terrible crimson creatures were landing. Runacar saw a woman-thing jeweled as if for Festival Fair grab the nearest Minotaur by the horns. One heartbeat, and she had ripped the horns from his skull. Two, and she had gutted him with them.

She was laughing.

She was still laughing when Runacar charged her, his sword in hand, his blade already swinging toward her neck. It rebounded off something he couldn't see—

Isn't it enough that they can fly? Must they be sorcerers too?

—and she pouted at him lasciviously.

"Not today, darling boy," she said, blowing him a kiss. "You stink of purity." She bounded into the air before he could shape another blow.

Think! Runacar told himself desperately. *These are no allies of the High King—they attack everyone here. We cannot prevail against a foe we know nothing of. What is left?*

Retreat. And to manage it was all but impossible—he wasn't even sure where they should retreat *to*. Nomaitemil would be as much of a trap for his army as it had been meant to be for Vieliessar's.

Melisha, where are you? Why didn't you warn me? Didn't you know?

Runacar's war-horn was slung across his surcoat like a baldric. An artifact of a simpler time, he'd used it to drill his army, and to teach them the signals of the enemy they would be facing.

The enemy he'd *thought* they'd be facing.

He raised the horn to his lips. *Retreat, retreat,* it sang. *Disengage, do not pursue, retreat, retreat. . . .*

His heart hammered wildly, and Runacar realized he was near to panic, his mind full of memories of the disaster at Daroldan. This time there was nowhere to retreat to, no Sea Folk to save them.

And then he saw *her.*

She wore no helmet, but if she had, it wouldn't have mattered. He would have known her even if he had been struck blind. She did not wear the bright armor and surcoat he had last seen her in—she was dressed like the rest of them, like a forester, her only ornament of rank a diadem of elvensilver Vilya blossoms that even now shone brightly in the twilight.

"*Caerthalien!*" she shouted. "*I am coming for you!*"

At her words, Runacar flung his war-horn aside and raised his blade. All he could do was meet her charge. The scrubby little pony she rode moved as if it were a destrier, and from its obliviousness to the carnage surrounding it, he knew she held it bespelled.

"*The thing that makes the Aesalions truly terrifying. . . .*"

"Vieliessar!" he shouted, as their blades rang together. (Pivot, strike, turn, disengage.) "Listen to me! The Aesalions! We must—" (Feint, feint, attack, disengage.)

"Do you think I need help to hate you?" she cried. (Pivot, strike, turn, strike, attack.) "You who do the Endarkened's work for them?" (Lunge, parry, disengage.)

With a chill, Runacar realized that the Aesalions' blood-frenzy had left her. Worse, he could sense she was readying herself to leap from her saddle to his, to drag him to the ground to finish this, and he spun Folwin out of the way. A Wild of Wulvers lunged at her. They were no more than shadows and gleaming eyes in the gloom, but she killed three of them in a heartbeat while her mount fought as if it were a destrier.

Which of my friends have you left alive? Runacar wondered bitterly.

Vieliessar's defense was in vain, for the rest of the Wild won through to her horse to pull it down with teeth and knives. Vieliessar jumped free as it fell and ran toward him. "Traitor!" she cried. "Abomination! I will see you in the Ghostlands before I die!"

Runacar swore under his breath as she made for him. Folwin was hardened to battle, but too old to fight. If he had been younger, Folwin would have been an additional weapon in this combat, one that would all but assure Runacar the victory, especially now that Vieliessar was unhorsed. But Folwin's power had diminished with age, and so Runacar had no choice but to join Vieliessar upon the ground.

She laughed when she saw him vault from Folwin's back, and paused her attack to salute him mockingly. In that instant he was on another battlefield, far away in space and time, and it was Serenthon Farcarinon before him, Serenthon who laughed, even though he knew that he and his cause were doomed. . . .

And now Runacar must join Serenthon's daughter in the same dance of death, for they were enemies far more than Bondmates—a thousand times more so now than when he had fought for the Alliance and she had led the Rebels. As they struck and whirled, their feet beating a private Challenge Circle into the blood-soaked grass, there was no world apart from this, a world inhabited by only two.

His tuathal hand gripped his dagger tightly though he had no need of it—if she struck him down, by the terms of the strange magic of their Bond, he would take her—his Bondmate—with him to whatever judgment lay beyond death.

And then, impossibly, Vieliessar stopped attacking.

She stared past him into the forest, her face blank with shock as her sword's point slowly lowered.

A moment, and then Runacar heard what she had heard. Felt it through the soles of his sabatons. Hooves drumming against the earth. And he knew, in the part of his mind that would always, ever and forever, keep track of every single element on a battlefield, that neither his army nor Vieliessar's had gotten enough cavalry into Nomaitemil to make that sound.

Even as he realized he could now see Vieliessar clearly, Runacar was turning toward the forest. Then the drumming and the brightness resolved itself into the impossible.

Unicorns.

⸻

It was a glory and a joy to kill the Gryphons. Those hateful altruists could almost always outfly an Endarkened hunting party, and when they could not, one or two of them would always sacrifice themselves so that the rest of the Ascension flew free. But tonight every single one of them would be the sacrifice, and none of them would fly free.

Despite their formidable size and their formidable talons, Gryphons didn't really weigh very much. Their bones were hollow, like those of the raptors they partially resembled, and those bones made a lovely popping sound when they were crushed. The wings came off easily, too, once you learned the trick of it.

Shurzul was already on the ground when the Aesalions attacked. She watched the beginning of the combat with interest to see which of her rivals would die here, easily shielding herself from the murderous bloodlust the Aesalions were broadcasting.

Perhaps . . . Perhaps the Aesalions can be brought to aid us. Anything that takes such a healthful joy in killing carries a spark of He Who Is *within it. I sense it. And how much more heartbreaking for the meat if their own allies turn against them?*

But that was a matter to consider once this delightful slaughter was over.

Shurzul climbed to the top of a pile of bodies to get a better view of the aerial combat. And so it was that, with the tiny spark of her attention that Shurzul kept focused on the hateful Absence at the edge of the killing field, she was the first to see the stygian unglow from deep within it. Shurzul barely had time to recognize the mystery—*What is it? Oh, what is it?*—when the first of the Unicorns breached the border of the void.

They were running directly at her.

Shurzul cried out and leapt aside, for all Endarkened knew that the touch of a Unicorn's horn meant death. And Shurzul did not have just one Unicorn to evade—she had *multitudes.* An army of Unicorns, rushing out of the Flower Forest that had concealed them from Endarkened senses, racing down the length of the valley. Their horns and their bodies glowed painfully bright in Shurzul's vision, and to breathe the air in the very presence of so much purity was sickening.

Shurzul was about to quit the battlefield—King Virulan would never punish her for fleeing from Unicorns, not unless he was bored—when the choice was taken from her hands. King Virulan crashed to the ground right in front of her, still entangled with the Aesalion who was his chosen prey. The Aesalion screamed in outrage and fury, but Virulan had a momentary advantage, and he took it. He plunged his talons through the Aesalion's soft unprotected belly and dragged its intestines from its body. A moment later Virulan was able to rip out its heart and spring to his feet.

There had been only moments between the Aesalion's fall and its death. Time enough for the Unicorns in their hundreds—*thousands!*—to issue forth from the terrible Absence, but not enough time for them to reach the place where Virulan and Shurzul stood.

Shurzul saw the astonishment on Virulan's face at the sight of them—it *must* be astonishment, for surely the King of the Endarkened could not feel fear—before he turned to her, and held out his hand. The message was clear: they would leave. Together.

Shurzul was just about to take Virulan's outstretched hand when a Unicorn—not black, but deep grey, melding into the shadows—ran directly at them both. Virulan saw it, and sprang aside . . .

. . . and so the glowing stormcloud horn of the Unicorn lightly scratched the King of the Endarkened instead of skewering him.

The strike was so soft and shallow that it would not have even killed meat. Nevertheless, the touch was enough, and Shurzul stared, too fascinated to flee, as Virulan slowly began to die. His back bowed, his limbs withered, his skin faded from glowing vermillion to the brown of old blood, his magnificent golden horns grew first dull and then crumbled to dust, his shining hair fell away from his skull in dull lifeless hanks. Suddenly Shurzul could imagine crushing his body between her two hands. How friable would this Light-polluted flesh be? How exquisite its inhabitant's pain and despair?

Virulan spread his wings to fly, only to have their sails shred away like rotted wood. His face contorted with desperate rage. And then . . .

The winds dropped, the air became lifeless. Virulan looked skyward, and Shurzul followed the direction of his gaze. Against the brilliant night sky was the shadow of a towering figure—or more truly, the shadow of the *absence* of all things, a great nihility that no dweller in the world of form and time could truly comprehend.

He Who Is had come to aid *His* creation.

Shurzul did not know whether to fling her body to the blood-soaked soil in worship, to seek out new prey to sacrifice in *His* glory . . .

Or to kill Virulan in this moment, while he stood weak and defenseless.

But Shurzul hesitated too long. Strengthened by the mere presence of their Uncreated Lord of Nothingness, the most powerful Sorcerer of the Endarkened did the impossible. From the presence of *He Who Is*, King Virulan drew power to weave the greatest spell the King of the Endarkened, Master of the Twelve, Blood Ruby in the Crown of Pain and Sorrow, had ever cast. From the bodies of the dying Endarkened, from the injured Elflings, from the wounded Otherfolk, Virulan drew power crafted from agony, hate, despair, and endless spilled blood—all the necromantic amplitude those creatures had to give. Dying himself— his death slowed, not averted, by the presence of *He Who Is*—Virulan wove that magic into a rope, a chain, a glorious river of Dark Void Magic that pulled him back from the abyss of Death even as he began to topple into it. Struck to his knees by weakness only heartbeats before, Virulan now rose to his feet, saved from death.

But not unchanged.

The Endarkened were ageless, but Virulan's form showed what age would bring, were it possible. His body had become nearly as barbarous a parody of the glorious Endarkened as were the bodies of the hateful Elflings. Wingless, hornless, toothless, his cankered skin slack in seams and folds over wasted muscle and twisted bones, Virulan mewled his cheated fury to the now-empty sky in a hoarse cracked voice from a toothless maw. He lunged for Shurzul, wrapping his arms and legs around her. The touch of his flesh made her shudder. His breath was the sour reek of the charnel house, but instead of carrying the delightful aroma of rot, it somehow managed to be . . . unnatural. Repellent.

"Fly," Virulan croaked, digging his crooked talons into her flesh. Virulan was the greatest sorcerer among the Endarkened. He had once again proved that. It would be suicidal of Shurzul to anger him, she told herself, especially now.

Shurzul thrust herself into the sky, her great ribbed wings straining. She could see the Unicorns below her, like stars come to ground. She shuddered at the touch of her lover's rotting flesh, and desperately tried to find something else to think about, lest he should punish her for her thoughts.

After this failure, after this curse upon him, Virulan will be unpredictable. All that I have done over the course of hundreds of Risings to gain status and power could vanish like the flame of a quenched candle, and once again I would have nothing. It is not fair!

There must be a way to turn this inconvenient disaster into sword and armor for her ambition.

Think!

This was all the Unicorns' fault. And suddenly, full-blown in Shurzul's mind like a dying star, was the knowledge of what she would do with Hazaniel. What she had taken the Elfling child for, nurtured him for, against this time of overwhelming need.

Grow fast, my lovely boy. Grow tall. Love me above all others, and when you are grown . . .

Bring me a Unicorn.

With Shurzul in the lead, the Endarkened fled northward. To Ugolthma, the World Without Sun.

Home.

And the river of Unicorns ran unchecked into the West.

⊰⧉⊱

The Unicorns leapt over the dead and the dying as effortlessly as if they had wings. Their horns lit the battlefield as brightly as if by Silverlight, the radiance too bright to look at directly, bright enough to cast shadows among the trees, upon the ground, and in that brightness Runacar could see that everyone on the field—even Elvenkind—had stopped fighting. Everyone made way for the Unicorns, and then turned to follow as if spellbound, whether ahorse or afoot.

As the first of the Unicorns passed him, Runacar saw an Elven child clinging to its neck. Behind the gleaming silver Unicorn stallion came black and bay and roan and chestnut; the pale gold of the new moon and the steel grey of the winter sky, a herd, a troop, an army, a glory, a Delight, more Unicorns than Runacar had ever imagined to exist. By the light of their bodies he could see that the smallest members of his army—Brownies and Fauns and Palugh and Wulvers—ran beside and even rode *upon* them: he glimpsed a bewildered-looking Elven child seated on the back of a black Unicorn, clinging to its mane and to the Palugh in its lap in equal measure.

"Come on!" Melisha's voice was high and sharp with pain, but Runacar would have recognized it anywhere. He found her in the press of moving bodies, and flung himself upon her back in the moment she paused just as if they had practiced it all the days of his life, so that the rhythm of her gallop was nearly unbroken.

"What are you doing here?" he shouted over the battlefield's din.

"Rescuing all of you—what does it look like?" she answered. "And striking the first decisive blow in this war, I might add. You have met Amretheon's Darkness at last, my darling—that which your Bondmate gave up everything to fight."

Runacar clung to Melisha with his knees, his hands fisted in her short bristling mane. The position was oddly precarious at the same time as it was utterly secure: Melisha was a tiny thing, far closer in size to a deer than a horse, and proportionately narrow. His feet would drag on the ground on either side of her if he let them, and the world rushed by at an angle he was not used to seeing it from. A thousand questions surged up in his throat at Melisha's words, but when Runacar could manage to speak, he asked none of them.

"Leutric isn't going to like this, you know," he said.

"What? That you've brought him new allies who actually know how to fight?" Melisha answered, courageous laughter in her voice. "Now hush, beloved. There's work to be done."

Runacar fell silent at once. He trusted Melisha in a way he had never trusted any other living thing. Once again he remembered what Andhel had said about the presence of the impure causing the Unicorns pain, yet here they were, in the midst of Elvenkind and Otherfolk—and if that was bad, how much more horrible must the presence of the Endarkened be? He felt strangely humbled at the scope of the sacrifice the Unicorns' presence represented.

From his vantage point on Melisha's back, Runacar could see that the Unicorns galloped down the valley as straight as an arrow might fly. A moment later he changed his mind: this was not an arrow's flight, but a trident's. The vast rushing multitude split itself into three prongs: one—Melisha's—headed down the center of the valley, the other two running close along the valley walls.

They are making sure no one is left behind, Runacar realized.

But the greatest miracle of the Unicorns was that their bat-winged attackers fled. A few Endarkened stood their ground, but as soon as one of the monsters was within reach, the closest Unicorn would turn toward it and lunge with feline quickness, horn lowered. Wherever glowing horn touched scarlet flesh, there was a stink of burning, a shriek of agony, and the winged enemy died.

The Western Gate loomed ahead—a starry gap in the night-dark wall of granite. "Hold on!" Melisha cried, and suddenly she was not running, she was *bounding*. Her gait was faster than the ravall; faster than Gryphonflight; faster than any horse Runacar had ever ridden. He could see landmarks whip past him at blinding speed, and at last he had to shut his eyes and simply lean against her neck.

Once he'd gotten used to Melisha's bounding gait, the rush of speed was intoxicating. Joy bubbled up in his chest, and Runacar found himself laughing—for their rescue, for his own reprieve from death, even for having seen Vieliessar once again.

He did not have to wonder where Vieliessar was in all this mad host of rushing bodies and unanswered questions. He knew precisely where she was, just as he knew that her heart burned with a chill wrath unchecked by the apparition of any number of Unicorns. If there had ever been any hope of sundering their Bond, it was gone forever: Runacar did not know whether he loved her or hated her, but to be in a world where she was not was unimaginable to him. Runacar had no doubt that the Unicorns had some larger plan in mind, and all he could do was hope that it would not meet an immovable object in Vieliessar High King.

What he would do about Vieliessar was yet another matter Runacar consigned to the future. For now, there was only the moment, the speed and the glory that sang through his veins like rare wine.

Perhaps this was what it felt like to ride with the Starry Hunt.

Suddenly he heard a crash louder than thunder, audible even over the galloping of thousands of creatures. It made the ground dance beneath Melisha's flying hooves, and made Runacar flinch.

The Earthdancers. I told them to seal the eastern pass as soon as Elvenkind were in the trap.

Apparently the arrival of the Endarkened had merely delayed them.

Runacar dared not open his eyes for more than brief glimpses while Melisha ran at this speed, but he knew everyone not riding Unicorns—Elvenkind and Otherfolk and the High King herself—must be far behind them by now. When he raised his head briefly to look forward over Melisha's shoulder, he saw Vondaimieriel rush up at him with impossible speed—the Unicorns would take less than a candlemark to cover the distance it had taken his army a full day to cross.

⊰⊱

Eventually Melisha slowed: from the bound, to the gallop, to the trot, and finally to a walk. Runacar sat up and opened his eyes. They were near the base camp from which Runacar had led his army to battle—two?—three? days ago. The glow of the Unicorns' horns had dimmed to the faintest glimmer, but even without the Unicorn version of Silverlight, there was still light to see by: the camp was lit with lanterns and torches.

Those who had remained behind gathered at the edge of the camp to stare at the Unicorns in wonder as they slowly passed by. Some of the riders—Runacar recognized several of the Woodwose—jumped down from the backs of the Unicorns to go to the camp, but when Runacar would have done the same, Melisha said: "Not yet."

Once they had passed the camp, the herd divided again. A group of the Unicorns continued further west. The others continued south, parallel to the Mystrals, until they reached the copse of trees where Runacar and Melisha had spent the night before the battle.

Runacar looked back toward the Dragon's Gate. From this distance, the road looked even more unnatural than it did up close; a wide artificial scar against the rightful shapes of the mountains. Clouds of Silverlight stretched nearly to the top of the pass. Lightborn work. *Vieliessar must be gathering her forces together before she descends. Leaf and Star grant that work takes her long and long to accomplish.*

The Otherfolk still descending the pass were harder to pick out—the majority were just black dots against the pale road. It would probably take most of the night for them to reach the place Runacar now stood.

And when Vieliessar's army follows, we will resume battle, and I do not know how to bring about any other outcome.

Melisha stopped at the very edge of what was now a rather large collection of Unicorns. (According to the enchiridions of venery, a grouping of Unicorns was properly referred to as a "Delight.") Some of the Unicorns knelt to allow their passengers to dismount, others stood steady as their riders clambered carefully down from their backs, and as he watched this, Runacar realized that all of the riders were children.

They gazed about themselves with wide eyes and an unchildlike grimness to their mouths, and touched each other's hands and faces as if to assure themselves they were real. Some clung to the necks or the legs of the Unicorns who had brought them to safety. And some simply sat down wherever they were, huddled in upon themselves.

There was a sound that should have been present, and wasn't, and after a moment, Runacar realized what it was. There should have been weeping, wailing, cries of fear—if not fear of the Unicorns (Runacar found it hard to imagine anyone could be afraid of a Unicorn), then fear of the plight they found themselves in.

But none of them made a sound.

"What now?" Runacar asked. He did not dismount so much as stood and swung one leg over Melisha's back. His muscles ached with weariness, and he stroked her neck and withers almost without conscious thought, the gesture made to take reassurance as much as to give it.

"Now I hope you are good with children," Melisha said, "for there are several hundred of them here and they will all want answers."

Hostages. He shook his head to dismiss the automatic thought, but it would not leave. *The ones I meant to spare after my army had killed their families—and the Elves carried them into battle.* All the children he could see were very young (young enough to trust a talking animal rather than to run from it screaming).

"She sent them into battle," he said softly.

"No," Melisha answered gently. "Your people did not intend to sacrifice their children, my darling. They were sending them to shelter. They know the Endarkened cannot enter the Flower Forests. The Flower Forests are where your people have lived since the day the Red Harvest began."

They aren't my people, Runacar thought in automatic rejection. *Once, maybe. But not now.*

"Where are their parents?" Runacar asked. The question he could not ask was far too cruel to voice: *Do their parents live?*

"Coming, we hope," Melisha said, leaning into him. "Those that can. But you need have no fear of some hidden Elven city that waits and plots to take revenge for what you have done this day. The folk you saw today—they are all that remain of the Hundred Houses."

At some level Runacar had already known this, but it had not seemed real until now. He couldn't decide whether to feel triumphant at Vieliessar's failure, or . . .

Ten Wheelturns. It has taken Vieliessar ten Wheelturns to bring her people from Ifjalasairaet to Ceoprentrei. Is this how the Child of the Prophecy battles her enemies and husbands her people?

"Tell me what to do," he said quietly.

"Come with me," Melisha said.

Only long acquaintance with Melisha allowed Runacar to shake off the effect of the mesmerizing beauty of so many Unicorns all in one place. As he and Melisha stepped through the ring of guardians—somehow Runacar had no doubt that this was exactly what the Unicorns were—one of the children stepped forward, a girl of perhaps nine summers, but certainly too young to fly her kite. She regarded him with chin raised.

"I am Princess Adalieriel, daughter of the High King and Warlord-in-Waiting to Lord Calanoriel, Heir-Prince, the next High King," the child said stiffly. "Disclose to me your name and your station, and tell me what ransom you will ask for our lives." Some of the braver children were gathered behind Adalieriel. She was clearly the leader.

Daughter of the High King? Lord Vieliessar's *daughter? But that's impossible!*

Once his brother Ivrulion had discovered Runacar's secret—and bound him with unbreakable *geasa* to prevent Runacar from telling anyone he was Vieliessar's Bondmate (or killing Ivrulion, for that matter)—Runacar's mad Lightborn brother had entertained himself by taunting Runacar with what he knew of the Soulbond.

It hadn't been all that much, but it was undoubtedly all there was to know. One was that the Bond provided a limited form of Heart-Seeing. Another was that each member of the Bonded pair could only beget—or bear—the children of their Bonded.

What had Vieliessar done? And *how*?

"Vieliessar Farcarinon is your *mother*?" Runacar asked, trying to stifle his disbelief.

"*Lord* Vieliessar," Adalieriel said reprovingly. "She who is High King over all the land. You are her subject."

Melisha cleared her throat slightly. (Surely Runacar had not heard her stifle a snort of amusement.) "*And* you are a bandit," Adalieriel added. "So we will discuss our ransom now."

"Well, actually, I am not her subject, and I am not a bandit," Runacar said. *Where is your brother, little princess? He would be at your side if he was here.*

"All the *alfaljodthi* are her subjects," Adalieriel said firmly. "Even bandits."

Runacar knelt down in front of Princess Adalieriel—not to do her fealty, but to place himself at her eye level. "I am Runacar of no House, Warlord to King-Emperor Leutric of the Folk, he who is Prince of all this land from the Mystrals to the shore of Great Sea Ocean, he who is counselor and friend to the Folk of the Sea, and likewise to the Folk of the Air, who do him homage." Runacar found it a little disconcerting that the titles and styles of the Hundred Houses still came to his throat so easily. "I do not hold you and your friends hostage, nor do I ask any ransom. I will return you to your people as soon as they arrive and are settled in place."

And as soon as I have somehow managed to keep them from killing everyone in sight.

"That . . . That is good hearing indeed," Adalieriel said, her majestic composure faltering. She glanced skyward apprehensively, reckoning the time. "We need to go to the Flower Forest," she said. "Right now. Enerwirchereth in Mangiralas is the nearest."

Vieliessar must have been desperate to risk such a journey, Runacar thought with an unsettling flare of compassion. *Even the border of Mangiralas is two sunturns' ride from here.*

"Fear not, my dearest." A chestnut Unicorn from the circle of guardians stepped toward Adalieriel and lowered his head. "The Endarkened cannot harm you while *we* are here."

Adalieriel flung her arms around the Unicorn's neck and hugged him close.

"I promise you, Princess Adalieriel, that you shall have no cause to take affright while you are under my guard, for here you will be neither imperiled nor disparaged. Here is Melisha, who will stand surety for my word," Runacar said, in his most formal mode. He had the unsettled sense Adalieriel was judging his performance as Leutric's Warlord and finding it wanting.

Melisha glanced sidewise at him with a faint smirk as she stepped forward to face Adalieriel, but when she spoke, her tone was grave and composed. "I promise you that all Runacar Houseborn says, he will do. He will guard your safety and your honor as his own until you are reunited with your family—and beyond."

This is flattering, Runacar thought, *but the last time I saw Vieliessar she was trying to kill me.* "Lady Adalieriel—is the Prince-Heir here?" Runacar asked. "I must be sure you are both safe."

"I do not know," Adalieriel whispered. "Githachi told me he was safe—but I do not know where *she* is either!"

"We'll know soon," Runacar said. "I will send word to you if I cannot bring it myself." Runacar matched her painfully maintained dignity with his own. It was the only gift he could give her. "My duties call me, Lady Adalieriel, but I will return as soon as I may."

"Will the Unicorns keep the Beastlings away as well as the Endarkened?" a boy asked, stepping forward to stand beside Adalieriel. "I don't want them to eat me."

Runacar winced. Too much to hope for that these children's minds had not been poisoned just as their parents'—their ancestors'—had been. He could not even imagine how to begin to convince them that the Otherfolk were not monsters.

"You will all be safe here," he said firmly. "The Unicorns will protect you from all harm. My word on it as Battlemaster of the King-Emperor." *And may the Great Bull and every other Power in the land protect me from having to explain what Leutric is the King-Emperor of.*

"But who are you, if you are not one of us?" the boy asked. "There *is* no one else."

"Be silent, Tuni," Adalieriel said sharply. "It is for the High King to question the bandit chieftain Runacar, not you."

"When you have been reunited with your own folk there will be much to see and to explain," Runacar said. He gestured toward the switchbacks leading up to the Dragon's Gate. "They'll be here soon."

"Those are *Beastlings*!" Runacar heard Tuni hiss into Adalieriel's ear. She shrugged him off imperiously, her gaze never leaving Runacar's face.

"You are all safe here, and will remain so," Runacar said firmly. Words repeated with conviction sometimes turned into truths, and he devoutly hoped this was one of those times. "Before I go, is there anything you or your companions need?"

"Bring us water and bread, and blankets," Adalieriel said. "For the night is cold—and the High King's people are hungry."

CHAPTER FOURTEEN

HARVEST MOON IN THE TENTH YEAR OF THE HIGH KING'S REIGN: THE REAL AND THE TRUE

Almost, it seemed during those strange and swiftly moving days, that the High King fought her own war, and there were three armies on the field instead of only two. What her object was remains unknown, for Lord Vieliessar has never spoken of it.

—Thurion Pathfinder, A History of the High King's Reign

"Coward," Melisha said comprehensively, as she and Runacar walked back toward the camp.

As they walked, Runacar glanced toward the pass. The Silverlight was all on the upper half of the trail, and there was a wide gap between the clusters of Silverlight and the retreating Otherfolk. The only group ahead of the Folk were the Elves' riderless horses, which had galloped wildly until exhaustion forced them to slow to a walk—the *geasa* upon them apparently being no longer in force.

His gaze turned toward his own camp. He'd order them to retreat to Vondaimieriel Great Keep. He knew it well, since he'd sacked the castel a few Wheelturns ago. It was defensible against Vieliessar's army . . .

. . . but not against these "Endarkened."

At least the Unicorns can kill them. And what else have you not told me, Melisha?

He stopped. They were nearing the edge of the camp; she wouldn't be able to accompany him much further.

He should be doing a thousand other things at this moment. Instead, Runacar stroked Melisha's neck absently, and stole this precious moment to plan. To choose the site of their next battle, for Runacar had no doubt there would be one.

But it would be on his terms.

When he'd been a boy, his elder brother still at the Sanctuary of the Star, and Farcarinon still Caerthalien's staunch ally, Runacar remembered many High Table conversations about Gunedwaen of Farcarinon, Prince Serenthon's Swordmaster. Most of those discussions were lost to him now, save for the ideas they had carried, but one comment had stood out from all the rest, and Runacar remembered it clearly.

"He schools the children who come to him until they are masters of war. Farcarinon can do more damage to an enemy while they're running away from it than any two High Houses attacking."

Very well, High King, Runacar thought grimly. *Let us see how well you can apply your Swordmaster's teachings. I will retreat and you can follow.*

⊰⊱

Everyone knew that the Children of Night were a myth. A myth, a wondertale, a legend for a Storysinger to beguile their noble patrons with on a dull winter's evening. Nothing more.

What use is an assassin whose skills are known and whose coming is foretold? For that was what the Children of Night were said to be: a guild of assassins. Expensive, unstoppable, and utterly indifferent both to the Codes of War and Mosirinde's Covenant. But if they existed it was because the clever War Princes of the Arzhana—in the days when both War Princes and the Arzhana existed—wasted no opportunity they saw for power or wealth. And even a broken tool is of use to someone who has none.

In the days before the High King came again, all the Hundred Houses gathered their children and Called the Light in them each Midwinter, and there were always those who, having been Called, did their Service Year in the Sanctuary of the Star and came home again. And while those of the Arzhana who took the Green Robe went to High Houses of the Western Lands to serve (just as the komen of the Arzhana served in those same High Houses), no one paid any attention to the fate of a failed Candidate.

But there was a thing that even Lightborn did not know: that some

were Called, and went to the Sanctuary, and went away again, Lightless, and then found—moonturns or Wheelturns later—that their Light
came at last. These Crofters, and commons, and Landbond were not returned to the Sanctuary of the Star to be trained—for that had been
proscribed in the reign of Timirmar Astromancer—nor could they be
left to exercise their untrained Gifts. If they were discovered, they were
killed. Or their Light was burned from their minds, and if it was, they
died soon after.

Except in the Arzhana, which tithed all its Lightborn to the West.

In the Arzhana they were prudent, and frugal, and did not discard a
tool simply because it was not as they would have it be.

❈

I'm cold, Dianora thought distantly. *Ridiculous. It isn't even the middle of Harvest Moon—unless I've lost count and we're already in Rade.
Hard to keep track of Harvest Fair when you haven't planted anything for
the last decade. Not that anything ever grew in the Arzhana. And not that
I would've been tending it if it had.*

Dianora chafed at her arms to warm herself, even though (she knew)
the night wasn't cold—not as cold as it was anywhere in the Arzhana
in this season, anyway. As she did, she listened to her own disordered
thoughts with a certain detachment. They meant nothing, after all: to
detach her true thoughts from the surface chatter of her mind had been
one of the first things she'd learned when she'd entered the School of
Night. It wouldn't do to have actual Lightborn know what you were
thinking when you were thinking something they wouldn't like.

The Arzhana's worth (though hardly wealth) was in its mines and its
horses. The bloodstock of the High Domains were no sleek petted darlings such as were proudly paraded at Mangiralas Fair: they were small
and hammerheaded; shaggy and goose-rumped and flint-footed—and
they could run forever, face down wolf and ice tiger and snow lion and
survive, live on fare that would starve the highbred darlings of the West.
And no one but the Free Companies—and the houses of the Arzhana—
wanted them.

But everyone wanted what lay beneath the earth in the foothills of the Feinolons and the Bazhrahils. Gold and silver, copper and iron, tin and lead. There were no Landbond in the Arzhana, for there was little land to farm. But there were mines. Their work was as hard and as brutal as that of the Landbonds to the West, but at least the miners were no komen's chattel.

When Dianora came home from the Sanctuary, Lightless, House Mallereuf gave her two choices: become a servant to some Lightborn to the west or to the east—or work the mines. Dianora had chosen the mines.

And three Wheelturns later, she lit a brazier just by glaring at it furiously.

Barely a fortnight later a stranger had come to the mine-head with a paper bearing the seal of War Prince Camrian Mallereuf, and a pack-pony laden with rich gifts for the mine's owner. Dianora had ridden away with the stranger that same sunturn.

The stranger's name was Arathiel, and Arathiel took Dianora to a place high in the Feinolon hills, a castel keep carved out of the rock itself. He named it as House Bulbaryat, just as if it were a domain, and took Dianora up to its highest tower. She stood upon the tower's parapet and looked out and down and saw a river roaring through a gorge far below. Then Arathiel told her what he was, and what she could be, and gave her a choice.

Stay and learn. Or see—right here and now—if she could fly.

(It wasn't a difficult choice.)

Dianora of Mallereuf was listed as dead on her family's Tablet of Memory, and Dianora of Bulbaryat had barely finished her training when Shanilya Thadan became lord of the Arzhana entire. Shanilya Thadan-Arzhana went to place herself, her vassals, and all her lands beneath the hand of the High King. For the honor of the Arzhana, Prince Shanilya took with her the finest komen, and the finest cattle, and the finest horses—and she had gathered up nearly all of the Children of Night as well.

Arathiel had been one of the chosen, and he said once—during the Wheelturns that House Bulbaryat had labored in Tildorangelor at Prince Shanilya's bidding—that to the Loremasters' list of the seven great battles that had won the High King her throne—Oronviel, Aralha-thumindrion, Jaeglenhend, Niothramangh, Cirdeval, the Barrens, and the Shieldwall Plain—they should add an eighth: Tildorangelor. Without their doing, there would have been no westward march at all.

Or its endless slaughter.

This morning Dianora had ridden out from Saganath Flower Forest with the Company of the Hare. Tonight she stood at the foot of Star-dock, surrounded by Unicorns who glowed in the dark and could kill Endarkened.

The Unicorns stood in a loose ring around the adults they had saved. The people here with her were those who had said *"yes"* when a Unicorn said: *"get on my back; I'll carry you to safety,"* because when the Endarkened were hunting, you said *"yes"* to anything that would get you away from them.

Dianora was standing near the edge of the group, her desire to get as far away as possible from *them* warring with her desire to get as far away as possible from *everyone*. Dianora was not entirely sure now that "alive" was better than a quick death in battle, though it was certainly better than captured alive by the Endarkened.

"We've got to do something."

The voice behind her summoned her attention. It was too dark for her to recognize the speaker, and his voice was unfamiliar. There was a low murmur of agreement from several of the other captives; through a combination of Light and training Dianora abruptly knew that it would take less than a tenthmark to make these people into a mob.

Mobs died.

"What do you suggest we do?" she said in a loud conversational voice as she turned to walk toward the speaker. "Fight with them for our freedom? Fight with *horses*?" (She thought she heard one of the Unicorns snicker.) The Unicorns didn't look very much like horses, but that was the point: to make the idea sound as ridiculous as possible.

"If we must," another voice said. "We have to get away."

"From things that can kill the Redwings? Now *that* is the stupidest notion I've heard in . . . quite a long time," a new voice said.

"Well met, Arathiel," Dianora said in relief. The Children of Night did not precisely have a leader, but if they did have, it would have been Arathiel.

"If anything can be well in these days," Arathiel said. "Certainly I agree that we should rejoin our people at once," he added blandly, now addressing the others. "Only . . . where *are* they, exactly?"

(This time Dianora was certain she heard a Unicorn snickering.)

"Up there." Someone raised their arm and pointed at the Pass Road, where balls of glowing Silverlight marked the presence of the Lightborn. Where the Lightborn were, the rest of the people must be also.

And the High King! Dianora told herself desperately. *If she does not live we are truly lost.*

"Excellent, my good Fenthor," Arathiel said fulsomely. "We shall depart at once. Only . . . what do you suppose those lights are between us and the road? Could it be the war camp we passed on our way here? Whose war camp could that be, I wonder?"

Out of the corner of her eye, Dianora could see that most of the Unicorns were now watching Arathiel with rapt attention.

"There can't be anyone there," Fenthor said. "They were all on the field. I saw them."

"The Beastlings," Arathiel said helpfully. "Who clearly meant to stop us at Ceoprentrei, and who would naturally leave their camp utterly unguarded."

"We have our swords," Fenthor blustered.

"And bows, and pikes, and knives, and anything else *none of you dropped in the retreat,*" Dianora interrupted in exasperation. "And you're going to do *what* with them? Kill the only things we've seen that can kill *them*? I don't know about the rest of you, but I'm on the same side as *anything* that can do that."

"I like her," said a voice from outside the circle. "She isn't stupid. Can I have her?"

She turned toward the sound of the voice. It was a raven-black Unicorn. He—at least the voice was male—was easier to see than some of the others; he was darker than the night.

Lessons from the Schoolhouse at Bulbaryat: *Black garments don't make you invisible: they make you stand out. If you can't wear what ev-*

eryone else is wearing, wear brown or grey or even green. At night, those colors fade into the shadows.

"That depends," Dianora said evenly. "What do you want me for?"

"Come with me and find out," the Unicorn answered.

And once again, Dianora made a choice.

⊰⊱

Vieliessar could feel the magic of the Prophecy pushing her, demanding of her, attempting to force her in the direction she must go. The sense of need that had been with her since she had first heard the sound of her war-horns was heavy and implacable, like the promise of a headache to come. She would have done its bidding immediately if she only knew what it wanted, but she dared not take the time to find that out while her people's survival was at stake.

The Endarkened had fled the battlefield in the midst of their victory. The Unicorns had taken the children. The Gryphons had taken her *alakomentai'a*. The army had lost its remounts, supplies, and livestock, and her forces were scattered all across the mountainside.

Her steps were laggardly; she knew that once she rejoined her folk she must have words for them that would make sense of this wicked day. She could think of none.

If Caerthalien's War Prince was in truth the master of the Beastling army, that changed everything. Could he be reasoned with? Could he be taken prisoner? Would the power of the *geasa* that surrounded her as Child of the Prophecy allow her to survive the death of he who was her destined Bondmate?

She rejected their Bond and distrusted any loyalty Runacarendalur might offer, but she knew she needed his cooperation. In one great rush the Unicorns had slaughtered—Vieliessar had *seen* them slaughter—more Endarkened than she and her people had killed in all the time since the Endarkened had first descended upon them.

What do the Beastlings want? Why did they gather to attack us? If they resume the attack, here or anywhere, can we prevail against them? Think! Your time is short! The only definition of a Beastling I know is Lannarien's: in his Book of Living Things, *he writes that a Beastling is a creature that speaks with Elven voice and pretends to think as if it is Elven. I heard the Unicorns speak when they came out of Nomaitemil. And that means . . .*

But even as she reasoned the matter out, Vieliessar rejected her own conclusion. If the Unicorns were Beastlings, and the Beastlings were Elvenkind's enemies, why . . . ?

The thing that had once so exasperated her War Council—Rithdeliel had told her so, many times, as had Gunedwaen *(Oh, brave heart! Too soon a Rider!)* and Thurion still teased her about it constantly—was the fact that, though komen and King, Vieliessar had begun her life as a scholar in the Sanctuary of the Star, and often her thoughts were not the thoughts of Warlords and komentai, but of a Lightborn steeped in philosophy and study. The arrival of the Unicorns did not make her act.

It made her *think.*

Did the Prophecy send me west so I could discover the Unicorns? Perhaps they are my answer, and not the Library of Arevethmonion. But they slew no Beastlings—they saved them just as they saved us. Once my people have gathered together the battle with the Beastlings will resume—and we cannot win it as we are now.

And yet, by what power I know not, Nomaitemil is now larger than any other in the Fortunate Lands, and the closest Flower Forest. A logical refuge.

Retreat? Press on? Fight? Think, Child of the Prophecy! Or you and all who look to you will die before Midwinter Moon!

The night air was bitter and sharp. Her teeth chattered with cold, interrupting her thoughts. After a long hesitation, Vieliessar cast Minor Cloak to warm herself, but she still shivered as she hurried her steps to catch up to the stragglers from her army.

Just as she stepped through the pass, she heard a strange wild shriek above her; like a hawk upon the wing, but deeper in tone. She stopped and looked for the source, and found it in the sky: two Gryphons, circling low above the valley, crying out as if they spoke to each other.

It was a sad and desperate song of uttermost sorrow that they sang, and Vieliessar remembered the sight of Endarkened tearing the wings from the Gryphons' backs.

They are mourning, Vieliessar thought in wonder. She had never known a hawk or falcon to care particularly about the fate of another hawk or falcon, and had assumed that Gryphons must be much the same. Clearly they were not.

What else have I always believed that is not true? The Beastlings can speak. Could we not speak with them? There is so much we do not know!

The Gryphons circled higher, until their lament quieted with distance and vanished into the noise of the people on the road ahead.

Automatically Vieliessar's gaze shifted as she searched out the Unicorns. She could see them on the road far below, still glowing as if they were made of Silverlight.

She had always believed that the Unicorn she had followed for so many years as talisman and guide was as singular a creature as the Unicorn Throne was a singular object. Instead, the Unicorns were as many as the horses of Mangiralas-as-was.

They can kill the Endarkened! It is a part of their nature! Ah, if only I knew how to use them—if they can be used at all. . . .

She stopped where she was and formed Silverlight above her head so that she was visible. The elvensilver Vilya she wore glowed like a captive star. Within heartbeats, globes of answering Silverlight rose up like bubbles through deep water along the road ahead of her, marking out the presence of Lightborn. Those she had followed from the battlefield turned toward her in astonishment and joy.

"The King lives!" several cried. From below she heard ragged cheering, and her people began turning back to rejoin her.

As if in answer to the cheering, there was a drumming of hooves behind her loud enough to break through the rest of the noise. It heralded the passage of a troop of Centaurs. The creatures passed her without a single sideways glance, their discipline as crisp as any cadre of komen, and she raised her hand to keep any of the folk who were with her from drawing their swords. As the Centaurs cantered on down the road, she saw her people make way for them.

"My lord, you must take my horse."

"Well met, Baureth. It is a strange day we find ourselves in," she said.

Vieliessar glanced at the tired knights on exhausted horses who were gathered around her; they were a company of pikemen who fought afoot, but were still granted the title of komen—a title that meant something much different than it had in the time of the Hundred Houses.

Each time I think of that as historians and scholars do, it hurts a little less. Someday it will cease hurting all together. . . .

Baureth had dismounted and was holding his horse's head as he awaited her. He had been born a Landbond and worked as a farmer now when he could, but there was no one among her people who did not fight.

The faint spark of a plan was growing in her mind, but she must first discover if she had the means to execute it.

"No day is strange while you yet live," Baureth answered valiantly.

She smiled at him and let him help her to mount his battlepony. The poor beast was trembling with exhaustion; she put her hand upon its neck and drew Nomaitemil's power into it so that it raised its head and sidled as if it had just come from its home *khom*.

"You have done me valiant service, Baureth. What shall I call my new friend?"

"His name is Crow, Lord Prince. And see—he gains strength from your very presence."

"So he does," she answered. She could heal one beast of its exhaustion—or even a dozen—but not every animal in her army. *Unless I bespell all of them and we ride them to death. Poor reward for these friends who have been with us in every peril.*

From her vantage point, Vieliessar looked down the mountain again. The Unicorns were far ahead, and the Beastlings followed. In places, Elvenkind and Beastlings intermingled along the road, but there was no sign of clashes between them.

Scattered among all three groups were horses, and sheep, and goats. Chickens flew through the night, squalling bitterly whenever they found a temporary roost. Herd-dogs circled tiny flocks of sheep, barking madly for aid. Goats were everywhere—many of them had chosen to risk the steep banks of the mountainside instead of following the road. Vieliessar did not need Magery to know that if the riderless horses and livestock were on the road and not sheltering in Nomaitemil, the *geasa* upon them had broken with their panic.

If we have lost the pack animals, we have lost everything! It would take the rest of our lives to gather them up again, and by then the Beastlings will already have eaten them.

She did not allow any of her dismay to show on her face; this was neither the time nor the place for a show of weakness. As word of her presence spread, her folk were turning back to join her. As they reached her, she greeted them by name and gave quiet simple orders. She could feel their confidence grow as they took their places in her array, but the more of them that came to her, the greater her uneasiness grew. None were *alakomentai'a*. None were children. Mounted archers, mounted infantry, yes—but no cavalry.

Vieliessar gave the same orders over and over—even as she knitted up the small injuries brought to her—broken bones, and deep bruises, and minor sword-cuts— orders she had not given since that last day on Ishtilaikh, for what she commanded now of her array was the organization of an Elven meisne in full battle groups, and the Endarkened had never allowed them to conduct that kind of war.

As she gave her orders most of her mind was elsewhere, for the plan that had been only an inkling a half-mark past was now in full flower.

"Always do that which the enemy will not expect." Gunedwaen had told her that over and over, and the repetition had maddened her, for of course the enemy always expected one to fight, so how was one to do the unexpected? Run away?

Yes.

The enemy would not expect her to retreat to Nomaitemil—they had fought to keep her from reaching the West and should expect her to press her advantage and move forward. Even Caerthalien might not expect retreat of her, for during the Winter War her tactics had been much different.

Nomaitemil held power of a magnitude Vieliessar had not touched since the very day of her Enthroning. Her folk could overwinter there. And in spring, Vondaimieriel would be a much altered battlefield.

Wide as it was and mild as was its grade, the pass road was no Battle City where she could assemble her folk in safety. They filled the road back to the mouth of the pass and past the first switchback; they must move *somewhere* soon. The road was filled with moving bodies traveling in both directions now—some terrible and misshapen, some dear and familiar.

We might as well have avoided all we have done this day, for it ends as it began, Light willing—with us cowering in a Flower Forest uncertain of what to do next!

At least it would be a different Flower Forest than it had been this morning.

So dense was the gathering around her that it took some time for Lawspeaker Commander Gelduin to reach her. Vieliessar's heart rose at seeing one of her senior commanders; he was spattered with blood—of what creature, the Light alone could say—but seemed superficially unharmed.

"My lord, I see that we do not advance. What are your orders?" Gelduin bowed fractionally from his saddle as he spoke.

"My Lord Gelduin, my heart is lighter for seeing you," Vieliessar answered, just as formally. "And you are correct: we do not advance. We shall retreat to Nomaitemil this night, and remain there until I and my councillors discover what this visitation of Unicorns may portend. And so I grieve that I have no choice but to lay a heavy task upon you. I must have my council—if you can find them—and my Lightborn as well. Say to all you encounter that the High King lives, and send them here to me," she said. "Say this also: we allow the Beastlings free passage on the road as if they were an enemy honorably retreating from the field under the Codes of War. Say that I will slay any with my own hand who flouts my word and make of them a hungry ghost to roam the Cold Dark forever." Her mild tone did not change from the beginning of her speech to the end.

Gelduin's eyes widened slightly, but he bowed his head in acquiescence. "I shall gather what commanders and Lightborn I can, my lord King. I shall give to all the words you have given to me. But the livestock, the remounts—" He gestured helplessly down the mountain.

"We do not concern ourselves with them this night," Vieliessar answered shortly. "Go upon your commission as quickly as you can."

Gelduin saluted and retreated. The press of komen and horses had eased as he and Vieliessar spoke together, but the position of her forces was still precarious. Vieliessar looked back over her shoulder and then to the sky. The Gryphons seemed to be gone. There was no fighting anywhere she could see. The strange truce that came from the intercession of the Unicorns still stood, even as Nomaitemil beckoned to her with the song of Light strong enough for her to sweep the Beastlings from the road below and obliterate them utterly.

If only . . .

If only I had not seen what I have seen. If only I had not been wrong about so many things. How can I now know what is true, and what has been the convenient fantasy of the War Princes? And yet— And yet—

At the Sanctuary of the Star Vieliessar had Healed so many injuries caused by Beastlings. But had any Lightborn Healed fewer or lesser injuries each time the War Princes took to the battlefield? She needed answers, and there would be no answers until long after she had to make her decisions.

If only—!

"The warrior who makes their home in *What Might Be* makes their home upon their pyre." She'd heard that homily in many forms, but the meaning was always the same: to act on the basis of what *might* come was to gamble with your life. And the High King held so many more lives than her own beneath her hand. She dared not wish—or hope.

She needed facts.

Grudgingly, her mind responded to her demands. The Unicorns carried Elven children on their backs. The Unicorns carried tiny Beastlings as well. The Unicorns spoke with Elven voices, just as the Beastlings— and the Endarkened—did, and that fulfilled Lannarien's Proof. But if the Unicorns were Beastlings . . . what did that make the *rest* of the Beastlings? She must *know* before she could act. She must have answers.

At least she was alive to need them—even if her present function was to sit her beast as if she were some icon that inspired those who gazed upon her by the mere fact that she *was*.

And the sense that there was some decision she must make—and that the time in which to make it was running out—grew.

❧

My lord King, I am here," Aradreleg said.

Vieliessar fought back the treacherous pang of relief to see Aradreleg Lightsister. Her face in the Silverlight was ghost-pale with exhaustion and the soul-anguish of exposure to the Endarkened. But she was alive. "The Healers?" Vieliessar asked quickly.

"There—below." Aradreleg pointed down the hillside, to where a cloud of Silverlight indicated a group of Lightborn and their Lightless counterparts. "All that I can find. My lord, have you word of Thurion? Iardalaith?" Minor Cloak shimmered about Aradreleg as well, a reminder that those who lacked Lightborn Magery had no warm cloaks or tunics in the raw alpine night.

"Not yet," Vieliessar said shortly. In this moment, she knew less than Aradreleg did of who lived and who had died. *Where is my Liri? Where is my Calan? Master Dandamir said they were both safe, but that was before the Endarkened attacked us. Then the Unicorns bore children away with them—I saw this myself.*

But I did not see them.

Vieliessar forced thoughts of her children from her mind. Many of her folk must have lost children this day; she was not unique in her grief. "Here are your orders; they are my orders to all the Lightborn: Use Nomaitemil as you like, for she is fresh and ready, but we dare not draw her down too far, for she is to be our refuge. Let it be known that all Beastlings are under my Peacebond and shall not be harmed this night. I shall deny the road to no one, but bring your Healers here to me as soon as you may. For now, choose a deputy from among them whom I may send back into Ceoprentrei to prepare the way for our return. More, I would learn if any of our folk upon the battlefield yet live."

Vieliessar had left wounded to the mercy of the Endarkened before, but this time, succor might be possible.

"You're not going *back* there?" Aradreleg's voice was horrified.

"No," Vieliessar said dryly. "I am sending one of my Lightborn."

Aradreleg stared at Vieliessar for a long moment, clearly wanting to tell the High King exactly what she thought of the idea, but at last she nodded mutely. "I go," Aradreleg said, and turned her mount back down the road.

Soon enough, Aradreleg's deputy arrived. "My King, how can I serve?" Pantaradet Lightsister asked. *I remember when you first came to me, Lightsister,* Vieliessar thought. *Caerthalien attacked Oronviel, and we routed them utterly. Such a long time ago. Such a short time ago.*

"Go into Ceoprentrei. See what obstacles may exist to bar our entry to Nomaitemil. Hiraen and her meisne will accompany you. Check the battlefield for wounded. If there are any, send a—"

Suddenly there was a rumble and crash from above, and the ground trembled. The sound was nearly buried by the sound of voices raised in fear and dismay, but, glancing upward, Vieliessar could see a plume of rock-dust coil slowly up to the sky.

"—and find out what just broke," she finished wearily. "We will retreat to Nomaitemil as soon as our forces are assembled here. Providing, of course, that Nomaitemil is still there," she added dryly, and was rewarded by wry chuckles from the knights gathered around her. "Hiraen, escort the Lightsister and see to her safety."

Hiraen saluted Vieliessar, and then reached down to assist Pantaradet to mount behind her. They were short on horses, and those they had were exhausted.

They would make do, just as they had learned to.

⊰⊱

Aided by Silversight and Farsight, Vieliessar scanned the road below to learn what she could. That they could retreat to Nomaitemil was an unexpected gift, but it was not forever. Moreover, if Runacarendalur had come to hold the position he clearly did among those Elvenkind had always considered abomination . . .

Could her people do the same?

Allies, she thought with a horrified thrill of realization that this, *this,* was what Amretheon's *geasa* was pushing her toward. *We can be allies. If we ally with them, and with the Unicorns, we can withstand the Endarkened. Together.*

"*If.*"

It seemed impossible, but as Vieliessar watched the road below, she saw moments of terrified chivalry between Elvenkind and Beastlings.

Here a Centaur, an Elven child upon its back, stopped to hand the child to a komen, all three of them equally afraid. There a komen stopped to scoop up a limping wolf-creature and carry it along to safety on her saddlebow. For this strange time out of time they were not Elvenkind and monsters, but all living things together, all survivors of the terrible delights of the Endarkened.

Suddenly there were screams from behind, and—without thought—Vieliessar turned her mount up the road and spurred it, followed by the meisne she had gathered to her.

Harvest Moon in the Tenth Year of the High King's Reign: Change is Only the Beginning

Harm to the enemy is only the second objective of war. The first is the preservation of your folk and your lands. It is better to be thought a fool and a coward than to be seen to do more harm to your own Domain than an enemy ever could.

—Gunedwaen Swordmaster, The Art of War

Pantaradet Lightsister had dismounted and stood beside Hiraen in the road. Hiraen's meisne stood facing six Unicorns who barred access to the Western Gate. The Unicorns ranged in color from a dark blue roan to purest white. For the first time, Vieliessar had the chance to study them, and saw that the Unicorns carved into the Unicorn Throne had apparently been sculpted from life, wholly accurate as to size and form.

But to see a Unicorn in the living flesh was entirely different.

They were glorious.

Lannarien said they had the heads of goats, but their heads were not precisely like that of deer, goat, or horse, just similar—in the same way a housecat resembled a snow-tiger. They were much the size of deer, their bodies covered with short plushy fur like a destrier in winter coat. Their stiff and bristly manes ran from poll to withers, and they had the tufted tails of lions. The Unicorns—*real* Unicorns, Vieliessar's mind could not help but add—looked nothing like their depictions in *Lannarien's Book of Living Things*. Lannarien had also written that the Unicorn, being made up from parts of wholly incompatible beasts—deer and lion and goat and serpent—and crowned with a single horn of miraculous powers upon its brow—was the symbol of the High Kingship. And utterly imaginary.

But the Unicorns Vieliessar saw had spiral horns that glowed as bright as sunlight seen through glass, a light so bright Vieliessar was tempted to shield her eyes against its intensity. The point of each horn looked as impossibly delicate—and as sharp—as a rose thorn. She could see the luminous sentience in their eyes, and had a sense that the Unicorns did not wish to be here at all.

Her assessment had taken mere heartbeats. Dust from the crash Vieliessar had heard moments earlier still hung in the air, but the Unicorns themselves were spotless.

"When we got here they just . . . appeared." Pantaradet Lightsister hastened to Vieliessar's side. Her gaze kept returning to the Unicorns as if she was unable to look away, and she swayed, just a little, as she clung to Vieliessar's stirrup-leather for support.

"Wait here, Tara," Vieliessar whispered to her. She gazed toward Hiraen and gestured to him with a small flick of her fingers. He looked relieved to be able to move his meisne away from the Unicorns. Vieliessar unbuckled her sword belt and gave sword and dagger both into Pantaradet's hands, then swung her leg over her pommel and dismounted.

"*No!*" Pantaradet cried, reaching for her. "You can't!"

"I must," Vieliessar said, her voice still low. "If we cannot return to Ceoprentrei we must go elsewhere." She turned to face the Unicorns, and took a step toward them as soon as Hiraen's meisne had retreated. "I am—"

"Oh, believe me, High King, we *all* know who you are," one of the Unicorn stallions, his pale coat spotted all over with black like the night sky in reverse, took an equivalent step forward. His nostrils flared wide, as if he smelled something foul. "But even *you* are not stupid enough to want to go backward when you have paid so many lives to come forward."

Vieliessar still found it jarring to hear speech from something that looked like an animal. If she had closed her eyes before it spoke, she might have thought one of her komen stood before her—if any of her komen would have spoken to her so.

Think!

"I am the Child of the Prophecy, tasked by Amretheon Aradruiniel, the last High King, to save my people when the Darkness comes." *Just in case anyone here has forgotten that fact,* she thought bleakly. "Was it you who sent the Beastlings to meet us in battle? Did you do it to keep us from crossing into the West? We will willingly oblige you; let us return to Ceoprentrei."

"To kill it, as you have killed so many others," the Unicorn replied, ignoring her questions.

"You know my name, and I do not know yours," Vieliessar said, ignoring the Unicorn's accusation in turn. "And yet, Nameless One, I say this to you: never have I or mine trespassed against Mosirinde's Covenant."

"Are you certain of that?" the Unicorn asked archly.

"I am certain that you are safe from the Endarkened and I am not," Vieliessar answered bitterly. "Now tell me why you bar my entrance to Ceoprentrei—or move."

"She gets over her awestruck worship rather quickly, don't you think, Belwing?" another of the Unicorns said. This one was colored in the fashion of a blood bay horse—flaming copper coat, black socks and mane and tail tuft—and horn. The sight was profoundly disorienting, since the Unicorns did not look like horses at all.

"Wasn't it you who first lectured me on how short-sighted Elvenkind are, Ringion? If she wants to go back to Nomaitemil, I say let her," Belwing said. "The Earthdancers will seal this pass too, and that will solve a number of problems at once."

"If you seal the pass before I and my people are all on the same side of it I do not think matters will go well," Vieliessar said mildly. "If you would bar us from Nomaitemil, you have the power, if not the right. But at least let us search the battlefield for our wounded while there is still time to save them."

The silence from the Unicorns took on a new quality, as if Vieliessar had said something extraordinarily wrong. It took her back instantly to her Sanctuary days, when her teachers had forever been exasperated with her and her imperfect grasp upon what she was meant to learn—

when they had not been utterly astonished by the use she made of her lessons.

"We thought you knew, Vieliessar." It was a white Unicorn who spoke now. A mare; she had been at the back of the party. Though her face could not show emotion any more than a deer's or a goat's, Vieliessar thought she looked compassionate—and sad. "They are all dead."

"Dead?" Pantaradet blurted out. "But they can't be—not *all* of them! Even if—"

"I am so sorry, child," the white Unicorn mare said softly. "The Endarkened King stole their life-force to keep himself from death."

"Which he should not have been able to do!" Belwing said irritably, shaking his neck. The gesture was so horselike it was jarring: were these animals—or *alfaljodthi* in strange bodies?

"*He Who Is* was on the battlefield tonight," the bay stallion answered. "And King Virulan is the most powerful sorcerer among the Endarkened."

They know things about our enemy beyond anything we have been able to discover! And they possess the secret of killing them! Involuntarily, Vieliessar took a step forward. The Unicorns backed away—as if she were a threat.

"You have not done your reading, High King," a blue roan Unicorn said chidingly. "Lannarien wrote that we are symbols, did he not?"

If their form and speech were disconcerting, then hearing them rebuke her about her mastery of the Sanctuary texts as if she were still a Postulant was a thousand times more so.

"Symbols of the High Kingship," she answered, and the Unicorn almost seemed about to laugh.

"No. Of *purity*. The touch of the horn of a living Unicorn—I said 'living,' so don't even imagine you can kill any of us and then use our horns for weapons—" This time it was Vieliessar who recoiled. She had never seen a dead Unicorn and she did not want to. "Where was I? Oh yes: the touch of a Unicorn's horn can kill one of the Endarkened, yes—because they are creatures as much of the Dark as we are of the Light—but that power comes with limitations. We are living symbols of purity, as I say, and as such, none of us is able to be close to those who are not both chaste and celibate."

I suppose I am not celibate, Vieliessar thought. Few who left the Sanctuary of the Star at the end of their training had been. *"Chaste" is debatable, though I had never imagined having to argue with a Unicorn about it.*

"Very well, Living Symbols of Purity, I will not approach you," Vieliessar said as she strove to keep both the mockery and the anger out of her voice. "Now. I wish to search the battlefield and to call my folk to retreat to Nomaitemil. Will you permit this?"

"To search the battlefield after we have told you there are no survivors indicates a lack of trust on your part," Belwing said blandly. "And since Nomaitemil is void, there is no reason for the Earthdancers to preserve it. You may imperil your forces."

"Don't talk to them, my lord King!" Pantaradet Lightsister said urgently. "They were sent by the Endarkened!"

"I would talk even to the Endarkened if I could," Vieliessar said quietly.

"Oh, well, yes, that makes all the difference," Belwing said mockingly. "My friends, she is only carrying out Amretheon's orders—and well we know how dear a friend he was to us."

"Belwing." The white Unicorn spoke again, this time reprovingly. "She cannot learn if we will not teach. There is still time."

"Then *you* teach her, Celebremen," Belwing said. "I no longer have the patience."

"In that, I am at one with you," Vieliessar said. "I have no patience for tricks and traps and riddles. I thank your kind for all the help it has given to me and mine in the past, but it cannot count against your present actions. Stand aside so I may pass. This is the last time I will ask it."

She took a step forward, deliberately, her eyes focusing on the Unicorn the others had called Belwing. One step, then two . . .

. . . and then, by some trick of the light, five of the six were gone and only Celebremen remained. The white Unicorn mare took two steps backward. Vieliessar stopped. And waited.

"Search if you must," Celebremen said resignedly. She hesitated for a moment, then turned and walked back through the pass. "Come, and see what you will."

Finally Vieliessar could risk a glance behind herself. The bottom third of the road was dark with retreating Beastlings—*so many of them all gathered together! What has Runacarendalur done?* The middle third was full of clusters of Silverlight moving slowly upward as Beastlings continued down; her people returning to the top of the pass. The dearth of them was a pitiful sight.

Vieliessar returned to the waiting meisne. "Pantaradet, go to Aradre-leg and say what has transpired here, and that the Lightborn must come up to Ceoprentrei as quick as they can. Hiraen, send your meisne to aid her; I know it is much to ask, but they must return here as fast as possible. Stop for nothing save aid to another of our people."

"But my lord, where will you be?" Hiraen asked.

"Here," Vieliessar said, and turned to walk through the pass.

⊰⧉⊱

The abrupt darkness and silence that fell as Vieliessar walked through the pass gate was profound and disorienting. The walls of the pass silenced the wind, and the living voices from the road, and the night was moonless. No night-creatures called or howled, no night birds sang. No rats scrabbled among the corpses; no dogs quarreled over meat.

The reek of the dissolving Endarkened bodies overwhelmed every other smell, even that of the Flower Forest. The psychic stink of the Endarkened did not survive their death—unlike their physical stench. Vieliessar pulled a scarf from around her neck and wound it over her lower face to cut the smell.

Anything spattered by Endarkened ichor was disintegrating. Vieliessar was careful not to touch those things; her people had learned that Endarkened ichor would burn the skin of any who touched it, as well as sicken them—sometimes to death. The Endarkened themselves—those that lay dead on the field—were already as liquid and misshapen as if their bones had been removed. Some had only the single puncture wound from the stab of the Unicorn horn that had killed them. All that would be left of them by morning was the terrible stench. She made a quick tally of the Endarkened dead and was astonished at the numbers. Dozens of the monsters lay dead.

At what had recently been the Eastern Gate, Celebremen stood near the foot of a great rockslide. The dust had not yet settled completely, and so the Unicorn appeared as if she were shrouded in mist. Vieliessar called up Silverlight, sending two globes down the valley to halt at the entrance of the impossibly expanded Flower Forest, setting two in the Western Pass, and keeping the other three with her.

Then she began to work.

She could not possibly check the battlefield physically in the time she had, but she did not have to. Vieliessar reached out, cautiously, and cast the weakest iteration of Knowing of which she was capable. Many Lightborn had no notion that a spell could be cast at varying intensities. They knew their spells, they cast them with all the power they could muster, and their masters never asked for anything more. But in the years she had spent first hiding her Light, then hiding its power, Vieliessar had learned the value of weak spellcasting. Knowing, if she cast it at full strength, would bring her every detail of every death here on the field—at once. Such a blast of terror and pain might well kill her.

But a weak iteration would merely tell her what she wanted to know.

She sensed Celebremen—a glorious bright blaze of Life—and shut the Unicorn from the spell's boundaries as she continued to search. She narrowed her focus to shut out Nomaitemil and the sides of the valley, she checked and rechecked her Knowing, until she had to accept the spell's information. *The Endarkened King stole their lives in order to live. I imagine he has little interest in keeping Mosirinde's Covenant.*

Vieliessar voided her spell, and then, driven by an emotion she could not put a name to, she began to bring order to the battlefield. She untangled bodies, both Elven and Beastling, to lay them out in a seemly and dignified manner, smoothed garments back into place, gently closed staring eyes. Even though some of the bodies had only minor wounds, all were dead. Soon her hands were wet with blood of a dozen colors, all mingled. It seemed to Vieliessar as if every race of Beastling that existed between Sword and Star had sent levies to this battle: among the Elven dead she saw Centaurs, Minotaurs, and Bearwards—Beastlings she could recognize from drawings and descriptions—but there were other bodies to which she could give no name.

Elf-shaped creatures no taller than her knee, garbed in miniature chain and coif, armed with swords the size of an eating knife. Child-sized creatures that seemed to be half-goat, half-Elf, with slings and daggers tangled in their lifeless hands. Tiny female-bodied creatures with dragonfly wings, those wings now crumpled and scorched. There were mutilated Gryphons, still twisted in their death agonies. Another creature that she recognized—only after long thought—as a Hippogriff. Strange wolves with the muzzles of bears and the hands of Elvenkind. Creatures whose shape could not be determined from the smears of blood and fur that was all that remained of their bodies.

Death upon death, until her mind and her senses were numbed to its immensity. No one deserved to die this way. Not Elvenkind. Not Beastlings. Not the least of the forest creatures. Even a chicken did not deserve this dreadful death. Vieliessar, Sanctuary-trained, interrogated her memories to find any living being that she would be willing to consign to this death by Endarkened.

There was none.

She had worked her way down the valley wall before she stopped her work. The battlefield was too great a task for one person. She found a bit of clean soil in which to scrub her hands, then wiped them dry on her thighs before turning to her second puzzle: the Flower Forest.

The Unicorns had said Nomaitemil was "void"—but void of what? Not Light, certainly, for she had drawn on it and so had other Lightborn. The Flower Forest's growth now completely filled two of the three valleys of Ceoprentrei but the trees that edged the expanded Flower Forest were as tall as if they had existed in this very spot for centuries, not Wheelturns.

And that, so far as Vieliessar knew, was impossible.

If its Light remained, what else was in a Flower Forest that might be removed? *I am too long out of the Sanctuary to enjoy such riddles,* Vieliessar thought to herself. She cast weak Knowing again, and cautiously focused it on Nomaitemil. The surge of life she had always associated with Flower Forests was absent—and so were its larger inhabitants. But . . .

There! Near the edge of the trees she sensed Life—but too much life. Living creatures. She cast Silversight upon herself again and saw . . .

Bearwards. Centaurs. Beastlings. Searching the battlefield for their dead just as she had searched for hers. There were few bodies at the northern end of the valley—most of the hard fighting had been closer to Nomaitemil. She watched them uneasily as her hand drifted toward her sword-belt, but she had disarmed herself before coming here.

Never mind; she had no desire to offer battle, and perhaps Celebremen would intercede if they attempted to attack her. Or she could—

Or you could help them.

It was a profoundly disorienting moment, as if everything Vieliessar had ever known was abruptly turned inside out and upside down. The Beastlings—these strange and exotic Elven adversaries—had been hunted as vermin and pests for as long as the Hundred Houses had existed. But they were not in any way kin to the Endarkened. The Endarkened were monsters. But the Beastlings . . .

I care not what they are so long as they are Good. I would recruit butterflies and earthworms if I could. I would take fealty from oak trees and vineyards if they would aid me against the Endarkened.

I will fight beside the Beastlings if they will have me. If they will not, I will aid them in some other way.

On legs suddenly unsteady, Vieliessar turned back toward Celebremen, still dazed with her new realization. A part of her wondered if she was simply so tired of the endless fighting that her mind searched for any pretext that would let her bring an end to it. Another part burned with the need to transform her hopes into truths. "If you wish to teach me something," Vieliessar called to her, "now would be an excellent time."

There was no response from the Unicorn, but the others had heard. They straightened and stood still, looking at her. The Minotaur had a Gryphon's wing in his hands, one of those that an Endarkened had torn from its owner's back. He had picked it up and gently folded it closed, and now stroked its surface as if it were a sleeping child. Vieliessar thought of the Sanctuary, of her Service Year, where Arahir of Hallorad—one of the other Candidates—had worn a Gryphon feather at her throat, taken from the wing of one she had killed. Domain Hallorad had been the most isolated of the Windsward Houses.

Arahir was dead.

Just as everyone in Ceoprentrei was dead.

"Mama! *Mama!*"

Vieliessar was running before she thought. Across the valley, the Beastlings had gathered around an Elven child. She saw one of the Centaurs pick him up, ignoring his struggles.

She had been wrong. There was one living thing worth salvaging here upon this battlefield.

Calan.

Her breath scoured her throat as she ran, and she tasted blood. A thousand spells came into her mind, ready to deploy, to strike down, to *punish* the creatures that held Calan.

She reached the group of Beastlings clustered on the gravel slope at the edge of the rock wall and stopped just out of sword's reach, willing her breathing to slow. Calan had stopped struggling when he saw her, and simply stared, wild-eyed and terrified. He was dirty, scraped, and battered—but he was alive.

And Celebremen would have it that there was nothing here for me, and had I heeded her words, what would have become of him?

"This is my child and heir, Calanoriel," Vieliessar said, when her breathing had slowed enough for her speech to be measured and calm. "I am Vieliessar."

"Everyone knows who you are," the Minotaur replied, his voice a deep rumble. He was frighteningly large, nearly a third again her height, and his wide sweeping horns were bright against the darkness. He was the one who had collected the Gryphon's wing and he was still holding it. Now he crouched to set the wing down gently on the ground. "Why should your child live when so many of ours do not?" he asked, straightening.

"Because you know who I am."

A sudden idea rose up in her mind, so audacious even she would call it lunacy. It was Amretheon's *geasa* pushing at her—but Vieliessar didn't care. She would have done what it impelled her toward regardless.

"You know I am the Child of the Prophecy and High King—Amretheon's heir and Pelashia's greatdaughter. I have said I was come to end the High House and the Low, and I have done so. I have said I was come to bring one justice to all my people, and I have done so." She took a deep breath. "And now I say there will be one justice for *all* people, no matter their form. The Endarkened must be fought, and there is only us to do that. Join me."

Madness. Insanity. Impossible. Somehow terrifyingly right.

She had asked so much of her people. They would not agree to fight beside creatures who were so *other*.

Yet, in memory, she could still hear the Gryphons mourning their dead in the sky above.

Any creature that speaks and weeps I will gladly enlist in my war against the Endarkened, for such are far more like us than they are like the Endarkened.

"It is as I have told you, Mindaso. All Elvenkind are mad," the Centaur said dismissively. He released Calan, and the boy flung himself into Vieliessar's arms.

"Githachi said to hide and she would come back but she didn't and then the Darkened came and the Unicorns came and everyone left!" Calan said in a rush. "And it got dark but I stayed where I was and then *they* came!"

"And now you are here with me, *kalaliel*," Vieliessar answered, and hugged him very hard. Calan trembled with the aftermath of terror. How long had he waited as he clung to hope, obedient, desperate in his fear? "I will not leave you." *Where is Helecanth? Where is Thurion? And where is your sister, my heart, because the one thing I do not see among the corpses upon this battlefield is children.*

She turned back toward Celebremen. "You! Unicorn! Did you know Calanoriel lived when you tried to deny me entrance to this battlefield?"

Once again Celebremen ignored her.

"Well, she doesn't lack for courage," she heard one of the Centaurs behind her say.

She turned back toward the Beastlings, trying to ignore the sense of unreality she felt. This morning she had stood in Saganath in Jaeglenhend with the last of the Lightborn and slew Endarkened with a spell. In the evening, she had passed through the Dragon's Gate and fought Beastlings—and Endarkened—with her sword. And now she must make sense of it all for the sake of all.

Calan squirmed in her arms, his terror set aside now that she had come. At the age of eight, he did not hold on to frights and hurts very long. Yet he was nearly old enough to take the field against the enemy. As the heir, they would protect him as much as possible. Nevertheless, her people had been schooled to one truth: *When the Endarkened come, you run. Or you die.*

"Thank you for the gift of my heir's life," she said to the Beastlings. "I do not know what your purpose is here, nor do I ask it, but I will say to you what the Unicorn Celebremen has said to me: no creature lives upon this battlefield, no matter how small the wound, for the Endarkened King stole all their lives to fuel his magic."

The Fauns looked up at her in confusion. "Everyone is dead?" one of them said. Despite their somewhat Elvish appearance, Faun ears were long and pointed, with tufts of fur at the tips, and they twitched as he talked.

"Yes," Vieliessar said gently. "They are all dead. I searched with my own magic and saw Celebremen was right. Everyone is dead."

"Then we should go," the Faun who had spoken said decisively. He looked up at the Minotaur. "Nothing to find," he said sadly.

The Minotaur reached out a hand to the Faun, and picked up the small being to set it on his shoulder. Other Fauns climbed up onto the Centaurs' backs, and the last of them climbed onto the shoulders of one of the Bearwards. Vieliessar watched them as they went toward the Western Gate, Calan's hand warm in hers.

"Creatures!" she called at the last moment. "I cannot call you beasts! What am I to call you?"

The small party stopped, and the Minotaur turned back to her. His booming voice carried easily across the narrow valley. "We are Folk," he said. "Just as you are. Call us Otherfolk if that would please you."

"Fare you well then, Otherfolk," she said, raising a hand in salute.

She watched until they had gone through the pass, and as she did, her anger grew. One learned control before all else at the Sanctuary of the Star, and she had witnessed the disasters caused by the intemperate fury of the War Princes. She tried everything she could think of to school her temper, for a star-forged rage was building in her, and she would not let it master her.

But the children had been at—and *in*—Nomaitemil when the Unicorns came. If they had gone with them, they would have been first down the mountain and would have turned back candlemarks ago to rejoin their families. Those who had not gone with the Unicorns would have been last out of the pass, and would already be among her muster. But she had seen no children anywhere on the Western Road.

"Where are the rest of the children?" she demanded of the empty air.

"We saved them. You're welcome."

Celebremen walked from behind two large rocks in the scrim of the eastern wall. The Unicorn's body glowed as if she were made of Silverlight, and despite her misgivings Vieliessar's heart lifted at the sight of her. *I wish I could believe that what is beautiful is also truthful . . . but I dare not, no matter how much my heart aches.*

Calan tugged at Vieliessar's hand, wanting to go to Celebremen.

"And since they're safe and nobody has eaten them, you can gather up your army and Runacar will gather up his and we can all have a lovely parley. Or didn't you mean what you said to Stephantes and Mindaso?" Celebremen asked.

It took constant effort for Vieliessar to concentrate on Celebremen's words, and not simply be spellbound by her beauty. Stephantes and Mindaso must be the Centaur and the Minotaur she'd spoken with. "I meant it," Vieliessar said raggedly.

Calan tugged at her hand again. Vieliessar put her arm around him, holding him to her side. He looked up at her, his expression troubled and disappointed. "Mama?" he asked. "Are the Unicorns monsters?"

Oh my child, how can I answer when I do not know myself? All I can say is that I feel no taint of Darkness here. And I am so tired of fighting losing battles.

But a child's questions could not be met with a scholar's equivocations. "No," Vieliessar said firmly. "The Unicorns are not the monsters.

They and the Otherfolk have come to be our allies. See? I even have Cele-bremen's image on my surcoat."

"Allies, you say?" Vieliessar felt acutely that Celebremen was trying very hard not to laugh. "Then how about this? You don't kill any more of my people, we won't kill yours, and we'll *all* kill Endarkened."

"For myself I can swear this now, and I will," Vieliessar said. "I can-not speak for my people, but I will ask them. And I will ask you—who *are* your people? For you say we are at odds, and never have I nor any member of the Hundred Houses offered harm to your kind."

She thought of what Thurion had said the first time he saw the Uni-corn Throne. *"I have always wondered why they are chained."*

"That you know of," Celebremen said on a heavy sigh. "But the Folk come in every shape you have seen upon this battlefield—and more that you cannot imagine."

"Then you say that you—Unicorns—are Beastl—*Otherfolk*," Vielies-sar said. "The . . . *Otherfolk* took the field today against us. Only the ar-rival of the Endarkened—and *your* arrival—ended that battle, and you rescued my people as well as yours."

"Would you prefer we hadn't?" Celebremen asked.

"I would prefer truth," Vieliessar snapped.

"Woe betide us that a Sanctuary scholar should be the Child of the Prophecy," Celebremen said irritably. "You would seek truth and an-swers even within the cauldron of war."

"Where better to find Truth than where warriors fight about what Truth is to be?" Vieliessar countered.

Celebremen huffed a sigh. "Truth, then. Because of the Red Harvest—what you, in your innocence, call the Endarkened's hunting—the Oth-erfolk now gather beneath the rule of an Emperor. However, my people have never agreed with Leutric's course. We pursue our own, as we have for more years than you might number, Star's Child."

"So you have betrayed the oaths you swore to this Leutric? Or did you refuse to swear to him?" Vieliessar desperately attempted to fit the Unicorns—the *Otherfolk*—into a picture of the world that had not until this moment held them.

"Oh, we never swore fealty to him," Celebremen said loftily. "And that's just as well for you, since Leutric's plan is to kill every single one of you—except, so I am told, your children—and ours is to make you see reason. When your ancestors came to this land, the Folk welcomed them willingly. Perhaps that was a foolish thing to do."

Despite herself, Vieliessar laughed harshly. "If that act brought us all to this hour, Unicorn, it was. My people have known nothing but war and slavery for a hundred—a *thousand*—generations. That is what we are. That is *all* we are."

"Perhaps you underestimate your people—and your ancestors," Celebremen said gently.

"I doubt that very much, Celebremen," Vieliessar said shortly. If anyone knew what her ancestors were capable of, it was she. "And now I ask—just as *I* will be asked—where are our children?"

"They are safe with us," Celebremen said. "We would never hurt a child—though your kind seems to see no difficulty in leaving them in the woods to starve to death."

When Vieliessar had still been at the Sanctuary of the Star, Celebremen's words would have puzzled her. Now she knew that the Crofters, the Landbonds, all the people she had raised up to equality with the Lords Komen, had often left their children in the forests to die because they knew they would not be able to feed them.

"If you would enjoy my patience, do not regale me with every nithling disgrace and small murder the Hundred Houses have committed, for there is no changing the past," Vieliessar said warningly. "The only purpose of such words is to enflame the present."

"So haughty!" Celebremen mocked, tossing her head. "O High King, where is your kingdom?"

"Here," Vieliessar answered simply. "Among the ghosts."

She lifted her hand from Calan's shoulders, and he ran toward Celebremen. She had sworn in her heart to make this folk her allies—and that was a promise that looked more unattainable every heartbeat.

"There is one thing we must—" she began, only to be interrupted by shouts from the Western Pass.

A great blanket of Silverlight hovered there like a strange, glowing (and flat) cloud. Its light was enough to illuminate the rank upon rank of horses and riders, and the infantry that walked between their rows as they came slowly toward Alpine Nomaitemil. Helecanth and Thurion walked in the first rank of the array, leading their flagging mounts, and called out for her. *As one would summon a straying sheep!* Vieliessar thought in exasperation. She looked for others who should be in the vanguard—Rithdeliel Warlord, Cirwath of Mangiralas, Mirwathel of Cirandeiron, Tagriel of Araphant, Otriam First Sword, Master Cegusara of the Scouts—and thought again of the Gryphons. If her commanders were dead . . .

I shall deal with that when I must. Just as I shall deal with . . . everything else.

She heard the sound of rocks shifting behind her. Celebremen stood a scant rod of distance away, her horn glowing silver and blue. Calanoriel was on her back. At the sight of him a murmur of voices—half alarmed, half amazed—came from the vanguard, and it picked up speed.

Vieliessar looked from the Unicorn to her army, and back to her heir. "Go," she said to Celebremen. "Carry my words exactly. Say to the traitor Runacarendalur that I will meet with him here a sennight hence. And one thing more: return to me all of my people including those whom the Gryphons carried off, or return to me their bodies."

"You are amazingly used to ordering people around," Celebremen said inscrutably.

"I have learned to be. Now go," Vieliessar said. "Calanoriel will go with you—he is my pledge of honor. Calan, my *kalaliel*, be worthy of this great task I set you."

His eyes grew round, and Calan nodded enthusiastically "I hear, and—and to hear—to hear is—"

"'To obey,'" Vieliessar prompted gently.

"Hear and *obey*! My liege!" Calan said.

This time Celebremen *did* laugh, blowing out her lips and shaking her neck. "Hold on tight, my little love," she said to Calanoriel, and bounded away up the slope.

It was several candlemarks past dawn by the time every horse and its rider were tended to, but at last the dreadful day was over, and the High King's people were safe within the bounds of Nomaitemil.

Despite their exhaustion, they made their encampment in the usual way: widely separated groups so that the monsters the Endarkened regularly sent against them would not be able to destroy them all in one fell swoop. In practice, this meant that they marked the bounds and then lay down to sleep just as they were. Everything else could wait.

The High King's own encampment was separate from all the others. It held only the High King, her guards, and what members of her Court she chose.

If this were any other day, her council, her generals, and her senior advisors would be with her, and together they would determine what their course of action should be. But this was no ordinary day, and those gathered with her were true friends and known allies only—Helecanth, Thurion, Aradreleg, Iardalaith, Shanilya, Tuonil, and a few more. Most of her senior commanders were still missing. That was a problem for another day. If another day came.

The year itself was about to become their enemy.

It was already Harvest Moon, and that meant the first winter snows in the mountains would fall within the fortnight. Snow Moon was only a little more than five moonturns away, and that was only Midwinter, not spring. Spring would come very late this high in the Mystrals, and most of the battleponies would drop foals in the early spring, and the folk desperately needed those foals.

Vieliessar had planned to be in Arevethmonion by foaling season, but Nomaitemil would do as a refuge for the broodmares just as well. The Flower Forest could provide ample food and water, though there would be no meat for Elvenkind unless they trapped and ate mice and squirrels. Any larger creature, from hare to deer, was absent.

Is this why Celebremen said Nomaitemil was "void"? What things do the Otherfolk know that we do not? And never forget that our children are in the hands of the Otherfolk.

Though Vieliessar had been awake as early and fought as hard as any of them, the possibility of sleep eluded her. She had bathed, and dressed in spell-laundered clothing. And now . . .

"Stop pacing," Thurion said from where he was tending the small fire. *She is my daughter too.* Vieliessar heard his thoughts plainly, as he had meant her to.

"If the High King did not think her heirs would be safe with the Unicorns, she would not have surrendered the Heir-Prince into the Unicorn Celebremen's keeping," Helecanth said. The formality of her words was the only indication Helecanth would give of her displeasure.

"You know that for truth," Vieliessar said to her gently. "I fear Calanoriel is far safer with Celebremen than he would be here."

"Once you have shared your thoughts with your council," Helecanth said, in the tones of one only finishing her liege-lord's thought.

"What's left of it," Thurion muttered under his breath. It had been a small matter for him, surrounded by an infinite bounty of Light, to create cups and a teapot from leaves pinned into shape then enchanted into shin'zuruf, and there had been several kettles among the packs. Now he shook some tea into the pot from a twist of paper, and poured water over it. "Now sit. It is only Sanctuary Blend, but we should not dishonor the crafting."

"You make me feel as if I am back in the Sanctuary myself," Vieliessar said. "Come, Helecanth. You can guard me just as well from the ground."

But if her words were light, her thoughts were not. Soon Vieliessar must return to the battlefield. Whether it was to be a battle of words or of swords, she did not yet know. Until this very day, she had never even seen one of the Otherfolk. Now she was asking her people to ally with them. She could name at least some of their races and their appearance, but that did not mean she knew them.

But.

The title that had been forced upon her—Child of the Prophecy— was no empty thing. Numberless generations before her birth, before the ages of darkness and chaos, Amretheon Aradruiniel, the last High King, had spoken a true prophecy. That prophecy had searched down the centuries until it had found Vieliessar, and from the instant of her birth had begun remaking her with dreams, with visions . . .

And with *luck*.

Sheer *luck* had saved Vieliessar's life a thousand times, as she grew from babe to child. *Luck* had bent the thoughts and emotions of others in her favor, had made them blind to reality when her survival demanded they should not see. Amretheon's Prophecy had been the featherweight in the balance—the *luck*—that tipped fate in her favor repeatedly. That gave her victories, if by the narrowest of margins.

That altered the thoughts of her friends and foes alike—without her will and sometimes against it.

Gladly would I rid myself of it, for I fear I am as much the pawn as everyone else whom the Prophecy has touched. But now I ask: Is Amretheon's magic enough to incline my people to my will? I do not know. And I do not wish to find out. But there is no way back, so we must go forward.

The *geasa* that Amretheon had set upon her, Child of the Prophecy, was pushing her to ally her people with the Otherfolk (and with Runacarendalur who led them). This she knew for truth. And if she could not manage to make them accept the idea, her folk would fight against the Otherfolk and the Endarkened both.

And die.

She sighed deeply, choosing a cup from those laid upon the floorcloth and holding it out mutely. Thurion filled it, his expression grave. She did her best to smile at him reassuringly.

"Say to the others that there is tea enough for all. If they are not asleep," Vieliessar said.

Never have I been able to command my people as the War Princes commanded them. No, I can do nothing but use reason, and logic, and debate with them until they see that my choice is good.

If they will.

HARVEST MOON IN THE TENTH YEAR OF THE HIGH KING'S REIGN: THE HOUSE DIVIDED

I swear before Leaf and Tree and Flower, before Fire and Moon and Star, that I am your vassal until both Leaf and Star have withered away, and my life and all I hold is yours to do with as you will. I will uphold this oath until I die, and with it I pledge to serve you above all others until Amretheon Aradruiniel returns, and to this oath I will be faithful.

— Elven Oath of Fealty

Glad I will be when the first brewing of ale is ready," Frochoriel Oronviel said, taking the gently steaming cup of tea. He had escaped the attack of the Gryphons by virtue of being thrown from his horse, which had panicked at the sight of them.

"And until then you will drink tea with gratitude," Shanilya Thadan-Arzhana said, smirking.

"I would even drink *water*," Frochoriel said fervently.

Iardalaith, Frochoriel, Aradreleg, Shanilya, and Tuonil had joined the others beside the tea-brazier. The rest of those folk who commonly frequented the High King's encampment slept, though a taille of the Silver Swords remained awake and watchful, providing such security as was needed in the middle of a Flower Forest—for any of the beasts Elvenkind had come to know and fear would surely have fled the sounds of battle.

Vieliessar was grateful beyond words to see those who had escaped the Gryphons. So many sorely missed comrades were unaccounted for. Moreover, tomorrow her people must bring themselves to search the battlefield, to tally the dead and missing—and to loot their bodies. In these dark days Elvenkind did not have the luxury of abandoning weapons and armor: to forge either required a great deal of time, a great deal of Magery, or both.

You might as well begin your debate with them, Vieliessar told herself. *If you cannot sway your dearest friends and comrades, you will not convince the rest.*

Once the second cups of tea had been poured, she spoke.

"You will have seen me accompanied by a Unicorn when you returned to Ceoprentrei last night. You will also have seen that Heir-Prince Calanoriel departed with her when she left—all praise to Komen Githachi of the Silver Swords for placing him in safe hiding when danger threatened, so that he might do so."

"More praise if he had remained with his people, surely?" Shanilya said blandly.

"And yet, it is a thing I chose, and a thing which I have done," Vieliessar said, shutting down that debate. She went on to summarize her meeting with the Unicorn Celebremen in Ceoprentrei and the Unicorn's offer: alliance with her and her "Otherfolk" against their common enemy, the Endarkened.

"You cannot possibly even be thinking of allying yourself with a pack of talking animals," Iardalaith said flatly.

"It's better than dying in the claws of the Endarkened," Frochoriel said.

"We *'ally'* ourselves with horses," Vieliessar pointed out. "We make partnerships with hawks and hounds. How is that different from fighting beside Centaurs?"

"Horses don't eat Elves," Iardalaith said flatly. "I beg you, Lord Vieliessar, heed the counsel of one born upon the Western Shore. We grew up fighting this monstrous vermin. They will bring an end to us as terrible as any the Endarkened may."

"The Unicorns can kill Endarkened," Vieliessar said, in the first of what she knew was to be many repetitions of that sentence. "Fifty Endarkened—perhaps more—met their deaths upon this battlefield—all at the horns of the Unicorns. Can any of us claim as many kills even through ten Wheelturns of fighting? In addition, the Endarkened King was badly wounded. Dare we spurn an alliance with his destroyer?"

"If it were merely the Unicorns," Thurion said, choosing his words with care, "that would be one thing. But that is not what we are being offered."

"No," Vieliessar agreed reluctantly. "Celebremen said that all those whom we fought upon the battlefield—save the Endarkened—are Otherfolk. And thus, all would be included in our alliance."

"Ally with those who sought our deaths less than a sunturn ago?" Aradreleg asked, her tone wavering between outrage and disbelief.

"Is such any different than what the War Princes did over and over each and every War Season?" Vieliessar asked. "Caerthalien made a thousand alliances and betrayed a thousand more, and never did I hear it said that Bolecthindial or Glorthiachiel were other than *alfaljodthi*."

"*No*," Iardalaith said flatly. "Listen to your own words, High King. *We fought them*. They *hid in Ceoprentrei* and they meant to slaughter us all. Where is the Eastern Gate now? Buried under an avalanche of stone! And we—"

"The Unicorns can kill the Endarkened," Vieliessar repeated evenly.

"Then ally us with the *Unicorns*!" Iardalaith shouted.

"*That is not the treaty we are being offered!*" Vieliessar shouted back.

Thurion closed his hand over his teacup. It broke with a small cracking sound, but faint as the sound was, it drew every eye to him. He looked around the fire as he tossed the fragments into the flames. "We have heard from princes," he said into the silence that filled the space. "Let Landbonds speak."

"I would speak," Tuonil said. "I would be heard, even by princes and Lightborn," the former Landbond said.

"You shall speak," Vieliessar answered steadily. "And you shall be heard."

"High King raised up Landbond," Tuonil said. "No more are Landbond given less worth than a fine lord's fine horse. It is our folk who become Light's Chosen—"

Here Thurion smiled slightly and bowed his head in acknowledgment, for he and Tuonil had both been born Landbond.

"—and then, in old times, did gifts and freedoms come to some of us, for fine lords would leash Light's Chosen through their kin. That day is done. Landbond are free."

"What are you—" Frochoriel began, and Vieliessar silenced him with a curt gesture.

"But I say these words: this day Forestfolk[1] fought and killed. Redwings came. Unicorns came. Forestfolk saved us when they saved their own."

There was a moment of silence when he had finished, for everything Tuonil said was true.

"This speaks to a matter that I have long held under my tongue," Shanilya Thadan said. "If the High King will permit?"

"Oh, let us have an end to courtliness and High Table manners!" Vieliessar begged irritably. "Do you see castels and finery here? Perfumes and sweetmeats? Let us be honest with one another."

Shanilya nodded, her face inscrutable. "Then I shall ask: Why do you take us into the West? We have paid out many lives to reach Ceoprentrei and Nomaitemil, and will pay many more should we choose to go on."

"The Domains of the Shore begged succor from their liege-lord," Iardalaith said. His expression was courteous and wary.

"Ten turns of the Great Wheel ago," Shanilya pointed out. "Their problems have undoubtedly ended, one way or another. Nor have I yet heard the High King's words, Daroldan."

Vieliessar pondered her next words carefully. It mattered less in her calculations that Thurion would sense a lie than that she had sworn she would always give truth to her people—even if not always the truth whole and entire.

Amrolion? Daroldan? My Lightborn whom I sent there so long ago? I know not what their fate may be, nor what I can do to change it. Perhaps there is nothing. Perhaps, all along, I have been a bellwether who thought she was a flock-guard.

"If they yet survive and are whole," she said at last, "they are the last intact domains in my king-domain, and we need what resources they can spare. Further, I have taken fealty of them, and they have a sacred right to my aid, no matter if I should believe it is not—or is no longer—needed. We all know that such tales of truth and honor belong

---

[1] The Landbond Elvenkind speak a slightly different dialect than the rest of Elvenkind. This is the Landbond word for Otherfolk/Beastlings.

in a Storysinger's tale, and not in the world—so while these are reasons, they are not the whole. Since we left Celephriandullias-Tildorangelor, we have not come upon any Flower Forest as vast and as powerful as she was, and that means our folk are always scattered across the lands we pass through. To search blindly for another such as Janglanipaikharain through the uncharted south is a risk we do not have the resources to take, but we know that in the West there are two: Arevethmonion and Delfierarathadan. Gain either or both, and perhaps it might be possible to create a stronghold that could defy the Endarkened."

"'Might.' 'Perhaps,'" Shanilya said dubiously.

"The Arzhana ever held beggar brats and backstabbers," Frochoriel commented.

"If either of you has a better idea, say so," Vieliessar snapped.

"Arevethmonion was never tapped during the war," Thurion said slowly. "But Delfierarathadan?" He looked around to the other Lightborn. Aradreleg deliberately avoided his gaze.

"We took Cirandeiron with her own Flower Forests," Iardalaith said. "It was deemed too dangerous to call upon Delfierarathadan, for fear of rousing the Beastlings there—which returns us to my original point: *you cannot make an alliance with monsters.*"

"Lord Shanilya, are you satisfied with the reasons I have tendered?" Vieliessar asked, ignoring him.

Iardalaith got to his feet abruptly and walked to the edge of the clearing, resting his forehead against the trunk of a gigantic uluskukad, which looked as if it had taken centuries to grow, an uluskukad which had not been here ten Wheels ago. The morning sun through its blue leaves gave him an eerie pallor.

"They are indeed good ones," Shanilya said, inclining her head. "The Arzhana is satisfied."

"Then we shall return to the main argument," Vieliessar said, continuing to ignore Iardalaith. "Tuonil points out that the Otherfolk—the Unicorns—saved our people when they might have abandoned them. The Unicorn Celebremen has offered us an alliance—"

"And Runacarendalur Caerthalien fights for them," Helecanth said gruffly. "We all saw him."

There was a beat of silence. Before today, only three people—Vieliessar, Helecanth, and Thurion—had known that Caerthalien lived. Now it could no longer be a secret. Aradreleg looked horrified. Shanilya looked intrigued. Iardalaith raised his head and looked grimly thoughtful.

"And many of us fought his damned Centaurs," Frochoriel said. "Say what you choose, but those murder-horses are the Rade Itself upon the field."

"Far better that they become *our* murder-horses then," Vieliessar retorted.

"And if in addition to their other faults the Beastlings hold a traitor and oathbreaker whose life belongs to the High King? Let them execute him and tender up his slain body before we contemplate yoking ourselves to these abominations." Iardalaith stooped down and picked up a handful of pebbles from the forest floor and began idly juggling them.

"I was not proposing that we ally with the Endarkened," Vieliessar said acidly.

Thurion raised his hand. "I am sorry to interrupt again, but while we are asking questions that must be asked, here is one: Why tell us? Shouldn't this matter be discussed before the whole council? And among the Guilds?"

"If I cannot convince even my friends, what luck will I have convincing my people?" Vieliessar said aloud, glancing toward Iardalaith. She did not want to lose him. Counselor, Lightborn, Master of the Warhunt . . . but friend before all of those things.

She rose to her feet, gesturing to the others to remain where they were, and went to Iardalaith's side. "Is there no way I can persuade you, my friend?" she asked softly. *You followed me to war and made of the Lightborn a thing never yet seen since the days of Mosirinde and Arilcarion. You sped my cause to victory. Do not abandon me now!*

"I was born a prince of Daroldan. My cousin swore fealty to you," Iardalaith said without turning to face her. "Will you give him the same choice you are asking us to make? How can he? How can *I*? I was born and raised upon the Shore. You were not."

"I was not," Vieliessar echoed. "I was born in the Sanctuary of the

Star and fostered by my dearest enemies in Caerthalien, those who slew Nataranweiya and Serenthon and stole from me every scrap of my inheritance. Yet when I gained power over Caerthalien, I slew none save those who chose death rather than fealty. And those I slew died with honor." She thought of the Challenge Circle at Ifjalasairaet. She thought of Glorthiachiel, proudly mocking her until the moment Vieliessar cut her down.

"You do not know what these monsters *are!*" Iardalaith said in anguish.

"*I know that they can kill Endarkened,*" Vieliessar answered. "My brother, I beg you: Can you not love this alliance for that alone? How can the Otherfolk be more terrible than the Endarkened? When this war is done . . ." Vieliessar's voice faltered and stopped, for she could not imagine that day. "I am the Child of the Prophecy," she said instead. "I must do all I can to save my people."

Iardalaith let the pebbles in his hands fall back to the forest floor. He turned to face her, a cold and feral smile upon his lips. "Then you may have my full support, *Child of the Prophecy,* at a price. You will name me your Consort Prince this day and we will wed at once. You will designate me your Heir and set aside Adalieriel and Calanoriel from the succession. *I*—and I alone—shall choose who is to be the next High King."

Vieliessar stared in shock. Behind her, she could hear the gasps and whispers as the others reacted, for it was impossible they had not heard. What Iardalaith asked . . .

Did not matter. Victory over the Endarkened was all that mattered.

"I agree to your terms and will give my oath," she whispered, bowing her head. She could not bear to look at him. Grief and betrayal made her blind and deaf.

She was startled by a gentle hand upon her shoulder. She looked up. Iardalaith's eyes were sad. "I only wanted to see if you would do it," he said in a broken voice. "I swear to you—"

"*I* swear to you, Iardalaith," Thurion spoke from behind Vieliessar, his voice cold with fury. "Threaten my children again and I shall kill you in the Circle."

Iardalaith looked past Vieliessar, and as he did she saw his sorrow turn to shock. The paternity of Calanoriel and Adalieriel had been the closest of close-held secrets: Vieliessar had said no one claimed their paternity because she had erased the father's memories. No one save Vieliessar and Helecanth—until now—had known Thurion was their father. And no one save she and Thurion and Helecanth knew—even now—that Vieliessar was not the children's mother. If *that* secret escaped, there would be war among her people once more, and Calan and Liri would be its first victims.

She drew breath to speak, turning to include the others in what she was about to say, when Helecanth forestalled her.

"My lord King. Someone comes," Helecanth said.

⌐日⊨

"A bsolutely not," Rithdeliel said flatly.

The Gryphons' Elven prey were restored to their fellow komen—without any Otherfolk involvement, and without injury. Bewilderingly, the Gryphons had simply plucked them from the field, flown several leagues across the Flower Forest, and dropped them—fairly gently, overall—into a large clearing.

And so the *alakomentai'a* who had been kidnapped from the field simply walked back toward the northern edge of Nomaitemil until they had encountered the Elven encampment and its sentries.

Once they had been recognized, the majority of them headed to their latest home places for rest and news, leaving Rithdeliel, Master Dandamir, and Githachi of the Silver Swords to return to the High King. Vieliessar told Githachi that Calanoriel was now safe.

She had been forced to say rather more to Rithdeliel—with the expected result.

"Can *you* convince her?" Iardalaith asked him. "Because *I* can't."

"You're *also* supposed to be on her side now," Thurion said acidly.

Rithdeliel looked at him in surprise. Thurion, more than most, affected the meek nonthreatening demeanor of the Lightborn. Until he chose to abandon that façade and reveal an inner core of iron.

"Very well," Iardalaith said. "I support the High King's decision—

because really, if she won't change her mind she'll go her ways and everyone else will go theirs, and we'll all be dead in a moonturn."

"*The Unicorns can kill Endarkened,*" Vieliessar said yet again. She was beginning to wonder if anyone was listening to her.

"So we raid the Beastlings—"

"Otherfolk."

"—camp, take the Unicorns captive, and use them!" Rithdeliel said, sounding as if it were the most reasonable thing in the world.

Vieliessar did her very best not to laugh, but it was hard. The others present who had seen the Unicorns—but not spoken with them—simply looked . . . surprised.

"I do not believe that will work, my lord Rithdeliel," Iardalaith said carefully. He looked very much like someone who had no notion of what his own thoughts were.

"The High King is not an idiot," Githachi announced loudly.

"I thank you, Komentai Githachi," Vieliessar said, bowing fractionally. Vieliessar wondered if it was going to be necessary to have to make her argument for alliance with the Otherfolk serially and singly with every single one of her people. They would still be arguing when the Endarkened came and killed them all.

"We all stand in fealty and love to the High King," Iardalaith said irritably. "What's your point, Silver Sword?"

"That the High King is not stupid," Githachi said promptly. "And yet she gave her child, Calanoriel Prince-Heir, into the hands of the Unicorn Celebremen."

"Assuming that Unicorns have hands," muttered Prince Arzhana Thadan.

"Therefore, if the High King has so acted, this act is not the act of stupidity, because the High King is not stupid," Iardalaith said. "I salute your logic, Lord Komen Githachi, even if you seem to believe that Unicorns have hands, but logic is not truth."

"Nor is truth logical," Thurion said instantly. "This is of no matter. What matters is our decision. It must be made soon. The High King and her council must speak with one voice."

"To imagine we have the unfettered freedom to make a decision is to imagine wrongly," Rithdeliel said. "We have no supplies and no remounts. Our flocks and herds are scattered to the nine winds. Our children—so I am told, and not merely Prince Calanoriel and Princess Adalieriel—are in the possession—thank you, Iardalaith Lightbrother—of the Unicorns and their bestial cohorts. Therefore, we *must* make the alliance."

"But you just said—" Iardalaith accused.

"Do I say I mean a true alliance?" Rithdeliel answered. "The Beastlings hold hostages. That cannot be changed. They ask that we swear to an alliance of peace and fellowship that we might together destroy our common enemy. Without giving such an oath, we will not be able to free our hostages, nor regain our *khom*. Without horses and supplies we cannot fight."

"I take it then that you are in favor of this alliance with talking bears and inedible cows, Lord Rithdeliel?" Frochoriel Oronviel drawled.

Rithdeliel bowed ironically in Frochoriel's direction. "I am. Firstly, Arilcarion teaches that forced oaths cannot be true oaths, as the oathgiver is compelled under duress to swear. Secondly, the Code of War was never meant to apply to animals, only to komen. Let us swear our oaths as they wish. Let us hold to this oath in every particular, as scrupulously as if it were sworn between princes. And let our alliance—sworn in this moonturn of Harvest—run until the beginning of Frost. No more."

Vieliessar held her breath and schooled her features to impassivity. Was it better to swear a faithless oath than to outright refuse this alliance? Three moonturns was an eternity in a land at war with the Endarkened. Anything might happen, from a sweeping victory to a crashing defeat—to a sincere change of heart among her people. Could being forsworn be worse than watching the whole of her people die before her eyes? Did the keeping of oaths even matter anymore? The Starry Hunt punished all oathbreakers with banishment to the Cold Dark, but if They had not answered any of her prayers in all this time how could it be that They would concern Themselves with anything she did?

She did not know.

But Rithdeliel's plan makes of the alliance oath something as soft and sweet—and as quickly gone—as Festival cake. The people will accept it.

*And thus we will be able to retain Nomaitemil as our refuge, while send-
ing a meisne across the Mystrals and into the Western Reach.*

And perhaps even to the Sanctuary of the Star.

The deception did not sit well with her, for she had spoken with Celebremen in honesty and with her whole heart. But she could see no other
way. Give her three moonturns to persuade her people, and the false
oath might—could—would—become true.

Vieliessar took a deep breath. "We must all be grateful to the Starry
Hunt for having spared Lord Rithdeliel to us, for it seems to me that his
plan is one we can all follow with whole hearts. Three moonturns is not
so very long—but it is long enough to make Nomaitemil a sanctuary,
and perhaps give us a Great Keep to invest and defend."

She gazed around herself at her impromptu council. Iardalaith
looked deeply suspicious. Rithdeliel looked relieved. Thurion looked
grimly thoughtful. Vieliessar wondered: Would she have to name him
King's Consort now? The secret of her children's parentage would not
remain secret for long, now that Iardalaith knew it.

That was a problem for another time.

"Now—as soon as may be—we must set those words before the whole
of my people and bring their words to me," she said firmly.

That alone should take us all of the next sennight.

⹌⹍

The chambers and passageways of the World Without Sun echoed
with uneasy celebration. There was not actually anything to
celebrate—since they had lost—but many of their fellows had been
obliterated on the battlefield and none of the Endarkened understood
the concept of mourning. Thus, to slake their dread, they drew lavishly
upon their stores of captive living meat, creating inventive and deadly
games for their hapless victims. Centaurs were ridden to death on race-
courses floored with razors; Fauns and Brownies were boiled alive; Wulvers forced to fight each other to the death. Every Brightworld creature
in the Endarkened's possession was being either tortured to death, or
used to torture others. It lent something of a carnival atmosphere to the

World Without Sun, one that all of the Endarkened were careful not to remark upon, lest someone ask what they were celebrating.

Shurzul walked through all of the uneasy festivity unmoved. Her destination was the throne room, though she did not wish any of her fellows to know that. She stepped delicately aside as a screaming Elfling, its skin sloughing away from the acid applied to it, lurched blindly down the corridor on the clusters of bones that were all that remained of its feet.

"Shurzul! Come and join us! Ashraq has had a wonderful idea!" Orbushnu cried. She was reeling as if half-drunk, her lambent yellow eyes slitted closed and her wings half-unfurled. "We shall find the nursery and send some of the meat into it. What do you suppose the spawn will do? It will be entertaining!" Even as she spoke, she reached out and toppled the maimed Elfling from its feet. It mewled and whimpered as it tried to crawl away.

Shurzul smiled at Orbushnu. "That is something I long to see," she said mendaciously. "I will come as soon as I have taken care of a project of my own. Fear not, I will not tarry." *It is just as I hoped—no one saw me bear King Virulan back here. No one but I knows he is injured.*

"Do not," Orbushnu advised, turning back to her captive.

There was a rising sequence of Elfling screams. It ended in retching, then silence.

⚏

"My lord? My King?" Shurzul whispered. "It is I, Shurzul, your most loyal beloved. Let me in, I beg you."

She had paused only to collect Hazaniel from her chambers and to drug him with a sleeping cordial—what was to happen if her plans went as she wished was nothing for a Brightworld child's eyes and ears.

Especially *this* Brightworld child.

You have a great destiny before you, my little sweetmeat, she thought to the sleeping boy. *Be sure I shall make you ready for it.*

She was not foolish enough to make her petition at the main door into the Heart of Darkness, but Shurzul had become privy to many of

Virulan's less-important secrets when she had been given the freedom of his private chambers. There was an entrance from his rising chamber to his throne room, and it was at this door she had scratched.

At last, as she had hoped, the scent of Elfling flesh roused Virulan. The bolts holding the privy door closed slid back as if by an invisible hand, and the massive nielloed silver door slowly swung ajar. Shurzul entered the throne room.

The walls were ornamented with torches of Unfire; a magical substance that created darkness just as fire created light. To any senses but those of the Endarkened, this chamber—just as most of those in the World Without Sun—would have been unremittingly black, but no darkness could blind the Endarkened. Shurzul and her kind could see a thousand shades of darkness, hues that no other race had words for. She could plainly see Virulan huddled on the Throne of Night.

The chamber itself had been changed over the millennia, and its walls were now of smooth featureless basalt—the Unfire torches the only ornamentation—arcing upward to a domed vault inlaid with figures from the alphabet of spells crafted of the darkest and most fulgent metals to be found beneath the surface of the Bright World. The power of those spells was vast: a sorcery crafted by Virulan himself so long ago that only the Dark Guard had existed. Even to look upon it made Shurzul feel slightly uneasy, though she had no name for that sensation.

The Throne of Night was made of iron and obsidian and it was inlaid with black pearls that had never been touched by the sun. No one had made it: the Throne and its chamber simply *was*. As far as Shurzul knew, the Throne of Night had simply grown there.

The floor of the Throne Chamber was a single polished block of black topaz, so smooth and flawless that the ceiling and walls were reflected in it as if in a mirror.

For an instant Shurzul stood frozen with astonishment, for King Virulan was here, but he was not—*quite*—alone.

He Who Is was present. Not in any soft foolish Brightworlder way, to offer strength and aid and healing, but as the very breath of the Void. *He Who Is* was . . . *regarding* . . . King Virulan. And while *His* attention was fixed on *His* servant, *He* might choose to do anything.

Anything at all.

To anyone.

Shurzul took a long, deep, careful breath and then took a slow and supremely cautious step forward.

"I see you have brought me dinner," Virulan said, in his cracked and whistling whisper. He smiled for an instant, pleased, then his toothless mouth folded in upon itself with petulant anger.

Virulan crouched upon the Throne of Night, clutching the Crown of Pain to him as if it were some peculiar plaything. He did not wear it, Shurzul understood, because his wracked and withered body would no longer support its weight. The King of the Endarkened was a pitiable sight—or so he would have been, if Shurzul were capable of feeling pity. The magic of *He Who Is* had allowed Virulan to survive the touch of a Unicorn's horn, but . . . it had not allowed him to survive unscathed. He became a hunched and wizened thing—hairless, wrinkled, frail . . .

Vulnerable.

To be vulnerable within the World Without Sun was to die.

"I have brought you more than that, my King," Shurzul said. She kept her voice and her words sweet and soft, for the King's temper was uncertain in the aftermath of his wounding. "My King, I have brought you a promise."

Shurzul gazed downward for a moment, fascinated by the image of herself and Hazaniel hanging suspended in the black void, crowned and surrounded by the deathly symbols of the blackest magic. Then she hefted Hazaniel higher in her arms, displaying him—but she was not so foolish as to come within arm's reach of Virulan.

"This Elfling child—beautiful, virginal, stainless, and *pure,* shall grow to adulthood knowing no other world than ours," she said. "We shall tutor him carefully, and when he is grown, we will send him back to the Bright World. To hunt for *us.*"

"I have thousands of subjects who can do that *now,*" Virulan whined pettishly. He shifted, and Shurzul knew his next words would be a demand to which she did not wish to accede.

"But you do not have any who can hunt Unicorns," she said in a rush.

There! That had gotten his attention. "Stainless and pure," she repeated. "Utterly loyal to me—to *us,* my King! He will go forth into the Bright World to bring us Unicorns. Not one or two—*hundreds* of them, for they will trust him as he trusts me. You will bathe in the blood of Unicorns and be fully restored to the pinnacle of your power and glory." She looked down at the Elfling child hungrily. "And that day will come soon. These creatures grow very fast."

Shurzul watched as Virulan assessed her words, believed them, accepted them. But as he hovered upon the threshold of trust, he seemed to withdraw, regarding her offer with suspicion and distrust that soared far beyond the boundaries of normal Endarkened paranoia.

"I beg you to believe me, my Lord and King!" Shurzul cried. "It is true that any of us would willingly slay you and eat your flesh to rule over our kindred, to wear the Crown of Pain and sit upon the Throne of Night. But we all know that only the strongest can ever hope to do so—and you still rule, my great and terrible Beloved, for *you* are the strongest. Even now, King Virulan! Even now. Why would I tell you a lie that was easy to disprove, Master of all Endarkened, when the truth will save my pitiful life? You bask in the regard of *He Who Is.* I can only believe *He* means you to do great things—and woe betide any of us who interfere in—or even try to guess—*His* ineffable plan!"

Shurzul waited. Terror filled her with its exhilarating pain. Virulan smiled, and knuckled the drool from his chin with a shaking gnarled paw. When he spoke, it was in half-gargled hisses. Shurzul tried not to shudder. "Yesssssssssss, my delicate firebrand darling. *Yesssss* . . . I will bathe in the blood of Unicorns. Your plaything will bring them to me. The blood is the life—and their magic can harm no one once they have died. I shall regain my power, and together you and I shall ssstand before *He Who Is* when all the land has been turned once more to sssterile and unliving sssand. It will vanish like sssmoke on the water, and we will rejoice. Now come," he said. "It is time to ressst. And to plan for the future."

On the third day after the battle, the Elves went to clear the battlefield of their dead. Before the salvage parties went forth, Vieliessar, with Gollor Law Lord beside her, called them together to order that there would be no looting of the Otherfolk dead. The bodies were not to be desecrated, nor mutilated for trophies. They were to be left to as much dignity as was possible to the dead.

Some of the agreement was grudging, but it was agreement.

And it was also—now—law.

The High King's law.

⚶⚶

The fallen Elvenborn were carried deep into Nomaitemil to rest eternally in the embrace of the trees. There were not enough resources to burn them appropriately, nor had there been for some time. The dead battleponies were skinned and butchered. Their bounty was set aside for further use, and prayers of gratitude and thanksgiving said for their death-gift.

The bodies of the Otherfolk were left on the battlefield where they had fallen, but arranged in as seemly a fashion as possible. The Otherfolk bodies were grouped together on the long grass by size and appearance.

Such ordering made it far too easy to count the slain—both Elven and Otherfolk. The number of fatalities was stunning. If not for the Unicorns' arrival, the whole of both armies would have been slaughtered on the field.

Fortunately there were no Unicorns among them. Vieliessar didn't think she could have stood it. Yet there was one thing more to be discovered among the bodies. Something more disturbing than even a dead Unicorn could have been.

Chapter seventeen

RADE MOON IN THE TENTH YEAR OF THE HIGH KING'S REIGN: WISDOM, MOURNING, AND FATE

Mercy is a misfortune promised to the future. Forgive an enemy today and he will take vengeance upon you for it later.
—Elrinonion Swordmaster of Caerthalien, The Book of War

These are not Elves." Aradreleg Lightsister looked up at Thurion from where she knelt beside one of the bodies. The names of all the known dead had been given to the Loremasters and Story-singers Guilds as the bodies were taken into the forest, for there were no more castels, let alone Tablets of Memory, upon which to engrave the names of the dead.

Those no one could identify were gathered together near the forest verge and left to the Lightborn, for Knowing would cause even the dead to give up their name and Line. Years of spellcasting had enabled the Lightborn to refine Knowing so that was *all* they learned: otherwise, they would have had to relive the deaths of everyone they bespelled.

"They are not Elvenkind," Thurion agreed. "And yet they are."

He looked down at the body in front of Aradreleg. The dead face was painted. The only injury on the body was a shallow cut to the upper arm. Like so many on this battlefield, he had died of Endarkened magic, not honest wounds. The hair had been sectioned with each plait dyed a different color and only a few allowed to retain their natural black. The braids were cut to various lengths with no rhyme nor reason to the cutting, and had been wrapped in dyed leather, or braided with feathers, or ribbons, or scraps of cloth. There were no bright colors used, no matter how elaborate the decoration, only greens and greys, browns and yellows.

None of the unknowns wore armor of any kind, not even a stiffened leather corselet. Some wore nothing but several layers of vests and tunics over their bodies; the weavings as coarse as hunting nets. Some wore short trews of leather or fabric, painted as their faces and tunics were. Most wore combinations of skins and cloth which had been treated in much the same fashion that their hair had been: painted, ornamented, and artfully tattered.

No two were dressed alike, and none was dressed like Elvenkind. The effect was remarkably unsettling.

"Shall I cast the spell, Rella?" Thurion asked.

Aradreleg shook her head. "It's a simple thing." She held her hand over the body's chest for a moment, then looked up again, eyes wide. "His name was Orthal. He called his people Woodwose. He fought for the Otherfolk."

"We'd better do the rest, then. The High King will want to know."

"And what do we do with the . . . ?"

"For that purpose, these are Elves. We will have them carried into the forest," Thurion said.

⟨⟩

In these difficult times, an inevitable clash with the Otherfolk only sunturns away, their children still held hostage, the King's council met daily for candlemarks, and Vieliessar exerted herself to give audience to anyone who wished it, for that was one of the few promises she had made at the beginning that she could still keep.

Her "palace" was beginning to take shape. Vieliessar had searched carefully, first for a spring (she did not find one), and next for where a spring could be Called without breaching the harmony of the Flower Forest. Her palace grew outward from that, as the petals of a flower grew outward from its center. Sleeping areas and cooking areas and audience chambers had been defined—and if the palace existed mostly in the minds of those who abided here, that was nothing new.

The news of these "Woodwose" had reached every encampment across Nomaitemil. Everyone wanted to know more about them—and Vieliessar had no information to give.

Yet.

At dawn on the third day after the battle at Ceoprentrei, a sentry reported folk—*their* folk—coming up the pass road, accompanied by a few horses and some straggling livestock.

"Do you think there are spies among them?" Iardalaith asked.

"They have creatures who look just like us. Of *course* there are spies among them," Rithdeliel answered testily. "The question is, what are we to do about it?"

"Nothing," Vieliessar answered. She was weaving lengths of bandage on a hand loom: there was always some need for them, and it occupied her hands. That it annoyed the Princes and Lords Komen on her council was an added bonus. They felt nobles should not toil, only fight.

But Lightborn live lives of toil, and though I was born a prince, I am Lightborn first of all things.

"Nothing?" Annobeunna asked doubtfully. "I doubt they're coming to swear fealty to us." Annobeunna Keindostibaent was one of the few surviving War Princes of the Uradabhur, and her calm good sense was a great treasure to Vieliessar.

"Indeed," Vieliessar answered agreeably. "They are coming to find out all they can about us and steal anything they can. We have nothing to steal, and we want to know about them too—if they are those we are making alliance with."

"If they don't slay us all in our beds," Rithdeliel muttered. "May we at least, O King, know which ones they are?"

"If you do not by now know all our folk by sight, you are amazingly aloof, my lord," Vieliessar said. "But my Lightborn will mark them out."

⫚⫛

A taille of the Warhunt, two tailles of the Silver Swords, and the High King's personal guard waited—with the High King—to greet the returning folk. It was a little past midday, and the returning Elves had been seen on the Dragon's Gate road at dawn, along with a heartening number of horses, dogs, goats, chickens, sheep . . .

And spies.

The sheep and goats arrived in the company of irascible herding dogs; the horses wandered back to the meadow in threes and fives, settling to graze as if nothing had happened, and the chickens hopped from the backs of goats and sheep to find perches in the trees, complaining loudly.

The most important thing Vieliessar's people must now do was to discover all that these "Woodwose" had to tell them about the Otherfolk Empire and its plans. That meant convincing them that their masquerade was successful.

No matter what Vieliessar had said to Rithdeliel Warlord in council, it was not entirely true that every one of her folk knew every other by sight. The komen knew each other across Houses and Lines, of course, and had from Before, but the layer of nobility was thin: her surviving folk were mostly Crafters and Landbond, who looked first to their family, then to their extended family, and then to their guilds. They would willingly believe the Woodwose were folk they did not know.

The fewer souls you knew to love, the fewer you would have to mourn.

The first group of captives were from the Arzhana, and known to Shanilya Thadan-Arzhana. Prince Shanilya greeted two of her horsegrooms, Dianora and Arathiel, with joy, and they were quick to step aside from the rest to give their story. Its particulars made Vieliessar sharply remember the days of the Hundred Houses, for there was talk of ransoms set (none), disparagement (none), forced oath-taking (none). The horsegrooms said they had been given wholesome food and adequate shelter, and had been guarded by the Unicorns for the entire term of their captivity. Around noon of the previous sunturn, they had been told they and their chattels were to be sent back to their families at sunrise, providing they did not now wish to stay behind. Before the sun had risen, other Beastlings—*Otherfolk*—began rounding up the Elven livestock that had fled through the pass and sending it up the road. At dawn, the Unicorns began choosing parties from the captives based on some mysterious criterion, and sent each group toward the road at halfmark intervals.

Some folk had hurried onward to tend to their beasts, or to return to Ceoprentrei as quickly as possible. Others had lingered to walk with those they knew. Between beast and Elf, the road to the Dragon's Gate was filled to fullness.

"What about the children?" Githachi of the Silver Swords asked. Vieliessar knew Githachi felt the absence of the Prince-Heir and his older sister as a personal failure. It was a beacon in the Silver Sword's thoughts, constant as a heartbeat.

"We saw no children, Lady," Arathiel answered firmly. "There was no one below twelve turns among us." More details would have to wait, as a party of sheep harried onward by exasperated herd dogs filled the pass; the noise made conversation impossible.

Goats, nimble and disgruntled. More sheep, ridden by chickens complaining loudly, and attended by dogs. A group of former captives, followed by a blessed *khom* of battleponies, heads high and eyes rolling. Pigs, always. Ducks. Geese. More chickens. More Elves. A pack of hunting dogs, busily seeking their masters.

Vieliessar watched it all, sitting her mount as silent and immobile as a statue. Though she feigned indifference, her whole concentration was on an elaborate webwork of spells she had spent most of the night constructing, a working that would allow her to shut out the familiar minds of her komen and advisors, and concentrate on hearing the thoughts of the returning folk. Some of Thadan's folk were telling the truth whole and entire—but others were not. Vieliessar would need more information there before she acted.

An unexpected pang of deep grief overwhelmed her. *Gunedwaen!* Her Swordmaster should have been here. He could have advised her. He could have taken up the tedious and vital work of intelligence gathering. She had never appointed a new Swordmaster after Gunedwaen's death: there had seemed no need, since all her people did was run away and spying on their enemy was impossible.

And now, when they needed the information a seasoned Swordmaster could provide more than they'd ever needed it before . . . she had no one to call on.

The Woodwose infiltrators Vieliessar had expected were among the second half of the captives. That was a masterstroke, as anyone watching for enemy spies should be careless and inattentive after so long. There weren't many, but Vieliessar took from their thoughts the fact that more Woodwose would also be entering Ceoprentrei by other routes than the Dragon's Gate.

Vieliessar let them all pass without comment. She Marked them, as she had told Rithdeliel she would, but it was a mark only Lightborn could see.

What they did—and what they did not do—would be informative.

⧏⧐

The Arzhana craves speech of the High King."

Shanilya Thadan-Arzhana stood at the edge of the clearing that had become the High King's throne room.

The Elves, from long practice, had quickly re-created their homes in this new Flower Forest. Vieliessar's Presence Chamber had neither walls nor doors nor even roof, but there were many loaf-shaped white stones laid upon the grass in a seemingly random pattern. Those stones delineated the boundary areas of various spells. Willingly or otherwise, all who sought audience of the High King were aware of the uses of Magery and spellcraft.

"Enter and be welcome," Vieliessar answered. There was no throne, of course, nor even a room, but there was a tea-brazier on a tray of stones, and a tea service set upon a leaf-basket Transmuted to shin'zu-ruf. She set aside the work of her hands—repairing the leather straps of a bridle—and set the coals beneath the tea-brazier alight. Even before the metal had time to warm, she filled the kettle from a waiting pitcher.

The burden of Amretheon's *geasa* had never borne down upon Vieliessar so heavily. It pushed her toward a true alliance with the Otherfolk—not the false alliance Rithdeliel had proposed. Vieliessar had as little choice in the matter as an arrow had to fly from the bow. She only hoped this was not the matter Shanilya had come to discuss.

"Will you sit and drink with me?" she asked, as Shanilya seated herself opposite her.

"I have always wondered what would happen if I said 'no' to such an invitation," Shanilya answered, and Vieliessar smiled.

"That is a tale for Loremasters and Storysingers, but it must indeed have happened. Somewhere," she answered.

"So it must," Shanilya agreed.

Vieliessar re-set her spells: Hush to make their voices inaudible, Warning to keep others from entering. Better those spells than Silence and Shield, uncompromising and easily seen. Subtlety, Vieliessar had found, was a general so able that he claimed victory without taking the field.

When the tea had steeped, and been poured, tasted, and praised, Shanilya was ready to speak of the reason she was here.

"For nearly ten turns of the Great Wheel we have been led through perils and dangers, always westward toward the greater Flower Forests that remain," Shanilya said in neutral tones. "And now we have reached the gateway to the West."

"We have," Vieliessar agreed. "And here we have found safety beyond hope. Nomaitemil is vast as Arevethmonion, and will serve us admirably."

"So it shall," Shanilya agreed. "And that it is available is a gift unlooked-for. Just as the arrival of the Beastlings is another sort of gift."

"Is it? I would say it is also a gift unlooked-for," Vieliessar answered smoothly. She continued with the courtly fencing automatically, but suddenly she could feel the touch of another's mind—not within this counterfeit presence chamber, but in the sheltering trees above.

"—that's her is it or one of them doesn't look like much rune hates her but he'll die if she does wanted us to see but there's nothing here to see—"

It was one of the Woodwose spies who had come with their repatriated captives. Andhel. Close to Lord Runacarendalur. His successor-to-be. The information Andhel contained sifted down into Vieliessar's mind like spice through hot wine, and Shanilya's words seemed almost an intrusion.

"Of information, surely," Shanilya said. "And the knowledge that any hope of saving the Western Shore is lost. It is a sad truth, but it occurs to me that it, nor the Flower Forests, had been your sole reason for going into the West."

I have always known this day would come. The reasons Vieliessar had given her folk for their westward course had always been as thin as new ice. That no one had questioned them was a combination of fear of the Endarkened and a belief—bordering upon worship—of Vieliessar High King, Liberator and Savior of the Downtrodden.

"It is true that I hoped for many things of the West," Vieliessar answered carefully. "The Sanctuary of the Star yet stands. I would warn it."

"Or claim it?" Shanilya asked, but once again Vieliessar's attention was summoned away by the thoughts of Caerthalien's spy.

"—going to smash it maybe winter big village send them to her have to feed them witches kill tear it down—"

"Perhaps another day—soon—would be more advisable?" Shanilya's voice dripped poisoned honey as she noted Vieliessar's inattention.

"A moment, my lord, if I may." Vieliessar raised her hand and Cast one of the layered spells the Lightborn had concocted in their long months of hiding: instances of Silence and Lesser Overshadow and Compulsion, all woven together, all Cast at various strengths.

There was a scrambling rustle in the branches as someone scurried along them, then the Woodwose Andhel, bespelled, fell the last small distance to huddle silently at Vieliessar's feet.

The officers of the court—and the High King's guards—rushed through Warning, ignoring its sting. Rithdeliel drew his sword, pointing it at Vieliessar's captive. Helecanth had also drawn her blade and stood warily before Shanilya, all her attention upon this potential traitor.

"Really, Lord Vieliessar, you don't have to go to such lengths to entertain me," Shanilya drawled, as if there were no sword at her throat. "The Arzhana was a small place, and poor. We did not look to gorge ourselves on great wonders."

"Peace!" Vieliessar cried. "Here is only a spy—we knew Caerthalien would send them. The child is harmless."

The flick of her fingers as Vieliessar disenchanted Andhel was mostly for show. Even in the Sanctuary of the Star the various gestures had been mnemonics, not spell components. Spells could not be written down, nor could the knowing of them be spoken into the ear. The shapes of the

Greater Spells could only be passed mind to mind, so that any Lightborn who wove and crafted a new spell must come to the Sanctuary to pass it to as many other Lightborn as possible.

Andhel stood before her, unshackled, eyes glittering with terror and hate. Her mouth worked as she decided what to say.

"I'll take care of this." Rithdeliel's tone held a narrow line between contempt and boredom. He took a step toward Andhel.

"No!" Vieliessar said strongly. "Let her be."

"Only a fool and a weakling leaves an enemy alive behind them," Andhel spat. "I will never—"

With another gesture, Vieliessar cut off Andhel's speech. "Leave us," she told Rithdeliel. "The Prince of the Arzhana has not completed her business with me. You will find it far easier to spy on me from here," she said to Andhel in the most patronizing tones she could summon.

"What *is* that thing?" Shanilya asked. "Not one of ours, surely?"

"They call themselves Woodwose, and live among the Otherfolk," Vieliessar replied. "Otherfolk take up discarded Elven infants, and raise them, so I have heard. Just as well, for when we are allied with the Otherfolk, we shall make up our numbers with them."

"If they will fight for you as savagely as our Landbonds did, then this is the second treasure of the West," Shanilya agreed neutrally. "But we were speaking of the Sanctuary of the Star."

"*—fool and monster that bed of witchlords and its king all dead walls slain blood fire sanctuary no more rune was to take it down why why how—*"

"We were," Vieliessar agreed calmly, though her heart sank at the thoughts shouted out by Andhel's mind. "My purpose was twofold: to gain Arevethmonion's shelter, and to claim the Sanctuary of the Star, for I felt it must hold the key to defeating the Endarkened."

There came a wordless howl of mixed derision and terror from Andhel's mind that nearly made Vieliessar flinch. *But the Great Library is underground, guarded by many potent and eternal wards. Surely it has not been destroyed. Please, Pelashia Flower Queen, let it still survive!*

"One tends to forget that you were raised in the Sanctuary of the

Star," Shanilya murmured. "You will have had time to learn the secrets we may only guess at."

"To learn that its vast library holds more learning than any person can discover in a lifetime," Vieliessar said.

"And dissembled . . . ?" Shanilya probed.

"You will be aware that most of my princes are not great scholars," Vieliessar said drily. "Did I tell them we went westward in search of scrolls, I dare say we would still be in Celenthodiel arguing over the Unicorn Throne."

"Ah," Shanilya said, bowing her head in acknowledgment. "Then the Arzhana is satisfied, Vieliessar High King."

Vieliessar inclined her head in return as Shanilya Arzhana rose to her feet.

⊰⧓⊱

I will never serve you!" Andhel burst out, the moment Vieliessar released her from Silence. "I will die first!"

"How very useful to me, considering I know perfectly well you will never harm me," Vieliessar said.

Andhel glared, fingering her knife, clearly at a loss for words either thought or spoken.

"Go where you will, question who you will, discover what you choose. Then return to Runacarendalur Caerthalien and see what he makes of your news."

"We don't call him that," Andhel said with grudging politeness. "We call him Rune Houseborn. And why should I believe you about letting me go?"

"You have seen the enemy we flee and you ask that?" Vieliessar answered, and Andhel was silent.

⊰⧓⊱

One sennight after the battle of Ceoprentrei, King Leutric's *alfal-jodthi* Warlord returned to the valley of Ceoprentrei with a hand-picked meisne and King Leutric's heir to await the embassy from the

High King of Elvenkind. Celebremen had told him that she'd made no specifications about who Vieliessar could bring to this meeting: the High King could show up with anything from a pet turtle to her entire army and not violate the terms of the parley truce, which did not improve Runacar's temper.

It was nearly Rade Moon, but here in the high mountains, the skies were achingly blue, the air was as sweet and crisp as the apples falling from the trees in every abandoned orchard in the Western Reach, the grass in the fields and meadows was as golden as firelight, and every breath Runacar took reminded him that merely to be alive was a wonder and a glory. It was hard to be in a foul temper on such a day. Runacar congratulated himself on his success.

To attend this parley, the King-Emperor's Battlemaster wore full battle armor and stood beside his palfrey, a grey gelding he'd named Folwin. He and Folwin were both caparisoned and emblazoned in the colors and insignia of a House that had never existed: a Vilya, proper, surmounted by a moon, argent, footed by a golden star and a single leaf—jaun and vert respectively—all on a cobalt field. There was no doubt the High King would see it instantly. What she would make of it, Runacar neither knew nor cared. There were more important things he should be doing than attending this ridiculous parley.

Runacar had thought he would be spending the sennight following the end of the not-exactly-battle at Ceoprentrei convincing his army to retreat from the foot of the Dragon's Gate. Instead he'd been arranging routes for their departure so that the warning about the Endarkened could be carried to the whole of the Western Reach. Now that the Endarkened had shown themselves, most of his people had but one thought: to get back to their families.

Leaf and Star, keep Rithdeliel Warlord from guessing most of my army has just gone home or he'll have a sortie party riding for our base camp by dawn.

At least a few members of his force remained—what Runacar thought of as his "core" commanders. He was just as glad of their presence, for this parley did not guarantee either peace or safety. If the Endarkened did not attack again immediately, the High King might decide to launch another assault on the Otherfolk rather than honor a truce made with "beasts."

If she could manage it. By the middle of Rade, snow would begin to fall in the Mystrals, and three moonturns after that the whole Western Reach would lie under a blanket of snow. Nobody fought in winter— except Elves driven crazy by prophecies, and the idiots who decided to chase them.

In a Harvest twelve Wheelturns ago the Hundred Houses lost its collective mind and decided to follow Vieliessar across the Mystrals. Runacar wished he could stop comparing today to the False Parley on the banks of the River Toharthay that had begun that disastrous chase, but its lesson remained achingly fresh in his heart: The best Warlords of the Hundred Houses had not been able to win against her because they could not predict her. And Runacar feared he might fall into the same trap.

He didn't even know what they were going to parley about, since Celebremen's demands—and therefore those he would present today— were for full partnership and agency and the High King could not possibly be considering treating the Otherfolk like people.

And yet.

Celebremen had chosen where Runacar and the others would wait to receive the High King's Parley Court; about two bowshots from the verge of the Flower Forest, and—therefore—directly in the middle of the battlefield.

What could have been a ghastly denigration of his party by forcing them to wait upon a battlefield strewn with rotting corpses . . .

. . . was not. In fact, the battlefield was sweet as a meadow and disturbingly empty. The Elves had removed their own dead of course—and taken away their slain horses for reasons Runacar could not imagine— but they must have burned their dead deep in the forest. The Woodwose dead were gone as well (hopefully mistaken for Elves), but that left hundreds upon hundreds of Bearwards and Brownies, Centaurs and Minotaurs, Fairies and Sprites and Fauns and more.

It was as if the Elves had decided to do their foes honor, something Runacar thought utterly impossible even as he stared at the proof.

Each body had been moved to the eastern edge of the narrow valley and laid out upon the grass with great care. Even the mutilated Gryphons and Hippogriffs were arranged in as seemly a fashion as possible, and some attempt had been made to match up severed wings to bodies. It was another fact to add to his list of facts both unwelcome and undeniable.

"I don't like this," Runacar said quietly.

"You wouldn't like it no matter what they'd done," Melisha pointed out. Audalo and the rest of the party were far enough away that the Unicorn was not discomfited; when the High King arrived, Melisha would depart and the others would advance.

"I wouldn't like it if they'd skinned every one of our dead—but I'd understand it," he answered. *This makes no sense. She cannot have brought her Lords Komen to agree to an alliance. She can't.*

No. She can. She can do anything. You saw that at Oronviel.

That was one of many reasons Runacar had favored the immediate release of all the hostages.

He'd lost: the children were to remain behind. The Unicorns guarded them, the Woodwose spoiled them, and the Wulvers, Palughs, and the Fauns had decided the children had been procured solely for their entertainment, a notion with which the children wholeheartedly agreed.

He'd even tried to enlist little Princess Adalieriel to advocate for the children's release. It hadn't worked, but it had led him to a surprising number of conversations with her. No matter who she had been born to, little Liri reminded him very much of her "official" mother, Vieliessar. She was grateful to have her brother and she would prefer to be with the High King her mother—but not if it was what Runacar wanted. Princess Liri was unshakable in her insistence that Runacar was a mere bandit chieftain, but despite that, she was happy to talk with him about nearly anything, and as they spoke together, a terrifying narrative emerged.

At around the time Runacar had first been captured by Leutric's scouting party, Vieliessar had begun her sweeping-up of the Uradabhur, which had descended into utter chaos because the Winter War had removed most of its War Princes. By the time Runacar became a courtier at the court of King-Emperor Leutric, she had consolidated her people

and begun forging them into the folk of one domain: the High King–
domain.

(Liri didn't mention the Grand Windsward. It was as if she didn't
know it had existed.)

And at the time in the West when Runacar began his tenure as
Leutric's Battlemaster, the day of celebration that would cap the long
moonturns of work—the Enthroning of Vieliessar Farcarinon as High
King—became instead the beginning of the Endarkened's Red Harvest.

Half of the High King's people died that day.

Liri hadn't even been born when these things happened, so she could
not tell him of them, but Runacar knew his people. Once the survivors of
the first Endarkened slaughter had gathered together and felt themselves
at least temporarily safe, Vieliessar would have been forced to fight her
wars for the Unicorn Throne all over again. Every surviving War Prince
would have been certain they deserved the throne instead of her.

Clearly Vieliessar had won the kingship yet again, and then her
people began the long, bloody, agonizing trek to the West. Adalieriel
didn't know why they'd come—it was as if the Storysingers and Loremasters among Vieliessar's people had all taken a vow of silence—but
the rest of what Liri had to tell was horrifying enough: a people harried from every refuge by monstrous enemies who could not be bargained with, could not be reasoned with, which had no understandable
goals . . .

And which never *ever* stopped coming.

"You're quiet today, Rune. No last-minute homilies so we don't fall at
her feet and worship her?" Tanet asked, rising up out of the high grass.
The Woodwose warrior was dressed in his usual tatters, camouflage,
and paint, and carrying a quiver full of the deadly javelins the Woodwose preferred. He was alone. Andhel had disappeared a couple of days
after the battle, and Runacar had a strong suspicion he knew where
she'd gone.

"Worship her if you like," Runacar said. "Apparently the Hundred
Houses do." The bitterness in his words surprised him.

"Was it magic then?" Tanet asked curiously. "To make them love her?
Everyone says she's a powerful witchborn."

"*Everyone,*'" Runacar said in his most blighting tones, "knows less about her than I do."

Tanet snickered, and after a few more moments spent intently watching the forest edge, he wandered back to the others, twirling one of his javelins across his fingers.

If anybody had just told me what was going on in the first place— If the so-called High King had ever bothered to explain why she wanted the Unicorn Throne—

"Look. Here she comes," Melisha said suddenly. "Remember to play nice." She rubbed her head against his arm—a quick caress—and sprang away.

A few moments later, Audalo moved up to where Runacar and Folwin stood. Further back, the Bearward Bearsarks were on his tuathal side, the Centaur war-band to the deosil, and the observers anywhere they chose to be. By the time everyone had settled into place, Runacar could see the flicker of movement through the forest. Then the first of the Elven party stepped out into the open.

Vieliessar. She wore robes of Lightborn cut, but white, and an elven-silver coronet of Vilya blossoms. Her hair was still cropped short, and she was afoot and unarmed. When she reached the open meadow, the sun turned her robes to a blinding column of white flame. She paced forward in lockstep, her face serene and distant.

Her Warlord rode at her tuathal hand—the only other person in all of Jer-a-kalaliel who had a suit of armor, and a destrier, apparently. His armor was enameled in the scarlet red of Oronviel over a golden pattern of waves. *That's Rithdeliel in the scarlet armor. So he's still alive? He must have the luck of the dead.*

On the High King's deosil side—the place of lesser honor—walked a formally robed Lightborn carrying a greenneedle branch. For an instant Runacar did not recognize him as such: his hair was long, caught back at the nape of his neck to fall freely and unbraided down his back. *The Lightbrother must be Thurion. At least she keeps her favorites safe; that's worth knowing.*

Behind him came the commander of Vieliessar's personal guard.

Like Rithdeliel, she wore full formal armor. Hers was Lightborn green

over a silver relief of stars, with a surcoat bearing the High King's device with the stylized crest indicating the wearer was head of the King's
guard, and the three gold stars on a field vert of Caerthalien, which must
(Runacar decided) be meant as the bearer's personal device. She was
mounted on one of the small horses most of the army had ridden, and
rode to the side of the others so that the High King's banner could be
easily seen: the device was a silver Unicorn on a field of Lightborn green,
with pennons to show that the War Prince (High King) was on the field
in person and that this was a conditional truce during wartime.

And the banner carrier is . . .

Helecanth.

She'd been the commander of Runacar's personal guard from the day
he'd received his first sword from his father's hands. He felt a wild uprush
of rage—that this pretender, this *mountebank,* should bring Helecanth
with her as witness to Runacarendalur Caerthalien's disgrace—

He forced himself to take slow even breaths. Vieliessar's Swordmaster had been Gunedwaen of Farcarinon. Undoubtedly Gunedwaen
had taught Vieliessar every trick he knew, and she was using them all.
Runacar had set Helecanth into the High King's hands himself. He
should be glad she had found a place of high honor with her new master.

But he would miss his friend.

Close behind the vanguard came the High King's armed escort. Their
mounts moved at a slow ceremonial pace, halting after each step. It was
familiar, but Runacar was momentarily puzzled. The pace-step was
taught to destriers, not palfreys, and twice not to these peculiar equines.

And then the riders, moving as one, drew the double swords they
wore and began brandishing and clashing them. The sound was an ancient wild sword-song calling komen to the battlefield. It woke long-
sleeping demons in Runacar's blood, demons he'd thought were safely
dead. He turned toward his palfrey. He would mount up, ride to Vieliessar's side, to his *Bondmate,* and . . .

Audalo put a gentle hand on his arm. "We will wait here, Rune. As
we all agreed." The silver cap-and-ball that replaced the horn Audalo
lost at Daroldan gleamed in the harsh alpine sunlight.

Runacar nodded shakily, patting Folwin on the withers. The old palfrey nuzzled at him hopefully, and Runacar stroked his nose, scratching him beneath the shanfron, which every destrier he'd ever ridden insisted itched. The clashing of swords went on, as inexorable as wardrums. Its rhythm—timed to match the horses' slow pace—implied that some relentless force approached, its will adamantine. Runacar had never wanted to flee a battlefield so much in his entire life.

When the last of the Silver Swords reached the open meadow, they began to fling their swords into the air, spinning them, catching them as they fell, all without missing a beat in the slow maddening rhythm.

"Why do they do that?" Pelere asked, trotting up to Runacar. The only emotion in her voice was a kind of dumbfounded puzzlement, as if she'd been told that trees were made of bread and that from now on the sun would rise in the west.

"It's how the *alfaljodthi* go to war," Runacar answered. An aching grief filled his chest. *I do not want that life back. I have renounced it. I have.*

"It's a good thing they only fight with other Elvenkind, then, isn't it?" Pelere said. "Andhel could put a dozen javelins into every one of them while they were still tossing their swords around."

Runacar just shook his head. He had no words that could explain the Elven war-making to Pelere, its glory and its horror. And its terrible efficiency.

Vieliessar reached his banner and stopped. The Silver Swords caught their swords one last time, resheathed them, and became utterly still. Rithdeliel, Thurion, and Helecanth dismounted. As the other two took up positions beside their horses, Helecanth walked forward to drive the stave of their own banner deep into the soil beside Runacar's and returned to her place. Thurion came forward, placed his greenneedle bough on the ground in front of both banner poles, and stepped back.

Before anyone else moved, Andhel stepped out of the Flower Forest to the left of the column of Silver Swords, and came trotting toward Runacar across the space between the two parties. Her hair was uniformly black, her skin unpainted. She was dressed in the fashion of Vieliessar's people: deerskin vest, woven tunic and leggings, sturdy horsehide boots, and a short cape of sheepskins about her shoulders. She carried an Elven bow, and a quiver of matching arrows was slung at her hip.

Oh, by all and any gods there are: she has been spying on them—and Vieliessar knows it.

"You missed the pretty part," Pelere told her.

Andhel snorted. "I've watched them practicing for almost a sennight," she said dismissively. "Rune, can we—?"

"Quiet," Runacar said. Elrinonion Swordmaster had always told him *"When disaster strikes, smile. And pretend it was your plan all along."*

Vieliessar came forward to stand beside the banners.

❖

She had done so many hard things in her life—hard, dishonorable, treacherous. She'd thought she was immune to shame, to fear, to grief. She had not known how hard this one small thing would be.

She did not know what was to come, save that there would be an alliance of lies made here today. Because Amretheon Aradruiniel had willed a true alliance in some long-lost eon. Because she was Vieliessar, High King, Lightborn, Child of the Prophecy. Amretheon's weapon. Amretheon's heir.

She remembered herself, the child of ten whose greatest ambition was to become a komen of Runacarendalur's meisne. She remembered the girl of twelve who had dreamed only of revenge upon House Caerthalien—and upon its Heir-Prince. She remembered the woman newly come into a Lightborn's power, who found that her dreams of revenge had somehow vanished when she wasn't paying attention.

She remembered the yoke of knowledge upon her shoulders, the yoke of prophecy shackling her to a future she did not want.

Once upon a time, Runacarendalur of Caerthalien Erased had been her true mirror. What had each of them become?

❖

Well met, Prince Runacarendalur Caerthalien, War Prince of Caerthalien, Emissary of the Otherfolk," Vieliessar said formally.

Runacar stared at her, unable to remember the ritual reply. In his heart, he'd never actually expected to *see* Vieliessar again, and nothing had prepared him for the reality of her: as bright and dangerous as a swordblade. *Say something, you cloudwit! We are operating under formal rules—if I offend her honor she'll have Helecanth cut off my head, and the Hunt will take us all.*

Desperately, he forced out the proper words. "Well met, Vieliessar Farcarinon, High King of Elvenkind. I am Runacar Houseborn, Battlemaster to King-Emperor Leutric, King of the Minotaurs, Emperor of all the Folk, who holds the fealty of the Folk of Land and Air, the kind regard of the Folk of the Sea, and the respect of the Brightfolk. You have come under a parley truce to speak of alliance, which the Folk have offered you. Will you speak with me?"

He saw her eyes flick to Audalo, then to Pelere, but her face was unreadable. "Ought I not speak with your master? Or with Celebremen?"

She has made up her mind to the alliance, Runacar thought in stunned amazement. He could think of no other reason for Vieliessar to even acknowledge the presence of the Otherfolk, let alone ask to speak to any of them.

"I do not know your name. Or those of the others with your Battlemaster," Vieliessar said to Audalo. "Will you share them with me?" Runacar gave her credit for actually addressing the Minotaur, rather than forcing Runacar to continue to act as some sort of wildly unnecessary translator. This was the dance of protocol Runacar had done his whole life. It was only the context that made it surreal.

"I am Audalo, called the Silverhorn, victor in battles, son of Hresa the great cow who has borne a thousand calves, nephew of Leutric the great bull who has sired a thousand times a thousand offspring, Heir to the House of a Thousand Doors, Heir to the Empire of the Folk, General of the armies of the Folk, Master of Runacar Battlemaster, and Prince-Heir to Leutric King-Emperor."

"I greet you, General Audalo, Heir to the House of a Thousand Doors, Heir to the Empire of the Folk, General of the armies of the Folk, Master of Runacar Battlemaster, Prince-Heir to Leutric King-Emperor, and offer you condolences on the possession of your Battlemaster," Vieliessar said, bowing as if to an equal.

Condolences? Runacar caught Vieliessar's gaze and raised an eye-brow. *I have the Western Shore and you don't.*

She looked away, her mouth quirked in amusement only he was meant to see. "There are—you will forgive my noticing this, Lord General—two persons here who have not been named," Vieliessar continued.

Audalo glanced toward Runacar expectantly. Runacar took a half-step forward.

"May I present to the notice of the High King the apprentices of General the Prince-Heir Audalo's Battlemaster, called Runacar Houseborn, who are Pelere the Centauress and Andhel the Woodwose? You will surely find them the equal of your own Warlord, should he chance to meet them on the field."

Pelere nodded graciously. Andhel snickered.

"You style yourself grandly, Leutric's Battlemaster," Vieliessar said.

"I had been given to understand that the position of High King was taken," Runacar answered drily.

"So it was," Vieliessar agreed. She smiled suddenly—a genuine smile, unforced and radiant—and Runacar felt its impact as if it were a blow given upon the battlefield. Up until this moment he had hoped there was some escape from this, some way to, well, *ignore* the Bond.

Vieliessar shook her head slightly, clearly answering his thoughts. A small rueful smile lingered on her lips. *"No. No, there isn't. We are Bound until the stars grow cold, you and I. And if I must, I will slay us both so that my people and yours may live."*

He heard those words as clearly as if she'd spoken them in his ear. She was his Bondmate—however little either of them desired that—and the Bond cut both ways. But before Runacar could react, Vieliessar turned toward Andhel. "You will be an ill-mannered losel to the end of your days, Woodwose brat, but I hope you now believe you did not need to come among us by treachery. Here and now, I speak as High King, and the High King says to Cadet-Warlord Andhel, I acknowledge you and your folk as kin, until the last sword is broken and the last star burns cold. You are children of the children left in the woods to die be-cause of the greed of the War Princes and the Lords Komen. That day is done."

She cannot possibly be trying to recruit the Woodwose to her cause in the middle of a parley truce!

. . . Can she?

Andhel glanced to Runacar for permission to speak and he nodded. If they were setting the protocols of the parley truce aflame and dancing in the embers, so be it.

"So that day is done, Houseborn King?" Andhel said. "And yet I see great lords follow you."

"All beneath my rule are subject to my law," Vieliessar answered, unfazed. "There is one law for great and small among all my people, and a guild of Lawspeakers to enforce it. We would welcome you—and all the Woodwose—should you choose to live among your kindred once more."

Andhel opened her mouth to reply once more. Runacar flicked his fingers at her. She sighed, and stood silent.

"We have not come here to discuss what you will do with people who are not your property," Audalo said firmly. "We have made an offer of alliance and given its terms. You have had a sennight to consider it, as your own preceptor of battles, who is Arilcarion War-Maker, has set forth in his works. Do you accept?"

"And I say again: Where is Celebremen? It was she who first tendered this . . . offer," Vieliessar answered obliquely. Runacar saw how she held herself still, keeping herself from looking for the Unicorn. He felt a pang of sympathy for her.

"Here."

Celebremen and Melisha stepped out of the tall scrub at the eastern side of the valley, far enough away that they could tolerate the decided impurity of both delegations. *"Not today, darling boy. You stink of purity."* For an instant of memory, Runacar saw the Endarkened female bare her fangs at him in a hideous parody of seduction. He shoved the thought away.

The two Unicorns' fur flamed white in the sunlight, and their horns flared with all the colors of the rainbow. Runacar thought he could smell their faint spice-cinnamon scent, and wasn't sure whether he was imagining it. Each Unicorn bore upon her back a rider whose smallness gave the illusion that the Unicorns were the size of horses, and which made the Palugh also on Melisha's back seem to be the size of a leopard. The two children were dressed as Woodwose children would have been dressed in some unlikely season, in bright-colored woven tunics, vests, and trews, sheepskin-lined boots, knitted caps, and long quilted vests oversewn with ribbons.

Calanoriel and Adalieriel. The High King's heirs.

The children sat quietly, waiting, but the Palugh jumped down from Melisha's back and trotted in the direction of the gathering, tail carried high.

"Can we go now?" Calanor meant to be quiet, but his whisper could easily be heard by everyone.

"No!" his sister answered, louder. "We're hostages! Mama has to ransom us!"

Runacar schooled his face to blankness, but when he looked back toward Vieliessar and her entourage, he realized he hadn't needed to bother. Every single one of them—even the Silver Swords—was staring at the Unicorns, mesmerized. It took time to become accustomed to the sheer beauty of Unicorns. It would be the perfect opportunity to ambush them—the High King was not even armed.

Then suddenly Vieliessar turned away from the Unicorns. Her gaze locked with his. In that moment Runacar felt on the verge of some momentous revelation.

Pelere picked up her left forehoof and delicately set it atop Runacar's boot. Then she leaned her weight on it.

"Stop that," Runacar hissed in what he hoped was a better undertone than Calanoriel had managed.

"Stop looking at her like she's a Festival banquet," Pelere hissed back.

"Upon the swearing of our alliance, all of the children of your people will be returned to you," Audalo said firmly. "As will any other persons of your meisne who are now under our care and protection."

"Since they are here, shall we begin with my children?" Vieliessar answered instantly. "I would ransom them before we speak of an alliance."

"And what ransom will you offer for them?" Runacar asked, when it was clear Audalo was still struggling to find a proper response. The idea of hostages and ransoms—something the Elves considered perfectly normal—was something Runacar had attempted to explain to the Otherfolk with no particular success.

Vieliessar pretended to consider the matter, though Runacar knew she would have planned out an entire series of possible ransoms to offer. Or her Swordmaster would have. Where *was* Gunedwaen anyway? Dead? Then who had replaced him?

"I shall offer your people the freedom of this, the battlefield, that you may claim your dead and provide to them what rites you choose. I have ordered that the bodies of the slain be held sacrosanct: if any of them has been despoiled by so much as a wing-feather, tell me, and I will punish the vandal," Vieliessar said.

"For how long and how far do you offer this freedom?" Runacar answered, his words coming now with practiced ease.

"The High King offers the—the *Otherfolk* the freedom of the battlefield for a fortnight, as the Codes of War specify," Thurion said, stumbling a little over the unfamiliar term (though the fact that he used it was another insight into the High King's mind). "They may go freely about the field, but the Flower Forest remains ours. Entry into it will be considered to be warhunting, an act of aggression."

Audalo looked at Runacar, and Runacar nodded fractionally. Freedom of the battlefield would make it much easier for the Woodwose to enter the forest. They might be Vieliessar's people by decree, but they'd been Runacar's first and their own before all.

"And when is this 'freedom' to begin?" Audalo asked dutifully. Runacar had reminded him over and over: specify everything. If something was not mentioned in an agreement, it was not part of the agreement. Many wars within the Hundred Houses had been launched through such loopholes.

"Tomorrow. At dawn. And for the freedom of the battlefield for any of your people who choose to avail themselves of it, you will return to me, now, my son and daughter—unharmed in any way."

"If they'll go," Runacar muttered under his breath.

"So agreed," Audalo answered, on familiar ground at last. "And should you swear falsely to any agreement with my folk, do not think the Flower Forest will protect you: that which you call Nomaitemil is Void, and I shall burn it down over you and the rest of the Children of Stars if you are playing games."

"That makes good hearing," Vieliessar answered pleasantly. "For it means I will not hesitate to turn it to ash as I turn the West and all your folk into something even the Endarkened would be sickened by. If we should come once more to be at war, of course."

"I shall send for the hostages at once," Audalo said, ignoring the rest.

He turned toward the Unicorns, but apparently their charges already realized they had been ransomed, for Adalieriel had slipped from Melisha's back to hug her fiercely. Calanoriel had dismounted as well, but his attempt to hug Celebremen was complicated by a pair of young Wulvers who were bouncing up at him from the grass and (to all appearances) trying to knock him over.

Runacar had been a treaty-hostage several times before he was old enough to become a Sword Page; he knew both children understood they should return to Vieliessar in a calm and formal manner. But the Wulvers circled them, shouting, *"Run! Let's run!"* and Celebremen cantered past them toward the Dragon's Gate. The combination was too much to resist. In moments both children came running toward Vieliessar at top speed.

Runacar winced inwardly when they reached her, for he well knew what would happen now—a sharp rebuke and a short lecture on the proper behavior of a prince of . . . somewhere.

But instead, Vieliessar swept Liri up into her arms and swung her around in a circle, hugging her tightly, and Thurion knelt to embrace Calan.

"He is a wicked bandit, Mama, but he is very nice!" Runacar heard Adalieriel say.

"You must decide whether he is more nice or more wicked, Liri," Vieliessar answered, "for I may yet have to kill him. Later you and Calan must tell me all that you have seen and heard."

Calan's eager words drowned out whatever answer Liri made. "My friends want to come with us, Mama. I said the High King must say about that but they can, can't they?" Calan asked, now with his arms around the necks of the two Wulvers.

"Of course they can," Vieliessar answered instantly. "They can be the first of my hostages, and they will sleep with you in your bed."

"I am going insane," Runacar said, very quietly. The High King of the Hundred Houses, Master of the Unicorn Throne, cuddling with her children in the middle of the meadow as if she were no more than a farmwife. "We expect them back unharmed!" he called to her.

She'd gotten grass-stains on her robe.

"You shall receive them just as they have come to us," Thurion said, getting to his feet.

"I thought all the Houseborn hated all the Otherfolk," Andhel said, mystified.

"Perhaps only the ones from castels do?" Pelere sounded equally baffled.

Vieliessar rose to her feet, setting Liri down and shaking out her robes. At her summons, Master Dandamir came forward to take the two children away into the Flower Forest. He clicked his tongue and gestured, summoning the Wulvers to follow as if they were his hunting dogs. Runacar didn't know what he should think about that. For that matter, he wasn't sure what *Audalo* thought of it.

"Perhaps now we will speak of the alliance the Unicorn Celebremen of the Otherfolk has mooted," Vieliessar said. Her tone was faintly reproachful, as if the delay had been entirely Runacar and Audalo's fault. "She spoke of peace between our people, and of forging a pact between us to destroy the Endarkened."

And did Celebremen tell you that Leutric's plan was to murder all of you save the children we already hold? Did she tell you what Melisha told me? Did Celebremen tell you that a very long time ago, one of the Bright-folk put on flesh and fur, hoof and horn, and stepped from the Flower Forest, and named herself Pelashia Celenthodiel?

Please, just this once, I hope you hear my thoughts. Because if she didn't, I have to. Because terrible and earth-shaking as that was, it was not the only thing Melisha had told him, or even the most crucial. There exists a way for us to have a chance of defeating the Darkness . . . and only the alfaljodthi *can wield it. Melisha said a star came down from the sky to become Amretheon Aradruiniel's bride. And Leutric called us "Children of Stars."*

For a moment Runacar's mind spun giddily, in a maelstrom of oaths, promises, loyalties. He would not betray Leutric, but—

Andhel kicked him. *"Rune!"* she hissed, when he stared at her in surprise.

"And do you say, Audalo Silverhorn, that you have the authority to offer this alliance and the power to hold all of the Otherfolk to it?" Vieliessar was saying. "Without . . . incidence?"

She was staring directly at Runacar, Andhel, and Pelere as she spoke.

"I extend to the High King my deepest apologies for any insult my apprentices might be deemed to have offered her person. I offer my own assurances that such an insult will not be repeated," Runacar said. He bowed, High House Warlord to reigning War Prince.

"So noted," Thurion answered, bowing fractionally in return.

"And the alliance?" Vieliessar asked. "It is a large thing to ask, Prince Audalo, when we know so little of you."

She has to be told. Melisha told me that story for a reason.

"How better to learn of us than as our allies?" Audalo said. "Our Battlemaster has been a fine ambassador for your folk."

"Before there can be an alliance, we must know what hostages you will offer," Vieliessar said patiently.

Sword and Star, I never until this moment realized how mind-numbingly pedantic *a parley truce could be!*

A moment later, Runacar realized he *liked* pedantry and boredom. Loved them. Preferred them to any other possible condition. In fact, he wanted to be utterly bored for the rest of his days.

Unnoticed in the high grass, a Palugh had crossed the distance to Vieliessar. Now he crouched and sprang into her arms. Vieliessar caught him reflexively. Her fingertips vanished in his long ticked fur.

"I, I, I," the Palugh sang, purring and kneading at her arm. "I am Pouncewarm. I am worth a thousand, a hundred thousand hostages. I will come. I."

Vieliessar looked down at the creature in her arms, enchanted and bemused in equal parts. She continued to stroke his fur. "Are you one of the Otherfolk?" she asked.

"The Otherfolk are many," Pouncewarm said. "I am the best of them. My brothers and sisters are also better than the rest of the Otherfolk, but not as wonderful as *I* am."

Vieliessar rubbed him under his chin with one finger. Pouncewarm closed his eyes in bliss. "I see this is true," she said gravely. "And I will be honored and delighted to have you as the foremost of my hostages. But sometimes a King must execute a hostage when her ally misbehaves, and I do not think I could execute you. So, you see, I must have more."

"Execute the Wulvers," Pouncewarm said instantly. "Nobody will miss them."

Runacar glanced at Audalo for permission to speak. He was comforted to see that Audalo was equally aware that negotiations had taken an . . . unexpected turn.

"We will give you one hundred hostages," Runacar said loudly. "You will give us the same. Of—"

"The choosing of hostages is a long and tedious business," Vieliessar interrupted. "Let us drink tea together, and we will discuss the matter."

Chapter eighteen

RADE MOON IN THE TENTH YEAR OF THE HIGH KING'S REIGN: ON THE TRACK OF THE SETTING SUN

To win decisively, you must control your foe's thoughts as you control the battlefield. A foe who thinks the cost of war too high will sue for peace instead of risking a costly defeat.

—Arilcarion War-Maker, *The Way of the Sword*

A stiff ground-cloth was brought, and standing braziers were set out to warm the air, for otherwise (as Thurion explained) the tea would cool far too swiftly. Once the braziers were lit, the rest of the tea paraphernalia was brought; it seemed odd to Runacar to see armed Elves in hauberk and helm carrying the formal cloths and trays and baskets containing the tea-brazier, the water kettle, the teapot, the tea canisters, the tea-sweets (Runacar had never seen anyone actually eat any), and the tiny, fantastically delicate cups.

Since it was autumn, the cups were lidded and slightly larger than usual, and despite the actual number of people present, there were twelve cups upon the tray since this tea was being served during a war parley. A woman came out of the forest to take charge of the brazier.

Vieliessar knelt upon the cloth, with Thurion—*and* Pouncewarm—beside her. Helecanth stood at Vieliessar's back, regarding the Otherfolk watchfully. Audalo, after a glance at Runacar, who nodded in response to the Minotaur's unspoken question, knelt facing Vieliessar. Runacar handed Folwin off to Pelere, and—blessing the silk-like flexibility of his multiply flanged Elven armor—reluctantly knelt beside Audalo, facing Thurion. Runacar had dealt with the mind-numbing boredom of treaty negotiations many times as his father's heir. It had involved drinking many tiny cups of hot water and listening to the negotiators from each side say "no" a lot. This would be no different.

I hope.

The service was set up in silence.

Runacar had a hard time keeping his thoughts in order while he waited. What Melisha had told him and whether he should tell it occupied the forefront of his mind, and he missed Radafa so intensely his whole chest ached with the loss. The Gryphon, with his infinite memory for history and lore, could have advised him on what to do, and kept secret the fact he had asked.

And there was no one else among the Otherfolk who would do that. Not even Andhel.

There was silence on the High King's side also during the lengthy and laborious process of preparing the tea. Vieliessar sat with her hands folded demurely in her lap, her eyes downcast. The Otherfolk behind Runacar spoke to one another in low tones. He heard the snap of wings as two Hippogriffs—plus probably Eltaor, the Gryphon observer from Marosia's Ascension—took to the sky.

"Rune." Andhel, who stood behind him, leaned down to whisper in his ear. "They're watching us."

"No, they—" He stopped. The High King wasn't watching them. Neither were the Silver Swords. But behind them, just inside the perimeter of the forest . . .

As if a veil had been lifted from his eyes, Runacar suddenly saw Elvenkind standing among the trees. Their clothing blended into the background just as that of the Woodwose did. They stood, or knelt, or gazed down from trees they had climbed, all of them still in a way that did not draw an eye. And every one of them was armed.

It is a violation to use magic during a treaty parley! Runacar thought indignantly. But (even if Cloak *had* been cast) it wasn't. There were no rules anymore except those the High King and the Otherfolk made. And he wasn't entirely sure magic had been used. Certainly, he'd seen the Woodwose vanish in plain sight often enough, and none of them were Mages.

"Yes," he said at last. "They are. Celebremen said she could bring any-one she liked."

So Vieliessar had brought *everyone*.

⊟⊨

At last, the water was boiled, the pot was warmed, the tea was steeped, and the tea was poured. Vieliessar reached out to remove one cup from the tray and upend it, pouring the tea out onto the grass before wrapping the cup in a napkin and crushing it in her hand.

"The sacrifice to the Silver Hooves," Runacar murmured for Audalo to hear.

Next, the small covered cups were arranged on a shin'zuruf tray which matched their design. An unspoken message passed between the High King and the Lightsister in charge of the service; she turned, moved forward on her knees, and held the tray in Audalo's direction.

The cups chimed faintly as her hands trembled. Her eyes were wide with terror.

Carefully, Audalo plucked up one of the cups between thumb and forefinger and stared at it. The Lightsister scuttled backward to present the tray to the High King.

"Once everyone is served, you drink it. Slowly," Runacar glossed in a near-whisper. He could almost feel Andhel's derisive gaze between his shoulder blades. If he'd had the least notion they'd be coming to a High House tea party, Runacar would certainly have warned Audalo what to expect beforehand.

Vieliessar was served next, then Thurion (a subtle insult; Runacar should have been next). There were seven cups remaining on the tray when the Lightsister moved to present the tray to Runacar.

Her hands did not shake. Her face held no expression. And her eyes gleamed with hatred.

Did you imagine they would love you? Runacar asked himself. He'd known the answer to that long before today. He just hadn't thought it would matter to him. He took the cup, and the Lightsister moved away. *They will not poison you at a negotiation,* he told himself. *And the High King knows she would die too. Drink the tea.*

As the Lightsister returned to the brazier, the High King summoned her over with a flick of her fingers before she could empty the remaining cups into the waste bowl. The High King took a cup from the tray and placed it before Pouncewarm. The Palugh inspected it critically, removed the lid, sniffed deeply, and sneezed.

Vieliessar actually looked *amused*.

The tea was drunk in silence. Normally there might have been idle conversation—about the tea, about the weather. Vieliessar's silence was a concession to Audalo's unfamiliarity with their ways. When the plate of tea-sweets was offered around, Audalo unwarily took one before Runacar could warn him.

Runacar decided he hated tea.

⊰⧓⊱

I shall waive the hundred hostages if you agree to exchange your Battle-master for mine," Vieliessar said conversationally.

Runacar opened his mouth and shut it firmly.

"No," Audalo said.

"Then perhaps our 'witches' for yours?" Vieliessar said with feigned ingenuousness.

"It would not be an equal trade," Audalo said. "And Rune tells me your folk are dependent upon your witches to build your fires and heal your hurts."

"And to do a thousand other things, I imagine," Vieliessar answered smoothly, "but I regret to inform you that he is completely wrong." She did not sound at all regretful.

"We will give you one hundred hostages. You will give us the same. Of the hundred we give, fifty will be of the Woodwose. Of the rest, you may choose twelve of the hostages you receive of us; the others we shall choose by lot. Further—" This time Runacar was *almost* permitted to get all the way to the end of his proposal.

"Your present captives must naturally be returned immediately, and before any hostages are exchanged. Should we agree to exchange hostages at all," Thurion Lightbrother said. This was the part of a negotiation usually left to the House Swordmaster.

Perhaps Gunedwaen is dead. Probably. He was not young even at the Breaking of Farcarinon. But where is his successor? I do not recall seeing his Cadet upon the field. Is it the Lightbrother? Another thing to find out. We must know who counsels her. Thurion? A Lightbrother who'd been born to the lowliest of Caerthalien serfs? I cannot quite make myself believe that.

"We do not ask hostages of you, for this is to be a treaty of peace, an alliance against our great enemy," Audalo said.

"Very well," Thurion said agreeably. "We agree that we will not give you hostages. What hostages will you give *us*?"

"The same number you give us—and we will keep the children now in our hands. All of them," Runacar interrupted sharply.

"This is fun," Pouncewarm announced, purring happily. Vieliessar idly stroked his fur.

⇥⊟⊢

It was true that Audalo had never done this particular sort of negotiation before, but it did not mean that the Minotaur Prince was unfamiliar with negotiating. The Otherfolk did not fight among themselves—at least not with sword and bow. They negotiated. They argued. (In the case of Centaurs, they also got drunk and broke a lot of furniture.) Today's discussion ran like xaique played at lightning speed, but even so, Vieliessar and Audalo were still haggling over hostages by the time the sun began to set.

During the afternoon, several more Palugh had come over to sit with the High King's party. Most clustered around the brazier. The Wild of Wulver whose youngsters had gone off with Calanoriel had joined them in the Flower Forest.

The lone Gryphon observer, Eltaor, had returned, moving to place himself between the two parties so as to watch everything. He seemed fascinated.

And probably there are hundreds of Brightfolk here that I can't see, and my only consolation is that Vieliessar probably can't see them either, Runacar thought.

"The hour grows late," Audalo finally said. "Let us agree to withdraw and continue our discussions tomorrow."

"At dawn your folk will possess the freedom of the field for two sen-nights," Vieliessar said. "Return if you wish."

By the horns of the Hunt—that's her plan. She's going to drag the par-ley out until freedom of the field is ended. She has no reason to conclude matters any earlier—and while we negotiate, she's learning as much about us as if she'd sent a hundred spies! Runacar nearly laughed aloud at the sweeping audacity of such a plan. It was beautiful. It was—

An ornament to the Sword Road, and by Land and Leaf, I have re-nounced that Road!

Everyone stood. Both sides stepped backward, away from the tea cloth. The Silver Swords marched forward, opening and closing their ranks around the High King's people with meticulous drilled precision. They pivoted in place and retreated into the forest, carrying the High King and her meisne with them.

It was very impressive.

Fauns loped after them. The Pounce of Palugh had gone . . . some-where.

"We need to go," Runacar said tightly. "Now." The verge of the Flower Forest was still filled with armed Elvenkind. And the freedom of the field began tomorrow, not today.

Blessedly Audalo did not doubt him.

⋞⧓⋟

R unacar did not breathe freely until they reached their temporary camp just outside the Western Gate. He saw with resignation and no particular surprise that the camp had doubled in size since this morning, a reminder—not that he needed one after this long—that Oth-erfolk did not think like Elves.

It was cold enough here on the high mountain road for most of the Folk to prefer shelters to the open sky. Runacar made quickly for the nearest fire.

"There," Runacar said, pulling off his gloves to warm his hands at a brazier. "We're safe now." He looked back up the road. Stardock's snowy skirts were colored deep blue and indigo with approaching night. Be-yond the pillars of the Gate, nothing could be seen.

"Would they really have broken a truce?" Pelere asked, sounding more curious than worried.

"There *is* no truce," Runacar said, trying not to grind his teeth. "Not yet. But beginning at dawn, they will refrain from killing us for a fortnight."

"They're all crazy," Andhel pronounced firmly.

"That's why so many of them are dead," Runacar answered.

❧❦

Within Ceoprentrei, the Silver Swords spread out among the trees almost at once—it was second nature by now for all of Elvenkind never to make paths across the forest floor for an enemy to follow. Their Arzhana horses—as superbly trained as the destriers they superseded—had flanked them as they marched, and now each sought out their rider.

"How bad?" Thurion asked Vieliessar.

"Worse than I could have dreamed. He—"

Bervaset Lightsister came down from her treetop perch to land with a soft thump upon the mossy forest floor. Though Overshadow was a common enough spell, it had been difficult to find anyone who bore it as a Keystone Gift among the surviving Lightborn, but it required Keystone Overshadow for someone to bespell a creature through whose eye she could watch the parley, and to hold it in thrall candlemark after candlemark. Fortunately Bervaset was gifted with such a spell, and today she had used it. Vieliessar wondered if the Otherfolk Warlord knew how thoroughly the Elves had violated the Code of the Sword today.

"As my King commands, I watch only those lands we hold," Bervaset said. "The Otherfolk have left them. All save this one, perhaps. What is it?"

"I," said Pouncewarm, stretching to arch his back and curl his tail. "Am beautiful. I am great. I, I, I, and *only* I, am first and foremost of the High King's hostages."

"A hostage?"

"As he says," Vieliessar answered. "I relieve you now. Go and rest," Vieliessar said. "I well remember how exhausting it is to hold a Casting for the whole of a day."

Bervaset nodded gratefully and turned away to seek her home camp.

"Before the Hunt!" Rithdeliel let out a sharp sigh. "I would challenge that gallowglass to the Circle if it would not taint my blade. Amrolion and Daroldan gone!"

"Worse than that," Vieliessar said to him. "From Caerthalien's thoughts I collect that the Astromancer has built himself a war city. But let us go—this news makes dreadful hearing. We will summon the council. I would not speak it twice."

⌘

I have to talk to her," Runacar said. "Now. Tonight."

"Why tell me?" Audalo asked. His pavilion had probably once belonged to some minor Elvenborn hedge knight, but it was large enough to hold a Minotaur. Even so, Audalo sat on the ground, lest an unwary head-toss bring the whole thing down around both of them.

"Because you represent my liege-lord," Runacar said wearily. "And I won't be unfaithful to the oaths I have sworn him."

"I liked it better when we were friends," Audalo answered wistfully. "You didn't care about these things then."

"I did care," Runacar answered gently. "But they didn't matter then. Not between you and me. But you outrank me now, and before you say that doesn't matter, think of what you'd say to Leutric if I ended up a prisoner of the Elves."

"I'd send Andhel to get you back," Audalo answered. "Then I wouldn't have to tell him anything." There was a pause. "Will talking to her do us any good?"

"Maybe. Yes. No. I don't know. But it will change things."

He wished he knew more than that.

⌘

With the whole of the council present, plus the Guild Leaders, the royal heirs and their personal guards, and additional Law Lords to make certain protocol was observed and the One Law was respected, the enclosure was overcrowded, but spells like Cloak and Shield and

Silence required defined boundaries for their casting, and the boundaries of the Council Chamber could not be quickly expanded.

It had been with an odd reluctance that Vieliessar had excluded Pouncewarm and the young Wulvers, Runfar and Birdleap, from the meeting. Although in the end, very little of this would be secret, Vieliessar did not want any gossip circulating among her folk. Nor among the Otherfolk.

Caerthalien's presence was a constant itch at the back of her mind. She had rarely noticed the existence of the Soulbond before, but now she was aware of his presence and even of some of his emotions in a way she did not seem to be able to shut off. She wondered if it was possible to open the Bond further—enough to Overshadow him, perhaps. But that was a puzzle best left for another day. And what if she couldn't close it down again?

The council meeting began with the reports of Calanoriel and Adalieriel and what they had seen and heard in their time among the Otherfolk. Calan's report had mostly encompassed the kinds of creatures he saw in the Otherfolk camp and what he was given to eat. Liri's was more detailed, beginning with the rush of the Unicorns out of the depths of Ceoprentrei. In Vondaimieriel, the children had all been kept together, and treated well. They'd been guarded by the Unicorns, and Liri remembered the names of many of the Unicorns who guarded them. She was also able to give a rough count of the numbers of the hostage children in the Otherfolk camp and most of their names: now the Royal Loremaster could begin checking them against the roster of those dead—or seen to be taken by the Endarkened—to come up with a list of the missing.

Fortunately, neither of the children was particularly disturbed by their kidnap (in Liri's case) and captivity (both of them). They had seen far too much of death, and of horrors beyond death, to hold on to unpleasant memories of something that had neither injured nor killed them. Liri was asleep, leaning into Helecanth, and Calan sprawled across Thurion's lap, snoring faintly.

Thurion next summarized the bad news—without explaining that Vieliessar had taken it from Caerthalien's thoughts through their

Soulbond—for those who had not heard it firsthand: the Domains of the Shore were erased and Hamphuliadiel had declared himself Astromancer Eternal and was building a gigantic War-Village beside the Sanctuary of the Star. Most of Vieliessar's councillors thought that the loss of the Shore was the worse of the two, and the Lightborn present didn't let them suspect otherwise.

"My condolences for this unhappy news, Lord Iardalaith. I suppose you are War Prince of Daroldan now," Vieliessar said.

"Unless there is some survivor who outranks me," Iardalaith responded. "I suppose it is a matter of interest to Loremasters and knights-herald, and to hardly anyone else now." He smiled crookedly. "But I need not explain to you the pain of having one's domain erased."

Vieliessar inclined her head in silent agreement.

"If we are to believe anything that traitorous young jackal said, the talking animals hold the whole of the West, save for the Sanctuary and its bounds. So. Are we to support Hamphuliadiel as Astromancer? Or . . . ?" Rithdeliel regarded Vieliessar with interest.

Vieliessar swept the council with a look that gathered them all in. "I intend to become Astromancer—*Eternal*—as well as High King," she answered. "If Hamphuliadiel will pass the ring to me and declare fealty, I will allow him his life—and no more."

Vieliessar had long been mulling the problem of how to avoid a future Astromancer becoming a rival in power to the Unicorn Throne. The counterargument that the dual title would render the High King too powerful was void, for any special knowledge the Astromancer might have been given by his predecessors would die with Hamphuliadiel, for he would surely refuse to recognize any other aspirant as Astromancer.

And of course, to *not* have an Astromancer was impossible, even though Vieliessar's people had gone back to the days of Mosirinde Peacemaker in their training of Lightborn. The Elven Loremasters and knights-herald still kept and curated the lineages of the Hundred Houses, even though some of the domains had but one member yet alive.

"Would you take away his Light?" Aradreleg asked, sounding shocked. "That seems—"

"Only fitting, when you consider how he's used it," Iardalaith interjected.

"A Binding at the least, for him and any Lightborn who choose to remain loyal to him," Vieliessar said firmly. "But this is to cook the chicken before it has been caught. We have more immediate concerns."

"Very well," Rithdeliel said briskly. "We will march west, sack the Sanctuary of the Star and its war-village, and overthrow the present Astromancer. No doubt the Vilya will contrive to flower appropriately when you assume the title."

"A great pity we didn't know all this before we came west," War Prince Frochoriel said. "We could all have stayed home. There's nothing in the West to either save, or to go back to, and now we're trapped in Nomaitemil with the Mystrals at our back and an army at our doorstep."

"An army that doesn't want to kill us, which is a nice change," Thurion said. "But I don't think they'll let us go without a treaty, either."

"With an enormous Flower Forest at our beck and call, we are in a position to force the issue in our favor," Iardalaith said. "My scouts have ridden south for three sunturns and not found Nomaitemil's further edge."

"They frighten me," Aradreleg said softly, looking down at the ground. "I fear what they will do to us."

Tuonil leaned over to speak softly in Thurion's ear. Thurion looked surprised, then nodded, and turned to reply. After a long moment, Thurion turned to Vieliessar.

"If I may interrupt the council to relate a story which might have bearing upon our deliberations? It is not likely to be news to some of us—but to others, yes." Thurion nodded in Aradreleg's direction.

Vieliessar frowned faintly. She could not read Thurion's thoughts clearly—not with so many minds around her shouting out their endless monologues—and while she trusted him with her life, the council was especially skittish over the Otherfolk treaty. "Speak," she said finally. "I do not think we will solve all of our problems tonight."

Thurion moved Calan to Tuonil's lap and got to his feet. "My Lord Princes and Lords Komen, when you look at Lightborn you see what we can do, but not who we were before we took the Green Robe."

("Not that anybody has had a proper robe in a taille of Wheelturns," Aradreleg muttered.)

"But I was born a Landbond, lowest of the low. And Tuonil, who was a borders Crofter, reminds me of something I once knew and had long forgotten. Great nobles such as yourselves"—Thurion's tone was lightly mocking, and Iardalaith flicked his fingers at him derisively—"do not see the world as your chattels do. You fight the Otherfolk, and see them as monstrous foes—akin to the Endarkened in their hideousness, if not their evil."

"Everyone knows that," Rithdeliel said sharply.

"Everyone does *not*," Thurion snapped. "We—not all the Lightborn, for Aradreleg and others think and feel as you do—but *our* people—the Landbonds, the Crofters—do not think of the Otherfolk as the enemy of Elvenkind. We . . . They . . ." He stopped, clearly at a loss for words.

"The Little Ones," Tuonil said quietly. Vieliessar held up her hand for silence. Tuonil had been born a Crofter, made cropped-eared, lowest of the low. It was a miracle that he was here, for there were too few like him. She could not change the facts. She could free them, but Vieliessar could not undo the beliefs that had been beaten into them for the whole of their lives.

Tuonil bowed his head. When he spoke, his voice was soft, and thick with the Landbond patois.

"Starry Hunt is far away. Flower Queen too high for such as we. Who will see us? The Little Ones see us. They bring luck. When we can, we leave offerings. When we have no food to give . . . we leave children. And this day—" He raised his head, pride now shining from his face and his voice. "And this day we, Landbond, know: the Little Ones save our children once again. They are kind. They are *here*."

There was utter silence in the Council Chamber. Thurion sat down again. Vieliessar glanced at the faces around her. War Princes and Lords Komen—she had been born a War Prince; Iardalaith had been a cousin of Damulothir Daroldan—and very few of "the lowest of the low" made up her council.

But if Tuonil was right, the army she led might be more willing than she had realized to make common cause with the Otherfolk.

"Gelduin, what were you before I made you a Law Lord?" Vieliessar asked. She knew the answer, but others needed reminding.

"I was a cordwainer, my lord King. A leatherworker. Craftfolk," he answered. "And my folk always said the ghostlights in the wood were help to the lost and injured. To see the forest lights brought good luck." *But we never sacrificed our children to them.* The thought was nearly as clear as speech.

"And this means," Vieliessar said forcefully, before either Frochoriel or Rithdeliel could say anything, "that we may now freely debate the merits of this treaty, knowing that our people will willingly accept whatever decision we render, for some of the Otherfolk are kin to them. We have much to thank the Otherfolk for."

"*Thank* them!" Iardalaith exploded. "After what they did on the Western Shore?"

"This was to be a sham treaty only!" Rithdeliel cried.

Everyone on the council began to shout at one another.

⌗

Vieliessar ended the gathering after another quartermark had passed. Rithdeliel held that since any truce had been merely a ruse to allow them to reach the Western Shore, there was no need for one now. Iardalaith said it would be easier to attack the Otherfolk from the position of false ally. Frochoriel said that since the Endarkened were killing all of them anyway, they might as well make a true alliance. "And so long as the High King does not have to make a marriage alliance with any of them, what's to complain of? Though I should like to see—"

"Enough!" Vieliessar said, rising to her feet. "Go your ways, my lords. We have a sennight to reach a conclusion. We need not do it tonight."

⌗

The Elven children had awakened at the first shouts, but having attended council meetings all their lives, had simply gone back to sleep again. When Vieliessar turned to wake them once more she found Pouncewarm curled up between them and purring.

"How did you . . . ?" she began. "Thurion?" He shook his head. He hadn't seen Pouncewarm's arrival either. Of course she'd undone the spells warding the chamber once the meeting was over, but . . .

Pouncewarm merely purred louder.

Vieliessar sighed. "I suppose you know all of this already," she said to the Palugh. "You might as well stay."

"My lord!" Helecanth protested.

"I know," Vieliessar said gently. "But the Palugh have never done any of us any harm, and they will gain little advantage from learning what little we know of their folk. Take the children and put them to bed—and if a pack of Wulvers wishes to sleep with Calan, then we may know him doubly guarded."

Helecanth picked up Calan and took Liri by the hand.

"And I, my lord?" Aradreleg asked.

"Bed," Vieliessar said firmly. "There is always work for the Healers. And I would know which of our Lightborn were born to Landbond or Crofter families."

"As you say, my lord," Aradreleg said doubtfully. Vieliessar could hear her next thought as clearly as if she had spoken it: *I thank the Light that I am not one such, for I was born a Craftworker's daughter!*

Once Aradreleg was gone, Vieliessar cast Silence upon the chamber once more. No Lightless would be able to sense its presence, and it would give those inside some semblance of privacy.

Thurion was kneeling over the tea-brazier, coaxing its coals back to life. Vieliessar sat down beside him and began hunting through the basket of tea canisters.

"I'd thought you must be holding something back," Thurion said. "But if we already know the good news, I'm not sure I want to know what it is."

"A mixed bag," Vieliessar said, as Pouncewarm stepped into her lap and grabbed for the canister she was holding. "You had this today, small one, and did not like it," she said, before closing the canister and choosing another. A Thousand Choices was not the tea for tonight. She needed one answer, not many. She finally settled on Rest after Sorrow. Perhaps it would come true. She passed the canister to Thurion after letting Pouncewarm sniff at it. The Palugh sneezed violently at the scent—but fortunately not into the tea.

"I'm not completely sure of what I heard from Caerthalien's thoughts at the tea ceremony," she said. "One item was clearer than the others, but still very murky, even though it was nearly all he thought about for most of the afternoon—that and how much he hates parleys. He feels he has urgent news that I must have." She shrugged apologetically. "But even he is not sure why."

Thurion raised his eyebrows in mock disbelief. "He *does* know we are enemies at the moment?"

"He does," Vieliessar said, sounding doubtful. "He says—rather, he believes, and has been told—that the Otherfolk possess a weapon that can destroy the Endarkened."

There was a long moment of electric silence. Thurion studied her face. "There must be more to it than that. You'd have told the council."

"I may yet have to. Apparently their King-Emperor would rather the Otherfolk all die than surrender it to us. When Caerthalien was not thinking about that, he was thinking about Pelashia Flower Queen."

Thurion blinked. "Well that's . . . unexpected. I shouldn't think he even knew Pelashia Celenthodiel existed."

"After the Windsward Insurrection the whole of the Hundred Houses could quote *The Song of Amretheon* from memory," Vieliessar said dryly. "But . . . still. I don't see what Queen Pelashia has to do with a Minotaur weapon."

"Perhaps Caerthalien will tell us," Thurion said.

"Perhaps he will," Vieliessar said. "He is coming tonight to see me."

CHAPTER NINETEEN

RADE MOON IN THE TENTH YEAR OF THE HIGH KING'S REIGN: PATTERNS OF FORCE

A commander faced with two bad choices, and no good ones, gains the victory by concealing that truth from the enemy.

—Arilcarion War-Maker, Of the Sword Road

It was nearly midnight by the time Runacar managed to return to the top of the pass, and this time he was wearing his heavy stormcloak. At least (he told himself) he wasn't going to freeze. *And if I weren't intending to skulk off here like the villain in a Midwinter Festival storysong, I could have slept in Audalo's tent and been actually warm.*

The discussion that had followed their return from the parley had been frustrating. Audalo was pleased to have come to the same conclusion as his former teacher about Vieliessar's delaying tactics, but saw no reason the parley should not go on for another fortnight. Should the Endarkened come, in Audalo's opinion they would simply all shelter in Nomaitemil.

If I can't teach the Otherfolk to think like Elves, it won't matter how well my people can fight. They'll still all die.

The Unicorns still held sufficient hostages that Vieliessar's people would not attack the Otherfolk tonight, and as of sunrise, her folk would be oathsworn not to attack them in the valley—but *only* the valley. So while it was tactically possible to evacuate the whole of the remaining Otherfolk to the Flower Forest in the event of another Endarkened attack, it would be useless if all that meant was that the *Elves* would kill them instead of the *Endarkened* killing them.

Which is the reason why Leutric is dragging his hooves about full cooperation: dead is dead, and if this weapon of his means that the Elves can kill the Endarkened, but then the Elves kill us, it's not much use handing it over from his point of view.

He attained the valley itself and moved down its western side. Once he was out of the wind, the still air gave the illusion of warmth—but the jagged cliff wall made it much harder to see. Runacar fished in one of the pockets of his stormcloak until he retrieved what he sought: a small hinged box. The Lightborn had made thousands of these; easier to use than a candle, and never used up.

When he opened it, Silverlight blazed forth from inside. Runacar lifted the box high, as if it were a torch.

The battlefield was clear. The Flower Forest glowed faintly in places with the distinctive moonlight glow of the uluskukad, but Runacar saw nothing that looked like watchfires. Apparently, the High King's forces had posted no sentries either. Perhaps the Flower Forest had powers of protection and defense unknown to mere komen.

Next, Runacar held the light-box down low, and angled it so that its illumination spilled directly on the ground. Closer to where he stood, the remaining dead lay in grotesquely organized ranks. He wondered if he would recognize either Radafa or Keloit in death. A Warlord was necessarily a master of weapons and tactics. In ten years, Runacar had become one. But there was no way for groundbound armies to fight a foe that could fly—Riann's Ascension and three Flights of Hippogriffs had proved that with their lives. Unless the whole of both their armies grew wings, they could not fight the Endarkened in their natural element.

"The Endarkened seek out Lightborn Magery, you know." Vieliessar's voice came out of seeming nowhere.

Runacar did not flinch. He closed the spellbox and slipped it back into his cloak. "Awkward," he said mildly.

The High King faded into visibility surrounded by a foggy nimbus of Silverlight. Runacar couldn't tell whether she'd been Cloaked before, or had been awaiting him. Her breath, like his, fogged the night air, and the proof of her corporeality was oddly reassuring.

An enormous furred stormcloak covered most of her body, its stripes and dapples providing a natural camouflage. Runacar gazed at it incuriously for several heartbeats before he realized he was looking at an ice-tiger skin. The stormcloak was fastened down the front by clasps made from the beast's claws, and beneath the stormcloak, he could see that Vieliessar was no longer wearing the flamboyant white robe of the afternoon's parley. She was dressed in tunic and vest, leggings and boots, all drab and colorless in the Silverlight. She wore no badge of rank, unless the fur counted as one.

"Are you alone?" Runacar asked, not moving.

"Are you?" Vieliessar responded.

"I have no idea."

"I do," Vieliessar said. "There's a Unicorn."

Runacar looked back the way he had come. "Melisha," he said. The Unicorn stood at the top of the valley, head high and tail curled as if she were posing for her portrait. Her coat glimmered softly, like the reflection of the moon in water, and Runacar could tell she was looking at him. Apparently he'd been wrong: he was going to see her tonight after all. *I wish she'd just come and tell the High King everything she told me.*

"But she probably won't, as Unicorns don't seem to want to tell me anything," Vieliessar said.

Anger and fear—*sorcery, witchcraft, forbidden*—warred with indignation: use of Lightborn Magery was utterly forbidden in battle or parley by Arilcarion and the Codes of War. "You're using Magery. You're reading my thoughts," he said levelly.

"Yes and yes," Vieliessar answered. "What do you expect? The Codes of War are elaborate playthings for bored War Princes. My Lightborn keep Mosirinde's Covenant. Nothing more."

Runacar took a few steps toward Melisha, then stopped. "I wish you had died in Nataranweiya's arms," he said, not moving.

"Not half as much as I," Vieliessar answered in the same flat tone. She sat down on a boulder and folded her hands in her lap, as if she were about to view a play.

"They call her Mosirinde Truefriend, you know," Runacar said idly. "The Otherfolk revere her."

"Why?" Vieliessar asked.

"I don't know. I suppose she must have been a Woodwose."

"I don't know if there were Woodwose in that time," Vieliessar answered, as if she were proposing to debate the subject. "Their families want to see them."

"Who? What?" Runacar stumbled over the non sequitur.

"The Woodwose are the abandoned children of Landbonds and Crofters. Their parents want to see their children again."

"Their children don't want to see them," Runacar answered. He stood now with his back to the valley wall so he could watch both Vieliessar and Melisha.

"Fine. What did you want to tell me? And more to the point: Why?"

"I don't know," Runacar said. He had the unsettling sensation of grasping for something just out of his reach. Not the Soulbond. He could feel it, like an infected thorn beneath the skin. But something had driven him here, and he did not know what it was.

"Then this conversation will be short," Vieliessar answered.

Confusion was replaced by irritation. "Misconstrue me if it amuses you. I had always thought it foolishness not to learn all I could of an enemy."

"'Knowledge.' Did I keep you here until sunrise, I could not enumerate the things I do not know and wish to. So. Let us begin your telling: What is this weapon that can destroy the Endarkened?"

With an effort, Runacar repressed his first impulse, which was to draw his sword. *She is goading you,* he reminded himself. *And she can hear your every thought. She wasn't negotiating at the parley today. She was spying. She said so herself:* "The Codes of War are playthings for bored War Princes."

"Melisha told me that much and nothing more. Leutric will not give it to you, and nobody else knows where and what it is." *He calls it the Bones of the Earth. Rocks are accounted the Bones of the Earth. Perhaps we should just throw rocks at the Endarkened? I do not think the Unicorns will consent to being launched from catapults, but I must ask Melisha about that. . . .*

Runacar allowed the surface of his mind to fill with insignificant chatter. Ivrulion had taught him to do so when Runacar was first old enough to attend Bolecthindial at his councils. The idea was to confuse

any Lightborn who might be eavesdropping. Runacar flinched inwardly
at the thought of his brother. Ivrulion had not cared for either Code or
Covenant in the end, only his vast and toxic ambition. . . .

"Did you come to speak of any other thing?" Vieliessar asked, as the
silence stretched.

"I came to ask you to surrender."

Her answering laugh was quick and sharp; a fox's bark. "I might ask
of you the same. But we are to be allies, instead, and coexist in peace. Of
course sworn allies never turn on one another."

As Caerthalien did against Farcarinon. He wasn't sure if she'd spoken
the words aloud, or he'd merely thought them. Could she steal his will
through the Soulbond, as his brother had through his profane Magery?

"Allies? Oh, do let us be as allies as if in a Storysinger's ballad,"
Runacar said venomously. "We will all hold hands and dance and sing
until the Endarkened come and slay us all. We are all, after all—" The
words choked him. He still couldn't say them aloud—not because of a
geasa such as he had suffered at his brother's hands. It was as if to speak
the words would make them true.

*The blood of the Otherfolk runs in our veins. Pelashia Celenthodiel
was one of the Brightfolk. She was the first of the Unicorns. She gave us
Magery. It all came from her and her children, and her children's children.
Melisha and I are cousins, just as you and I are.*

"You were not there to see, I think," Vieliessar finally said. She spoke
as quietly and as simply as if they were two old friends exchanging tales
of their long time apart. "There was a pass in the cliffs of the Shieldwall.
Dargariel Dorankalaliel our ancestors called it—the Fireheart Gate. If we
had not been able to open it by Pelashia's blood, we would have died on
Ifjalasairaet, and you . . . would have lived until the Endarkened came.
But we did not. When we had won, we took possession of Amretheon's
ancient city. *Kalalielahwyr.* Heart of the World. We called it Celephrian-
dullias, because of the Flower Forest, but that wasn't its name. Not really.
Inside *Kalalielahwyr* was *Parman Paramad,* White Jewel. Amretheon's
great castel. It had no bastions or curtain walls, no defenses. One day I
climbed the spire to see how they had lived in that time so long ago. I
never went back.

"It was utterly in ruins," Vieliessar went on, still in that quiet confidential voice. And for the first time, Runacar truly understood what her being Child of the Prophecy, touched by High King Amretheon Aradruiniel's own hand, meant. It did not just set her apart from the common run. It yanked her away from them.

"There were no walls, no defenses. What had once been the gardens of *Parman Paramad* had been overgrown by a forest of ancient trees. The trees had destroyed nearly the whole of the city, because it had been built without magic. Amretheon's people knew nothing of magic."

"Only Pelashia's children did," Runacar said. They were both speaking in hushed tones, like mourners at a death.

"And so *Dargariel Dorankalaliel* was sealed with magic during the escape of Pelashia's children, for after Amretheon died, there was war. In his time, Ifjalasairaet was called *Ch'rahwyr-thrawnzah*, Border of the World, because Elvenkind had never ventured any farther westward than that. Pelashia's children fled into the unknown west, pursued by great armies. Their mother had granted them magic, and the gift of her own long life, and against those things Amretheon's people could not prevail." Vieliessar spoke as simply as if she'd been there.

"And then Pelashia's children turned on each other because we were all the High King's heirs," Runacar said, taking up the thread of the story. "We've fought for centuries to get back something that was gone before we began to fight." The devastation Runacar felt was sickening. *Everything has been for nothing. Everything any of us has ever fought for. And now we will all die together, Pelashia's people and Amretheon's people, united at last in death.*

"Yes," Vieliessar said simply. "We all fought over the Unicorn Throne, as if it would . . ." She shrugged, at a loss for words. "As if having it would *give* us something. And it won't. We are not Amretheon's heirs, no matter what we say. Compared to his people, we are . . . not even Beastlings. We are *beasts*."

"*You* wanted it. You wanted the Unicorn Throne. You wanted to be High King."

"Because of the Prophecy." Though she still spoke softly, Vieliessar's voice was almost a wail of despair. "I knew some great Enemy was coming against whom I was to fight. I didn't know what the enemy was, or when it would come, or . . . All I knew was that if the Hundred Houses met it as a hundred quarreling princes, we would lose."

"And now most of us are dead, and no matter how many Unicorns fight for us, they can't fly and the Endarkened can, so we're all going to die anyway," Runacar said. He felt oddly light, as if to speak the truth had lifted the weight of failure from his shoulders.

"Well, *there's* a heartening forecast," Melisha said.

The Unicorn had come as close as she could as they were talking. Now Runacar went to her and put an arm around her neck. He could feel the tension in her muscles, and walked away with her to where he could feel that tension ease. Vieliessar stayed where she was.

I can do this and you can't. I have Melisha and you don't. Melisha loves me and not you. The thought was humiliatingly petty, and Runacar did his best to be ashamed of it. But he could not bring himself to pity Vieliessar Farcarinon.

"Do you have a better one?" he asked Melisha.

"Goblins!" Vieliessar said, lunging to her feet. *"Run!"*

For an instant Runacar almost thought it was an answer to his question.

"I will warn the others!" Melisha cried, wrenching away from him and sprinting toward the pass.

Vieliessar clapped her hands sharply, obviously doing a spell. A phantasmal bell began to toll, and suddenly the whole of the Flower Forest glowed with Silverlight. She ran to Runacar before she raised her hand as if clutching at air. Her sword flew from nowhere into her grasp.

"They'll start with the dead. That gives us a chance," Vieliessar said. She grabbed Runacar's wrist with her free hand and yanked hard. "I said *run!*"

⊰⊱

She managed to drag him several steps before Runacar wrenched his arm out of her grasp. *If I die, so does she,* Runacar thought angrily. *But I'm damned if I'll jump at her word like a Sword Page at their first war.*

"Come-come-come!" Pouncewarm appeared out of nowhere, crouching on Vieliessar's shoulder. "The goblins come! I, I, I can protect you—but not for long!"

"Protect *him*!" Vieliessar snarled, glaring at Runacar. She scooped Pouncewarm off her shoulder and tossed him at Runacar. The Palugh landed, claws out, and scrambled up Runacar's chest.

Pouncewarm was heavy, and his claws were long. His tail lashed repeatedly across Runacar's face as he dug his hind feet into Runacar's shoulders and his paws into Runacar's scalp. Runacar suddenly regretted wearing only his aketon beneath his tunic and not his armor. The thick braid Runacar wore his hair in gave Pouncewarm excellent purchase, and gave Runacar no protection at all.

Vieliessar turned again and ran. Pouncewarm bit Runacar's ear. Hard. Runacar swatted at the Palugh, snarling, and ran after Vieliessar. She hadn't thought to have her Silverlight follow her, and Runacar tripped and stumbled over the uneven ground in the darkness, unbalanced by the growling weight upon his shoulders.

Then Runacar caught his boot on something and fell, full length, onto the scree. The suddenness of it kept him from catching himself, and he went down hard, knocking the air from his lungs and hitting his chin on a rock. Pouncewarm leapt from his back, bounding on ahead.

As he struggled to his knees, coughing and gasping, Runacar saw that the dead were moving, as if some scavenger was shifting their weight. He winced as he heard the distinctive snap of a cannon bone breaking. Something had just bitten through one of the dead Centaurs' legs.

There was a squealing and chittering as of a hundred rats fighting over their meal. Then one of the creatures climbed to the top of one of the corpses—and for the first time Runacar saw what Vieliessar was running from.

It was small and hairless, and its head seemed oversized for its small body. Its frail arms were longer than its short bowed legs. Its enormous eyes were round and bulging like those of a frog, and flared silver even in the dimness of the battlefield. The goblin drew itself up to its full height and hissed defiance. Runacar could see that its mouth was very large and its teeth were very sharp.

Other goblins swarmed after the first, but not to fight. Instead they began devouring the dead, biting gobbets of flesh from the bodies and bolting them whole. It did not matter to them whether it was flesh, bone, hair, or cloth that they ate: the only things they spat out were objects of metal and stone.

And they kept coming.

Suddenly a movement far nearer caught Runacar's attention. Right before him, a goblin swam up through the surface of the ground as if it were water. It pulled itself free of the soil, standing on its bowed mis-shapen legs, and looked about itself, blinking. Then it saw Runacar, and its jaws opened wide.

The sky above flamed as bright as day.

The goblin gave a piercing wail and sank into the ground as fluidly as it had emerged from it. Runacar, as blinded by light as he'd been by darkness, ran for whatever safety the Flower Forest could give.

⌘

The Mageborn sky-flare slowly dimmed as Runacar crossed the perimeter of the forest and caught his balance against one of the great trees. It looked to him as if the High King's army was attempting simultaneously to break camp and take the field. Some of them carried bundles. Others quickly armed themselves. And all with a discipline and speed Runacar had tried in vain to impose upon his Otherfolk army.

"Move the horses back—they're sure to have Watchers with them!" someone cried.

"Get the children up *high*!"

"Can the talking dogs climb?"

"*Move*, catling!"

Runacar stepped away from the tree. He needed to find Vieliessar.

Something heavy—a Palugh—dropped from above to land on his shoulder.

"You are fast, but I, I, I am faster," Pouncewarm sang happily. Runacar was about to explain to Pouncewarm that biting off his ear while providing absolutely no information was not the way to endear himself to anyone when he was interrupted.

"You! Idiot War Prince! Come with me!" A hand clamped over his arm.

Runacar turned quickly into the grasp as his Armsmaster had taught him to, to find himself facing someone who was disorientingly familiar. Lightborn, judging by the green armband with its embroidered silver star that he wore over his tunic, but . . .

"Thurion of Caerthalien, very much not at your service," the Lightborn said swiftly. "Come on." He released Runacar and turned away. Pouncewarm jumped down again and ran on ahead.

"Just— Wait! You— Am I a hostage? I've given you no parole. . . ." Runacar knew he sounded witless, but all of this could be some trick, some ruse to gain advantage.

Thurion turned back and gave Runacar a look of withering contempt. "We don't play High House games here, witling. Now come *on*."

Runacar came. As he followed Thurion deeper into the forest the light dimmed even more, until the starlight shining through the breaks in the canopy above was the whole of the illumination. Runacar realized that the shouts and the signal calls had ended. The tumult had been a thing of moving combatants to the line and moving supplies out of the strike zone. He knew it as clearly as if he had given the orders himself. This was war as he had first learned it.

Even to think such a thought seemed disloyal to his adopted people, as if it might mean he would abandon them at the first sight of something homely and familiar.

They stopped in an open space. Runacar automatically looked skyward. From the position of the stars Runacar could tell that First Light was at least six candlemarks away.

"She's coordinating defense along the eastern wall," said a new voice. A sphere of Silverlight hovered over the unknown's head. Now Runacar could see the newcomer wore a Lightborn badge, but his hair was long and braided instead of closely shorn. Most of the braid was unreadable— though it was elaborate enough to be a true Honor Braid—but two of the plaits were easy to read.

War Prince. Daroldan. This must be Iardalaith Daroldan.

"Did she cast Flare all by herself?" Thurion demanded.

"Probably. Go yell at her for it. I'll watch Prince Precious," Iardalaith said. He stooped to stroke Pouncewarm, who arched his back in pleasure.

Thurion vanished into the underbrush and was invisible within a few strides.

"Do I get to ask what's going on?" Runacar asked evenly. "Or do all of you just intend to run me around in circles for your amusement?" The ear Pouncewarm had bitten was still bleeding, and the claw marks he'd left were sore.

"*My* amusement would involve flaying you alive," Iardalaith said. "And I am here to keep anyone else who recognizes you from doing that. Now. We need to go further into Nomaitemil, because goblins don't come this far from home without orders—and minders. That means they probably have Lesser Endarkened minions with them that can breach Nomaitemil—or even just loose some fire arrows."

"Thank you for that information," Runacar said, schooling his voice to neutrality. "Is Liri safe? And her brother?"

Iardalaith gave him an odd look. "Let's hope so. Vielle's using the talking animals to guard them."

After perhaps another quartermark of walking, the track opened out into a clearing once more. Iardalaith stopped. Pouncewarm bounded on ahead, leaped at a tree trunk, and scrabbled up into the branching green canopy.

All was quiet.

Runacar had the unmistakable sense of being watched. He looked around, then upward. Many pairs of eyes glowed from behind the shelter of the leaves. More Palugh than one, and possibly Wulvers, too. The sight didn't bring him much comfort, even though both Palugh and Wulver were (technically) on his side.

Iardalaith snapped his fingers and pointed, and flames kindled in a firepit. In the brighter light, Runacar could see that the firepit had been dug down, then lined and floored with stone. There were several benches and stools set around its edge. A bucket was hung over the fire on a tripod. From somewhere nearby Runacar could smell the unmistakable scent of horse.

"The Silver Swords' encampment," Iardalaith said. "As good a place to put you as any—most of them are off supporting the King." He went to the edge of the clearing and returned with a large covered basket. "We need a little more time to make the place homelike," he said, sitting down on one of the benches, "but we weren't expecting company. Tea?"

"Answers would be better," Runacar said, trying to keep the anger out of his voice. The sense of being watched was growing stronger, and it made his skin crawl. As the Prince-Heir of Caerthalien, Runacar had certainly gotten used to having enemies, and many of his enemies had disliked him very much. But the experience of being so cordially and universally hated that he needed to be provided with a Mage bodyguard was outside his experience, and he didn't think he cared for it.

He let his stormcloak fall, and sat down on a bench opposite Iardalaith. Unwarily he reached up to his ear, and winced as his fingers encountered the bite.

"Everyone says those things are cats, but they're more like forest lynxes, if you ask me," Iardalaith said, catching the movement. "Sharp claws. *Long* sharp claws. And they're vermin!" he called upward. Something unseen sneezed in reply. "You'd better let me Heal that."

"No!" Runacar recoiled.

"Now hold still, brother dear—not that you could move if you wanted to, actually—and let me work. This won't hurt at all. Oh, wait. That's completely untrue. It's going to hurt a great deal. . . ." Ivrulion. His brother. The Banebringer.

"No," Runacar repeated more quietly. He realized he'd drawn his dagger and was clutching it.

"All right," Iardalaith said quietly. The jeering undertone in his voice was gone, and his eyes held something like—understanding? Whatever it was, Runacar didn't want it. "But I was serious about the tea. And you should at least poultice that. It's going to fester if you don't."

"I think—" Runacar began. An arrow sang past his ear. A second one embedded itself in the bench beside him, and suddenly the world turned a bright glaring purple. *Daroldan's cast Shield around me,* he thought.

Iardalaith strode from the clearing, leaving Runacar on the bench in his small purple box. *Damn all Lightborn to the Cold Dark. But who's shooting?*

After a few more heartbeats the purple vanished. Iardalaith returned.

"I assume that was one of the many people who want to kill me?" Runacar asked levelly.

"Probably, since she was one of ours," Iardalaith said. He pulled the arrows free from the wooden bench and returned to his tea preparations. "You wanted answers," he said. "Ask your questions."

"How do you kill goblins, what are they, why are they here, you said they needed minders," Runacar answered, in the swift staccato with which he would tender a scouting report. "How do you know the Endarkened aren't with them, what's a Lesser Endarkened, and why wasn't anyone protecting the High King tonight?" The last question surprised even him. Runacar hoped he didn't look as puzzled as he felt.

"Have you ever *tried* protecting her?" Iardalaith demanded. He shook his head. "She should be safe enough with Nomaitemil to draw upon. As for the goblins . . ."

Iardalaith's explanation was also as brisk and neutral as if he was briefing a sortie party. The goblins were creatures of the Endarkened. They'd eat anything they encountered, even their own dead. They spat poison and could move through rock as if it were air. Their ichor was as corrosive as their poison, so it was better not to use a sword against them. Anything could kill goblins, because they were physically fragile and extremely stupid, which also meant someone had to order them to go somewhere, and keep them from leaving until they'd done whatever their master wanted. That was usually one of the Lesser Endarkened: grotesque creatures who were servants of the Endarkened, but which lacked both magic and the power of flight.

"But the worst thing about goblins is that no matter how many you kill, there are always more, and they never stop being hungry. So while the freedom of the field you negotiated will stand, I don't think your furry friends are going to have any dead to collect."

"And you *fight* those?" Runacar asked.

"No," Iardalaith said. "We run from them. Unless we're in a Flower

Forest. Then we hide, and watch out for someone setting the forest aflame. Goblins don't come out in daylight, which is the only reason so many of us are alive."

"So you don't really need to fight them tonight," Runacar said questioningly.

"If we get them all, it will take a while for another wave to come. And when we're attacked, there's always a risk of fire. When the snow comes, that won't be as much of a worry." Iardalaith spoke with the calm assurance of one who had fought this foe more times than he could number.

The tea was brewed. Iardalaith poured two mugs and passed one to Runacar. The scent and taste of the tea was another thing that was homely and familiar. The Otherfolk used tea, but it never tasted like this.

Iardalaith took a length of cloth from his shoulder bag and poured the rest of the pot into it, then scooped out the wet tea-leaves to add to it. He folded the cloth neatly into a pad and offered it to Runacar silently.

"Do you really want an alliance with us?" Runacar asked, taking the poultice. He gingerly applied it to his ear, and then to the gouges in his scalp.

"Me?" Iardalaith said. "No. You and all of your flea-bitten abominations can go down into the Cold Dark forever and I will rejoice. But the King wants the alliance, and I am oath-bound to support her wish in this."

"The High King wants the alliance," Runacar repeated. "Then why didn't she just say so this afternoon?"

"Because she can't just wave her hand and have everyone do her bidding," Iardalaith said with patience. "Not during the Short Peace, and certainly not after Enthroning Day. Right now the guilds are still discussing things; it will probably be Woods Moon, before we have their answer. And if you want to know anything else, you can ask her yourself; she'll probably tell you."

"I'm not sure I want to see her again," Runacar muttered under his breath.

"Get used to living with disappointment," Iardalaith replied.

"What about the—the Otherfolk in the negotiating party?" He'd been about to say *"my friends"* but Iardalaith had made it fairly clear what his feelings were about Otherfolk. "Melisha went to— That is to say, will the goblins attack them?" Runacar meant to gain information, not give it—even in as small and seemingly harmless a matter as a name.

They already know what they're facing. Melisha told me so, didn't she?

"It depends on who's driving them." Iardalaith thought for a moment. "How many Unicorns do you have with you? If they can kill Endarkened, they can probably kill goblins. If the goblins know that, they'll stay out of their way."

Runacar shrugged.

And so much for my chance of having a quiet talk with the High King. Do her followers know their King is mad? After what I've seen of her tonight, I think she might be. Or has Amretheon Overshadowed her from beyond whatever place his kind go to, and there's no Vieliessar at all? The Soulbond says otherwise, but . . .

I don't know. I wish I did. I need to, for Leutric's sake. For the sake of all the Otherfolk. Maybe even for hers.

Runacar and Iardalaith sat in silence. There was a yowl, abruptly ended, as a Palugh disputed territory in the trees. There was a yelp and a thud, and Stormchaser limped slowly into the clearing.

"What are you doing here?" Runacar demanded. He'd left the Wulver back in camp.

Stormchaser flattened his ears and allowed his tail to droop, the very picture of misery. "Elves said we can't chase the goblins." He looked expectantly at Runacar, clearly hoping he would contravene the order.

"You wouldn't like it if you caught one," Runacar said. "So, no. You can't chase the goblins."

Stormchaser sighed deeply and took a place by the fire. "Runfar and Birdleap say they want to be hostages, too," he said. "What do Elves feed hostages?"

"Whatever they feed them, those two will say it's not enough," Runacar said. "Not that there seems to be anything to eat here besides horses."

"And mice," Stormchaser said instantly. "But Pouncewarm won't share. He says he saw them first—but he can't have seen the mice and the tamias and the escurials *all* first, can he?"

Runacar ruffled Stormchaser's ears. "Solve your own problems, my friend. Nobody wins an argument with a Palugh."

("That's truth," Iardalaith muttered.)

In ones and twos the Wulvers came down from their hiding places to share the fire, until Stormchaser's entire Wild—roughly fifteen Wulvers—was there. Runacar wondered why the Palughs had ceded the warmth of the fire until he looked around and saw five of them sitting on the empty benches, looking like large furry loaves of bread. Peculiar bread, granted, but . . .

Iardalaith left the clearing twice more, and on a third occasion simply pointed his finger until something—some*one*—screeched and fled. Once, Birdleap and three of the other Wulvers got to their feet, growling, hackles raised, staring into the darkness for an interminable moment before settling again.

Runacar's sense of being watched by unfriendly eyes never diminished.

CHAPTER TWENTY

Harvest Moon and Rade Moon in the Tenth Year of the High King's Reign: A Kind of Wild Justice

"Why" is not the business of scholars, scouts, or spies.
—Harwing Lightbrother, *The Blade with Three Edges*

The best thing about impersonating Hamphuliadiel of Bethros, Lord of Areve, Astromancer Eternal, and now Extremely Dead Former Lightborn, was that the things Harwing Lightbrother said didn't have to make any sense. He could probably have announced that goats were to be inducted as Lightborn, and everyone would just nod and agree and go get the goats so they could be Called to the Light. (While it was useful, there was hardly any sport in lying to people who had no choice but to believe you.)

With the Otherfolk attackers "driven off," the people of Areve turned wearily to retrieving what they could from the wreckage of their village.

Harwing Lightbrother, in his secret identity as Hamphuliadiel of Bethros, Astromancer Eternal, announced that all of the fallen, regardless of birth, would receive the sacrament of a pyre. He sent his Lightborn into Areve to make sure that any who had been injured were Healed, and opened the stores of the Sanctuary to replace the lavish feast that had been lost in the Bearward/Hippogriff attack.

Which you caused in the first place.

Once Harwing (in the guise of Hamphuliadiel Astromancer) was sure the salvage-and-rescue operation was proceeding as he wished, he went back to the Sanctuary. He snarled at those he could not avoid, and only drew a full breath once he had locked himself into the Astromancer's Tower. *Safe. For now. But oh, the cost in blood and souls of this night . . .*

It was as if he had just awakened from a raging fever. *You knew there would be deaths. You didn't care who died, or how many, so long as you could kill Hamphuliadiel.*

"And I still don't," he said aloud. "In fact, I have quite a list of folk who are going to the Cold Dark before the end of Harvest Moonturn."

After indulging himself in a quartermark of self-pity, Harwing finally looked around.

What in the name of the Void and the Cold Dark has that idiot done to this place?

The tower looked as if it hadn't been cleaned since Inderundiel Astromancer's reign: dust and cobwebs everywhere, baskets of mouse-nibbled scrolls, and even the Silverlight orbs in the walls dimming to darkness. The astrolabe, armilaries, and other instruments for studying the sky and the stars were covered by dust-sheets that were themselves covered with dust, the windows were shuttered and barred, and the staircase that led to the roof was currently being used as a bookcase.

I wonder if he or Celelioniel ever came up here at all? Certainly they didn't have any interest in finding out what the stars said.

Harwing concentrated for a moment, and then Fetched. Apparently, the one thing Hamphuliadiel hadn't changed when he remodeled the Sanctuary was the location of the cleaning supplies. A bundle of soft rags, a scrubbing brush, a pail full of water, a cake of soap, and a large tub of polishing wax appeared.

Harwing got to work. The scrubbing was soothing and mindless, just as it had been in his Candidate days, and the menial task gave him a chance to think.

Item: Go or die. In the virtuous treacherous bargain he had made with the Otherfolk, Harwing had promised Deornoth and Frause that in exchange for their help in killing Hamphuliadiel, he would evacuate the population of Areve, the Sanctuary of the Star, and Rosemoss Manor by Rade. Evacuating a population implied taking it somewhere, and if the Western Reach and the Western Shore were closed to the *alfaljodthi*, that meant going over the Mystrals.

Spellmother Frause had told him it was unsafe to travel in winter now that the great hunters—ice tigers, snow lions, and frost bears—had been driven down out of the Mystrals into the West. She'd actually sounded sorry about it, but Harwing knew that made no difference. Anyone still at Areve by Rade Moon would be slain.

Dying here would be much less work than a forced march through winter snow, but he'd made a promise, and Harwing had been raised in Oronviel's stables. His father had taught him that no matter what one said to komen, one must never lie to horses, hounds, or hawks. He supposed that meant half-beast Otherfolk, too.

Item: Nobody here, Lightborn or Lightless, would follow Harwing Lightbrother. (Or Harwing *Astromancer,* come to that.) But they'd listen to Hamphuliadiel Bethros: Prince Hamphuliadiel, Lord of Areve, Astromancer Eternal. Hamphuliadiel could tell them he was turning Areve to cheese and feeding their children to wolves and the villagers wouldn't even run away. Where could they go? The Sanctuary and Areve were *all that was left.*

(That meant continuing his impersonation of Hamphuliadiel. That would cause problems of its own. But at least everyone would be alive to *have* problems. And that would be later.)

Item: Hamphuliadiel had gathered to himself a large number of people who were complicit in his debasement of the Light. Harwing needed to get rid of them immediately. Even if his voice was Hamphuliadiel's, his words would be his own, and for that reason it wouldn't really be possible to fool those who had known Hamphuliadiel well. Not for very long.

One way or the other, we'll all be dead by Frost. That's comforting, I don't think. "All right," Harwing said aloud. "Let's make a list. Who dies first?"

It was no violation of Mosirinde's Covenant for a Lightborn to kill, after all.

⊰⊱

By the time dawn had come, the Astromancer's Tower gleamed and Harwing had found some previous Astromancer's stash of spell-preserved teas and sweets. Their exquisite tea set—deepest blue lacquer studded with stars that seemed to hang in a sky of infinite depth—only saddened him. It was a thing that belonged to the Old World. It had no place in the new.

By the time dawn had turned to day, Harwing was ready to leave his aerie and continue his masquerade. He had a list of Hamphuliadiel's closest Lightborn cronies and would do his best to avoid them. With Arevethmonion to draw upon, and the Warhunt's training, Harwing's illusions would stand against any assault.

For a while, anyway.

⌗

The very first thing he did that morning was to interrogate the survivors of Daroldan—who had arrived at Areve just in time to see it sacked by monsters. Fortunately, that was something they were used to at this point. There were no Lightborn among the Daroldanders—Momioniarch Lightsister said she'd "taken care of them" and Harwing didn't dare ask what she meant.

Fortunately none of the refugees had ever met Hamphuliadiel, and Harwing had been able to kick Hamphuliadiel's cronies out of the room (and to the other side of the privacy wards) without arousing suspicion. After that, it was a simple matter of shameless eavesdropping on their thoughts combined with leading questions. The refugees were all more than willing to talk—except Lady Carath, the young War Prince of Daroldan, who looked ill and stricken and whose eyes were red and swollen with weeping.

What Harwing learned was disturbing. Not because their stories were anything new to him, but because everyone here was about to learn that Runacarendalur Caerthalien was fighting on the side of the Otherfolk, the Shore Domains had been erased, and the Sanctuary would be attacked next.

There had been Warhunt Mages traveling with the Daroldanders until they reached the Angarussa, but the parties had split there. There were only about twenty in the other party, and these people had forgotten (or never known) their names. Except for one.

Rondithiel.

Rondithiel Lightbrother had died at the Angarussa.

Harwing did not dare let anyone see his grief. *Is Isilla alive? Is Dinias? Are any of my friends alive?*

Fortunately, wrapped in their own sorrows, nobody saw anything amiss. Harwing sent the Daroldanders away with some pompous and meaningless platitudes and spent the rest of the day hiding from Momioniarch in the Astromancer Eternal's insanely luxurious private quarters. He tweaked the room's wards until he was satisfied with them and then searched Hamphuliadiel's chambers. The Astromancer had hidden away enough delicacies here for Harwing to be able to withstand a small siege, as well as a number of bottles of extremely potent cordials. Harwing uncorked each one in turn and sniffed at it experimentally: it seemed Hamphuliadiel had been having trouble sleeping.

In which case I have done him a very great service, for he will never wake again.

Once he was certain that Hamphuliadiel's chambers held no surprises—and unfortunately Hamphuliadiel was not the sort of person to leave a useful diary of his plots and schemes behind him—Harwing summoned a young Lightbrother named Erendor. He'd chosen Erendor because Erendor had been Called to the Light after the Winter War and knew no world other than the one Hamphuliadiel had created. Harwing felt it would be instructive to familiarize himself with Erendor Lightbrother's thoughts and dreams.

Besides, Harwing felt that "Hamphuliadiel" would need new henchmen. Soon.

Through Erendor, he ordered the Sanctuary to open its larders to the villagers to make up for the feast spoiled in the Otherfolk attack. Next, he demanded a complete list of everyone in the Sanctuary, Rosemoss Manor, and Areve. The third thing he called for was a store of blank vellum and a stylus.

He promised a major announcement at the evening meal.

⊰⊱

This has been the most boring battle I've ever been to, Runacar decided. Sitting and waiting was only endurable when there was something at the end of it that wasn't sitting and waiting.

Eventually Iardalaith yawned and stretched, looking up at the sky. "Dawn," he said. "Which means for the next fortnight you can go anywhere in Ceoprentrei unmolested. Let's go see what the goblins have left us."

Iardalaith took the most direct way to the edge of the Flower Forest, which meant the path was unfamiliar to Runacar. He stared out at the meadow, unmoving, when suddenly Iardalaith shoved him—*hard*. Runacar took two long steps to regain his balance. After the warmth of the Flower Forest, the air was like a slap. Runacar realized that the sense of hostile eyes upon him was gone for the first time. The relief was almost painful—but the sense of something wrong remained.

"Now you go back to your new friends," Iardalaith said helpfully.

Runacar wasn't listening. His gaze roved over the meadow ceaselessly, never finding a place to rest. He finally realized what he'd first taken for ice and rock was mud and bits of metal. The bodies of the dead were gone. Even the grass was gone, save for a few withered tufts. The goblins had eaten every living thing.

"And on today's ever-expanding list of things the Lightborn must do immediately is extend the bounds of the Flower Forest to the whole of the valley and put the grass back so we won't be drowning in mud next springtide. You're welcome. Now *go away*."

"Where is—?" *Where is Vieliessar?* Runacar meant to say. But Iardalaith wasn't there.

A flicker of movement drew his eye. Melisha was standing just inside the Western Gate. At the sight of her, the Wulvers raced toward her. Runacar pulled his cloak tight and followed them.

⌘

"My dearly beloved children of the Light. It is with heavy heart I come before you, sick with the heartache of my failure."

It was apparently unusual for Hamphuliadiel to make speeches to the whole group of Lightborn, but not completely unheard-of. Harwing had dressed in Hamphuliadiel's finest regalia (and, Hamphuliadiel had a great deal of fine regalia) to bolster his illusion of being the Astromancer before going forth to make the first move in his endgame. *Be proud of me, Be-*

loved. All I do, I do in your name. And with the weapons you first put into my hands.

The evening meal tonight was relatively lavish: meat in the stew, bread to accompany it, and as much honey for their tea as the Lightborn might want. In Hamphuliadiel's guise, Harwing presided over the High Table with Momioniarch and Galathornthadan on either side of him. Orchalianiel acted as server (disturbing, as Harwing knew that Orchalianiel's specialty was undetectable poisons), and Sunalanthaid simply . . . hovered.

Once the meal was over, Harwing got to his feet and addressed the Lightborn in his best approximation of Hamphuliadiel's rhetoric.

"I have recently received disturbing word from a scouting party I sent forth to gain news of the Western Shore. And since I love and cherish you all as a father his children, once I heard this news, your beloved Astromancer had no choice but to—as I will shortly do—send forth an even larger party to aid and rescue poor dear Harwing Lightbrother and his companion, the well-beloved Ulvearth Lightsister. By now you have all heard the story the pitiful survivors of the Shore—who have come among you at vast and perilous risk to themselves—have to tell. If those I send forth may succor any other survivors of the Beastling atrocities at the Western Shore, it will be a great and glorious day indeed. And of course we must discover what insane treachery the traitorous and unregenerate Caerthalien prince is plotting."

Poor imperiled Harwing Lightbrother. Alas for his probable demise! Harwing thought.

The Lightborn listened in utter silence. Harwing congratulated himself on crafting a speech that told its listeners several times that something utterly horrible had happened and *did not tell them what it was.*

"It is time for our enemies to know that the Sanctuary of the Star will not permit transgressions against the Light to go unpunished. I am therefore sending against them a far greater force of Lightborn and komen than before. I know that all of you would volunteer if you could, so I ask for no volunteers. Three sunturns from now I shall announce who is to become the Sword of the Light. Until that day, cherish our vengeance in your hearts, just as I cherish each one of you."

With a sweeping gesture—Hamphuliadiel's robes seemed to have been specially designed for sweeping gestures—Harwing strode from the Refectory. He was only a few paces down the hallway before he heard the whispers explode behind him with a noise like surf against the rocks. Harwing strode faster, hoping he could manage to get back to the Astromancer's private chambers before any of his acolytes caught up with him.

※

Unfortunately, by the time he reached Hamphuliadiel's suite of rooms, Galathornthadan and Sunalanthaid were awaiting him outside the door.

"And how can I *further* serve you this fine evening?" Harwing asked. The pettish surliness was properly in character for Hamphuliadiel, and neither of the others seemed surprised to hear it.

"It was a great surprise to learn of this proposed expedition," Galathornthadan (born Galath of Haldil, Landbond) said. "I wonder that you did not seek counsel."

"From whom should I seek it?" Harwing snapped. Out of the corner of his eye he saw Sunalanthaid (Sunlan of Haldil) place his hand upon the door. Sunalanthaid's great gift—and a Lightless one at that—was to be inconspicuous to the point of invisibility. Harwing watched him all the more closely because of that. "Lightbrother, you do not have my permission to attend me privately."

"My deepest apologies, my lord, but we felt it would be better to hold this discussion discreetly," Galathornthadan said. "If we could but—"

Most of the sentence had been uttered to Harwing's retreating back, for Harwing had turned away and made for the Astromancer's public Audience Chamber.

※

I never realized what a difference a little elevation can make when you want to look down on someone.

The enormous chair, with its verdant silk cushions and its soft and opulent footstool, made an excellent place from which to review the situation. It was also the only place in the room to sit. Harwing was tempted to try to bring it with him when he left.

Momioniarch and Orchalianiel (Orchal) had joined their comrades as fast as possible. All four of them looked cross as well as nervous.

"I am here," Harwing said, sweeping his arms wide. "Since you feel you have the right—nay, the *obligation*—to interrogate me, do please feel free to begin."

"Lord Astromancer, please forgive Galathornthadan for his graceless lapse," Momioniarch murmured, eyes demurely downcast. "It was only his zeal for your comfort and safety that spurred his unwise words."

This is the dangerous one. She thinks. And she is as ambitious as Hamphuliadiel himself. I do not need Heartseeing to know that, Harwing thought to himself.

"They *were* unwise," Harwing agreed, still feigning Hamphuliadiel's anger. "But I am certain it will relieve him considerably to know he will shortly have the opportunity to redeem that lapse."

"Yes—of course, Lord Astromancer," Galathornthadan blurted out. "But this expedition—"

"In the wake of last night's attack, do you dare to say we do *not* need more information on our attackers and their plans?" Harwing demanded.

"But my lord—Harwing and Ulvearth are dead. Why mention them at all?"

Harwing stared at Momioniarch for several heartbeats as he decided on his response. Of these four, only she wore the name she had been given at birth. Momioniarch had also been born of Haldil, but as the daughter of a castel servant rather than as a kitchen slave. Harwing suspected that she had never quite forgiven Hamphuliadiel for being placed above her by fate.

"I mention them because there are many among us who would prefer to think we are sending a rescue party to our own rather than preparing for a war." *That we could never have won and, in fact, have already lost.* "It will also allow us to—shall we say—exert a more appropriate level of control over our new arrivals as well as some of the more turbulent folk among our own people."

The tense atmosphere in the receiving chamber immediately eased as the four Lightborn were presented with an explanation that made sense to them.

Too trusting, Harwing thought to himself. *But I suspect Hamphuliadiel preferred gullibility to doubt.*

"Of course, my lord Astromancer," Galathornthadan said. "Who will be sent?" His *second* demand for information in a quartermark did not seem to indicate a strong sense of self-preservation on his part.

"*You* will be leading it," Harwing said flatly. "I have long thought that a person of your abilities needed a wider scope for his talent."

Galathornthadan looked pleased. Momioniarch looked disquieted.

Yes—she is the smart one. I shall have to deal with her carefully. But I have just the plan . . .

⌿⌐⌐⍀

Three days later, the expeditionary force departed the Sanctuary of the Star. "Lords" Morenthiel, Girwing, Brenonor, and Alarilla, the false lords and ladies from Daroldan, had been "asked" to accompany the others (so "Hamphuliadiel" said) because it would be foolish to send only Lightborn on such a crucial mission. Since nobility must have servants, Harwing had chosen the cruel, the thievish, and the greedy out of Areve to perform the needful work. He chose no one who would be mourned by anyone left behind.

And since Lightborn, lords, and servants must all be protected, Harwing emptied Rosemoss Manor of its so-called komen to safeguard them. Most of the "komen," as he'd discovered, weren't true komen, but pretenders to the name—former horsegrooms or armsmen or servants who had realized, just as the Daroldanders had, that there would be no one in this new world to challenge the stories they told about themselves.

As for the Lightborn to be sent, there was really only one set of candidates. Harwing had attached all four of Hamphuliadiel's minions to the party by using a set of spells that combined compulsion with susceptibility in a way the Sanctuary Lightborn would never have imagined.

One of the great strengths of the Warhunt had been its innovation.

The Warhunt had not merely raced to devise new weapons and tactics for their battles. They had made it a *game*. Vieliessar had freed the Lightborn from the shackles that had been placed upon them by greedy War Princes, and they had finally learned to play.

But this was not a time for play.

You knew there would be deaths. You didn't care who died, or how many, so long as you could kill Hamphuliadiel.

And I still don't.

The Magery had only worked because Harwing added a sleeping potion to the wine he'd served at the leave-taking party for Galathornthadan. Once the three Lightborn were bespelled, he'd "suggested" that Orchalianiel and Sunalanthaid go along with Galathornthadan to provide support, and asked Momioniarch, as a special favor to her beloved Astromancer, to accompany the party for the first day or so as his observer.

The private orders "Hamphuliadiel" gave her were to watch for signs of rebellion. There wouldn't be any, but it was a lie Momioniarch would accept. Any Lightless who disagreed with the manner of Hamphuliadiel's reign had long ago found themselves victims of tragic accidents.

Just as this is to be.

Harwing was a little sorry that there would be nobody he could tell about this. Tragic accidents were difficult to arrange, especially for a group of more than sixty people.

But possible.

Oh, yes, they were possible.

As the supplies for the journey were assembled and the provisions bespelled, Harwing tainted every single food item. The meat, the bread, the ale, the wine . . . every edible thing the party carried with them. Even if Galathornthadan—or, Light forefend, *Momioniarch*—was suspicious, Magery would detect no poison. There *was* no poison until two or more of the tainted foods were combined. One might healthfully survive quite a long time on bread and water—if one drank only water from springs and streams. But the moment one took a drink from a water-cask or a stoup of ale or cup of wine to go with that bread, they were doomed.

Slowly, of course: Harwing didn't want any word of their deaths to get back to Areve.

⊰⊱

It was long past midnight. The "rescue party" had left at the previous dawn. No lights shone in either Areve or the Sanctuary. The waning moon had set long ago, but the autumn stars shone brightly enough to illuminate the low mist that rose over the fields and the pale clay of the Sanctuary Road.

Harwing heard the sounds of the riders long before he saw them. As the riders came into view, he, still in the guise of Hamphuliadiel, greeted them cordially.

"Momioniarch, have you learned so much so soon? And Galathorn-thadan, I see travel does not agree with you. Sunalanthaid, Orchalianiel, naturally there was no reason to stay once Galathornthadan had left, but I do wish you had tried harder to persuade him to remain."

"I think I have learned that which you sent me forth to learn," Momioniarch said.

"Then come, and we will speak together," Harwing said, as he turned his mount eastward.

⊰⊱

When the creation of Areve had eliminated the need for a dedicated Farmhold to serve the Sanctuary's needs, Rosemoss Manorhouse had been converted to housing for Hamphuliadiel's new komen. None of these changes showed in the building's exterior, and Harwing thought, briefly, of the happy Midwinters he'd spent here, celebrating the Return of the Light among those of his fellows who had dared Mistress Maeredhiel's displeasure to sneak out of their Sanctuary dormitories. Those days seemed like a sweet fever-dream now.

He dismounted in the dooryard and sent his palfrey trotting into the paddock. He would rather have untacked and stabled her, but it was not in character for Hamphuliadiel Astromancer, puffed-up and power-mad former scullion. He strode into the house without looking to see if the others followed, brightening the Silverlight disks set into the walls and ceiling with a flick of his fingers.

The empty rooms already seemed as if they were filled with ghosts.

The other four Lightborn followed him toward the farmhouse kitchen, where the long wooden table had been covered with a fine linen cloth and laden with fresh hot bread, roast pork, summer fruits, cheese, cider, and wine, not to mention a platter of sweets that most of the folk of the Sanctuary and Areve now tasted only in memory. There was even tea, though it was nothing more esoteric than Sanctuary Blend.

"It seems we were expected," Galathornthadan said, regarding the table.

"The Astromancer knows more than you can imagine. And the stars hold all secrets." Harwing seated himself at the head of the table and lit the coals beneath the tea-brazier with a gesture. "Sit. And say what you would have me know." His manner was as offhand and casual as his beloved teacher could have hoped for, but behind that façade, Harwing felt a cold chill of dread. *They know!*

But *did* they—and if they did, *what* did they know? *"It is always better to panic after you know a good reason for it than before,"* he reminded himself.

"Do you mean to tower over me like cruel tutors over an erring student?" he asked. "Sit and eat. I know not where you have ridden from, but I know it must be far for you to gain home in deep night."

Grudgingly, the others seated themselves. Galathornthadan was the first to reach for the food, though the other two Lightbrothers quickly followed suit, filling their plates and their wine cups. Only Momioniarch refrained, pouring herself a cup of cider and selecting an assortment of sweets, all of which lay untasted before her.

"Momioniarch, has our expedition proved fruitful so quickly? Have you found my lost children?" Harwing pressed. Impatience was in Hamphuliadiel's character—that, and an unwarranted sense of invincibility.

"Perhaps, my lord. But first, I would beg of you an indulgence: Harvest Home ends with the telling of old tales, and there was no chance to do so this Festival. I would remedy that lapse tonight."

There was a flurry among the other Lightbrothers that reminded Harwing of doves disturbed by a cat. Either they didn't know whatever Momioniarch knew, or they had not expected this deviation from their plan.

"And as you surely bring welcome news, I am minded to indulge you, Lightsister. But let there be only one tale," Harwing said warningly.

Momioniarch inclined her head in acknowledgment. "Indeed, my lord. Thus shall it be." She looked around the table at her fellow conspirators, clearly willing them to silence. "Once there was a girl-child who should never have been born, never survived her birth, and never returned to the Sanctuary of the Star."

The water in the iron kettle was roiling now, and Harwing poured the teapot full, letting the water warm the clay.

"If she had not, all our lives would have been simpler, for—as you know, my liege—Celelioniel Astromancer studied the ancient texts of prophecy until all thought her mad—save her dearest acolyte and intended successor: Hamphuliadiel of Haldil."

Once Momioniarch had begun her tale, Harwing had realized the reason for it. While she spoke, the others were probing at his shields, trying to find and destroy the spells he had wrapped himself in. They might have overcome him if all four of them had worked their Magery together, yet the idea had clearly never occurred to them. *Orchalianiel is attacking this time, I think. They're taking turns. How sweet.* The Warhunt Mages had resurrected the Wizard-wars and Mage-duels immortalized in the Storysingers' repertoire as a form of teaching and play, and Harwing had skills they could not begin to counter.

"Surely I know the whole of my own story—and dear Celelioniel's too," Harwing scoffed. "It does not explain why the four of you have returned here so quickly."

"Of course," Momioniarch agreed blandly. "But a story that would become a Storysinger's song must be retold many times. And so, knowing the truth of Celelioniel's researches, and knowing that the child uncannily born from the storm heralded the arrival of disaster, Lord Hamphuliadiel made his plans."

"*I* made my plans," Harwing corrected quietly. Momioniarch inclined her head again. Harwing picked up the pot, swirled it to be sure the water warmed it thoroughly, and then poured the waste water onto the floor. He reached for the canister of Sanctuary Blend. Momioniarch resumed her tale.

"Whatever fell danger was coming to them, it could not be met by a hundred domains squabbling over precedence. The last attempt to choose a High King had been in Serenthon Farcarinon's time, and it had failed. The Astromancer knew a new attempt would fail as well. And so he conceived a daring plan."

"How audacious of me," Harwing murmured. The water came to its second boil. Harwing carefully measured loose tea into the pot and filled it, setting the teapot carefully back onto its tray so its contents could steep.

The magical probing continued.

"It was a thing that must be done slowly and carefully so that the War Princes would not suspect," Momioniarch resumed. "Nor was it a thing certain of achievement. But their forces must be united, and only a leader wholly disinterested in lines of succession and personal wealth could unify the Hundred Houses. Hamphuliadiel knew the War Princes would be far more willing to follow him than one of their own, for a Lightborn could not come to rule over their lands."

This is the most outrageous nonsense I have ever heard. So Hamphuliadiel is to be the valiant hero? That would be almost enough to bring Arilcarion War-Maker down from the stars again.

Momioniarch continued, and so did the probing of "Hamphuliadiel's" shields. None of the Lightbrothers was making even a pretense of eating now; they stared fixedly at him as they cast their spells and Momioniarch told her meandering tale.

"Slowly, the Astromancer gathered the threads of his weaving into a skein from which he would weave a rope strong enough to be a noose for ambition."

Harwing raised his hands in silent applause. "My dear Lightsister! Threads and skeins and ropes! You have missed your greatest gift! Such words show you were meant to be a Storysinger yourself!"

Again the calm nod of acknowledgment as Momioniarch once more resumed her tale. She told of Vieliessar who, discovering her part in Amretheon's Prophecy, believed herself to be the destined High King, and of noble Hamphuliadiel, who had tried time and again to woo her to his side to aid him in the battle to come.

Harwing rinsed and warmed a teacup and poured his tea. He set five honey-disks to float on its surface one after another, placing each gently onto the surface of the liquid when its predecessor had melted away to nothing. When all were dissolved, he raised the cup to his lips and drank.

"Never did Hamphuliadiel suspect that the child Vieliessar would be mad and imprudent enough to go to war against the Hundred Houses when another peril lurked upon the horizon, yet she did. And the Astromancer discovered that her insanity had turned nearly all the Lightborn against him, crushing his hopes of victory on their very doorstep."

If his attackers had known Harwing was not Hamphuliadiel they should have slain him immediately. He'd wondered why they chose to follow him so tamely back to the manor house, but now he realized it fit into their plans as well as it did his. He wondered what they were looking for. Proof? Revenge? An offer of alliance?

"Yet I fought on, alone and reviled, with the hand of every lord and noble komen against me, to build once more the defense Vieliessar's recklessness had denied me, la, la, la," Harwing interrupted. "We all know how this story ends, so I ask, Momioniarch: Why tell it now?"

Momioniarch lifted her cup of cider, hesitated, and set it down untasted. "Because the story ends with a death, as is proper to this season. One day the Astromancer sent forth Lightborn to see why the great Flower Forest of the West had burned. When they vanished, he sent more. Now, here is the part that might surprise you. Before the second party of Lightborn departed, unbeknownst to anyone, one of the Lightborn made spellbirds that would fly to the Astromancer's side wherever he lay, so that he would have timely word of whatever occurred."

I knew I should have Dispelled every single one of those damned wagons. But they'd have noticed at the first stop. Ah, well, Harwing thought wryly.

"But that evening, when I set them free, they went nowhere," Momioniarch said softly. "They would only circle about me, over and over again. Their destination could not be found. But this could."

Momioniarch drew an item from the pocket of her robe. She held her closed fist over the table and then opened her fingers. An object fell to the table.

It was a ring. An enormous cloudy blue cabochon stone in an ornate elvensilver band, said to date from the time of Mosirinde Peacemaker. The band was carved to resemble a Dragon, but the ring had no more magic in it than any other pretty trinket. Nevertheless, the ring was a mainstay of Storysingers, appearing in many of their tales to mete out justice, accuse evildoers, and prove the noble rank of orphans.

The Astromancer's ring.

"I Called this jewel to me. Can you say how it came to lie where I found it?" Momioniarch asked.

"I was careless," Harwing said blandly. "As you were." *How was I supposed to know Momioniarch's hobby was looting the dead?* He reached out his hand. "Give it to me."

The chairs scraped and clattered as the four Lightborn stood.

"What have you—? What?" Galathornthadan sputtered, swaying unsteadily.

Momioniarch tried to pick up the ring but instead her shaking fingers closed on a ripe berry, crushing it. Its juice stained her fingers like blood.

"You can't have . . ." she said thickly. "There was no poison. I . . ." She fell back into her chair, her face twisted in confusion. Her soiled fingers made dark prints on the front of her robe as she pawed at herself dazedly.

"No poison," Harwing agreed. "Just a Haste spell. You didn't notice because a weak instance of Haste feels very similar to a Preservation spell," he said to Momioniarch. "Don't blame yourself. You'd already been poisoned by the provisions I sent."

"Combinations." Orchalianiel's voice was slurred as he spoke. "Elegant." He clutched at the edge of the table, managing to convert his fall into a slow kneeling. Galathornthadan simply fell.

"It was," Harwing said. "And you're the only ones I can tell." He got to his feet. "And now all of you die and are never seen again, and everyone I sent out with you will also die, and this is where your story ends. May the Cold Dark take every one of you for what you have done to profane the Light."

There was no answer. By now Harwing was speaking to himself alone.

RADE MOON IN THE TENTH YEAR OF THE HIGH KING'S REIGN: MEMORY, TRADITION, AND DREAMS

A war is not a warrior, and no commander can force the world to follow their whim as if they wear the cloak of the Starry Huntsman.

—Arilcarion War-Maker, *The Way of the Sword*

I thought that becoming one of the Lords Komen would be more fun than this, Isilla thought. But there was nothing about this that was fun: not surviving the fall of Daroldan, not losing Rondithiel to some horrible Beastling sorcery, and not the split of the survivors along partisan lines: the Daroldanders choosing to seek refuge at the Sanctuary of the Star, and the Warhunt Mages intending to cross the Mystrals in search of the High King.

And no matter how small the party, someone had to make the decisions. Isilla sighed. She'd long since given up wondering why that someone had to be her. She had leaves in her hair, they'd run out of tea a fortnight ago, they'd covered less than a third of the distance to the Dragon's Gate, in a sennight or two they were going to have to find a safe place to overwinter, and the others had anointed her *komentai*.

Taking a circuitous route through Domain Rolumienion would add another two days of travel before they could double back to enter Arevethmonion Flower Forest, but if they stayed on the road they would reach the Sanctuary of the Star by midmorning. Everyone had agreed that they must avoid being seen by the Sanctuary at all costs, but of course an argument about raiding the Sanctuary village for supplies had been inevitable. Lightborn would argue about anything.

"I say we sneak in and loot them," Pendray Lightsister said.

"There won't be much sneaking involved with the Daroldanders having already warned them about us," Isilla said.

"Maybe we all died on the road," Dinias argued. "Or they did. Or they didn't mention us."

"Why raid with Arevethmonion right there?" Tangisen objected.

"Arevethmonion won't have new boots—and I need some," Dinias said promptly.

"And when you're caught?" Isilla demanded. "*They know we're out here.* Harwing went to the Sanctuary. And he never came out."

"That was ten years ago," Dinias protested, but more slowly. "A lot can change in ten Wheelturns."

"At the *Sanctuary*?" Isilla demanded.

"Who can say what normal is—especially in these dark times?" Alasnch Lightsister said piously. She clutched her remaining rolls of vellum protectively to her chest—her stores had been drawn upon by the others to make everything from tea bowls to skinning knives in the three moonturns since Daroldan had fallen.

"If they already know we're here, we should definitely raid them," Pendray Lightsister said immediately.

Isilla stopped and flung her hands in the air. "*Enough!*" she said. "Who has Overshadow—besides me?" Isilla's Keystone Gift was Overshadow, but that didn't mean she was the only one who could use the spell. It only meant her Casting of it was strongest, and a strong instance wouldn't be needed today.

"I do! I do!" Pendray sounded positively gleeful.

"Oh good," Tangisen said. "*You* can find out what the goats and chickens are thinking."

"They're thinking about breakfast. I would be," Dinias said instantly.

("*Children,*" Alasneh Lightsister muttered.)

Pendray sat down in the middle of the road, and the others gathered around her in a protective circle. Long moments passed.

"You are not going to like this," Pendray said, not opening her eyes.

But why would they just *go*?" Pantaradet Lightsister said bewilderedly, touching her fingers to the walls as if she hoped they weren't actually there. It had always been as bright as summer noon here, but now the Silverlight was gone, wiped away.

The party was gathered in what had once been the vestibule of the Sanctuary of the Star. It had been a vast circular domed chamber containing the inner and outer doors through which all Lightless and Candidates entered the Sanctuary.

Things had changed.

Now the antechamber to the Shrine was merely a narrow corridor that ran the length of the building. Where the great bronze doors to the Shrine of the Star belonged, there was only a smooth sheet of marble.

Isilla took a deep breath. Now was not the time for panic and mysteries. Now was the time to decide whether being able to sleep out of the cold and wind was worth remaining in this haunted place. *Harwing, dear brother, where are you? I left you here, but I have come back to find you gone. Have you no word for me?*

"It does make it easier to loot the place," Pendray said optimistically. "The trouble is, it doesn't look as if there's anything *to* loot."

"I just wonder how they managed to take the Shrine with them," Dinias said. "Or . . . Wait." He placed his hand against the wall where the Shrine doors should be. The marble began to sublimate, melting away as if it were smoke.

"Stop that!" Isilla cried, but too late. Dinias's Keystone Gift was Transmutation, and it was only heartbeats before the wall dissolved. Isilla caught him as he sagged forward.

"Idiot!" she said fondly. "Arevethmonion is still bounded."

"I just remembered that," Dinias said faintly. He took a deep breath and shook himself, putting aside his momentary weakness and stepping away from Isilla's support. "Oh, well, what's a day in the Warhunt without using up all your reserves of the Light, I always say. And look!"

Through the gap in the wall, they could all see the familiar doors of the Shrine an arm's length beyond. The bronze relief of the Rade was dusty with long entombment, but at least it was still where it had always been.

Only now the doors were chained shut with massive iron chains.

"Hamphuliadiel," Tangisen said bitterly.

"Or Beastlings," Isilla said. "It doesn't matter. We should—"

"But Hamphuliadiel isn't Astromancer any longer," Dinias said, sounding both confused and triumphant. "The Vilya in the garden has fruited."

They'd all seen that, of course. But the urge to get inside had taken precedence, and then the vandalism of the Shrine distracted them.

"Huh," Pendray said comprehensively. "Then who is? And where *is* everyone?"

"Maybe they left a message," Alasneh said. "The Library would be the logical place. I'll go and see."

"Be careful," Isilla warned needlessly. They had all been Candidates here; they knew that secret passageways existed within the walls.

"She just wants to get her hands on some more parchment," Dinias said confidentially.

"We should look everywhere for a message, not just the Library," Isilla said. "Herchet, Dovelock, Dinias—you all have Keystone Transmute. If something was left locked, I'm sure you can open it."

"Everywhere?" Jorganroch Lightbrother asked, sounding scandalized. "Even the Astromancer's private rooms?"

"Everywhere," Isilla said. Now that they'd learned that all the Flower Forests were infested with Beastlings, Arevethmonion didn't seem as welcoming as it had in memory. Perhaps there would be no harm in staying here for a few days, but Isilla intended to be sure of that before she agreed to it. "The Astromancer's Tower overlooks the village—we should be able to look down into it from there," she said. "That will be a good place to start."

"And if the new Astromancer minded us poking through their things, they should have stayed here to tell us so," Dinias said. "If there isn't a new Astromancer, who cares what Hamphuliadiel thinks?"

"It isn't there," Alasneh said, returning.

"What?" said Tangisen. "The—"

"The Library. It isn't there," she repeated.

"The Library's *gone*? How?" Dinias said. "Is it behind a wall?"

"I don't know how, but—"

"Are you sure you—?"

"Not even the *stairs!*"

"I don't think that—"

"*Quiet!*" Isilla shouted, silencing everyone. "We don't know what's going on. We don't know where everyone went. We don't even know who's Astromancer now that the Vilya has fruited."

"In short, we don't know much," Tangisen said. Isilla gave him death-eyes.

"So we are going to search the Sanctuary for answers—and for anything we can use," Isilla continued doggedly. "And after we've done that, we'll decide what to do next."

⊰⊱

Jorganroch and Bramdrin refused to enter the Astromancer's Sanctum, and since Bramdrin's Keystone Gift was Knowing, Isilla suggested that Bramdrin, Jorganroch, and Kathan should make a search of the public rooms of the ground floor to see what they could discover. Isilla warned them not to split their group. She, Dinias, Tangisen, and Pendray would investigate the Astromancer's Tower. Pantaradet, Seragindill, and Ghendanna agreed to investigate the other two floors, which were—except for the Long Chamber—entirely composed of dormitory cells.

⊰⊱

The Astromancer's Tower was as tall as the curtain walls of the great castels. Its entrance lay behind a door at the far end of the West Wing.

The bottom door was not locked or warded, nor was the one at the top. The windows of the Tower had been shuttered but not Transmuted: the first thing Isilla did was to open them. But the tower room contained not one scrap or scroll of writing, even though traditionally the Astromancer kept an account of their reign. *Celelioniel did, poor thing, even as she went mad. Those scrolls should be in the Great Library, along with all the other accounts. But we can't even find the Library.*

"Well, this is useless," Dinias said, turning in place to see everything.

"But really *really* clean," Pendray said, running her fingers across a countertop. She poked curiously at an object made of interlocking rings; its rings spun liquidly until there was a loud "clunk" and the ball in the center fell out and rolled away.

"Uselessness depends on your definition," Alasneh said haughtily. She got to her feet, her arms full of scrollcases she'd found in a lower cabinet. "Ells and ells of parchment—and all unused!"

"Tea," Tangisen said, gesturing toward the shelves behind the desk.

Teas and pots and kettles, cups and sugars and no sign of anything written down. Why? Isilla wondered. "Well, I hope we can find more, because I intend to personally drink everything here."

Tangisen poked at a long metal tube. It turned and pivoted, and there were measuring marks on the tripod that implied it could be set to specific positions, but what it was *for* was a mystery.

"I'm sure all this junk would be useful if I were Astromancer. But how do they know what it does? Nobody trains them. The previous Astromancer goes home as soon as the Vilya fruits."

"Perhaps there's a book," Alasneh said hopefully. "But if there is, it isn't here," she added.

"Come on," Isilla said, setting her foot on the lowest tread of the spiral stair that led to the roof, "let's get a good look at the village."

Dinias was the first to follow her. The circular door in the ceiling slid easily aside when she reached it, and Isilla surmounted the last few treads and stepped out onto the roof.

"It's cold up here," Dinias complained instantly, following her.

"Shield yourself," Isilla said.

"I'm too cold."

Isilla put an arm around his shoulders. "We'll unbind Arevethmonion as soon as we go down."

"We probably should," Dinias said in an odd tone. "Look."

The village below was still and quiet. There were no fires, no scent of smoke in the air, and nothing moving, not even a stray animal.

And unless its inhabitants were all hiding in their cellars, it was completely deserted.

"Byres and folds and pens and styes and coops and cotes are all empty," Isilla said. "And I think the storehouses must be too. But it's almost *Rade*. Where's the harvest?"

"This is creepy," Dinias said, as Tangisen and Alasneh climbed up to join them. "People don't just walk away from their homes—especially this close to winter."

"It could have been earlier," Tangisen said. "Moonturns ago."

"No." Alasneh's voice held certainty. "The Daroldanders—War Prince Carath and the others—if they'd come here and found everything empty, they would have stayed."

"Or doubled back looking for us," Isilla said. "Because they'd probably decide it was our fault."

"So everyone has to have left after they arrived—and went with them," Alasneh finished. "A moonturn, perhaps. Harvest Home or just before."

"Which doesn't tell us where the harvest has gone. Or the livestock."

"Come on," Tangisen said. "Let's see what the others have found."

⊰⊱

By the time Isilla's group had descended from the Astromancer's Tower, Pantaradet, Seragindill, and Ghendanna had finished their survey of the dormitories. The rooms had been stripped of everything but the wooden bed frames, Pantaradet reported. The windows had been sealed off for quite some time. As for the Long Chamber, it had been empty for more than a decade of Wheelturns.

Once Bramdrin, Jorganroch, and Kathan rejoined them, Isilla reorganized the Warhunt Lightborn into different groups—to keep eyes fresh—and sent them to search the Named Chambers, the Refectory, the kitchen—and the servants' loggia on the lower level. She herself searched the Mistress of Servants' desk with the mysterious wall of keys behind it. The keys were there, but the supply of teas, herbs, and incenses—Maeredhiel's special hoarding—were gone.

At least we have the tea from the Tower, or I do not think I could manage to go on, Isilla thought as she sat down behind the desk to begin a detailed search of its contents. It was only half a joke.

And when the others returned from their searches—having found nothing in the servants' quarters, the kitchens (and the Refectory), and the Infirmary—it was time to do what none of them wished to do. They must search the Astromancer's rooms, public and private.

⊰⊱

They started with Hamphuliadiel's bedchamber, in the faint hope they wouldn't have to search the rest of his rooms—if Hamphuliadiel had been keeping any secrets, he'd have been keeping them here.

For the thousandth time that day, Isilla wished Harwing were here. He was more than her friend; he was Gunedwaen Swordmaster's brilliant apprentice, and he had precisely the sort of mind needed to deal with this collection of random facts and make a true-tale of them. The Lightborn had clearly left the Sanctuary of the Star in an orderly fashion. They had taken away everything they could use—clothing, blankets, food. What they could not take, they had—presumably—sealed away. That could explain the "disappearance" of the Great Library and the Shrine of the Star.

And then there was this.

Hamphuliadiel's rooms looked as if the Astromancer had just stepped out a moment ago. The bedclothes were rumpled. A tray filled with exquisite dishes that still contained the remains of a meal had been shoved aside onto a low bench. A cup of tea, unfinished, was balanced on the edge of a window—and the spells that kept the tea hot and the winter outside the window were still in effect. This chamber looked as if it had been left utterly untouched.

To see the Astromancer living in such opulence—silk sheets and thick furs and soft mattresses upon his bed, shelves of perfumes and cosmetics and lotions, jars of rare incenses, racks of sumptuous garments in linen and wool and brocaded silk, identical in their materials to those the highest War Prince might wear—to see stacks of books and piles of scrolls and pictures displayed only for their beauty, cabinets filled with cordials and sweets, delicacies and rare spices all for his pleasure, others filled with nothing but canisters of tea, to lift the lid from fine shin'zuruf pots and find them filled with gemstones—disturbed all of them.

We all knew Hamphuliadiel was crazy, and rotted through with ambition, but . . . he was living in state as if he were a War Prince himself. Why did no one stop him? Isilla thought.

"So many *things,*" Alasneh said wonderingly. "When did the Astromancer come to live in such luxury?"

"As soon as he could get away with it," Pendray said promptly. She picked up a pot of perfume from a table—one of several pots and several tables that cluttered the room—and set it down again. "But I don't think it made him happy."

"What it did make him was *rich,*" Tangisen said disgustedly.

"Too bad there wasn't anything left by then to buy," Dinias answered.

"Well at least we can all get a change of clothes out of this," Tangisen said, waving toward a clothespress. "And yes, Dinias, boots."

"If you want to cross the Mystrals barefoot, I don't," Dinias replied, poking through a large standing wardrobe chest. "And vellum boots wear about as well as . . . vellum. *Aha!*" He pounced on a pair of boots— bright green, fur-lined, and stamped with a design of stars and vines in elvensilver—with a cry of delight.

"I don't actually want to cross the Mystrals again at all," Tangisen said. "Twice has been twice too many. And this is just one more mystery to add to the High King's silence."

"Perhaps this one can be solved," Isilla suggested. "Who wants to cast Knowing?"

Bramdrin Lightsister agreed to be the spellcaster. She cast Knowing over a number of objects in the Astromancer's chambers, but all she could determine was that Hamphuliadiel had suffered from bad dreams. At least she'd found what had been a secret entrance to the Shrine of the Star, but it had been sealed shut, Spell-locked, and had an enormous chest shoved in front of it.

"I guess he decided he really really *really* didn't want to talk to the Starry Hunt."

<hr />

Beginning the day after the inconclusive goblin attack, the High King met with Audalo for at least half of every day—and for endless tiny cups of tea.

The first meeting naturally focused on the disappearance of the Otherfolk dead, but as the first negotiating party had seen that the Elves had done their best to honor them, Vieliessar was able to settle that point to most of the Otherfolk's satisfaction fairly quickly.

Unfortunately, that was just about the only thing to happen quickly.

Their second meeting had been completely disrupted by the arrival of the Unicorns with the rest of the children they had saved, and—it seemed—half the Otherfolk.

("Manostar isn't that far away, you know," Melisha said to Runacar that evening.)

Palugh, Wulvers, Fauns, and Brownies joined the Elves in Nomait-emil, some visibly, some clandestinely. The adults seemed to regard their children's Otherfolk playmates as animate dolls, rather than enemy agents. Of the four races, the Elves were familiar only with the Fauns. There was no history of bloody conflict and betrayal between them and the Palugh, Wulvers, and Brownies.

Either the High King has utter control over her people, to force them against their natures, or she has no control over them at all, Runacar thought, seeing that. *I only wish I knew which of those two notions is true. Besides that, the Elves regard the Unicorns with a veneration near to worship, and won't do anything against them. They'd probably do whatever the Unicorns told them to do. It's just too bad that no one in all of Jer-a-kalaliel can tell the Unicorns anything.*

The Endarkened did not return. They did not send any of the beasts or creatures the High King's army had previously fought. There were no clashes between Otherfolk and Elf.

The negotiations—though it might be better to call them meetings, as nothing was decided during them—continued through the whole period of the Freedom of the Field. Runacar was on edge during that entire time, awaiting a fresh attack. But he was the only one. Neither the Elves nor the Otherfolk behaved as if they were anticipating a new attack. It was as if the Endarkened had never existed.

It took Runacar most of the sennight to deduce their respective reasons. He wasn't sure he was right, but his conclusion *felt* right.

Vieliessar's people had constantly been fighting the Endarkened for over a decade of Wheelturns. When they weren't fighting, they didn't waste time anticipating the next battle or remembering the last: they grasped at the sweets of Life as they could.

And the Otherfolk simply expected to die.

Since before Runacar was born, since before Caerthalien was founded, since before Amretheon had wedded Pelashia, the Otherfolk had lived with the knowledge that the Red Harvest would bring with it the death of everyone. Even Leutric, with all of his plans and connivances, had only hoped to delay that final battle—not win it.

Runacar had never managed to make a dent in that fatalism, but for the first time, it didn't matter. Vieliessar had defied every prediction of her future—and then she had gone on to defeat the Hundred Houses in battle. They all might die, but Runacar knew one thing for truth: Vieliessar would never give up—nor would she ever acknowledge defeat.

If adamantine stubbornness and stone-cold courage could defeat the Endarkened, there was no question of defeat. The Elves—and their probable allies—would win.

⊰⊱

The World Without Sun continued along its own path, its rhythms alien and unknowable to the Light and the living. Since the beginning of time, the Endarkened had only truly been interested in their own world. Now, in the wake of their inglorious defeat among the Dragon's Bones, they fought one another not only over the spoils of that battle, but for the possessions—and slaves—of the dead Endarkened.

Never before had there been so many dead. Never.

And the Unicorns—!

Since Silver Life was raised up out of the ashes of Green Life and Red Life, the Endarkened had chanced upon the accursed creatures now and then. But they had never thought there could be more than one or two. Now they had seen there were thousands. The thought was unbearable. Something must be done.

A hundred revenges were devised for slaughtering the Unicorns and feasting upon their flesh. A thousand stratagems were created to drive the Elflings mad with sorrow as their race died. A million ideas for scouring the Elflands to bare rock within a single night were hotly debated.

But none of those plans was brought before Virulan, for the King of the Endarkened had hidden himself away, with only *He Who Is* for his constant companion.

Now it was Shurzul who forced peace upon the Endarkened when they quarreled, Shurzul who gave them games and contests to distract them.

And if no one saw King Virulan, no one was foolish enough to remark upon that fact. When the Endarkened wondered aloud about the absence of their King, their words were fawning and honeyed. Virulan was preparing some mighty new sorcery that would render their enemies helpless. Virulan was going to slay the Unicorns from his throne in the Heart of Darkness. Virulan was preparing some other masterstroke of sorcery and war.

All of them could feel the pressure of the dark regard of *He Who Is* upon their King. And nobody wanted to interfere with anything *He Who Is* might be doing.

It was why the ambitious among them, like Uralesse, did not attempt to kill the King and take his throne. It was why everyone deferred to Shurzul, and followed her orders. They dared not attack King Virulan. And they dared not return to the Bright World without his permission.

So the Endarkened waited, entertaining themselves with torture, gluttony, and pleasure.

CHAPTER TWENTY-TWO

RADE MOON IN THE TENTH YEAR OF THE HIGH KING'S REIGN: IN WINTER'S SHADOW

*Bring me a blade that will cut the wind, that will sever the shadow
from the body or the scent from a flower. With one stroke of such
a blade I will slay all my enemies and all their unborn children.
With two strokes I shall slay their ancestors and all their kin. And
with three and four and five I will slay all the living things of their
land, wild and tame. I will turn the rock to sand for the wind to
blow away.*

—Arilcarion War-Maker, *Of the Sword Road*

The fire leapt and crackled. Outside the window—its opening filled with small pieces of glass instead of Lightborn Magery—snow sifted down from the sky as it had for all of the past fortnight. The room was filled with scents of wet wool, damp fur, horse, and leather, for Runacar had just come back from a ride through the woods. There was no more game in the woods than there had been back at the beginning of Harvest, but the destriers Atishinan and Folwin, as well as the grey palfrey Stormcrow, required exercise and conditioning, and hunting made a good pretext.

It was the end of Rade. A full moonturn since the Battle of Ceoprentrei. At this time of year Runacar was usually in the Bearward hidel that was home to Frause and her family. That had been home to his foster-brother Keloit.

Now both Keloit and Radafa were dead, in the battle that Runacar had expected to end his life as well. That he lived seemed unfair—to him and to them.

"Rune is brooding again," Stormchaser said, lifting his head.

The rest of the Wulvers ignored their brother, the dozing Wild squirming and nudging one another in an attempt to get closer to the fire. If there had not been a trestle-bench for Sundapple to absorb his share of the fire's heat, Runacar would have had to referee a dozen fights each day.

"I am not brooding," he said.

"Are," Stormchaser answered, lifting his head.

Runacar didn't know how he'd ended up with a Wild and most of a Pounce as house mates. Usually he enjoyed—or at least tolerated—their companionship, but there were other days when his mood matched the weather. He picked up an object from the table beside him. It was a silver buckle. The metal was worn and pitted now, but the design—*ceriss* trees in flower—could still be seen. He'd given it to Keloit on some occasion long ago. Now it was all that was left of the Bearward.

Properly it should go to Helda, or to Frause, but Runacar could not bear to relinquish it. Keeping it meant keeping the guilt he felt fresh and new. No commander worthy of the title ever forgot the mistakes they'd made in battle, nor did they wish to.

If the Unicorns had not come that day—if they had not been numerous beyond dreams—everyone in both armies would have died. And no matter how Runacar turned the matter over in his mind, he could not think of anything he could have done before the battle began that would have changed the outcome.

Except to have made use of a Swordmaster's skills, and not danced onto the field like a maiden knight come to their bridal.

"Should have, could have, would have"—the three sisters who haunt every commander's dreams. If I'd really been serious about stopping Vieliessar at Ceoprentrei, Runacar told himself, *I should have slit my own throat.*

And would that have stopped her mad Lightborn? Would it have stopped Rithdeliel?

He knew the answer.

Stormchaser pricked up his ears, lifted his head, and gave up the battle for hearth-space. As he got to his feet, the rest of the Wild began moving as well. "Someone's coming!" Stormchaser said. "Isn't that wonderful? Visitors, Rune! New people!" The rest of the Wild was equally ecstatic.

(It was no use attempting to strangle Stormchaser: that cheerful excitement and optimism seemed to be baked in to all the Wulvers.)

Runacar got to his feet and went to the door. When the Centaurs of Smoketree had graciously disassembled one of the empty houses and had it moved to the river edge—something they seemed to consider as simple as moving a war-pavilion and which Runacar felt to be the next thing to magic—he'd made sure that the main door was on the opposite side of the house from the prevailing wind, which was the only reason it was not covered by a snowdrift. The knocking began just as he reached it. He slid open the spy-hole, but all that he saw was two fur-swathed and snow-covered shapes, one of them a Centaur.

"Open the door!" the other one demanded. She began to kick the door.

The voice was familiar—and so was the impatience. Runacar opened the door.

⚎

"So we knew you were lonely, and when Pelere stopped by Blackwheat I thought we should come and see you," Andhel said.

He was mulling a pot of cider over the fire; three mugs stood ready for it. He sat on one of the settles to watch it. "You were living in my *house*?" Runacar demanded. Blackwheat Gate was his manor house in Cirandeiron.

The coats and hoods of his visitors hung on drying racks in the kitchen. The three Palugh had relocated to the cross-beam above and gazed down through slitted yellow eyes. Runacar had shooed the Wulvers away from the fire with the bribe of a bag of sugar candy from his larder. They'd creep back, of course, but meanwhile Pelere and Andhel could get warm without having to fight Wulvers for hearth-space.

"You weren't using it." Andhel cast him a provocative look. "What was I *supposed* to do?"

With the change of the season, the Woodwose's garb had changed as well. She had bleached her hair white, and tied ribbons and scraps of cloth into it. Her clothing, while warm, gave an appearance of tattered scraps and rags. She would vanish instantly in any winter forest.

"Meanwhile, despite my oft-praised great and resourceful imagination, I cannot *imagine* Pelere on the back of a Hippogriff," Runacar said, "which means you had to walk all the way from Cirandeiron to Mangiralas to interrupt my day. Or are you going somewhere else and—?"

"Stop it!" Pelere cried, stamping her foot. The Centauress was in full winter coat, as thick and plush as a Bearward's fur and much the same color. "Stop *playing!*"

Runacar sat forward, instantly all business. "Pelere? What's happened?" *The High King's people can't have done anything—they're snowed in until Rain Moon. And if the Endarkened had been sighted, Andhel wouldn't have been entertaining herself by dancing around the point.*

"The Shrine at Arevethmonion is deserted, and so is the village," Pelere said bluntly. "They've all left, even the witchborn. I asked the Hippogriffs, and they say the Elves are heading east. Probably toward the pass. Two groups."

"Oh," Runacar said.

The only direction they could be heading was toward the Dragon's Gate.

Toward Vieliessar.

Freed of his chief troublemakers, "Hamphuliadiel" could work toward his necessary goal: being gone from here by the end of Rade Moon.

Harwing thought—he *hoped*—the Otherfolk would give him that long before coming to wipe them out. What the Bearward sorceress had told him was simple enough: one moon, and after that all remaining in the Sanctuary and the town would be slain.

Unfortunately, there was more for Harwing to do than simply announce that fact.

First, in the name of occupying them and keeping them out of mischief, "Hamphuliadiel" called all the Lightborn together to order that they must search the whole of the Sanctuary for any object or garment made from the bodies of Beastlings. (Naturally the Astromancer would selflessly search his private chambers himself, a symbol of his eternal toil and care on behalf of the Lightborn he served.)

When the search was complete, Harwing was frankly astonished—and sickened—at the number of items the search produced. He had the items taken to the field behind the Sanctuary garden, and there he sank them—furs and feathers, leathers and scales, bones and ivory—deep beneath the soil. It didn't make him feel any better, but then, he hadn't thought it would.

Now that he had the Lightborn completely confused, Harwing proclaimed that the gates and walls of Areve must be removed, not rebuilt. When he was questioned—Ilmion Lightbrother couched his question *most* submissively as "what do we tell the Lightless?"—Harwing announced that the stars had confided a great secret to him, which he would reveal in due time. (Harwing, in possession of the Astromancer's ring and his wardrobe—but not the secrets passed down from Astromancer to Astromancer—had no idea if that was possible. However it was *plausible*, and that was enough.)

Ilmion pretended to accept that, fulsomely praising the Astromancer's wisdom and knowledge and power. Harwing did not have good feelings about Ilmion Lightbrother: he was ambitious, and now that his superiors had been removed, he saw a chance to take their place. But Gunedwaen had once told Harwing that sometimes it was enough to postpone disaster for a sunturn, or even a candlemark, and Harwing heeded.

The Lightborn began dismantling the wall.

As for the Lightless . . .

Since the departure of the rescue party (followed by the mysterious conflagration that had burnt Rosemoss Manor Farm to the ground), Harwing had been freed to behave in un-Hamphuliadielian ways. "Hamphuliadiel" had made daily distributions of teas and cordials from the Sanctuary to every household. He'd lifted the ban on slaughtering livestock for personal consumption. He'd revoked the law against distributing measures of flour, ale, or bread to any who did not toil.

And most astonishing of all, "Hamphuliadiel" decreed that anyone who wished could take their share of the harvest in full and at once.

Part of this stunning generosity was meant to make the villagers well-fed enough to survive a long journey. Another part was about drawing down their stores to the point they would starve if they tried to remain here.

"If you are giving someone a choice," Gunedwaen had always said, *"make it an easy one."*

And once the wall was disassembled, Harwing ordered another feast, this one to be shared by Lightborn and Lightless alike.

As befit his impersonation of the pompous ass Hamphuliadiel had been in life, Harwing remained in the Sanctuary alone while his Lightborn dined with the villagers. Tonight he would announce their exodus, and either they would agree to come away . . .

Or he would see how many Lightless he could place under *geasa* at the same time.

Harwing was fairly certain the Lightborn would come with him on no more than his word of command: the world Hamphuliadiel had created was strangely disturbing. It was almost as if Hamphuliadiel had worked to make himself—and it—the antithesis of Lord Vieliessar and her people.

Before the time of the High King, Lightborn had been valued and sometimes feared, their persons sacrosanct, their lives spent as diplomats and couriers, mediators and Healers. And sometimes—especially if they served in the household of a War Prince—they could hold themselves equal in rank to the Lords Komen.

But almost all of the Lightborn had been born as serfs and as slaves, and even while the Sanctuary of the Star trained them in use of the Light, it taught them that their role in the world was one of service. They might be given gifts of wealth and land by the lords they served, but they could not make an inheritance of their wealth. Lightborn moved through the Cold World like living ghosts, and could only hope for better from the Warm World after their deaths.

Hamphuliadiel had turned that upside down. In his tiny domain, the Lightborn were the superiors of the Lightless. They moved through the world he had made mantled in privilege, regarded with fear by the Lightless. Their word was law, their judgments irrefutable . . .

And their arrogance limitless.

At least half the Sanctuary Lightborn had been no more than Candidates or Postulants at the start of the High King's War. Perhaps another fifty or so had been Called to the Light from Areve. It had been simple for Hamphuliadiel to twist them in the way he had wished: fawning and servile to him, arrogant and vicious to the Lightless. Any who had mastered the first half of the unwritten law but not the second had their failure overlooked—at least temporarily.

Harwing didn't much care about reforming the corrupt Lightborn.

He just cared about getting out of here alive.

⊰※⊱

It was time to make his appearance. "Hamphuliadiel" wreathed himself in Silverlight, doused himself with scent, and descended from the Sanctuary of the Star to the fields of Areve.

The tables were laid out just as they had been for Harvest Home, and tonight the whole of the space was surrounded by curtains of amaranthine fire to preserve the diners from autumn chill.

The villagers looked puzzled but well fed.

"My dear and beloved children," "Hamphuliadiel" began. Silverlight glittered off the velvet and gems he wore. "I have promised you a revelation, and tonight I shall deliver it."

There was a flurry of expectant murmuring, quickly stilled.

"As we all now know, the Domains of the Shore have been erased, but long before that terrible day, your princes and komen deserted you, so that I alone remained as a bastion of safety and truth. Why have the folk who owe you their care and their protection deserted you? Long I sought some answer, and at last I was vouchsafed it—by *the very stars themselves!*"

"Long live the Astromancer! A thousand years of his glory!" Ilmion rose to lead the cheer, and the other Lightborn joined him.

Harwing raised his hands for silence. Just as he began to think really *really* hard about using Thunderbolt against Ilmion, it finally descended.

"What I now ask of you is hard, my people, but I know it is not beyond your power. With Lightborn and villager striving together, working side by side, our success is assured. We are protected by the stars themselves from any assault by Beastling or brigand. Now hear my decree: we will leave Areve and the Sanctuary of the Star. We will journey eastward until we reach the High King. When she stands before me, High King Vieliessar will acknowledge my authority and her responsibility, and golden years of peace and plenty for everyone will be assured."

The Lightborns' expressions seemed to indicate that Harwing *had* struck down Ilmion with Thunderbolt. The Lightless merely looked puzzled. Taking advantage of the moment, Harwing turned and made his magisterial way back to the Sanctuary.

⫘

The following day was filled with Lightborn implying to "Hamphuliadiel" (in the very most tactful fashion possible) that he could not possibly be serious about leaving on this mad quest. To most of those he gave tasks of preparation for the journey. To some he confided that he had received a visitation from the Silver Hooves, and that any *alfaljodthi* here at the end of Rade Moon would be taken by Them in sacrifice as They rode forth to cleanse the land of the Beastlings. By the end of the day, he almost wished Momioniarch Lightsister were still here. At least she would have kept everyone from badgering him.

⫘

They left Areve at dawn on the last day of Rade. Harwing's heart wept at the leave-taking, for since its founding by Mosirinde Peacemaker at the dawn of the Hundred Houses, the Shrine of the Star had never been without its Lightborn guardians. He wondered whether any of the Lightborn Hamphuliadiel had made felt the same.

Everyone was shivering in the cold, and Harwing was grateful that the journey to reach Arevethmonion was as short as it was. The Lightborn led, the wagons followed, and the herding dogs and what livestock the villagers had retained followed the wagons.

Harwing walked at the head of the procession in Hamphuliadiel's gaudy Astromancer regalia. Its crowning glory was a stave of unbreakable ahata-wood inlaid with a pattern of vines and stars in elvensilver, and holding at its apex a perfect fist-sized sphere of clear crystal that had been in some irremediable way bespelled with Silverlight. (Harwing had tried to break the spell for three sunturns without success.)

Just the thing to have when going somewhere inconspicuously, Harwing grumbled to himself.

But of course it wasn't possible to leave the staff behind; he needed all the help random props could give to shore up his impersonation of the Astromancer Eternal. The Lightborn would follow no one but the Astromancer, and as for the villagers . . .

They have been whipped, scorned, and abandoned, and I do not think they could choose a leader for themselves if they tried. If they did, he would not be a good one.

The major drawback to his masquerade was that Harwing must do as Hamphuliadiel would have done, and that meant leading the procession instead of following it.

Following it would have been much more useful.

By the midday halt, the caravan had already lost over a hundred people. Some had chased after livestock that had escaped into the forest and never returned; some were off searching for children who had inexplicably gone missing.

Some had decided they didn't want to go after all and doubled back to the village.

The Lightborn were able to find those and bring them back.

They didn't find the children.

❧

By the end of the second day, Harwing would gladly have led the caravan out of the Flower Forest to take their chances in open country. Unfortunately, Hamphuliadiel would never have considered it. Even more unfortunately, there was no way to leave the Flower Forest except by the road—at least not for a score of heavy ox-drawn wagons, livestock, and innumerable handcarts—and backtracking would bring them back in sight of Areve. Harwing did not think there were enough spells in the entire world to force the farmers and the villagers to leave it a second (or third) time.

Children continued to vanish.

First "Hamphuliadiel" ordered all of the children to ride in the carts. Then "he" ordered all of them *tied to* the carts. The Lightborn were ordered to walk beside the carts and in the fantail of the array to keep any of the Lightless from being taken.

It didn't work.

Their food supplies dwindled far faster than they should have. During their third night on the road, every single one of the chickens silently vanished.

Anyone (and any *thing*) that vanished into Arevethmonion could not be traced. Not by Lightborn spells, and not by dogs' noses. The only way Harwing could get the parents of missing children to come away was to bespell them into obedience. He only tried it a couple of times. It was useless. Worse than useless. The moment the spell was lifted, they returned to the search.

No one blamed the Astromancer for any of this, not even in the privacy of their thoughts. Harwing blamed himself enough for all of them. He went over in his mind the bargain he'd made at Centaur Newtown. He thought now that he'd missed something, and flagellated himself all the more for his mistake.

He'd understood that if he would evacuate Areve and the Sanctuary, and leave the West entirely, the Otherfolk would spare their lives. Apparently, what Vithimir and Frause had actually meant was that the Otherfolk *wouldn't kill them in battle.*

And does Vithimir speak for all the Otherfolk, whoever and wherever they are? You didn't ask. You were so happy to make your bargain with them that you didn't care about the details. And now it hardly matters if you'd all stayed there until Woods Moon. The people are disappearing. Probably dead. Probably by the time you leave Arevethmonion, you'll be the only one left.

—※—

In the beginning, the *alfaljodthi* who had survived Enthroning Day had no choice about leaving Tildorangelor, for when the Flower Forest was drained of its Light the Endarkened would have entered it and killed all of them. They might have husbanded its resources enough to remain there longer, but they had been fighting one another incessantly.

It was a mistake Vieliessar never let them make again. The cost of making it even once was ruinous, for there had been no other shelter nearby—and the Endarkened had been waiting.

Yet many of her people *had* survived. They had been running and hiding ever since. Vieliessar's ultimate goal was the Sanctuary of the Star, and Arevethmonion was the largest remaining Flower Forest anyone knew of, able to shelter all of the High King's people. It was Thurion who had made that point to the rest of the council over and over: in the West there was safety.

Unfortunately, he'd been wrong.

The Otherfolk forces held them in Ceoprentrei, and without the Unicorns, the Endarkened would have killed all of both armies on the spot. Discovering that Nomaitemil could shelter them for Wheelturns to come should have been a joyful occasion for all.

It should have put an end to any need for Vieliessar to go to the Sanctuary of the Star.

In the first place, Hamphuliadiel had gone mad years ago, and might have destroyed whatever information was there. In the second place, the Unicorns constituted a weapon that *would actually kill Endarkened*. And in the third place, the Minotaur King-Emperor *had* a weapon that would kill Endarkened.

But Vieliessar still meant to go to the Sanctuary of the Star—herself—*alone*—and Thurion couldn't think of any way to stop her. The only thing that *might* do so was the details of the great weapon that the Emperor of the Otherfolk possessed.

There was no help for it. He was going to have to go talk to Caerthalien.

Thurion cast a strong instance of Door, drew the Light of Nomaitemil around himself, and stepped through.

CHAPTER TWENTY-THREE

RADE MOON IN THE TENTH YEAR OF THE HIGH KING'S REIGN: TRANSIT OF LIES

There is little difference between lies and truths. Neither are facts.
—Thurion Pathfinder, Epigrams

When Thurion reached the door to Caerthalien's dwelling-place, he could hear multiple voices inside. Caerthalien wasn't alone. He was about to retreat, when a scrap of over-heard conversation stopped him.

"—the Shrine of the Star is *gone*?" Caerthalien's voice carried through the door even over the sound of the wind. Thurion stepped closer and cast Hearing.

"No—" It was an unfamiliar voice. "Just empty. The witchborn have all left."

Empty? That doesn't sound good. Thurion touched the door. Knowing combined with Fetch would allow him to unbolt it, Shield would get him inside without any betraying gust of air, and Cloak would keep him invisible.

But abruptly a gabble of Wulver voices erupted within, just as a heavy living weight dropped across his shoulders. "First!" the Palugh crowed. "Mine!"

There was really no point in Cloak after that, so Thurion dropped the spell just as Caerthalien opened the door. The two of them stared at each other for a moment.

"Why not come inside?" Caerthalien asked, stepping back. "Everyone else has."

Sundapple purred loudly. Thurion shrugged (as best he could under the weight of a Palugh) and entered.

—⊰⊱—

The Wulvers rushed up to Thurion while Caerthalien closed and bolted the door again. They searched him thoroughly while greeting him joyfully, and Thurion was quickly relieved of his eating knife and his possibles pouch, as Sundapple swatted at them and insisted Thurion belonged to *him*.

"I'll want those back," Thurion said mildly.

Caerthalien just snorted and walked toward the hearth, gesturing for Thurion to follow.

Caerthalien's house was certainly not Caerthalien Great Keep, but it had walls and a roof, furniture and a great stone hearth, so Thurion counted it as luxury. It looked like something Thurion would have expected to see in a Farmhold, though the proportions were subtly off. Wide shallow steps to Thurion's right led up to what might be a sleeping loft; two more Palugh were perched on the loft railing. At the far right of the chamber stood a sandtable and beside it a desk covered with scrolls, wax tablets, and other arcanum. (Runacar had gotten the Hippogriffs to bring him some of his materiels from Blackwheat Manor before the weather closed in completely.) At the near leftward end was the hearth, with stools, chairs, and benches clustered around it. There was a cauldron of cider heating, and another worktable nearby holding hoofpicks, cloths, brushes, jars of oil, and the pieces of a disassembled bridle. The room smelled wholesomely of leather, spices, wet Wulvers . . . and horse.

Caerthalien's guests stood in front of the hearth: a Centauress and a Woodwose. After a moment, Thurion recognized them: Andhel and Pelere, Caerthalien's *alakomentai'a*.

"I apologize for intruding upon what is clearly a private meeting," Thurion said, reaching up to stroke Sundapple. "I did not come to spy."

Andhel laughed. "Of course you did not, Houseborn! You came only to visit Rune, for he is accounted your dearest friend."

"Let's kill him and get on with it," Pelere said.

Runacar shrugged. "Witchborn," he said, as if that was an explanation. "If we tried it, he'd probably just smash the house to bits. And I'm fond of it."

"As I said," Thurion repeated steadily, "I did not come to spy. I came to speak to Caerthalien Warlord. If you will permit, I will return another time."

"Sit," Runacar said, indicating the empty settle facing the hearth. "Have some cider. And call me by my proper name and title: I am not Caerthalien's Warlord, nor her War Prince. I am Runacar, Battlemaster to the Otherfolk. What I've just been told isn't exactly a secret, and we probably need a Lightborn perspective."

Thurion sat. Sundapple slid from his shoulders to his lap, purring loudly. The two other Palugh—their names were Cloudfoot and Shadowdance, if he remembered correctly—crossed the room and sniffed at Thurion disdainfully—as if he were somehow inferior goods—before jumping up onto the settle to sit on either side of him. Thurion stroked Sundapple absentmindedly. Caerthalien swung the pot away from the flames and ladled out cider into three large wooden mugs. He sent one of the Wulvers off to the kitchen for a fourth mug, filled it, and parceled the rest of the cider into a dozen wooden bowls. The Wulvers took possession of them greedily, but there was not the snarling and snapping there would be with a pack of hunting dogs. The Wild leader, a female with the grey muzzle of age, took her own dish first, then made sure the rest of the Wild each received one.

"What makes you think the Sanctuary of the Star and its village are deserted?" Thurion asked, once everyone had a chance to drink. He glanced toward Caerthalien. "I was outside the door. You have a very loud voice."

"Spying," Andhel said with satisfaction.

"I went inside," Pelere said, after a glance toward Caerthalien. "I was taking the long way around the Pesthole—through Rolumienion, as you would call it—and realized I had smelled no smoke, though the wind was from the south. So I went to see." She shrugged, looking as much confused as troubled. "They took down the wall around the town, and took many of the buildings apart as well. No one was there. Even if they'd been hiding in the ruins, they would have attacked me—or run."

"And the Sanctuary?" Thurion asked. It was an effort to frame the question. He really didn't want the answer.

"As you know, we Centaurs cannot use magic, though it can be used upon us. I had never thought I would want Drotha by my side—I was certain I was walking into a thousand traps! But no: the garden gate was open, and the door that led inside. I did not go far. But the building was empty."

"Now *you* talk," Andhel said, rounding on Thurion.

"There is . . . There is a spell we have that can transport us from one Flower Forest to another—or from a Flower Forest to elsewhere. I used it to come here. The Lightborn of the Sanctuary could have used it. But they could not have transported all the Lightless with them."

"No bodies," Caerthalien added. "And before you blame any of my people: yes, the Sanctuary was to be my next campaign. It seems unlikely any of my people would anticipate me, but I tell you no secrets when I say we are very loosely organized."

"Why work when a Houseborn will do it for you?" Andhel snarked.

"No bodies, no battles—they just walked away," Pelere said. "And I don't know where."

"Arevethmonion," Thurion said absently. "It offers shelter and a good road."

"I did not ask there," Pelere said to Runacar. "I am sorry, Teacher."

"Better to live bringing a handful than die bringing a sackful," Runacar answered. It had the sound of a proverb. He got to his feet and began to pace, talking half to himself. "What would make the villagers flee? No, forget that; they'd do as the Lightborn ordered. What would make the *Lightborn* flee?"

"They wouldn't," Thurion said. "We would never leave the Shrine unguarded no matter how great the danger we faced. We have been there since Mosirinde Peacemaker founded the Sanctuary."

"But if refugees from the Shore reached the Sanctuary, you might find yourselves tempted," Runacar said.

It was still difficult for Thurion to believe the Domains of the Western Shore had fallen. They had all been counting so much upon the resources of Amrolion and Daroldan, only to find them snatched away and burned to ash. But . . . yes. If refugees had reached the Sanctuary and told what they knew . . . Hamphuliadiel's first priority would be to save himself.

"Does the timing work?" Andhel leaned forward, her eyes sparkling with the joy of a problem to solve.

"Daroldan fell at the end of Sword," Runacar said. "The soonest anyone could have reached the Sanctuary would be . . ."

"Fire Moon," Pelere said. "Or the beginning of Harvest."

"And right now it is . . . ?" Runacar asked.

Light and Leaf! He is training *them. I should have seen it when the Centaur called him "Teacher." They are* still *his students.*

And he loves them.

I never imagined a prince of Caerthalien could love.

"The end of Rade," Pelere answered obediently. "Eight sennights after the end of Fire."

"Which means . . . ?" Runacar prompted again.

"That we know nothing," Andhel answered. "We do not know how long it took them to pack."

"We do know I saw no sign of fresh wagon ruts," Pelere said. "I would say that means they are at least a fortnight upon the road."

"We know one other thing too," Runacar said, flinging himself down beside Andhel with a deep sigh. "We know I am going to have to go tell all of this to the King of the Witchborn. And *you're* going to take me to her," he said to Thurion.

⟝⧓⟞

It was cold, it was snowing, and they'd have to start rationing food before they were across Domain Caerthalien Erased, because whatever had stolen their children in Arevethmonion Flower Forest had managed to steal a lot more than that: bags that should have contained grain and turnips, when opened, were found to contain only leaves and rocks. Some of the spellbound provisions had been tainted, and the idiot Lightborn who'd discovered that simply threw them away before Harwing could discover if they were salvageable.

He'd known even before they left that there was no hope of getting across the Mystrals even at the speed he'd imagined they'd be traveling. They'd lost precious time in Arevethmonion: in less than a sennight the snows would start; the ground was already furred with frost even at midday.

Caerthalien, Oronviel, Araphant, Ivrithir, Aramenthiali, Vondaimie-riel.

But Harwing's destination had always been the Mangiralas foothills south of Vondaimieriel. The Caves of Imrathalion were a vast series of limestone chambers that wound under the Mangiralas foothills, extensive enough to have held the number of people he'd started out with and more than adequate for the survivors. An entire Great Hall could have fit into just the main chamber and left room for half the castel besides. Disks mortared into the walls still shone with Silverlight, illuminating the space and causing the crystals embedded in its walls to sparkle. When Mangiralas had still been a domain, the locals had used the caves for aging cheese and wine as well as for storing fodder. He remembered a spring being there as well, and if not, the Lightborn could create one. There they could outwait Winter High Queen and her *komentai'a*.

Assuming they could get there. That seemed less likely every day.

It wasn't as if the Lightless of Areve were unused to either hard physical labor or the cold of winter. But farming and herding, and ending each day in your own bed, was far different from trudging all day through bitter cold while mourning the children—and spouses, and animals—you'd lost.

The Lightborn, naturally, rode instead of walking—at least those they had horses for, which was only about a quarter of them, since Harwing had sent the rest off with the doomed patrol. So far the Lightborn were still terrified enough of their Astromancer that the grumblings were faint and sporadic. So far they did what "Hamphuliadiel" told them to do.

So far.

Harwing was exhausted by playing Hamphuliadiel, but there didn't seem to be any way to stop. It wasn't that he cared about any of these people particularly, but if he just walked off—if "Hamphuliadiel" mysteriously vanished—he didn't know what they'd do.

(He *did* know: they'd all die, either from turning back to Areve, or die from trying to go on.)

When we get to Imrathalion, Harwing promised himself. *I'll think of something then.*

⚜

In the World Without Sun, after what was to have been the final flight against both Red Life and meat itself, nothing changed, though the skin of every Endarkened crawled with the presence of *He Who Is*. *He Who Is* had held Virulan within *His* dark regard since the battle against the Unicorns. (Since the moment Virulan had been injured, though the fewer of his subjects who knew he was vulnerable, the better.) Despite the constant attention of *He Who Is,* Virulan was not healed.

He Who Is had no power to heal.

To buy time, Virulan had given out that he communed with *He Who Is,* for no one would dare to disturb him then.

Virulan had Rested, and Risen, and Rested again. It brought no healing to him.

Nothing did. Not baths in fresh Brightworlder blood, not feasts of soft delicacies ripped from Brightworlder wombs. But before *He Who Is* turned *His Dark Regard* elsewhere, Virulan must be whole again, lest his subjects—lest *Uralesse*—tear him to shreds to claim the Iron Throne of Night.

Only Shurzul was privy to Virulan's secret, and she was loyal to him only because she was too weak to hold the Throne herself, and she knew it. The next ruler of the World Without Sun would not allow Shurzul to retain her titles and her privileges. And perhaps, not even her life.

The prospect of being tortured to death for the Court's amusement was a more powerful motivator than even death itself could be, and so Shurzul did all that she could to conceal Virulan's weakness. It was Shurzul who gave Virulan's orders to the nobles of the Endarkened Court; Shurzul who endured Uralesse's silent knowing mockery. It was Shurzul who sent hunters forth from the World Without Sun with only one order: *Bring me Unicorns.*

But there were no Unicorns to bring. And Virulan constantly became more impatient.

⇥⊟⇤

S hurzul. Thirdmost. Beloved of Darkness. *Where are my Unicorns?*"
Where once he would have bellowed, now the ancient desiccated
form of King Virulan—wingless, hornless, hairless, toothless, skeletally
gaunt, his skin browned and flaking and covered with pustules oozing
rot—wheezed pettishly and glared up at her from his bed of furs and
silks. His retiring chamber was only a few steps from the throne room
and the Throne of Night; a secret place of mechanical locks and magical
wards.

Shurzul went instantly to her knees, bowing her head and furling her
wings submissively. The presence of *He Who Is* was palpable: a burning
weight of oblivion. It was terrifying. It was exalting. Shurzul could not
really decide how it made her feel.

"My lord, a thought has come to me," she said meekly.

She heard grunts of effort as Virulan attempted to sit upright, and
failed. "'A thought,'" Virulan said contemptuously. "My Beloved has had
a thought. Perhaps she would condescend to share this thought with
me?"

"My lord, the Unicorns hide themselves because they are weak and
fearful. But they are not the only creatures who possess that which you
desire. With the power in the blood of the Elfling Mages, you will surely
be healed," Shurzul said. She feared the desperation she heard in her
own voice, but knew Virulan was too weak to notice. "Their magic is
kin to—"

"To the Unicorn who nearly extinguished me," Virulan said testily.
"Do you think I don't know what a Unicorn is?"

"Of course you do, my dread lord, for you know all things," Shurzul said hastily. The Endarkened had known about the existence of the
Sanctuary of the Star for a very long time. It contained the only Light-
shrine in all the land that was not protected by a Flower Forest, for the
Elflings had cut back the Flower Forest until the Shrine stood outside

it—after which they had built their Sanctuary around it and filled that Sanctuary with Mages.

"I am certain that will work," Shurzul said, though she was certain of no such thing.

"You do not believe," Virulan accused, in the hissing rattle his voice had become.

"I am only the shadow to your eclipse," Shurzul answered meekly. "All truth is that which you decree." The Endarkened had been saving the debasement of the Shrine as a special treat for themselves, the last object they would destroy. But now . . . Perhaps the blood of those unnatural Elfling wizards would return King Virulan to health. Shurzul was, in the most literal way, betting her life on it.

"Your wisdom and power is far greater than mine, my King, my love. All that you say must surely come to pass."

Virulan laughed wheezily, exposing blackened and slimy gums. "Surely it must! So come and kiss me, my darling, and we shall go to our rest in expectation of a glorious Rising."

Cringing inwardly, Shurzul did as she was bid.

As Heir-Prince of Caerthalien, Runacar had traveled many times by Door. He always found it disturbing, as if his mind knew how many steps he should have taken to get from one place to another and wished to bedevil him with a full accounting of What Ought to Have Been.

But to travel to Nomaitemil without using magic would take at least a sennight, and could not be done at this time of year anyway, so Runacar made no demur as Thurion Lightbrother led him and Andhel away from the house to a place suitable for casting the spell. Runacar had sent Pelere to warn the village of Smoketree that trouble might be coming, and kept Andhel by his side. He also wanted Pelere to find out if anyone had seen the Areve villagers and their Lightborn, and try to discover why they had fled the Sanctuary onto the very doorstep of winter.

If they fled because the Endarkened had somehow managed to strike at them through the Shrine itself . . .

Runacar shuddered.

"*Now,*" the Lightbrother said, and the banks of the river abruptly became a dense forest. Runacar's stomach lurched, and he took a deep breath.

"Huh," Andhel said, sounding faintly surprised. "Findar can do this. But he falls down afterward."

"He should count himself lucky that that's all he does," Thurion said mildly. "That's a powerful spell to cast without training. Tell him to come to us. We'll make him better at what he does."

"I don't like this place," Andhel said, not answering. "It's empty."

"But I, I, I am here!" Sundapple announced from above them. He walked daintily along the tree branch, and then leapt into Thurion's arms. Thurion caught him, staggering only a little.

"I thought you said you could only bring the two of us," Runacar said. To his complete lack of surprise, Cloudfoot and Shadowdance came wandering over to them from the bushes.

"I did," Thurion Lightbrother said. "But I've been watching them. The Palughs can work a form of Door."

"He lies!" Cloudfoot said instantly.

"Betrayer!" Shadowdance added. "Betrayer of secrets! Nasty witch-boy! Traitor!"

Sundapple jumped down from Thurion's arms to hiss and growl at the other two.

"I don't care about your secrets, fuzzballs," Runacar said. "I need to talk to the High King. Where is she?"

"You're never going to find *anyone* in a Void Flower Forest," Andhel said, sounding halfway between smug and irritated. "Or any*thing.*"

Thurion turned away, touching several of the tree trunks as a musician might finger the keys of their instrument.

"If you mean by 'Void' a Flower Forest that isn't full of twinkly colored lights and extremely large bugs that sting," Thurion said, over his shoulder, "my answer is: 'I can't believe you rely on bugs to do your scouting.' This way." He picked up Sundapple and walked away.

⊣⊟⊢

They found Vieliessar in the middle of a clearing. She was sitting cross-legged on a thick woolen horseblanket completely alone and unattended, at least in the sense that there were no other Elves anywhere in sight. Pouncewarm was curled up on her lap, and a Wulver Wild lay in a tumble at her back, all blissfully asleep. As Runacar and the others approached, one of the Wulvers raised their head and regarded them with amber eyes.

Vieliessar did not seem to be aware of their presence. Her eyes were vacant and staring, fixed on something none of them could see.

Runacar thought back to the night of the goblin attack. He'd wondered then whether Vieliessar was mad or sane. He wondered the same thing now.

"This is not good," Thurion muttered under his breath. "My lord," he said, louder, "here is "

"What's going on?" Andhel demanded. "Is she drunk?" The Woodwose walked past Runacar and Thurion until she was standing halfway between them and Vieliessar. She peered in Vieliessar's direction. "I'd certainly want to get drunk if I had to live here, but—"

All the Wulvers were awake now.

"Go away." The eldest member of the Wild spoke, a grizzled male whose face was nearly white with age.

Vieliessar still sat, silent, motionless, blank-faced, hearing none of it.

It was that eerie death-like trance which made Runacar do something he'd sworn he would never do. He scrabbled in his mind for the Bond that tied the two of them together, and when he found it, he yanked on it as hard as he could.

Vieliessar's eyes cleared, and she flashed all of them a look of pure rage.

It's an act. Runacar couldn't help that reflexive response. He could feel grief through the Bond, and shame, and certainly irritation . . .

But the rest was an act, meant to cow and bully them. Why?

He felt his puzzlement reflected back at him for an instant before Vieliessar slammed the connection between them closed as hard as she could. The act gave Runacar a piercing headache.

"Thurion, that is *Caerthalien*," Vieliessar said tightly. "He does not have the freedom of the forest."

"He also isn't Caerthalien," Andhel said. "We renamed him." She beamed at the High King as if she were utterly cloudwitted. "His name is Runacar Houseborn."

It seemed that every encounter he and Vieliessar had was doomed to be somehow ridiculous, at least when they weren't trying to kill each other. "Look. I'm sorry to disturb you. You need to—"

"The council '*needs to*,'" Vieliessar interrupted, getting to her feet. "Whatever you have to say can be said to everyone."

She picked up Pouncewarm and walked away. When she passed behind a tree, it took Runacar several heartbeats to realize she hadn't come out the other side.

The younger Wulvers began playing tug-of-war with the blanket.

"Well, that wasn't creepy or weird at all," Andhel said.

"Is she possessed?" Runacar asked bluntly. "Is she fit to rule?"

"No one else is more fit," Thurion said, which wasn't really an answer.

"I know *I'd* follow her anywhere," Andhel drawled sarcastically. Runacar gestured to silence her, but her expression plainly said: *you know perfectly well I'm right.*

Thurion ignored both of them. It should have been the normal *I am invisible* deference Runacar unconsciously expected of a Lightborn, but it was more akin to the *you are utterly beneath my notice* that Runacar had always gotten from his own superiors. Runacar reminded himself that Vieliessar's people were as alien to him as the Otherfolk once had been.

"You! Runfar! Birdleap! Tailchaser!" Thurion called to the Wulvers. "Leave that alone and go summon the council!"

The Wulvers choodled joyously at being given a task and bounded off in several directions at once. As they ran, Runacar could hear them calling out: "A message from the High King!" "A message! A message!" "I will be first to deliver it!" "No! I!"

Runacar suspected his hunting dogs had been saying something similar in the heat of the chase, if he'd only had ears to hear.

Thurion picked up the blanket, rolled it, and flung it over his shoulder. "Let's go," he said.

Runacar shrugged and motioned for Andhel to follow.

⊟⊟

The "Council Chamber," Runacar discovered, was nothing more than a space marked off by a set of carved wooden screens in the middle of a glade.

Thurion folded back a panel of one of the screens to allow them to enter. Inside, the ground was covered with rugs and skins, and atop the rugs were low wooden stools and cushions for seating, but no seat was grander than the rest. The only piece of actual furniture the space contained was a tea-table with its pot and brazier.

The council had already gathered. Even the young princes were here. Runacar recognized less than half of the rest, and assumed they were members of the council only because there was no other reason for them to be present.

There were several Lightborn, including Iardalaith Daroldan; someone in the livery of the Silver Swords; two of the High King's new Lawspeakers; and others who were clearly former Landbonds and outlaws. Barely a handful of the Lords Komen were in attendance: Annobeunna Keindostibaent, Frochoriel Oronviel, Shanilya Thadan, Rithdeliel of Oronviel . . .

Helecanth.

Rithdeliel's face was a mask of professional indifference. Helecanth wore her helm, making her face invisible.

Sundapple flung himself down on his side at Runacar's and Andhel's feet, rolled over their toes, and began to purr loudly. Runacar wondered if the Palugh was here in an official capacity, then ruthlessly suppressed the thought. It was a route to madness.

"I am here."

Vieliessar must have used Lightborn Magery, for she simply appeared in the middle of them all. She now wore garments fashioned in the style of Lightborn robes, but hand-painted in a dozen different shades of green and grey and rust like Woodwose garb. An elvensilver diadem of Vilya sat strangely upon her shorn scalp. She wore no weapons, nor other jewels.

"Who shall set the wards that guard us?" It was the female Lawspeaker who asked. The words had the sense of a ritual.

"I shall set the wards, and when they are set, nothing we speak may be heard outside these walls; nothing we do shall be seen," Thurion answered. He did not move, except for a slight twitch of his fingers, but everyone seemed to accept that some Magery had been worked.

Vieliessar took her seat. The rest of the council sat as well, and there was a bustling adjustment of position. Adalieriel and Calanoriel came to sit one on each side of Vieliessar. Helecanth moved to stand behind her. Thurion went over to the Lawspeaker and knelt beside her. Runacar and Andhel remained standing.

Whatever Thurion said to the Lawspeaker was muffled by Lightborn Magery. When he sat down the Lawspeaker rose to her feet.

"I am Arwaen, Lawspeaker General, Master of all who keep the High King's laws and place them before the people. Before us are those whom some among us might name enemy, and so I will judge what best befits the Law. It is my ruling that since there is neither treaty with the Otherfolk, nor *absence* of treaty with the Otherfolk, these persons can be neither ally nor enemy to us. Therefore, we advise the High King to grant parole to these persons, so that they may safely return to their own lands when their business here is done." Arwaen sat down once more.

Vieliessar rose to her feet. "They are trespassing," she said flatly. "Thurion Lightbrother brought them, so Thurion will stand surety for their behavior. There need be no parole."

Runacar saw Thurion wince ever so slightly. Standing surety meant that whatever Runacar and Andhel did, Thurion would be held responsible for it. Clearly Vieliessar was still furious: Runacar wondered how many of those present could see it. He wondered if even *he* would have been able to see it without their Bond.

He wondered how many of her people knew she was Soulbonded. And to whom.

"No, no, no need for parole. Rune is pretty. Rune is kind. Rune

brings news he need not bring. But he is loyal. Rune is loyal-*l-l-l-l*."
Pouncewarm appeared out of the shadows and walked into Vieliessar's
lap. He made a loaf of himself, purring, and Vieliessar began to stroke
him absently.

"His loyalty would seem to be a flexible thing," Vieliessar said. But
this time she sounded amused. "Very well, 'Pretty Rune.' Tell my council
why you have come."

"My scouts have brought word that both the Sanctuary of the Star
and the village of Areve have been deserted and stand empty. Their inhabitants are heading eastward along the old Sanctuary Road. I thought
you might like to know," Runacar said briefly.

⌘

There was the usual moment when everyone began shouting at once.
To Runacar's surprise, the High King did nothing to quell it; she sat
with her arms around her children and the Palugh Pouncewarm in her
lap, and waited.

The first rush of accusation and counter-accusation ended quickly, and
Runacar braced himself for the inevitable spate of unanswerable questions. But it didn't come. The council began talking among itself, with
occasional appeals to the High King. None of its members asked him any
more questions, and several moments later Runacar realized the High
King's council was in the midst of planning a raid. Or a rescue. He wasn't
quite sure.

"Wait," he said. "Here now. Stop that. You can't be serious."

He glanced at Andhel. She looked only a little less bewildered than
Runacar felt. "You don't even know where they *are*," he said.

"We know they are east of Arevethmonion." It was War Prince
Shanilya who chose to answer. "They will be heading for the Dragon's
Gate and following the Sanctuary Road. And so we will find them."

"Finding out what they're running away from would be a nice thing,
too," Iardalaith said. "A building full of Lightborn is hard to breach.
And if *we* knew that, *they* knew that. Of course, Hamphuliadiel may
have decided to become High King."

"His opinions are of no matter," Vieliessar said. "I am Astromancer now. We leave in three candlemarks. Lord Houseless, you may return to your people and say to them what I will do."

"No."

Everyone broke off their conversations and stared at him. Even Andhel and Sundapple stared at him.

"I'm riding with you," Runacar said, into the silence.

"Agreed," Vieliessar said, before the shouting could begin. "Mistress Githachi, we shall ask for the help of the Silver Swords upon this rade. Cegusara, will your scouts work with the Wulvers?"

"Gladly," Cegusara answered.

"Then go ask of the Wilds who will come." Runacar supposed the wards had been dissolved, since Cegusara folded back one of the wall panels and left immediately. "My Lord Rithdeliel, I charge you with the hardest duty: to remain here."

Vieliessar rose to her feet; Helecanth moved to gather up Calan and Liri. Helecanth took the children each by the hand and walked through the gap in the screens Cegusara had left.

Vieliessar approached Rithdeliel. There was a brief conversation between them, too low for Runacar to hear. Vieliessar looked sad; Rithdeliel looked resigned. She touched him on the shoulder; he stepped back and bowed, then turned and left.

By now the Council Chamber was nearly empty. Vieliessar approached Runacar and his companions.

"Hello, Sundapple," she said, squatting down to bring herself closer to the Palugh's height. "How fare you, regal one? Does your companion vex you overmuch?"

"He is young, he is foolish, but he can learn," Sundapple said, purring loudly.

("Thank you—I think," Runacar muttered under his breath.)

Vieliessar rose to her feet. "*Alakomentai* Andhel, will you bear word to the King-Emperor that we go only to bring home our lost ones and mean no harm to your Otherfolk?"

Andhel seemed taken aback by Vieliessar's courtly courtesy. "Maybe," she hedged. "I can tell Mayor Lydkarl in Smoketree that you'll be riding out looking for some other Houseborn. And I'm coming with you."

"You are not," Vieliessar replied. "You are not trained in our ways of battle."

"Meet me on the field and say that again," Andhel said darkly.

"No!" Runacar took a sideways step, thrusting out his arm to push Andhel behind him. "She is not making a formal Challenge, Lord Vieliessar." He'd seen bored komen push an unintentional turn of phrase into a Challenge Circle duel before. He wanted to hope that wasn't something that could happen here, but he *simply did not know.*

"Peace, Battlemaster Runacar. Did I want to kill any of your folk I would not need to hedge the murder around with formality and law. But I will not have her," Vieliessar said.

"Andhel." Runacar made a half turn and forced Andhel to meet his gaze. "Go back to Smoketree. Tell everyone what's happening. Get a message to Leutric if you can." He cudgeled his brains, trying to remember what new settlements lay along the road between Arevethmonion and the Dragon's Gate. He didn't think there were many—most of the settlements, old and new, were south of the bounds that marked the edge of the Western Reach. A party of refugees was unlikely to run into them, and probably the only settlements they would recognize as places of the Otherfolk were the Centaur villages. "We don't want to fight them."

Andhel took a deep breath and held it for a long moment. "Ai, *Alakomentai,*" she said at last, reluctance plain in her expression.

"I will return you to Smoketree now, if you permit," Vieliessar said, holding out her hand. Andhel hesitated, glancing toward Runacar, but placed her hand in Vieliessar's without his encouragement.

Runacar blinked at the space they had occupied. He looked around. Neither Sundapple nor Pouncewarm was here now, but Palughs came and went as they pleased.

"Come, then, Lord of Nothing," Lord Shanilya said to him. "We must outfit you and find you a mount—and neither of these things will be as simple as they once were."

⌖

The shift from Flower Forest warmth to the biting cold of winter was abrupt and shocking. Vieliessar was glad she wouldn't be staying long; it was still snowing, and a storm was on its way. She moved to draw her hand free of Andhel's, but the Woodwose grabbed her wrist.

"You don't hurt him. You hear me? You *don't*," Andhel said fiercely. "I know all about the Soulbond and the rest of your stupid Houseborn things. There's more ways to hurt someone than by just killing them."

Vieliessar yanked her hand free. "Yes. There is exile," she said. She stepped through to Ceoprentrei before Andhel could say anything more.

The morning after the Warhunt Mages arrived at the Sanctuary of the Star, Herchet and Dovelock went to Arevethmonion to Dispell the border stones—a simple matter once they'd located one stone, since the Law of Contagion enabled them to Fetch all of the others. Once the Warhunt Mages possessed the Flower Forest's Light to draw upon, the Astromancer's chambers—both public and private—were thoroughly Dispelled, then looted of their treasures. There were warm clothes and winter cloaks for everyone now, and new boots without holes in them—or at least, with new soles and warm linings. There was enough tea to last them, individually and collectively, a lifetime (as well as honey and tea-sweets and Preserved cakes). That night there were warm baths, and warm blankets, and perfume for skin and hair.

But if the young Lightborn reveled in luxury, it was an uneasy festival. No one wanted to be the first to make long-term plans. Especially not after they discovered what was in the Astromancer's Tower.

Isilla nagged Bramdrin Lightsister until she cast Knowing over the chamber at the top of the Astromancer's Tower. With Arevethmonion open to her, Bramdrin had all the power she needed to Know everything that had taken place in the Tower all the way back to Hamphuliadiel's accession and perhaps beyond.

But there was nothing *to* know. The chamber had been scrubbed as clean by Magery as it had been by soap and water.

And after she cast Knowing over Hamphuliadiel's bedchamber—again at Isilla's urging—Bramdrin flatly refused to do it anywhere else. All she would say was that toward the end of his time here Hamphuliadiel had been insane with fear and drugging himself insensible.

On the third day they were there, the Mages searched Areve for information—both by spells and mundane means. That proved as useless as searching the Sanctuary: all that could be determined was that everyone was gone, and they had left little behind them when they went.

But a little could be a lot by the standards of those who had begun with nothing. There was a salt-cake they'd found in one of the cow-byres. And there were some winter crops that had not been harvested. A steady diet of turnips and parsnips and onions might be boring, but it was better than hunger.

No one felt quite brave enough to enter the Shrine and ask the Starry Hunt for a Telling.

And days passed.

⚜

At the end of their first sennight at the Sanctuary of the Star, the Warhunt Mages had gathered together in the Common Room at twilight. Even after only a few sunturns, it had become a custom.

"All right," Isilla said briskly. "It's the middle of Woods and Sister Alasneh says the winter is going to come early and hard. We can almost certainly hold the Sanctuary against a Beastling attack. Do we go—and where? Or do we stay here—at least until spring?"

She gazed at the faces around her. *I am not going to be the one who makes this decision. I'm not,* she told herself fiercely.

She knew what the truth would be, if her friends were brave enough to speak it. Alasneh Lightsister had found a broken handcart and mended it—for no particular reason, she had said, save that Mend was a very underrated spell and she wanted to practice it. Dinias had taken all the carpets from the Astromancer's Audience Chamber and was trying to make them into a pavilion. Pantaradet and Jorganroch had been gathering herbs and simples from the edge of Arevethmonion. There were enough pretty glass bottles in the Astromancer's bedchamber in which to store them (so the two of them said).

All of the Warhunt Mages had been doing things "for no particular reason" since they'd arrived, and all of them were aimed at leaving here. Soon.

The silence stretched.

"Are we really going to do this?" Ghendanna Lightsister asked.

"Leave known shelter to march an unknown distance through a mob of hostile enemy monsters to an as-yet-undecided destination?" Pendray asked instantly. "Why not?"

"In winter," Dinias added. "You forgot 'in winter.'"

"And insufficient supplies," Jorganroch said.

"Our destination isn't 'undecided.' It's 'unknown,'" Tangisen commented pedantically. "It's very difficult to know when you've reached an unknown destination."

Dinias snorted. Pendray smacked him.

"I'm in," said Alasneh. "But you bandits leave my writing materials alone this time."

"So," Isilla said briskly. "We leave at dawn tomorrow?"

Smiles and nods—and a wave of relief—were her answer.

⊰⧉⊱

It was barely a candlemark past dawn when the small band of Warhunt Mages stood on the Sanctuary Road once more. The fields were still heavy with mist and the whole world was dull-colored. The air smelled sharp and wet, and Isilla automatically contrasted it with the morning smells of the Western Shore.

When there'd *been* a Western Shore. And now, it seemed, the Sanctuary had fallen as well, for they—its last possible defenders—were abandoning it.

It was nice while it lasted, Isilla thought to herself. *Or maybe it wasn't. I never thought I'd feel happy to leave the Sanctuary, but I do.*

A short distance ahead, the Sanctuary Road entered Arevethmonion Flower Forest. They had decided to make for the Dragon's Gate for lack of a better goal. If the people of Areve and the Lightborn of Sanctuary were going anywhere, they were going east, and they were traveling on the Sanctuary Road. The pass through the Mystrals would be closed by the time they reached it, but that just meant they'd be easier to catch up to. But what route should they take?

The route through the Flower Forest would be fastest—and warmest. But now that Isilla really knew what lived in a Flower Forest, she was hesitant to enter it. There were water spirits, pond spirits, tree spirits, and every other thing in Lannarien's book. And the Beastlings had shown so horribly that they could reach out from anywhere to kill.

If they detoured around Arevethmonion through Domain Inglethendragir, they could pick up the road again after it entered Farcarinon Erased. But . . .

"Isilla. Look up," said Tangisen. His voice sounded odd.

"Oh," said Pendray.

"Uh-oh," said Dinias.

Isilla looked up.

There was an entire Flight of Hippogriffs in the western sky—and it was clearly heading right for them.

⊰⊱

Lord Shanilya led Runacar away from the "Council Chamber" to a clearing that seemed utterly uninhabited—until he thought to look up. Even then, for a moment, he was not sure of what he was seeing, but then his vision seemed to sharpen and suddenly he could see that the trees were studded with platforms, some walled. Some were linked by ropes, and some were not.

And they have made this in less than a moonturn. Just as they have made all the rest of it.

"It is simpler to keep our materiel reserves in one place," Shanilya told him. "And desirable to make it hard to despoil. Really, some people just have *no* manners." She stuck two fingers in her mouth and whistled. "Hende! Here is someone with need!"

"I am *busy,* my lord prince," an irritated female voice responded. "The High King goes to make war."

"The High King goes to make peace," Shanilya called back. "I have here a komen who must go into battle naked if you will not help!"

"It is simpler when they do because that way they do not come back to vex me!" Hende appeared in the doorway of one of the tree-rooms.

Her tunic and trews owed far more to Woodwose fashion than to that of the Hundred Houses, but the long braid that cascaded over her shoulder and dangled to her knees was crow-wing black.

Both of her ears were cropped short. Poaching. Two offenses. It was obvious that Hende had been born a Landbond: a third offense would have meant her death. Yet a War Prince—of the Arzhana, true, but still a War Prince—was bandying words with her as if between equals.

As if any scrap of The Way of the Sword *still exists in this impossible place.*

"Ah!" Hende said, seeing Runacar. "It is the Last Traitor, brother to the Banebringer—of course! To equip him will be an honor."

Runacar couldn't tell whether she meant that sincerely or ironically, but whichever it was, in short order she provided a heavy quilted under-tunic, stiffened with panels of boiled leather over the lower back; a mail shirt, split for riding; and a thick woolen tunic to cover it. His trews were deemed sufficient, but his boots were not: Shanilya demanded he exchange his for a pair with strong metal plates covering the toe, the instep, and armoring the lower leg much as a pair of greaves would. It would not be a particularly effective defense against a sword-blade, but it might buy the wearer precious time if they were attacked by some wild creature.

To assemble this collection, Hende had to visit several of her caches, which meant climbing between the trees on rope bridges so exiguous that at first Runacar had not even seen them. She greeted the discovery of each new item with a glad cry of welcome, moments before it sailed through the air to Runacar's feet.

"You won't need this, either," Shanilya said. She scooped up Runacar's stormcloak and tossed it aloft to Hende. Hende snatched it out of the air with a wild yip of glee and thrust it behind her.

"Hey!" Runacar said reflexively. "That's a good cloak!"

"You aren't going to be riding a High House destrier," Hende said, laughter bubbling below her words. "This will suit you much better."

She tossed what looked like a bale of sheep's wool over the side of the platform. Shanilya caught it, shook it out, and tossed it in turn to Runacar. "Better," she agreed.

He took it gingerly. It was goatskin on the outside, the shaggy grey pelt blotched further with artificial browns and greens. Upon examination, this was a more complicated design than his stormcloak: there was a wide raised collar lined in boiled leather that closed around the neck with a toggle-and-loop, to protect the throat when one's quarry attacked. The goatskins were sewn, rough to rough, to sheepskins. It was longer in the back than the front—though not by much—and seemed designed to be worn closed. He cudgeled his memory at the familiarity of it, then remembered that the older style of hunting cloak found in Araphant had been made this way. The cloak's hood was narrow and close-fitting, and it did not merely pull up: it pulled up and then over the whole face in the fashion of a mask, leaving no more than a slit to see through. There were two openings in the front panel that would allow him to put his hands through to grasp a set of reins, but little more. Once the toggles were closed and the hood in place, the wearer would resemble a shaggy conical object inexplicably on horseback.

Runacar regarded the cloak with disfavor. He couldn't imagine wearing it; in the case of an ambush, it would take far too long to free his sword.

"Give me your sword," Shanilya said, as if she had been reading his mind.

Resentment and obstinacy made Runacar unwilling to obey. His sword had been in his possession since even before he was old enough to lift it. Its hilt was enameled in Caerthalien green and gold, the three stars of the Caerthalien device picked out in gemstones. The motto of the house was engraved on the blade: *Caerthalien to the highest.*

His father had given it to him. It was his last link to his family.

"I will keep it," he said firmly.

"I will return it to you unharmed," Shanilya said with quiet sympathy. "If you go among us so armed, you may well find your liver entertaining someone's dagger. You'll hardly need a sword to defend yourself from a bunch of farmers. And it will do you no good against Lightborn."

Runacar had already been told that the Endarkened were attracted by the presence of Lightborn. It had made him wonder why Vieliessar was sending the Warhunt to search for the villagers. But Pelere thought it wasn't just villagers coming east, but everyone, including the Lightborn of the Shrine. If the Lightborn meant to fight, the Warhunt was the only battle element that could oppose them.

"And if the Endarkened attack us while we ride?" he asked evenly.

"Then your sword will come to you," Shanilya answered. "My oath and my honor upon it."

It was an unlikely promise—there were limitations to what the Green Robes could Fetch—but Runacar supposed this was the best he was going to get. Reluctantly, he began to unbuckle his swordbelt.

"Now come," Shanilya said, when he handed belt and blade and baldric and scabbard to her. "Let us do something happier. We will find you a mount."

⊰⊱

Here, in the mountains far above Smoketree, winter had fully conquered her realm. The snow lay thick and heavy across the alpine valley, muffling and distorting all sounds. In the distance, Runacar could see a herd of horses. They were in thick winter coat, with ice clotted in their manes and tails, heads down as they pawed at the snow.

"The valley is not large enough for the whole *khom* to winter here—and as you say, the Endarkened may come—but each of the herds gets a few days in the meadow in turn, lest they lose all their winter conditioning when we need it. We are fortunate that it is Penyamo herd that is here and not Oiloisse."

Runacar never did discover why Penyamo was better than Oiloisse, for Shanilya put two fingers into her mouth and whistled.

Immediately one of the horses raised its head, ears swiveling as it sought for the source of the sound. Then it began to gallop toward them.

The rest of the herd followed. Their hooves threw up a spray of snow like the spume of the ocean, and they churned through the areas of unbroken snow as if they were not even there. When they stopped, Shanilya walked toward them, greeting the leader first and going on to greet the others. The animals lipped at her hood and her cloak, nudging one another in an attempt to get closer.

As if they were hounds, or housepets. Not horses.

"These sluggards are of Gatriadde Mangiralas's breeding," Shanilya said proudly. "He died to save the bloodline from the Endarkened. Now Fierdind, who served as Gatriadde's Cadet Horsemaster, continues his work."

Runacar hoped his face showed nothing of his thoughts. He'd caught glimpses of these animals during the battle at Ceoprentrei, but this was the first time he'd had any leisure to inspect one. Compared to destriers, they were the size of small ponies. All had black stripes along their spines and dark striping along their haunches and withers. They were all varying shades of dun. Their manes were long enough at the poll to nearly cover their entire faces. Runacar could have looked any one of them squarely in the eye.

Any Horsemaster who brought them to Mangiralas Fair would have been laughed out of the domain: the beasts were hammerheaded, ewe necked, goose-rumped . . . They were the ugliest horses Runacar had ever seen.

"Aren't they beautiful?" Shanilya asked. "They can run all day and all night too, and fight like wildcats at the end of it. Live on scraps I wouldn't eat, and they're clever. Much too clever to want to work today—but you, my darling, have no choice."

The animal she addressed was a mare. She was white-faced with a pale dun coat. The rest of the herd was dismissed with a few slaps on rumps and shoulders. They wheeled and trotted away a small distance, then stood looking at the Elves.

"You've ridden mares before?" Shanilya asked him.

"I am Caerthalien." The title he had spent the last decade refusing to claim hung between them in defiant challenge, and Runacar was too angry to regret it. "Try me."

"Don't say I didn't warn you. This is Kishmiri," Shanilya said, holding out a piece of bread to the mare. Kishmiri took the bread delicately from Shanilya's fingers. In full winter coat, she looked less like a living thing than like some enormous child's doll. "I ride her full brother Malice. This is a strong line. She will bear you well."

Runacar regarded Kishmiri with what he hoped was a noncommittal expression. It must not have been as noncommittal as he'd hoped, as the mare snickered and tossed her head.

"If she will bear me at all, I'll be satisfied." He reached into his vest. He still had some sugar lumps left over from treating the Wulvers—was it only this morning? He held one out on the palm of his glove and approached her. "Kishmiri, you say? I suppose you have siblings named Rage and Fury and Mild Irritation?" he asked the mare. The name meant "Anger" in the Old Tongue.

Kishmiri lipped at the sugar and condescended to take it, her ears flicking with interest.

"Oh, no," Shanilya said, amused. "We lost Mild Irritation to an ice tiger a few turns of the Wheel ago; she simply wouldn't stop going after the things and she fell off a cliff."

"Unusual names," Runacar said, reaching out to scratch behind Kishmiri's ears.

"The children name the foals. Calan named the High King's mount—but in his defense, that was a long time ago."

"And he either named it 'Good Dog' or 'Total Annihilation,'" Runacar guessed.

"Nearly." Shanilya smiled. "He named her Assar." *Death.* "Now come: we must fit you two out with saddle and bridle, and there is little time. We ride before nightfall."

CHAPTER TWENTY-FOUR

RADE MOON TO WOOD'S MOON IN THE TENTH YEAR OF THE HIGH KING'S REIGN: LIKE A BRIGHT AND TERRIBLE MACHINE

One is naturally tempted to remove those beasts which can speak from the catalogue of creatures of venery, but that would be as foolish as insisting that birds were Elves because both could sing.

—Lannarien's Book of Living Things

D o we run?" Tangisen asked, staring skyward.

"And die tired?" That was Pendray.

"Wait for them to attack," Isilla said. "There's no point running back inside the Sanctuary now that they've seen us. And in case they brought company, try not to use any spells that can be seen from a distance."

Like Shield. Or Thunderbolt. Or anything that would be effective.

⚜

B ut the Flight of Hippogriffs landed more than a bowshot away, and only the Flight leader came toward them.

Lannarien's Book of Living Things had noted that the Hippogriff was seen in an assortment of colors (unlike Gryphons). Only the Hippogriffs' shape was consistent: the front half of an eagle (more or less; just as with every other Beastling, their shape was not identical to that of the true beast they resembled) conjoined with the back half of a horse(ish). But Lannarien's notes really hadn't prepared Isilla for the reality. The beaks and feathers of the Hippogriffs came in every possible shade and color: bright red, sky blue, yellow, vivid green. Where feathers became hide, their horse parts were in every color a horse could be, but none a horse could not, so Isilla assumed that somewhere in the world there must be bright red and green birds.

She would rather be looking at birds than Hippogriffs.

"Cloud and Wind!" the Hippogriff leader said as it approached her. Its voice was a raspy squawk, such as an echobird—a very *large* echobird—might make. The Flight leader had snowy-white feathers on its neck and chest and wings. Its head was grey-blue, the feathers mottled and stippled with black, and its beak was a disturbing flower pink, as was the skin on its taloned forelimbs. Its horse-half was piebald, black and white, and its tail was as white as its wings.

"And Rune says *we* are featherbrained! You're supposed to be going east, you witches! You don't have the time to dawdle around—the truce isn't forever, you know."

"Truces never are," Isilla heard Dinias mutter.

The Hippogriff swung its head to look at him and laughed, making a sound like a very large crow and exposing a curling black tongue. "So hurry along, little witches—and tell your King, when you see her, that Hyrann of the Hippogriffs showed you mercy."

"We will," Isilla said fervently.

"Good." The Hippogriff—Hyrann?—turned around and trotted back to its Flight. Isilla thought the Hippogriff moved amazingly well for something whose legs were so mismatched. A few moments later, the Flight was airborne once more.

"Well," Isilla said, into the stunned silence. "You heard . . . Hyrann. We have to catch up with the others. Whoever, wherever, they are."

"It said the King is alive," Pantaradet Lightsister said quietly. "It said we would see her."

Isilla took a deep breath, and gathered everyone in with her gaze. "I don't know whether she's alive or not. I don't think I'd trust some kind of crow-pony to tell me the truth even if it knew it. And I'm still not walking through Arevethmonion. So when we catch up with . . . whoever we're supposed to catch up with, we can ask *them* why the Hippogriffs think there's a truce."

"Good luck getting an answer to that," Tangisen said.

⊰⊱

I t took the Warhunt very little time to overtake the refugees, for the Sanctuary band moved very slowly, barely covering a taille of road each day. To the Warhunt's faint surprise, there was a demi-taille of Lightborn with them, apparently led by the Astromancer himself.

He had a very large hat and the end of his scepter glowed.

⊰⊱

S neaking along behind Hamphuliadiel was certainly better than facing Hamphuliadiel. But as the days passed, Isilla found it increasingly odd that he hadn't *noticed*.

She was missing something. She knew she was.

⊰⊱

R unacar had once told his army: "*Elvenkind begins to train for war the moment they can walk. They make war all their lives: it is their sport, their worship, their reason for being. Vieliessar was skilled enough to destroy the combined forces of the Hundred Houses with an army of rabble, and she has had ten turns of the Wheel to make them even better.*"

Those had not been empty words when he had spoken them. But now Runacar saw for himself what that meant.

The High King's search-and-rescue force was riding out through the Dragon's Gate less than three candlemarks after Runacar had brought Pelere's warning to the Elven Council. The elements Lord Vieliessar had chosen to bring were her Warhunt, the Silver Swords, and her personal bodyguard: less than two grand-tailles. Vieliessar led the vanguard, a white shadow on the white mare named Assar.

The risk of the High King leading a sortie such as this in her own person was terrifying, but no one else could. Pelere had said that both Areve and the Sanctuary of the Star stood empty, and that meant that when this array found the villagers and the Lightborn, they would find Hamphuliadiel Astromancer. Lord Vieliessar's authority was the only one higher than that which the rogue Astromancer claimed for himself.

She was the only one who could speak with the Lightborn and have any hope of being heeded.

If her authority were rejected, she would have to fight. Being War Prince—or High King—was like being locked in a cage filled with wild beasts. If any one of them challenged you, that challenge must be met with immediate force—or else they would *all* attack.

His purpose for being here, Runacar decided, was to convince any Otherfolk their paths crossed that the High King and her forces were on a peaceful mission.

It was slightly better than thinking of himself as a hostage.

⊣⊟⊢

Virulan needed to rest more and more frequently, and his Risings came further and further apart. His behavior and his needs were endlessly bizarre to their only audience. The Endarkened were immortal and ageless. None had ever died of sickness or age—those were things that *meat* did. For Virulan to bear such a resemblance to *meat* unsettled Shurzul profoundly—and made her even more certain that no other Endarkened must see Virulan as he was now. When she gazed down at the rotting body of her King and lover, she thought longingly of dismembering him as he lay insensible. She was the only one to revive when the King lay dormant: the other Endarkened would lie insensible until Virulan finally Rose. She only wished she could take it as an omen that counseled rebellion. But Virulan's death would mean her death as well.

Death would not be such a source of terror, Shurzul told herself, if only she could be certain it was a final dissolution. Would *He Who Is* accept her back into his glorious sterile oblivion? Or would her animating spark be spurned by him in death? Would that homeless spark take root in some Brightworlder body? Even if she freed herself from that prison by death—what if it only happened again? She was one of the Twelve, Created by *He Who Is*, Changed by Virulan. She had brought Life forth from her body. She was monstrously and irrevocably tainted by that act.

Surrounded here by *He Who Is*, Shurzul begged *Him* and petitioned *Him*. But she perceived no reply—only that endless curious contemplation of King Virulan in his altered and diminished state.

Was *He Who Is* studying King Virulan? Did *He* mean to infect all his beautiful children with this same crippling rot in punishment? How many more Risings would Shurzul see before she began to weaken and some other Endarkened murdered her?

(What would happen to Hazaniel?)

Shurzul wondered about these things, even as she lay by King Virulan's side, his stench in her nostrils. She dared not go elsewhere, lest he Rise in her absence. So she endured, hating him with every insensible breath he took.

⊰⊱

When Virulan Rose at last, he gave the command to hunt the Elfling Mages, though only Shurzul heard his cracked and petulant voice. It was Shurzul who took Virulan's word to all of his subjects, but Shurzul did not take Virulan's word to his subjects wholly unmodified.

They were (so Shurzul told them) to fly forth to seek the Elfling Mages. All would fly; all would kill. But every Elfling Mage must be captured alive and brought to the World Without Sun unharmed.

And (Shurzul continued), not only were they to harvest the Elfling Mages, they were to kill or destroy every single thing in the Bright World. This would be the last flight of the Endarkened, the last slaughter, the end of the Red Harvest. When they were done, the Bright World must be nothing but stone and smoke, dust and ash.

Such a momentous occasion (so Shurzul said) deserved a special celebration to mark its beginning. There were great banquets held, displays of exotic finery, exquisite slaughter to empty the slave pens for their witchling victims. It was *carnival*, the feast of the flesh. Even the children of the Endarkened in their hidden nurseries were fed to full measure.

She needed time to plan.

⊰⊱

It was the first time Runacar had ridden in a High House war party since the Battle of the Shieldwall Plain, and though nearly every detail now was different, the few that weren't filled his mind with unquiet ghosts. They could not be exorcised by prayer or magic, so he filled his mind with details, as if there were someone still alive to whom he could report them.

Helecanth rode on the High King's tuathal hand, leading her taille of the Kingsguard. Runacar rode between the Kingsguard and the High King. On Vieliessar's deosil side, Iardalaith led the Warhunt. Behind both elements, rank on rank, were the Silver Swords. *She must be planning to turn and run at the first sign of trouble, using the Silver Swords as her tuathal and deosil flanks and retreating through them. That's the only way their position makes sense.*

In the scant time since the Battle of Ceoprentrei, Lord Vieliessar had already begun integrating the Otherfolk into her army. Pouncewarm was riding with her; Runacar saw a few other Palugh among the riders. There was at least a taille of Wilds running along beside the war-ponies. A Wulver Wild was not a set number, but there were still over sixty Wulvers present.

In short: the whole of my Wulver cadre has gone over to the enemy. Except they aren't the enemy, are they?

Runacar knew now that no matter what happened in the sennights and moonturns to come, he would never meet Vieliessar in battle. He was surprised at how much the thought hurt; as if he'd lost something precious. Something—some*one* he'd never really had in the first place.

The Hundred Houses will never rise again. Even if the Endarkened vanished from the land in this very moment, neither the beauty nor the horror we created will come again.

Runacar had always believed himself to be a scholar of war. Unlike many Heir-Princes, he had wholly followed the Sword Road, and studied the details of battles he had not been able to see. He had spent hours with Lengiathion, Heledor, and Elrinonion—Swordmasters and Warlords of House Caerthalien—re-creating famous battles on the sandtable in Lengiathion Swordmaster's chambers. From childhood, Runacar had wanted to know how to win every battle, and more: to win it beautifully, as an act of homage to the art of war. He wanted to be Arilcarion's perfect knight: skilled in war and in poetry, in music and dance, able to forge a sword as well as wield it. He had yearned for the ancient days when—as the legend went—the komen of Domain Araphant were so puissant that the enemy surrendered the moment they took the field, weeping for the beauty that defeated them.

His three elder brothers had thought his interest a harmless quirk, and certainly not something worth emulating: their doctrinaire tactics served them on the field just as they had served Caerthalien's greatsires. Power triumphed and elegance was needless.

But now, at last, Runacar saw power and elegance together.

Vieliessar's army moved like the fingers of one hand; understanding of their purpose, their goal, and their tactics seemed to flow among them as if by Magery; the moment she was in the saddle the coterie began moving, separating into its elements and subelements, forming on their commanders.

If the tears would not have frozen on his face, Runacar could have wept at the beauty of it.

The High King's party rode through the night. Walk, trot, gallop; a quartermark of rest every two candlemarks, a halfmark every four. It was a method taken from the oldest scrolls, from before war had become a game with elaborate rules. When dawn came, Vieliessar called for a rest as the Lightborn searched the skies with their Magery to discover a flying thing they could use to scout with. Everyone dismounted, taking this opportunity to stretch cramped muscles and to feed and water their horses.

"There's nothing with wings and within range except some Hippogriffs," Iardalaith said in disgust. He looked toward Vieliessar.

"Mosirinde forbids the enchaining of that which speaks," Vieliessar answered, almost wistfully.

"Then why don't we just send them an invitation to come and *help*?" Iardalaith asked with poisonous sweetness. "After all, are we not *allies*?" He stared at Runacar, his gaze cold and hostile.

"If they see me from the air, they will land to investigate," Runacar said levelly. "Pelere and Andhel have already notified the nearest village—so if you would be so kind as to not blast the first Otherfolk you see, we might get some assistance."

Iardalaith turned and led his horse away without speaking. A halfmark later, Vieliessar gave the command to mount and ride once more.

And because it would have been extremely convenient to make contact with any of the Hippogriff Flights, none came near.

The night and the second day was like the first. Runacar began to develop a keen admiration for the Arzhana halfbreeds they rode: the shaggy little beasts were utterly sure-footed, and even in the face of the brutal pace Vieliessar set, they seemed tireless.

Of course, Kishmiri attempted to take the bit away from him on a regular basis. She was always testing him: Runacar thought it was because she knew that horse and rider depended on one another for their lives in battle. *I will not fail you, little Fury.*

Exhaustion was beginning to take its toll on everyone; they rode in a weary silence, grateful for the breaks that gave them a chance to stand instead of sit, to gulp down mugs of sweet steaming tea. Gallop had been removed from their repertoire—it had become walk, trot, lead their beasts on foot. Fortunately the snow wasn't heavy here—it was only Woods Moon, after all—and Runacar suspected that at some point in the past, the entire Sanctuary Road had been bespelled, for even when the snow flurried around them, it didn't stick there.

When he realized that Vieliessar meant to ride through the second night as well, Runacar very nearly rebelled. What was the purpose of killing themselves and their mounts with a hellride when Hamphuliadiel's merry band was safe from anything but the return of the Endarkened?

If the Endarkened did return, all they would be able to do was to die together unless there was a nearby Delight of Unicorns that was feeling generous. Short of that, any Otherfolk who crossed the path of Hamphuliadiel's band of farmers and Lightborn would be in more danger from those farmers and Lightborn than those farmers and Lightborn were in danger from anything.

(Except the Endarkened.)

The children of the Endarkened were grouped roughly by size, and raised in a series of nursery chambers in the deepest levels of the World Without Sun. They did not occupy this precious location because they were valued by those who had created them but because that meant none of the adult Endarkened would accidentally see them.

(That would not end well.)

The children were attended by the Lesser Endarkened. They guarded the youngest children carefully, but the older they got, the more they were left to fend for themselves.

⊰ ⊱

The child Savilla only knew her name because her nursemaids needed something to call her. She had no idea how old she was, only that it would be a long time before she left the nursery, for her wings were still small and her body unripe. But there were things Savilla learned without needing anyone to teach her—the first thing, the thing that kept her alive, was the knowledge that not every child delivered to the Black Nursery by its mother left it again.

(No one cared.)

The second thing Savilla learned was how to hide. While the others near her size huddled together for safety, Savilla chose hiding places where she could spy unobserved; hiding places it was difficult—to say the least—to remove her from. Her greatest treasure was the obsidian blade she had found deep in the matrix of tunnels that made up the Black Nursery. Even if someone did find her, they would have to be *very* sure it was worth the trouble to pry her loose.

The third thing Savilla learned was that knowledge was power.

⊰ ⊱

Since the Black Nurseries must not be brought to the attention of the adults, the Lesser Endarkened could only bring their charges what the adults discarded. Their limbs were clothed and warmed by fabric torn from the bodies of captives. Their food was only what the Lesser Endarkened could grow or forage for unnoticeably: pale glowing fungi, strange insects, blind eyeless fish. Never flesh, unless a group of the older children could catch a younger child alone.

There was constant hunger among the children. They learned early to steal from one another. To scavenge. To betray.

(Not every child delivered to the Black Nursery left it again.)

Then all at once everything changed. The Lesser Endarkened came to the nursery tunnels laden down with delicacies most of the children had never tasted. Fresh white bone, jellies of new-curdled blood, ropes of intestines stuffed with eyes and spices. And not just scraps, but *meat*. Lots of it. Whole Centaurs. Casks full of pickled Fauns. Long strings of pixies hung up by their heels and smoked to death over a slow fire, their bodies still faintly glowing.

At first the children fought over the food, but there was so *much* of it that they realized how ridiculous fighting was. They gorged themselves beyond satiety. They ate until they were clutching their bodies in pain, and still they tried to eat more.

The wiser ones, those too near adulthood to be able to fit themselves into the smaller tunnels, carried food to their private hiding places, storing it to eat unmolested. Safely.

But even they did not wonder why the food came to them.

Savilla did.

⊰◗▤◖⊱

To leave the Nurseries and the meager protection of the Lesser Endarkened was dangerous, but Savilla had done so many times. Bitter experience had taught her that both the slave pens and the gardens were watched over carefully, but the same was not always true of the kitchens that served the Court. Now there was no need to steal scraps from the kitchens, for food was abundant, even in the Nurseries. But food was not knowledge, and Savilla hungered for that even more than she hungered to fill her belly.

Savilla crept through long-disused passageways, moving carefully, always ready to retreat. But she hadn't needed to bother, because the adults were intent upon their own pleasures.

There was gluttony, and sadism . . . And waste. So much *meat* spoiled and discarded. Savilla fed well on the scraps left behind, but food was not what she was after. So she waited, and watched, and learned.

⟊⟊

They will ascend to the Bright World soon, and this time the Red Harvest will come.

After that, there will be no more flights. Our purpose will be fulfilled. What then?

Savilla didn't know. She was not privy to the mutinous whispers the Born passed among themselves. The only thing Savilla knew was that once the Bright World had been cleansed, there would be nothing more for the Endarkened to hunt.

Except other Endarkened.

⟊⟊

When the celebrations were done, when the larders were empty, the beautiful children of *He Who Is* left their citadel, soaring wingtip to wingtip in their thousands until the whole of the brightening sky in the world above turned blood-red with their bodies.

Every single one of them carried a sheaf of unlit torches.

Shurzul led the formation. She had expected that place of honor to go to Uralesse, but he was not here. She fretted over his disobedience to Virulan's wishes, but she didn't really care what he was plotting. She was too busy making plans to keep herself alive.

Shurzul did not really believe that the blood and magic of all the Elfling Mages that were now or had ever been was enough to heal Virulan. What she *did* believe was that Virulan should be dead. Not because she hated and feared him—though she did—but because his continued existence was unnatural—and if one of the Endarkened found something to be unnatural, that thing was loathsomely impossible to both Darkness and Light.

If the others die in battle, it will not matter. Only let Virulan die somehow—and Uralesse too—and there will be glorious war as we, the Created-and-Changed, slaughter every one of the Born. He Who Is will have to love us then, for we will be all that's left.

As the Endarkened flew south and west, grass and bushes replaced the beautiful sterility of rock and sand on the ground below. Dying Flower Forests dotted the land, stubbornly clinging to life.

The Endarkened lit the torches they carried and tossed them down at the trees as they flew.

Soon the sky was filled with the smoke of burning.

⌁⌂⌁

By now Harwing had lost track of how long they'd been on the road, and as "Hamphuliadiel" he didn't dare ask. He wished heartily that he'd brought along some of the cordial Hamphuliadiel had used to dispel dreams, for the dreams Harwing had were about attempting to shed the mask of Astromancer Eternal and discovering it had become his own skin.

That was a problem for the future.

Today—a few hours before dawn—he'd awakened feeling ill, and neither hot tea nor strengthening cordial were any help. Heal didn't work, and Knowing failed to pinpoint the source of the problem.

He ordered the march to continue, but barely a candlemark later he heartily wished he hadn't—and whatever the malady was, it had spread to all the Lightborn and several of the villagers.

Oh. Okay. Now we're all going to die of plague. That's fine. But if this was the Otherfolk's plan all along I wish someone had told me before we'd left Areve because I would much rather die in front of a warm hearth!

There was another halt while the afflicted were loaded into wagons—ones drawn by the villagers, as the ox-carts were already overloaded and fodder was scarce. Harwing attempted to cast Shield as protection from the sharp winter wind, and found he could not. It took all the strength he had left to hold the illusion of being Hamphuliadiel Astromancer in place. And if he got sick enough, that illusion would come to an abrupt end.

And then there'd be *real* trouble.

The wagons started forward again. Harwing was the only one of the Lightborn still on his feet, and every step was anguish. The convoy barely managed another candlemark before Harwing called a halt. It took his last strength to terrorize the suffering Lightborn enough to get an ice-wall erected around the camp.

Harwing had never before been more grateful that the perks of being Astromancer Eternal included a private tent. He crawled inside as soon as it was set, wrapped a fur blanket around himself, and held on grimly to the web of spells that sustained his impersonation.

It has to be plague. It's not a spell or a ward. I could sense those, and the other Lightborn probably could too. They're piss-poor Lightborn, and they've all been brainwashed, but their basic teaching was sound. Poison? We're all eating from the same cauldrons—and why poison the Lightborn? If it were a vendetta, we would know—I use Heart-Seeing a dozen times a day, and the others probably do the same. Impatient Otherfolk? Maybe. But why not poison everyone?

Oh, Flower Queen, what is going to happen to us?

⊰⊱

The stars above were brilliantly clear and the wind was correspondingly cold. Outside the dim sphere of Silverlight enclosing them as they rode, there was nothing but darkness: no distant spark of campfire or lanterns; no sound save that of the wind and sometimes a hunting owl. His cloak kept Runacar magnificently warm, especially with the hood in place, but he felt—looking at the night—as if he *ought* to be cold.

Kishmiri, of course, seemed tireless.

If the High King were an ordinary bandit, chasing after an ordinary prize—a supply train, say—Runacar would be able to predict her tactics and perhaps even improve upon them. But he could not make her tactics make sense—of course, she wasn't telling him everything, but he had enough of the facts to deduce the rest.

Only none of his deductions led him to an answer.

One of the Silver Swords—the woman who'd been in the council; Githachi—led her gelding over to him at one of the rest stops. Runacar was rubbing Kishmiri's ears and feeding her slices of dried apple. The mare leaned her weight against him, her heavy head thrust against his shoulder. He wondered—when this was all over . . . if they lived—if he could get Vieliessar to give her to him. Kishmiri had become dear to him in a handful of candlemarks.

"We will rest tomorrow," Githachi said.

"Doesn't she mean to run us until we drop?" Runacar asked, raising his eyebrows to take the sting out of his words.

Githachi smiled. "Us, certainly—but the horses? Never. Tomorrow and even the night after, we will stay in one place." Githachi sounded remarkably cheerful about it.

"Then why hurry to get as far along the Road as we have?" Runacar asked. "We have plenty of time to find them. We could even let them come to us."

If there was to be a battle, Areve and the Sanctuary had the numbers on their side. If this was a rescue, why couch it in terms of a battle? Exposing themselves to a possible Endarkened attack was risk without reward.

Except that she has very few Lightborn. And Lightborn take Wheel-turns to train.

That's what Vieliessar wants. That's why she brought the Warhunt.

That is going to be an amazing mess, Runacar thought.

"'Who chooses the battlefield chooses the victory,'" Githachi answered, quoting Arilcarion. "While we hope the party has remained upon the road, we do not know. Hamphuliadiel was always an enemy whose actions were hard to predict."

She makes it sound as if he's a War Prince who issues challenges every Sword Moon, Runacar thought. He remembered Hamphuliadiel as being annoyingly pompous, but little more than that.

"So the High King has ridden so hard to get to the battlefield first?" Runacar asked.

"When is that ever a bad idea?" Githachi answered merrily. "But come—the tea and the hot mulled ale are ready. And tomorrow we sleep."

But it was not to be.

⌑

Runacar roused from a dismal upright half-sleep as Kishmiri stopped.

Everyone had stopped.

It was the chilly, foggy part of dawn—the part he'd found most depressing during the Winter War, as it had presaged a long day of work in the most brutal sort of cold. Some of the Warhunt Mages were down lying on the frozen ground, their mounts led away from them by members of the Kingsguard. As Runacar looked on, the Silver Swords pulled back to form a picket wall around the rest of the band.

What in the name of Sword and Star . . . ?

Runacar drew his sword as he swung his leg over the cantle, wincing at his stiffness. Kishmiri waited for him to release her before she moved—once he'd given that command, she wandered a few steps to look for tufts of grass, her tail switching eloquently.

Runacar looked in all directions and saw nothing he could identify as a threat, though everyone else certainly seemed to sense one. They were near the eastern border of Aramenthiali, if he was reading the landscape correctly. They must have crossed most of Vondaimieriel already—it was a long but narrow domain that hugged the foothills and shared a border with Mangiralas.

He headed toward the Warhunt. Iardalaith and a handful of other Warhunt Mages stood over their fallen comrades. Several of those afflicted were trying to get to their feet. The High King was kneeling beside one of the fallen Mages. Pouncewarm sat upon the Mage's chest, and Runacar could see that all of the Palugh and Wulvers were active.

Inside the boundary set by the Silver Swords, most of the Palugh were walking in an elaborate pattern, tails high. The Wulvers were grouped closely around the fallen, warming them, while others stood watch, tails down and ears pricked.

"—worst possible time," Runacar heard Iardalaith say as he approached.

"Is there *ever* a good time, Arda? At least it means the Astromancer's force will be down," another Warhunt Mage answered. Their breaths smoked on the chilly air.

Vieliessar got to her feet, turning toward them. Through the Bond, Runacar felt a momentary surge of sickness and terror, before Vieliessar did something and the sensation vanished. She regarded him with the weary expression of a commander taxed to her limits who was faced with yet one more problem. Before he could say anything, she turned away, giving orders.

"Siona, the Caves of Imrathalion are perhaps a league and a half from here. It will at least be more defensible than open ground. Go now, and you can make it before *they* come. Take the Otherfolk Warlord with you; he can—"

"No," Runacar said. "I am still more use here than—"

"Don't you understand, Prince Idiot?" Iardalaith said, rubbing at his eyes as if they hurt. "The Endarkened are coming. Now. Here."

"I am *so* very sorry to hear that," Runacar answered in the most insufferable tones he could muster. "But it changes nothing. It is *still* true that Caerthalien once held Bethros in clientage, and that Hamphuliadiel served in Caerthalien Great Keep until he was released to the Sanctuary. He will know me by sight."

And they will bow down to a prince of the Hundred Houses where they will not truckle to one of their own.

He was needed here—especially since the High King's Warhunt Mages seemed to be failing her. Runacar remembered the Battle of Shieldwall Plain, remembered his brother summoning the *mazhnune*. Nearly all the Lightborn on the field had fallen in that moment. Apparently, the Endarkened affected the Lightborn the same way.

Siona and Iardalaith both looked toward Vieliessar.

"Stay if you choose. But I tell you this plainly: you will die here today," she said to Runacar.

At least Andhel and Pelere are safe. "Fine," Runacar answered. "Now let's summon some reinforcements to make this more interesting."

⊰⊱

As the Warhunt moved slowly toward the Caves of Imrathalion, Runacar walked in the opposite direction. His boots crunched over frozen leaves and frozen grass, and his breath made Dragon-clouds on the air. He couldn't be sure how far away was far enough, so his best guess would have to do.

He wanted to tell himself he didn't know what he was asking of the folk he led, if any of them should answer. But he did. He was asking them to die. *Vieliessar always knew that. She knew that from the beginning. War is not a game. War is death.*

There was no choice. Leutric had done everything he could to keep the Endarkened from crossing the Mystrals. Now they would. Runacar and his Bondmate would almost certainly die. He found himself wishing—to his surprise—that the High King's regency council could hold her people together. And that they would ally with his. With Leutric's. With any living thing that wasn't Endarkened.

Kishmiri broke off from her foraging and followed him. Runacar stopped and made shooing motions, and he could have sworn the mare simply laughed at him. "Fine," he said. "Do as you please."

A few paces more, and he reached the place he'd spotted from the road: the stump of a tree taken down long enough ago that its bark had weathered away and its wood had turned grey. If he didn't look back the way he'd come, he could imagine himself to be utterly alone. The sky had lightened even in the short time since they'd stopped. In perhaps a candlemark, the sun would rise over the Mystrals, and the day would begin.

And may the Silver Hooves bring all the fallen safely away with them in death, whether komen, or Lightborn, or Otherfolk.

"Melisha," he said. His voice was a hoarse croak. He swallowed hard, and tried again. "Melisha. Please come if you can. The Endarkened are coming, and we're in a stupid mess. I just hope that —If you want to . . . Melisha, please come. I—"

The sense that someone was listening, was about to answer, was strong. Then Kishmiri nudged him in the back and the moment was gone. Runacar took a deep breath. He didn't want to admit, especially to himself, that for a moment he'd thought it had worked. That Melisha had come.

Wishing is for children, he told himself brutally. *Generals plan.*

He hoped this plan was a good one, because it was all he had.

Runacar scrubbed the tree stump free of snow and began to gather tinder and tufts of grass. As his bundle grew, he added twigs and branches from the bushes. When he had enough, he took up a position where he could watch the mare and set his harvest of tinder carefully on the stump.

Kishmiri looked from him to the stump with interest.

"Take one step closer and I'll feed you these," he warned, reaching into one of the pockets of his borrowed cloak to pull out a small, tightly sealed glass jar. It held a number of small grey pebbles that rattled—innocuously—as he shook it. Carefully, he pried the wax seal away and pulled out the stopper, shaking a single one of the firestones into his hand.

Firestones had been one of the magical conveniences Lightborn had made for those of rank or favor who might not always have a Lightborn close at hand. Abruptly, sharply, a memory of his sister came unbidden. He'd been a child as he watched Ciliphirilir tossing hundreds of firestones into her bath to heat the water. She'd laughed to see it come to a steaming boil in moments, and swept him up in her arms, swinging him around and threatening to drop him into it. He'd clutched at her hair, shrieking in delight and terror.

She'd died in the field. Ullilion? Maybe. And the chamber, and the castel it had occupied, were gone, and there was no one left to remember Ciliphirilir of Caerthalien but him. All the things of those days were gone, except the firestones, created in such abundance that there had been literal casks of them left in the storage rooms of the Great Keeps.

Kishmiri continued to regard Runacar watchfully, her nostrils flaring. He placed the firestone carefully in the center of his nest of twigs and grass, then uncapped his canteen and splashed a generous amount of water on it. The moment a firestone touched water, it would burn.

The stone ignited with a huff of flame. Then it tried to ignite the sodden vegetation around it. Smoke immediately began to curl skyward from the wet tinder.

That was the point.

Runacar stepped back to watch as a thin column of smoke rose skyward in the still air of dawn. If he was lucky, the firestone would ignite the dead stump and the fire would burn for candlemarks.

Someone would see it. Someone would investigate. He hoped.

He turned away and led Kishmiri back to the others.

CHAPTER TWENTY-FIVE

WOOD'S MOON IN THE TENTH YEAR OF THE HIGH KING'S REIGN: A PAST WITH NO FUTURE

We had believed, even through the long Wheelturns of war, when entire households could be born and die never knowing peace, that the world we made would be familiar. It was not. Had the Light-born known how the campaign would end, I think we would all have flocked to Hamphuliadiel, base and corrupt and self-serving as he was.

—Anonymous, A History of The Lightborn, from Mosirinde Astromancer to Hamphuliadiel of Bethros, With an Appendix Summarizing the First Wheel-turns after the Western Objective of the High King's War

W hat's that?" Pendray Lightsister asked nobody in particular, gazing toward the distant pillar of smoke. "Someone really bad at building a cookfire?" She rubbed her forehead absently. She felt achy all over, and found herself dreading the day to come. The villagers and Hamphuliadiel's pampered Lightborn traveled at the speed of . . . rocks. Rocks that were not moving. Very stupid rocks.

Adding to her bloodthirsty mood was the fact that it was too early on another cold miserable morning, and she'd drawn the short straw last night, so she was the one who got to set Shield and Cloak and kindle a fire for tea and keep the Astromancer's people from seeing anything that might let them know that the Warhunt was following them. They seemed to be preparing to move out on schedule, which was too bad—though the speed they moved at meant Pendray and her friends could have a leisurely breakfast before catching up. It also meant they would have to be on the road instead of spending the day huddling in a nice warm hole in the dirt.

Not that there wasn't enough cover for the Warhunt to follow almost openly. Traditionally, the vegetation had been kept cut back a bowshot's length from the edges of the Sanctuary Road, but ten Wheelturns was a long time. The grass was long now, and sapling trees and berrybushes had crept in among it.

"Not a cookfire," Tangisen said, crawling out of the trench to stand beside her. "A beacon." He closed his eyes for a moment, as if listening. "And kindled by Magery."

Pendray knew he'd know. Tangisen's Keystone Gift was Fire.

"Am I the only one who feels like the Starry Hunt rode over me in my sleep?" Isilla asked, joining them. Tangisen shook his head. "How far?" she asked next.

"Not quite two leagues," Tangisen answered, shrugging.

"Maybe we should go ask Hamphuliadiel if he has any Healers with him," Pendray said. She was only half joking.

Isilla looked at her, then sighed, rubbing her temples. "We'll be lucky if this is just a winter cough. And not Bearward poison. Or worse."

"What could be worse?" Pendray asked, frowning. They'd set wards, of course, but everyone knew that wards weren't impenetrable—especially by Beastling magic.

"'Worse' would be something we've never heard of before," Isilla said pragmatically. "Get the fire started—after we have tea, we're going to go see who set that beacon."

⌐⊣⊢

"With me." Vieliessar summoned Runacar with an imperious hand gesture. To his weary amusement, Runacar found he was too tired to resent it.

He patted Kishmiri apologetically on the shoulder and swung into the saddle once more. Whatever kind of war the High King's people had fought, they had trained their Arzhana ponies to the same commands as the destriers.

For the last 'mark he'd watched Vieliessar disposing her forces and dispatching scouts in the direction of Hamphuliadiel's party. Apparently there was no Mage Door powerful enough to take all of them back to Ceoprentrei, or Runacar thought she might have sent her folk to relative safety. (Considering the extent of her available resources, a miracle might have occurred and Vieliessar would have gone herself.)

Only her personal guard and Iardalaith Lightbrother were with her: all the rest had been given their orders and dismissed. Runacar could see how the battle would play out against a conventional force, and knew, as the High King must know, that those tactics would fail. She'd deployed her elements along the route to the caves, separating the Warhunt Mages from the others so that they would draw the Endarkened. Those of the meisne who had been "adopted" by Palugh were designated as messengers between the battle groups, and except for Runfar and Birdleap, she sent the Wulvers to Imrathalion, telling them to stand guard.

None of the elements needed to hold for any length of time. In fact, they'd been designed to collapse into one another as they were attacked. It was a masterful example of a fighting retreat that would have cost any High House battle group dearly for every cubit of ground gained.

And it would be almost completely ineffective against an enemy with wings. There was no point in setting the elements of the force in cover, because they would be visible from above. There was no point in further disguising them—or even making them invisible—because the enemy had magic.

And there is no hope of damaging the Endarkened to the point they withdraw.

The cold calculus of battle offered up only one answer. They would die here—even if the Otherfolk army joined them. Or the Unicorns would come. Or the Starry Hunt would pluck them up alive and set them among the stars. There really didn't seem to be a third option, and only one of the three was likely.

"We will proceed south," Vieliessar said when he reached her side. "Iardalaith, you and Helecanth will ride for the Caves of Imrathalion."

"My lord King!" Helecanth protested. "My place is with you!"

Vieliessar locked eyes with her guard commander, and even though he was not its focus, Runacar felt that impact of the High King's will as he would have felt a blow. "Your place is where I say it is," Vieliessar said inexorably. "With Thurion on the Regency Council—if you can get back to Ceoprentrei. Tell the Warhunt to use Transmute to expand the cave system—Imrathalion should be able to reach Ceoprentrei." She leaned over, and—to Runacar's surprise—kissed Helecanth upon the lips, lord to liege. "I need you to live, Cantha."

Helecanth nodded stiffly—unreconciled—and turned her mount eastward, brandishing her sword for Iardalaith to follow her. The Lightborn glared at him—though personally, Runacar thought himself blameless—before turning his mount to follow Helecanth.

Now, all that remained was the King-Emperor's Warlord, the High King, and a taille of her personal guard.

And one more.

"Silly, silly, Elvenborn. Are you to have fun but not I?" Pouncewarm said, appearing from nowhere. The Palugh bounded up to settle on the cantle of Vieliessar's saddle, then leapt again to her shoulder. She reached up a hand to steady him; Pouncewarm was not small.

"I told you to stay where it was safe!" she said in exasperation.

"I am the greatest of hunters; the greatest of warriors," the Palugh replied serenely.

"You are a great deal of *trouble*," Vieliessar said scoldingly. She set Assar moving forward at a slow walk. Runacar fell in beside her, and the taille followed. Runfar and Birdleap trotted along happily at Assar's heels. They'd know where they were going once the scouts rejoined them. Until then, there was no need for hurry.

"I am leaving the Warhunt Mages behind because we know the Endarkened always attack Lightborn first," Vieliessar said, almost as if she was merely speaking her thoughts aloud. "It could split their attack. If the Lightborn are fortunate, they can retreat to Imrathalion under the cover the Silver Swords will provide. We have never seen the Endarkened fly through a solid object—if they have not brought goblins with them, the cave should be defensible."

Only if you seal it shut, Runacar thought. "You're talking as if I will survive this day," he said.

"My mother lived a full day after Serenthon's death," Vieliessar said. "Telthorelandor managed a moonturn. You may be stubborn enough to exceed him. It does not matter, so long as you survive long enough to teach the Woodwose our tactics. They will find them useful."

"Now you're talking as if *anyone* will survive," Runacar pointed out. It was odd, this sense of camaraderie he felt with her. He still believed High King Vieliessar was a dangerous lunatic at best, and a mad sorcerer possessed by ghosts at worst, but he also still trusted her—which only confirmed his belief that magic was useless at best, dangerous at worst.

"Child of the Prophecy," Vieliessar answered with a small smile. "It provides a few advantages. Now come—either our scouts are returning or we are about to do battle."

Drawing her sword, she spurred Assar to a trot.

⁂

Isilla's party, by virtue of not having stopped for an astonishingly inappropriate midmorning nap, was not merely a good distance ahead of Hamphuliadiel's people when they saw the company of riders, but moving salient to the Sanctuary Road. Everyone had Cloaked at the first sound . . .

And then, even without banners and heraldry, Isilla recognized their leader.

"Vielle!" she shouted, dropping Cloak and waving frantically. "You're alive!"

Vieliessar turned toward the sound of the familiar voice and leapt from Assar's back before the mare could begin to slow. "Isilla! Tangisen! Jorganroch! Praise Sword and Star that some of you survived!" Vieliessar cried. She reached Isilla and hugged her tightly. "I thought you lost when I heard tell that the Shore Domains were gone."

"Then you know most of what I have to report. Is Harwing with you?" Isilla asked hopefully. Vieliessar shook her head.

"I sent him with you. If—"

Isilla shook her head. "We knew that Hamphuliadiel never bore any great love for you, but it seemed he was the only real power left in the West. When we first reached the Sanctuary, Rondithiel wanted to call upon the Astromancer formally, but Harwing convinced him to first send scouts. Harwing convinced *me* he should go alone. He did. He never came back."

The rest of the party was dropping their own instances of Cloak and gathering around Vieliessar.

"Where is Rondithiel now?" Vieliessar asked.

"Dead," Isilla said bleakly. "Dead by Beastling Magery."

"We came looking for you once Daroldan fell," Tangisen blurted out. "Why did you take so long to come back? We could have stood if you were . . ." He stopped, staring toward Vieliessar's escort. "It is Caerthalien." He lifted his hand to Cast. Vieliessar seized his wrist and Dispelled the instance before it had fully formed.

"He has sworn fealty to an ally. You will not act against him," Vieliessar said firmly, and waited until Tangisen reluctantly nodded. "His tale is too long to tell just now. In scant candlemarks Amretheon's great enemy will reach us. We ride to seek those folk who have latterly abandoned the Sanctuary of the Star and the village called Areve."

"We've been following them for a fortnight or so," Isilla said. "We got to the Sanctuary just behind them and found everyone gone—and the Shrine chained and sealed behind a wall. They are stopped a few 'marks behind us. Vieliessar—Hamphuliadiel leads them."

"Jusserand, give Isilla Lightsister your mount, for I will have need of her. The rest of you go as quickly as you can toward the caves of Imrathalion. Spells are useless against the Endarkened, but stone may serve where spells do not. And mark this well: the Otherfolk—the Beastlings—are on our side."

"You've gone mad," Tangisen said in a voice of discovery. He recoiled with a strangled yelp as Pouncewarm placed soft paws upon his knee, stretching.

"I, I, I tell you this is not so," the Palugh said merrily, clearly inviting Tangisen to share the joke. Tangisen regarded him as if a stone—or the squirmy things under a stone—had spoken.

"I am the Child of the Prophecy," Vieliessar answered in an iron voice. "And you are sworn to *me*. The scarlet bat-winged creatures are the enemy—the *only* enemy. They will strike within the candlemark. Now *go*."

Isilla felt the High King's will crest over them all as she mounted the strange shaggy pony. It was no *geasa*, nor any spell, unless the mantle of Child of the Prophecy was itself a spell. *Do as she says,* she mouthed silently at Tangisen. His mouth settled into a grim line, but he nodded. The talking cat—surely Isilla would remember if she had read of such a thing in Lannarien!—bounded across the road and leapt to the back of the High King's white pony. Vieliessar followed only a bit more slowly.

"Come on," Isilla heard Dinias say as she and the other riders started forward. "I'm the leader now."

⊰⊱

Harwing was roused from a painful doze by terrified shouting. He groped around until he found the Astromancer's ridiculous hat, and pulled the brightly glowing staff out from under the nest of blankets he'd shoved it into, then crawled (with great dignity) out of the tent . . .

Into chaos.

Their encompassing walls of ice were only at half their original height and despite the temperature were melting like an ice subtlety in front of a fire. Several instances of Shield—of varying strengths, none of them shielding the whole circumference of the wall—sparked and sizzled as they bumped into one another. That was barely the leading edge of the Magery being wielded; Harwing could sense Fetch, Cold, Fire, and Send as well as others too blended and contaminated to identify. Fortunately or otherwise, most of the Lightborn were casting Shield, which did not permit most things to pass through it—including Magery. Those who had unwisely chosen another spell found it absorbed by the nearest Shield if they were lucky—and ricocheting off if they were not.

From the smoke in the air, things had been set on fire already.

The (former) villagers ran in all directions, their arms filled with provisions from the wagons—although where they might go with them was an interesting question. The Lightborn were in utter disorder—some trying to stop the villagers, others trying to build the ice-walls back up, still more casting truly context-inappropriate spells. The oxen were bawling. The dogs were barking. The people were wailing. They'd lost all the goats and chickens in Arevethmonion, and Harwing had never been more grateful for that fact.

It was all almost enough to take his mind off his headache.

"What is the meaning of this?" he demanded. Voice assured that everyone could hear it. He simply didn't have the energy to cast a useful level of Dispell.

"She comes! The Mad Witch has come for us!" Kasevien Lightsister came running to him. She had been Chief Lightborn of Laeldor until Vieliessar had conquered it. Harwing had considered executing her, but she was merely vain and greedy, not evil. "It is the Landless Witch, the mooncalf, Darkspawn, the mother of Dragons!"

"Does this person have a *name*?" Harwing demanded in frustration. The bells on his hat jingled. He forced himself not to wince.

"It is Vieliessar of no House!" Ilmion Lightbrother joined Kasevien, with Uldreyn hurrying after him. Harwing couldn't imagine Kasevien making common cause with Ilmion. Ilmion talked anyone's plans to death—Harwing suspected it was why Hamphuliadiel had favored him. (If Ilmion had been in charge, they'd all still be forming committees back at the Sanctuary.)

"What are your orders, my lord Astromancer?" Uldreyn Lightbrother asked. Harwing felt like hugging him. A good minion, he'd come to realize, was key to being an evil overlord. Perhaps he'd been too hasty in executing Momioniarch and the rest of that cabal.

"Shut those people up. Put out the fires. Stop everyone casting those dark-damned spells. And . . . Just let me think." Harwing didn't care right now whether he sounded like Hamphuliadiel or not. "Go." He gestured the three of them away.

When they were gone—indicating that they'd at least heard his orders if they didn't intend to carry them out—Harwing walked behind his tent. Now he could find out what was really going on. The ice-wall was barely a handspan above his head, though it had started at two cubits thick and eight high. (Obviously there was Magery afoot, but the question was: Whose?) He pulled off one of Hamphuliadiel's gauntlets and placed his hand against the ice. The cold felt good, and he leaned his forehead against the ice as well. (His hat fell off and landed behind him.) Then he reached out, through the ice, to the spell that was destroying it.

Every Lightborn's casting was unique to them, just as any cooper's or

wainwright's or blacksmith's or jeweler's work could be told from another's. The Hundred Houses hadn't thought detecting that signature was a
thing worth training—but Vieliessar had.

Vieliessar. Harwing felt the shock of recognition. It was her.

*Kasevien Lightsister has finally been right about something. It is the
fulfillment of a prophecy: the High King has returned to us at last. Although this isn't really the best time, what with the Otherfolk throwing us
out of the West and so forth.*

Harwing added his meager available Light to Vieliessar's. The ice-
wall melted as quickly as snow before a bonfire.

Perhaps Harwing had been expecting the traditional panoply of the
War Princes, but what he saw was the High King and a taille of
komen all dressed as if they were unsuccessful bandits, riding animals
that looked more like some strange species of Bearward than like horses.

And no less than Caerthalien himself was mounted beside her.

For a moment, all Harwing could see was the brother of the man
who had slain Gunedwaen. The prince who fled rather than swear fealty
to the High King. "Murdering scum!" Harwing snarled, taking a step
forward.

"Cease! This man is under my protection," Vieliessar announced.
"Hamphuliadiel of Bethros Erased, I am the High King, sovereign over
all the Hundred Houses by right of battle, and by right of—*Harwing*?"

Harwing suddenly realized that she had cast Dispell to negate whatever spell the "Astromancer" might be readying. It had stripped away his
careful impersonation.

"Where have you been?" Harwing demanded. "You *left* us!" (He
hoped nobody from the camp was actually paying attention, though
that was unlikely. At least they were too far away to see anything but the
Astromancer robes.)

"Why is he impersonating the Astromancer?" Harwing heard Caerthalien ask.

"That is *unimportant*," Vieliessar replied. "Harwing: Are you their
leader?"

"As Hamphuliadiel. I mean, since Harvest, and . . . Yes."

"Then resume your glamour. And swear to me as if you were he. The time of the Darkness of Amretheon's Prophecy is upon us. It will launch its latest attack within candlemarks. Your folk must come with me to have any hope of survival."

The Darkness of Amretheon's Prophecy advances toward us? Arriving today, and it's clearly worse than the Banebringer.

This is not good.

Harwing struggled to pick up the many threads of his impersonation, but he was ill and tired. All he could manage was Cloak, and that wasn't particularly useful. Vieliessar dismounted and walked unerringly to him. She clasped his hands between hers.

Harwing felt warmth and strength suffuse him, as powerful as if he'd drunk an entire bucket full of Healing Cordial. She smiled at him encouragingly, and Harwing felt a helpless love for her, the prince who did not forget the least of her servants. The lord who had inspired Gunedwaen's fierce loyalty. Now, the familiar spells he needed came quickly, and he pulled Hamphuliadiel's seeming about him.

"Hail, Lord Vieliessar, High King, Master of the Hundred Houses and rightful possessor of the Unicorn Throne!" Harwing cried, casting the strongest instance of Voice he ever had. Hamphuliadiel's oleaginous phrasing came easily to him after so much practice. "Long have we awaited your coming so that I, Hamphuliadiel, Astromancer Eternal of the Sanctuary of the Star, might bring the folk I have shepherded in your name under your wise care and insightful guidance." *And may all of Hamphuliadiel's illegitimate and misbegotten Green Robes choke on your laws!*

"Long have I yearned to see your face," Vieliessar answered in the same courtly register. "I pray you, Lord Astromancer, swear now your fealty to me, for I am High King over all who dwell in the Fortunate Lands."

"I shall." With painstaking caution, Harwing knelt before her, his hands clasped in hers. He took a deep breath as he summoned the form of the fealty oath. Would she cast Heart-Seeing over him? Did it matter?

"I, who carry with me all there is of Hamphuliadiel of Bethros, last

Astromancer of the Sanctuary of the Star, do swear before Leaf and Tree and Flower, before Fire and Moon and Star, that I am your vassal until both Leaf and Star have withered away, and my life and all I hold is yours to do with as you will. I will uphold this oath until I die, and with it I pledge to serve you above all—" There was a moment's pause as Harwing stumbled over the words, revising them as he went. "—above all things save the Light itself and the teachings of Mosirinde Peacemaker, until Amretheon Aradruiniel returns, and to this oath we will both be faithful."

Harwing breathed a sigh of relief as he felt the slight tingle of a true swearing. He hadn't been certain his revised phrasing would pass muster. He got carefully to his feet again, still holding Vieliessar's hands. She was his liege-lord now. Somehow, it made a difference.

There was a pause: Harwing suspected Vieliessar of mentally revising her own oath as well.

"I, Vieliessar, accept this oath of you, who carry the mantle of the last Astromancer of the Sanctuary of the Star, and pledge to you before Leaf and Tree and Flower, before Fire and Moon and Star, that I accept your service, and that your life and all you hold—save your Light, which cannot be taken nor given—is mine. For your tendering of this oath of fealty I swear I will not allow you to lie unransomed—that I shall seek to keep all harm from you, and to uphold your dignity and honor in your life and death. This oath shall bind me until I die, and with it I pledge to you that I will never ask of you the disparagement of Mosirinde's Covenant, and to this oath I will be faithful."

There was only that one slight bobble as she swore, and Harwing was fairly sure that the part about ransom and dungeons didn't apply to the Astromancer—or to anyone these days. But he had certainly caught the careful phrasing of the rest of the oath. *"Seek to uphold your dignity and honor in life and death"? That's not disturbing at all.*

"I delight to place myself and all who follow me beneath the hand of the High King," Harwing Voiced. If any of his people couldn't hear him that was not his fault. "And thus, in token of the end of the old ways, I render up this sign of office."

The Astromancer's ring was said to date from the time of Mosirinde

Peacemaker: he tugged a little at his left forefinger, prying the ring free, and held it out to Vieliessar on the palm of his hand.

Vieliessar took the ring and slipped it onto her own finger. "I accept this in token of the sovereignty and equality of all Lightborn, though I give my word that Hamphuliadiel of Bethros, Astromancer of the Sanctuary of the Star, shall always be first among equals."

"Then I go now to prepare my people to come beneath your hand."

Harwing turned away with Hamphuliadiel's ponderous theatricality, and Fetched the ridiculous hat to him.

It was wet, dripping, and muddy. He heard a snicker from behind and whirled around again. There were two misshapen dogs sitting on either side of the High King and laughing at him. Probably more Otherfolk.

"All right, fine, Otherfolk are swearing fealty to the High King now, why did I ever imagine my life was going to be normal again," Harwing muttered under his breath, turning his back on them. He Sent the water and debris from his hat and jammed it ruthlessly onto his head before he strode back to his people.

Hamphuliadiel's people.

⋈

Of course Ilmion and Kasevien were at the vanguard of the Lightborn gathered to greet him. Kasevien was leaning on a staff for support, and Harwing noted that even the arrival of the High King had not gotten some of the Lightborn out of their beds.

"My dear children," Harwing boomed at them. "You see how the High King in her wisdom has favored me above all her nobles! Now at last I can share with you the great secret that occasioned our departure from your warm and comfortable homes. It is indeed a glorious day for us all, for the High King has come at last to take us into her gentle and victorious care!"

He could feel Vieliessar glaring at him even without turning around. But if she wanted these people to do anything other than panic, she would have to reconcile herself to the fact that the Astromancer Eternal never passed up any opportunity to make a speech, and that was what these people expected. "I say to you this, my children: take up only what you can carry and leave the rest behind: we will depart at once to the warm and comfortable shelter she has prepared for us."

I am certain that the Vale of Celenthodiel is warm and comfortable, so I am not precisely lying to them.

"We will *not!*" Kasevien Lightsister responded. "Never has the Sanctuary bowed to any Prince! Nor has the Astromancer set himself below princes," she added dangerously. "The Mad Witch has ensorcelled you!"

I was wrong: I should have had you killed, you meddling self-important cloudwit! "If you want to stay right here, Kasevien, I can arrange that," Harwing snarled. He glared at Kasevien so venomously that she recoiled.

Harwing took a deep breath and tried again. "My beloved children! My Lightborn; my dear and beloved commonfolk! You may imagine I have humbled myself—yet I say to you I have not! I have bowed down to the High King as the War Princes have bowed, nothing more! I am the equal of mighty Caerthalien, of haughty Aramenthiali. Now let us—"

"Why didn't you tell us in the beginning you were taking us to *her?*" someone shouted out of the crowd. Harwing recognized her from his walks around Areve. Munariel—the komen *Steward* of House Inglethendragir. She had kept her son with her in Arevethmonion by the expedient of laying him in chains and standing over him day and night.

"The High King has many enemies, Lady Munariel, and I would not make them a gift of such knowledge. You yourself know that knowledge can be a two-edged sword, do you not? Be grateful that the High King extends amnesty to all, and calls you to take up your proper rank and title once more." There were about a taille of folk of noble or knightly rank hiding among the villagers: exposing them should make everyone stop thinking for long enough to get them moving. It also caused Komen Munariel to shut up (good), and the rest of the Lightless to temporarily forget they were in the presence of their beloved Astromancer (bad). Everyone began talking at once.

He felt a tug on his robe. He looked down. One of the Otherfolk wolves was sitting on its haunches, tugging at his garment with distressingly Elven-looking hands. "The High King says if you don't have them moving within the next eighthmark, she will strike you down and become Astromancer herself."

"If she wants the job, she's welcome to it," Harwing growled. "Go away!" He took a deep breath. "I bring you even more glorious news!" he shouted at the top of his lungs, wading into the melee before him. "The High King has conquered the Beastlings! They are all now her vassals!"

It didn't shut anybody up. Harwing was contemplating whether it would be possible to place a *geasa* on several thousand souls at once, when he heard hoofbeats behind him. He turned.

It was Caerthalien on his shaggy scrub. The animal trotted past Harwing.

"Dark take you, you useless spavined pack of jumped-up inbred Landbonds!" Caerthalien bawled in a voice that could clear battlefields. *"Stop this right now!"*

The Lightborn and the Lightless froze in fear. But Ilmion was apparently not merely immune to fear, he had seemingly appointed himself the Astromancer's spokesman. "And who are *you*, my good komen?"

"It is Prince Runacarendalur of Caerthalien!" Kasevien Lightsister cried.

"My father rides with the Hunt," Runacar snarled. "Now, do as I say. You! Lightborn. What is your name?"

"Ah, er, um . . . I am Ilmion Lightbrother, my lord. I was born in Cirandeiron."

"I do not care if you were born on the moon," Runacar answered in deadly tones. "Take charge of these damned Lightborn and get them moving. *Now.* Or I shall ensure that they do not move at all. Are we clear?"

Harwing was caught between his hatred of Caerthalien and his deep satisfaction at seeing Ilmion so summarily dealt with.

They think Caerthalien represents safety and security; the time of the Hundred Houses come again. Hamphuliadiel made them believe that was possible. I think that was his greatest cruelty.

The Lightborn quickly shuffled into a sort of marching order and began moving forward; Harwing moved toward the Lightless. Most of them were still standing frozen like rabbits. Harwing singled out those who were not.

"Munariel! Hathrion! Carthiel! Daramarth! Malathier! Come forward and lead these folk to safety! Take up your custodianship of those below your station in fealty to Prince Vieliessar, High King over the Hundred Houses!"

"Mama! I am going to be a knight after all!" a young voice cried excitedly.

A few people laughed. And everyone began moving.

⊟⊟

Harwing walked beside Vieliessar, still feeling as if he was suffering from every deep-winter malady there was. All of the Lightborn were feeling it now: the terrible oppression that was the harbinger of the enemy Harwing had not yet met—the Darkness prophesied by Amretheon Aradruiniel. Lord Vieliessar said the misery was a thing that diminished slightly with familiarity, but none of "Hamphuliadiel's" Lightborn were familiar with it, and that meant the High King had been forced to put as many of those not already mounted as she could on horseback in order to bring them along.

Harwing would rather be riding too, but the Astromancer had a place of honor beside the High King, and that meant walking. Right now, Harwing regretted every stitch of the green, high-heeled boots he was wearing: they were meant for riding, and they pinched.

The Lightless trailed behind the High King's household guard in a shuffling, quietly miserable, coffle. Without the komen behind them, many of them might simply have sat down in the road and waited for death. Just as Harwing had ordered, the only things they'd brought with them were what they could carry. Children who survived Arevethmonion; puppies, cats, elderly dogs—all that lived and could not keep to a marching pace were carried.

All but the oxen. They moved far too slowly, so they had been unyoked from the wagons, unharnessed, and left to their inevitable fate.

The small cruelty of abandoning the gentle patient creatures to terror, starvation, and death nagged at Harwing in a way his murders had not. The beasts did not deserve the end he suspected they would get.

In the name of the Light, we owe our protection to all who are weaker than we, to all who have given us their trust, to all who are put in harm's way because of actions we take. This is the true Covenant, I think, and oh, we broke it so very long ago. . . .

If not for what he knew now to be Wulvers, Harwing would have at least tried to go back: a quick and gentle death was better than death in terror and pain. But the Wulvers trotted around the perimeter of the entire party as if they were Otherfolk flock-guards. The High King had also brought with her enormous cats that talked, just to confuse matters. One of them rode across her shoulders, regarding Harwing with lambent green eyes and purring.

"I can hear you thinking," Vieliessar said quietly. "We are the chosen target of the Endarkened. Everything else will be safe. For a while."

"And what about after a while?" Harwing could not stop himself from asking.

"They will die, just as all life everywhere will die at the hands of the Endarkened," Vieliessar said matter-of-factly. "For us, it will probably be today."

"Then why did you make this whole Festival Fair of sweeping down on us? The oath of fealty, and . . . everything?" Harwing demanded in exasperation. "I could still be asleep!"

"Because some of you may survive. And—" Vieliessar broke off with a startled gasp. A wave of nausea swept over Harwing. On the road ahead, he saw several of the Lightborn fall from their saddles.

It had been a race against time. And they had just lost it.

CHAPTER TWENTY-SIX

WOOD'S MOON IN THE TENTH YEAR OF THE HIGH KING'S REIGN: DEATH IS THE HUNTER

It is—and was—impossible to fight against the Endarkened with-out taking on some shadow of their character. All that the High King did—even before Oronviel—can be seen as coming from that aspect of the war. For all of us, the war was fought on two battlefields—the fight against the Endarkened and the fight against ourselves. That the High King survived both battles is testimony both to her character, and to the power of the geasa that Queen Pelashia cast millennia before.

—Thurion Pathfinder, A History of the High King's Reign

Around her, Vieliessar heard the signals of her people mounting and deploying. Assar nudged her, wondering why Vieliessar was not in her saddle. Pouncewarm stepped lightly from her shoulders to Assar's saddle as Vieliessar scanned the sky for the enemy.

There.

At first, she could not credit what she saw. She had told Caerthalien they were coming in numbers. She had not realized how vast those num-bers were. It was as if all the birds in the world had gathered together to fly west—as if the whole inhabitants of a Great Keep had been trans-formed into monsters and given wings.

Vieliessar took a slow deep breath. She'd hoped that at least some of the rescued could win free, but . . . no. This was the end. They had no hope of defeating the Endarkened—or even driving them off. Even if the Unicorns had been here, Vieliessar did not think they could have helped: she had never seen this number of Endarkened together—not even on the day of her Enthroning.

"Go to Ceoprentrei," Vieliessar said urgently to Pouncewarm. "Find

Thurion. Tell him the Endarkened are coming. Stay with him." She knew that Palugh had a form of Door that made them excellent messengers—at least until they got bored. And she desperately wanted to save at least one life from the coming slaughter.

"I, I, I am a great fighter," Pouncewarm said, flexing his long sharp claws against the cantle. "I have been in many battles and I won them all: I."

"The Endarkened will kill you," Vieliessar answered, gentling her voice with effort.

"Never kill I," Pouncewarm said serenely. "Nor any of we."

She felt a tiny breeze, and Pouncewarm was gone.

She began to breathe a sigh of relief. She turned to Harwing. "Now here is what—"

"*Here!*" Pouncewarm *mrrted* cheerfully from behind her, bounding to Assar's back once more. Vieliessar gritted her teeth against what she might say.

"Stay, then." She put her foot into Assar's stirrup and swung her leg over the mare's back.

"Are we going to die here together?" Caerthalien asked brightly, riding up beside her. Birdleap and Runfar trotted along on either side of him—the rest of the Wild had gone with the others. "How romantic. I'd thought you took no delight in Storysinger tales."

"I am here to draw the first attack of the Endarkened," Vieliessar answered brusquely. "Since you will be useless, I suggest you find some other location in which to die."

"How long will you have after I am dead?" Caerthalien said after a moment's pause.

Vieliessar blew out a harsh breath. "I don't know. Now *go!*"

⊰⊱

Turning away and leaving Vieliessar behind was one of the hardest things Runacar had ever done. It was the Soulbond, he told himself. Nothing more.

Trying to believe a lie made nothing easier.

He spurred Kishmiri to the gallop and the little mare responded eagerly, lengthening her stride and stretching her neck out. He could hear her rhythmic hoofbeats upon the road . . .

. . . until he couldn't. Around him the landscape flickered and changed. Runacar was back where they'd stopped this morning.

And so was everyone else.

No wonder she studied the landscape so carefully! She used her Magery to Send me to Imrathalion!

Her Household Guard appeared out of nothingness. Several tailles of the Silver Swords. The false Astromancer, mounted and surrounded by the Sanctuary Lightborn.

They were still some distance from the caves, but now they had a chance to reach them.

Except for Vieliessar. Vieliessar had remained behind—*alone*—to fight.

"Void take you, you insolent Lightborn sow!" he roared in fury. "This day you will see how a son of Caerthalien dies!" He turned Kishmiri's head back the way they had come, and spurred her to the gallop.

When Audalo returned from Ceoprentrei, Leutric discovered that—even though the casualties were vast; even though the Endarkened had appeared upon the battlefield and taken the lives of thousands—his people had gained a victory more precious than a mere battlefield victory. High King Vieliessar had met his gaze, Audalo said, and regarded him without flinching.

This was a gift unimaginable. If the High King was truly able to see the Otherfolk as Pelashia's Children and her own cousins, Leutric might at last be able to give up his great secret into another's keeping. Such a hope could not wait for spring thaw to be realized, so in the waning days of Rade Moon, Leutric gathered up his court and headed for Ceoprentrei and Nomaitemil.

And two days before they could reach Smoketree and send a messenger to Nomaitemil, the gain and the hope was obliterated by harrowing misfortune.

The Endarkened had crossed over the Bones of the Earth.

Today was the end of the world.

⁂

Once her last instance of Door had been cast, Vieliessar took a deep breath and closed her eyes, willing her heart to slow and her pulse to steady. As she did, the whole of the battlefield appeared in her mind. The transported refugees from Areve and the Sanctuary, fleeing toward Imrathalion. The cave mouth, where Helecanth and the Warhunt waited. The battle elements she had placed this morning retreating in good order, just as she had planned.

And east of Imrathalion . . .

Endarkened. Thousands of them. Too many to kill.

She saw the whole battlefield—and its near future—in her mind.

From Smoketree, a large Centaur war party was heading north toward the Sanctuary Road with *Alakomentai* Pelere leading them. They would all be slain in the Endarkened attack upon Smoketree. She could *see* it.

Gunedwaen alone had known she could do this. Even Rithdeliel had not been told. The ability to see the whole of the battlefield as it was during the fight was a priceless gift to any commander, especially if they were a good one.

Vieliessar was better than good. She was the Child of the Prophecy, anointed by Amretheon Aradruiniel himself. That meant—that *must* mean—that she would prevail again today.

If I am to fail, do not let me be taken alive by the Endarkened. Pelashia, Aradhwain, do not let me be taken alive!

The Endarkened would overfly Imrathalion and Smoketree. They would ignore the caves—for the moment. A few of them would shear off to destroy the village, and the Centaur war party heading toward the battlefield, but the main force of Endarkened would continue westward. They would see her. It would be a battle she could neither flee nor win—and it would be brief. Once they were done with her, the Endarkened would proceed along their original line of flight. She could See that clearly.

But why . . . ?

Vieliessar drew a sharp breath of despair as the answer presented itself to her.

From the West came a small army of Otherfolk. A dozen races together. They bore bright banners, and marched to the sound of drums, but not as if they were prepared to fight. Audalo was among them, but Audalo was not their leader.

Then who . . . ?

It is the King-Emperor. He is coming to meet me. Himself and all his court.

The horror of it turned her blood to winter rain. She remembered Audalo saying repeatedly during the negotiations, that there were matters he could not speak to because he was not King-Emperor Leutric.

And now, for that very reason, Leutric and all his court have come. And they will be slaughtered by the foe, and when the Endarkened destroy them their deaths will be laid upon our shoulders, and any hope of an alliance will be over.

"Not that it will matter much, since all of us *everywhere* will be dead," Vieliessar muttered aloud. Assar shifted her weight uncertainly at the sound, ears flicking, and Vieliessar stroked the white mare's neck reassuringly.

"*Any plan, no matter how abysmally stupid, is better than no plan. And no plan, no matter how stupid or brilliant, survives the first clash of swords.*" That saying, in infinite variation, had been Gunedwaen's favorite.

Just as well I don't have a plan then, Vieliessar told herself mordantly. *My own folk could retreat alone through Imrathalion until the Endarkened lost heart for the chase—or at least lost their way. We might even find some route back into Nomaitemil in our seeking.*

That path is closed now.

She turned her attention back to her inward sight, watching as her choices spiraled outward. There was no way to save all of Elvenkind, but if Vieliessar drained Arevethmonion near to a ghostlands—or risked linking to the Shrine once more—she could open multiple strong instances of Door wide enough to get Harwing's Lightborn and many of the rest of her folk to Nomaitemil. Those of her folk who could not be transported directly might have the time to make it into the caves while the Endarkened were distracted.

Cheated of their intended prey, the brunt of the Endarkened's fury would fall on the King-Emperor's embassy and the meisne from Smoke-tree. Vieliessar had seen the Otherfolk in battle: they were slow in comparison to her mounted Elvenkind, particularly the Minotaurs. Even Wulvers could not outrun Elven-bred steeds.

Simply put, my people can run away faster than anyone else.

With both the King-Emperor and his heir dead, Leutric's hard-won alliance of Otherfolk would fracture into its original component parts. They could all go on fighting in the ways they always had. And if they did, they would die. All of them. Every bird and leaf, every beast and flower, Bright Folk and Otherfolk and Elvenkind. All and Everything.

Gone.

But if her Elvenkind stayed on the field and covered the retreat of the Otherfolk into Imrathalion . . .

At least a third of us slain, and probably closer to a half. Nor have we prepared for this. Yet it must be done. Pelashia and Aradhwain guard me this day, that I do not go into Their hands alive! she begged again.

Suddenly the earth roiled under the impact of Earthdancer magic. Assar side-stepped uneasily, but stood her ground. The Otherfolk coming from the west had seen the enemy, but there was no Flower Forest they could flee to within the next candlemark. The spellcasting Vieliessar had just experienced was a valiant effort by the Minotaur Earthdancers, but shaking the earth wouldn't thwart an enemy that could fly.

But there was one spell every being with wings must bow to.

Storm Strike.

The idea for it had come from the Silver Swords, whose home had been Penenjil in the Grand Windsward, where such storms were common. In the long Wheelturns of their journey to Ceoprentrei, the Warhunt had experimented with the spell, but had never cast a strong instance of it. Now Vieliessar would see if it was actually useful.

She reached out for Light, and could sense several sources: Enerwirchereth, Nomaitemil, even Saganath in the east. The two strongest were Lady Arevethmonion and the Shrine of the Star. She had sensed the Light of the Shrines many times before—all Lightborn could. They were taught that it was identical in kind to the Light of the Flower Forests, but they were also taught never to draw upon it. Compared to the Light of the Flower Forest, the Light of a Shrine was a furnace-forge to a candleflame.

Vieliessar hesitated—then reached for the power of the Shrine. *Defend yourself through me, Eternal Light, for your vilest enemy draws nigh!*

The power of the Shrine of the Star ripped through her, hot and vast. It flooded every part of her being and filled her as a wineskin was filled—a wineskin that could burst at any moment. *Was this how Ivrulion felt just before the death-magic took him?* A question best left unanswered. She must send the energy that filled her somewhere—quickly—or she would die.

Call Storm.

Clouds boiled across the sky impossibly fast, running west to east and turning the noonday to twilight. Thunder rumbled in the sky and the stormwind struck the forward ranks of the Endarkened, scattering them like autumn leaves. They regrouped quickly, but Vieliessar wasn't finished. Any Lightborn could Call Storm, for weather was always present and always changing, but to turn the wind into a weapon . . .

That took the Warhunt.

Call Storm Strike.

She set her Magery against the great mass of clouds she had summoned and *shoved*. The sky darkened further, and the wind began to roar as if it were an array in the heat of battle. Rain mixed with chunks of ice sheeted down; in moments, she and Assar were soaked to the skin, and Pouncewarm scrambled beneath her cloak. The mass of water-heavy clouds began to yield to Vieliessar's demands, to turn like a mill wheel, to spin faster, to tower higher . . .

And suddenly a dark whirlpool of air dropped from the clouds to touch down in the skirts of the Mystrals. Storm Strike, in strong instance, had been successfully cast.

In that moment, the power she had channeled from the Shrine leapt from her as the arrow leaves the bow, and in its aftermath, Vieliessar felt small and cold and—not alone, but *separated*. She watched, dazed and half-deafened by the howling roar of the whirlpool wind, as it swallowed up everything it could reach. Everywhere it touched ground it tore great furrows in the earth. Everything it tore loose, it sucked up into the sky. Endarkened vanished, like autumn leaves, into the spirals of wind.

One coil became two, then six, and then propagated too quickly to number. Once she had cast the spells that set the storm in motion, it drew its power from natural law, and it grew stronger—and more uncontrollable—with every heartbeat.

"Pouncewarm!" she shouted over the roaring wind. A moment later, she felt his paws on her shoulders. His whiskers tickled her neck as he peered past her. She could feel him rumble into a purr.

"Now all the Darklings blow away like leaves, yes? Fun to chase."

"*Not* fun to chase," Vieliessar said quickly. "But can you go to Caerthal—" She broke off; Pouncewarm didn't know him by that name. "To *Runacar*. Tell him it was I who called the storm but we are not safe yet."

"I, I, I seek. I chase. I find."

She was about to tell him to stay wherever Runacar was if he found him, but she was too late. The Palugh had already vanished.

The whirlpool winds heading into the foothills of the Mystrals did not like the terrain. The smaller and weaker whirls devolved into turbulent air, but the initial instance of Storm Strike remained strong.

Suddenly all of the whirlpool wind hopped back into the sky, and all that remained was the black storm clouds in their slowing aerial spin. Lightning chased itself through the whirling air, never touching the ground.

Thank the Light that's over, for I do not . . .

Vieliessar could almost hear the mocking laughter of the Ghostlord Indinathiel greeting her optimism as the whirlpool-wind spawned itself again, larger and more powerful than ever. And this time, when it touched down, it was moving toward Vieliessar faster than a running horse.

She was too weary to rage against her luck. Too weary to call upon the Shrine's power a second time, lest she lose control of it. Though it was an inanimate construction of power and will, the storm seemed to

Vieliessar as if it were mocking her, taunting her with the fact she had evaded one doom only to summon another. If it continued west, Leutric and his embassy would be destroyed.

The storm *had* to be stopped.

Once more, Vieliessar summoned up the harsh discipline that had governed every moment of her life. This time she wove her threads of power from Arevethmonion's Light, praying she would not need to take more than the Flower Forest could give. The power felt distant—or perhaps pulling from the Shrine had numbed her. Her first attempt to stop the storm failed: her spell was no match for its power and it came apart before it was fully cast.

The spinning column of black air swayed drunkenly as it veered southward. With each moment, it grew larger.

"If you face power greater than yours, think: how can you weaken it." She could no longer remember who first said that to her. Gunedwaen? Rondithiel? Magic and war were the same thing: an exercise of power.

She readied herself to Cast again. She could see distant trees tossing like stalks in a wheat field as the whirlpool-wind Storm Strike drew closer. She must succeed. There would be no chance for a third try.

Drain was a little-used spell, one that most Lightborn viewed as pointless, since the energy siphoned off by means of it could not be used by the caster. There were simpler spells to use if one wanted to quench a fire or shift a storm.

But if one could do neither . . .

Vieliessar cast Drain directly at the funnel cloud itself. Suddenly her perception of it expanded dizzily from the tail of the whirlpool near the ground to the spinning clouds on high that channeled force to the winds. She pulled on that energy, pulling it away, making the storm slow. Making it tired. Weak.

Its energy passed through her and dissipated, leaving nothing behind but her weariness. The winds dropped to nothingness. The storm clouds broke up as unnaturally as they had appeared. The east was clear. She began to walk Assar toward Arevethmonion and the Otherfolk delegation. She ached in every limb.

Then she looked skyward again.

The Endarkened were still coming. She had scattered them. She had forced them back. She had stopped many of them. But she had not discouraged them, for as she watched, they slowly re-formed their flight patterns and continued westward. All she had done had only bought her people some time.

She took a deep breath and placed her hands on each side of her mount's neck. Healing what she could, energizing what she could. When Assar moved out, she did so at the gallop.

West. Toward Leutric.

CHAPTER TWENTY-SEVEN

WOOD'S MOON IN THE TENTH YEAR OF THE HIGH KING'S REIGN: THE UNICORN RIDERS

Pretend to be weak, that your enemy may grow arrogant. If his forces are united, separate them. If his forces act in harmony, sunder it. Always attack where he is unprepared, appear where you are not expected.

—Arilcarion War-Maker, *The Way of the Sword*

I f we wait much longer, it's going to be too late!" Dianora said urgently.

"If we don't wait until at least half of the Endarkened are on the ground, it will be too late for *everyone*," Sondast answered unyieldingly. He tossed his head, and the dark spiral of his horn gleamed with hints of red and blue.

"Well, couldn't they land *now*?" Denelorn asked impatiently, and Sondast snorted rudely.

Dianora slapped her partner on the withers reproachfully. It was small consolation that Sondast knew as little as she.

The Unicorn had woken her in the middle of the night and said they had to go into the west *now*. Dianora remembered little of the journey, only that it involved a twisting path and a road through the Mystrals that had been so narrow that the riders all had to dismount to get through. On the way, all Sondast would tell Dianora was that it was "time"—to do what, he didn't say.

Since that moment at the foot of the Dragon's Gate—when she had chosen this, not knowing what she chose—Dianora of Bulbaryat, Daughter of Night, had entered into a stranger alliance than any she had known before. She'd never managed to make an accurate count of the Unicorns who had solicited partners. Perhaps a grand-taille. Perhaps more.

Perhaps a *lot* more.

Counting herself and Arathiel, there were twenty Unicorn Riders from House Bulbaryat—all the Children of Night that were left out of hundreds. Shanilya Arshana had used them and their arts to keep the High King on her invisible imaginary throne, but even Shanilya did not know about *this*.

The other Unicorn Riders came from every House and none. Lightborn, Landbonds, even komen—the Unicorns had chosen each of them by their own inscrutable standards, which they had never explained. All that those chosen had to do was say "yes."

And Dianora—and the others—had.

Since the day of their choosing, all of them, Unicorns and Elvenkind, had trained and practiced, hammered out tactics, designed and crafted weapons. The Riders did not carry sword, mace, or even dagger. The foe they were training to fight was no traditional one.

The Unicorns had chosen their Riders to fight the Endarkened.

The Riders carried a special weapon: a quiver of light ahata-wood javelins, each with Unicorn hair braided and inlaid all the way down its length. If the Riders could strike the Endarkened with those weapons—so the Unicorns said—the creatures would burn. Sondast said that Unicorn hair would hurt the Endarkened almost as much as the touch of Unicorn horns (though not enough to kill them). She hoped he was right.

If this worked, they were yet another weapon to place into the hands of the Light.

If it didn't, at least the rest of the Unicorns might survive.

W hen they reached the West, the Unicorn Riders sheltered in a rotting tithe-barn in sight of the Sanctuary Road. There was the scent of cookfires in the wind, and Golden Droullim, with Marwen her rider, had cautiously reconnoitered . . .

. . . Only to discover that the High King and the Silver Swords were riding directly west—toward King-Emperor Leutric and his court. And with the Astromancer and a pack of farmers inexplicably in between.

⊰⧏⊱

Leutric's Court huddled around him, struck numb and still by the sight of the Endarkened against the sky. Since the death of Pelashia the Fair, the Endarkened had been the dark eidolon that haunted the nightmares of the Folk—the end that would come despite their attempts to warn Elvenkind of the danger. When the Royal Witchborn had raised the whirlwind, some of the Folk had dared to hope it would be enough.

It wasn't.

The Endarkened were still coming. There was nowhere the Otherfolk could go for shelter. Arevethmonion was days behind them, Enerwirchereth nearly a day ahead. And to reach the sanctuary of either Flower Forest would only postpone the end.

But whether they went to Herdsman or Huntsman, Great Bull or Forest Lord, they would not tamely wait to die.

"Ivory Claws," Leutric said. "Find me a road to Enerwirchereth."

"I and only I," the Queen of the Palugh answered, vanishing.

⊰⧏⊱

Vieliessar crouched low over her mount's neck as Assar galloped westward. Suddenly a voice spoke from behind her.

"I, I, I could not tell Pretty Rune about the bad nasty wet rain," the Palugh reported merrily. "Pretty Rune follows you. He is angry."

"And he is going to be *dead*," Vieliessar snapped, slowing Assar to a trot and straightening up. "Pouncewarm, can you go to Leutric and tell him to head toward the Caves of Imrathalion? Then tell Githachi to hold her positions until the Otherfolk arrive. The Silver Swords are to retreat with them."

"So many words," Pouncewarm said disapprovingly. "All wrong. You should use Wulvers."

"Ah, but no Wulver is as clever as you are," Vieliessar said, stifling a laugh despite the direness of the situation. "Nor as beautiful."

"I go. I, I, I go," Pouncewarm said. "To the King-Emperor, to the Dragon's Bones, I."

"What?" Vieliessar said, but it was too late. Pouncewarm was gone again. She patted Assar on the neck and picked up the pace again. *I have no idea where the Dragon's Bones might be. At least I will get to Leutric before anyone else does.*

She was wrong.

⊰⊱

She reined Assar in once she sighted the party, and as she did, her heart sank. The Otherfolk were clustered around Leutric, and none of them was moving.

The Minotaurs were the tallest of anyone there, and so Leutric was easy to spot. The grey around his eyes and mouth betokened great age, and his horns were not only painted, but gilded and jeweled as well. He wore a cloak, a pleated kilt of embroidered linen trimmed with gold, jeweled bracers and armbands, high leather boots . . .

And he was robed in a mantle of compelling dignity, for he, like Vieliessar, had seen the horror that was to come and spent untold years bringing his folk together to fight it. In that moment, Vieliessar could not imagine treating him or his kind as beasts of venery, as she knew her ancestors had done.

"Go," she said, waving toward Imrathalion. "Just go. We have a truce, your folk and I. Go to Imrathalion. We'll protect you there, but you have to move!"

The King-Emperor and his court slowly moved to obey.

Abruptly an Endarkened female landed in front of Vieliessar, her scarlet wings spread wide. Vieliessar felt a stabbing pain lance through her defenses at the sudden proximity, and ruthlessly forced the sensation away. The monster was clad only in ornaments both exotic and somehow profane, and her red skin glowed like molten iron in the pale winter's light.

"I am Udbaukh, daughter of Luharzal, daughter of Xennara, sired by King Virulan, and today you will lay down this foolish life of yours in the service of my dread and terrible King!" the monster crowed. She towered over Vieliessar by a cubit or more. A longer reach could be either an advantage or a hindrance. It depended on whether Udbaukh meant to attack with spells or blade.

"Many have said that. Never yet has it been true," Vieliessar replied grimly. "Come, hellbeast. Dance with me."

⊰⊱

I wish anything the Endarkened did made sense," Dianora said forlornly. They were still inside the barn, waiting. Though for what, Dianora could not imagine, since the Redwings were already overhead.

"If we knew why they did anything, this battle wouldn't be unfolding the way it is, so we should be grateful," Arathiel said, peering out through a crack in the weathered wood of the rotting barn.

"They're just slaughtering everyone," Teias protested. He'd been a Sword Page before joining the Unicorn Riders.

"They're not killing as many of the Lightless as they could be killing," Arathiel said. "They're ignoring them to get to the Lightborn. Where in the name of Queen Pelashia did all those Green Robes come from? They act like they've never seen a Redwing before."

"They probably haven't," said Marwen. "They're the idiots who decided to leave the Sanctuary of the Star just as winter was coming."

"Well, this should teach them not to do that again," Arathiel said, and several Riders blurted out a laugh. "For some reason, it looks like this time the only thing the Endarkened care about is the Lightborn. Everyone else is just in the way."

"*We're* Lightborn," Dianora said glumly. All the Children of Night had been drawn from the ranks of "failed" Lightborn. "They'll get to kill us first."

Sondast nuzzled her cheek. "That's why I love you, darling," he said. "You're so optimistic."

"That's probably why the Unicorns wanted us especially," Arathiel said.

"A 'Unicorn' is right here, you know," Iskilsa said to Arathiel in mock resignation. "You needn't pretend you're talking among yourselves." In the gloom of their hideout, Iskilsa's horn glowed with a pale violet light.

Her mane and tail-tip and socks were black, but the rest of her coat was a stippled blue-grey color. Dianora sometimes wondered if it bothered Arathiel that Iskilsa was so . . . *showy*. At least with Black Sondast Dianora had a fighting chance of blending in.

Yes, she told herself. *He'd blend in just fine at the bottom of a mine at midnight when nobody was looking at him.*

"You'll certainly get their attention when we go, my dearest. But not yet." Sondast tossed his head. "Have patience."

⊰⊱

It was not possible to kill one of the Endarkened with a simple blade, and no spell of the Light could slay them. Even if one managed to land a blow, their skin was tough and their shields tougher. And if one managed by some miracle to wound them, the creatures either fled instantly or healed themselves by drawing all the life force from their hapless assailant. The only thing to slow them down was dismemberment, and as far as the Elves could tell, they eventually healed from that too.

But a spell did not have to slay—or even harm—to be effective.

With her deosil hand, Vieliessar wielded her sword: cutting, parrying, blocking. With her tuathal hand, she cast spell after spell: Wind, Silverlight, Fetch, Send, Fire, Cold. Not one of them harmed Udbaukh, but the Endarkened flinched cravenly each time. It was the cold mercy of Aradhwain, Bride of Battles, that Udbaukh was wholly concentrating on Vieliessar instead of turning on Leutric and his companions. The longer Vieliessar could keep Udbaukh's attention on her, the more time there would be for the Otherfolk to flee.

Slash, parry, duck. Vieliessar made a flying dismount from Assar's back, and the mare immediately rounded on Udbaukh, attacking her with teeth and hooves. It gave Vieliessar a momentary breathing space— enough of one to let her know that her life was measured in heartbeats. She was only grateful that she wasn't facing more of the Endarkened, but one of the things Elvenkind had learned about its foe was that Endarkened were jealous of their prey, defending it even from one another.

And, when there was time, the Endarkened liked to play.

Vieliessar speeded up the pace of her attacks, intent upon manipulating Udbaukh into making a mistake. But even at her fastest, Vieliessar was not as quick as one of the Redwings. Udbaukh—clearly tiring of her game—seized Vieliessar's wrist and whiplashed her away.

Vieliessar tucked herself up as tightly as she could, and managed to land in a crouch. She instantly Called her sword to her—but she knew the unequal contest was nearly over.

She looked around and up, searching everywhere for her enemy.

Abruptly, Udbaukh dropped to earth.

Equally abruptly, Udbaukh's head vanished in a spray of ichor.

Vieliessar stared as she saw Udbaukh's head go bouncing into the road, the Endarkened's lips writhing as she silently screamed curses.

"This," said Runacar, holding the most enormous axe Vieliessar had ever seen. "*This* is how you stop them."

Udbaukh's body had already gotten to its knees. With each exhaled breath, ichor sprayed from the stump of her neck, but the body was blind and soon to enter a deathlike coma that would render it a non-combatant.

"That shouldn't have worked, you know. But thank you," Vieliessar said gravely. "Where did you get it?"

"The axe? I passed Leutric on the road. Why send him to Imrath-alion?" The striking side of the blade was slimed with ichor and already dissolving: Runacar sighed and tossed it away.

"Because none of *us* will live to reach Imrathalion and it's the only shelter there is," Vieliessar said. Assar came up to her and nudged her hand.

"Shouldn't we be arguing now?" Runacar asked.

"Why?" Vieliessar answered, turning away and preparing to remount Assar. "Because you were an idiot and didn't do what I told you to?"

"I rarely do anything anyone tells me to. You should try it some-time," Runacar said.

"You're mad," Vieliessar declared.

"Said the blacksmith to the forge."

"Mount up. We still have to get to the caves."

⊰⊱

It's time," Sondast said, with what sounded like a sigh of relief. Dianora stroked his neck, downy-soft like a baby chick's, and took a deep breath of his clean spicy scent. This might be the last moment she could simply *be* with him.

She wondered if Unicorns ran with the Starry Hunt.

You will know soon enough.

Sondast stamped his cloven hoof meaningfully, and Dianora swung her leg across his back. Most of learning to ride Sondast had involved forgetting everything she knew about riding horses. Unicorns weren't horses, or anything like the size of horses. Dianora pulled up her knees and stuck her toes through the loops of leather riveted to the strap buckled around his barrel; the result left her almost crouching on Sondast's back as if she were a tumbler. She pulled one of the javelins from the quiver she wore.

An inaudible *something* seemed to pass among the Unicorns as the last of their Riders mounted. They moved toward the doorway of the ruined barn that had concealed them, and as they left it, they formed into a column, widening their ranks until they stood five abreast. The first four ranks held the Children of Night. Dianora hoped what they had would be enough to draw the Endarkened's attention.

She looked up for the first time. Ahead lay the battlefield—and the Endarkened. Hundreds of them.

Oh, Sword and Star, there are so many more than we thought!

It was her last coherent thought before Sondast began to run.

⊰⊱

The Unicorns moved as if they were all one creature. Sondast's horn glowed like a live coal, and Dianora looked away to keep from dazzling herself, only to see that all the Unicorns' horns were blazing scarlet.

And then they were among the Endarkened.

The red of the Unicorns' horns seemed to vanish against the scarlet flesh of the Endarkened. Even the merest touch of the Unicorns' horns slew the enemy; and if an Endarkened clutched at a Unicorn's head or legs or tail, the Endarkened's scarlet flesh burned.

Whirl and slash. If not for her grueling training, Dianora would have had no chance of staying on Sondast's back. *Leap and stab.* Her skin burned and itched where ichor from Endarkened wounds had spattered it. *Jump and turn and kick.* Endarkened shrieked—in anger or fear. Some of them ran. Some bounded into the sky to flee.

Dianora readied her first javelin and flung it. The light spear with its braid of Unicorn hair sank into her target's flesh as if the creature's body were made of warm suet. The Endarkened howled and thrashed and— for the first time at Elven hands—*died.*

More of the enemy took to the sky, circling like vultures over a dead cow.

Dianora had several javelins remaining.

⊰※⊱

The only direction the Warhunt could retreat to was toward the Caves of Imrathalion, where they would only be attacked from one side. It seemed preposterous that to reach safety they had to run toward the main group of Endarkened, but the monsters were swarming the cave's entrance. Still more of them wheeled and turned in the sky above.

"They're ignoring everyone who isn't Lightborn," Tangisen said, as if this was a matter of only mild concern. His companions saw the same things he did: the arrival of the Unicorns; the Endarkened scattering; some turning away from their siege of Imrathalion to seek easier—but still Lightborn—prey.

Like them.

They all saw the group of Endarkened turning in their direction.

"I wish Isilla was here," Dinias said mournfully.

"Quiet," Pantaradet said tensely.

And then the sky was filled with screaming. Gryphons, Hippogriffs, and an impossibility of eight Aesalions. They struck the Endarkened from above, and every one of them had learned from the bitter lessons of Ceoprentrei. Strike and flee. Turn flight into ambush. Force the Endarkened to choose between them and Lightborn.

It worked miracles where none had done before. It *confused* the Endarkened. And that confusion cost them dear. Aesalions happily beheaded them, then Gryphons carried their heads far away to hide them.

Runacar's call had been heard.

The Otherfolk had come to help.

It would not be help enough.

⧊⧉

The air was dense with the residue of useless spells. The Warhunt Mages were bunched together for whatever protection physical proximity could provide, while a group of Endarkened bounced around them like hideous puppies eager to play. Four of the Warhunt—Kathan, Nindir, Annandil, and Pendray—linked their Magery into an augmented strong instance of Send to move the enemy. The first time it didn't work. The second time Kathan picked up a rock, threw it at the Endarkened, and cast Send on the rock. It struck its target with the speed of an arrow and the force of a mountain. The Endarkened flew apart, its sundered pieces twitching and clawing.

Better.

Not good enough.

It didn't help matters that the proximity of the scarlet bat-winged monsters was in itself a form of attack. The Endarkened radiated death and pain and sickness—and, worse, they radiated malice, and cruelty, and sheer elemental evil. The Warhunt Mages fought to stay alert, to deflect the attacks of monsters too powerful for them to successfully assault.

To stay alive.

But their best still wasn't good enough.

Alasneh Lightsister screamed as one of the Endarkened dragged her out of the group of Warhunt Mages and leaped into the air. The female did not flee with its prize, but held Alasneh tantalizingly just out of the others' reach. Jorganroch lunged, trying to grab her ankle. A wingtip. Something.

"Oh, my lovely ardent boy," the monster cooed. "So eager to come with me? Take my hand, darling child."

Dinias flung his dagger at the Endarkened, using Send to hurl the only physical weapon he had with enormous force. It struck the Endarkened squarely in the face—or it should have—and the creature simply laughed. She spread her wings wide, preparing to depart with her Elven captive.

"*Alasneh!*" Jorganroch screamed in desperation. His gaze found hers, and he saw the anger and determination there. *I love you,* she mouthed silently. Then:

"*Burn,*" Alasneh whispered.

In an instant, Alasneh's entire body was engulfed in flame as her death-spell turned her to a blazing cinder. Jorganroch screamed in shock. There was a hideous scent of burning meat. The Endarkened dropped Alasneh's burning body, howling her anger, and dove at him.

Dinias grabbed Jorganroch and dragged him backward, certain that the next thing one or the other of them would feel was the claws of the Endarkened shearing through their flesh.

It wasn't.

The earth around them boiled as if it were a pot of water, and out of the earth a *thing* rose up as if ascending some chthonian staircase. It was Elven in shape—in the sense that it had a head, a torso, and arms and legs—but the head and body were as featureless as if it were a gigantic doll formed of mud.

Unfortunately for the hovering Endarkened, the newcomer was stronger than dirt. It reached up to snare one Endarkened by its ankle, then grabbed another by its barbed tail.

"Angarussa, Angarussa, Angarussa." Dinias didn't realize he was chanting the word aloud until Tangisen grabbed him, pulling both him and Jorganroch into the center of the group. *This is Angarussa all over again. The Beastlings—the Otherfolk—turning earth and water into our deaths.*

The earthling creature swung one of its captives around by its tail until that tail separated from the Endarkened's body and the screaming monster went flying. The mutilated Endarkened flapped desperately to turn its trajectory into an ascent and fled, squalling in rage and pain. The other Endarkened had been unable either to harm the creature or to free itself; the earth-creature's body turned black, or burned, or crumbled away as the Endarkened's sorcery lashed out at it, but the earthling seemed to have an inexhaustible amount of body mass to take its place.

The earthling tossed the tail away.

WHAM.

It began to hammer the ground with the other Endarkened's body.

WHAM.

The gold and gems the Endarkened wore sprayed out across the ground at the impact.

WHAM.

Its sword went spinning from its grasp.

WHAM!

It yowled in protest and redoubled its attempt to escape.

WHAM!

Patches of ground bubbled and turned to glass.

WHAM-WHAM-WHAM-WHAM—*WHAM!*

It wasn't fighting back anymore. The Endarkened's skin burst and bled, spraying the ground with ichor. Its wings were tattered and broken by multiple impacts with the ground. Fragments of its broken bones speared through its scarlet flesh. Its horns had been shattered and its lower jaw was gone.

The earth-creature dropped its plaything and reached into the ground to draw out an enormous slab of rock as a Craftworker might draw a tool from a pocket. With the first real effort it had exhibited, it lifted the slab above its head, holding it there for a moment.

Then it dropped the stone on the motionless Endarkened. There was a tiny popping sound from the body as it . . . squished.

Still silent, its task complete, the earth-creature sank back into the earth from whence it had come. The ground ceased to boil. In moments everything was just as it had been before.

"Well," Dinias said, "I guess whatever it was, it's on our side."

⊰⊱

Hunund of the Bearwards, Chosen Son of the Forest Lord, had come with Leutric on this embassy because Helda had asked him to, and because he respected Helda. And when the Witch-King of the Elvenborn told Leutric and the others to flee—and took on one of the Demons to make it possible, Hunund had been . . . impressed. They'd managed to reach Imrathalion, there to discover unimaginable allies. The warriors of the Witch-King were mixed among the ranks of Otherfolk—not to fight them, but to fight *beside* them. To do everything they could to clear the way for the others—for the *Otherfolk*—to reach Imrathalion.

Hunund did not believe the Caves of Imrathalion would protect them, or that most of those now fighting could reach them alive. But it was the only thing they could do, and so they were trying.

They'd managed to get Leutric into the cave with the Earthdancers' help, but more than half of the Otherfolk were stranded outside the entrance. The Endarkened swarmed around the entrance like maggots on a corpse, and the rock face above and around the opening was covered in a living, pulsing carpet of Redwings. A troop of Unicorns with Elven riders drove the cluster of Redwings away from the cave mouth again and again, and in each brief respite, a few more of the Folk, a few more Elvenborn, gained sanctuary.

But too few, too slowly, to call it victory.

The vast chaos of battle surrounded the Elven knights, witches, and Folk. Magical and practical weapons—flashes of light and fire; hammers, maces, axes, swords—each made its own tumult.

And none of the weapons affected the enemy.

From where he stood, Hunund could see Queen Ivory Claws of the Palugh and King Leaps the Moon of the Wulvers clawing and biting like mad things with a troop of Fauns acting as their honor guard. The only reason any of them—Folk and Elvenkind both—had survived even this long was that the only prey the Endarkened seemed to care about were the Elvish witchborn. Time and again the monsters turned away from some other battle to chase down and capture one of them. The witches in long green robes screamed and flailed and begged for rescue. The witches in armor fought back in grim silence. Either way the outcome was the same: the victims were carried off into the sky alive.

At least it meant fewer of the Demons were here.

Hunund roared in fury as a Demon dropped down directly in front of him and turned its back on him to seize one of the witches in their bright green robes. Hunund had no love for the witches—who among the Otherfolk did?—but being ignored made him angry.

He grabbed the male Demon by its long ornamented hair and yanked it back, away from the Elvish witch. The Bearward and the Demon were much the same height, but the Demon had the power of its magic to augment its strength. Hunund could pull it off its feet, but it would quickly retaliate.

But a body was only as strong as its bones and sinews. Hunund knew what had happened to the Gryphons in the great battle at the Dragon's Gate. Hunund liked Gryphons. He grabbed the Endarkened's wings in both hands and pulled with all his strength as the Lightborn he had saved ran toward the cave mouth.

He hoped the Unicorns would return soon.

⧽⧼

Dianora had been in many battles against the Endarkened this last decade of years, and in one thing this fight was like all the rest.

It was loud.

She could hear the furious shrieks of Unicorns, the mad howling of Endarkened, the cheers and screams from the other riders. All the sounds wove themselves into a tapestry whose design Dianora could not yet see. *Let it be victory! Oh, Lady Aradhwain, Queen of Night, let us triumph this day!*

It helped that the Endarkened couldn't touch the Unicorns without injury, and that the Unicorns could easily kill them. But there were thousands of Endarkened, and only a few of them. They could save the Lightborn only by becoming a more desirable target themselves.

The strategy worked.

At a cost.

Dianora clung desperately to the strap around Sondast's neck, feeling as if it—and he—were the only real and solid things in the universe. The Unicorns ran a pattern against their foe—from the barn to the Sanctuary Road, south to Imrathalion, across the face of the rock and the cave mouth, then back to their starting point, always moving fast enough that their speed might—just, barely—protect them from Endarkened retaliation.

Fewer Endarkened fell to their attacks on each pass, and time and again Sondast saved the two of them by the most desperate evasion.

Others were not so fortunate.

As the first rank of the Unicorn Riders raced toward the road for the third?—fourth?—time, Dianora glanced at the Unicorn running beside Sondast. Golden Droullim ran alone, her rider missing.

I will see you in the Vale, Marwen, my sister!

⚓

Vieliessar pulled Assar to a stop and Runacar stopped with her. It was already late afternoon. There were only a very few candle-marks remaining before the swift winter twilight. In the distance—half a league, little more—they could see the battle.

Its end would come long before nightfall.

Imrathalion could shelter them all—if it were actually an impassable defense—but it could not take all of them into itself at the same instant.

The largest element on the field was the Lightless villagers of Areve, and even the Endarkened avoided them, as they were nothing but a pan-icked, terrified, Lightless mob. They were a danger. Vieliessar wondered if the Endarkened knew how to manipulate them. She had never seen much strategy from the Endarkened in all her clashes with them. They'd never needed it.

She glanced sideways at Runacar. They were each trained to read a battlefield, he and she: Vieliessar was sure Runacar saw what she did: the swarming cluster of scarlet monsters—their numbers innumerable—trying to get at the people sheltering inside the cave. The Endarkened had not been able to break through the defenders, but in fairness to them, they really weren't trying—all they seemed to want was the Light-born, and there were enough of them outside the caves for the Endark-ened to go after Hamphuliadiel's Lightborn, the easier prey, first. The few Endarkened who left the battle did not do so in capitulation; each one carried a captive Lightborn with them. *Alive.*

Seeing that made her heart burn with rage, even though she was sure that every one of them would have killed her if they could.

"I am fortunate that Hamphuliadiel collected so many Lightborn at the Sanctuary of the Star," Vieliessar said aloud. "They distract the Endarkened."

"And buy time for the rest of you to escape." She could hear Runacar's thoughts as clearly as if he spoke aloud. *"Did you always plan for things to end this way?"*

No. They are my sacrifice, but I did not will it. They are my people. They are all my people.

"You fought these things for ten years?" Runacar asked aloud. "In the name of the Rade: *How*?"

"We ran away," Vieliessar said simply. "There is nowhere for us to run this time. Thank the Light the children are safe."

"We will care for them as our own," Runacar said. *"For as long as we can. At last I believe what everyone has been telling me: there will be no one left alive in all the land once the Endarkened are done."* The coda to his words came clearly once more.

And if I had gone to each of the Hundred Houses and begged them to unite in the face of this monstrousness, the outcome would have been the same: they would not believe. Not until it was too late.

"It is as if the enemy always attacks from our blind spot," Runacar said quietly, still looking toward the battle. "And we cannot follow them when they retreat."

"And so we lose, and go on losing. This will be my only chance to beg Leutric to place that weapon which he guards into my hands so I may wield it. If I reach him alive. And *he* is alive," she answered.

"You already know all that I know of it," Runacar said without rancor. Vieliessar knew that the knowledge that she had used her Magery to spy upon his inmost thoughts had once infuriated him. Now he seemed to understand how desperate she had been.

"I do," Vieliessar said. "I think I might have convinced Leutric to trust me if I had only had a little more time."

"'Time is a bandit who always fights on the enemy's side,'" Runacar misquoted, and Vieliessar gave a sharp bark of laughter. *Gunedwaen said much the same thing!*

"At least we've made them work for their victory." There was a beat of silence before she spoke again. "And you will wish to die among your own. Go south toward Smoketree. Your apprentice is leading a band of Centaurs toward Imrathalion."

Runacar stared at Vieliessar as if he could not imagine who or what she was talking about, then: "*Pelere? Pelere is leading the war-band?*"

"Yes. Go to her, that she may know your fate and you hers. For you to reach her in time, I must bespell Kishmiri, poor beast. She will run until she dies. You can guide her, but no more. Do you consent?"

"*She will run until she dies.*" If he said yes he would be consenting to Kishmiri's murder. He loved her. Even now he could dismount and set her free; the Endarkened would probably ignore her.

But I am selfish enough to want to die among my friends.

Runacar nodded sharply, and a heaviness settled in her chest.

"What about you? We never ——" he began. "*We've never spoken of the Soulbond. About living with it. Dying with it. Because we—*"

She stopped him with a gesture. "You go to die among your people, Leutric's Battlemaster, and I with mine."

She raised her hand toward Kishmiri, and vibrating energy instantly took the place of valiant exhaustion in the mare's body. Kishmiri tossed her head and danced for a moment, as fresh as if she'd just come from a months-long rest in the pastures, and then began to run. Runacar pointed her head in the direction of Smoketree.

She would run until she died. He had consented to that because he must, but his grief and despair pervaded her senses. Vieliessar felt a helpless sense of loss, and was not herself sure which coming death she mourned: Kishmiri's, or Runacar's.

Or Assar's.

CHAPTER TWENTY-EIGHT

WOOD'S MOON IN THE TENTH YEAR OF THE HIGH KING'S REIGN: A COLD AND LOGICAL SLAUGHTER

Oh Lord of Battles, precious to Aradhwain and Manafaeren, let me come to you before I know my death. I have given you blood to drink, Hunt Lord, let me ride first in your train. Lead me to your khom *as my heart still pumps, and let me come to you while I still savor the sweets of battle. Take me up and protect me from hungry ghosts, from the Void and the Darkness, that my name will always shine silver upon the Tablets of Memory . . .*

—Author Unknown, Sacrificial Prayer to the Starry Hunt

Vieliessar sat perfectly still on Assar's back. She watched Kishmiri run, felt the faint autumn sunlight warming her shoulders. Pouncewarm was braced between the front of the saddle and her knees; he rubbed against her in silent sympathy and she stroked his head. The spell had been Iardalaith's creation, she remembered, a spell to replace a cordial they'd no longer had the resources to concoct. They had used it in Jaeglenhend to lead their pursuers astray, their horses running faster than anything the Alliance could claim. That seemed as if it were a thousand Wheelturns ago, instead of a mere decade.

When Kishmiri and her rider could no longer be seen, Vieliessar turned her attention from the south to the east.

There, the battle went grimly on—Endarkened swirling through the air, flashes of Shield or Thunderbolt bracketing them. Just as often the target of the spell was the Lightborn some Endarkened held. They did not carry the dead away with them as she had seen them do so often before. When cheated of a living captive, they simply threw the body away.

"*What do you want of the battle to come?*" The Masters of War who had taught her always began with that question.

I want peace. "You will never have it," she said, rebuking herself aloud. "Not even the peace of the dead."

"Silly Witch-King. Pretty Rune is gone; that is what makes you sad. But I, I, I am here."

She ran her fingers over the top of the small furry skull. Pouncewarm flattened his ears in pleasure.

"I am going into battle, small one," she said. "You should go elsewhere."

"I will stay," the Palugh said serenely.

"As you wish," Vieliessar said, too weary to argue, and turned her attention again to the battlefield.

It did not seem as if it could be physically possible to pass through the swarm of Endarkened to get into Imrathalion. As soon as they had harvested the last of Hamphuliadiel's hapless Lightborn, the Endarkened would redouble their efforts to reach the Lightborn and Warhunt sheltering inside. Some of them would seek out anyone else with the Light. The Children of Night, of whose existence she was not meant to be aware. Anyone.

Herself.

Child of the Prophecy, she thought bitterly, and froze as terrible inspiration took her.

She had been born a nexus of Magery. Amretheon's hope. Pelashia's magic. Power strong enough to warp not just Elven minds and hearts, but the weft of What-Might-Be itself. To keep her alive where logic and reason said she should die.

If that power beat strongly enough in her veins—

If she was truly Pelashia's greatdaughter—

I must reach Imrathalion, and then call all the Endarkened to me after the mouth is sealed. I know how vast the cave-system is—if I can get deep enough into the mountain, they will follow along outside, I think, hoping for another way in. Once everyone else is inside and the entrance is sealed . . . we should be safe.

And I must do it as fast as I can.

"I am sorry, my dear one," she said to Assar. "I wish I did not have to do what I must do now."

There was a moment as Vieliessar tried to find another answer— another *way*—and could not. She could not cast Door and risk arriving on top of—or *inside*—another person or object. And Assar had little more left to give.

She dismounted and put her arms around Assar's neck. The battlepony was foamy with sweat, and Vieliessar could feel the mare's exhaustion everywhere their bodies touched.

You are innocent. You cannot consent to what I am about to do to you. But I do it for all things living.

The saddlebags remained on Assar's back, for there had been no reason to remove them. She reached into one and removed several of the trail-bars the Elves used to make soup. She fed them to Assar as she fought back her tears.

Then she kissed Assar on the forehead, and rested her own forehead against Assar's for a brief moment. There would be time later to mourn properly. Or she would be dead.

"I am sorry," Vieliessar repeated, and swung herself into the saddle as she cast the spell.

The mare's head came up, and her body thrilled with false energy. She bounced forward in a series of hops, as if she could not decide whether to keep her rider or not. On the last hop she sprang into a leap, clearing the ditch beside the Sanctuary Road and settling into a ground-eating run.

⊰⧲⊱

The one thing Gatriadde of Mangiralas had not been able to give this new breed of warhorse he had created from the Arzhana ponies was the ravall, the floating gait that carried an Elven destrier across the ground so fast it could cover more than two leagues in a quartermark. The battleponies made up for this by their hardiness and stubbornness—it did not take Magery to make them run until they dropped.

It only made it easier.

Assar ran flat-out, her neck and flanks covered in foam. Vieliessar crouched low upon her neck, coiled around Pouncewarm to protect him, the pommel of the saddle digging into her ribs. If Pouncewarm found himself uncomfortably squished, he did not comment on it.

They reached the leading edge of the battle. Vieliessar saw the Endarkened still carrying away fresh victims. Nearly all of them wore the green robes of the Lightborn who had come from the Sanctuary of the Star.

As soon as she crossed the invisible boundary of the battlefield, Vieliessar felt the attention of every Endarkened turn to her with the force of a blow. Those with captives dropped them.

Now Assar ran through the tangle of battle, using her hooves and teeth to clear her way. Vieliessar held her blade naked in her hand, ready to fend off Endarkened. The attack she expected didn't come, and as she looked around herself, seeking a reason, she saw an astonishing sight.

"See?" Pouncewarm said. "You are best as I, I, I am best."

The Endarkened were fighting with each other. The Endarkened were fighting with each other *over her.*

Vieliessar did not know what this should make her feel. All she needed to know was that this was an opportunity to *make them do what she wanted.*

She was near enough to the cave opening that she could see Helecanth standing within it when she hauled Assar abruptly sideways, veering off at a tangent. It seemed she could hear the wings of the Endarkened rustle like dead leaves as those not already locked in combat with one another prepared to follow.

Her generals would take proper advantage of the opening she provided. She tried for a moment to wish, but could not think who she wished saved if everyone couldn't be.

A mob of Endarkened landed, blocking her way.

If I lose control—

She had time for only that unfinished thought as she reached for the power of the Shrine Itself.

And Cast Sunstroke.

Her body was on fire. She felt blisters forming and breaking beneath the leather of her aketon. She was far closer to the Endarkened than they had all been at Saganath, and this casting had more power.

Scores of Endarkened were blasted away to bone and ash. As always, when any of them was injured, the others fled. But it was only a temporary respite. They would return.

I could—she thought in excitement and hope, but already she knew she could not. No one but the Child of the Prophecy—a *Lightborn* Child of the Prophecy—could have managed what she had already done—to continue making herself the focus of the Shrine's power would kill her.

Assar stumbled.

The mare ran on, but soon she would fall a final time. Vieliessar turned her once again, heading back for the cave entrance. The boldest of the Endarkened had already returned. They wheeled above her, snatching at her clothes, her arms. They would have grabbed her by the hair except that she had never let it grow beyond Lightborn length.

One of them got her cloak. The Endarkened's closeness terrified and nauseated her, and she found herself reciting a familiar litany in her mind.

Oh Lord of Battles, precious to Aradhwain and Manafaeren, lead me to your khom *as my heart still pumps. Let me come to you before I know my death. I have given you blood to drink: Hunt Lord, let me come to you while I still savor the sweets of triumph. Take me up and protect me from hungry ghosts, from the Void and the Darkness, that my name will always shine silver upon the Tablets of Memory . . .*

She had recited it many times when making the luck-sacrifices before a battle. Arilcarion had written it—so they said.

Oh Lord of Battles, precious to Aradhwain and Manafaeren—

Assar's breath made a strained whistling sound, and bloody foam dripped from her jaws.

Protect me from hungry ghosts, from the Void and the Darkness—

And suddenly, just as upon the night of the battle of Ceoprentrei, she was surrounded by a living river of Unicorns. Dusty and battered and even wounded, the magical creatures ran on either side of her, shielding Vieliessar from the Endarkened as much as they could.

And every one of them had a rider.

She did not have time to ponder what she saw, for suddenly the Unicorns sheered away from her on both sides, and Assar ran alone. The opening of Imrathalion loomed before her; she could see Leutric there, and Helecanth. The cave entrance was a wide low opening; the Endarkened were still scattered and Elvenkind and Otherfolk rushed to safety while they could. Freed of their riders, battleponies ran from the field; they had been untacked before being released.

Someone must have done a great work of organization to move people into Imrathalion so quickly . . .

Then suddenly there was a whistling sound behind her, and a sick stabbing pain in her temples. Vieliessar did not even need to look back to know there was an Endarkened behind her.

"You! You! You!" she heard Udbaukh scream in glee.

Someone must have found her head.

Pouncewarm vanished, and Vieliessar flew over Assar's neck as if the animal had been frozen in place. Assar screamed in agony, the sound going on and on.

Again, Vieliessar tucked her head and shoulders to break her fall. The impact was still bruising, but she was up and moving immediately, just as Rithdeliel had taught her. As Gunedwaen had taught her. As had everyone who had given their skills and their lives so that she could reach this day.

I will not disgrace them!

Vieliessar put together what had happened as she ran toward Assar. The Endarkened had seized Assar by the tail, yanking the mare out from under Vieliessar, and then swung the battlepony through the air as if the beast was a child's toy. Assar landed hard, all four legs broken, screaming horribly as—obedient to the spell cast upon her—she still tried to get to her feet and run.

With a reflexive spell Vieliessar ended Assar's agony (a strong instance of Fetch, to rip the heart from her body, and avoid the dangers of using the Light to kill directly). Turning again, she managed two strides toward the cave entrance before the Endarkened's claws ripped through her tunic and found purchase on her belt. A backhand blow sent Vieliessar sprawling again; she rolled, and managed to loosen her belt and struggle free. She staggered to her feet, looking around herself to know which way to run. She saw Imrathalion. Too far. In another moment the Endarkened would have her.

Vieliessar scrabbled for her dagger.

Udbaukh howled with laughter.

And Pouncewarm appeared, shrieking like a falcon, wrapping himself around Udbaukh's face with all four sharp-clawed feet, kicking and biting and wailing. Tears filled Vieliessar's eyes as she floundered gracelessly into a run for Sanctuary.

I cannot waste his death in tears!

She reached the mouth of the cave, not knowing if the Endarkened would follow her. Imrathalion was filled with defenders, and Leutric was among them. He took one long stride from the mouth of the cave to seize her, then turned and simply flung her deeper into the cave.

The roaring of the battle was magnified inside the cave, as if the whole of it was a gigantic sounding board. She tried to brace herself for impact, but before she could hit the ground, a Bearward plucked her from the air and broke her fall.

Pouncewarm!

"Stop!" she cried. "I have to go back!" Knowing it was useless, knowing Pouncewarm was already dead. But the Bearward stopped, and set her on her feet.

"Wait," he said.

A second Bearward appeared. "We have him, Frichist."

At first, Vieliessar thought the Bearward carried a wad of bloody rags—but then she saw that it breathed. She stretched out her hands. "Please," she whispered. "Give him to me." *He fought to save me. He set himself against the Endarkened to save me.*

"There is nothing to be done save ease his death, Lady," the second Bearward said gently. Pouncewarm's blood stained the golden fur on Helda's arms as she placed the tiny body in Vieliessar's hands.

"I," he whispered, opening his eyes to regard her. "I, I . . ."

I will not let this happen!

She had never loved. She had never had anything *to* love. When she had set her foot upon the road to the Unicorn Throne she'd found comrades, liegemen, allies. Even some who called themselves "friend." But every relationship had been transmuted by the alchemy of princes into something that had to be weighed and measured, rationed out, defended against. Or used. Even her love for her children had not been selfless and absolute.

But Pouncewarm had never cared about what she thought or could do and be. He simply loved her. And she had loved him as utterly as if a soul-deep starvation could be fed by giving. And now . . .

Because of me. Because of me. Because of me—!

Grief and loss were scoured away by the cold rage that filled her: implacable, all-consuming, demanding that her wish, her word must become the world's truth. Because she desired it. Because she willed it. Because Creation itself must bow to the will of the Lightborn—and she was both Lightborn and King.

She would win, or she would die. She would not fail.

She sank to her knees, careful not to jar her precious burden. And began.

"*To the Lightless, our Healings seem instantaneous—a touch, a gesture, and it is done.*" Lightsister-Healer Hervilafimir had said. "*In truth, the Healer must first see their subject whole and unmarred, and next, eliminate the discord between their self as it is, and as it has been and will be. This is why we study bodies when they are whole and unharmed, so that we may make them so again.*"

Vieliessar called the Light to her as a falcon to her glove, hearing the words of her teachers in her mind as she had when she trained as a Healer, so very long ago. She must work blindly—but she must work. And she must prevail.

Someone placed a pad of sheepskins on the ground before her. She laid Pouncewarm on it gently.

"*Magery is not without cost. Magery is never without cost. The Flower Forests feed our spells, and through our studies the Light is ours to command, but to control its power requires the strength and stamina of riding a destrier and making the beast's will align with your own,*" Nithrithuin Lightsister had said. "*Know that no matter what the Lightless will say, every spell—every Healing—is a success if you survive it. If one of you must die, let it be your patient. You must always keep back enough power to heal your own hurts, even if your patient must die."*

Never!

Vieliessar filled Pouncewarm with Light, stopping his pain, strengthening his body.

Then she stepped inside him, into an unknown world.

Lightborn spent Wheelturns learning the structure of the bodies—Elven, equine—that they healed. She had no time for that. Her patient was heartbeats away from death.

She could feel the slime of Endarkened magic upon him, and laved it away with Light until his tattered body was clean. The Endarkened had ripped Pouncewarm from her face with her talons, crushing him in her grip before she dashed him to the ground. His body bore a report of each injury: broken bones, torn muscles; worst of all, the bleeding, blood that drowned and crushed lungs and heart even as it starved them. Each vessel must be found, each break healed, fluid drained from where it should not be. That must be first.

Next, the organs of the body. Each one must be known, tested, examined for wrongness before she Healed it or moved on. Over and over Vieliessar checked her work, terrified of failure, but all the time knowing that this work must be done quickly.

Bones. Joints must be set right, bones returned to their proper places, shattered fragments dissolved or removed before she rebuilt the bones they had come from. Only when the bones were in their proper places could she repair muscles, tendons, ligaments. Only then could she command heart to beat and lungs to fill.

And when he was whole . . .

Brightness beyond sun, beyond fire, beyond the naked blaze of the Shrine of the Star, filled her senses, rushing through her to Heal her patient. It seemed as if her own Light, her own strength, would follow the power of the Healing, draining her until there was nothing left. In that moment, it seemed the Light had voice, a living consciousness like her own. *"This is what I give, if you are strong enough to take it. But gift must be repaid in gift . . ."*

Freely given, she thought. *Freely given!*

She felt Pouncewarm breathe in and begin to purr. She touched his blood-matted fur, just to prove to herself that he was here. Whole, alive, a beating heart.

"I," he said, bristling his whiskers and yawning sleepily. "I who am First."

"You, you who cheat at xaique," she whispered to him through tears. He purred louder.

"Your witches told us they could not do this." It was the female Bearward who spoke.

"Do what?" Vieliessar looked up at her. She knew her words sounded slow and stupid. The Healing had taken what strength she had left from the day of battles. If she had been in the Sanctuary, after a Healing such as this Vieliessar would have gone to her chambers to eat—and probably to sleep the clock around.

"Heal '*animals.*'" It was the male Bearward who answered. Frichist's voice was thick with contempt.

That's ridiculous; the Lightborn are trained to heal more than Elven-kind—we would be of no service to the War Princes otherwise . . .

"Take me to your wounded," Vieliessar said, staggering gracelessly to her feet.

<hr />

Everything was burning. The smoke made her eyes burn too, and it was so thick Dianora could not see the Unicorn running beside Sondast—if there even was one now. Landmarks appeared briefly through the smoke and were snatched away again.

They'd had to change their pattern. The old barn had been set afire. Everything seemed as if it had been set afire.

She and Sondast were going to die. Everyone was going to die.

Dianora saw an Endarkened using one of the Unicorn Riders—Tiriane—as a club to bludgeon Tiriane's mount—Kellen the Grey—to death. Dianora could not tell whether Tiriane was already dead. She hoped so.

Ysance fell, one foreleg shattered by a thrown stone. Celegal crawled back to her side and pulled the Unicorn to her feet. Together they limped—slowly, hopelessly—toward the safety of Imrathalion. An Endarkened lunged toward them, only to be obliterated from sight by Thunderbolt.

The Riders were an easier target than their Unicorns, and when the Endarkened finally figured that out, the Riders suffered accordingly. Again and again Dianora saw Unicorns standing over their riders, desperately trying to protect them until rescue could come. She hoped it would, but she didn't know; she and Sondast were doing their best to make up for the absence of the fallen. As one of the Children of Night, Dianora was a powerful lure, drawing the attention of the Endarkened away from the other riders.

It was the plan. It always had been.

She did not know where Arathiel and Iskilsa were.

She was so tired.

⊰▤⊱

Another pass. Another glimpse of Elvenkind and Otherfolk fleeing the battlefield. You did not win a battle with the Endarkened: you survived it. But even though the smoke still covered the battlefield, Dianora thought that there were fewer of the monsters visible now, and she began to hope this would be over soon and she and Sondast would still be alive.

And then the twilight winter sky abruptly turned brassy and white. It was like a summer sky, a storm sky, but the light that shone down made everything look flat and strange. There was no color anywhere— even the pools of blood had been leached of their redness. Across the winter landscape, everything touched by that light had withered if it could, turned to dust if it could not.

I am dead, and this is the land of the hungry ghosts, Dianora thought, clutching her last javelin. But no: this was all too terribly the real world, deranged by a war of magics fought by a god against mortals. It was even hard to breathe, as if the very air resented being used to sustain life.

"*He Who Is* has come," Sondast whispered. "I am so sorry, Dia." He came to a stop, simply standing there. Dianora barely noticed. She was struggling for air as if she was drowning.

"What—? Sondast, what—?" she gasped.

"The Greater Power that made the Endarkened has come to the battlefield. It strengthens them."

And they are already too strong for us, Dianora thought miserably.

"Go," Sondast said hoarsely, and Dianora readied herself once more. She only had one javelin left. Perhaps this would be the last pass they would have to make.

Perhaps they'd die and she could finally get some rest.

⊰⧣⊱

The attack upon the meat should have been a glorious triumph of killing that went on until no Brightworlder was left to kill. It ought to have been simple to gather up the Elfling Mages Virulan had demanded. There were no hateful Absences for the Elflings to hide within—not that weren't on fire, at least—and if the meat chose to hide in the cave, they would only be herding themselves into a group for easy collection.

Even the unexpected sky-storm did not faze the Endarkened. Those who survived regrouped, and the great aerial sea of Endarkened in their vastness set the land afire from the mountains to the sea. Their power was incalculable and their speed faster than any other creature of land or air. Rimroheth, Angoratorei, Eldanwarasse, Taziridan, Mornenamei, Arevethmonion—each of the great Flower Forests of the West turned from blossoms of Light to blossoms of purgatorial flame beneath their hands.

There were Brightworlders in abundance, but none of the Endarkened stopped to slaughter them for fear the rest of their comrades would reach the most desirable prey first—and Endarkened did not share. But of the Mage-meat that had not hidden, Shurzul and her comrades were able to collect a mere handful, and those all ceased to live almost at once, their Light wasted upon death.

What had begun as a glorious campaign of erasure, the culmination of their very reason for being, had become a treasure hunt for very high stakes.

The combined power of the Endarkened could have easily forced the cave and clawed loose their recalcitrant prey—but once again Unicorns

came who fought by the side of the Elflings. And if that were not astonishing enough, the most delicious prize of all, the burning bright Elfling
Queen appeared, she who was spoken of in whispers and known by rumors. She who shone more brightly than a thousand Mages.

To bring her back—*alive!*—to the World Without Sun would be to
gain more power than any other Endarkened—more power (perhaps)
than Uralesse—

They should have regrouped, they should have made a new plan,
but none of the Endarkened would follow anyone's orders save the
King's—or perhaps Uralesse's—and Virulan (at least) wasn't here.

They should have retreated, but no Endarkened wanted to give up
their chance to take prizes. Especially the most delicious prize of all, the
Elfling Queen.

Shurzul's fellow Endarkened should have captured the Queen (instead of fighting over whose prize she would be). The Unicorns should
have been easily slain, or carried off, regardless of the pain.

And none of those things happened.

That was when *He Who Is* came to the battlefield, and Shurzul
thought that now all would be well. Even if she could not capture the Elfling Queen, if she could bring even one living Unicorn back to Ugolthma,
then surely King Virulan would forgive her for the loss of the Elfling
Mages.

But as *He Who Is* had come, so had the Great Power the Elflings
worshipped. The Starry Rade whipped its hunting pack across the sky,
and *He Who Is* left *His* children as inexplicably as *He* had come to them.

As the balance of power shifted above them, it started to rain, show-
ering the battlefield with fat black drops that were as much soot as water.

It was time to go.

Shurzul did not know what she would say to King Virulan, but it was
a time-hallowed maxim among the Endarkened that the first to tell the
tale was the one who would be believed.

And spared.

All that remained behind in the World Without Sun was a scattering of slaves, some *meat*, and the children of the Endarkened, who cared for nothing beyond their daily survival. But even so, the halls of the deep earth were not silent. Without the chatter and the screams of its inhabitants, without the relentless noise of movement infinitely magnified by their echoes, the true music of the World Without Sun could be heard.

There was a faint susurration as of breathing, as air was pushed into the underground chambers and sucked away again by the winds of the World Above. As the labyrinth settled into its waiting silence, the faint dripping of liquid, the scurrying of insects, the swish and splash of blind fish moving through the water could be heard. From the inhabitants of the slave pens, standing near empty now in anticipation of the harvest to come, came a hopeless crooning. Underlaying all other sounds was the scrabbling of the Lesser Endarkened going about their mundane tasks.

Without the press of furnace-hot bodies, the mindless stone began to cool, to seek its own equilibrium, never aware that no present moment could continue forever.

In his hidden chamber behind the Iron Throne of Night, Virulan heard all these sounds and more: the high soft keen of the Obsidian Spire, the mad whispers from the artworks in Garden of Tears. But at the moment Virulan dismissed all these sounds from consideration, there came another.

Footsteps.

I am dreaming, Virulan told himself comfortingly. *No one would dare defy me and remain behind. They just wouldn't. Really.*

He was certain that must be true. He, Virulan, Lord of the Twelve, Master of the Dark Guard, first creation of *He Who Is*, would never be defied by his Endarkened subjects—not while he was held in the explicit regard of *He Who Is*. His orders to his people had been simple and precise: everyone must go upon this hunt.

But *He Who Is* was no longer here. *He Who Is* had turned *His* attention elsewhere.

Virulan was alone.

No! It is not true! It is the sickness that makes it seem so! He Who Is—*Is here! Here!*

Virulan huddled deeper into his nest of silks and furs. The furs did not warm him. The silks did not comfort him. They weighed down his withered limbs until he could barely move. Since he had been touched by the Unicorn's horn, all Virulan had felt was weakness, pain, hunger.

Just as if he was one of those unspeakable maggots who lived in the Light above. Unclean. *Impure.*

He held his breath, listening. The sound of footsteps continued. Faint scrape of talons against the floor. Fainter sound of the ruffling of great leathern wings, the soft muffled clicking as wingtips touched the floor.

It is one of the children, Virulan thought. *Yes. That is it. Clever animals—they've realized everyone is gone, and they've come looking for food.*

Nothing could come in here. Nothing would dare. Besides, this room was a secret. No one knew about it. The footsteps didn't matter. (Why were they so slow?) Virulan scrabbled at the fur coverlet, pulling it up over his head. Now no one could see him even if they found his hiding place. Not that he was hiding. He was King of the Endarkened and he did not need to hide.

He heard the sound of the great doors to the throne room open. He heard them close. He heard the sound of feet moving over the polished jeweled floor.

He tried to hold his breath, but that made his chest hurt. He was cold. Why was he cold? He was the King—he should not have to be cold! When Shurzul came back, she would warm him. She would bring him Elfling Mages to devour, and he would be more powerful than before. Then he would hunt down all the Unicorns. They would pay for what they'd done. He would sacrifice every one of them at the Obsidian Spire and take their power into himself until he became the most powerful being in the World of Form.

But he was so *cold* . . .

He heard the click as his secret door was opened. He heard the faint scraping sound as it slid back.

Virulan tried once more to hold his breath. So occupied was he in the attempt that the sound of the intruder's voice caused him to emit a faint mouse-like squeak.

"Now here's a pretty riddle, one which, I believe, the King of the Endarkened would approve."

It is Uralesse! Uralesse has returned! Or maybe Uralesse hadn't left at all. *Traitor! Monster! Your death will encompass eternities!*

Beneath the covers, Virulan held very still.

"The ruler of the Endarkened is the most powerful of us all," Uralesse continued. "And that is as it should be, for that is how *He Who Is* ordained it should be. But what force is it that makes our King so strong? Why, the regard of *He Who Is.*" Uralesse yanked the coverlet away, pulling it easily from Virulan's desperate grasp.

"You dare?" Virulan wheezed. He'd meant his words to sound intimidating, but when he spoke he began to cough. The combination of fury and breathlessness made him light-headed.

Uralesse regarded him, lip curling in distaste. "You look like one of the Elflings now," he said. "But fear not, my brother. You will not have that problem for much longer."

"*He—He—He—*" Virulan was coughing and choking too hard to get the name out, but he knew Uralesse knew what he meant to say. He Who Is *will defend me.* He Who Is *loves me best!*

Uralesse leaned down to whisper in Virulan's ear. "*He Who Is . . .* has left you."

Virulan whimpered, trying to scrabble away from Uralesse. Uralesse, the second-born of *He Who Is.* Uralesse, the only other one of the Twelve unchanged by Virulan's great spell.

Uralesse, Virulan's equal in cunning and cruelty.

"Now, my brother. Here is your final lesson in kingship." Uralesse extended one taloned finger and rested the point at the base of Virulan's throat. Virulan began to scream.

Virulan stopped screaming very shortly afterward.

⊣⊒⊨⊢

Vieliessar had worked in the Healing Tents in the aftermath of hundreds of battles as she fought her way to the Unicorn Throne. The fight against the Endarkened was not precisely a battle, and there were no tents, but all else was the same.

There was something not right though. Not out of place; something that should be here and wasn't. But just as she grasped the answer, a wave of choking foulness broke over her, so vile that for a moment Vieliessar was certain the Endarkened had broken through the defenses. She fell to her knees, blind to everything around her.

Vileness . . . darkness . . . void . . . It was Ivrulion at Ishtilaikh, raising his *mazhnune* army from the bodies of the dead. It was Enthroning Day in the Teeth of the Moon, when the sky was red with Endarkened and the ground was red with blood. It was a power as vast and terrible as that of the Silver Hooves, but there was nothing clean or honest about it. It was the ultimate expression of the Darkness that she had fought against since the day of her Enthroning.

Vieliessar struggled against the very presence of it. She could hear screams from elsewhere in the caverns as Lightborn did their best to breathe against the terrible wave of oppression. *Nothing can shield us from* He Who Is, *but we can have Light . . .*

She drew upon burning Arevethmonion, much of its vastness still whole, and pure cold Silverlight seemed to well up from the stone, cascading in ripples from her hands where they were pressed against the floor. The light raced along the floor, rose up through the walls, cascaded over the ceiling. It outshone what it replaced until the entire chamber was as bright as a shadowless noonday.

Oh Lord of Battles, precious to Aradhwain and Manafaeren—

Never before had Vieliessar had the sense of speaking to . . . if not an equal, then at least an ally. She had seen the Hunt Lord at the end of her Novitiate, and had made the prescribed sacrifices at every moonturn and before every battle.

But this one.

In this battle, her people were the sacrifice. Assar. Kishmiri. Beloved war-ponies. And Palugh. And Wulvers. Every living thing she or some other had brought to the battlefield. All were sacrifices.

I have given you blood to drink, Hunt Lord. Take me up and protect

*me from the Void and the Darkness, that my name will always shine silver
upon the Tablets of Memory* . . .

Oh Lord of Battles—

The tightness eased within her chest, and Vieliessar forced herself to
stand. Frichist was staring at her, clearly baffled. Vieliessar took a deep
breath.

"The enemy has brought reinforcements," she said briefly, turning
her attention to the scene before her once more.

In a cavern within Imrathalion, on pallets or blankets or litters or
piles of furs, the wounded lay, Bearwards and Centaurs, Fauns, Wulvers,
Minotaurs.

But no Elves.

No Elves—and no Lightborn Healers. Only Otherfolk—Lightless—
Healers

When she finally spoke her voice was mercilessly even. "Frichist, I
pray you of your courtesy, send someone among my Lightless to find
any with Healing—we call it *nursling*—skills, and tell them in my name
to attend these wounded here. Say to Iardalaith and Helecanth that I am
well and safe, and that those who require orders must report to them, for
I will be occupied. Tell Helecanth that Caerthali—that *Runacar* comes
with a meisne from Smoketree, and she must send them aid if she can.
Send Iardalaith to go among my Warhunt Mages and the Sanctuary
Lightborn and tell him to bring any who are able to Heal, whether Warhunt Mage or Lightborn. Do not move the Elven wounded from where
they lie, but bring all the newly injured, whether Elven or Otherfolk, to
this one place. Say to any who oppose you that I, Vieliessar of Farcarinon, Lightsister, rightful High King over the whole of the Hundred
Houses by both battle and lineage, swear upon my Light and my Kingship that I will slay them with my own hand for such defiance of my will.
Now. Who are your Healers?"

"I am one," said a female Bearward, stepping away from the patient
she had been tending. She looked tired—as far as Vieliessar could read
the expressions on Otherfolk faces. "My name is Helda," the Bearward
said. "You murdered my mate Keloit at Ceoprentrei."

Vieliessar took a quick breath, wanting to protest the unfair accusation. But this was not a time to sort out whose fault—or loss—was greater. No one could change the past.

"Then now I can aid your people in his name. First do this," she said, holding her hands out before her. "Here are the three hands of Aradhwain the Mare. In one, the first, She holds those who will live to see another dawn even without help. In the second, She holds those who will die within the sunturn if they are not aided. In the third"—now Vieliessar brought her hands together, cupping them—"She holds those who will die within the quartermark without succor. Your wounded are not organized in such fashion. Do so. We will begin by Healing those in the third hand of Aradhwain."

Helda looked over Vieliessar's shoulder at Frichist. Whatever she saw there made her flatten her ears in conciliation. "Come then, Lady. All shall be done as you say. Now, there is a patient you must see."

⁂

The battlefield had become a deranged xaique-board of fire and half-melted pillars of Mage-created ice. The smoke-filled air was stifling. Coughing was sheer torture, and Dianora had never been so tired as she was this day, not even when she toiled in the mines. It was as if the air held no health, only poison. She thought she might happily die if it meant she could only stop moving and *rest*. The dreadful yellow sky, the oppressive presence of *He Who Is,* took a monstrous toll upon every creature of the Light who toiled beneath them.

There was no sun in the glaring saffron sky. Only death.

"They're afraid," Dianora said. "The Endarkened. Afraid." Her voice was raw with smoke, and her chest ached with the struggle to breathe.

"Yes." Sondast's chest worked like a bellows as the Unicorn gasped for air. "They know something and it worries them. But I doubt that thing is us."

Each time she and Sondast scattered the Endarkened from the entrance to Imrathalion—and then turned away from that refuge—Dianora's heart ached with loss. Each time she told herself: *Just one more run. Just one. You can do one . . .*

There was no longer any pretense among the Unicorns of maintaining formation. Now they ran as a line, a troop, a herd of flashing horns and gleaming hooves. No living thing—not even the stainless, glorious Unicorns—could keep up this grueling pace forever.

Even Sondast was tiring. Dianora could feel it.

"Sondast—Sondast, *stop!*" Dianora gasped. Over the sounds of Sondast's ragged breathing and her own, she could hear the cries of the Celestial Pack as the Starborne Hunters rode above the battlefield. The dank airless presence of *He Who Is* was washed away by a dry, freezing wind that bit the lungs like a swordblade. Dianora sucked in the icy air greedily. It was as painful in its way as the other had been, but it meant *life*. She buried her face against Sondast's neck. It was said that to see the Starry Huntsman was to join him, and suddenly Dianora wanted very much to live.

Sondast stopped where he stood, falling to his knees. His whole body shuddered with weariness. Dianora slid off his back and put an arm around his neck. Her last javelin was gone; she couldn't remember using it.

Her heart hammered in her chest; she wanted to ask Sondast what they should do now, or even just to say something. Anything. But she could not imagine what to say about a world where gods fought in the sky above her head.

Then the glassy yellow bowl of the sky shattered, and between the cracks there was the flaring red and gold of sunset. Black clouds starred with lightning—*normal* clouds with *normal* lightning—swarmed against it until the sky was twilight-dark. The Endarkened cried out angrily, and when the rain began to fall, they fled as if the sky were raining fire instead.

Did we win? Lady of Battles, Lady of Night, Blessed Aradhwain, please let it be so. At least for today. I do not ask for more than a day . . .

The cold rain was black with smoke and dust.

It was glorious.

CHAPTER TWENTY-NINE

WOOD'S MOON IN THE TENTH YEAR OF THE HIGH KING'S REIGN: A HOME UPON THE PYRE

The storysongs tell us that when Queen Pelashia was murdered, her death curse reached out to the animals of the forest, giving them minds to think, tongues to speak, and hands to kill. From that day to this, the Beastfolk have carried out Pelashia's curse. Whether there is truth in the storysongs or not, there is one thing I do know. To treat the Beastlings as our equals is madness; to make them our allies is to open our armor to the knife.

—Rithdeliel of Farcarinon, Private Journal

Body after body came beneath Vieliessar's hands. As her Healers arrived, she showed her work to them so they could duplicate it: the hale and whole bodies of Bearward, Centaur, Minotaur, Wulver, Palugh—all the races of the Otherfolk that had found themselves embattled this day.

The departure of *He Who Is* was like a drink of cool water. She valued the respite it gave, for too few had joined her. Vieliessar set that problem aside; she could not take the time to deal with it now.

She gave orders without knowing to whom she spoke, her attention always on the body beneath her hands, the body she must learn and Heal. There could be no Vieliessar Lightsister to ache and thirst; only the Light, flowing from the Flower Forest into her children.

It was easier that way.

Vieliessar had come to this work already exhausted, but to Heal the wounded Otherfolk was its own sort of war, and one she dared not lose. *Let no one say Elvenkind was set above Otherfolk, or Otherfolk set above Elvenkind. Let us all remember what we forgot long ago: that we are all Pelashia's children. . . .*

Each time weariness threatened to overwhelm her, Vieliessar drew again on Lady Arevethmonion's grace to lend her strength. She dared not draw upon the Shrine for Healing as she had drawn upon it to attack. The Shrine of the Star was far too powerful to use in Healing frail living bodies.

The first time she took note of her surroundings again, it was because a pair of Palugh sat, warm and purring, one on either side of her. She had lost track of Pouncewarm, but now, each time she looked, there were more Palugh in the Healing Chamber. They sat silently in the shadows, their eyes flashing red and green and coin-gold.

A delay during a Healing gave Vieliessar a few moments to rest. Dinias worked beside her, carefully washing the intestines of a Bearward who had been disemboweled, healing tiny tears and plucking out stones and grass. Dinias must finish his work before she could resume hers. As she waited, Vieliessar drank thirstily from a tall mug of tea someone brought her. The tea had a homely and familiar taste—it was one of the Sanctuary's recipes. She hadn't known anyone had it with them.

Those wounded held in the First Hand of Aradhwain had been moved to another chamber, for their care was fully within the capability of the Lightless *nurslings* and the Otherfolk Healers who did not have magic. Those of the Third Hand were also absent: their Healing having been accomplished, they had been taken elsewhere to rest and recover. A number of the Second remained—but there were few Lightborn available to tend them. She saw Harwing (as himself, not as Hamphuliadiel), Isilla, Tangisen, and perhaps a dozen more. She did not expect to see Iardalaith, for he would be among the *alakomentai'a* if any of the Warhunt Mages were still on the field. She remembered vaguely that she'd heard Iardalaith shouting earlier, and was distantly glad he was alive.

Please, Pelashia Flower Queen, tell me this is not the whole of my brothers and sisters left alive!

Night had fallen as she had worked on the injured, and, with the departure of *He Who Is,* the weather had changed; Vieliessar could smell the hard rain, and the added damp made the mineral scent of the cavern overpowering. But if she could smell the rain, she could not hear it; sounds and shouts echoed off the walls, losing all identity and becoming a featureless wall of noise broken only occasionally by high squeals that could mean anything—joy or pain or rage.

"Where are the others?" she asked, taking care to keep her voice low. "The Warhunt? The Sanctuary Lightborn?"

"Shielding Imrathalion," Dinias said absently, finishing his work. "Those who aren't just puking their guts out. And helping to move the last few hundred idiot villagers out of the entrance cavern so we can get the Unicorns in. If there are any left."

"Then we here must do all else," she said. She took the Bearward's intestines carefully in her hands and let the Light fill her once more. *Hale and whole, hale and whole*—the words filled her mind like a chant.

Like a prayer.

Carefully, she set the intestines back in their place, making certain they lay correctly, that they were without flaw. Then she pulled the edges of the opening together and closed it. As she sat back, darkness bloomed before her eyes. Vieliessar took a deep breath, and drew once again upon Lady Arevethmonion for strength.

Rondithiel would scold me if he were alive to know of this. It is dangerous.

"Have this one taken to the Spellmothers and Healers," she said to Silverclaw, the Palugh acting as her messenger. "He is whole, but say they must watch for wound-sickness."

"Yes-yes quick-quick-quickly I go," Silverclaw said.

A few moments later, the litter the Bearward lay on was lifted away. Nothing replaced it.

"Bring me work!" Vieliessar demanded harshly. She could not fight and she could not defend Imrathalion, for the sight and sense of her would drive the Endarkened into frenzy. If she did not have the Healing to occupy her mind, she thought she might go mad.

"I have work," a new voice said.

Alakomentai Pelere stood in the doorway of the cavern. Runacar sat upon her back, sideways, as if Pelere was a chair, one arm slung across her shoulders to keep himself upright. Vieliessar could not see any blood, but his face was grey and pinched with pain and nausea. *He lives! He fought his way across a battlefield of Endarkened and he lives!*

"Pelere, as soon as I can stand, I will kill you," Runacar said.

"He is of the First Hand. The Second at most," Vieliessar forced the words out through a throat gone suddenly dry. The plaits of his hair had come unbound. His battle-braid was simple, with function over ornament, unlike the elaborate braids komen and princes had worn when the Hundred Houses still stood. Her fingers itched to gather it up, to braid it again. Properly.

"He's our Battlemaster and he needs to be able to fight *right now,*" Pelere said. "So Heal him or I'll tell all your Elves what Andhel told me. I think it's a stupid thing, but I'll tell them."

"Pelere!" Runacar attempted to shout, but all he did was trigger a spasm of coughing.

"I think she means she'll tell everyone that you and Caerthalien are Bondmates," Dinias said, whispering in a low voice no one else could hear. Vieliessar whirled on him; Dinias performed his best look of wide-eyed innocence. "Is it true? There's gossip. But I don't think anyone actually cares by now," he added confidentially.

She gave him as much of a murderous glare as she could summon, but Dinias didn't look especially worried, possibly because Silverclaw had begun walking back and forth in front of Vieliessar, purring, and pausing occasionally to head-butt her knees.

"Bring him, then," Vieliessar said to Pelere. "But were I you, I would be the last Healer you brought him to."

"And you would be the last I would go to," Runacar responded hoarsely. "Because you're mad, you know. I can't think why no one has noticed."

Helda came to help Dinias lift Runacar from Pelere's back. Helda had brought an empty litter with her; they laid him down as carefully as possible, but Runacar's face was ashen by the time they were done.

She could not refuse to Heal him; the training of the Sanctuary ran deep. But neither could Vieliessar begin until she saw the damage. *"Better not to Heal at all than to Heal a cased knight or a clothed servant,"*

Hervilafimir Lightsister had told her when Vieliessar began her apprenticeship as a Healer. *"Armor is armor and flesh is flesh, and to meld the two together would be truly lamentable."*

Like everyone in her war party, Runacar had been garbed in aketon, tunic, trews, mail shirt, leather bracers, basquinet, battle cloak, and heavy boots. Vieliessar already knew he had broken bones; there would be no way to Lightlessly remove his armor and clothing without causing him agony, even if she and Dinias simply cut them off.

Vieliessar looked away from Dinias, Sundapple, and Runacar. Harwing was staring at her from several rows over with a peculiar expression on his face. He looked like a spirit from another time in his elaborate Sanctuary robes, even with the makeshift apron over it. Vieliessar turned her gaze elsewhere—she did not dare look at Dinias—and saw that the Cadet Warlord had not yet left.

"Before you go, *Alakomentai* of the Otherfolk," Vieliessar said, with the most lordly disdain she could muster, "you may tell me how this komen came to be injured."

"I can speak for myself," Runacar said in irritation.

"I can pickle you in dream-honey so I don't have to listen," Vieliessar snapped.

"He talked back to an Endarkened. She broke his ribs and both his legs and smacked him in the head," *Alakomentai* Pelere said. "But we escaped."

"That is a thing fortunate, for it takes many Wheelturns to make a Warlord," Vieliessar said.

"He said it would be easier just to breed one, and it would be faster, too. They say your kind lives forever if you do not die," the *alakomentai* added.

"We live long," Vieliessar agreed. "Since you will not leave, come and help."

The Centauress came forward, and knelt with surprising grace next to Dinias. She frowned fiercely at Runacar. "Oh, hold still, Rune—the Great Herdsman would suppose you have never been injured before!"

Runacar glared at her wordlessly.

A strange sort of compassion—awareness of the horror of being in thrall to an enemy, even if that enemy was his ally and Bondmate—overcame Vieliessar. "Rune, I cannot Heal your hurts until you are uncased," she said gently. "You know this is no lie. That cannot be done without pain unless you sleep. Will you permit it? I can send for a different Lightborn to Heal you. Or here is Dinias beside me. He is very skilled."

Runacar took a deep shuddering breath and met her eyes. She forced herself not to look away. Where Runacar could not see, Dinias touched Vieliessar's hand lightly with his fingertips and nodded—very slightly—toward Caerthalien. *"Take him now."* She heard his unvoiced words—as he had expected her to—and reached out for Runacar's hand, clasping his fingers with hers.

She realized it was the first time she had ever touched him. *There will be no hope of setting aside the Soulbond if I Heal him.* His hand was cold and rough with sword-callouses, and the electricity of the connection raced through them both, salving aches and exhaustion far better than either sleep or medicine could do. Only together were they whole. Only Bonded were they each all that they could be. She was his Bondmate, and he was hers, and not even the Starry Rade could tear them asunder.

I might as well order the wedding feast and call up my levies!

She wasn't sure whether it was his thought or hers.

Do what you must.

She bespelled him into unbreakable Sleep.

Dinias didn't bother to cut away Runacar's clothing. Dinias's Keystone Gift was Transmutation—he turned Runacar's garments into skeins of linen thread and wool yarn. The metal became ingots. The leather became scraps of unsewn hide.

"Show-off," Harwing commented, gesturing the orderlies to remove his patient.

"Now you know why everyone doesn't do this," Dinias responded. "The sound of the applause would disturb the wounded."

"I could have done the same thing with my skinning knife," Pelere scoffed. "Rune was right about you—witchborn never do something by hand if it can be done by sorcery."

And there are better uses for a Flower Forest, Vieliessar added mentally, before turning her focus to her patient.

Runacar's body was covered in bruises. Some were ancient and pansy-colored, some dark plum-black (some misadventure, but what?), some the deep red of strawberries—those he must have gotten today. *Ribs and legs and a blow to the head,* Alakomentai *Pelere said. You must begin with the head—if that is left untreated, any damage could kill him, now, or a Wheelturn from now.*

Vieliessar closed her eyes. Compared with others she had Healed this day, these were truly minor injuries: broken bones, wrenched muscles, strained tendons. In the days of the Hundred Houses, komen had bragged of such hurts as these, for their wars had been only games, and war's consequences a thing to be wiped away by Lightborn Healers.

She and Runacarendalur Caerthalien had each spent many Wheelturns learning otherwise.

⊰ 🝮 ⊱

As *Alakomentai* Pelere had said, Runacar's legs were broken cleanly, high on the long bones. In addition, his collarbone was broken, his ribs both sprung and broken, his left shoulder dislocated. The armor's underlayments had protected Runacar as they were meant to, but even good armor was not proof against Endarkened strength.

Vieliessar closed her eyes to look deeper with Healer's sight, and read a whole library of the damages done to his body, the marks of wounds long-healed and invisible to outward sight. However the hurts had been dealt with, no Lightborn magic had simply willed them away. She wondered how he had gotten them, and forced the question from her mind.

I do not care, she told herself determinedly.

One of the other Lightless Healers—another Bearward; her pelt was darker than Helda's was—brought a blanket to cover Runacar. It must have somehow come from the Sanctuary, for it was cross-woven with elvensilver and sang gently with the song of previous bespellings. With the touch of Light, it began to radiate warmth like gentle sunlight. Vieliessar spread it carefully over his body.

"How is he?" Dinias asked quietly.

"I think the Endarkened must have used him as a laundry-bat," Vieliessar said. "Gladly I would leave him his hurts to counsel him to prudence when he is next upon the battlefield."

"Except he won't be prudent, and just about everyone wants to murder him, and that won't do much good for your Treaty. I would have said that was a stupid idea until I saw the Endarkened, but . . ."

"And so I begin," Vieliessar said, cutting off further speech, and closed her eyes again.

"To begin, you must see the body hale and whole . . ."

Hale and whole . . .

Vieliessar thought of a day many Wheelturns ago, before she had been taken to the Sanctuary of the Star, before she knew who she really was. Aramenthiali had sent two great-tailles to try Caerthalien Great Keep when Bolecthindial and Glorthiachiel were away on Spring Procession. Prince Runacarendalur had carried the day, returning from a decoy ambush to defend the castel and rout the enemy. The feast that had followed was one of the times Vieliessar and the other noble children were let into the Hall, and there was Prince Runacarendalur seated at the High Table in jewels and velvet, Ivrulion Lightbrother beside him. Ivrulion had said something and Runacarendalur had laughed, toasting his Lightborn brother with his jeweled goblet.

In that moment it had seemed to the child she was that Runacarendalur was the most glorious thing she had ever seen, the crown of knighthood, and Vieliessar had dreamed of the day she would gain spurs and sword and bear his standard into war . . .

The dream-image shimmered and vanished.

You know better than to wander in dreams while you are Healing! Vieliessar told herself fiercely. To become lost in dreams was to replace What Had Been with What Might Be, and that could be fatal for both Healer and patient. She brushed the memory aside with irritation, reaching again for the map of Runacar's body and the marks of its damages.

But once again the Magery slipped from her grasp, this time to show her an unknown Light-shrine in an unknown Flower Forest.

And Caerthalien—Runacar—*Rune*—stood on the far side of the

Shrine, beneath a Vilya tree in flower. The symbolism was not lost on her. But this time he was not garbed in glowing enameled armor and velvet surcoat. This time he wore leather armor over chain, both items scarred and worn with use.

"I'm glad you're here," he said simply. "I have missed you."

"Missed trying to kill me?" she asked. She tried and failed to banish the vision, instead remembering the moment when she'd seen him across a battlefield; when she'd looked at him and *known*.

"My father would have called it courtship," Rune said with a smile. "Mother raised half the domain in revolt when Father's envoy brought her his proposal of marriage. The war lasted all summer, but they were married at Harvest."

"I do not play such games," Vieliessar said. *The Child of the Prophecy does not play such games.*

"I know," Runacar said quietly. "Nor I. But I would know at least . . . are you happy?"

"What does that matter?" she asked blankly. "I do what must be done. That does not include wedding you." For the first time, she felt unsure of that.

"I suppose I would rather have Melisha's company than yours," Runacar answered, shrugging.

"I would make the same choice," Vieliessar answered truthfully. Oh, to speak as a friend to a Unicorn. To *touch* one!

Once more Vieliessar realized that she was lost in dreams and visions—but this time, they were not of the past—nor could they be banished.

"Why are we here?" she asked.

"My brother would have said it is caused by the Soulbond. Toward the end, that was his answer for everything—at least to me." Runacar followed her change of subject easily. "I have seen you here before, I remember now—you asked me to wait for you."

Vieliessar looked around herself in curiosity. *Asked him to wait?* She remembered no dreams of him—and if she had, she certainly would not have asked him to wait for her. *To what end?*

"Soulbonded or not does not matter. Soon we will all die, and I will not consent to a betrothal while I must wage this war—especially with one who claims allegiance to another prince."

"That would be me," Runacar answered, sounding amazingly cheerful, all things considered. "Your council must have demanded—or I should say, requested very politely—that you wed."

"I made a bargain. Heirs, but no marriage."

"And while I confess that if I were free I might consider marrying Adalieriel some day—if only I could convince her I am not a bandit—I am understandably curious about her lineage," he answered.

So he knew. Those who were Soulbonded could only make a child with the other half of their pair. Vieliessar opened her mouth to reply— the same artful misdirection she had fended off Iardalaith and so many others with—and abruptly realized that in this timeless unreal space she could not tell so blatant a lie.

"They are Helecanth's and Thurion's. I would have borne them to him myself, but I could not." *And much good may it do you to hold this knowledge!* She stopped before she said more, before she told him of the politics that lay behind that decision, the weighing and measuring of alliances and factions, the knowledge that she could wed none of her nobles without starting another civil war.

That she loved Helecanth's children as much as she could, and knew it was not enough.

"Then the Unicorn Throne will be Caerthalien's in the end," Runacar said, his expression coaxing her to share the joke. "Bolecthindial would have been so proud."

"It will belong to no one. The Endarkened smashed that throne on the day of my Enthroning," she said.

"Then we must make a new one, you and I." The breeze shook a Vilya flower loose from its branch to land upon Runacar's head. He plucked it loose and regarded it. "Your mother named you for the Vilya, you know. Vielle. The tree of Light and of Law. I'm not sure it suits you, but it is a pretty name." He held the flower out to her. "Here. You should take it."

Belatedly she felt a surge of warning caution. When entranced, gifts were dangerous things. She stepped back. "Nataranweiya also named me for Death," she said warningly.

... and she was back in Imrathalion's Healing Cavern, staring down at Runacar's—at *Caerthalien's*—body. Not even the bruises remained.

Hale and whole, hale and whole . . .

⊰⊱

Before Vieliessar had quite oriented herself after Runacar's Healing, Helecanth came hurrying into the chamber. "My lord, we have carried the day," she said, dropping to one knee. "The Endarkened have surrendered the field. Their Dark Power has fled from the hounds of the Starry Rade. And there are Gryphons," she added, sounding disgruntled. "They brought rain."

"And we didn't bring them anything," Harwing said idly, walking over to Vieliessar and sitting himself unceremoniously on the floor beside her. "So we're mostly alive and so is the King of the Otherfolk and his friends. What next?"

"I know not." Vieliessar looked to her patient, and was relieved to see that Runacarendalur was deeply asleep, as was proper for a Lightless who had just been Healed. Despite the odd invigoration of the Healing she had just done, Vieliessar was still bone-weary. "I suppose we will never know why the Endarkened attacked as they did today, nor truly why they left. But at least it is over for now," she answered, stretching long-cramped muscles.

"For now," Harwing agreed. "I regret to inform you that Hamphuliadiel Astromancer met a glorious death upon the battlefield, fighting valiantly to save his people. He bequeathed me his clothes, and if anyone wants to be Astromancer now they're probably crazy."

Helecanth's expression suggested that *all* Lightborn were crazy, whether they wanted to be Astromancer or not. "And you, my lord, must come away. There are other hands to do this work—and none but you can do the work of the High King."

Harwing made a vague shooing motion as he stood, reaching down a hand to help Dinias to his feet. "*I* am going to see if there's anything to eat. And after that, I'm going to look for a hot spring. There must be one in here somewhere."

CHAPTER THIRTY

WOOD'S MOON IN THE TENTH YEAR OF THE HIGH KING'S REIGN: RUNNING AFTER DREAMS

Peace had been tried oh so many times. The last attempt followed the birth of Vieliessar Farcarinon and the erasure of Domain Farcarinon, a peace lasting less than ten Wheelturns. While the greatest Houses of the Western Reach gagged down their spoils and the lesser quarreled over the spilth, one truth became clear to some of the brightest minds of the age, and it was simple, and terrifying: without the eternal battles, they would all starve.

Without war, they had nothing. War Season gave them the excuse to enrich the Craftworkers, for destriers must be shod and armor created. Armies needed to be fed, so the Farmholders and their Landbonds were assured of a domain which would take in all that they could grow or breed. Those who could neither make nor grow could train for the coming conflict and be assured that their contributions were vital. And of course the Lightborn, upon whose oblivious shoulders the whole framework of the Hundred Houses rested, were kept from any useful tasks by War Princes who collected them as if they were so many gaudy toys.

In short, because of "war," everyone ran around performing useless tasks, save for the Lightborn, who were kept from doing much of anything at all. The whole of the Hundred Houses was teetering on the brink of collapse when Aramenthiali broke the Long Peace—had they but held off for another Wheelturn or so, the slide into oblivion would have gained too much mobility to stop.

If Aramenthiali— If Glorthiachiel Ladyholder— If Vieliessar— If the scattered nobility of Farcarinon— If—

But none of them did. And so, rather than the healthful collapse of a fractious Empire in revolt against itself, we endured another decade upon decade of bloody and incomprehensible slaughter.

*There was no peace in the early days of the High King's reign ei-
ther, but there did seem to be an end to the antic creation of outside
forces to justify an economically invigorating martial campaign.
Then we encountered the Otherfolk once more.*

— Thurion Pathfinder, A History of the High King's Reign

By the time Vieliessar and Helecanth reached the corridor that
led to the Outer Chamber, Vieliessar had already dismissed the
Healings she had done from her mind. As Helecanth had said,
now she must be High King.

The great cavern which opened to the outside world was so vast its roof
looked low. It blazed with the Silverlight she had awakened. The strongest
scent in the air was that of fear, for the outer cavern was packed with
bodies.

There were roughly a half-dozen Endarkened still close enough to the
cavern mouth for its light to shine upon them. Vieliessar had a sense of
others of the monsters waiting behind them in the dark, but not many.
A fraction of what had first come against them.

*Fortunately all that have remained here are young ones. They are just
as unkillable, but far more easily tricked. Their nursemaids are the true
threat . . . if they have come as well.*

The sound that had drawn her had been caused by one of the juvenile
Endarkened trying to rush in, and being repelled by the whole mass of
the Unicorns.

Even she could tell the Unicorns were exhausted.

Why does no one do anything?

She looked around the cavern once again. The villagers of Areve were
gone somewhere further in to the Caves of Imrathalion and most of the
Sanctuary Lightborn had gone as well, though there were three or four
of them standing at the opening to the Healing caverns, their bodies
slumped with weariness and their faces lined with horror.

Of the Warhunt Mages, only Iardalaith was there. He was as far from the Otherfolk as it was possible to be, and she could not see his face, but she knew his feelings about the Otherfolk quite well indeed.

There was perhaps a demi-taille of Silver Swords also present, their mounts beside them. All were standing to horse, their gaze fixed on the fragile Unicorn line and their bodies utterly still.

The rest were Otherfolk, a great-taille and more, a few whose shapes she did not recognize. Their stillness was not readiness, but the terror that holds the rabbit motionless in the falcon's gaze. She saw Leutric and Audalo; Audalo was trying to speak to Leutric, but kept breaking off to stare fearfully at the Endarkened.

What I would not give in this moment that Runacar was hale and wakeful and could give the orders that must be given!

But he should sleep for most of a day after such a Healing. And she must solve this now, before the Unicorns collapsed and the Endarkened swarmed into the caves. They would slaughter the sick and the helpless with ease; the komen and Mages were too exhausted to even attempt to fight them. The cavern opening must be sealed. Quickly.

She must see if the Otherfolk King-Emperor would give that order. Or if she must disparage him before the whole of his court left alive.

As Vieliessar started across the chamber, a familiar weight descended upon her shoulder. "I, I, I am first and best. I am hero of a thousand battles, victorious I."

She lifted Pouncewarm from her shoulder and held him in her arms. The Palugh smiled up at her, bristling his whiskers. His fur gleamed, silken-soft and clean with no trace of blood. The warm body she held was hale and whole. "You were *lucky*," she said fiercely. "You nearly *died*. You saved my life, but—"

"First among hostages, first among warriors," Pouncewarm sang serenely. "Pretty Rune. Brave Vielle. Victorious Pouncewarm! And here is Leutric, Emperor and King, to praise me."

She had not precisely been unaware of his approach, but now Vieliessar gave Leutric her full attention.

King-Emperor Leutric, King of the Minotaurs, Lord of the House of a Thousand Doors, Emperor of all the Folk, General of Armies, Lord of the Folk of Land and Air, Kindly Regarded by the Folk of the Seas and the Waters, and Respected of the Brightfolk (to give him his full honors and titles), was a formidable individual. His hide bore the marks of many battles, and his face had turned white with age at eyes and muzzle, but his carriage was as straight as that of Audalo beside him.

The other Minotaur accompanying Leutric she had met before; Leutric's queen, Hresa. Hresa's skin was brown and white; Vieliessar had been told she was an Earthdancer, one of the Minotaur Mages. She wore gems and jewels, but if she wore signs of rank, Vieliessar could not read them, and she had already discovered to her vast annoyance that—with the exception of the Woodwose, of course—she could not hear the thoughts of the Otherfolk.

The last of the party, and clearly present as a guard, was an enormous Bearward. For now he walked on both hands and feet, but if he stood upright, he might be taller than Leutric. He carried no weapon, but his foreclaws had been polished and sharpened and capped with gleaming steel.

He is one of the Bearsarks, the Bearward clan that devotes itself wholly to battle. At Ceoprentrei they went through our defenses as if they were butter.

Vieliessar was abruptly aware that this was the meeting of two kings of vast king-domains, ancient foes to one another, and Leutric had come wearing jewels and gold, accompanied by attendants and guards, and she, High King of Elvenkind, lord of the Unicorn Throne, was wearing muddy buckskins covered in other peoples' blood, and holding a Palugh.

It seemed an unfortunate imbalance of dignity.

Pouncewarm squirmed around in her arms until he could rest both paws on her shoulder and look behind her. "Iaaaar-r-r-rdalaith!" he chirped happily. "Greenrobe Witch, and Landless King, and—"

Vieliessar squeezed Pouncewarm as hard as she unobtrusively could before he added to the catalog of Iardalaith's virtues the fact that Iardalaith would happily slit the throats of every one of the Otherfolk, including the ones who stood before her.

Iardalaith draped a cloak over her shoulders. He must have gotten it from Harwing, for it was heavy velvet in Lightborn green, its hem encrusted with embroidery and jewels (and fortunately, not adorned with any Otherfolk body parts). "Sorry I'm late," he said, for her ears alone.

"Indeed, you have done well, small one, in this great work of bringing our two peoples together," Leutric said to Pouncewarm. "I am certain King Vieliessar has benefited greatly from your wise counsel."

"You have spoken truth, lord King-Emperor," Vieliessar said. "But now there are matters more pressing, if not more important." (This last was to Pouncewarm, who purred enthusiastically.) "We were to seal the opening when all the folk had reached Imrathalion," she said mildly. "Why has it not been done?"

"We . . . we are not sure they have," Leutric began. He stopped, and started again. "There may be others still alive out there. We cannot abandon them. We must wait to be sure."

Vieliessar tried not to show the horror she felt. Her people had learned—in the hardest and bloodiest school of all—that turning back to rescue one comrade led to the death of a hundred others. If you did not abandon a comrade upon the field, then you died with them. There could be no pity, no kindness, when your enemy was the Endarkened.

"How can you weigh their lives against those who are here?" Vieliessar blurted out. "The Unicorns cannot hold much longer. We must seal the opening—"

Suddenly she felt a sharp pang in her chest, and heard Iardalaith sigh brokenly. "Arevethmonion," he whispered.

She could feel what he felt, hectare after hectare of forest turned to ash and blown away by the fire's updraft.

"We must seal the opening at once," Vieliessar continued, her tone turning harsh. "The Flower Forest Arevethmonion is burning, and soon we may no longer draw from her."

"We do not need witches to say a thing must be done and when we must do it," Hresa said, tossing her head proudly. "I can move that rock with a mere gesture, as my sisters did in the High Valleys!"

And you—and your sisters—would survive any collapses you would cause here, and we . . . would not, Vieliessar thought.

"You do not care whether you live or die," Hresa said triumphantly. "But we will not abandon our own."

"Your own what?" Tangisen and Isilla had joined Iardalaith. "Corpses?" Tangisen, too, had just come from the Healing Chambers. The tunic he wore was soaked in blood that was still fresh. "Admittedly I have only now faced the Endarkened, but I have had vast experience of the great mercy the Beastfolk show their enemies."

Isilla placed a hand on Tangisen's arm, and he stopped. Isilla shook her head resignedly at Vieliessar.

"I do not believe there is anyone left alive outside," Vieliessar said to Leutric, as if Tangisen had not spoken. She could feel the rage and grief radiating from the three Lightborn, the emotions strong enough to bring with them jumbled images of the battlefield they had recently left. "We must think of the lives we can save—those of the Unicorns and their companions."

"Elvenkind!" sneered Hresa.

"I have lost more of my folk today than you did." Vieliessar felt herself filling with the vast cold rage that could not be bargained with, the anger that always brought disaster in its wake. "They died saving *you*, at my orders. Perhaps this was a mistake that should be rectified. Now. If your folk will not freely depart this chamber so that the Unicorns may retreat, I will compel them."

Pouncewarm butted her chin with his head. Hard enough that her teeth snapped shut. Vieliessar stroked his head absently, then handed him to Iardalaith, who assisted the Palugh to mount his shoulders with the ease of long resignation.

"My lords, I am sorry," Vieliessar said. "If any of the Folk, yours or mine, remain outside, they are dead. And the Unicorns must be brought to safety."

She held out her hand to Leutric, willing him to understand.

"To *where*?" Tangisen gibed. "Do you see any place in here they can go and not be up to their little Unicorn noses in the Impure?"

"Find one," Vieliessar snarled, turning on him. Tangisen flinched back, his eyes going wide, and left quickly.

Leutric was staring at the hand she had extended to him as if it held a dagger. He took it between thumb and forefinger and turned it so that the Astromancer's ring she wore was uppermost.

"We must speak of this," Leutric said, indicating the jewel. "But for now, let us save our cousins."

⚜

If she had ever attempted to herd cats—a task which, after getting to know Pouncewarm and the other Palugh, Vieliessar was not inclined to undertake—that task would have been quicker than moving everyone out of the main cavern.

And deciding what to do next, before we all starve here.

The only delay was in finding a haven for the Unicorns and their riders, and Tangisen, well-motivated, found one within the quartermark. It was the furthest anyone had so far gone in Imrathalion: an enormous cavern nearly the size of the Dragon's Gate, and it held an equally enormous lake. The Unicorns and their riders needed more than that—as everyone here did—but at least they would no longer be holding off the Endarkened.

If they could be gotten inside.

Four tailles of Lightborn were lined up against the walls of the cavern, all touching rock and all as far away from the Unicorns in the doorway as they could manage. Kathan Lightsister had Keystone Transmute, and would be their focus. Vieliessar took the deosil terminal of the line, the place farthest from the Endarkened.

"Not you." Iardalaith plucked her loose and carried her to the far back of the cavern. Here the walls were ribbed with stone daggers that glistened like polished glass.

Vieliessar was so astonished that she stood rigid in his arms as if she were one of the stalagmites herself.

"Before you utter a single word," Iardalaith said as he set her down, "know that I am doing exactly what Thurion would do if he were here. You rode all night and fought all day and, if that were not enough, you did Magery at puissant strength and *then* decided it would be fun to spend four candlemarks bringing people back from the dead."

"I did no such—" she began, and was suddenly distracted. They both were.

The Lightborn had begun the Working.

⊟⊟

First thing: push back the Endarkened.
    Cast Cold.

The Endarkened smashed through the first four ice-walls the Lightborn built. The fifth held. There was sudden silence within the cavern as the sounds of rain and of Endarkened howls were blocked from hearing.

Then the Unicorns entered.

They were few, barely a double-taille in number, and to see such beauty muddied and bloodied and wounded by battle reduced the onlookers to tears. Many of the Unicorns had Elven riders who dismounted (those who could) the moment they reached the interior of Imrathalion. They staggered in slow progress beside their partners, their boots leaving dark sticky traces upon the stone.

Slowly, in double column, the Unicorns and their riders retreated along the path a suitably "pure" Lightborn directed them down, the arrhythmic click of hooves fading into soft overlapping echoes as they left the chamber. None was capable of more than a staggering walk.

Vieliessar could feel the anger well up where before there had only been terror: a desire to kill, to smash, to spoil those creatures who had so despoiled the Unicorns. She was not alone in her rage, and the Lightborn made certain the anger funneled itself into their Workings.

Second: seal cavern mouth.

The ice rushed into the cavern opening, sealing it shut.

Cast Transmute (strong): Ice to rock.

Ice faded to seamless stone in just the way the last ember from a fire dwindles into darkness, and the Silverlight on the walls slowly trickled down to cover it. Beneath the Silverlight, the new-made stone thrummed with Warding, strong and complex, that was slowly spreading to the stone around it.

The sense of the Endarkened's presence was fading as the spell spread. The people—Elves, Unicorns, Otherfolk—were safe. The spell was a success, but no one felt it was.

Arevethmonion was still burning. Even in the rain, Arevethmonion was burning.

The aftermath of any battle was always the same: count the costs, heal the wounded, praise the victory, and prepare for the next fight. Iardalaith went to succor the Lightborn who had lent their energies to the spell, and Vieliessar looked around for Helecanth. She wished desperately to simply lie down and sleep, but there were too many things she must do—like discover how Leutric had come to wear a copy more than twin to the Astromancer's ring.

She must be awake, alert, and for those things she needed Light. To draw from the Shrine directly was—as she had told herself over and over this day—unutterably dangerous, yet Vieliessar . . .

I have a choice, and I choose this. My work this night is not yet done.

As she pulled the wonder of the Shrine's harsh inexhaustible power to herself yet again, Vieliessar could feel something that was almost a presence, shielding her from the Shrine even as it compelled her to tap it. Its power wiped away hunger, hurt, and exhaustion, it left her mind clear and decisive and her body eager for work. Whatever price it asked for this bounty she would pay, so long as it gave her the will to carry Amretheon's *geasa* forward in the now.

For the first time in her life, Vieliessar could sense that *geasa* as something separate from herself. Its weight had never been harder to bear, and the demands it made were so absolute and extreme that they left very little room for her own volition. Its demand was clear: she must fuse their two races, Elvenkind and Otherfolk, and make them one. In all the turns of the Wheel she had planned to reign as High King, in all the Wheelturns she *had* reigned as High King, she had never considered sharing her power with someone—no matter their race or lineage—she must treat as equal.

But as she looked around the now-quiet, now-empty main chamber, she could tell that—save within the Healing Chambers—Elvenkind and Otherfolk had separated themselves as fully and utterly as if it had been both ordered and ordained: the Otherfolk to the deeper deosil caverns and shafts, Elvenkind to a series of tuathal chambers that connected to the Healing rooms. Even though this in itself was progress toward alli-

ance on a scale Vieliessar could never have hoped for even a moonturn
ago, it was far from the goal she saw in her mind. For that, she must
meet, and soon, with Leutric so that they could decide—jointly—how
they were to proceed.

"My lord, your bath is ready." Helecanth returned and touched Vieliessar's shoulder gently. "And suitable clothing has been found. Come.
You need not stand about like the last of the *khom* at Festival Fair."

"A *hot* bath, I hope," she said, and Helecanth smiled.

"One of the Lightborn has sunk a hot spring in one of the empty
chambers. It gives a welcome heat to cold stone. Come," Helecanth repeated.

The hot spring was large, and occupied by a taille of Lightborn—all
Warhunt—who ignored Vieliessar and Helecanth aside from making
space for them in the pool. Every face was drawn with weariness—
Tangisen, Dinias, Pendray, Harwing—and some were streaked with
tears.

The water felt so wonderful Vieliessar nearly sent word that Leutric
should meet her here, but she supposed it was beneath the dignity of a
king to do something like that. Dinner was served (as Harwing said) *sar
abadzh*: above (or with) the water. There was soup made from trailfood
(held in mugs Transmuted from cloth), and the villagers had been induced to share their provisions, so there was bread and cheese and tea
as well. Pouncewarm, Shadowdance, and another Palugh named Cloudfoot stalked back and forth along the edge of the pool, making grumbly
mutters of disproval at this unseemly form of bathing.

One by one the other Lightborn exited the pool. But no more persons
entered, and Vieliessar knew full well that even if there were a dozen hot
springs, they would all be empty.

It was time to go.

As Vieliessar climbed out of the pool, the Palugh—their numbers now
increased to six—retreated to resume their pacing and complaints at a
safer distance. Isilla came forward with a towel. Vieliessar's eyebrows rose
in surprise at the sight.

"It's astonishing what the Lightless carried with them as they fled
from certain death," Isilla said, blandly, as she wrapped the cloth around

Vieliessar's shoulders. "I appointed Jorganroch as Quartermaster, since they will all defer to a Lightborn—poor thing; he needed a distraction: Alasneh is dead."

"Are you certain?" It was instant, automatic, the first question the survivors of an Endarkened attack asked. *Are they dead? Are you sure? Did you see it?* Death was a blessing compared to what captivity might offer.

"She burned herself to death as that *thing* tried to fly away with her. Are these what Amretheon sent you to destroy?" Vieliessar heard the words Isilla didn't say: *How are you going to defeat them?*

"They are indeed the Darkness against which Amretheon Aradruiniel warned us in a spectacularly unuseful fashion," Vieliessar answered bitterly. "And which he somehow assumed I could easily defeat. It was perhaps a fraction optimistic of him."

Isilla's expression was halfway between a smile and a wince. She turned away to collect the extravagant robes Vieliessar was to wear, now cleaned and (where necessary) mended by Magery.

Stockings, garters, high-heeled embroidered slippers, first undergown, second undergown (both transparent silk), long tunic, first sash (both samite), short tunic (fine wool, embroidered with silver and pearls), long open robe (fine wool with appliqué work), second sash (linen, embroidered in colored wool and elvensilver sequins), long outer robe (silk velvet) . . . And every thread of it (save some of the embroidery) was virulent Lightborn green. Vieliessar was developing a distaste for the color—awkward, as she had taken it for the High King's color as well.

She had never worn such robes in her days as Lightborn: such elaborate garb might possibly have been suitable for a Lightborn acting as envoy between fractious High Houses, or to the Astromancer presiding over the springtime sacrifices at the Shrine of the Star—but she had seen Hamphuliadiel and many Lightborn performing both offices (before she had fled the Sanctuary) and none had worn anything like this. She wondered if these elaborate garments were a symptom of Hamphuliadiel's madness. She was certain the ridiculous hat had been. Fortunately, it seemed to have been a casualty of the battle. She only wished the stave had been lost as well. She had no intention of carrying it.

But as Vieliessar donned the extravagant robes of office, she discovered that she *really did* need the Astromancer's stave. The world spun crazily as she raised her hand to turn a section of the cavern wall into a mirror. Isilla grabbed for her with one hand and the stave with the other.

Vieliessar snatched at the power of the Shrine, only to find it slip through her grasp as a ribbon through cold-numbed fingers. Perhaps there was some maximum amount she could draw from it—and that maximum she had already passed. Or perhaps she was simply too benumbed by exhaustion to capture the power of the Shrine as she had before.

She could not even feel Arevethmonion now.

But she could move, and think, and speak. And so she must go on for as long as she could. Tomorrow's problems were as urgent as today's.

Helecanth took charge of the Astromancer's glowing stave in an eloquent silence. She too was dressed in clothes that had been made new and clean, though not in finery to rival her mistress's.

"I know you are High King and cannot stop and rest now and there are many things to do, and the Beast King has come so you must speak with him, but you *must* have rest, and—and—and *tea*!" Isilla said.

"As soon as I may," Vieliessar promised. "Don't worry, sister. I am tired, nothing more. And if I am tired, you must be exhausted."

Her answer was a rude snort. "I walked all the way from the Shore to the Sanctuary on winter roots and bits of boiled rabbit. I have new standards for tired and hungry, I assure you!"

"I think we both must have." Vieliessar hesitated. "Silla, you have been at the Shore this past decade, where you fought the Otherfolk. You return to discover we are making an alliance with them. Does it not bother you?"

Isilla had been trying to coax Pouncewarm into petting distance. She straightened up quickly, looking guilty. "I am from a Landbond family, my lord King," she said at last.

Vieliessar remembered a time long ago, and a conversation she was not meant to overhear.

"Says the gentle Craftworker's daughter," Isilla jeered.

"*Have you yet washed the mud out of your hair, Landbond brat?*" Aradreleg instantly responded.

"Did your family leave out offerings to the Little Gods?" Vieliessar said softly.

"Yes. It is why I live," Isilla said. In quick words, she told the tale: the fourth child, left in the forest in hopes the Little Gods would take them in, for the family could not feed them. When she was born, her father took the infant Isilla to the place the Landbonds left their meager offerings for the Little Gods, only to find there a gift instead.

"There were blankets and swaddling-bands—Oh! You have never seen work so fine!—and a honeycomb, and *meat* . . . My father brought me home again, and my parents kept me."

"And then you became Lightborn," Vieliessar said.

"Yes," Isilla said. "And here we are. And how *could* you?" Isilla said, sounding slightly hurt. "You could have told *us*. Not the komen, of course. But we're Lightborn. We're your family. We would follow you even if you were Soulbonded to a-a-a *Bearward*!"

If the Lightborn know I am Soulbonded, do they also know I cannot have borne my heirs? Vieliessar thought wildly. Outwardly she showed no sign of panic. She had learned impenetrable poise in the hardest of schools. "It is bad enough that it is Caerthalien," she said, hugging Isilla to her. "I knew anyone I told would have been in danger, even if only from those who knew there was a secret to be had. It was not *your* knowing I feared."

Isilla sighed resignedly and forced a smile. "Then all that needs be done is for everyone to become Lightborn, and the world will be much more civilized."

"I shall tell Leutric you have said so," Vieliessar said. "And should it be that the madman who is my Bondmate tries to leave the Healing Chamber, get his Cadet to come and sit on him. She is a Centaur. That will serve."

"I will." This time Isilla's answering smile was unforced.

Helecanth, go you ahead and see if you can find where the King-Emperor's embassy lies. If there are Lightborn in the Great Chamber, send them elsewhere: we wish the Endarkened to grow tired of waiting for us."

"Iardalaith has said they have not confined their destruction to us. They also lay siege to Nomaitemil, but so far they have had not success."

Vieliessar had known that might happen. In fact, she had based some of her strategy upon it, for a divided enemy was a weakened enemy. She nearly asked Helecanth why so many of the Endarkened had simply left—rather than besieging either Imrathalion or Nomaitemil—before she stopped herself: neither Helecanth nor Iardalaith could know the answer to that question.

Helecanth and Isilla both having left upon her orders, Vieliessar left the hot spring cavern and started down the narrow cross-passage that led back to the main chamber. Behind her she could hear the faint homely whuffle of bodies moving in the direction of the hot spring, now that she had removed her royal self from it.

To be the High King affects the lives of others even when I do or say nothing, for my people have their own ideas of what a High King should be and will not rest until I agree with them. I fear that Pelashia will come again ere I do.

The passageway back to the main cavern, though brightly lit, was narrow, and so it seemed to be both bright and dark at once. When Vieliessar first heard the sound, she thought someone must be singing and an auditory quirk of the caves carried the sound to her so clearly. Unconsciously, she found herself stopping to listen.

It was a strange music. It fell upon the ear as if into silence, rich and haunting and unknown. Who was singing? Why? Whoever they were, the song was one Vieliessar had never heard before and could not recreate. Each note vanished from the mind as quickly as the song vanished from the hearing, leaving behind only the yearning to hear more.

She stood spellbound. She must know who was singing, and why.

Then out of the corner of her eye she saw a shadowy shape rush toward her. She spun instantly, drawing her dagger, and barely stopped herself from murdering a young Lightborn.

"Vieliessar Lightsister!" Erendor gasped, clutching at her robe. "I'd hoped you might be— Is it true? Is he dead? I must know!"

Her attacker was no attacker at all—merely a very young Sanctuary Lightborn who had been desperate to speak with her. He could barely have been a child when the High King's War began.

"Gently, Erendor Lightbrother," she said, removing his hand from her sleeve. Vieliessar was more amused than anything—despite the gravity of the situation—that in his distress Erendor had apparently forgotten she was High King. "Our teachers would censure both of us to see you in this state, for truly they have said: *'The Lightborn calm by their very presence. In war they are serene. In conflict they are tranquil. In argument they are silent.'* Now tell me, what is this matter that distresses you?"

The boy gazed at her with wide panicked eyes. "It is my lord Astromancer—I have been searching for him since I got here. I can't find him anywhere!"

A number of different thoughts flashed instantly through Vieliessar's mind. Harwing had been working—as Harwing—in the makeshift Healing Chambers. He had announced to her that Hamphuliadiel had died gallantly in battle. Even if she chose to repudiate the story for some other, Harwing could not be expected to carry on the Hamphuliadiel masquerade. The Otherfolk might not even see the illusion; their magics ran far differently than that of the Lightborn. And in addition to all other things, Vieliessar needed the Sanctuary's Lightborn's allegiance focused on her, not Hamphuliadiel.

"I bring to you sad and glorious news, Erendor Lightbrother," Vieliessar said gravely. "Some of what I would say must forever remain our secret. Will you hear my words?"

Erendor gulped and nodded.

"Hamphuliadiel of Bethros, last Astromancer of the Sanctuary of the Star, has gone to live in the Warm World," Vieliessar said gently. "He need not have died, but he sacrificed himself to save others. I myself fought beside him against the Endarkened. Over and over I urged him to seek safety, but he said to me that he would go only when all his Lightborn were safe, for he was always a one to place all others before himself."

"Yes, that was always his way," Erendor agreed shakily. "You— You knew him well, Lightsister?"

In the back of Vieliessar's mind, there was a whisper of mocking laughter, as unlike the singing as honey to salt.

"I served at the Sanctuary for nearly all of his reign, Erendor, and he was often in my thoughts," she answered truthfully. "And today, when at last he reached safe haven, he went straight from the battlefield to the Healing Chambers to succor the wounded. No one who saw him there realized he had been injured on the field. Having given so much of himself, he only thought to give more. He died as he would have wished, helping others to live."

Erendor nodded, gulping as his eyes filled with tears. "But— But— Lightsister, why may I not say to the others that he is dead?"

In truth, Vieliessar couldn't think of a single good reason. She'd only hoped that swearing Erendor to secrecy would keep the story from spreading before she'd warned Harwing. But now inspiration struck.

"There was no one present when he collapsed," she said. "Only Harwing Lightbrother and I. When we reached his side, we discovered he was dead. As we touched his body, it began to glow, and soon it was too bright to look upon. And then he was gone. The Light took him into itself, and now they are one."

"I—I think I understand," Erendor said slowly. "He would not want tales of miracles to make us think of him and not the Light. But I—I thank you for trusting me."

"I do not think my trust is misplaced," she answered solemnly. "Now I must go. And you must sleep. Fare you well, Lightbrother."

Erendor bobbed his head and stumbled off. Vieliessar gazed after him for a moment in bemusement, the laughter of a woman ten thousand years dead echoing in her ears.

❧

Iardalaith, Helecanth, Githachi, and Pouncewarm were waiting for Vieliessar in the main chamber, which was otherwise empty save for some Wulvers who were obviously in charge of making sure the Endarkened didn't manage to burrow through the Mage-created rock, and two of the Silver Swords there to keep watch over the Wulvers.

Helecanth stood impassively, Githachi sat on the floor, and Iardalaith paced back and forth like an irritated cat, followed at every step by Pouncewarm.

"I bring you miraculous tidings," Vieliessar said. When she stopped, Pouncewarm bounded over to her and began stropping himself against her ankles as if he were a cat in truth. "Hamphuliadiel Astromancer has gone to the Warm World." She drew the Astromancer's ring from her finger, and tossed it into the air, catching it and replacing it on her finger. "With his dying breath, he begged me to serve as his successor."

"Harwing will hold Festival Fair when he hears," Iardalaith commented.

"I am pleased to hear it," Vieliessar said. "Githachi, how fare your horses?"

"Well enough," the Commander of the Silver Swords answered. "We managed to save most of them—and so, most of our supplies, but that is fodder for a sunturn or two. A sennight if we are very careful."

"I can hope we find a way out of here before that," Vieliessar answered. *And that the rain quenches the fires the Endarkened have set, for we dare not attempt to work the weather from here.* She did not have to ask to know Arevethmonion still burned; she felt the ache in her chest like a fresh bruise. "We shall begin tomorrow. Helecanth, how are the Lightless villagers?"

"Panicked and squalling like kittens," Helecanth said. "I have guards posted on them. About half of them made it to the caverns, but that's still a sizable number of people—they outnumber the rest of us more than ten to one. They have water and braziers and a few blankets, but nothing much in the way of food."

"Will they follow orders?" Vieliessar asked.

"Probably," Helecanth said. "Whether they will follow them *well* is another matter. Most of them lost children in Arevethmonion—I'm told they simply vanished in the night."

"The Woodwose might have taken them," Githachi said hesitantly.

"I wish we could be sure of that. We could tell them so. But I don't want to lie to them." *Only to Lightborn like Erendor.* "Just tell them we will search for their children as soon as it is safe—and that if those children are within the Flower Forest, as we presume them to still be, they are wholly protected from the monsters that attacked us today."

Iardalaith smirked. She knew what he was thinking. *"As opposed to the monsters we're allied with."* But his heart wasn't in it, she could tell.

"How many Lightborn are ready and able to fight?" Vieliessar asked him.

"Of the Warhunt, maybe half—if you ask tomorrow. Of Hamphuli-adiel's precious pets, it's hard to say. Give me a moonturn to work with them and I can give you a better answer."

Vieliessar sighed. It was what she'd expected. The Lightborn who had spent the last decade fighting beside her—and being free, and allowed to do whatever research in Magery they chose—were a far different thing from the Lightborn Hamphuliadiel had crafted to serve his whim.

"How many are affected by the burning of Arevethmonion? And by the presence of the Endarkened?" Through the wards, through the stone, she could still feel them, though faintly, like an old bruise.

"In the fight? A third of the Sanctuary Mages were too incapacitated to defend themselves; a third could run away, but little more. The last third could fight back—because they were utterly terrified—but they didn't seem to know a lot of the basics. They had Lightning, but they had to Call Storm to use it. I didn't see any of them Cast Thunderbolt. Now? None of them can sense anything through the wards, Arevethmonion's burning included."

Vieliessar did her best not to sigh aloud. "Githachi, see you to your komen and your horses. Iardalaith, make sure there are no surprises—guard the Lightless, watch over the wards, and do not permit trouble to arise between our folk and the Otherfolk." The Sanctuary Mages had seen Hamphuliadiel pledge fealty to Vieliessar earlier in the day, but a lot had happened since then.

"A promotion." Iardalaith bowed. "I must see about asking Adalieriel for her hand in marriage."

Vieliessar wasn't sure whether to be irritated or charmed by that.

She settled for being weary. "If there is trouble, find me. For now, I shall be with Leutric. I shall send word when that changes. Helecanth, walk with me."

⧓

There were two sets of passages leading out of the main cavern—the ones on the tuathal hand led into the network of interlocking chambers that had been converted into Healing and recovery areas, while the deosil side held a lengthy corridor. Someone had clearly done a great deal of work on these caves—and not merely to make them more useful for aging wines and cheeses.

Like so many things lately, it was a mystery Vieliessar did not have the time to unravel—even though its solution might well be the thing that could save her people.

Their peoples.

The walls glowed, of course—whatever its former use, these chambers had become well used to Elven Magery, and had eagerly drunk from the Lightborn to refresh themselves.

Pouncewarm bounded ahead, stopping intermittently to sit and stare back at them. His eyes glowed green in the dimness of the cave passageway.

"The, ah, the Court of the Otherfolk lies ahead," Helecanth said awkwardly. "The majority of them are gathered by race, most being Centaurs and Bearwards, along this sequence of chambers. I do not know how many they began with, but a great-taille and five remain. Leutric holds court in the outermost chamber of *wusha tawilat*."

String of pearls, Vieliessar thought. *Connected chambers.* They could probably put together enough of the Old Tongue to converse in, and the Otherfolk were unlikely to know it. And: *Seventeen tailles. About two hundred people. Their losses were proportionate. But ours were far higher.*

"Heeeere!" trilled Pouncewarm, stopping before an opening in the rock.

"My lord," Helecanth said, stepping back so that Vieliessar could enter first. Pouncewarm trotted importantly behind her, then bounded ahead.

❧❦❧

There were several large carpets laid out in the middle of the chamber. Their work was fine, but the colors and symbols were wholly unfamiliar to Vieliessar. Leutric and Audalo sat in their center—putting them roughly at eye-level with her—and behind them was the Bearward guardsman. Hresa and her Earthdancers were nowhere to be seen.

Around and behind them were Otherfolk she did not know, but clearly royalty of their kind. There was a black Palugh wearing a pendant necklace, a Wulver and his lady, two Centaurs—one of whom was Pelere—Fauns, a single Hippogriff looking very out of place underground, a young Woodwose whose winter tatters served as good camouflage here in the cave, and a cluster of tiny creatures who looked like Elves but stood less than five hands high.

The braziers that had been left here by the previous users had been filled and lit, and there were torches in the wall brackets, so the chamber was filled with the homely scent of wood smoke and spices. Lightborn might say that Silverlight was better, but Vieliessar preferred the honest red-gold glow of true fire.

"Greetings, Lord King-Emperor Leutric," she said.

"And greetings to you, too." Runacarendalur Caerthalien had been hidden by the bulk of the Minotaurs until he got to his feet. "I thought it would be unchivalrous to let you be the only War Prince working themselves into an exhausted coma," he added. "And by the way, here are Queen Ivory Claws of the Palugh; the Wulverking Leaps the Moon and his lady, Guards the Fire; Llydlis, Foremost of the Hippogriffs; Torvald, War-born of the Centaurs; Ranolf, Lord of the Bearwards; Jinxt, Mischief in Chief of the Fauns; Quickneedle, Planmaker of the Brownies; and Tylor, Speaker for the Woodwose. All are sworn in fealty to King-Emperor Leutric, King of the Minotaurs, Lord of the House of a Thousand Doors, Emperor of all the Folk, General of Armies, Lord of the Folk of Land and Air, Kindly Regarded by the Folk of the Seas and the Waters, and Respected of the Brightfolk."

Pouncewarm danced forward and began to climb Runacar as if he were a tree. Runacar hissed at the pain and picked Pouncewarm up and set the Palugh on his shoulders.

Vieliessar opened her mouth to answer, then shut it again. She bowed low to all the company, acknowledging their status, then directed her attention toward Leutric.

"I see your Battlemaster continues to be valuable to you," she said.

"Indeed he has been, and we thank you for caring for him as you did. The speed of your peoples' healing arts is impressive to us. We do not possess its equal."

"The Bearward Healers brought me back from the dead after the siege of the Shore though," Runacar said helpfully. "So don't assume you're better than they are."

She could feel through their Bond that he was reasonably content: not afraid, not in pain, neither cold nor hungry, and just as much in the dark about why Leutric had summoned him to be here as she was. She favored his comment with a basilisk glare that would have done credit to Lannarien's possibly imaginary creature. "I need only be acknowledged better than *you,* and I will be quite content," Vieliessar answered tartly. "Emperor Leutric, we will be happy to share any arts we possess of Healing—and our Healers as well. It is not impossible that some of your people might become Lightborn—we are all one kin, as you must know."

There! She'd said it. Or at least implied it.

"Come. Sit," Leutric said kindly. "These are matters that must be discussed, truly, as well as the final terms of the alliance that we both hope for. But I would begin with the matter of the ring we both wear."

At his invitation, Vieliessar sat facing Leutric. The Lightborn robes made this easier than if she wore full armor, though armor would have been more soothing. Helecanth took up a standing pose behind her, hand on her sword.

"This?" Vieliessar asked, tugging the ring off her finger again. "It's traditionally worn by the Astromancer, but it's just a keepsake, really. It doesn't even have any magic."

"So you're Astromancer now? That's convenient," Runacar said.

"Far more so than leaving the authority in the hands of one whom I would then have to fight," Vieliessar answered. She held out the ring to Leutric, who took it carefully.

"And did you?" Audalo asked, speaking for the first time.

"No. He was already dead before I had the chance," Vieliessar answered regretfully. She was not certain she would have killed Hamphuliadiel—but she would certainly have burned his Magery from him, and laughed as she did it.

Leutric took off his own ring in turn and held them side by side. The Astromancer's ring would pass easily through the band of the other, yet the stones and mountings were entirely the same. Even the stones were the same size. "No magic, you say?"

A thrill of warning passed through Vieliessar's body. Leutric knew something.

"None," she said. "It is a mark of rank only."

"Then you shall try mine, and I yours, in token of alliances yet to come." Leutric held out his ring to her.

It's only a ring, she thought. It was still warm from his hand. She held it for a moment, then slipped it onto her forefinger, closing her hand into a fist to keep it in place.

"Little barbarian," Lady Indinathiel hissed in her mind. *"You'll be wearing a bit and bridle next!"*

The ring on Vieliessar's finger slipped sideways—as she had expected—and then it . . . fit. She looked up. Leutric was wearing her ring on the littlest finger of his left hand, just as he had his own.

"It is only a minor instance of an Adapt spell," she said gently, not wishing to upset him. Nearly every Lightborn had dealt with the need to disillusion someone who came to them with a family heirloom that they were certain was a powerful object of Magery. "It—"

It means nothing, she'd been about to say. But suddenly she realized she was hearing music again—had been hearing music for some time before she had become consciously aware of it—a haunting exotic melody that did not resolve into a tune. Just as if the sound had only been waiting for her to notice it, it grew in complexity and volume, disclosing itself to be a song sung by . . .

Who?

No one else reacted. Not even Runacar. Vieliessar was the only one who heard the singing. If she had not heard the same singing in the corridor where she met Erendor, she would instantly have suspected a trick related to the exchange of rings—if not something more sinister. She glanced past Leutric toward the back of the cavern, where a narrow opening was visible. Was the singer there?

"Oh come now, girl, you've been 'hearing voices' for nigh on to a dozen Wheelturns now," Ghostlord Zenderian whispered to her. *"Give up and let us rule you. You will be happier."*

Never! she thought back.

"—It does not mean the ring the rings—are of any great power," she finished clumsily. "I cannot imagine that the hundred Astromancers who wore this one would have failed to discover its power."

"The Elven Witchlords are not the source and destination of all Magery," Runacar said with fake pompously. "Oh, forgive my manners: *surely* I meant to say 'the Children of Stars.'"

"*Surely* you meant to say nothing at all, Runacar Battlemaster," Vieliessar retorted. "*I* say that all Magery, whether *alfaljodthi* or otherwise, can be sensed by another Mage. If it could not, the Endarkened would not be able to strike us down by their mere proximity."

Vieliessar knew she was perilously close to arguing with Runacar, and that was not what she had come here to do. If she could not put an agreement to a simple truce into place this night, tomorrow their peoples would be at daggers drawn.

It would be a simple matter if the only Elves here in Imrathalion were the Silver Swords and the Warhunt—they were already coming to accept the Otherfolk, and would certainly cooperate under these circumstances. But there were the villagers and the Sanctuary Mages—who greatly outnumbered those two elements of her forces—to consider. The villagers might be easily cowed to obedience, but it would be the Sanctuary Mages who cowed them, not the High King—and all that the villagers knew of the Otherfolk was that they were the monsters of their nursery tales.

She wished Thurion were here. He was full of good common sense, and not in the least overawed by the mantle of *the Child of the Prophecy* she reluctantly wore. She wanted to look over her shoulder at Helecanth, to get some sense of what her friend—and the Captain of her personal guard—was thinking, but she could not do so without seeming obvious about it.

"There is much I wish to tell you," Leutric said. "But first, I am advised to present you with tea."

I will flay you alive and roll you in salt and honey before I stake you out on an anthill, Prince of Caerthalien! She glared at Runacar. He smirked as he picked up a large basket from behind Audalo, and set it down in front of her.

"It's much more fun than you might think to sack your own castel," he said brightly. "Caerthalien Great Keep itself had been taken—several times—and was standing open, but I knew the layout and previous thieves didn't. I found a number of useful things in the sub-sub-sub-cellar. Including a tea set."

While she had been distracted by the byplay, the singing had stopped again. She turned her attention to Runacar's offering. She expected it was meant to annoy her—he seemed to have a gift for it.

The basket was of commonplace everyday woven reeds; sturdy and disposable. She opened the lid. The first item that met her gaze was a simple woven straw case, of considerably finer workmanship than the basket that contained it. Inside the straw case were eight round cherry-bark canisters with corkwood tops, and they were true treasures, glorious beyond price. She picked one up and tilted it; the torches in the chamber were not quite strong enough to illuminate the surface, but as she turned it inquisitively in her hands she was rewarded by a flash of elvensilver. The costly metal had been applied so delicately and sparingly to the bark of the canister that it was barely visible, using the grain it adorned to create an image that would only reveal itself fully after long and careful study. She opened it and sniffed the tea inside: Fog and Moon. She quickly examined the other canisters one by one. All contained tea, and costly and rare blendings at that: Bright Mornings. Autumn Wood. Rest after Sorrow. Night Forest. First Snow. Accession.

And Accession is made with Vilya fruit, which means these blendings may be more than a century old—but as fresh as the day they were prepared!

She replaced the canisters in their places and set the straw box aside. Beneath the padding that concealed the next layer were six shin'zuruf cups and their matching pot. The tea-set must have been ancient—the War Princes had lost interest in the way of tea long before Luthilion Araphant had leapt his fire. When she held one of the cups up to the light, the delicate bone-clay revealed an image. It was too dim to make out in this light, and she quickly set the cup back into its place. She prodded the lambswool wadding hopefully, but the rest of the pieces—the discards bowl and the sweets plate, the poison-tasting spoon and the indoor serving tray—weren't here. Even so, each single cup was a treasure worth a blooded destrier.

"I wonder who explained to you that this was beautiful," she said. She had meant only to prick him a little, but instead the barb struck deep. She saw Runacar's face go still, and felt his sorrow.

"He's dead. Never mind," Runacar said. Through the Soulbond she caught a glorious sensation of flight on golden wings and a name: *Radafa.*

"I am sorry," she said truthfully. "I must always remember that we all have lost friends in this war."

Runacar turned his face away, unwilling to speak. *We only seem to hurt one another, don't we?* Vieliessar thought. *Better we spend the rest of our lives far, far apart, my Bonded.*

She returned her attention to Leutric, as she must. "I thank you for the opportunity to see such a treasure, but I do not know if there is time tonight for tea," Vieliessar said regretfully, replacing the padding and the straw chest and closing the basket.

"I suppose not," Audalo said regretfully, glancing toward Leutric. "I have come to enjoy the experience of Elven tea very much."

"Should you wish to perform tea as well as drink it," Vieliessar said, "I myself will be honored to instruct you."

"If we don't all starve to death down here or get lost in the caves," Runacar muttered.

Leutric and Audalo both burst into startled laughter. The sound boomed from the walls of the chamber. Runacar looked as puzzled as she.

"Lost! In a *cave*!" Audalo could barely get the words out. He took several deep breaths to compose himself. "Oh, Rune," he said at last. "After all this time: *Really*?"

"Our kind does not get lost in the House of a Thousand Doors," Leutric said kindly, to answer Vieliessar's confusion. "So you may rest easy. The way may be long, or blocked, or simply impassable, but it can always be found—and reshaped by our Earthdancers, as necessary."

"That makes good hearing," Vieliessar said. "I hope you and your folk will be willing to show us a way through Imrathalion to Nomaitemil. Many of my folk are old, or sick, and unprepared for a winter march. And yet even this is less important than that which I sought you out to learn."

"The rings," Leutric said, nodding. "My father, and his father, and his, down an unbroken line to the morning of the world, told me there had once been two, but that the other was lost. It was said they belonged to Mosirinde Truefriend and her consort, Arilcarion War-Maker. It was she who gave her ring to my great-sire. There are legends surrounding the two, of course. I think perhaps they are meant to be together."

He removed his ring and held it out to her. She took it and slipped it onto her finger beside the other, and as before, the ring adapted to her finger. She gazed down at the two translucent blue stones. She felt as if they were becoming transparent beneath her gaze, as might a Scrying stone. It was with an effort that she returned her attention to Leutric's face.

"If they are, then it is with you they must lodge," she said regretfully, removing both rings. She offered them to Leutric, who shook his head slightly, and so she set them on the rug in front of her. Pouncewarm poked at one of them speculatively, then sat back, unimpressed. "It was not the rings that concerned me, though they are indeed a riddle I would wish to solve—and given time I would wish to learn more of your legends. I came to speak to you of the weapon you hold in trust—the one only Elvenkind can wield. The one that can defeat the Endarkened."

"Go on," Leutric said neutrally.

I wish now I had agreed to the tea, she thought unhappily. *It would have given me more time to assess my . . . opponent.*

"It has been said that you would rather all of the Otherfolk die than give Elvenkind this weapon. You believe that no matter our intentions—*my* intentions—it would fall into the hands of those who would use it to harm you more terribly than we already have. I could promise that we and you would live as we did before the first Red Winnowing, but such promises can only be proven over time, and we do not have time. Here and now the Endarkened are more than legend and history preserved by your Loremasters. You have seen them, and seen what they can do. Is it not worth risking the future to save those who suffer in the present?"

There was silence for a long moment, then Leutric spoke. "You promise we would live as one people. Horse and hawk and hound live among you. Do you treat them as you would your brothers?"

"Better, usually," Runacar said. "The beasts are of some use. Our children are not."

"The Lightborn—most of us—know well what it means to be valued as beasts are valued, for their parents were chattel of the War Princes. I have freed both Landbond and Lightborn, and I have set beside them my Law Lords, who enforce my laws over highborn and low. I have sworn that there is one justice for Lord and Landbond, and none shall own another, and I have kept that promise these many Wheelturns, even as we were hunted and harried by the Endarkened and a return to the old ways might have seemed easier to many. Your folk would receive the same justice as my own. Prince Calanor will rule my people after me. I vow that he will be taught to accept you for what you are: our cousins. I will ensure it, by any means required."

"You would bargain away a child's future for a weapon?" Audalo asked curiously.

"No child has any future now," Vieliessar answered. "Calanor is to be High King. He knows already that the Kingship is a thing of duty, sacrifice, and service."

"Yet children change as they grow, and forget old friendships. Alliances—and treaties—are built on more than the light loves of childhood. You spoke once to Audalo of hostages. What hostages will you give for what you seek?" Leutric asked.

Vieliessar felt a thrill of excitement. Here, now, in the worst possible time and in the worst of places, the true treaty would be made. There would be no pomp, no ceremony, no crowds of witnesses—only two kings, thinking and speaking as kings must. As emperors must. As the Child of Prophecy must.

Celelioniel worried that my birth was omen of the end of our people. The Starry Hunt said I had come to end it. They may both have been more correct than I knew. . . .

"You already have the greatest of my hostages," Vieliessar said steadily. "Runacarendalur Caerthalien, your Battlemaster, is my destined Bondmate. We are Soulbonded to one another and there is no breaking that tie. If one of us dies, no matter how far separated we are, the other will die as well. Within sunturns at least. Moonturns at most. Possibly within candlemarks. My parents, Serenthon and Nataranweiya, were Bondmates. Lord Serenthon was slain by one who had broken faith with him—"

"She means my father," Runacar interjected.

"—and Nataranweiya lived barely long enough to reach a place to birth me where I would not be immediately slain," Vieliessar finished, as if Runacar had not spoken.

"Is this true?" Leutric asked Runacar.

"It is," Runacar said. "And before she offers you any of her children, my lord, know that they are not her children. Bondmates only bear to each other. 'Her' children are a trick she played on her nobles to ensure their loyalty."

She had thought once that she could no longer be surprised—or hurt—by anyone she knew. Not because they loved her, or were loyal— she had learned to the last measure how flexible both love and loyalty could be. But because they were *known* to her, in all their aspects.

She had thought Runacar would not use the truths she had given him against her.

"Yet I have loved them and raised them and treated them no differently than I would treat a child of my body. *They are my children.* And I would sacrifice them to the Starry Rade with my own hands if it would buy me victory over the Endarkened. This is a thing a king must do—that a prince may be ignorant of," she added, regarding Runacar stonily. *You are no king. You are a king's hound.*

"Then for this weapon you say I possess, were I to offer it to you, you would give these children to be raised in my court?" Leutric asked.

"I would. I would hope that you would not mistreat them—but even if you told me I condemned them to a lifetime of slavery and abuse, I would still make that bargain. I am the king of *all* my people, and we will *all* die if we do not have a weapon against the Endarkened. Including those children, *Leutric's Battlemaster,* whom you say are not mine."

Runacar regarded her unflinchingly. The Soulbond roiled with emotions, but Vieliessar could not say whether they were hers or his. She pushed them away as best she could.

"And if I told you this weapon which you seek is no weapon but a curse?" Leutric said, his tone still mild.

"I would say to you that I am Child of the Prophecy. The whole of my life has been a curse. Death turns aside from me to take instead those who love me—who have been *compelled* to love me, against their wills. Amretheon's *geasa* rules my life, rules everyone and everything I know. Curse me as you wish, Lord Leutric. Your curse cannot be more terrible than Amretheon's."

She had risen to her knees as she spoke. Behind Leutric, the Bearward, too, rose to his full height. Vieliessar heard a scraping behind her as Helecanth loosened her sword in its sheath.

"Rune is pretty. Vieliessar is valiant. Leutric is wise. Why fight?" Pouncewarm sneezed vigorously several times and trotted away from Vieliessar to leap into Runacar's lap.

"'*Rune*' is pretty—and in love with a Unicorn," Vieliessar agreed dryly. "Else I would have offered up a child of my body and his begetting."

Inwardly she fumed: Pouncewarm had interrupted when she had

512   MERCEDES LACKEY AND JAMES MALLORY

nearly coaxed Leutric to commit himself. She would have to begin all over again. "*Vieliessar* is fighting a losing war. And Vieliessar is cold, and hungry, and very tired. Give me the weapon or say you will not! And if you will do neither, kindly allow me to go and get some sleep."

She could not believe she had spoken those words. They were not pacific, they were not conciliating . . .

And they were not what I meant to say! This time she was not sure whether there was singing, or merely a ringing in her ears. She shut it out ruthlessly as she settled back into position. King Leutric would not negotiate now, but if she could salvage the situation, she might be able to bring him to negotiations again.

And I pray the Light that would be soon, for we are out of time.

Her head hurt. She wanted some target for her anger and frustration. Runacar would do nicely, but that would only offend Leutric even further. If she had even offended him just now. Runacar would know. He should be on her side—*at* her side, aiding her . . .

I do not want him! I do not want the Soulbond!

She gathered herself together in preparation for standing, organizing in her mind the words that would allow her to end their conversation gracefully and leave open the promise of another meeting.

"My first condition: both of your children to be fostered at my court until they are adult, beginning at once," Leutric said abruptly. Vieliessar took a deep breath, trying to mask her shock. She could not believe that Leutric had chosen this moment—*this* moment!—to begin negotiating in earnest, but she would not waste this chance. "I give no assurances as to their treatment," he went on, "but should they die, my House will pay a penalty to be negotiated later."

"Agreed," Vieliessar said instantly. "Their parents to accompany them: Komen Helecanth and Thurion Lightbrother."

"Agreed. All of your people's children to be fostered among the Woodwose," Leutric said next.

Vieliessar wished she could read his expression. Or his mind. "No. The Woodwose are our children and our siblings. Send them to live among us, that they may know their brothers and sisters."

"Agreed. Your marriage to my Battlemaster, to seal the alliance between us."

"No," Runacar said, just as Vieliessar said: "Agreed." She took a deep breath, willing herself not to laugh: all these battles and plots and plans, and she ended up nearly where she began. "Announce it as you will. Ceremony when you choose. Consummation—if required at all—only after the Endarkened are defeated."

"I would rather bed an Aesalion." Runacar's thought came through the Bond crystal clear and furious. Vieliessar wondered what Aesalions were like. She only had *Lannarien's Book of Living Things* to go by, and she knew that to be astonishingly inaccurate.

"Agreed," Leutric said.

"No!" Runacar said again, this time more insistently.

Leutric turned to look at him. Beside Leutric, Audalo also looked toward Runacar, but though she could tell that both Minotaurs were in the grip of some strong emotion, she could not tell what it was. Anger? Sympathy? Amusement?

"Are you no longer my vassal, Runacar Houseborn, Child of Stars?" Leutric asked softly.

The eldritch music Vieliessar alone could hear changed, into one single high wail of warning.

"Do not ask this of me, my lord," Runacar said, as if it was an answer. His gaze met Leutric's. Vieliessar and Helecanth—and the others—might not even have been in the room.

"I will have from my vassals what I will have from my children: obedience," Leutric said, his tone still mild.

There was a long tense pause. Vieliessar found herself trying to send reassurance to Runacar through the Bond. But his emotions—and hers—were too turbulent for her to know if her attempt had any effect. She wondered if he was about to kill himself—or her—or either of the Minotaurs. She wondered if the Bearward would stop him. She wondered if she'd be alive after the Bearward had.

"I will do as you have ordered, my lord," Runacar said at last. His voice was utterly even, without emotion, and his face was expressionless.

The emotions of a moment before were gone from the Soulbond as if they had never been.

Leutric turned away as if the interruption had not occurred. "The west from the mountains to the shore is ours and will remain so," he said.

"Agreed," Vieliessar answered. "Do you reserve it to your sole use, or may Elvenkind live upon it as well?"

"If you will live in peace, at peace with us, and recognizing our laws, customs, and prior claim to these lands, then yes. If not, you will be banished from them."

"Then we will take, reserved to our sole use, the Teeth of the Moon and the Vale of Celenthodiel, Tildorangelor Flower Forest, the city Cele-phriandullias, the plain of Ifjalasairaet, and the Ghostwood once known as Janglanipaikharain," Vieliessar said instantly. "These lands to be in-violate and ours alone from the moment you and I are sworn, whether we live upon them or not. In exchange, we cede you suzerainty, domin-ion, and prior claim to all the rest, from the snows of the north to the deserts of the south, from Stardock to Great Sea Ocean, from the Grand Windsward to Greythunder Glairyrill, from the Eastern Plain to the Sea of Storms."

"Agreed," Leutric answered.

Runacar watched the quick exchanges with puzzled distaste. Offer and counteroffer were like the beats of sword blades wielded in the Challenge Circle. The High King conceded lands, children, alliances as if none of them mattered—or as if her concessions were meaningless. Helecanth stood stoically as the High King bargained Helecanth's life away as if she were mere chattel, and never once moved a muscle to indicate she heard any of the words spoken. It was as if the two rulers—High King and King-Emperor—were archers shooting at the same target, alternating releases to cause the greatest destruction.

Or victory.

WOOD'S MOON IN THE TENTH YEAR OF THE HIGH KING'S REIGN: DANCE OF EQUALS

When disaster strikes, smile. And pretend it was your plan all along.

—Elrinonion Swordmaster of Caerthalien, *The Book of War*

Runacar dared not interject himself into the mercilessly swift negotiations between Leutric and the High King. Not when he had just come so close to being turned out by his liege-lord. That stung. His concession was only bearable because it would be a marriage in name only. But the habit of loyalty was bred in the bone, and he ached to warn Leutric about the peril he saw. Only what could he say?

Don't trust her! She's lying! I don't know how, or about what, and . . .

The trouble was, whether the High King was lying or truthful or planning on murdering the whole of the royal family *didn't matter*. After the Endarkened attack at Ceoprentrei, Runacar knew that neither Elvenkind nor the Otherfolk could defeat the Endarkened by themselves—or even keep from being obliterated. But what if Leutric's fears were correct? What if delivering the weapon he guarded to Elvenkind really *did* mean they would use it to destroy the Otherfolk and the Brightfolk. How could either of them know that wouldn't happen? How could the *alfaljodthi* set aside centuries of hatred as simply as Vieliessar's blithe negotiations implied?

She speaks like a mooncalf, a fool, promising things she can never deliver. It's a trick—I know it is! And I still can't find the lie.

At last, and far too quickly for Runacar's peace of mind, Leutric said: "We consent in theory to your possession of the lands you have previously named, once the Endarkened are utterly destroyed—and if we cannot agree to live together in peace. And until that day? What say you, High King?"

Runacar held his breath.

"I agree, in principle and in fact, on behalf of the whole of my folk who are now alive, and for all my folk as yet unborn, that I and they shall keep the terms made known to me by the Unicorn Celebremen, and by King-Emperor Leutric, King of the Minotaurs, Lord of the House of a Thousand Doors, Emperor of the Nine Races, General of Armies, Lord of the Folk of Land and Air, Kindly Regarded by the Folk of the Seas and the Waters, Respected of the Brightfolk, and agreed to by us both."

Leutric held out one enormous hand. "Come to me, High King, and swear your oath in blood as I shall swear mine. And together we and our armies shall go against the Darkness—for all of Pelashia's kindred are Creatures of the Light."

She won't do it, Runacar thought hopefully.

Vieliessar got to her feet. (Runacar realized that not only was he holding Pouncewarm in his lap, he had been for some time.) The ornate and luxurious robes she wore sat oddly on her body: she was meant to be garbed in stark and simple armor, her only ornament the sword she bore.

All Runacar could do was bear witness as Vieliessar took three steps forward, and Leutric and Audalo rose to their feet to meet her.

When she stopped, Vieliessar drew a tiny knife—no longer than her finger—from the sash of her robes. She displayed it to the Bearward, who nodded assent, and then sliced the delicate blade across the palm of her deosil hand. She held out her hand, palm up, the blood slowly pooling in the palm of her hand. And waited.

Leutric closed the distance between them with one step. He took his own dagger and slashed his palm. His blood welled up, a brighter scarlet than Elven blood, and for an instant Runacar believed this final manifestation of *difference* would stop her.

But she unhesitatingly reached out to Leutric. They clasped hands, palm to palm, Vieliessar's hand swallowed up in Leutric's. Their mingled blood oozed along the line where their two hands met. Blended. Neither one shade of red nor the other.

"I, Leutric, son of the Great Bull of Heaven, Architect of the House of a Thousand Doors, Husbandman to the Meadows of a Thousand Herds, King-Emperor of the Folk, do swear to Vieliessar High King that none of my folk shall harm any of her folk, and together we will fight against the Endarkened until they are erased from the world. May Leaf and Star, Blood and Bone, Earth and Sky turn against me, and upon all in whose behalf I swear, if we break this oath."

There was a pause. *Someone will speak out to stop this,* Runacar thought wildly. Helecanth must. *The High King will not swear so binding an oath to a Minotaur. She won't!*

"I, Vieliessar, daughter of War Prince Serenthon Farcarinon and Nataranweiya of Caerthalien and Farcarinon; Greatdaughter of Pelashia Celenthodiel, Lightsister at the Sanctuary of the Star; Lightsister by trial of the Shrine of the Star and by the Starry Hunt; Child of the Prophecy by decree of Amretheon Aradruiniel; High King over *Parman Paramad*, the White Jewel; War Prince of Farcarinon and Oronviel; and High King over all the Hundred Houses, swear before Leaf and Tree and Flower, before Fire and Moon and Star, and by the Light Itself, that there will be true and honest alliance between your folk and mine, so that together we shall fight the Endarkened. Never shall I harm your folk by spell or weapon or any other means, nor shall I permit any of whom I hold fealty to do so, nor shall I scruple to punish any of my folk who transgress the particulars of this my sworn oath, or the laws I have made for them, or the customs held within your lands when they are there. I further swear before Leaf and Tree and Flower, before Fire and Moon and Star, that I will uphold this oath until its term is run, or until Amretheon Aradruiniel returns, or until I am absolved of it. All this I swear freely, and on the following condition: that our two folk will fight as one body against our mutual enemy until the threat of the Endarkened is gone forever."

As he listened to the sonorous phrases of the most binding oaths his people knew, a cold realization filled Runacar. Vieliessar had said so herself: Amretheon's Curse worked through her, without her consent or control, on everyone with whom she came in contact.

This treaty was not her choice. It was not Leutric's choice. It was the work of an ancient Power working through—and *on*—both of them. He found himself clutching Pouncewarm so tightly that the Palugh was forced to extend his claws. Runacar loosened his grip with an effort.

Leutric kissed her upon both cheeks, king to king, prince to prince. "It is done," he said.

It is a terrible mistake, Runacar thought.

⊰⊱

The conversation among the others in the room—Leutric's court and vassals—was a low susurrant hissing behind them. Runacar tried to listen—Leutric had no Swordmaster so his Battlemaster must serve—but he could not concentrate.

"*Now* we will have tea," Audalo said firmly.

"And we will speak of that which we have held in trust for you, Child of Stars," Leutric said. He guided Vieliessar to a place beside him on the cushioned floor: now that she had done what the Powers she served had brought her here to do (Runacar thought uncharitably), the fire seemed to have drained from her body, and every line of it spoke of weariness. Audalo left the chamber—probably to find tea-water, Runacar thought. He found himself layering confusion over his thoughts just as he would have at a parley truce. To protect himself from his Bondmate? That was impossible. To figure out how to warn her without letting the Power that held her noticing? To warn Leutric? Even if they believed him, he didn't think they'd care.

She was right: the life of the Child of the Prophecy is cursed.

"Rune, Rune, Rune, Pretty Rune. Not to worry. Not to fear. I, I, I shall protect you," Pouncewarm half-sang as he kneaded Runacar's thigh. The Palugh managed to speak at the same time as he purred loudly; the riddle of how he managed it was enough to distract Runacar for a moment.

"The weapon," Vieliessar said, and Runacar's attention snapped back to her.

"Again: not a weapon, but something that can be used as one." Leutric held out his wounded hand to her—as if he had every right to do so—and the cut healed immediately, leaving nothing behind but the drying blood.

"By Elvenkind alone," Vieliessar responded. She brushed her hands together, trying to clean away the drying blood on her own hands, and finally gave up and wiped them on her robe. She looked oddly wistful, as if her thoughts were years and miles away.

"So I was told," Leutric said. "You must remember, King Vieliessar, that guardianship of the Bones of the Earth has been a duty passed down from father to son since long before your people came west: a thousand thousand generations of duty. In such an expanse of time Truth itself might grow weary. When I have told you all I have been given to tell you, it may be that you know no more than you do at this moment."

Runacar watched her turning over Leutric's words in her mind, but when she spoke, the question Vieliessar asked was not the one he expected.

"How long do your people live, King Leutric?"

Leutric smiled at her, as if he were a tutor whose pupil had asked the right question. "I have seen sixty summers since I was born. I do not expect to see even half that again before I go to the Great Bull."

"Except for the Gryphons, the Minotaurs are the longest-lived of the Nine Races," Runacar interjected. Pouncewarm purred even louder in approval. "Some of the Brightfolk might live longer. I don't think anyone's really sure."

It had shocked and saddened him when he'd first known. And it was a terrible twist of fate that of his friends and companions, it was Radafa—with a lifetime of centuries before him—who had been the first to die.

"The fairies' life is but a cycle of seasons," Leutric said, taking up the thread of the conversation again. "A Dryad's, as long as her tree. The Unicorns are secretive, and will not tell, while the oldest of Fauns never sees the end of their third decade. Each of us must be content with what the Great Powers have given us."

Vieliessar was still looking thoughtful, but Runacar did not trust her *geasa* any more than he would trust one of the Endarkened. He could see Leutric bending to her will, charmed by what he saw as modesty and honesty—even after she had warned him explicitly. *"I am Child of the Prophecy. Amretheon's* geasa *rules everyone and everything I know."*

"Why did Queen Pelashia give us long life and not you?" Vieliessar asked at last.

"You are her children. We are her cousins. To us, the Great Powers gave other gifts, in accordance with Their will. I am at peace."

"Then Audalo will succeed you, and long before I might die of old

age. Ought I swear to him as well?" Vieliessar asked. She sounded curious, nothing more.

"Lord Vieliessar, I truly do not think any of us will live long enough
for it to matter, Bones of the Earth or no," Leutric said, very gently.

⊰⊱

Vieliessar looked up as Audalo reentered the room, this time bearing a large wooden chest and a homely and commonplace wooden
bucket. Tomorrow (ah, *tomorrow!*) she must order an inventory done
of the possessions her folk—and the Otherfolk—had at their respective
commands. No matter how well Imrathalion was sealed and warded and
barricaded, they could not stay here long, not when there were thousands to feed instead of hundreds. The Endarkened might return at any
moment. She thought they had all gone now, but that was no guarantee
of their *staying* gone. She had thought they would reach Nomaitemil
safely, after all.

She realized she was tired, wrung out, as if some driving force that
had propelled her onward had abruptly ceased. And then she realized
that it had, and what it was. At that discovery, she nearly wept.

Madness to come west in search of the villagers of Areve. Madness to
come myself. Yet I insisted on doing so, against all argument. If we had
not come—if I had not come—the Endarkened would have had Leutric
and his heir, and all the Otherfolk who came with him. And probably the
Lightless of Areve and all the Sanctuary Mages as well.

I did not come west to save anyone, not even the King-Emperor. I came
west to make a promise to Leutric, and I could not make that promise to
him if he were dead.

As Audalo opened the chest and began setting out its contents,
Runacar moved from where he'd been sitting to help. Pouncewarm, dis-
lodged from Runacar's lap, walked over to the chest to peer inside. He
sneezed his disapproval and sauntered to lie down at Vieliessar's side.

She risked a glance toward Runacar. His face was blank and still, as
if he had been dealt some grievous wound. She ached to see him like
this, just as she would sorrow for Thurion's pain, or Helecanth's, or that
of any of the folk who were closest to her. *I must think of a way to make*

this bearable to him, she thought, before her attention was summoned by Leutric once more.

"The first thing I was told, when my father, King Otrund, initiated me into this ancient wardship, was that the rightful possessor of the Bones of the Earth would bear the ring," Leutric said, reaching out to pluck up the two identical rings from where Vieliessar had left them. "Since we did not know that one of the two had remained with Elvenkind, this was something we found hard to interpret, and many Guardians speculated about what it truly meant. Perhaps donning the ring would be the final test. We did not know."

"You had me do it anyway," Vieliessar pointed out.

"So I did," Leutric said. "And now both together are yours to bear. I believe the rings will lead you to the resting place of the Bones of the Earth. The lore says that once you reach that place, our part is done."

He handed both rings to Vieliessar. She regarded them dourly and then slipped them on, one on each forefinger. She no longer remembered which of them had been originally hers. They were utterly alike.

Audalo had set up a tea-brazier and iron pot, and filled the pot with water. The earthenware teapot that followed the iron pot out of the basket was sized and shaped for Minotaur hands. Its proportions looked oddly distorted to Vieliessar, but the glaze covering it was beautiful. The teacups were tall and narrow, flaring out at the bottom.

"Everyone drinks tea," Audalo said. "But not in the same way. The Great Powers rejoice in our differences, and so do we."

"Of course, he's leaving out the Centaurs," Leutric said, with mild amusement. "The Centaurs have little use for tea when they can have beer."

Audalo spread out a clean white cloth and placed a pot of butter, a pot of honey, and a compact round loaf of dark bread upon it. Next, he removed an elaborately stamped and gilded leather pouch from the chest, and offered it to her. Vieliessar opened the pouch gingerly and sniffed at its contents. The smells were unfamiliar, but it was definitely tea. She handed it back, nodding her approval.

"The Bones of the Earth lie in Stardock's roots," Leutric said. "Imrathalion might lead you there—or she might not. Beyond this, I know nothing, though I and mine will aid you in any way you ask."

Pouncewarm flopped onto his side, legs stretched out stiffly and claws unsheathed as he stretched. "I, I, I will accompany you," he said. "It is withouuuuuut question," he trilled.

"It is the only thing that is," Vieliessar said under her breath. She stroked Pouncewarm reflexively. Her mind was filled with a thousand conflicting needs: to claim the Bones of the Earth immediately, to bring the refugees she had saved home to her people, and to return to them herself to prepare them for the initiation of her treaty (and for the influx of Woodwose). To remain here to keep quarrels between Elvenkind and Otherfolk from burgeoning into riot. She had never felt so alone and so indecisive. Which of these tasks was the most urgent?

In the beginning, everything was simple. The longer I continue upon this path, the harder it becomes to see my way. No. It is simple. The first thing is—

She was distracted (yet again) by the scent of tea. Audalo was pouring from the kettle to the pot.

"Tomorrow you'll know how many of the wounded can be moved. You can't make decisions until then," Runacar said bluntly.

"Says the High House Warlord," Vieliessar grumbled, and Runacar gave a sharp bark of laughter.

Audalo cut the loaf into six Minotaur-sized portions and slathered each one with honey and butter. He passed the slices around, including Helecanth and the Bearward but not Pouncewarm, and then poured the oddly shaped cups full. Vieliessar motioned for Helecanth to seat herself, and they both waited until Audalo had taken the first bite of bread and the first drink of tea before joining him.

"Nobody's going to poison you," Runacar said waspishly. "Not that I'm not tempted."

"Apparently that would be quite in line with High House courtship customs," Vieliessar said. "I am grateful I was raised as Lightborn."

The tea itself was . . . interesting. It had much more body than the teas she was used to. Not unpleasant, but different. An earthy taste, resolving into an echo of sweetness, yet with a sharp, almost acrid note that encouraged the taster to drink more.

"What does that mean, 'to be raised as Lightborn'?" Audalo asked. "Rune has said he doesn't know."

"Komen were never really interested in us or our ways," Vieliessar answered. "Though they should have been—for tactical reasons if nothing more."

Leutric joined the conversation with another question, and suddenly the three of them were deep in a discussion of the ways the culture of the Lightborn differed from that of the War Princes. She had missed this sort of discourse since she'd left the Sanctuary of the Star: conversation for its own sake, and the pure exercise of imagination. Their talk lasted until the whole of the pot of tea had been drunk, and Vieliessar got reluctantly to her feet.

"It will be dawn in a few candlemarks, and there is much that must be done. I must, unwillingly, ask that you excuse me now, but be sure I shall return to you as soon as I may. I have much enjoyed our talk tonight."

Audalo and Leutric stood as well. "Be sure that a guest of whom one regrets the leaving is a guest who will be doubly welcomed the next time."

Vieliessar smiled up at him. Her teachers had told her that a word spoken was a weapon in the hand of an enemy, but she did not feel it was true here and now. She realized that no matter how hard and how long she had striven to be only one among many Lightborn, and how carefully she had built up her Law Lords to ensure that any one of her people could approach her as a near-equal, this was the first time since her victory at If-jalasairaet that she herself felt like one among equals. Leutric did not care how many warriors she could put into the field, and he didn't care how strong her magic was, or what she looked like. It was wonderful.

It was dangerous.

If the Otherfolk aristocracy would not use her inattention to remove her from her nonexistent throne, then there were a few of her own folk, even now, who would happily take that advantage. She must be careful and watchful, just as she had been since she first set foot over the threshold of the Sanctuary of the Star.

Pouncewarm had been teasing Runacar, and headbutted him several times before turning away to launch himself at her shoulder. Vieliessar staggered slightly with the impact, then reached up a hand to steady the Palugh.

"I do not know what leave-taking rituals exist at your court, King

Leutric. For that I apologize," she said. (It was difficult to concentrate on what she was saying—or to look dignified—when she was trying to keep Pouncewarm's plumed tail out of her face.)

"I must disappoint you when I say there are none," the Minotaur answered. "It shocked our Rune to his heart to hear of it."

"Then I will simply say fare you well, and a peaceful rest to all," Vieliessar answered.

⊰⊱

Stepping into the outer corridor once more was like traveling into a different world. Vieliessar realized how much she had enjoyed the few candlemarks she had spent with King-Emperor Leutric—whose story must be the mirror of her own, if he had managed to unite all the Otherfolk beneath his banner. She hoped this meeting would be the first of many . . . and not the only one before death and war claimed them all. She could even forgive him her betrothal to Runacar, though it added a hundred thousand complications to her life. Runacar must swear fealty to her before they could be either betrothed or wed, and she imagined Leutric was hearing about that just now and for the very first time.

"Perhaps between the battle fought and the battles to come, the High King would consider sleeping?" Helecanth suggested, rousing Vieliessar from her abstraction.

"When we are home, safe, and alive," Vieliessar said dismissively. She looked at her hands, and the rings upon them. "It is hard to believe that these will lead me to a weapon powerful enough to destroy the Endarkened."

"It is even harder to believe that Lord Rithdeliel will not die in his tracks when he discovers you are to wed Caerthalien," Helecanth said.

"I suppose I—" Vieliessar began, when the light was abruptly blocked by someone entering the passage from the main cavern. ("Someone" as in "Minotaur"—the horns made that much identification easy.)

Helecanth stepped forward to tell the Minotaur to make way for the High King, but Vieliessar put a hand out to stop her. At Vieliessar's silent gesture, they both stepped back to the corridor wall. They would not give way, nor ask the other to do so. *Politics! And I long for the day I am free of it.*

The Minotaur was Hresa. The markings on her hide, the designs on her horns, the snow-white face, all made identification simple. Did she already know about the oath her king and husband had sworn? Elven-kind knew so little of the powers their new allies could call—a hundred generations of war had seen to that.

What was not a matter of ambiguity was Hresa's contempt for Elven-kind. Even without experience in interpreting the expressions on Oth-erfolk faces, both Vieliessar and Helecanth had no trouble recognizing the long look of smoldering hatred Hresa gave them. Vieliessar took a long breath of relief once Hresa had gone.

"It seems this alliance has the potential to be as tempestuous as any Caerthalien ever forged with Aramenthiali," Helecanth said dryly. "Per haps you will wish to have been rested before you participate in such excitement?"

"The list of things I must see to has not shortened since the last time you counseled rest," Vieliessar said, stepping away from the wall. "And so I fear you must be unsatisfied."

"Perhaps tomorrow," Helecanth said.

"Perhaps," Vieliessar agreed.

⚜

The Elven female and her servant left the chamber, and the three of them shared the corridor for a moment.

They do not even do me the courtesy of acknowledging me!

Hresa stood as they passed, then, schooling her whole body, horns to tail, to an expression of meekness and deference, she entered the Court chamber, kneeling submissively before her husband. Leutric touched his forehead to hers in gentle greeting.

"This is no time for formality, my first above many!" Leutric told her. "The treaty with the Elves is made, and will be sealed with a marriage to my Battlemaster."

She had not been invited. She had not even been consulted!

"So now we only have one enemy. Excuse me: *still* only have one enemy. But I am certain our new allies will erase them, though they be as numerous as flies in the spring," Hresa said.

Leutric looked confused, uncertain of whether to take her meaning from the words or the tone of her comment.

"And better even than that!" Audalo leaned forward. "If the time of their prophecy has come, as the Elves say it has, then so the end of our guardianship has also come."

He flicked his ears back and forth in delight. Hresa stared at him in horror, then looked down at Leutric's hand.

It was true. The ring was gone. The Great Secret had been profaned. The Elves would turn it on her people as easily as they would turn it on the Red Winnowers, and all the Folk would be destroyed.

Hresa had never wanted this alliance in the first place. She had never wanted Leutric to become Emperor. Let each of the Folk go their own way. It was what always had been done.

"As you say, young cousin, this is a time of strange and wonderful things," Hresa said, bowing her head again. "And I wish to think about them. I will walk the cave."

At Leutric's nod of approval, she rose to her feet again and walked to the back of the cavern. A few of her dancers rose to follow her, but Hresa waved them away. This was one dance that must be danced alone.

⚜

The path that led from the Court Cavern was narrow, and many times her horns scraped along the roof of it. Hresa walked through utter and absolute darkness, but her senses led her, at last, to the vast open cavern she'd known would be there. She could feel the cavern branching out beside and beneath her, extending for ten paces outward. One might even cross the mountains here—with available supplies, and with a map of where they were going.

Neither of which Hresa needed.

Hresa was an Earthdancer.

⚜

Each of the Folk, save the Centaurs, had a magic uniquely their own. Among the Minotaurs, cave-kenning was held by both male and female, but Earthdancing belonged to females alone.

Dance, and the earth danced with them.

Dance, and rock tumbled to the ground at their command.

She regretted the death of her sisters, but there was no avoiding it. Perhaps they would be able to escape once it began. But that would be an escape into the claws of the Red Winnowers, and death would be preferable.

Hresa extended one long graceful leg. Her iron-shod toes tapped the rock. The rock shuddered, just a little. Hresa tapped it again: twice, a pause, then a long intricate pattern that broke off as she leapt into the air and came down hard on both feet. She could feel the heartbeat of the living rock around her.

Soon it would answer her.

⚓

The sun rose outside the sealed caves as Vieliessar located her people and set them to work. She established temporary chains of command: Iardalaith to lead the Warhunt Mages, Harwing to lead the Sanctuary Mages, each to choose their own subordinates (a temporary matter for both groups of Lightborn); a courtesy visit to the Silver Swords, since the Silver Swords were a full military unit with its chain of command in place; Helecanth in charge of Vieliessar's personal guard (no change there), and all four commanders to report directly to Vieliessar. That only left the Areve villagers and the Unicorn Riders absent from the command hierarchy.

Vieliessar had known sennights ago that a Delight of Unicorns had moved into Nomaitemil. She had even known the Unicorns were training some of her Elvenkind as a cavalry unit. It hadn't occurred to her that the leader of the unit would be one of the Unicorns until Tangisen told her.

"Black Sondast. His rider is Dianora of the Arzhana." He shrugged. "I helped this one here get everyone Healed and settled. I recognized several of the riders."

"Helped! You watched from the doorway!" the Lightborn Tangisen had said accusingly. She was the only one of the Sanctuary Mages here, clearly at Tangisen's insistence. "They were so beautiful . . . it is an offense against the Light Itself to injure one of them!" she added, looking fierce, and—to Vieliessar—about the age of her daughter Adalieriel.

"What is your name, Lightsister?" Vieliessar asked.

"Daeriel, my lord High King majesty." Daeriel added a rather muddled court bow; if Leutric kept no great state and ceremony, clearly the opposite had been true of Hamphuliadiel.

("This is why you always bring heralds to a war," Isilla whispered to Dinias.)

"Lightsister Daeriel, will you serve me by being my envoy to the Unicorns? And can you be loyal to me and not to Black Sondast?"

Daeriel gazed at Vieliessar with very wide eyes. "I-I-I-I will try, Lord Majesty."

"Choose four subordinates whom you can order in my name. Say to Sondast that all the Riders have sworn fealty to me, and I expect to find them arrayed with my forces—as much as possible—if the need should come. You know the magical proscriptions of the Unicorns by now. See to it that everyone does, and that they are respected."

"Yes, my lord." This time Daeriel's words were accompanied with a shaky curtsey, confirming Vieliessar's guess that she was probably commonborn but not Landbond. Possibly the child of a Crofter or a lesser Farmhold family. She would have been very young when the West went up in the flames of war. "I want Tangisen, please, Majesty."

"You may have him," Vieliessar said.

"And he will tell you that you may address your King as 'Lord Vieliessar,'" Tangisen said, putting a hand on Daeriel's shoulder.

"But the rest of us will have to be from the Sanctuary, because Lord Hamphuliadiel—peace and joy be upon him as he walks in the Light of the Warm World!—told us we must remain pure as the Light Itself is pure—"

It had lacked only that, Vieliessar thought to herself. The pleasures of the flesh had often been the only consolation during the long years of discipline, training, and lessons the future Lightborn endured.

"—so I will accompany her to the dormitory of her similarly un-slaked Lightborn peers, and assist her to choose my fellow lackeys," Tangisen said.

"Thank you, Lord Vieliessar!" Daeriel said.

"A Lightbrother of the Sanctuary named Erendor has come to my attention," Vieliessar said. "If he is otherwise suitable, I would suggest him as one of your assistants."

(She saw Tangisen give Isilla a theatrically agonized look. Apparently Tangisen had already met Erendor Lightbrother.)

"Yes, my lady—lord—*King*!" Daeriel said. Vieliessar waved her and Tangisen away, her mind already turning to the next problem.

The villagers. She did not want to put a Lightborn in charge of them: the Sanctuary Mages would only reinforce Hamphuliadiel's suspect teachings, for those were all they knew. One of the Warhunt Mages would be forced to deal with both the almost superstitious reverence of the Lightborn which Hamphuliadiel had instituted, as well as the fact they were an outsider. Any of Vieliessar's Lightless would face the same problem.

Either overlord could not hold command if the villagers realized they were here (and so many of them were dead) because Harwing (or Hamphuliadiel) had given their village to the Otherfolk and agreed to vacate it. The story that Harwing (or Hamphuliadiel) had been bringing them to a reunion with the High King was stupid, but at least it wouldn't cause a rebellion.

And for all those reasons, her liaison would have to be one of the Lords Komen in hiding she had identified yesterday morning. She would send—

"My lord!" The urgency of Dinias's tone grabbed her attention at once. "Something is happening in the stone!"

Dinias Lightbrother's Keystone Gift was Transmutation; Dinias had a special affinity for rock and stone. He had his hand on the cave wall.

Other Lightborn were touching the cave walls, trying to feel what he had sensed. Vieliessar was more efficient: she touched Dinias.

Through him she felt the long patient life of the stone, its movement so slow that Time was its only possible dancing partner. She touched, as he did, the heart of the stone, where granite and limestone became a field of blazing golden motes that could be changed—or moved.

Someone was moving them.

She felt a faint infinitesimal tremor through the soles of her boots.

"We have to make this stop," she said. They were in no shape to go out into the storm: half the wounded were asleep, the other half had received Lightless Healing only. And the Endarkened would slaughter them all if even only one of the monsters remained.

There was another tremor, stronger than before, and suddenly, over everything, Vieliessar heard the eldritch singing once again.

This time its tone had changed. Before it had been wild and sweet. Now it held a note of mockery—and malice.

"Helecanth, go to King Leutric and make him aware that there are tremors in the stone—he has Earthdancers who may be able to help stop them." She scooped Pouncewarm off her shoulder and thrust him at Helecanth. "Tell Runacar he may act with my authority—" As she spoke, Vieliessar was unknotting the leather cord that held the elvensilver Vilya blossom in place. "Helecanth, you will aid my Soulbonded and Betrothed in this." She thrust the badge of authority at Helecanth. "Isilla, you are in charge here. Make the Healers understand!"

"As you command, Lord Vieliessar," Isilla said.

"And you?" Helecanth asked. She held Pouncewarm and the Vilya token, regarding Vieliessar with grave suspicion.

"The weapon," Vieliessar said, low.

Helecanth's eyes widened, and she opened her mouth to protest, but Vieliessar was already running.

She followed the singing.

※

Every time, Vieliessar thought in exasperation, *every time I garb myself in courtly attire a disaster happens! Never again! Runacar must wed me in armor or rags if he weds me at all!*

She flung off the layers of the Astromancer's highly ornamental regalia: over-sash and over-robe and sash and vest and tunic as she dodged among the corridors of the labyrinth, barely remembering to retain the tiny knife from the hidden pocket of the over-sash. When she was down to undertunic and shift she paused long enough to knot the undertunic up over one hip so that it would not trip her. At least her boots were good and sturdy.

The path she followed had gotten progressively dimmer and narrower, until it became nothing more than a rough fissure in the rock. The first slight tremors had become a constant shaking, and she feared that the rock would simply close upon her, obliterating her utterly—and leaving her people and her allies to the Endarkened.

She did not cast Silverlight. Someone might be following her who would see it, and Silversight—though it presented the caster with a faintly distorted landscape—would show her the way more clearly.

But it had its shortcomings, as she found when she placed her foot on what she thought to be a pool of water reflecting the ceiling above.

It wasn't.

She recoiled, praying for balance and clutching at the rough wall beside her. Fortunately she had not fully committed her weight to the phantom image, and was able to get back to sound footing once more.

The rock trembled.

Now Vieliessar cast the strongest instance of Silverlight she could. Its day-bright brilliance raced across the vault of the cavern—proof that someone had cast the same spell on the rock in the past—and showed her that the narrow defile she had been following stopped abruptly, opening out into a cavern so vast and so deep that the Great Keeps of the twelve High Houses could have been dropped into the chasm and barely filled it. As the eldritch radiance slowly claimed more stone as if it were honey dripping down the sides of a stone jar, and she could see that across its floor great points of stone rose up, like spears set in the bottom of a trap. The vault above mirrored the chasm below, as if she were within the maw of some incalculably vast creature.

There was nothing but a sheer rock face to the left and the right of the narrow path she had been following. There was no passage across the abyss.

I must find one!

She searched through her mind for a spell that would serve, but Light had been so difficult to Call that she was not entirely certain she could cast one if she could think of one. Arevethmonion was still burning, and though it would be sunturns before the whole of it was consumed, the part that had become accustomed to answering to Lightborn commands was already ash.

Transmute? Shield? Fetch? None of those seemed remotely usable. No matter what the Storysingers said, Lightborn could not fly. Door would require too much power when departure and arrival points were both outside a Flower Forest—

The earth-tremor had been a constant background sensation, a thing Vieliessar hardly noticed. Now there came a crack, like wood pushed beyond its limits. The stone spears of the ceiling swayed above her head. Several broke loose and fell, falling to the bottom of the cavern with a resounding echoing crash.

They took a very long time to reach the bottom.

The temblor ceased, but the groaning of the rock went on. Vieliessar wished for Dinias's familiarity with stone—no matter what she might sense, interpretation would inevitably fall behind.

But she must go forward. Somehow. Even now the song grew fainter, as if there were some corporeal singer who was drawing farther away.

Behind her, she heard a scuff of a boot against the stone.

She whirled to face the intruder, cursing the fact that she hadn't thought to bring her sword. Who could have followed her—and how?

Runacar stepped forward, Pouncewarm in his arms.

"I brought your necklace back," he said. Pouncewarm leaped from his arms to the ground and trotted over to Vieliessar. "You must have dropped it somewhere."

Silently, Runacar held out the Vilya blossom.

"So I must," she answered, holding out her hand.

The elvensilver blossom was warm against her skin as she tied it back into place around her neck. *Kingship is a thing not lightly surrendered.*

"As you see, a necessary journey," Runacar said. "And yours?"

"I must have Leutric's weapon before it is buried in stone! But—"

"I, I, I know!" Pouncewarm sang. "I, I, I know who shakes the stone! I know how to find the way! I who am cleverest. I who am chosen. I!"

"Then—" Vieliessar began, but Pouncewarm had already gone trotting off along the deosil face of the stone. What had at first looked flawless was in fact possessed of a ledge. No wider than her hand was wide, it ran horizontally across the face of the stone. Whether it vanished or ended she did not know, for the rock face curved away and she could not see beyond its horizon. Pouncewarm trotted along the tiny ledge with as little concern as if he were walking down the middle of the Sanctuary Road.

It did not seem possible that anything larger than a Palugh could follow.

"I am sorry," Vieliessar said. She had come to suspect that even if Runacar died, the mantle of Child of the Prophecy would save her life. It was indecent to test that by luring him into peril. "You should go back," she said seriously. "The way is straight."

"You sent for me," he repeated, folding his arms over his chest for emphasis.

"I did not! I gave you my authority and you came chasing after me to return it! You are mad!"

"*I* was mad?" he said in exasperation. "*You* are definitely mad. I cannot imagine you successfully organizing a Kite War, let alone defeating the Hundred Houses. I am coming with you as the voice of common sense and reason!"

"You will be the voice of the *dead* if we do not find a way forward," she snapped.

"He's *your* Palugh. Follow him."

The cavern shook again, and more stone fell from the ceiling.

CHAPTER THIRTY-TWO

WOOD'S MOON IN THE TENTH YEAR OF THE HIGH KING'S REIGN: THE LONG WALK

Though she had plotted and schemed almost since she was a girl to become master of the Unicorn Throne and High King of all Elven-kind, what the reign of King Vieliessar the First (and last) is best known for is the dismantling of the hundred noble houses she had conquered and the destruction of her kingdom. Though the title of "King" remained, the realm her successor inherited was a shadow kingdom, with a ruler who could not command, only entreat.

Thurion Pathfinder, Private Journal

If not for Pouncewarm, Runacar would never have made it this far into Imrathalion. He'd had no Silverlight charm to light his way, nor advance knowledge that the crack in the stone would lead him directly to his goal. Pouncewarm had come for him—Helecanth hard upon the Palugh's heels bearing the High King's message—and Pouncewarm had led him to this path. Runacar had followed the Palugh by touch and by sound.

It had seemed urgent and right to go to Vieliessar, but once he had, he couldn't imagine why he'd come.

She was wild-eyed and disheveled, her hair a spiky mess despite being shorter than a Landbond's. Sweat and dust streaked her skin, and she was clad in nothing more than boots and tunic. A less kingly figure he could not imagine, and yet, the air of command she wore, like a suit of the finest armor, cloaked her in regal grace.

"I'm not sure I—" Vieliessar began. She gestured at the abyss behind her.

"Your rings are glowing," Runacar said, very quietly.

Vieliessar looked down at her hands. Two rings, both identical, one on each forefinger. A cloudy translucent stone of a color similar to *pirozaduta,* the sky-stone, but there the similarity ended. One ring had been proven over thousands of turns of the Wheel to have no particular innate magic. The other . . . ?

"Leutric said the rings must be brought together as the first step toward gaining the Bones of the Earth," Runacar said. "Maybe that's why they're glowing."

"That's not how Magery works," Vieliessar protested.

"Nowww-w-w-w!" Pouncewarm called.

Runacar pointed silently.

Vieliessar stepped to the edge of the abyss to regard the narrow shelf of stone. Pouncewarm was far ahead, his tail drawing pictograms in the air.

She had to believe this was a path she could follow. Transmute might save her if she fell. She set first one foot, then the other, onto the path, digging her toes into the crack. Her heels hung off the edge of the ledge. She gripped the rough stone tightly, digging her fingers into any handhold she could find.

It seemed to be a very long way down.

The part of her mind unoccupied by holding on and moving forward was frantically sorting through spells. There didn't seem to be any that were useful in this context.

"If you're going to follow me, try not to fall," she said tightly, taking another sideways step.

"Good advice," Runacar answered.

She could not turn her head to see if Runacar followed, but she was certain he did. His presence was like a warm hand in the dark. She did not know what she would do if he—if either of them—slipped and fell.

Pace, and pace, and pace. The scuff of Runacar's boots echoed hers. The rings on her fingers gleamed. Her nails broke, her fingers grew bloody as she forced them into cracks in the stone. When the shaking of the stone grew stronger, all she could do was clutch the stone face tightly and wait for it to ease. Pouncewarm was a small figure in the distance, grey on grey, still moving forward, marking out the distance she must traverse.

Then Pouncewarm abruptly disappeared.

She gave a cry of protest and heard Runacar swear breathlessly.

"Heeeeere!" trilled the Palugh.

⊰⊱

The crack in the stone widened just past the curve of the rock face, producing a space barely large enough for the three of them to stand together. Vieliessar scooped Pouncewarm up and held him. The whispering of her ghostlords had stopped while she made her way across the rock face, but now it had resumed. She could barely hear his purring over the song and the whispers.

"I am going mad," she said quietly.

"I am delighted to hear that you agree with me at last, future spouse. A marriage is much more satisfying when both parties share the same view of reality, don't you think? Speaking of which, what do we do now? You will notice that there's no way forward."

Runacar sounded as cheerful and calm as if he weren't trapped in a collapsing cavern with his worst enemy while questing madly for some object that might not even be here. She knew his mien was a façade—a trick of command, to seem unruffled while disaster unfolded on every side. It still helped.

"Yes, I did notice that. I don't think we go forward. Now move."

She passed Pouncewarm to Runacar and got down on her belly, then pushed herself as far over the edge as she dared. The rock face was rough under her hands, but not rough enough for them to climb down. Was there another way across? Or down?

There was a child's game called *palawan*—sticks and plates—played with wooden pegs and a board covered with holes. The pegs were of different lengths, the holes of different depths, and the game had no fixed rules. Dori'chi, one of the servants at the Sanctuary of the Star, whose mind had never grown beyond that of a child, had loved it—and played it compulsively. During her Service Year, Vieliessar had often been the one tasked with taking the board away from him so he would work, or with finding the playing-pieces when (as was inevitable) he lost them. There was no "proper" way to play the game, but when putting it away, Vieliessar had always paired the longest rods with the deepest holes, so that the surface was even. Dori'chi had always done the opposite, delightedly turning the board into a thing of jagged palisades.

The ground below her looked very much like Dori'chi's game board. Here, the great pillars formed by water and time did not rise to points. They were broken off at various heights.

The closest pillar was several cubits distant. The jump might be managed from a standing start, but the landing would be rough, the target small, and the penalty for failing an almost-certainly-fatal fall.

"What do we do now, you furry oracular pest?" she heard Runacar say, and: "Crrrross!" Pouncewarm replied.

"He's right," Vieliessar said, getting to her feet. "I think we can manage it. There are stepping stones—of a sort."

She had barely finished speaking when the cavern shook again. It was far worse than the previous times; the stone spears of the ceiling chimed against one another like bells as they shook.

And swayed.

And fell.

The rock shook and tumbled and ground itself together as dust billowed upward from the floor of the chasm. Vieliessar held Pouncewarm, and Runacar held them both. Vieliessar cast the strongest instance of Shield that she could with Arevethmonion in the state she was, and while they would not be able to breathe inside Shield for very long, at least they could breathe right now.

But Shield would not keep them from falling.

Vieliessar could hold Shield through a fall, but in the end, if you fell from a high enough place, it did not matter whether the stone you landed on was rough or smooth. If Magery could save them, Vieliessar had only seconds to come up with the spell.

There was none.

"I think we're going to die," she said quietly.

"Don't be such an optimist," Runacar said. Tendrils of hair floated about his face from his half-undone braid and she could feel his breath against her cheek. He smelled of leather, and horse, and the lambsgrease everyone used on their stormcloaks. She could see the pulse in his throat beating frantically with the terror of their predicament, she could feel his fear through their Bond, but his voice was even and his tone light. "It's more likely we'll just break every bone in our bodies and die slowly and—"

His last words were cut off by a strangled yelp of surprise. The rock under their feet crumbled away and they fell.

Transmute: strong instance: precise boundary: rock to water.

Shield, detached from the rock, reverted to its natural spherical state. (All instances of Shield were shaped like one or more segments of a sphere; it was why student Lightborn studied geometry.) The rock face sprayed outward as if a battle-ram had struck it from behind. When it collapsed, the ceiling collapsed as well, and its destruction took Silverlight with it.

The sphere of Shield fell. But it did not land. It splashed into the lake that had been the cavern floor, bounced back to the surface, and spun crazily. Pouncewarm howled his displeasure and Runacar swore. With Silverlight gone, the only illumination was the glow of Shield itself, and it shone more within than without.

Shield bobbed and rolled and spun until Vieliessar began to believe death would be preferable than being here. But relief was at hand, from the cave itself. Slowly and ponderously at first, then faster and faster, like powdered honey poured into milk, the rock of the collapsing cavern flowed into the abyss. There were bright flashes as parts of the ceiling landed on Shield's upper curve; some bounced off, some slipped off, to sink into the slowly thickening mud. At last, enough of the rock had fallen into the water to thicken it, and the bubble of Shield lay half-buried, rocking gently. Vieliessar suspected they were going to be *completely* buried when the cavern finished collapsing. She expanded the instance of Shield while she still could, but Shield had not been designed to use as a battering ram. The increase would buy them some time, that was all.

Runacar looked at her, his face still and calm, waiting.

"I am very sorry," Vieliessar said, "but it is possible we are all about to die. I do not think so, but when the air in here grows foul enough, I will not be able to hold the spell any longer."

"So much for Amretheon and his Prophecies," Runacar said. "And I assume that if you had any witchborn Magery that could save us, you'd use it."

Vieliessar wrinkled her nose. Of all the titles she had fought to gain, "Witchking Mage" had not been among them. "Amretheon is why I think I may live. I don't think the Prophecy cares about either of you. Go home," she said to Pouncewarm. "You can save yourself. Go home."

Pouncewarm's eyes flashed silver in the purple light. "I, I, I am first and best. I stay."

"You are first and best," she agreed resignedly, holding out her arms to him. Pouncewarm climbed delicately into her lap. It was beginning to get uncomfortably warm inside Shield.

"I know this is a ridiculous time to bring this up," Runacar said, "but Pouncewarm *did* mention he knew why Imrathalion was collapsing."

"Who stands closer to a king than his shadow, and so is unseen by him but not by all?" Pouncewarm answered merrily.

"What?" Vieliessar said. "Is this a riddle?"

"Didn't you know? They're famed for them. They go everywhere and see everything, but if you ask them about it all you get are riddles," Runacar said.

"You shouldn't have mentioned it if you didn't intend to tell us," Vieliessar said severely.

"Tell him you're the High King. That always works," Runacar said.

"When I say that, someone usually tells me I'm not," Vieliessar answered. "But *why* Imrathalion quakes doesn't make a difference to the fact *that* it quakes, does it?"

"Only if we get out of here alive," Runacar said.

"Ah, another murder attempt," Vieliessar said. "How refreshing."

"Not murder, silly wise one!" Pouncewarm said indignantly. "Hresa dances so there is no alliance."

There was a pause. "Queen Hresa is smashing the caves flat so that there will be no alliance?" Runacar asked incredulously. Why had Hresa done this? She was proud and arrogant, to be sure, but the Otherfolk simply didn't think that way. To do what Pouncewarm had said would be perfectly sensible to Elvenkind . . .

. . . But not to Otherfolk.

"Are you sure?" Runacar asked urgently. "That this is Hresa's idea, and she hasn't been—"

"Overshadowed?" Vieliessar said instantly. "Not by any Lightborn. Not even— Wait. Something's happening."

The moment Vieliessar spoke the stones in the rings she wore flared too bright to look at. There was a boom (sound didn't penetrate Shield, but vibration did), and a shivering crackling crumbling. Her Shield-sphere began to move again, this time in a wide circling motion, rolling as it did. There was something familiar about that, but this was not the time to puzzle the riddle out.

Hresa might smash Imrathalion, but Imrathalion decides how it dies.

Vieliessar quickly shrank Shield so that she and Runacar could brace themselves against its walls, while Pouncewarm clung, all claws, to Runacar's chest. The coruscating light caused by their touching of the walls of Shield was marginally better than being flung around in the dark like dice in a cup.

"Whirlpool," Runacar announced suddenly.

Yes! She thought again of her Service Year in the Sanctuary of the Star, of draining the enormous copper tubs in which clothing was washed. The tubs were too large and heavy to move, so a plug was opened in the bottom.

And if I had been a small glass bubble, I would have swirled around the drainhole just this way. . . .

Shield spun faster and faster as they were sucked toward the center of the whirlpool.

Then they fell for a very long time.

⇥⇤

It had been a very long day for Harwing Lightbrother. First there'd been those blood-red horrors from the sky—oh, wait: they'd come *after* he/Hamphuliadiel had pledged his fealty to the High King—after which there'd been a long hike with a lot of running, hail, fire, Thunderbolt, rain, horrors, Unicorns, and the manifest presence of not one but *two* Great Powers over the battlefield.

After which he'd been herded into a cave and told to Heal people, which meant he was at least absolved of caring for upward of five thousand of the Western Reach's greatest simpletons and lackwits—his (Hamphuliadiel's) Lightborn and the villagers he exploited.

After all of that, he thought he deserved a rest.

He wasn't going to get one.

He'd just settled down to a hopeful sleep—among the Warhunt, they who were more family than any other kin he might claim—when he was awakened to a gaggle of confused voices and someone shaking him.

No. Not someone. Some*thing.*

"Wake up," Dinias said urgently. "The rock's moving."

"Where's it going?" Harwing mumbled, still not quite awake.

"Nowhere we'll like," Dinias answered grimly. "Come on; I need to find the others with Transmute so we can link up."

Harwing got to his feet as Dinias moved away. "I suppose you think that makes sense to anyone but you," he muttered under his breath, reaching down to gather his blanket around him.

What Harwing had taken for smoke in the air wasn't smoke. It was dust. As he looked around for the source there was a squeal from shifting rock. Across the cavern Dinias whirled away from Isilla and slapped his hand against the nearest open face of rock. Harwing saw his eyes go wide with pain, and then close, as Dinias attempted diligently not to scream.

Harwing ran toward Isilla. She was standing at the center of a small group of Warhunt Mages—everyone who'd got back alive from the Western Shore.

I could have been among them. Or dead, Harwing thought. *If I hadn't been enslaved by Hamphuliadiel Astromancer.*

"I don't know what's out there and I need to know," Isilla was saying as Harwing reached her.

"Not the ones with Transmute!" Dinias moaned. "You guys—over here!"

There were seven among the Warhunt who either had Transmute as their Keystone Gift or who worked with the spell frequently. They approached the rock face. Isilla approached Dinias.

More dust filtered down. There was a squealing sound accompanied by a tremor louder than the first, and a tiny pattering as of rain as the first larger pebbles struck the floor.

In the distance, echoing off the stone, Harwing heard screams.

"What's going on?" Isilla asked Dinias.

Dinias's face was nearly grey with horror and strain. "All the rock in Imrathalion from the cavern mouth to Stardock is about to turn to liquid and *settle*. There are some clear passages a few stadia to the east, but we won't have time to get anyone through them. *Zir-zamin a'wusha tawilat* is going to come down and we're all going to die."

"What? Who? *Why*?" Isilla demanded.

"Somebody doesn't like us—by which I mean an angry pot-roast, because this is Minotaur magic. Earth magic . . ." His voice trailed off into a groan, and Harwing could almost feel the strain of pushing back against Otherfolk sorcery.

"Pendray, go tell Lady Helecanth what we're facing and that we have to open the main cavern again. Tell her to send the Unicorns through first. We're going to have to cast Calm over every living thing in here to get them to do what we want," Isilla said grimly.

"Tush," Harwing said. "This is no time to be negative about things. Go tell the Sanctuary Lightborn that Shield will protect them. That way you can keep them back until the end. Then go to Leutric and tell him somebody has Mad Cow disease. Unless it's him, in which case he probably already knows."

The cavern opened, and sharp winter cold entered. Harwing almost imagined he could hear the click of Unicorn hooves on stone as they ran through the opening. Lovely things. He would have been sad to have missed them.

"And what are you going to be doing?" Isilla demanded.

"Oh, I'll be here. Singing sad songs of the death of kings," Harwing said, flourishing an abbreviated bow.

"Jackass," Dinias gasped. "I don't—suppose you could be—useful?"

"Probably," Harwing said. "Here, Dinney. Take my hand."

Dinias raised one shaking hand from the rock face, and Harwing clasped it tightly.

Suddenly it seemed to Dinias that he was standing in a shallow sheltering alcove, while just beyond it the Light blazed, scouring everything until its surfaces blazed like the Light itself.

There was a figure standing in the full of that wonderful terrible Light, a figure dressed in Lightborn robes as white as the Light itself.

"If you link directly to the Shrine—" Dinias was jarred out of his vision by Harwing's voice. Harwing was striving for pedantic, and not making it. "—you get more power than you do from a mere Flower Forest."

"*Harwing—!*"

"Draw through me, Dinney, and you and the others will be safe. Now, come on!"

"Warhunt! To me! *Link*!" Dinias cried.

In the distance there was the clatter of hooves, the scrape of leather.

⚜

It was dark, and something was patting at her face. "I come, Mistress," Vieliessar muttered groggily. If Maeredhiel had come to wake her in person, she must have overslept badly.

The patting continued—now with the barest whisper of claws—and Vieliessar jerked upright with a gasp.

There was no light, save for the moon-moth glow of the stones in her rings. The air was cold, and the thin clothing she wore was sodden with water.

—*Rune?*

—*Alive.* The response through their Bond was quick and sure.

She groped around until she found his unconscious body. *That is it, then. The Bond is made, and will endure until I die. Or he does.*

She turned him over, her hand lingering on his shoulder in exasperated affection, and shook him until he roused. He sat up, groaning. He was just as wet as she was.

"I am *not* leaving here the way I came in," Runacar announced. He sat up with a groan. "It's dark," he added unnecessarily. "Where is that damned cat?"

"Cold and wet," came Pouncewarm's disgruntled answer. "*Cold!* And wet, wet, *wet*!"

With more effort than she liked, Vieliessar raised Silverlight again and Cast it into the stone. It showed a length of passageway (more tube-like than otherwise), with a hole in the ceiling at one end—they'd obviously dropped through that; it was still dripping—and at the other end, a rock-fall.

She had disjointed memories of a long (long!) fall and then a splash into another torrent, fast-moving with the water it had drained from the collapsing cavern above. She had put Pouncewarm into Sleep quickly, to spare him the worst, but she and Runacar had held each other's hands as they whirled through the dark, gasping for air and holding on to consciousness as long as they could.

And now they were here.

The rock-fall looked almost like a wall some Farmholder or hedge knight might build: a myriad of small round stones, water-smoothed. But how these had come here and how they had come to be placed in this fashion must remain a mystery.

Runacar got stiffly to his feet, and approached the side of the tunnel, touching it experimentally. "We're a long way from Imrathalion—if there's anything left of it. And somewhere far to the east."

"Why east?" Vieliessar asked curiously.

"Because we're in a hole in the ground, and the land isn't right for that west of Mangiralas. All that land is built on bone-stone—it's why their horses were so spectacular. But east of there? Not so much. Half of Jaeglenhend was solid granite; that's why Nilkaran spent so much time tithing the caravans; he could grow little and breed less. So. I wouldn't be surprised to find us sitting right under Old Man Stardock."

"It's going to make it difficult to get out," Vieliessar said, standing up.

Runacar walked down to the hole in the ceiling. He caught the dripping water in his hands and drank. "For what it's worth, I think we can climb up through this hole. If we can get out . . . well, that's another matter entirely."

"Pouncewarm?" Vieliessar asked. The Palugh was a sorry sight, his thick fur soaked through. He was visibly shivering, and looked more miserable than she'd imagined a Palugh could look. She put her hands on the tunnel wall once more and cast Fire into the stone until a section of it radiated heat like a good stove. Pouncewarm crept stiffly over to it to bask in the heat. "Better," the Palugh said forlornly.

"Can you . . . get out?" Vieliessar asked gently.

The Palugh's ears flattened and swiveled sideways. "Too far," Pouncewarm said, very quietly, and said nothing more.

Runacar returned, pulling off sodden layers of clothing to spread them out before the heat. He'd lost his cloak sometime after Shield had vanished, and his hair was a tangled mess that he shoved back impatiently. "As soon as everyone's dry, we can start back," he said.

Vieliessar didn't answer. The whispering had stopped—not gone, but waiting—and beneath it, so far and faint that it might almost be her hope rather than reality, the singing endured. She was still going in the right direction. Forward, not back.

"I must go on," she said.

"I, I, I too will go on," Pouncewarm said, his voice a hoarse croak. He sneezed, and crept even closer to the stone.

"You are killing Pouncewarm," Runacar said, speaking slowly and forcefully. "*He fought an Endarkened for you.* And you are killing him now."

Vieliessar lowered her head, wishing she could weep. But that wasn't something that prophecies did. "I must go on," she repeated, closing her eyes.

There was a long period of silence. Only the breathing of the three in the passage could be heard. Then Runacar knelt before her, gently touching her face.

"I can't imagine anyone pitying you for what you are," he said quietly. "You terrify me. I will ask you this only once: are you *sure* this is the way to the Bones of the Earth? Vielle, are you *sure*?"

"All I am sure of is that this is the way I have to go."

"Then we'll all go," Runacar said.

※

Harwing could feel the Light rushing through him as if he were a drain pipe—no, a straw; that sounded better. Into Dinney and the other Warhunt Mages. They healed the stone constantly. It wounded itself again. All they could do was hold the cavern steady until everyone was free.

Harwing felt as if he were being slowly overheated from the inside and abraded on the outside. His grip on his personal shields was fading; soon the whole contents of his mind would be available to everyone in the link.

If anyone had the time and energy to look.

"How many are left?" he asked, to distract himself. He could feel Dinias send his consciousness racing around the caves, touching every place touched by a living thing.

"Only a few. Less than a candlemark. Can you hold?" Dinias sounded breathless.

"Till the end, my brother. Don't worry about me."

"Ah—! We can let the tuathal caverns along the northern side start collapsing soon," Dinias said. "And maybe collapse one on whichever witchbeast is doing this to us."

"They call *us* witches, you know," Harwing said. *They were kind to me when they did not have to be.*

"*Focus,*" Isilla demanded.

⚬⫚⫛⚬

When Pouncewarm was dry, though still rumpled, Runacar put him next to his skin to keep the Palugh as warm as possible. Vieliessar wore Runacar's now-dry tunic over her rags; Runacar wore his undertunic and leather jerkin, his chain mail over all. Another tremor in the rock made them all freeze in place.

"Do you think it's going to collapse on us?" Vieliessar asked, with the idle curiosity of utter exhaustion.

"I know it's going to collapse on *something,*" Runacar answered.

Vieliessar reached the face of the blockage. She touched the surface of one of the rocks, one-fingered. It was covered with fine grit. She ran her fingers over the boulders in the landslide—they were all the same, except in size—and cast Knowing, though doing so made her eyes water in pain. At least she could still Call Light; the thought of being trapped down here without Silverlight was terrifying.

Pouncewarm struggled free of Runacar's shirt to investigate for himself. He jumped up onto the rocks and tread among them delicately, picking up pebbles and inspecting them.

Runacar picked up a rock about the size of a small melon. "These don't belong here," he said, hefting it. "It's almost as if this was made by someone. Just don't ask me who."

"By whomever does not wish us to continue," Vieliessar said absently. The small rocks could be Transmuted singly—using a weak instance—or the whole of the rockfall could be Transmuted as a strong instance.

Only Vieliessar wasn't sure she could cast a strong instance of *anything*.

They had to bypass this barrier, but she didn't know how: the rockfall barred their advance, and there might not even *be* a tunnel past this point.

Runacar tugged one of the smaller rocks free, only to start a small avalanche of sand and pebbles. He glanced at her. "Can you hold it back with a Shield spell if I try clearing it?"

"Let me see how it's balanced first. I wish Dinias was here; he'd be in his element. Transmute is a gift that doesn't require power as much as it does intelligence. You can spend a lifetime learning how to use it best."

Vieliessar placed her hands delicately upon the stone once more. She sensed no magic, and pushed her senses to sink deeper, learning the structure of the rock and the position of each stone in the rockslide. The process was similar to the beginning of a Healing, when the Healer assessed the structure of the patient under their hands. She could feel the stresses in the rock: the pieces balanced on one another, the large stones whose weight held the whole mass together. Over and over she calculated probabilities and each one ended the same way: the rocks fell and they all died.

Behind her, she heard Runacar clear his throat. "I don't know whether or not this is important, but the rock's glowing."

Not all of the rock was glowing, but at the very top deosil edge there was a faint blue-green glow coming from one stone. When Vieliessar cautiously cleared away the smaller stones, she saw that the glowing stone was flat—as if crafted—and contained a dimpled impression in the center. As if she had pushed the Astromancer's ring stone-first into a brick of wet clay.

"This is not how Magery works!" she announced, irritated. She'd seen—and made—hundreds of spell-locks and even spell-locked doors. The lock wasn't placed on a random piece of rock in the middle of a pile of rubble. What would she get if she unlocked it? *Two* piles of rubble?

"Clearly they should have consulted you," Runacar said. "Why not try it anyway? What harm can it do?"

"Those are the last words of many a Candidate," Vieliessar muttered, even as she was pulling the ring from her finger. She picked it up gingerly and settled it into the impression on the stone.

The stone and the ring vanished, taking their eldritch aquamarine light with them. Once they had, the rest of the rockslide slowly vanished, as if turning to mist, hard though it was to be sure of anything when the light was so dim.

But the light was bright enough to show that the barrier was gone. The tunnel that lay revealed was smaller than where they were, but still passable.

"What did you do?" Runacar asked. "Were the rocks real or not?"

"I have no idea. All I know is that I've just lost the Astromancer's ring."

"Or Leutric's."

"There's that."

Pouncewarm jumped to Runacar's shoulder, and they went on.

⊟⊨

The singing grew louder, though no one but Vieliessar could hear it. No matter how hard she tried, the stone around them would not hold Silverlight for long, so in frustration she sent balls of it floating down the tunnel ahead. The light was dim and uncertain, and she had to keep renewing the spell, as if there was something down here that ate Magery.

The tunnel didn't run straight; it ran in long curving arcs, always heading downward. At first the grade was too insignificant to notice, but slowly it increased enough for them to know that for every ten cubits forward, they went one cubit down.

More and more Vieliessar had the sense of something watching. She caught silvery flashes out of the corner of her eye—as if there were side-tunnels where there obviously were not—but there was never anything visible when she looked, and she had absolutely no sense of any form of sorcery or spellcraft being present. Nor did she have any idea of how long they'd been walking. They were not dead of hunger or thirst, so that argued three sunturns at most—or had it merely been candlemarks since she had begun her descent into the darkness? She knew Imrathalion had been at the edge of collapse when she had begun—had anyone escaped? Did her folk in Nomaitemil mourn her—or were they arming for war? Had the Endarkened returned to finish burning down the Flower Forests?

Were the three of them the only ones left alive anywhere in the Fortunate Lands?

Runacar shuffled along beside her, as exhausted as she. They took turns carrying Pouncewarm in their arms; it was a mark of the Palugh's exhaustion that he allowed it.

They had to stop carrying him when the passage became so constricted they had to crawl forward on hands and knees. When it became even more cramped, Vieliessar took the lead, crawling forward on elbows and toes. The sense of the weight of living rock above her was utterly oppressive. Silverlight was little use here, but Vieliessar kept casting it just so they all wouldn't be crawling down into the dark. She began to imagine she heard creaking in the rock. Surely it would collapse soon. When the rock collapsed, would death be fast or slow? Would the three of them be immediately obliterated, or slowly crushed?

The size of the space they must pass through continued to shrink. Now the rock brushed against her on all sides, and Vieliessar had to grip the sides of the passage to pull herself forward, handspan by handspan. It was difficult, as the rock was nearly smooth, as if it had been shaped by Elven hands. Rune said that an *audtiraq* from a *tehukohiakhazarishtial* had shaped it long ago. Apparently making these tunnels was a thing they did. It was odd to contemplate Stardock fountaining out molten rock as if a crucible pouring forth molten metal.

She was tired, Vieliessar realized, for her mind to be turning upon irrelevancies like this. It was not like a battle. No matter how tired you were, someone trying to kill you kept you alert.

And her teeth were no longer chattering. The stone she crawled over was warm. It had been warm for a while, as if the cold of the upper galleries had only been some passing season, and here the summer had come.

But no matter how hard or easy this long painful slog, she'd held out hope that it would resolve itself in her favor. In the Child of the Prophecy's favor. That the tunnel would widen again.

Until she saw what was ahead. "Runacar?" she whispered. "Pounce-warm?"

"I'm here," Runacar answered instantly. "I, and I. I," said Pounce-warm, an instant later. The Palugh sounded utterly exhausted. Vieliessar hoped Rune was carrying him. Somehow.

"The passage narrows up ahead," she said, and heard Runacar laugh. "What a peculiarity! Who could imagine such a thing?"

"And after that it's impassable."

"Maybe there's another lock? You still have a ring left."

He was right. She pressed her forehead to the stone beneath her, breathing carefully, then squirmed forward as far as she could. She might gain a few more handspans beyond this, but she was already fighting against the panic of being entombed. It was like being encased in badly fitting plate armor: she could not breathe except shallowly.

And if she forced herself much further forward, she did not think Runacar could pull her free.

Vieliessar exhaled as completely as she could, filling her mind with the first of many evocations the Lightborn used to conjure up quiet and repose out of panic and fear. When both body and mind had stilled, Vieliessar stretched her arm out as far in front of her as she could reach.

Her fingers touched . . .

Nothing.

The passage went on, only now it was the width of a draining-pipe, if that. And nowhere on its walls was there anything in the shape of the first spell-lock she'd seen.

"I can't get through," she said simply. "The passage goes on, but it's too small for me."

She relaxed against the stone. Sleep would be wonderful, and she was so very tired.

She thought she did sleep then, if only for a few heartbeats. She awoke to Runacar waggling her ankle, trying to get her attention.

"Back up," he said. "I've got an idea."

WOOD'S MOON IN THE TENTH YEAR OF THE HIGH KING'S REIGN: PERPLEXED IN DARKNESS AND ENTANGLED IN RUIN

Do not waste your tears on the truth. Save them to ornament your lies, so they will be believed.

—Arilcarion War-Maker, *Of the Sword Road*

They had to crawl backward a substantial distance before the tunnel was again wide enough for the two Elves to sit up, and even so, the stone still brushed the tops of their heads. The thought of having to retrace the whole of their way was too exhausting to contemplate.

And the faintly felt tremors that continued to reach them hinted that it might be impossible.

Pouncewarm stepped up into Vieliessar's lap, and she combed her fingers through his fur, smoothing and straightening it as much as she could. "When we are free I will give you brushes of fine silver and combs of pearl, and you shall have a seat on my council and be my most trusted advisor."

"You're getting soft in your dotage, O High King," Runacar said, his tone as affectionate as it was mocking.

"I learned mercy in a hard school. It is not a quality the War Princes prize."

"I am not a War Prince," Runacar answered. "I'm not sure I could have been one. If I were, at Ifjalasairaet I would have sworn fealty to you and then killed you in your sleep."

"Fortunately, I rarely sleep."

Runacar raised his eyebrows, indicating he wasn't sure whether she was joking or not.

"And I, I, I am her guardian, Pretty Rune. I!" Pouncewarm blinked up at Vieliessar, eyes luminous in the dimness. "I, I, I am first and best. Best hostage. Best warrior. Best." But it seemed to Vieliessar's ear that Pouncewarm's cheer was forced.

"You are," she agreed. "And now Pretty Rune must tell us his idea, for surely such a puissant prince and knight can solve all our difficulties with a single word."

Now Runacar was sure she was joking. If sarcasm counted as joking.

"Pouncewarm," he said. "He can go further along the tunnel than you can. He can tell us what he sees. If this route is really impassable, we can . . . think of something else."

"Will you do that for me, my brave heart, my lion? Go where I cannot, and see there what I cannot see?" Vieliessar asked.

"I will go," the Palugh said. "I."

She pulled the remaining ring from her finger. "Take this. Use it if you can." She held out the ring. Its stone glowed more brightly than any of the Silverlight she had been able to make.

Pouncewarm reached out to take it. He held it in both hands and regarded it doubtfully, then slipped it onto his hand. Vieliessar blinked as it became a bracelet. *It changes for every wearer.*

Pouncewarm rubbed the side of his face against her hand. "Vielle is wise. Rune is pretty," he said with effort.

Then he walked off down the tunnel, tail drooping, the gleaming ring around his wrist. The two Elvenkind watched until the light vanished, cut off by the curve of the passageway.

"What shall we do now?" Runacar asked. They could do nothing until the Palugh returned, and without something to occupy his mind, Runacar would think of a number of things he'd rather not. "I'm afraid I don't even have a *gan* set with me."

"I never liked *gan*," Vieliessar said idly. "It's nothing like real life."

"Then xaique," he said easily. "Which I also do not possess."

"What do you think will happen?" Vieliessar asked.

Trust her to ask the question no one wants to think about. "To us, to him, or to the world?" Runacar countered. "For the first, I hope your weapon is small."

"Leutric called it the Bones of the Earth," Vieliessar said. "It's probably the size of a Great Keep."

"And if he finds nothing?"

"Then . . ." Runacar watched as she sighed and rubbed at her face. He was filthy and cold and tired and hungry, and if he was, so was she. "Then I suppose I must figure out some other way to get through this tunnel."

"Since that's impossible, why don't we—"

"Wait. Something's happening."

⚓

The air in the side-chamber was thick with rock dust, and rank with the scent of fear and exertion. Harwing did not know who came intermittently with a basin and bowl to wash his face and give him water to drink, but he blessed them, for it almost made this bearable. There'd been pain at the beginning, when he'd linked, for the raging power of the Shrine of the Star was not something mortal flesh was built to bear, but Dinias's hand was warm and strong in his, and Dinias took the power Harwing pulled from the Shrine and passed it to the others linked to him, and so the power was worth its pain.

This is my execution. But that's all right. I have blood on my hands. This will be its expiation.

Harwing's mouth tasted of blood, and the tears running down his cheeks were amaranthine until the dust clotted them.

There were seven of them, all Warhunt, all holding hands and pressing their bodies against the rock face as if mere Elven strength could keep these caverns from collapsing. All linked: Harwing could catch random scraps of their thoughts and emotions as they struggled against the stone.

Their enemy acted and they reacted, their xaique pieces balances and faultlines and incalculable weights of rock. But the Warhunt held. Imrathalion held.

"Ware slip!" someone called, and the chamber was suddenly flooded with harsh sunlight and winter air as the whole of the rock casing Imrathalion's entrance became sand. Harwing could almost feel the relief in the stone as it fragmented into new and different lines of stress.

"The last of the wounded are out." Dinias sounded a little breathless, and the hand that clutched Harwing's trembled.

"Delighted," Harwing answered, his voice ragged. His free hand left bloody prints on the rock as he clutched at it to keep himself upright. "Is it possible that the rest of our merry band could consider *hurrying*?"

"It's a lot of people to move," Dinias said conciliatingly. "Harwing, you have to stop this. Arevethmonion—"

"Is far away, is burning, cannot spare us the power to do this," Harwing snapped. "And don't try to stop drawing from me, because I will know—in the scant instants before the roof of this Dark and Void mountain falls on all of us."

Harwing could hear Dinias thinking about how to get the taille of Mages—and Harwing—out alive. But the power Harwing drew from the Shrine was used by everyone. He must stay behind so that the others could go.

Unbidden, Harwing's mind offered up the memory of Hamphuliadiel clawing for his last moments of life as he drowned in the mud of the Harvest Festival; at Momioniarch, Orchalianiel, Sunalanthaid, and Galathornthadan, as they sat around the table he had prepared for them, a table laden only with death. *Don't worry about me, my brother: I'm not nearly noble enough to live into your new world.*

Distantly, Harwing could feel Dinias's shock and horror.

"Harwing, how could you? Why did you? When—"

Hush. Just hold the rock. Harwing turned his mind to the enemy. *I swear by Light and Void, by the Cold World and the Warm, I shall outlast you.*

All that mattered was drawing Light from the Shrine and passing Light to the others.

⊰⊱

New Mages came to replace those who were exhausted. They came bearing water and tea and scraps of news. There were no more of the Endarkened to be seen.

And everything in the outside world seemed to be on fire.

Dinias groaned at the news. Harwing squeezed his hand tighter. "We'll deal with that when we have to," he croaked aloud.

Only he and Dinias had been here from the beginning now.

⌑

Miraculously, the cavern system they had claimed at such high price half a day before was nearly empty again. The villagers, the Sanctuary Lightborn, the Silver Swords, and the Otherfolk who had entered the cavern were retreating to what would be a safe distance if the entire hillside came down.

"Who's left?" Harwing's voice was an abused whisper now.

"They say the Unicorns have vouched that the caverns are clear," Dinias said, "save for one to the north that was opened and is now sealed."

"It is where your enemy lies. Shall we have someone assault it?" a new voice asked brightly.

"No," Dinias said firmly. "The rock that comes down will squash them."

There came a snort in response. Harwing wondered who had been speaking.

If they'd won, it didn't feel like it. The High King was missing and so was the Banebringer's brother. The Minotaur Earthdancers were trying to kill everyone. Everybody who had run here to hide not a sunturn ago would now have to retrace their steps to where "Hamphuliadiel's" people had been encamped only yesterday, reclaim the wagons and supplies (if any were left), and head in the direction of the Dragon's Gate. Or Arevethmonion, if they could get the fire out.

Not that you'll see it either way.

"Come *on,* stupid two-legs!" the voice demanded. "Come on and do it fast."

Harwing leaned against the rock. Dinias clutched his hand.

"Aranor; go first," Dinias said.

⌑

One by one, Harwing heard the shuffle-steps of the Warhunt departing. He felt it as each link in the chain was severed, as those who remained took up more of the strain. Dinias let the caverns behind them collapse, and rock dust once more roiled through the cavern, this time so thick that Dinias cast Shield over those present so that they could breathe.

At last only the two of them were left.

"Harwing," Dinias said. "Go—"

"Now to the Warm World, where Pelashia will forgive my necessities." Harwing cut him off ruthlessly. "Get out of here, Dinias. My hands are bloody—" He laughed, croakily, at the metaphor that was more than truth.

"I can—"

"Go. Tell Isilla enough and no more."

It was an effort to relax his hand, to feel it empty, to know that Dinias's grip was the last touch he would ever feel.

Now I am alone in holding up the rock. And I vow I will make a better death than Hamphuliadiel did.

And everything was the bright white of the Shrine, and then it was dark.

WOOD'S MOON IN THE TENTH YEAR OF THE HIGH KING'S REIGN: THE LORD OF THE FOUR QUARTERS

Peace is nearly indistinguishable from war; it merely has fewer casualties. The wise komen can turn war into peace in such ways as to baffle his enemy, who will then exert his force against nothing.

Arilcarion War-Maker, *Of the Sword Road*

The moment Runacar spoke, she felt it. And heard it. A steady vibration. A sound almost like tearing cloth. Then impacts, one after another, like heavy flat weights falling.

We are trapped down here forever!

"Pouncewarm!" Vieliessar cried, her shout mixing with his yowl of victory. The sound echoed back up the tunnel, and then the cramped space began to . . . melt away. In moments, though they had not moved, they discovered that they were now sitting face-to-face on the floor of what seemed to be a very large space. The Silverlight vanished, and Vieliessar recast it yet again. The globe she conjured was only a faint shadow of its usual self: instead of being silvery-white, it was the color of stormclouds. But it was better than the blackness.

With the light to guide him, Pouncewarm bounded over to them, his exuberance restored.

The ring she had given him was gone.

"I, I, I, only I could have done this! Pouncewarm Victorious! Pouncewarm Adventurer! Pouncewarm Hunter! I!"

"Yes, you," Vieliessar agreed, getting to her feet. It was sheer joy to raise her arms above her head as far as she could and stretch. "But what did you do, small *alakomentai*?"

"Long tunnel, small tunnel," Pouncewarm said. "And then a lock. And now, no lock!"

"That seems simple enough," Runacar commented, standing up as well. "And I hope this is our final destination, because we are fresh out of magic rings, not to mention the fact that your lights keep going out. If we can find something to burn, maybe we can get a look at your prize. And possibly find a shorter route out of here."

Vieliessar let him ramble, not really paying attention. It was all meant as a distraction, after all. The walls on either side of this new space were too far away to touch, and Pouncewarm had come running toward her over a considerable distance. She thought they must be in the same place they had been—and the illusory/not illusory rock had all vanished, leaving them . . .

Where?

"I think you're right about being under Stardock," Vieliessar said musingly. "It will be a long walk home either way."

The first thing to do is find the wall. The next is to follow it around.

She stumbled as she moved, feeling off-balance and clumsy. It took her a moment to realize why. The silence. The voices were gone. So was the singing. She was alone in her own mind.

She took a deep breath, orienting herself once again, and took another step forward.

"What in the name of the Void are you doing?" Runacar's exasperated voice came clearly, though he was visible only as a dim shape.

"I'm going to find the cavern wall, and see if I can figure out where we are. And maybe find those torches you're after."

Suddenly, two enormous lanterns appeared right in front of her. They were round as melons, their color the featureless gold of burning coals, and they shone brighter than the Silverlight. For a moment Vieliessar thought her evocation of Silverlight might have triggered some other lighting spell, but then the lanterns began moving, rising higher and higher and higher.

"Who has come to awaken me and my children?" a voice demanded.

Leutric had not mentioned that his weapon could talk.

"I am Vieliessar High King. I seek the Bones of the Earth."

"Why?" the voice asked. Vieliessar could tell nothing about it save its apparently female gender. That, and that something very *very* large was speaking. Was this some guardian she must overcome? Something Leutric had also not mentioned? She knew Runacar knew nothing more than she.

"I am the Child of the Prophecy, and this is the time of the Red Harvest. I come in the name of all living things, and I tell you this truly: if you do not aid us, the Endarkened will kill us all."

"Not *us*," the female voice said assuredly. "They will not find *us*. Pelashia, go back where you belong. We will not rise for such as you."

If she had possessed less self-control, Vieliessar would have gasped out loud. It had never occurred to her that when she found the weapon, it would refuse to be used. And to call her by the name of her long-dead ancestress . . . ?

She felt the faint disturbance of the air that meant Runacar had come to stand beside her.

"She isn't Pelashia. Pelashia has been dead for ten thousand years," Runacar said. "Vieliessar is Pelashia's greatdaughter, and I am Runacar, Battlemaster of the Folk, and I say Vieliessar is telling you the truth. Now reveal yourself at once, and surrender the weapon we need to destroy the Endarkened."

"Or risk your wrath?" Vieliessar asked him before she could stop herself. They were here facing an unknown creature, and Runacar had sounded *precisely* like some High House komen who could not imagine anyone would dare to defy him. She wanted to giggle, and knew that if she began to laugh she'd never stop.

"I have a great deal of wrath," Runacar said indignantly.

"And we have Pouncewarm," Vieliessar said. "Pouncewarm's wrath is to be feared."

"I!" The Palugh's voice echoed in the darkness. She couldn't tell where he'd gotten to. "I am fierce and terrible! I! Slayer of thousands! I! Watcher in the dark—*I*!"

"There," Runacar said with satisfaction. "We are all wrathful and terrible, and we demand your surrender."

"Are you mad?" the voice from the darkness demanded, sounding astonished. "Do you not know I could destroy you in an eyeblink? Why aren't you afraid of me?"

("Because we can't see you," muttered Runacar.)

"Destruction is easy," Vieliessar said. "My people spent many years waging war upon our own kind. We covered the ground with the dead from our wars, and killing was our pleasure and sport. We thought ourselves masters of the world until the Endarkened came. They kill as easily as they breathe, and we have no force that can withstand them. If I had known I would have to argue with Leutric's weapon, I think I would not have bothered to come."

"'Weapon,'" the voice said, sounding insulted. "You do not even know what I am." Suddenly the cloud of Silverlight above Vieliessar's head vanished, and the chamber walls began to give off a bright blue green glow.

"I, Children of Stars, am a *Dragon*."

CHAPTER THIRTY-FIVE

WOOD'S MOON IN THE TENTH YEAR OF THE HIGH KING'S REIGN: A SWORD OF LIGHTNING

In size, it is similar to a large horse. Its skin is red and thick and hairless, and its wings do not function, and are merely an ornamental crest along the spine. The Dragon is almost definitely an imaginary creature, for its form conflicts with the laws of venery. It is to be considered as the personification of the knight who fights with great force but without elegance.

—Lannarien's Book of Living Things

Lannarien's Book of Living Things said that Dragons "were almost definitely imaginary creatures." Of course, Lannarien also said *Unicorns* were imaginary. You really couldn't trust what people put in books.

The Dragon looked very little like Lannarien's description. She was pale as elvensilver, white as the moon; her alabaster scales were opalescent, shimmering with every color that could be found in the world, iridescence dancing over them like rain on glass as she breathed.

Oh, Radafa, I wish you had lived to see this!

She was also somewhat larger than Lannarien's estimate. Her head alone was longer than Runacar was tall; a thing of sword-bright planes of chitin that gleamed like snow and ice and metal. Her jaws were enormous, and her long sharp teeth were very *very* white. She had a long sinuous neck with ventral scale-plates like the faulds in a suit of armor, and dorsal ridges that went from small to large from her neck to her shoulders. Scales covered her body in sizes ranging from the breadth of his hand to the diameter of wagon wheels. She was winged. Her wings weren't feathered like those of the Gryphons and Hippogriffs, but were vast sails of skin and bone, with every color there was shimmering over their opalescent surface. Her tail was easily twice the length of her entire body, ending in a long flat barb similar to the ones young girls attached to their kites.

It must be for balance when she flies.

Her front legs ended in Gryphon-like claws; she could probably pick up rocks and throw them if she wanted to. Runacar could not imagine her ever *needing* to.

"Beautiful pretty pretty *pretty* one!" Pouncewarm sang. He skittered across the floor until he was practically underneath the Dragon, then settled there, looking smug.

"And what good is a Dragon?" Vieliessar asked bluntly.

"What she means is that you are beautiful beyond dreams and her delight in beholding you makes up for all the pain and anguish she endured to reach your side," Runacar said hastily. Diplomacy was not among Vieliessar's skills, apparently.

"I meant what I said," Vieliessar said stubbornly. "What do Dragons *do*? You are very large, and your teeth are very sharp, but I have seen the Endarkened kill Gryphons and Aesalions and Hippogriffs more easily than I would kill a chicken for the pot. They would probably kill you just as well."

The Dragon lowered her head down to their eye-level. She sighed deeply, and Runacar felt a rush of warm air spill over him. The chamber was filled with a pleasant and unfamiliar spicy scent that must be the scent of Dragon, and Runacar thought suddenly of Melisha. Where was she? Was she safe?

Would he live to see her again?

"Only one of you is a Mage," the Dragon said, sounding long-suffering. "But I see that the two of you are Bondmates. That isn't something in your favor, by the way. We Dragons have been fated to Soulbond only with Elven Mages—until the day comes when a new form of magic enters the world, the magic of Men."

"If 'Men' is not fighting for the Endarkened, there will be plenty of time to find him and learn his Magery," Vieliessar said. "But how can you Soulbond? That is for Elvenkind alone."

The Dragon heaved a deep sigh. "Elvenkind! Always placing themselves at the center of everything. You Soulbond with one another because the day would come when one of you must Soulbond with me. Or with one of my brethren."

You have brethren? Runacar thought, then: *I do not want to be Soulbonded to a Dragon.*

Pouncewarm pulled himself up onto the Dragon's foreleg, then began the long ascent to her shoulder. Runacar watched him in fascination as the Palugh gained his goal, and gazed out in triumph from the Dragon's dorsal ridge—after which he began walking along her neck to her head, his plumed tail now held jauntily erect.

"Each Dragon—and we are the only ones, we thirteen who were born when this world was born, the Light's echo of something you don't really need to know about—is fated to Soulbond with one *particular* Elven Mage—after which, that Mage becomes incredibly powerful, having an endless supply of Light to draw on. I am a repository of infinite Magic that is my Bonded's to wield however they choose—if I find someone to Bond with, which is looking increasingly unlikely. I think that's just as well, since my life becomes tied to my Bondmate, just as theirs does to mine. Unless my Dragonmage Bondmate can manage to cast the spell to transfer my Dragonbond to another Mage before they die, when their heart ceases to beat, so does mine. I'm afraid there's nothing for the Dragonmage save death, if I die first. Don't worry. My kind is very hard to kill."

The Dragon drew breath to go on, but Vieliessar spoke first. "Forgive me for mentioning this, but there doesn't seem to be much advantage to this relationship for the Dragon."

It seemed to Runacar that the Dragon's expression softened, and she blinked her great golden eyes slowly. "Without the one with whom we may Bond, our lives are empty. Our Bondmate is the expression of our magic, our heart's fulfillment, the one to whom our lives and hearts are forever linked."

"Until you die. Or your Bondmate transfers your Bond to someone else," Vieliessar pointed out.

Pouncewarm had reached his destination. He put both paws on the crest of bone that protected the soft vulnerable place where neck met skull.

"I suggest you find yourself a suitable successor quickly," the Dragon snapped, "because I don't think you're going to be around for very long."

"Wrong!" Pouncewarm said in delight. "Old sleeper, here is Vielle the clever, who has fought a thousand battles. She! And solved a hundred thousand riddles! She only! She is peerless, unparalleled! Much better than Wulvers! Almost as good as we! First Dragonmage! Queen of Legends!"

The Dragon looked more irritated than convinced, though not quite cross enough to simply shake the Palugh from her neck.

"Me?" Vieliessar asked blankly. Runacar had never imagined seeing her so flabbergasted, but he supposed it was justifiable under the circumstances.

"Why do you suppose we've been having this conversation?" the Dragon demanded. "I've just woken up and I'm *hungry* I'm not going to find dinner sitting around in here. You! Child! Explain this to her!" The Dragon pointed at Runacar with her folded wing. It had a sort of clawed finger at its joint, and Runacar realized that Dragons were six-legged creatures: the wing was simply a strangely-distorted forelimb. *I wonder what you call a collection of Dragons? A herd? A tribe? A flock?*

Or maybe just . . . a lot of trouble.

"If this is the Bones of the Earth," Runacar said, speaking to Vieliessar, "then this—"

"My *name* happens to be Tannatarie!" the Dragon huffed.

"—Dragon, whose name is Tannatarie, is what—*who*—you can use as a—I mean, will be your ally against the Endarkened. If you Soulbond with her. And then I suppose you don't have to worry about whatever Lightborn use to power their magic anymore."

"You don't know anything either," Tannatarie said with a disappointed sigh. Pouncewarm chirruped encouragement to her.

"If you and I Soulbond, Tannatarie, what happens?" Vieliessar asked.

"Try to pay attention this time, Child of Stars. As I have told you—"

"No," Vieliessar interrupted. "To *him*."

"Oh, he'll probably die," Tannatarie said offhandedly. "You're very small. You don't look as if you could Bond to two people at the same time."

Vieliessar glanced toward him. Runacar knew there was nothing to stop her: nobody would question his disappearance when she came back with a Dragon. She could say he'd died in the cave-in. It would even be true, in its way.

"I don't believe I wish to kill him at this time," Vieliessar said consideringly. "His life isn't really a fair trade for just one Dragon."

"*One?*" Tannatarie sounded as if she couldn't decide whether to be outraged or amused. "Brothers! Sisters! Awaken! It is time! Our long sleep is ended!"

⫘

All of Runacar's attention had been on Tannatarie, because she was beautiful and dangerous—and also because she was the brightest thing in the cave.

But suddenly the cave grew brighter still, the green-glowing walls paling in color as if some mysterious chthonian sun had just risen. Pairs of golden eyes opened in what he had thought were outcroppings of rock. Heads rose up on sinuous necks. Color flooded into what had been grey rock, filling the chamber with living jewels. The underground chamber (which he'd already thought to be enormous) now seemed to extend forever.

"Rise up, Black Sorgane! Rise, Lianor the Beautiful! Awake, Rimanet the Clever! Steadfast Elderin, rise! Come Herianne and Araneida, come Elokai and Telleval! To me, Kallon, Oziana, Miravant, Balorak the Cerulean! It is time to rise up from your slumbers!"

Dragon eyes opened and Dragon limbs stretched. Dragon tails lashed back and forth, or curled around Dragon feet. In only a few heartbeats, Runacar and Vieliessar were standing at the center of a wheel of which Tannatarie was the hub.

And there were twelve enormous Dragons around the rim, all gazing down at them.

They were all the shades of color it was possible to imagine: brilliant many-hued blue; glorious green; enchanting violet; fire-bright scarlet; opalescent *pirozaduta*; the dark blue-violet of encroaching twilight. And gold and silver, copper and bronze: where the other Dragons' colors were shifting and opalescent, their scales gleamed as brightly as mirrors and crystal and gems reflecting lightning.

"Thirteen Dragons, then," Vieliessar said, unimpressed.

"You are going to get all three of us killed," Runacar told her.

"Optimist," Vieliessar answered.

There was a long pause—Runacar would have been delighted to allow it to continue for several days, really—before Vieliessar spoke again.

"Exalted Lady, Tannatarie the White, whose scales teach the snow to shine and the foam upon the ocean wave to mimic the moon, great one who is as wise as she is beautiful, as intelligent as she is fearsome, I beg of you your wise counsel in this my hour of need," Vieliessar said.

Pouncewarm beamed. Runacar stared. Tannatarie's face was not made to show expression, and Runacar was doing his best not to look at her anyway.

"Better," Tannatarie said grudgingly. "But you don't really mean it."

"Of course I do, you ridiculous lizard! I don't know what a Dragonbond is, and you're clearly not weapons, but I will do anything I must to save my people—to save all of Jer-a-kalaliel—from the Endarkened. There are many Elven Mages among my people. Come back with me to Nomaitemil and you will have all of them to choose from. I swear this by the Light. Only fight beside us against the Endarkened!"

Long necks coiled and twined at the rim of the circle as the Dragons whispered among themselves. Runacar thought it was just as well that he couldn't hear what they were saying.

Tannatarie cocked her head, studying Vieliessar. "Very well," she said at last. "Kill your Bondmate and I will give you power beyond your imaginings."

It was as if suddenly all time stopped. He wouldn't fight her. Runacar swore that to himself. He'd expected to be dead in Harvest Moon; that he would die in Woods Moon instead didn't change the fact that he had already made his peace with the leaving of life. And if he did not die in battle, did not receive a pyre, did not go to ride with the Hunt for all Eternity . . . well, he had forfeited that right many Wheelturns before.

"No," Vieliessar said. "I am a Child of the Light. One of the Children of Stars. Pelashia Celenthodiel's greatdaughter. I will not profane my honor or my Magery for your power, if this is the price you ask. No."

She turned to face him. Runacar could see her rueful expression quite clearly. "I am very sorry," she said apologetically. "But I really don't feel like killing you today."

"Ah. Well. I think it would be more appropriate after we are married, of course. Traditional. It would be wrong to anticipate our pleasures."

"So it would," Vieliessar said gravely. "Perhaps we must call you Rune the Wise."

"No! No-no-no-*not* wise! Rune is pretty! And Vielle is *usually* wise."

The Palugh bounded down from Tannatarie's nose and came trotting toward Vieliessar from between Tannatarie's forelimbs. He bounded into her arms and Vieliessar set him on her shoulders.

"Not wise today?" she asked Pouncewarm. "But really, it doesn't matter whether I slit his throat or simply Dragonbond with Tannatarie. Pretty Rune will die."

"Child of the Prophecy," Pouncewarm sang. "Chosen of Amretheon and Pelashia! Rare and impossible, unique and strange!"

"I think he means I'd survive," Runacar said.

"I suppose you might," Vieliessar said, grudgingly accepting Pouncewarm's logic. "But I would have to have a Dragon with which to make this Soulbond, and no one here has offered."

"You are so very young," Tannatarie said, sighing. "Come, Child. Look at me. Look closely. See my eyes."

⋰⊟⋱

The great white Dragon lowered her head until her eyes were level with Vieliessar's. The end of her nose poked Vieliessar in the stomach, and Vieliessar reflexively reached out to Tannatarie to steady herself.

She looked into Tannatarie's eyes.

"I have slept since the beginning of the world," Tannatarie said aloud. "And in all my dreams there was no moment of joy until I saw your face."

It was true. Vieliessar did not need Magery to know it was true. For an instant the memory of that long-ago Oronviel battlefield rose up in her mind: Runacar, splendid on his gleaming stallion, his golden armor radiant in the rays of the setting sun. She'd looked into his eyes, and in that moment knew there could be no other for her.

But there was. There was Tannatarie.

This was a mother's love. A sister's. Love Vieliessar could otherwise never have had, for she had chosen safety for her people, and power could not command love. She would love Tannatarie, and Tannatarie would love her, and their hearts would beat together for the whole of their conjoined lives.

And Runacar would live. Runacar loved the Unicorn Melisha, and Melisha had chosen to love him. Theirs was love without constraint, and it would endure between them no matter what his Bondmate did.

I love you, Vieliessar said to Tannatarie, astonished.

And I love you, my darling, the great Dragon replied. *I have awaited you since before Time began. Let us now become one.*

Power filled Vieliessar's senses, and magic. Her body was filled with Light, and with joy, and for a time she knew nothing more.

WOOD'S MOON IN THE TENTH YEAR OF THE HIGH KING'S REIGN: A SHIELD OF BROKEN GLASS

No komen can engage in honorable battle with wind, and dust, and sand. Be sure, when you go to fight, that you know how much victory you need. Or you may receive far more than you want.

—Arilcarion War-Maker, *Of the Sword Road*

Vieliessar came back to herself lying against Tannatarie's neck, with Pouncewarm curled up against her. Tannatarie's wing was cocked forward, shielding them both. She reached out carefully with her senses. The Dragonbond with Tannatarie burned hot and bright, and unmistakable.

And the Soulbond she shared with Runacar was also there, a glowing moon to the Dragonbond's refulgent sun.

"Pretty Rune? Bondmate? Are you here?" she asked, sitting up.

"If you're going to call me that all the time, I am going to go live with the Gryphons," Runacar announced.

Tannatarie raised her wing so Vieliessar could see him. Runacar was sitting on the cavern floor with his folded tunic as a pad, attempting to untangle his hair with his fingers. From the look of it, he had been engaged in this losing battle for some time.

"I see I'm going to have to gift you with a comb as well."

"And a seat on your council?" he asked instantly.

"For my Bondmate and the Battlemaster of the Otherfolk, of course."

⁂

Runacar wasn't sure he'd even met this woman. For the first time, Vieliessar looked *happy*. She kept her hand upon Tannatarie's neck, her need to constantly touch an echo of the way Runacar had seen lovers behave. But if this was love—and he believed it was—it was the same sort of love he shared with Melisha: a love of mind and heart and spirit to which bodies were not admitted.

"You're being remarkably agreeable," he said. "What about the rest of your councillors?"

"Oh, they'll object," Vieliessar said, airily. "But everything is different now. They'll have to see that. Don't you understand? *Now we have a fight we can win.*"

Runacar found himself smiling back at her. "I see only one impediment to our upcoming campaign," he said gravely. "We're all still in here."

"Oh," Vieliessar said, her eyes dancing, "is that all?"

Runacar watched as she concentrated. She seemed to be listening for something—or looking for it with senses he didn't have.

"Yes, darling," Tannatarie said. "Won't that be a lovely surprise?"

Vieliessar laughed, and suddenly a part of the chamber wall . . .

Vanished.

Cold winter sunlight spilled into the chamber, the scent of new snow mixed with the scent of green growing things, of flowers and the springtide, all overlain by the scent of burning. Runacar thought of the Western Shore, when they had set Delfierarathadan alight. Another Flower Forest was burning here.

Runacar got to his feet. There was a streak of fur as Pouncewarm bounded past him and through the doorway. "Aiiiiiiiiiiiiiiiiii! *First!*" the Palugh chortled.

"Haven't you ever seen a puissant instance of Door before?" Vieliessar asked amusedly. "Go on. It's safe. I can hold it for candlemarks."

"Is that Arevethmonion?" he asked.

"Yes. If anyone got out of the caves before they collapsed, they went toward Arevethmonion. You'll step out onto the Sanctuary Road," Vieliessar said, her Dragonbond giddiness suddenly lessening. It was a sobering reminder of the fact that this enchanted interlude was over, but Runacar knew he would carry the memory of it in his heart forever.

"After you," Runacar said, flourishing a bow, but Vieliessar only stepped back to let the Dragons lead.

Runacar had expected Tannatarie to be first, but it was Sorgane who led the exodus. The great black Dragon got to his feet and stepped carefully over to Door. A few more steps, and he was through. The ground trembled as the Dragon walked—just as it would have when heavy dray-horses pulled their loads—and then the trembling stopped.

One by one, the other Dragons followed Sorgane out onto the Sanctuary Road, until only Tannatarie and the two Elves remained.

"Well?" Tannatarie said. "Are you coming?" The white Dragon walked through Door. Vieliessar followed, her hand on Tannatarie's side.

The brightness of the chamber walls had begun to fade, first to white, and then to grey. As he headed toward Door, Runacar took a last look around. All there was to see was an enormous round domed chamber, its floor covered with the eggshell-like stone casings that had once held thirteen Dragons.

⊰⊱

Runacar turned around automatically as soon as he felt the road beneath his feet, just as he always did, but Door was gone, just as it always was. He could see he was inside a Flower Forest, but he couldn't tell Arevethmonion from Nomaitemil by sight. At least the road was familiar, and the surroundings didn't seem to have taken too much battle-damage. And if this was Arevethmonion, Smoketree was a few leagues northeast of here; the Dragon's Gate and the (former) Caves of Imrathalion further still.

Vieliessar and Tannatarie were standing, alone, in the Sanctuary Road. "Sky and wind," Tannatarie sighed. "At last."

"Where are the other Dragons?" Runacar asked. He couldn't believe they'd already gone so far into Arevethmonion that he couldn't see them.

"There," Vieliessar said, pointing toward the sky.

Runacar looked up.

Wheeling slowly through the sky, like the most fantastical of kites, were the other twelve Dragons. They were high enough in the sky that the colors of their bodies could not be seen, but the membranes of their wings glowed like colored glass. The Dragons swirled one last time, and then departed in every direction.

"Well, Tannatarie says she's hungry," Vieliessar said, "and though I am not sure there is enough game left in the land to satisfy the tastes of one Dragon, let alone thirteen, I imagine they're going hunting." Vieliessar put her arms around herself and shivered, in a very non–Child of the Prophecy, non-Dragonmage way. "And I am cold and hungry as well, and have been for longer than I like, so find the others. I have set us as near Imrathalion as I may, but the road veers toward the Dragon's Gate there," she said apologetically. "As soon as you can find them, find Pouncewarm, before he tells anyone what he told us about Hresa. Leutric should hear it first—if at all. Also, let them know that the Dragons are *our* Dragons, and not some new trick of the Endarkened."

"And where are you going to be while I'm doing all your cadet-work?" Runacar asked.

"There!" Vieliessar said, nodding skyward.

Tannatarie put her belly on the ground and cocked the elbow of her near foreleg. Vieliessar scrambled up onto Tannatarie's back and seated herself at the base of her neck. Tannatarie stood, then lowered her head to Runacar's level.

"Shoo," she said. "I don't want to step on you by accident."

Then she turned away and began to run.

⚜

Vieliessar held on to Tannatarie as tightly as she could. She'd expected it to be more difficult, but the Dragon's gait was smooth, as well as faster than that of the fastest horse ever foaled.

Tannatarie's claws squealed on the patches of ice under the trees, and her feet kicked up drifts of snow. It sprayed in all directions, and Vieliessar was glad she'd thought to cast Shield. She would already have frozen to death if she hadn't.

Tannatarie had been running with half-open wings. Suddenly she lifted her head high and opened her wings wide for the very first time.

They left the ground.

It's like flying, Vieliessar thought, before she corrected herself: *It is flying!* She could feel how much Tannatarie gloried in the freedom of the sky, and suddenly Vieliessar remembered a day many Wheelturns ago, when the child she had been stood upon Caerthalien Great Keep's topmost tower and imagined herself free to fly on eagles' wings, becoming one with the wind and the sun.

Tannatarie banked, tilting her wings so that she alternated gaining speed and gaining height. Finally she was high enough that she could catch one of the crosswinds from the pass itself.

Upward they soared, and still upward. The other Dragons joined them, flying dazzling and complicated patterns around Tannatarie. She sailed through all of them magisterially, her wings spread and her flight even, out of care for her Elven rider.

I need a saddle, Vieliessar thought. *Or some other way to hold on. And warm furs to wear over armor.*

Through the Bond she could feel Tannatarie's laughter, and as they rose even higher it seemed to Vieliessar that they were not Dragon and Mage, but one being. One thought.

The joy died quickly, though, when she looked below.

Arevethmonion stretched south, farther than Vieliessar had ever imagined. It was still burning there; the Endarkened had clearly ignited the widest possible north-south band. Some areas were already merely sticks and stones and black ash; others were clusters of Light-bearing trees. Vieliessar moaned aloud at the sight of it. How many forestfolk had died without knowing why the fire had come?

::*Well, you're the Dragonmage. Fix it::*

"How?" Vieliessar asked, still stunned by the scope of the destruction.

::*Still the Dragonmage. We are magic itself, my darling, but we are not spellbooks::*

She sounds like Arelinn Lightsister from my Sanctuary days. A spell, then.

Vieliessar held out her hand reflexively—the young Postulants had spent moonturns mastering the complex and meaningless gestures that signified to the Lightless that great Magery was being done—and in a blinding rush of power, the fires in the Flower Forest were quenched. The smoke began to clear.

It was as if she had once more linked herself to the Shrine. But—

More power, no damage, endlessness . . .

::If it is endless, it had better be dinner:: Tannatarie commented.

::You'd better go fishing then. Just don't eat anything that can talk::

They raced on through the sky. The land was filled with fire; apparently the Endarkened had circled around, trying to burn as much as possible. Here Ullilion. There Cirandeiron, both robed in snow and cinders. A few slaughtered Otherfolk in their farmsteads and villages, but fewer than Vieliessar expected; the Endarkened truly had sought only the Lightborn this day. Some of the Dragons had hunted the stampeded farm animals and made them Dragonfood.

Tannatarie flew on.

The riverbed that had once held the Angarussa was dry, and Delfierarathadan Flower Forest was gone, a thing of charcoal and harrowed earth, hideous and terrible to behold.

Making a wide circle over the ocean, Tannatarie turned north, skirting the edge of the Medhartha peaks. They had come at them upwind, for their greenneedle forests were burning.

"I think you ought to dismount for the next part," Tannatarie said. "At least until you get that saddle made."

Vieliessar agreed, for further out, she could see Dragons circling over the water and diving into it to rise with great silver fish in their mouths. Hunting.

Tannatarie landed at the edge of a cliff, and Vieliessar climbed carefully down from her back.

Then Tannatarie got to her feet, spread her wings, and jumped off the edge.

Vieliessar barely had time for a startled gasp when the great white Dragon rose up like a kite, turning and rising until she was flying higher than the tallest tree Vieliessar had ever seen. Suddenly she folded her wings and dropped like a sling-stone, not snatching prey from the surface of the water, but diving so deep even her tail vanished. When she surfaced, her claws were deep in a fish larger than any Vieliessar had imagined; a fish nearly as large as Tannatarie herself.

But she won't be able to get into the air again!

But the Dragon didn't have to. Holding on to her prey, she swam with wings outstretched, using them as oars. When she reached the shallows she spread them wide, shook them, and folded them neatly into place before beginning on her meal.

Vieliessar stared down the cliffside at her with a mind so full of questions and thoughts she would have to meditate for candlemarks to put them all in order. She stood upon the site of Daroldan Erased, an Otherfolk triumph certainly well remembered by both sides, even if they were former sides. Hresa had worked to break that treaty, even at the cost of the lives of Leutric and all his allies—as well as herself. What would happen when he found out about that? *If* he did—but he must know the cave collapse had been created by an Earthdancer, and Vieliessar knew that all the others had escaped.

Unless the Endarkened had come back again and eaten them all.

That dark thought led immediately to another. How would having the power of Dragons change the theater of battle? Could they at last trace the Endarkened to their lair and put an end to them? How would her folk—the Guilds, the Law Lords, the Lightborn—react to the presence of Dragons? Would they accept them? What would happen—now that thirteen Lightborn must be set above everyone else?

But most of all . . . who would become the other twelve Dragonbond Mages? Lightborn released from the need to draw power from the Flower Forests. Able to wield as much power as if they linked themselves directly to the Shrine Itself.

::*You don't have to worry about that, Beloved. We are the ones who choose*::

::*But I'm the one who knows them*:: Vieliessar countered. She attempted to consider all of her Warhunt Mages, and even the Sanctuary Lightborn, and decide who would be the worst and best Bondmates to Elokai, Rimanet, and the rest, and gave up. There were far too many variables. She would have to wait and see who the Dragons chose.

::*Yes*:: Tannatarie said, finishing the last of her feast. ::*Tomorrow is for work. Today is for joy*::

"Today is for war," Vieliessar corrected her. Gunedwaen's words echoed in her mind: *"If there is something your enemy wants, deny it to them. If there is something your enemy needs, destroy it. Terrain is a weapon. Supplies are a weapon. Take enough from him and he will be defeated before he steps onto the field.*"

The land they had flown over was still scarred from the war two decades ago. Flower Forests were diminished and even missing. The Endarkened could not enter Flower Forests. What could enter there could be killed. "Come, sister. We have work to do."

Vieliessar ran down the beach to Tannatarie, who walked onto the sand to meet her. She climbed onto Tannatarie's back once more, and once more the Dragon took flight.

First a wide circle over the Western Shore. There was the ruin and desolation of Amrolion; the shattered stones of Daroldan Great Keep lying in the sea, but nothing worse. Nothing dead. She gazed eastward, but there was nothing in the sky. They rose higher, and she could see what had once been the entrance to the Caves of Imrathalion. It looked as if it had been turned to sand. Before it, she could see a dotting of figures heading south, and others heading west, but she was too high up to see whether Pouncewarm and Runacar were among them.

They circled back west, over the absence of Delfierarathadan, over the great wasteland the West had become, studded with its tiny islands of village and farm. She reached for Tannatarie's power, and it was there just as if Vieliessar had been born with it.

Live!

On the Western Shore, across the Western Reach, there came a roaring crackling sound, as if a wildfire had Bonded to a thunderstorm. It was the sound of growth, fantastically accelerated. Trees went from seed to towering giant in a heartbeat. Delfierarathadan raised herself up from the ashes, flinging her borders wide. She crossed the streambed of what had once been the Angarussa and flung herself across Cirandeiron only to meet herself there as lesser Flower Forests came back to life as well. In the East, Arevethmonion burst her bounds and roared over both the ashes of the Sanctuary of the Star and the foundation stones of the village that bore her name. She brought life, health, shelter, peace. Like a thousand rivulets running to the sea, Flower Forests in the Western Reach grew until the land was not covered by many, but by one. The magic Vieliessar unleashed roared up over the golden hills and down into the valleys.

Vieliessar gazed yearningly eastward. If she could but cover the whole of the land with Flower Forests, they could win a breathing space—for themselves and their allies.

::And themselves and their allies will be at each other's throats if you don't turn up soon:: Tannatarie commented.

"True," Vieliessar said. "Land as close to Rune as you can, then take flight again. We can decide together when it's safe for you and the others to come down."

::Unless they kill you. Then, with my dying breath, I'll fall on them::

Vieliessar snickered. "I'll definitely mention that if it comes to an insurrection."

The Dragon made her descent, with Vieliessar wedging her body between two of Tannatarie's dorsal spines as hard as she could. As soon as everything stopped moving, she slipped down the Dragon's side, landing with a huff of air. She paused to hug Tannatarie's head fiercely, then turned away. Tannatarie located the Sanctuary Road, and began her run-up to flight. As soon as the noise of her departure faded, Vieliessar could hear a Palugh singing.

"Rrrune is prrrretty, prrrretty is Rrrune, Rrrune, Rrrune, Rrrune . . ."

Runacar walked out of the bushes toward her, with Pouncewarm (looking much less rumpled) at his side. "What did you do?" he demanded. "One moment I'm looking for the remains of your army and the next I'm being attacked by a goldenberry bush!" He looked skyward reproachfully. "This was more of your damned magic, wasn't it?"

"Mine and Tannatarie's," Vieliessar said. "The Endarkened can't enter the Flower Forests. So I made them larger."

"You'd better hope the Brightfolk don't mind, or you'll never have a sound night of sleep again. Have you seen Imrathalion? Did anyone get out?"

"Most of them, by the look of things. Your folk are heading south, more or less. I can take you to them." She glanced skyward. "It's only a little past midday, but there is much to do."

"Sleep," Runacar said uncompromisingly. "Eat. See to the wounded, sew this damned cat in a sack—"

Runacar was still enumerating tasks when he, Pouncewarm, and Vieliessar walked through Door deeper into the Flower Forest.

They reached the Otherfolk refugees. Their column was a pitiful sight; walking wounded lurching forward, more severely wounded being carried on stretchers, or pulled on travois by Centaurs.

Runacar didn't see Leutric anywhere.

"There's Audalo," Vieliessar said, pointing. They both hurried to his side.

"Where—?" Runacar asked.

"Gone to the green fields, the Great Bull guide him now," Audalo said.

Dead? Vieliessar wondered in giddy horror.

"Then you are my liege-lord now," Runacar said steadily, "and I would swear to you."

"And be tugged between sun and moon? Leutric is dead, as is the treaty. As is the alliance. Let these things rest together until the time of growing things has come."

"Explain this to me," Vieliessar said, more sharply than she'd intended.

Runacar turned toward her. "Leutric is dead: the alliance he crafted and the treaty you and he swore both end with his death."

"But that's not how treaties work," Vieliessar said hoarsely. The world spun around her. Runacar caught her arm.

"Don't faint," he said. She glared.

"Have they found his murderer yet?" Vieliessar asked. "Was he—"

Was he trapped in the cave? Was he killed by Hresa?

Runacar stared at her in surprise. "*Murderer?* Leutric was *old.* It was the running and fighting that killed him."

But he told me he had seen only sixty summers. Vieliessar herself could expect to see another seven hundred or more Wheelturns if she were not killed on the field.

"They don't live that long," Runacar said quietly. "None of the Nine

Races do. Except the Gryphons, for some reason. And maybe the Aesalions, though nobody really knows. No one knows about the Brightfolk or the Unicorns. Or the Stone People. Any of the Elementals, really."

"Then we must now go forward," Vieliessar said resolutely. She turned to Audalo once more. "Treaty or none. Lord Audalo, my condolences on the death of your king and the head of your Line. I bring you good tidings in this sorrowful time. That with which your people were entrusted has been found and has passed into our care. Know that we mean to use it for the good of all who partake in this alliance."

"There is no alliance," Runacar said again. "There is no treaty."

"Then what am I to tell my people?" Vieliessar said, utterly lost. "Are we to be at each other's throats once more?"

"Tell them that what withers can bloom again," Audalo said gently. "Rune Houseborn, escort the High King back to her people. They will have need of her."

⊰⊱

Vieliessar had no choice but to accompany Runacar along the Sanctuary Road eastward. The Otherfolk line of march was wildly scattered, and now she knew why.

Leutric was dead.

"Tell them—any that you can—that we hold a peace in effect, and will aid any of their folk we find in distress," Vieliessar said.

"I can't say what reaction you'll get," Runacar answered. He slowed until they both stopped. Runacar continued speaking. "You don't understand how Otherfolk society—*societies*—function. You don't understand how the Otherfolk *think*. They pledged loyalty to Leutric *personally,* and with him gone, Audalo is King and nobody is Emperor," Runacar said.

Vieliessar had been thinking about this since the moment she'd learned the alliance was in shards.

"Runacar, would the Otherfolk accept *me* as Emperor?" Vieliessar asked quietly.

Runacar stood quietly, neither accepting or rejecting the idea out of hand. At last he spoke.

"I don't know. Audalo was serious about everything stopping for winter. I don't know if the Endarkened will attack again during winter; your guess would be better than mine. That might make a difference."

Vieliessar made a bitter face. "They attack as they choose, without rhyme nor reason. Winter will be no bar to them. What I do not know is whether they will begin to attack your folk as well. They seem to prey on anything that lives."

"Then maybe thirteen Dragons will tip the odds. But if we're all alive in Rain Moon, you can try reviving Leutric's alliance. You'd have to be extremely polite, not to mention grovel, but you already know that. The question everyone will ask is: What is this alliance for, now that they have all seen the Endarkened and know they are going to die?"

"For information, so they do not die," Vieliessar answered instantly. "I want to know how to kill the Endarkened. Unless we can kill them, we cannot win. And how to make all of us truly one folk," she added quietly. It seemed inconceivable.

"There are folk to ask," Runacar said. "About killing those things, or making them easier to kill. The Gryphons, mainly. You'll have better luck coming to them as High King-Emperor."

Runacar resumed walking, and she followed.

"We are barbarians now," she said, sighing.

"It's a new world," Runacar answered.

"I wish I'd never created it."

"You didn't really," Runacar said. "That world was balanced on a sword's edge. It only fell."

"And now it's broken beyond repair."

"But not beyond remaking. If you know what you want."

⊰⊱

The World Without Sun was dark and quiet. Once she reached the bottom of the entry-shaft in Ugolthma's walls—a vertical fall of over a mile—Shurzul ran toward the Heart of Darkness. Her heart was racing, but she knew she was first to reach here.

And first to bring the tale . . . lived.

It should have been simple to gather up the Elfling Mages and return to the World Without Sun. The meat had split itself into two groups: one had left the Absence; one, the larger group, had left the Unspeakable and its little town. Divided, they should have been even easier to harvest.

But the Endarkened had been able to collect a mere handful of Elfling Mages—rather than the hundreds Shurzul had hoped for—and those had all ceased to live almost at once, while the Lightborn who remained alive hurried to concealment under the mountain.

And if that were not offensive enough, the Unicorns once again fought by their side.

That was when *He Who Is* had come to watch over the battlefield, and Shurzul had thought their luck might have changed. If they could bring with them even one living Unicorn, then surely King Virulan would forgive them—forgive at least *her*—for the loss of the Elfling Mages.

But even with *He Who Is* to draw strength from, they only managed to kill some of the hateful beasts. The rest of the Unicorns retreated into the cave before one of them could be captured, and *He Who Is* left the battlefield as inexplicably as *He* had come to them.

Shurzul did not know what she would say to King Virulan that would explain their ignominious retreat—and at such a high cost to their own.

Fortunately, she didn't have to think of anything. From the far end of the hall, Shurzul could see that the doors of the throne room stood open, its expanse flooded with the refulgent blackness of Unfire.

And Uralesse, not Virulan, sat upon the throne, the Crown of Pain nestled between his gleaming horns and Hazaniel sitting on his lap. Shurzul didn't know whether to try to run or sink to her knees . . .

Or scream.

"My dear Shurzul," Uralesse said genially. "Of course you would be first to arrive, so eager are you to greet your new King and Master."

❦

When they had been sent forth upon this crusade, so many had filled the Presence Chamber that the chamber had overflowed with celebrants. This time, the first to follow Shurzul into the Presence Chamber attempted to retreat at once, only to be held in place by the force of Uralesse's will.

Those who followed them were even more reluctant to enter the Presence Chamber. This time, everyone tried to huddle at the back. This time, the chamber was barely filled by the Endarkened who remained. The ones at the front hissed and scratched at their neighbors, trying to get behind them.

"I believe it is possible that at least a few of you may have noticed that in our recent encounter with the Elves, *we lost*?"

At King Uralesse's feet sat the only surviving Endarkened that had been created by *He Who Is*. Shurzul held an Elfin child in her arms, more to keep him from wandering near anyone who would eat him than out of excessive fondness. Hazaniel was not disturbed by the lightlessness of the chamber in which he sat, for Uralesse with his own sorcery had crafted the helm the child wore, the helm that turned stygian ultradark into day for a Brightworlder's eyes.

And which hid some things completely.

As Hazaniel played happily with his toys, oblivious to anything around him, the Endarkened shuffled nervously. All knew they could die in the next instant; the new King's temper was uncertain.

To say the least.

The Endarkened at the front of the room tried to cringe back. Those behind them were determined to show loyalty and refused to let them. Uralesse continued.

"We lost," Uralesse went on. "Against a collection of *meat* which until now has lost every fight against us."

Uralesse arose from the Throne of Night and began to pace, his tail lashing.

"And did any of you think to bring Unicorns back for your poor dying King? Yes, *dying*! Of fury and shame at the thought of you! And with his dying—or his something, anyway—breath he begged me to avenge him. And who do you think he meant?

"Not you, you self-obsessed gluttons! Virulan begged me to take up the task set us by *He Who Is,* and also to avenge his noble and valiant death. I am only grateful he did not live to see the day when the Brightworld Queen woke the Dragons' Bones. The fact that all of you are alive is disgusting. The thought of having disappointed *He Who*

Is, of having left *His* task unfinished, should be enough to kill you with shame!"

Uralesse stared down at them from the plinth on which the Throne of Night rested, his pupilless gold eyes glowing as if he would set all of them on fire. It was fortunate his audience couldn't follow the logic of his argument, because there wasn't much of it. What existed for them was terror so numbing that all any of them wanted was for the speech to stop so they could run away. Finally Uralesse flung himself onto his throne once more and glared balefully at them.

"The Dragons are powerful, though not as powerful as we. The Elves are the Dragons' weak point. We must exploit this in every way possible. We have sworn to cleanse this rock of all life, and twice has *He Who Is* overseen our failure.

"If we fail again, *He Who Is* will condemn us to endless life, walking the Bright World forever. We must not fail. Our task is more perilous than ever, and that means we must all act as one. Cabals and infighting—if there are any of you left alive to engage in them—will be severely punished. Most of all, there is to be no more cannibalism. *All* Endarkened lives are precious now that we have lost so many."

He reached down and picked up Hazaniel, setting the child upon his knee again. Shurzul, taken off guard, looked alarmed.

"We will fight with guile now. When this beloved child is grown we will launch our next—and last—full-on assault upon Elvenkind. Until then raids, random attacks, small tricks at your whim, certainly. Amuse yourselves—but plan for the future. Yes, the Elflings have awakened the Bones of the Earth, but everything that lives can be suborned.

"Everything."

Uralesse held out his hand, and an Aesalion padded into the chamber through a side tunnel to join him. The enormous creature ruffled his wing feathers, clearly not at all bothered by the place he found himself.

Manticores had rarely graced the Endarkened's larders.

Drotha smiled at the Endarkened, exposing fangs which were far larger than theirs. "We're going to have so much fun."

WOOD'S MOON IN THE TENTH YEAR OF THE HIGH KING'S REIGN: OF RIBBONS AND RAZORS

One law for all.

—Attributed by historians to Great Queen Vieliessar Farcarinon

Vieliessar walked toward the Sanctuary Road, turning over in her mind the information Runacar had given her. Just as at the beginning of her campaign, she didn't wonder *if* she could do a thing, but *how.*

Who will join you? The Centaurs are a lot like our Landbonds once were, if a Landbond were free. The Woodwose are already Elves and the only problem there is convincing them of that fact.

The Bearwards? Perhaps. Best to begin with Helda, she holds sway outside her own forest, and she knows you. The Minotaurs . . . it depends on Audalo. At the moment the Earthdancers have no queen, so at least he'll have one less advisor. I don't know what grudge they may bear you for Hresa's death.

If the Hippogriffs join your meisne, they will remain true. The Gryphons won't ally themselves, not after so many of them were slaughtered at Ceoprentrei. The Unicorns will say yes and mean no, which comes as no surprise to me at this point, make of that what you will.

That leaves Runacar. I believe him when he says he can lead Otherfolk and I cannot, so I will have to have him, but how do I get him? If our marriage sealed the treaty, and the treaty is void, are we still expected to marry?

::*We'd all like to know the answer to that*:: Tannatarie said, breaking in to Vieliessar's thoughts.

And shall I marry him, to gain his army? I don't think he wishes it, and for that matter, I don't think all the power of the Hundred Houses at their greatest would be enough to stop the Endarkened. So. We gained the Bones of the Earth from Leutric, and Dragons are not enough to defeat the Endarkened. And oh how I miss Leutric, for I know he would be a wise counselor to me in this desperate moment!

::You need the Otherfolk alliance to wage a peace. But that is something entirely different from waging a war:: Tannatarie said.

What do I want and what do I need? Most of all, what can I have? What I want is for the past two decades of Wheelturns to have not been for nothing.

The Otherfolk and I have—or had—an alliance. It is not enough to defeat the Endarkened.

We have to have an enemy we can kill. And I see no way to achieve that. The Endarkened cannot be killed. And an enemy who cannot be killed cannot be defeated.

::Killing is often the best way to stop people bothering you:: Tannatarie agreed.

⊰∃⊱

Isilla was the first to see them. She ran toward Vieliessar, not noticing the white Dragon in the sky above.

"Oh, thank Leaf and Star you are safe! We were so worried! We barely got the wounded out in time, and the Unicorns, and—"

"And all the other things we can tell her once we're encamped for the night," Iardalaith said. "Wherever that is. I don't think there's one among us who can even cast Fire right now, let alone Door."

"Just get everyone moving in the same direction," Vieliessar said. "And leave the rest to me."

The day was edging toward the swift winter twilight; Vieliessar intended to be back in Ceoprentrei before night fell.

::I could land and give them something to not talk about:: Tannatarie said.

::I somehow suspect it would not daunt them in the least::

She created an instance of Door wide enough for ten people to walk through. It would serve for now.

The villagers and the Sanctuary Lightborn were satisfied with the answer that the radiant growth of the Light Forest was merely Eldritch Magic to protect them from the Endarkened. The Warhunt—who knew it was far more than that—she had to put off with a promise. To Helecanth she told the truth—the "weapon" Leutric had given up to her was a large talking Dragon that was an infinite reservoir of Light.

But the most urgent question the majority of her new subjects had was: *Where were their children?*

⧰

"We are a solid sunturn from the Sanctuary Road, and two more until we cross the old borders of Arevethmonion. There is no point in looking for anyone here," Isilla said wearily, as she escorted the latest runner back to the road. The woman was big, and had the shoulders of a blacksmith. Her mouth was drawn in a hard line.

"When we reach the road, I'm going for him, and you won't stop me then," the woman said flatly.

"Fine," Isilla said. For all of her, every single one of the villagers could go galloping off into the woods right now. Maybe they'd vanish again and take the mythical people they were searching for with them.

⧰

Dinias watched with exhausted apprehension as Isilla rode toward him. He knew what she wanted and he hoped he would never be so base as to give it to her.

They rode east in silence for a while, a silence broken only by the frantic cries of villagers dashing from the path and the bright excited commentary of the Wulvers chasing them. Even the Hippogriffs and Gryphons were walking, because in a Flower Forest they were safe and in the sky they were not. He could almost forget it was winter outside the forest borders, because in here it was spring. Eternally.

The perfumes from various bushes and trees were strong in the warm air. There would be fresh fruit with dinner—or would possibly *be* dinner—for all the usual bushes that grew in a Flower Forest were in fruit. So was the Vilya tree, but eating Vilya just to stop your stomach growling seemed insulting in a way Dinias couldn't quite name. He supposed War Princes did it all the time.

Had done it.

When there were War Princes.

Tangisen joined them, saying nothing, and soon the very last survivors of the Western Shore were gathered together in silent mourning.

Eight, where there had once been one hundred.

Then Isilla spoke, and even though it was not to him, what she said jarred Dinias out of any sense of peace he'd been able to gain. "Tangisen, have you seen Harwing? I've been looking all over for him. I wouldn't be surprised to find he's swapped clothing with one of the villagers in order to blend in. In fact—"

"You won't see Harwing," Dinias said quietly, then quickly cast a weak instance of Silence to cover all of them. "Ever again."

Isilla pulled him to a stop and gazed into his face. "You were supposed to be the last two out of Imrathalion. *You're* here . . ."

She let the silence hang as an accusation and finally Dinias broke it. *"Tell her as much as she needs to know. No more,"* Harwing had said.

"Harwing was tapping the Shrine in the first place so we could do our work. Nobody could call Arevethmonion in that mess." Two stark sentences, and Dinias's throat closed before he could say more.

"A charming story. What a pity it isn't true," Isilla said evenly. "Now do I have to rip it out of your mind or will you tell me?"

"Yes, we both might have gotten out. Yes, it was more logical for me to stay—Keystone Gift Transmutation and all. But Harwing stayed behind so that I could get out. For either of us to have a chance was for one to hold back the stone for as long as possible and he . . . He was uneasy in his mind about what he'd done to free the villagers. As—"

"As in, he'd killed Hamphuliadiel," Isilla interrupted.

It was a statement, not a question. For a moment Dinias's mind filled with the image he'd taken from Harwing's mind, of Hamphuliadiel drowning in the mud, begging for mercy as Harwing gloated over him.

"For whatever cause, Hamphuliadiel is dead and we are here," Dinias said. "So we will light a pyre to Harwing as soon as we can, for he is in the Warm World now."

He hardly recognized the sound of his own voice. He wondered if Harwing had known himself, before the end. He wondered if anyone here would know or recognize themselves by the end.

⊰⊱

Vieliessar was a little surprised to see the villagers and the Sanctuary Lightborn were not only gathered together, but intermingled with Wulvers and Palughs, dogs, chickens, and even Fauns. The Warhunt stood in a loose circle around them; she could see purple flares of Shield at the back.

"I am your King," she said, even though it seemed a ridiculous remark coming from someone dressed in mud and tatters. "I will lead you to safety."

"What about our children?" someone cried. A moment later everyone was demanding the answer to that same question, until Vieliessar had to use Voice to be heard.

"Your children are safe! They were taken in error by the Woodwose— the little gods! They thought they were saving them! You will be reunited with them soon."

⊰⊱

She was relieved to discover that the villagers could not tell one part of the Flower Forest from another, so she was able to tell them that they could soon continue the search for their missing children. As for the Sanctuary Lightborn . . .

I am very nearly certain that Hamphuliadiel did not teach them any spell they might raise against him, so I don't think they will recognize Door, and certainly won't be able to cast it.

She called all of what she (still, always) thought of as her own people to her side. "I am going to open Door and bring everyone through to Ceoprentrei from here."

"You can't do that," Iardalaith said quietly. He glanced around himself, as if to see if anyone had heard.

"I can and I shall, Arda," Vieliessar answered. "Watch me."

The act itself was utterly anticlimactic; one Flower Forest looked very much like another, and only the Warhunt could tell whether Door was present or not. Vieliessar led the Lightborn, the Lightless, and several hundred instances of livestock through it to the edge of Round Lake.

And they were home.

The only thing Vieliessar did that anyone near to it could have seen was filling the Western Gate with an ice sculpture of running Unicorns that blocked it utterly.

❦

The villagers she was speaking with had almost entirely come from among the Crofters and Landbonds, for the great lords, thinking to return to their Great Keeps in a moonturn or two, had left them nearly empty, and likewise stripped the manors and Farmholds under their hand of useful servants. All that had been left on the land had been the Landbonds.

This time she could pick out a few words and phrases from the great susurrus of talk.

"—the Little Gods—"

"—the Small Gods—"

"—fight beside her—"

"—ally—"

"The Otherfolk are our allies," Vieliessar said strongly, hoping it was true. "They will fight at our side. They will live where they choose. If for no other reason than that King-Emperor Leutric, lord of the Otherfolk, has presented me with the token to unlock great powers of war.

"After the Astromancer's gallant and terrible death, I had donned the Astromancer's ring for safekeeping, and then Lord Emperor Leutric gave me one that had long been in his keeping as well, for it was a legend passed down from his greatfathers that the one who held the ring and entered into Imrathalion would awaken the Bones of the Earth, and discover a true aid against the Endarkened. This has been done, through the bravery of the Palugh Pouncewarm, Runacar Battlemaster, and myself."

By now she did not have to wait for silence; the hush was complete.

"I will show to you what we found in a moment. But I must say that I view the disappearance of the Astromancer's ring as an omen. There will be no more Astromancers. Astromancer and High King shall be one."

The audience began another round of grumblings.

"And now," Vieliessar said, in a voice she knew no one could hear, "here is our promised deliverance."

A dot in the sky swirled itself into size, then shape, then landed upon the grass beside the lake, running forward a few steps before she stopped.

The ground trembled as she landed. It trembled again as she walked forward. The great white Dragon—like a dune of snow and ice—lay down, folded her front legs, raised her head up, and regarded the Elves expectantly.

"Hello," she said aloud. "I am Tannatarie the White. I do hope *all* your livestock hasn't run away. I'm tired of fish."

I have brought you all to the Flower Forest of Nomaitemil in the valley of Ceoprentrei in the Dragon's Gate Pass. Here no enemy can attack you, and by my word as your king, you will attack no one, for all here live under my peace. There is no point in looking for anyone here. I have made my own arrangements to return your children."

There was a murmuring from her audience that grew steadily louder. A woman shouldered her way to the front of the villagers. She was big, and had the shoulders of a blacksmith. Her mouth was drawn in a hard line.

"I'll look for him even if I have to smash up your pretty ice door to do it, and you won't stop me," the woman said flatly.

"I'll see if I can find you a hammer, then," Vieliessar said mildly, and some of the villagers laughed. "I told you: the Woodwose have them, and they're perfectly safe. They thought you were going to take them out into the blizzard."

"And they thought they'd never seen such a harvest of babies since the time of Great Queen Pelashia Celenthodiel," Dinias murmured in Isilla's ear.

"Come on," Isilla said. "Let's find food and somewhere to sleep."

There. That's done, Vieliessar thought wearily as she curled up under Tannatarie's wing to sleep.

::*Building a king-domain is not for those who fancy a solid night's sleep*:: Tannatarie pointed out.

::*Or any sleep at all*:: Vieliessar responded. ::*I thought I would have the whole winter to prepare for this! That I could parcel out some of the work to my Warhunt Mages. Instead I have but a handful of them, and I didn't expect Dragons at all!*::

::*And Hamphuliadiel is dead, and Leaf and Star know what he has done to those poor children, but whatever it is, it will be a thing you must contend with. And now, tell me all you know of your world and your land, for I know little of it*::

⊰⊱

Niviel Lightsister had seen five summers when she lost the second of her parents to an Endarkened attack. All of the Elves parented the orphaned children in various ways. It was better than nothing, Niviel agreed, but not as good as having your own mother and father.

But once her Light had begun to manifest—early, but the Warhunters said it was coming in Candidates earlier and earlier every year—her de facto parents became the Warhunt Mages who oversaw her training and warned her constantly that the Endarkened liked to capture Mages more than anyone else and so she must be more careful than anyone else. And nobody knew what the Endarkened did with the people they took away with them, except that it was probably worse than what they did to those they met on the field.

When it was five Wheelturns after Niviel had lost both parents, she could no longer remember how they looked or how they sounded. She decided she didn't really want to grow up, and since *Ashabi mu Arnab* were always happy to have Lightborn help, she joined them.

She hadn't been meant to come west. There were plenty of other Warhunters to ride with the King, and she had not officially joined the combat meisne yet. She was sure that if someone had actually noticed she was in the meisne she would have been sent back to Nomaitemil, but no one did until they were all down the mountain and then there was no choice for anyone but to let her ride on with the rest of them.

And now it was the middle of the night, and she'd gotten soup and some apples and a blanket because the villagers felt sorry for her (Niviel tried not to laugh; it was rude) and all those things were good but then she woke up and couldn't get back to sleep.

(Had someone called her name?)

She stared up at the winter stars. They were blazing and bright in the thin cold air of Woods Moon. That was disconcerting in the warmth of the Flower Forest. Not that she was complaining.

(There. She hadn't heard it again. It was a very loud sort of silence.)

Niviel Warhunter got to her feet quietly, careful not to disturb anyone. She folded the blanket carefully and wrapped it around her shoulders as a shawl. Then she cast Silversight over herself and summoned up all she knew of tracking.

⟊⟊

Large glowing golden eyes—moon-glowing, not cat-glowing—opened an instant after Niviel realized there was a large thing here that wasn't part of a Flower Forest. Her heart raced and she wondered if she could outrun it.

"I mean you no harm," a voice said.

"Are you Otherfolk? Or a Dragon? What are you doing here?" Niviel asked.

"It's safer than the sky."

Dragon, Niviel decided. "What's your name?" she asked, taking a cautious step closer. The Dragon was so large that Silversight had failed her; it—he?—looked like a hillock or maybe even an entire hill.

"A gift for a gift," the Dragon said, sounding amused. "What's yours?"

"I am Niviel Warhunter," Niviel said proudly.

"Very well, Niviel Warhunter. I am Telleval the Blue."

"Something called me here, Telleval the Blue," Niviel said, which was the truth. The High King had spoken to the Warhunt and the Sanctuary Mages separately from the Lightless and explained all about the Dragons and the Dragonbond. She had stressed that the Dragon chose, not the Mage. So (Niviel told herself) she wasn't exactly trying to Bond with a Dragon here. She was just looking.

And something *had* called.

"And I am Rimanet, called the Crimson, and if you mean to Bond or otherwise, go elsewhere. Some of us are trying to sleep." The voice sounded as if it came from very far up.

"And some of us have had quite enough of sleeping," Telleval returned mildly. There was a huffy ruffle of wings as Rimanet tucked her head under one of them and strenuously ignored Telleval.

Telleval blinked his eyes slowly, looking at Niviel. "You cannot have come to ask me about it, because you didn't know I was here. So what do you wish to ask, Niviel Warhunter?"

"I want to know how to Bond with a Dragon," Niviel said in a rush. "I want to touch you. I want to fly. I want—I want—I want someone who won't die and leave me!" She hadn't known she was going to say any of that. It had all just come out in a rush. She cringed in humiliation. "I'm sorry, Telleval. I shouldn't have said all that. It's rude."

"If you think that's rude, I can see none of use are getting Bondmates anytime soon," Telleval said wryly. "Poor child. I imagine it is hard to get used to being left."

"We didn't get a choice," Niviel said, taking a few steps closer to Telleval.

Seen by Silversight, the Dragon was a strange and beautiful sculpture of swooping planes, writhing coils, and the glitter of scales. Each time he inhaled, a ripple of light ran over them, making them sparkle. She wondered what color he would be in daylight.

"My father died in the Succession Wars. My mother died . . . somewhere along the way." Niviel shrugged.

"Well, let's give this Bonding thing a whirl," Telleval said. "Come over here."

Niviel came over and stared fixedly into one of Telleval's eyes, then the other, then seated herself cautiously on his nose and tried to stare into both of them at once.

"Nope, nothing," she reported.

"Well, Niviel, there's always—" Telleval said.

"*Will you two ever shut up?*" Rimanet hissed. She reared up, flinging her head high, and then dropped down onto all fours to thrust her head directly and menacingly at Niviel. "Little Elven child," she began and stopped. When she spoke again, it was in a completely different tone. "Little Elven child," she said. "Come to me."

Niviel didn't think much of that idea, but Telleval was right here and would probably stop Rimanet from eating her. If Dragons ate people. The High King said they didn't.

She took a few steps closer. Rimanet was still looking at her, almost . . . hopefully? Niviel put one hand on the end of her . . . nose? Muzzle?

And gazed into her eyes.

::*I have been waiting for you so long*:: Rimanet said. ::*Never leave me?*::

"I never will," Niviel said. "I will stay with you until the day I die."

⊰≣⊱

Vieliessar awoke before the sun had risen. She wanted to be up and alert before anyone else. Up was no problem. Alert would have to wait.

The last camp the Arevians had made before the Battle of Imrathalion was roughly two candlemarks' walk to the west of it, a single footstep out of Tildorangelor by Door. She wanted to see if anything salvageable was left there. She cast Door and stepped through. For the moment, she would leave the ice-barrier across the Western Gate intact. It would be a mistake to say that a Flower Forest was always the same. Flower Forests had their seasons, both of sunturn and moonturn. Early morning was not precisely crisp, but it was cool enough for a cloak—and also to raise mist from the ground.

::*Good morning!*:: Tannatarie chirped inside Vieliessar's mind. ::*Four new Bonds last night; so amazing. I am truly impressed by your people's ability to not run away! Oh, and you have visitors. Shall I come down?*::

"No," Vieliessar said quietly. "Wait."

She looked around. The carts and wagons had been charred, but the fire had been fast-running and they might still be salvageable. The oxen might have survived as well. Easier to search for them from the air.

In the mist, Vieliessar saw people. The "visitors" Tannatarie had mentioned. Woodwose. They waited silently, most of them holding small bundles. When one of them realized she'd noticed them, he set down his bundle and came walking toward her. Vieliessar awaited him with wary caution; from everything Runacar had said about the Woodwose, they had not been eager to embrace the treaty.

"Good morning, High King Lord Vieliessar the Child of the Prophecy," the Woodwose said. "I am Baenor. I have come to speak for my people."

Baenor was dressed in typical Woodwose fashion, so far as Vieliessar could tell; rags and feathers and twigs, all meant to lead the eye away from the person underneath them. When Woodwose stood still, they were nearly invisible.

"Have you the right to speak for your people, Baenor of the Woodwose?" she asked warily. She was still mindful of what Runacar had told her: the Woodwose had no king. At best they followed the order and customs of those they lived with. But that wasn't the same thing at all.

Now it was Baenor's turn to look wary. "I have a baby," he said, as if that was an answer to her question. "It came from the forest when the Elves were riding through it."

"I believe the Elves would have preferred to keep their children with them rather than having them taken," Vieliessar said.

"They were going to take the babies out into the blizzard. We only meant to keep them safe in Arevethmonion. We wouldn't hurt them. And Rune Battlemaster said we could have the babies if we came with you," Baenor wheedled. "So we will."

Rune Battlemaster has something to answer for. ::*And so do you*:: Vieliessar thought toward Tannatarie.

::*You needed the sleep. And it wasn't really an invasion*:: Tannatarie said placidly. ::*You wanted Woodwose. Here they are*::

Vieliessar looked up and around. Woodwose everywhere, and all with babies. She made a quick count. At least a grand-taille of Woodwose, and more than that of toddlers and infants. She knew older children had vanished, but they weren't here.

"I accept that bargain," Vieliessar said quickly. "And as you are their King, I expect you to go and bring with you all of the children—Woodwose, Elven—who are not here—and the rest of the Woodwose as well."

"That sounds like a very hard task," Baenor said.

"And yet it is *your* task," Vieliessar said mercilessly. "Further, you must speak to their parents and their kin about being with the children. And you must come with us to Nomaitemil to live. There is room for all of you there."

⊰⊱

She coaxed the Woodwose through an instance of Door that would lead them back to their families.

Some of them hesitated at its threshold as if they were actually aware of its presence; the children old enough to walk simply ran through unheedingly. The stolen children ranged from babies to toddlers to youngsters old enough to be put to a task; they were running through Nomaitemil, obviously looking for their parents. The older children—those of fighting age, Vieliessar's mind irrelevantly supplied—were standing with the Woodwose, in a half-moon on the camp's western boundary, distinguishable only by their difference in dress.

The villagers woke slowly, groaning from a night spent on the ground, and then saw their children and called out to them. Some stood. Some knelt. Some found their children at once. Others had their children passed hand over hand to them, for everyone had been sleeping close for reassurance and warmth.

When they found that the children standing with the Woodwose were not coming to them, the cries reached a sharper—*angrier*—pitch.

"*Cease this!*" Vieliessar cried. "*Silence, I say!*"

Enough people became silent that she could speak without using her battlefield voice.

"The Woodwose thought they were saving your children, because when you left the forest you would be riding out into a winter storm. And so—".

"Who are you, saying we should just forget the whole thing?"

With a silent apology to Rondithiel of the Warm World, who had been her teacher in Mosirinde's Covenant, Vieliessar cast a minor instance of Silence, a medium instance of Compulsion, and a strong instance of Belief.

The combination of spells worked well—the people believed her, felt compelled to do as she asked, and didn't want to discuss it.

"I am High King; I need be nothing more. In this place you might meet your lost kin, for the Woodwose are kin to you as much as your children."

Then the trees rustled mightily as something very large approached.

Vieliessar turned to see the three Dragons—Elderin, Rimanet, and Telleval—walking toward them. Niviel was riding on Rimanet's back, looking both excited and scared. Iardalaith walked beside Elderin and Isilla by Telleval.

Bonded.

But I see only three, and Tannatarie said there were four . . .

Up until this moment, Vieliessar hadn't entirely realized what the Dragonbond meant. Any of the three Dragonmages was as powerful in Magery as she was. Any of them could take her throne away from her if they chose.

"And are you the only ones of my people who have anticipated me so?" Vieliessar asked dryly.

"My lord King, I heard someone calling me," said Niviel, "so I went looking for what it was, and . . . I didn't think this would happen."

"I heard two of your latest pets arguing," was Iardalaith's only comment. "I wish I'd had Elderin in Celenthodiel. I'd have given you a run for your throne."

"Noted," Vieliessar said. "Now here are my orders. You will make a permanent enclave in the south part of the valley. I do not think I have convinced the villagers that the Dragons are harmless and friendly, and so I don't want anyone attacking anybody until I am there to make them stop."

"Saving the fun parts for yourself?" Iardalaith asked.

"Figuring out how to keep you and the Dragons safe since I can't build a Flower Forest in the *air*!" Vieliessar snapped in exasperation.

Iardalaith's expression instantly turned contrite. "I'm sorry," he said. "And then?"

"Report to"—she cudgeled her brain for her most senior officers and finally settled on—"the council. Tell them everything, including that we are to make these folk—refugees, kidnappees, hostages, whatever—feel safe and at home. Our senior Lightborn are to get their hands on the Lightborn trained at the Sanctuary—don't listen to anything they say about Hamphuliadiel; it will be easier on all of you."

"And you?" Isilla asked, speaking for the first time. "What are you going to be doing?"

"Retaking my kingdom," Vieliessar said, with a knife-edged smile. She opened Door again, this time at the far end of Nomaitemil, and watched as the three Dragonbond Mages stepped through.

CHAPTER THIRTY-EIGHT

WOOD'S MOON TO COLD MOON IN THE TENTH YEAR OF THE HIGH KING'S REIGN: TO SURRENDER IS NOT THE SAME AS A BEAUTIFUL RETREAT

Suddenly Vieliessar felt a familiar brush at her leg. "I, I, I, will help. I am first and best. I have slain monsters," Pouncewarm said.

"Where have you been?" Vieliessar demanded. The Palugh had disappeared when it ran from the Dragon chamber, and she hadn't seen him since.

"I, I, I, was on a quest! Brave Pouncewarm! Heroic Pouncewarm! I!"

("That's all very well," muttered Vieliessar, "but I was hoping for an answer.")

The Palugh had clearly been somewhere, and was now back safely, but asking him was unlikely to put either her worries or curiosity to rest.

"Are we flying or are we talking?" Tannatarie asked.

"Flying," Vieliessar said, trying not to think of the hundred things she needed to have so she could fly more comfortably. At least today she had a warcloak to pad the space between the spines on Tannatarie's bony neck, and another to wear. Pouncewarm jumped happily into her lap as soon as Vieliessar had wriggled into place.

⊰⊱

A Dragon trying to get off the ground without being able to jump *down* into the wind gave an incredibly bumpy ride, as Vieliessar had reason to know. But this time, Tannatarie didn't even move. After a long moment, the Dragon turned around and looked at her.

"'Send' would be good," she said mildly. "'Door' to the coast? Or—"

Clenching her teeth, cheeks burning in embarrassment, Vieliessar lifted Tannatarie several hundred feet into the sky.

"That's better," the Dragon said patronizingly. "Here we are." She spread her wings wide, and suddenly they were flying.

Vieliessar regarded the ground dubiously, and kept Pouncewarm from walking up to Tannatarie's head to get a better view.

::I know what I want to do now:: she thought.

::Then let us begin, darling::

The old Flower Forest of Delfierarathadan, she had touched when she rejuvenated it, but Izalbama that rose up the slopes of the Medhatara and Sahullanath whose tall cedars covered the rolling hills of the south, were simply ordinary forests.

Vieliessar forced magic into them as a War Prince might pour liquor into beer. She held her breath for several seconds—waiting, hoping—until they too sparkled into enchanted life.

Vieliessar turned her attention eastward. Tannatarie made long swooping circles as Vieliessar knit together the forests of the West from Delfierarathadan to Arevethmonion and then spread them wide, until they ran up the skirts of the mountains—north, south—and into the southern foothills.

And the spread of the Flower Forests, the return to their ancient majesty, did not stop at the edge of the Mystrals. As she soared over it, the whole of Ceoprentrei became one vast forest; borders and boundary lines vanished under the growth of trees and vines.

Grow!

They crossed the Mystrals, seeding sheltered mountain valleys with vast fortresses of trees. The Magery raced onward. Jaeglenhend vanished beneath a canopy of green. Every forest her people had ever called upon—for shelter, for food, for survival—was repaid for those gifts a thousandfold. The Ghost Forest whispered back to life, its astonished resurrection a song in her ears. Tildorangelor filled the whole of the Valley of the Spire once more, climbed the Teeth of the Moon, forced itself through the mountain crevasses as the inexhaustible Dragon-magic ran ever eastward.

Once she stopped to let Pouncewarm down for a short span of time. Once she stopped to eat wild grapes. But she always flew eastward.

The sun set over the Mystrals and the moon rose winter-bright as Vieliessar worked. Tannatarie flew on, untiringly, as the land unspooled beneath her, recalled from death with each beat of her wings.

Now the Bazhrahils at the far end of the Uradabhur took on new life. The Arzhana became a garden, and still the tide of life and growth and magic raced ever eastward, across the Feinolons into the Grand Windsward. Dead lands cursed by the Endarkened rose up again. Dead grasses cursed by the creatures of the Endarkened crumbled to dust as new shoots reared up to claim their forfeited places. The starving Flower Forests were fed with pure Light, and the grasslands turned out-of-season green as the tide of Magery, of healing, raced eastward. It paused at the edge of Greythunder Glairyrill, but only for an instant before it swept on. Every shoot, every berry, every blade of grass that had ever belonged to the Light or worshipped the sun became new again. Stronger, braver, protected, championed and ready to fight.

Vieliessar and Tannatarie reached out to pour more power into the famished land. To heal the world. To push back against all the gains the Darkness had claimed in its long Wheelturns of battle. Its creatures her people would deal with at once, and once they had won—

But if the Dragon had infinite resources to draw upon the Mage did not. Vieliessar slipped from Tannatarie's back and began to fall.

❈

When she awoke, it was to Pouncewarm patting at her face.

"What—? Where is this place?" It was night. Sea air was in her nostrils, and she heard the crashing of waves. The ground was ice-hard, but there were no deep drifts of snow. She could feel both worry and reassurance through the Soulbond—that was Runacar—and concern and relief through the Dragonbond.

"Another tiresome ocean shore," Tannatarie said. "But seals. Yum. You were expending a great deal of power, my darling girl, and I should warn you that while I can never be exhausted by you drawing on my power, *you* can."

"You might have mentioned that sooner," Vieliessar grumbled, sitting up. She sent reassurance to Runacar—she couldn't send him verbal messages, not easily—and looked up at the sky, measuring the time.

"I *did* catch you as you fell."

"That's something," Vieliessar admitted. It was well past midnight, and even if the sun turned at a slower pace in the east, her absence had surely been noted.

She got to her feet carefully, for she and her Warhunters had all learned the painful consequences of grabbing or being grabbed while falling, and was pleased to note that her body had very few complaints. She stood up, placing a hand on Tannatarie's neck. *This is probably the last private moment I shall ever have. We* shall have, she edited internally, thinking of her Bonded partners. Tomorrow was clearly going to be a day of soothing the villagers and making sure the Sanctuary Lightborn didn't try to kill them all.

And to figure out what would come with spring, for when the snows melted, her king-domain and Leutric's Empire would no longer be separated by the Dragon's Gate, and who knew what would happen then?

"I love you," she said to Tannatarie. It seemed important to say, somehow.

"And I you," the white Dragon answered fondly. "And kindly remember that I am only as immortal as you are, and almost certainly less invulnerable."

"Scales."

"Armor. And persistence. So kindly arrange that any hostilities that open end well?"

"I am the High King," Vieliessar said, knowing she sounded outraged, unable to stop. "And my folk shall obey me."

"Of course, dear one. Just as they always have. Come now, and we will go."

Vieliessar looked outward at the ocean. No light showed, and the far shore was unguessable.

"That is where we came from," Vieliessar said. "From somewhere out there. And we are no more of their kind than they are of ours now. What will they say when they meet us?"

"Very little," Tannatarie answered. "Your ancestors exterminated all the Mages among them and when the Endarkened fell upon them, there was neither force nor curiosity to keep the scarlet monsters at bay."

Once again Vieliessar made the laborious climb to the Dragon's back and looked around, casting a ball of Silverlight to do so. At the edge of an unfamiliar sea, a golden rim of new sea grass sprouted up through the broken dusty grey remains of its predecessor. Half a rod away, the trunks of an ancient and venerable—and *new*—Flower Forest stood, their trunks lined up like cavalry at the charge.

A forest she had created out of light and magic.

Vieliessar took a deep breath, absently stroking Tannatarie's scales. The only thing she could compare them to was gems: smooth and glowing and lit with an inner fire. Then she sighed.

"Pouncewarm?" she called quietly. The Palugh had vanished again. She was about to call a second time when there was a flurry of sneezes from the direction of the shore and Pouncewarm streaked toward her. The Palugh glared up at her momentarily and then climbed to his usual spot. He was wet, but only the front of him—as if he had looked into a waterspout.

"Let us go away from here at once. The food is very bad and perhaps poisoned," he said.

⋉⊨

"Are you sure that's it?" Vieliessar asked, though the wide white scar of the western Dragon's Gate and the sharp peak of Stardock made it obvious. She was used to taking a bird's eye view of a thing; it was the easiest way to view an incipient battlefield—or an enemy about to treat a place as one.

Now the Flower Forest filled the whole of the three linked valleys and climbed up much of the inner walls of Ceoprentrei. Just as in the smaller Flower Forests, there were glades, and each of those had been crisscrossed by footprints that showed against the snow. The Elves had colonized much of the forest border; now, watchfires sketched an outline of the border-that-was—probably because everyone here was awake.

"Do you land, or do I just jump off?" Vieliessar wondered, looking down.

"Patience, child," Tannatarie said. She made a last pass over the forest and then dropped directly into a clearing. "Here we are. Just don't ask me to do that very often."

The Kingsguard burst out of the woods, led by Helecanth. She dropped to her knees before Vieliessar, head bowed. Vieliessar looked away for a moment, surprised, and saw that the whole of the Kingsguard had joined her.

"Is it well, my lord?" Helecanth asked, head still bowed.

"It is well," Vieliessar said firmly, taking Helecanth by the elbow and raising her to her feet. She kissed her liegeman as she had upon leaving, directly upon the mouth. "You must say to me how it has been here."

"Now that you have returned, all is well," Helecanth said. The rest of the company rose to its feet. "Lord Rithdeliel has been his delightful self," Helecanth said dryly. "As the candlemarks mounted, he said we must presume you missing, nor did he care much for the Dragons." She gestured in the direction of the valley rim, hidden by the trees, where, presumably, the Dragons were resting.

"I must meet this person," Tannatarie remarked.

"The villagers? The Lightborn?" Vieliessar asked.

"Safe and well," Helecanth reported. "Naturally you must call a council tomorrow and tell everything of what has happened, so that everyone can shout at the same time and feel ill-done-by in company. But what *are* we to do with these people? They cannot plow their fields—there *are* no fields, just to begin with."

"There will be many skills they have that we do not, and they will teach them to us. Further, Tuonil will teach them to farm as he farms, which is good, since at the moment I see no day upon which we can leave these forests," Vieliessar said. *But the Endarkened have wings, and torches . . .*

"Then it is good he has a Dragon beside him, for Black Sorgane will help him in encouraging them to pay his words a useful attention."

"A Dragon?" Vieliessar asked blankly. "Tuonil has a Dragon?" She had known, of course, about Iardalaith and Isilla and Niviel, and when Tannatarie had said four were bonded (yesterday morning as it was now) Vieliessar had counted Tannatarie among them. "But . . . But he doesn't have Light!"

"Black Sorgane has said he will have Tuonil and no other as his Bondmate, and that he will teach him Magery as required. Perhaps your Dragon could change Tuonil's Dragon's mind," Helecanth said. "I do not think so. But come, my lord, we must get you before a warm fire and food and tea."

"And sleep?" Vieliessar said hopefully.

"Dawn comes soon," Helecanth said, with the faintest air of getting her own back. "Many will question."

"And few will get answers they like," Vieliessar muttered. "Say to the council and to the people there will be a general audience before the council meeting."

⊰⊱

The Audience Chamber was vast, but not so vast as to include all of Vieliessar's folk. She had included delegates from Areve: the whole of the former nobility who had hidden there, for the way she ruled would be good for them to see, and the *Ifanbigan* of Areve. She'd wondered who could be the highest-ranking among the surviving Sanctuary Lightborn now that Hamphuliadiel was gone, then, in her position as Astromancer, chose Elderin as her Deputy Astromancer, at least partly because the Unicorns had liked him. What these folk would make of things, she had no idea, but they were here and they could speak out and they could tell their fellows what they'd heard. Tannatarie was here as well, at the far side of the Council Chamber. Even as large as she was, it was not easy to see her.

For the rest, the open space was held by the Guilds and Societies. Before she had won the Unicorn Throne Vieliessar had sworn to replace the rule of might and privilege with law and justice. And to keep that vow, Vieliessar had turned to Guilds and Societies, social systems that had already been in existence for grand-tailles of Wheelturns. Once she had confirmed the continuing existence of those, she added more. The

Guild of the Lawspeakers had been formed almost simultaneously with the Lightborn Guild, and over time every one of these Guilds and Societies had made and remade itself a hundred ways. Vieliessar could argue against the changes and even abolish them—but even she had to answer to the Lawspeaker General if complaint was brought against her.

And if the Lawspeaker General found against her, she must lift her demand—or her people would plunge into civil war once more. That had always been the force behind her rule: two entities, each bound to the other and standing at the edge of a cliff, each holding a knife at the throat of the other. If one stabbed, both fell. If both fell, both died.

It inclined Vieliessar to rule by persuasion.

The "chamber" was already packed with the full hierarchies of every Guild and Society, and as many more as possible. Woodwose, endlessly curious. Palughs draped around shoulders like fashionable scarves. (*Heavy* fashionable scarves.) Wulvers climbing into unoccupied trees to get a better view. Behind the throne, the semicircle of Court stood ready to be enchanted, and the attending officers of the Court stood waiting behind the throne.

Vieliessar, wearing tunic, trews, and boots, walked through her Court under Cloak to avoid having to speak with any of them. The color of her garments—Lightborn green—and the elvensilver Vilya flower she wore at her throat were the only signs of rank she bore.

Now, as she crossed the perimeter, she saw the chair from which she must speak for the first time.

Isilla, Dinias, Tangisen, I know you have a part in this! she thought, and tried not to laugh.

Since she was about to hold a public audience, the High King needed a throne, the logic behind this object clearly went. And thus, the Lightborn had entertained themselves by creating a throne that would not have looked out of place in any of the High Houses in which many of them had served. It was made of wood and jewels instead of marble, and sat on a platform Vieliessar would have to walk up three steps to reach. Magery had gone into every aspect of its building, from the scrolled armrests shaped like Unicorns, to the carved Dragons intertwined on the back. The artisans had taken advantage of the reborn Flower Forest to show off their skills with inlay and sculpture; the Unicorns glowed in uluskukad-wood, and the Dragons were the deep purple of sedulu.

The frame of the chair, and the settings for the gems, were made from ahata, stronger than any blacksmith's steel and harder to work, for it must be done by magic.

Hamphuliadiel, she was sure, would have loved it.

And that was the point, really. To mock the despot in death, to rejoice in the fact that they were all alive, and to laugh about a chair that Vieliessar was certain she was going to have to sit on for the rest of her life.

She mounted the steps and seated herself on the chair, and then dropped Cloak. The Warhunters clapped ironically at the showiness of the act while the Lightless gasped in wonder and delight at the Magery of it.

"I am here, my people, to speak with you and to listen to you. With the help of the Dragon Tannatarie, of whose arrival I shall tell you soon, I have covered the whole of the Western Reach and the Uradabhur with Flower Forests, and the Endarkened cannot come at us through them. But while that is true, it does not make us truly safe. We have all been harassed by goblins and Lesser Endarkened before, and certainly the Endarkened will now find new horrors to send. But at least we are reunited with our lost kin: the children of starving Crofters and Landbonds, abused by rich *komen*, left in the woods to die, were taken up and parented by the Otherfolk. By treaty with the King-Emperor of the Otherfolk, these Woodwose are among us and we will become known to each other.

"Next, any of you who didn't believe in ancient prophecies, and bet on that, have now lost your bets. I, Vieliessar Farcarinon, Child of the Prophecy, have fulfilled the foretelling passed down through generations not only in the *Song of Amretheon and Pelashia*, but by foretellings of the Otherfolks. It has long been foretold to Leutric, King-Emperor of the Minotaurs, that someone of Elvenkind lineage would come to claim the powers he held in trust. This I have done. The power held in keeping is that of thirteen Soulbond Dragons who will choose their Soulmates and lend their power to the fight. Four—*five*—have already done so. It is that power I used to render us all, if not safe, then safer.

"And last, the Sanctuary of the Star is no more. We will train any Lightborn-to-come as we have been doing, as Mosirinde trained the first Lightborn. There is hope that there are some things within the Sanctuary and its library that can still be salvaged. The coming days will tell.

"That is all I have to speak to you. Question me how you will."

Wheelturns of meetings such as this had taught her audience silence as she spoke—it had been broken, this time, by the voices of the outsiders. And now they spoke first.

"What of the komen? I, Munariel of House Inglethendragir, was *darabinat* to War Prince Sierdalant, and in the absence of any of higher rank before me, I claim his lands and chattel for my own! And take my son, Raneriliet, for my heir!"

The members of the Komen Guild began shouting loudly.

Several more komen—all from the Western Reach, who had been pretending to be commonsborn in Areve—began moving toward Munariel, all shouting their claims on abeyant Domains. Some of the Lawspeakers followed to keep the peace.

"*Hear me!*" There were times Vieliessar thought that she had kept her place because she had the loudest voice. "I am the High King, and Inglethendragir is mine by right of conquest. The last War Prince of Inglethendragir swore an oath of fealty to me upon a battlefield where the dead had lately walked. I am the Child of the Prophecy, chosen by Amretheon Aradruniel." Vieliessar got to her feet. "Will you stand in the Challenge Circle against me now, or will you go to the Komen's Guild first, and the Lawspeakers second?"

"You can't do that!" Munariel cried.

"Do you think I'm on this throne for Festival Fair? I am High King over all the Hundred Houses, and I can do whatever I choose!"

General laughter at the newcomers' expense greeted that comment. Munariel's face darkened, and she pushed her way toward the back of the crowd.

"I speak for the people of Areve!" The woman's voice nearly drowned Vieliessar's out. "I am Cereniel, *Ifanbigan* of Areve, and I demand to know *what's going on*! The great Astromancer Lord Hamphuliadiel promised us safety! He promised he would rule over this false High

King—that she would swear herself to him! Now he is dead and she is here, and further, she is engaged in a monstrous and unnatura—"

"But did you have a *question*?" Iardalaith asked, smiling sweetly. He'd already learned that these villagers were easily terrorized by anyone wearing the green robe, and used this knowledge without mercy.

"What is to become of us?" Cereniel asked brokenly, her anger turning to grief. "What do you mean to do to us? We have no riches with which to bribe you—we have nothing. Hamphuliadiel told us much about you—but I no longer know what to believe."

"You are our kin," Vieliessar said simply. "Further, you are farmers and Craftworkers, and we need both greatly. I need some way to ride my Dragon without fear of falling off, and who is to provide that? Not me!"

Again the general laughter from her long-ruled subjects. "Show us your Dragon!" someone else shouted.

::Well?:: Vieliessar asked. ::Are you ready?::

::If you *are*. Now lift me up—and carefully. You won't like it if you drop me:: Tannatarie answered.

With an effort, Vieliessar kept her fingers from twitching in the meaningless gestures meant for the sight of the Lightless. Tannatarie stood up on her hind legs and stretched out her neck, then her wings. She continued to rise—magisterially—until she was above the trees. Higher, higher . . .

And then she was airborne.

Her audience was entranced. It was always springtide in the Flower Forest, but there were a number of peepholes in the leafy canopy through which to watch the display of Dragonflight. When Tannatarie landed again, there were disappointed groans from her watchers.

Even with the strangers—and a Dragon—present, the audience went much like any other, with questions like "When will we defeat the Endarkened" and "Can goblins come this far into a Flower Forest," until it came to the question she had been dreading.

"What about our children? You promised to give them back. Now these creatures have them and say they've been promised them! Well, I like a good nursemaid as well as anyone, but why should we share our children with those vermin?"

"Some of them have fleas!" someone else shouted, and there was general grumbling among the villagers.

Areve had been a village of perhaps five thousand souls, more than half of them women. Mortality in childbed had been high, since Hamphuliadiel had forbidden Lightborn to act as midwives, but that still meant the caravan had left Areve with roughly 1,500 infants and toddlers.

All of which had been gone in the first sennight of travel.

Baenor hadn't come back with all of them, or with anything like one thousand babies. Collecting them from the West would be the work of seasons, as it would be to collect the Woodwose themselves.

"These 'vermin' you so lightly speak of are your children, the children of Landbonds, servants, the Crofters who worked the borderlands farms. They were left for dead as their families could not feed them. The Otherfolk took them in and raised them. These Woodwose have little desire to be among us, but there is much they can teach us about survival, and much we can teach them. Remember: they want your children because they love them, and they thought they would die when the wagons left Arevethmonion."

There were more questions about the missing children, mostly redundant. Vieliessar made a mental note to send two Lightborn into the West, so as to be able to use Door to bring back any children and Woodwose as they came across them.

And to bring back information.

The next collection of questions were of the usual sort: memorial services for the dead, Loremasters to remember them, a section of the Flower Forest to be dedicated as the grave grove if they could not find the location of the one they had built here after the Battle of Ceoprentrei. Most of these were as easy as referring the questioner to the appropriate Guild, or asking a Guildmaster who felt they could deal with the problem to step forward. Some questions were personal: Was she all right? Could they see the other Dragons? (Could *they* have a Dragon?) Others entered into the realm of rumor: Was it true she was to marry Leutric? (No, she was not going to marry Leutric, and left it at that.)

The people had their right to see her and question her, for she had

known since the slaughter at her Enthroning that her people must be her
allies, and know her to take responsibility for the preservation of their
lives. Nothing else would have kept them with her during the sunturns,
sennights, moonturns, wheels of their flight. She must always be seen,
always available to be questioned.

But at last Perandor—her steward—stepped forward, carrying a long
staff that must have been made at the same time the throne had, for it
was glowing and baroque and jeweled. He banged the end upon the bottom step three times and announced this audience was at an end.

Vieliessar promptly cast Cloak.

⊰⊱

Her personal guard formed a line between the back of the throne
and the Council Chamber. The twelve of them—plus Helecanth—
were not a particularly powerful barrier to anyone attempting to rush
the council, but anyone trying to intrude upon the High King when
they'd just had the chance to question her publicly was unlikely to be
met with sympathy. Vieliessar, still invisible, walked around the end of
the line of komen and into the space designated as the Council's Chamber.

Her councillors awaited her standing before their seats. There had
apparently been time between her flight from Imrathalion—and the
subsequent expansion of the Flower Forests—and the council meeting
for today to also create seats for the council. These were less showily
ornamented than her "throne," but each bore on its backrest the individual's symbol: for Githachi, two silver swords, crossed; for Rithdeliel, the
High King's arms caparisoned, for he was her Warlord; to Helecanth,
Commander of the Kingsguard, the same, but with a gold caparison
instead of red and silver.

The rest bore devices instead of arms: Tuonil's, a cluster of acorns
and berries; Thurion, Iardalaith, Aradreleg—all Lightborn—green
and silver for leaf and star, but they reported to three different masters
whom their devices showed plainly. And Gelduin, Lawspeaker Commander, displayed a device that showed him as equal in power to the
High King herself, for even she must bow to the Law. In the midst of

these was Vieliessar's chair. She dropped into it with a sigh, dropping Cloak as she did so.

As her councillors followed Rithdeliel's lead in making obeisance—since they could hardly avoid it if all of them were standing—Vieliessar looked around the spellbound chamber. Githachi looked weary and concerned, for she already knew her horses did not take well to the Dragons. Tuonil sat beside her, looking equally concerned about having to retrain a large number of truculent farmers in wildgathering. Iardalaith looked sardonically amused, probably at the prospect of terrorizing a collection of untrained teenaged Lightborn.

Vieliessar gestured that they should begin.

"What shall we do with the Dragons?" Annobeunna Keindostibaent asked. She was not only one of the few surviving members of the nobility, she was also one of the few surviving War Princes who had not risen to that position due to all of their upline being dead.

"Say, rather, what they will do with us," Iardalaith said lightly. "As four of us here are Dragonbonded, and another among the Folk."

"You're wrong about that; there are only three of us from the council—including our gracious lord—and the others are Isilla and Niviel, both Lightborn of course," Thurion said innocently.

At the word "Lightborn," Rithdeliel shot Tuonil a poisonous glance. "Regardless of the wretched beasts' opinions, what are we to do with them? Or feed them? We can barely feed ourselves."

"They are free agents," Vieliessar said. "They will feed themselves—from the oceans, I hope—until the lands can return to fruitfulness. And that will require our constant watchfulness—and that of our allies, the Otherfolk."

"Are *you* a free agent?" Rithdeliel asked directly. "I have heard madness and nonsense and rumors—which, somehow, you did not address when you spoke to the folk. I would hear the truth from you in plain words, Mother of Dragons."

"The truth is simple and plain. I brought us west for two reasons. One, if we did not come west, the Endarkened would kill us all. Two, to reach the Great Library at the Sanctuary of the Star, for if we knew our enemy, there might be information there we could use."

"And not," Rithdeliel said, "to raise the siege of the Western Lands."

"Now, knowing the strength and numbers of the enemy, no. My only hope would be to raise Door drawing on Arevethmonion and bring as many here as I could, but you know as well as I that this would doom us when we exhausted her. This is now the largest Flower Forest in the Western Reach. I did not know then that Delfierarathadan had been destroyed, but that was of no matter: It would be moonturns on foot to reach her, and hard winter when we arrived."

"Well, here's hard truth, and hard changes. And unanswered questions: What does it mean that some of us have Dragons? You say they are only for Lightborn, yet my friend Tuonil here has one, apparently. And there is the matter of the rest of them. How shall they be apportioned?" Annobeunna asked practically.

"*We shall not be apportioned.*" Tannatarie reared back, letting them all see her enormous size, then came down to stare directly into Annobeunna's face. The spells of the Council Chamber writhed and crackled around her. Vieliessar hastened to restructure them to admit Tannatarie. "*We shall choose. And if we wish, we shall leave.*"

Vieliessar knew this was only the truth, and that even the Bonded Dragons might go, though she hardly knew what that meant. She struggled to keep her face from showing the anguish she felt at that possibility.

"Then what use are you?" Rithdeliel said evenly, just as Vieliessar shouted "Stop!"

Everyone looked at her in surprise. Tannatarie lay down on her side, like an enormous cat, and began flicking the very tip of her tail against Shield, which popped and crackled at each touch. Vieliessar scrambled to weave words together before she began to speak.

"Yes, we have Dragons—or rather, they have *us*. Leutric didn't know that. He believed that what his family guarded was weapons, which is what the Dragons actually aren't. I think they may be something even more powerful than mere weapons, if they and we can work together to discover what it is. What we know is this: Dragons are creatures of the Light. They can make the Dragonbond with any who have the Light *or the potential for it*. One who is Dragonbonded no longer needs the Flower Forest to power their spells, and can cast all spells at puissance level, as if each spell were their last. Tuonil, can you tell me whether the Light was Called in you?"

"The answer to that is 'no,'" Thurion said, from his place between Tuonil and Vieliessar. "No one came to their croft most years, and it wouldn't have mattered anyway, since the family hid from strangers if they possibly could. But after Sorgane announced the Bond, I Tested Tuonil. He is Lightborn. Sorgane says he will train him. With luck, we can learn Sorgane's spells from Tuonil."

Tuonil did his best not to look terrified of the concept, but it was the only way. Spells like Fire and Silverlight had once been learned from proximity to the walls of a chamber upon which they had been cast unknown times. But even though those walls were gone, the small spells could be coaxed to manifest themselves in a Postulant's mind.

But not the Greater.

For the Greater, there must be a link between minds while the spell was cast. The Greater spells could not be written down—there was no language that could describe them. Before the war—before Vieliessar and the Warhunters, before the Enthroning, new spells were few, and the ones who created them kept them close until they could pass them to as many Lightborn outside their own House as possible. Even so, many spells had been lost, surviving only as a description in a scroll in the Great Library.

If the Great Library itself even remained in existence.

"Start from scratch then?" Aradreleg asked. "I don't really want to keep the other Lightborn away from, well, us. Or from the villagers either. But while both groups are going to be hard to fit in—and the Woodwose, well!—if one of the Sanctuary Lightborn Dragonbonds . . . He could kill us with a Fire spell."

"The Silver Hooves save us from our allies," Rithdeliel muttered.

The rest of the meeting was a matter of who and what and when, and after a certain point even admitting that just before the caves of Imrathalion had collapsed she'd made a binding treaty with the Otherfolk (without awaiting the consent of her subjects), *and* had agreed to marry Rune Battlemaster (formerly Runacarendalur Caerthalien, and technically a ruling War Prince), to seal it *and* enduring the shouting and arguing and "discussion" that followed was not enough to keep Vieliessar awake. Smothered yawns turned to moments of sleep and then longer moments, until Tannatarie pushed her nose between Vieliessar and the back of her chair and easily sent her sprawling onto the grass.

"Nothing can be decided when she's asleep," the Dragon said ruthlessly. "If you want to argue, do it without my Bonded. *She* is going to sleep."

"I am sorry, my lords and ladies," Vieliessar said, getting to her feet. "I do not treat your wise counsel with the gravity it deserves, but—"

"But my lord has not slept in a sennight, and spent most of that time fighting and laboring," Helecanth said ruthlessly. "Let us heed the Dragon's advice."

"Oh yes," Tannatarie said, "let us heed the Dragon indeed. For she is a very hungry Dragon, you know."

⟊⟊

Well, that solves one problem. Tannatarie spoke true: the Dragons choose Lightborn. We shall have to give them the opportunity to inspect all the Lightborn here," Thurion said.

"Yes to the first," Iardalaith said. "As for the second, can't we just tuck a few of those yammering half-cooked sausages somewhere the Dragons won't—" He broke off with an expression that indicated he was listening. "Look, I know you're perfect, but it's not as if *you* choose either," he said, now addressing Elderin. "Look at the Soulbond, and what a mess it's made. Now we have to spend the rest of our lives *not* killing Caerthalien."

"Spoken like a true War Prince," Thurion teased. "But you're Bonded, Iarda—how hard are the Dragons looking for partners?"

It was a few sunturns after the council meeting. The three Lightborn were sitting at the edge of one of the small clearings in Nomaitemil Flower Forest, gazing cautiously skyward. After ten horrific Wheelturns where the sky meant the most terrible form of danger, it was hard to believe they were safe—or, at least, differently in peril.

"Most of the Unbonded are finding places to den up," Iardalaith said meditatively. "There's a lot of Nomaitemil now and we don't use most of it, so why not? They're hunting—Vielie told me the Centaurs' herds are off-limits, so we're all having to be creative in finding hunting grounds. But the short answer to your question is 'no'—the Dragons aren't looking right now, but that doesn't mean a Bond won't find them."

"Speaking of things that won't find us, or rather will," Aradreleg said, "what about the Endarkened? I can't imagine how horrible for you it must have been."

"I can't imagine how horrible it must have been and I was there," Iardalaith said lightly. Of the three of them, only Iardalaith had seen the combat at Imrathalion. "When their Greater Power took the field to help them . . . that was bad."

"But you won," Aradreleg said doubtfully.

"But something that was not us made them all leave before they'd killed all of us and the talking animals, too. I have to say, though . . . watching a Bearsark fight is magnificent," Iardalaith said.

"The Bearsarks were magnificent and the Endarkened still won," Thurion said, keeping them on track. "With the Dragonbond we have a more powerful way of casting the same old spells that *aren't doing anything*. Sure, we're safe in here and that's wonderful, but we're only safe from the Endarkened, really. A Flower Forest stops goblins, but it doesn't stop everything. And some of those other things are—"

They all fell silent, thinking of the battles they had faced in their westward journey. The Endarkened delighted in taking creatures and . . . *twisting* them. The Bugbears had been made from Bearwards—their fur black as if with old blood, eight legged, with bulging red eyes, and long glassy claws. The Bullroarers began as Minotaurs; their roar was stunningly loud, coming from a throat so wide it could swallow a whole pig. When it opened its maw, its lower jaw dropped to the middle of its chest, and the whole rim was lined in dagger teeth. And there were the Serpentmarae, whose genesis no one could agree upon—whether it was horses, or Centaurs, or possibly some unknown species. Superficially they had the semblance of flesh-eating horses, but in place of a tail was some long prehensile tentacle that could stun a foe until the Serpentmarae could turn on them and trample them to death with its many-toed feet.

"Frightening. And lethal. And then there are the Lesser Endarkened.

Who *can* enter the Flower Forest. With encouragement." Iardalaith lay down on his back and stared up at the sky through the trees. "This does not look like a game we can win."

"So we all die, and our allies with us. Even with the Dragons to help us." Thurion's tone was flat and disinterested.

"In theory we could kill—or at least dismember—all of them, but it's hard to know when you've won when you don't know how many of the enemy there are," Iardalaith drawled.

"Then we'll have to count them," Thurion said.

One of the Dragons, far above, crossed the patch of open sky, and all three Lightborn flinched.

Three days after they returned to Nomaitemil, the Warhunt lit the funeral pyre for Harwing. There was no body, of course—that had perished in the collapse of Imrathalion—but a pyre had been built of fragrant woods and oils and draped with green silk. The Warhunt stood about it, waiting for Vieliessar.

"I have stood beside the pyre of too many of my kindred," Isilla said sadly. "I had rather not do so again."

Dinias watched Isilla from beneath his lashes. This was a hard going-forth: he could not decide whether to be glad that Harwing was dead, or sorry he'd died so soon. Certainly he had done things which warranted death—the betrayal of the village of Areve to the Otherfolk, just to begin with, when another moonturn would have seen them safe. The murder of Hamphuliadiel and his followers; he had not used the Light to kill any of them, but it was horrific just the same.

Vieliessar came through the forest at a near run, her green robes shushing against the bushes and other low growth. She looked harried. There were always too many calls on a ruler's time. When might Vieliessar go as Harwing had, and use the Light to make her life . . . easier?

"I worry about what the Lightborn are becoming," Dinias whispered to himself.

"Other than free?" Tangisen asked.

"Freedom is a costly luxury," Dinias answered sadly.

"I am sorry to have kept you all waiting, though I cannot say it was without cause," Vieliessar said to all of them. She stretched out her hands—to Pendray on the right and Isilla on the left—and her hands closed over theirs.

"We come to celebrate the leave-taking of one of Pelashia's Children. Harwing of Aramenthiali, you have served long in the Cold World. Go now to the Warm World, where it is always summer, and go with joy."

Everyone there knew that with Tannatarie the White to draw upon, Vieliessar did not need to draw upon their linked power, but she did so that it was their joint effort that caused Harwing's funeral pyre to vanish in a flash of light.

Vieliessar was gone again before their vision cleared.

⊰⊱

Hearth Moon became Frost Moon, and the small area outside the Flower Forest was covered in deep snow, for here in the Mystrals the winters were bitter. The contingent of Woodwose that had come with Vieliessar's people had been standoffish at the beginning, feeling that they had been tricked into imprisonment or perhaps slavery, but when all that happened was that Elves came to them to learn about camouflage and foraging, the atmosphere between the two groups warmed considerably, even among those Elves whose children the Woodwose had stolen. Especially when the Elves learned that *every one of the Woodwose could do magic.*

It did not require the Light to be Called, it did not require years of training at the Sanctuary of the Star, it did not end in a life of bondage. It was just *there:* the ability to see and hear the Brightfolk. To speak with them. To kindle fire, to call, and to find.

The Woodwose had Called the children old enough to come to them, and silently stolen the rest, and seeing what came after that, their parents found it harder and harder to begrudge them.

As the various groups slowly merged, they spread out through the Flower Forest. The farmers were as traumatized by their brief exodus and long persecution as those who had spent ten years fighting for their lives. Now, they were shocked to find they had the right to choose a Guild other than the one they had been ordered into. They had so many rights that they found themselves dizzy with them, and the thought that their kindred had spent ten Wheelturns trying to rejoin them sealed the friendship.

Some of the villagers had carried seeds in their pockets, and tiny plantings of wheat, of barley, and of rye began to appear in the smaller clearings of the Flower Forest.

Over the sunturns, the Elves moved north through Nomaitemil, toward the center of the Flower Forest. Here they found a clearing far larger than any they had found before—large enough to be dangerous—with a lake in the center. It filled most of the center of the valley, and on each side, there was a series of shallow dead-end caves in the valley walls, many (on the east side) now filled with Dragons. The Elves used the ones on the west side for storage, as a Flower Forest was wonderful in many ways, but it did not keep off the rain.

Vieliessar spent much of her time training—or, rather, *re*training, the Lightborn the Astromancer had collected. She never spoke the truth about Hamphuliadiel to them or to anyone else. Let that one truth die with Harwing and with her.

By inalterable custom, the High King's throne room remained where it was, a creation of spells, imagination, and baroque chairs almost two leagues away from current Elven settlement. But for their own uses, the Elves built sturdy, warm, and dry homes in the trees, so artfully concealed that they might almost have been a part of the trees they filled.

A deep, long-unfed hunger caused a flurry of building: traditions, lives, homes. Nor was there any less need for komen now that the Elves had found this sanctuary, for too many of the Dark's creatures still stalked them. Children harvesting mushrooms were accompanied by Woodwose with their deadly javelins; the only ones who did not receive an armed escort were those old enough to defend themselves, and they went in packs.

It was strange to have a home one did not expect to leave. A home with chairs and beds. A home with Silverlight coins in wooden boxes so you could see at night if you wanted to, and it was safe to see, and boxes full of heated stones so you could stay warm. The weavers constructed their large looms from memory and reassembled the small ones, and soon the Woodwose were able to add well-woven wool tunics and hose to their wardrobes, and bright rugs under their feet. The potters found deposits of clay and began to make jars and pots and lanterns, and from the willows growing at the side of the streams the weavers could create baskets, chairs, and many other things. Carpenters, accompanied by Woodwose, sought through the Flower Forest for trees they could safely fell, and so there was wood for houses, for furniture, even for barrels and casks. With all the fruit of the Flower Forest to draw upon, the Elves began to make wine and cordials again.

The only crafts that required Light were drawing gems and metal out of the earth, and the making of vellum and leather, for what sheep remained must be kept alive to increase the flocks. When the Endarkened did not come with that small use of Light, the burgeoning community was divided between joy and deep suspicion.

Everyone knew the Endarkened would return, for the Endarkened had promised to destroy everything, and Ceoprentrei and the Western Reach were still here. For now, all the Dragonmages could do was warn the western settlements of incursion; the eastern lands, from the foothills of Jaeglenhend to the shores of the Cold Ocean, had become a sterile wilderness again despite the Dragonmages' best efforts: all that remained was wind-blown ash, scorched earth, and lifeless stone.

⁘

U gh." Vieliessar squatted down to the ground, sifting its dirt through her gloved fingers. She'd asked Tannatarie to dig down through the snow to reach the soil, for here in the Uradabhur, Winter High Queen ruled with ruthless force. Vieliessar had used Magery to recreate the Flower Forests twice over from the Uradabhur to the eastern shore, and each time they had not only died, but vanished to the last stump.

The air and ground were thick with snow, without Flower Forests to keep them away. Feeling the current flurries, Vieliessar realized she'd never thought she would come to miss winter, but she did: the sharp scent of the air, the snowflakes that landed against her skin like weightless touches. The Flower Forest had nothing similar, and the Elves dared not make their homes outside it.

"Nothing's left," she said to Tannatarie. "And I don't know why. Goblins would eat wood, but they can't get in. Bugbears and Bullroarers only eat meat—as do the Serpentmarae, I think. Well, I shall tell Iardalaith—if he's up there—to raise it again, then a nice flight for the three of us, what do you think?"

Whenever she could steal a moment from her other duties—most of which seemed to involve sitting in a chair listening to someone—Vieliessar took to the sky with Tannatarie and Pouncewarm. Her cordwainers had created a riding seat for her upon Tannatarie's back—not quite a saddle, but a place to keep her warm and safe and in place. Several stormcloaks had been repurposed to add thick leggings to each saddle, for Tannatarie had told Vieliessar that the air high in the sky was always winter-cold, and Vieliessar herself had found it to be true. In place of straps, each saddle had a sort of vest that could be buckled shut. There were stirrups on the saddle-girth, but they were meaningless, as she could no more control Tannatarie by force than she could the moon.

It could hold three, the other two riding before her, since Adalieriel and Calanoriel constantly begged for rides, and Tannatarie was happy to provide them.

Most of all, Vieliessar craved the opportunity to drop her many masks: High King, Astromancer, Child of the Prophecy, Lightborn. She did not know who she was without them, and on Tannatarie's back she did not care.

She glanced skyward and saw two other Dragons—only dark shapes against the sky—circling there. She thought she might see if the Otherfolk would allow her to send Dragonmages west—not just to aid their allies and tighten bonds, but for faster reporting in case of another Endarkened attack.

No, not "in case." They have vowed to come at us again and I believe them.

Pouncewarm jumped down from the saddle and minced delicately across the exposed soil. It more resembled cinders and ashes than soil—ashes, Vieliessar could understand, since these forests had burned down several times in the last few months—but these spongy friable remains dwindled into dust if handled too roughly.

"I suppose we had best be on our way, and I shall ask Iardalaith to raise it up again. But I do not understand. Why does it not *stay*?"

Suddenly Pouncewarm gave a fearsome shriek and bounded to Tannatarie's back. He reared up, plucking at his hands and pulling at them before turning his attentions to his feet.

"Unfaaaaaaaaaaaaaaaair! It bites! I, I, I am virtuous and innocent, I! Not capable of wickedness, I!"

Vieliessar ran over to Tannatarie and caught Pouncewarm as he was about to fall from the saddle. She ran her fingers over his hands and feet and realized both were covered with large bumps, black and welling with blood.

"Hold still, small one. I think I can free you," Vieliessar said. Pouncewarm uttered another earsplitting shriek, but at least he stayed where he was.

The bumps, she found, were some sort of insect. She pried them loose one by one—using a touch of Cold to numb Pouncewarm's skin and make removing them easier. She moved her fingers over his injuries—they looked like tiny bites—healing and soothing them as she worked. She tossed each insect to the ground as she finished—they were all over the bare skin of his hands and feet and she'd even found some crawling up his legs—but saved the last one to study.

She inspected it curiously—or did until it flipped itself over onto its stomach and gave the base of her thumb a ferocious bite. She plucked it free and held it between thumb and forefinger.

"So that's what's been eating my forests," Vieliessar said.

"Poor Pouncewarm," said the Palugh mournfully. "Harried and bitten and *sore*!"

"I bet you are," Vieliessar agreed. "Now stay up here. I think they're leaving me alone because of the thick boots I'm wearing, and maybe Tannatarie doesn't look that edible—"

"Thank you for that," the Dragon said.

"—but you, my furry warrior, are on their menu. If they catch you again. Which they won't, because after I prove my theory I am going to make them wish they were never born."

Forcing a plant from seed to maturity in an instant, or to create a healthy plant from its remnants, was actually a simple Lightborn spell, since the War Princes had wanted flowers in winter, and fresh fruit as well.

No longer, Vieliessar thought with grim satisfaction. *The day of the War Princes is done—and the day of Lightborn being in thrall to any frivolous whim with it.*

"And of course they always thought that spell-made fruit was somehow better than fruit that had been put into stasis moonturns ago, because they were all idiots," she muttered under her breath as she worked.

She rummaged through the bag that held her lunch and dropped a piece of dried fruit on the ground. A blackberry bush sprouted up out of the ashes. In a few seconds it was swarming with beetles, which ate every part of it but the stems and thorns, and then ate them too. Vieliessar dug around the base of the bush. No roots were there.

"Well," Tannatarie said briskly, "what are you going to do now? They're in the soil all the way to the Cold Ocean, and when your perfectly ordinary brambles and vines come over the mountain in the spring, they will eat them up and then eat *you* up."

"Charming," Vieliessar said drily. "I know: I'll appoint a committee to study the problem. But"—she kicked at the ashy friable soil that concealed so much disaster—"why haven't they come west already?"

"Probably because the mountain wall stops them," the Dragon replied. "And also probably because the Endarkened seeded them in a very narrow area."

"The Flower Forests of the east," Vieliessar said. "But they'll spread. They'll eat everything. Unless they're stopped."

"What a very good idea, darling," Tannatarie said pertly. "Who do you suppose is going to do that?"

"Probably me," Vieliessar said with a sigh. "And then seed a sample Flower Forest here to see if it will last. And then worry about what comes next. If the Endarkened are going to attack us with little things like these hellgrammites we're in trouble. It's almost better when they send us nice big monsters—but we can't fight what we can't see and we don't know where the Endarkened are so that we can fight *them*—not that we could defeat them anyway! Tannatarie, do *you* know how to make them vulnerable?"

"If I knew, I would tell you at once, darling," the Dragon said gently. "But all I know is that it is something you must discover, and soon."

"Or not even Dragons can help us," Vieliessar agreed. She kicked at the dirt, frowning, thinking of the beetles that had bitten Pouncewarm. All she needed to do was create a thousand tiny Pouncewarms to hunt them and eat them—and anything else the Endarkened created.

Bugbears and Nightwolves and Bullroarers and every other type of horror—I wouldn't create something like that even if I could.

But perhaps I can do the opposite . . .

She pulled off her heavy flying gloves and opened the pack Tannatarie carried. She pulled out a few more berries and dropped them on the ground, and when the hellgrammites swarmed them she plucked out a handful of them, then wrapped them in a protective sphere.

Now to find out what you do and change it, only a little.

She let herself drift into the light trance of a Healing, as she inspected the beetles. It was much like inspecting a wounded komen, or an injured horse, except that the beetles had behaviors built into them as well, so it was much like studying someone under a Compulsion spell. *That's it,* she thought, and burrowed deeper.

Here were the orders the hellgrammites had been given: to breed, to burrow, to eat anything living—or once living—that they could. She changed the orders built into all three: eat hellgrammites.

When she opened her eyes and looked down at them, the beetles in her hands were no longer black, but instead a pearly white, like Tannatarie's scales.

"Hmph," said the Dragon, nearly blowing the beetles from Vieliessar's hands with her snort. "Why won't the black beetles just eat the white ones?"

"Because on the list of things the black beetles are tasked with eating, other beetles are not on the menu."

"Can we go somewhere else now?" Tannatarie said. "I was promised a day of flying—and hunting, though I'm not expecting much there. Are you sure you can't trade with the Centaurs for a measly little cow or two? It's not like you'd be stealing them."

"In the spring," Vieliessar said, climbing into the saddle. "Everything changes then. Now you, you lazy lump, have no fear of running into a tree here. So run."

❦

Frost Moon became Snow Moon. In Snow Moon the Elves—or most of them at least—would celebrate Midwinter together.

And at Snow Moon, children would be Called to the Light.

❦

It is not enough to hide behind our . . . forests," Rithdeliel said. "Even if half our Dragons are unavailable—"

And pacifists, and not technically "ours," Vieliessar added mentally. Though she didn't really believe that. What she knew was that the Dragons were as different from the Elves as the Endarkened were—though the Dragons seemed far kinder.

"—we have five Bonded Dragons, and should be able to take this war to our enemy."

"Wherever they are," Iardalaith said sweetly.

Another council meeting—this, the first of two scheduled for Snow Moon—and after a handful of sennights of comparative safety, the debate was going about as well as Vieliessar had expected. Much as she had expected, with safety—or the illusion of it—her people had once more splintered into a thousand factions.

"Easy enough to find—"

"Perhaps you could delay the matter until we have finished committing our dead to the Tablets of Memory!" Thurion snapped.

"My lord Rithdeliel, do not force me to speculate that your eagerness for battle is so that I may die in it," Vieliessar said icily, more out of irritation with Rithdeliel's opinion that the lair of the Endarkened would be easy to find than out of belief in her own words.

"My lord King!" Rithdeliel came instantly to his feet to kneel before Vieliessar, the nape of his neck exposed and his helmet tucked beneath his arm. "Take my—"

"Oh stop it, all of you!" Annobeunna got to her feet. "Am I the only one here who has actually ruled over a Great House?"

Yes, Thurion mouthed silently at Vieliessar. She did her best to keep from laughing aloud.

"The decision to begin a campaign is not a matter of shouting at one another over the course of a council meeting whose more proper purpose is to discover who can remember the recipe for alzipayn. This may be a war we can win—with the Dragons' help. Or we may have to resign ourselves to living under bushes in a small corner of lands we once ruled. My lord High King, let us defer any discussion of war until Flower Moon, its rightful place," She sat down again.

"Thank you, Mistress of the Robes. My lord Warlord, rather I would lose my good right hand than you, but to attack our enemy without knowledge of him surely means defeat. What we must do is seek out other creatures like the hellgrammites and ward ourselves against them. Now. I have served some term of sennights in the Sanctuary of the Star's kitchens, and I remember some recipes. Other Lightborn may surely remember more."

"How could you—" Rithdeliel said incautiously. *How could you know any recipes? You are High King.*

"Because we were *slaves first,*" Thurion snapped.

"*You* perhaps, Landbond," Rithdeliel said. "But—"

Thurion snapped his fingers and an icy green glow began to play over his hands.

Annobeunna got to her feet.

And at that point the Wulvers could not contain themselves any longer. They leapt to their feet and began jumping as high in the air as they could, shouting "Fight! Fight! Fight!"

"Silly Wulvers. Useless Wulvers. I, I, I, am far better."

"And far quieter," Vieliessar said, lifting Pouncewarm down from his perch at the back of her chair. "But it seems that safety, no matter how little, is more frustrating than flight."

She regarded her council, noting, not for the first time, how it had divided itself. Thurion, Tuonil, Aradreleg, Mistress Githachi, and Lawspeaker Commander Gelduin sat to her deosil hand. Helecanth, Rithdeliel, Annobeunna, and Iardalaith to her tuathal. It was lords versus vassals even now; both Githachi and Gelduin had been ennobled by their appointments, but the Elves would, now and forever, prefer the sword to the law.

"If we might continue?" Vieliessar said, as the Wulvers collapsed in a heap, panting. "We must consider Nomaitemil and the assistance of the Dragons an opportunity to replenish our losses. To train more komen and Lightborn. We know it to be a haven for us by treaty with the Otherfolk, and though I have now told you in confidence that it must be renegotiated again it is possible that after that we can open trading negotiations with the Centaurs, who seem to be most like us, for other things we need."

Vieliessar held her breath, but the anticipated explosion from comparing Elves to Centaurs did not come. Perhaps everyone was tired.

"Get bees," Thurion said, not looking up. "I'm tired of keeping notes on bits of bark."

"So," Vieliessar said. "It is in my mind that before even considering moving against the Endarkened, we consolidate our gains. If, two Midwinters from now, we can figure out how to call the Endarkened to the battlefield and chop all of them into small pieces, we will plan a campaign. Today we will plan a meal. Alzipayn requires almonds. Have we any?"

⊣⊨⊢

The sun was just rising when Vieliessar came to the Round Meadow in Nomaitemil. Tannatarie was waiting for her, curled up around herself, her paws crossed over Vieliessar's saddle like a cat with a mouse.

"Good morning," Vieliessar said politely.

"And good morning to you," Tannatarie said. She yawned hugely, then stretched out her neck for Vieliessar to drag the saddle free and then climb up and settle the seat upon her back. Tannatarie raised herself for the yoke and the girth to be fitted, then settled back down again.

"It would be nice to have a comfy cave up there," Tannatarie said wistfully, looking toward Stardock. "Taking off would be no problem."

"Just as it would be no problem if you were willing to climb the valley wall, lazy slug," Vieliessar answered, climbing up the Dragon's side and settling herself into place. She pulled on her cap and her long mittens. Only her eyes showed now. Then Vieliessar cast Rise, and she and Tannatarie began to rise slowly into the sky.

The Flower Forest dwindled below them, until its whole shape could be seen. There was a waterfall at the north end, the source of the several streams within the Flower Forest itself. Then came the three valleys that gave the place its name, then the Dragon's Gate. The eastern side of it had been shattered and sealed forever by the Earthdancers; the western still stood as it had been made.

Vieliessar relished the sense of motion, the sweep and fall of flight. Tannatarie said there were currents in the air just as there were in the sea, but the only experience Vieliessar had of the sea was knowing it was there, and she could not see the currents in the air.

She thought about riding Tannatarie into battle. There would have to be armor, of course, but beyond that, what Thurion had said was true: the Dragons only allowed them to cast more powerful instances of spells that didn't work now. A targeted instance of Sunstroke might burn a single Endarkened so badly it was out of the fight, but the creatures simply *could not be killed*. And while Sunstroke was happening a dozen other Endarkened could come for the caster.

And other spells simply wouldn't work—even cast at puissance strength.

Every single one of her councillors had firm ideas of how to proceed—all conflicting—and she had none.

She pulled a face and looked down. The sweep showed her a small but spreading Flower Forest, and she exclaimed in barbaric glee. "Go down, Tannatarie. I want to see."

⌐⊨⊨¬

It was a copse of strong mature trees, surrounded by saplings, bushes, and grass. When she poked at the grass, Vieliessar found soil underneath, so she poked at its edges until the soil stopped and became the crumbled ash again.

Here, hellgrammites and pearl beetles swarmed turbulently through the mixture; the hellgrammites trying to reach the plants, the pearl beetles voraciously holding them off. Their numbers had increased hugely since she had created them, until they swarmed the fertile earth with Light itself. Vieliessar looked down the whole length of the Uradabhur. All the land, she knew now, was tainted—and what if the Endarkened sent further plagues?

Still, she had to try.

She took several bottles from the pack strapped to Tannatarie's back and squatted at the verge of the grass, where the concentration of pearl beetles was largest. Carefully she plucked them up by fours and fives before placing them into each bottle. Some for Nomaitemil. Some for Arevethmonion. Some to scatter across the Uradabhur, in hopes their numbers would grow so great the hellgrammites would be devoured.

It was a start.

⌐⊨⊧

After a formal visit to Audalo's court, Runacar went home to his lodge near Smoketree. He was grateful to leave; the knowledge that the Red Harvest had come and the enemy was so overwhelming caused people to resign themselves to death, to squander their resources in licentious revels, to demand of Audalo what he was going to do to save them . . .

Or all three at once. The Otherfolk had never held strong cross-species bonds, it was more in the nature of "I will leave you alone so long as you leave me alone." Runacar had changed that—at least for the persons in his army. Leutric had gotten everyone to point themselves in the same direction against a common enemy and permit Runacar to direct the fight, but little more than that. Well, it was all Vielle's problem now. At least watching her would be entertaining.

Such were Runacar's thoughts as he headed homeward. It was hard finding his way across a land so changed; he wished he'd kept the battlepony Vieliessar had tried to give him.

He wished any of his own horses were still alive.

It was odd to watch the brief days and long nights pass against the backdrop of fruits and flowers and warm perfumed air. But even if he'd wanted to leave the Flower Forest there was nowhere else to be: trees grew across the entire Western Reach. Only the Northern Trunk Road, the Sanctuary Road, was spared, and the road itself was crossed with vines. Eventually some of the larger trees would get their roots under the road's hard-packed surface, and it would become just another part of the forest.

In the back of his mind, like a constant comforting bell-tone, was his Soulbond with Vieliessar. He tried to decide whether or not to mind it—it would be worse if she could nag him or even speak to him, but it was only the sense of how she felt (frustrated, with blinding flashes of exasperation, and candlemarks of great joy, which must be time spent with Tannatarie).

He wished her well, he found. He just didn't ever want to see her again, and Runacar wasn't quite sure why. She worried him. She disturbed him.

Best not to think about her then.

Runacar was not alone on his journey homeward. The Wulvers of what he (and they) thought of as his personal pack came with him, as did the Palughs whom he had invited to overwinter with him, even though there was no longer need for protection from the cold. But while the Wulvers ran ahead, or trotted along beside him, or chased one another through the trees, the Palughs simply appeared on tree branches along the way. (Sometimes they brought him dead escurials to add to his trailfood.)

He would have had a lot of time to think, if he had anything to think about, Runacar told himself. There was no more war, unless you considered trying to stay alive when the Endarkened came at you. He would serve as Audalo's Battlemaster, training the Otherfolk to fight effectively at need. He would marry Vieliessar if he must. Let her bed him if she must. But he did not see anything in that future to *care* about.

You're tired, that's all it is. A few nights' sleep in a proper bed will set you right.

But upon arriving at his lodge, Runacar discovered that a sleep in a bed was going to be unreasonably difficult to achieve.

When the Flower Forests had sprouted magically, they had grown out of the edges of the existing Flower Forests, until the Flower Forests had all run together. But the running together had not respected things in its way. There was a full-grown oak tree in front of his door, its trunk large enough that he could not clasp his arms around it, and the doorway was completely blocked.

At least you now have a project.

"Gracious Palugh, Mighty Palugh, Noble Palugh, I would beg a boon of you."

One of the Palugh on the lowest branch of the oak tree—Embereyes—stretched out a long paw toward him, and gave a frustrated sniff to discover Runacar was too far away to sink claws into.

"I, I, I, can think of no r-r-r-rrrreason to helll-l-lp you. But magnanimous I, kindly I, noble I, will tell, I. To answer you, first answer me, what runs, stands still, and hurries to the sea?" asked Embereyes in return.

Fortunately a simple one, Runacar said to himself. *Flattery does help.*

"A river," Runacar answered. "Now, best and most valiant of Palugh, go inside and open the shutters. After that, O wise one, O pretty one, you could build up the fire?"

With that, Runacar began his walk around the house. It seemed like an age rather than three days of battle and a fortnight at court since he'd been here. There were bramble bushes he would need to dig out, and the inevitable vines, and a small copse of saplings would also need removing, but no more large trees either beside the house or in it. He'd have to make the hike over to Smoketree to see if anyone there could tell him whether there was a Dryad in the tree (probably), and any other of the Brightfolk here, and if so, what could be done about matters.

It will be easier to move the house than to move the tree, if I know Centaurs. And I only meant it as a temporary shelter, anyway.

Soon he smelled the smoke rising from the chimney—it might be spring in the Flower Forest, but eternal springtide was matched with eternal rain as the falling snow melted—and levered open a window. He was still impressed that the unmagical Centaurs had found a way to block a window and still let light in with their clear discs made of sand.

He lifted each Wulver over the sill before climbing over it himself, then closed the windows again. He didn't close the shutters; it was warm enough not to need them.

"All right," Runacar sighed. "Let's see what sort of disasters a fortnight have wrought. Then I'll see what provisions I have left. I'd tell one of you lazy lumps to go hunting, but there isn't a whisper of game from here to the Sanctuary of the Star unless we catch and eat Areve's oxen. And I'm pretty sure something's already done that."

⌗⌗

The discovery of other enemies followed the hellgrammites, and many of these were able to climb over—or through—the eastern wall. There was a sort of orange winged flutterbye, very pretty—and toxic. It sought out old and ill trees, and settled into a place on their bark. Then it fed the tree with sap and flew to another spot—and the tree eventually smoldered into flame.

They found an eel that befouled the streams it occupied with its waste, killing and eating everything in them and making the water undrinkable.

A leaf-cutting beetle that could strip a tree of leaves in a sennight.

An urthwyrm that rendered soil unfit for life—and which was venomous besides.

It seemed an eternally growing list, and if the new vermin were not stopped in the Uradabhur or Nomaitemil, they would advance through the Dragon's Gate and into the Western Reach. Fortunately they only occupied a small area of the first valley at the moment, and nothing of the Uradabhur, or Vieliessar's baby Flower Forest would have been dead long ago.

The Lightborn killed them singly, which was useless. They tried casting an instance of a spell that would kill all of one specific type of being, but nobody could make it stable or keep it from fizzling out after a dozen or so—even with Dragonish help. They fought anyway, because to surrender was to admit they would lose the forests.

Vieliessar taught everyone who would learn it (Hamphuliadiel's Lightborn were still afraid of Magery) her Deep Changing spell. The fire-flutterbye transformed into a blue-winged creature with a taste for the original's eggs. For the eels, they morphed an eel that was highly seductive (at least to other eels) and whose offspring would be sterile.

For the leaf-cutting beetle, another beetle-eater. For the loathy urthwyrm, one that ate it, and went on to enrich the soil as well.

The former Landbond had never seen any creatures like these, and Vieliessar wondered if Nomaitemil had them in such merry abundance because the Flower Forest was Void or because they really were an attack by the Endarkened. If that was so, the springtide would put an end to them, for the pixies, fae, and Dryads would colonize the new forest and do whatever they did with them. And if that was not so, Nomaitemil would be whittled down to leaf and bone.

And then they would all die, because the Endarkened would come back and they would have nowhere to hide.

⇥⍿⇤

In the largest of the northeastern caves, Vieliessar and her court kept Midwinter. Her folk feasted around her—even the Woodwose, who had never heard of the notion but felt that a chance to eat a great deal of food was a good idea.

The gathering of the delicacies had been the work of more than a moonturn, for while Nomaitemil fed them well, she did not feed them traditionally. But the Dragons had provided enormous fish from the Cold Ocean—

(*"Did it say anything?"* Iardalaith demanded. *"We can't eat it if it can talk."* *"Why don't you ask the next one?"* Green Elderin suggested tartly. *"All this one said was 'glug.'"*)

—And the Elven bakers had found many ways to counterfeit flour and butter, and so there were bread and cakes and pies as well. They had found trees here in Nomaitemil that were new to them, trees that bled sweetsap, and had taken advantage of the fact to make candies and syrups. Even the hoped-for alzipayn had been created.

The cave was crammed, not primarily with the highest ranks of Vieliessar's people, as it would have been in the days of the War Princes, but with the Lightborn who would shortly be called to work. What space there was after that her princes and Guild leaders could occupy. The tables of the rest of the Midwinter feasters were concealed in the trees around the Round Meadow, for even though they had not been attacked since the battle of Imrathalion, Vieliessar felt somehow that being out in the open would be tempting the Endarkened too far.

But there were delicacies beyond counting—even some of the precious goats and sheep had been slaughtered—and the stars shone in their proper places in the winter sky, and Loremasters and Storysingers told the old tales and sang the old songs.

It was enough.

A place for an enormous fire had been built in the meadow in front of the High Table. It was piled high with enough wood to burn until dawn, and surrounded by a thick stone ring. When it was lit, the children who were to be Called tonight would use it to navigate through the forest to reach the High Table.

Vieliessar remembered lying dreaming beneath Tannatarie's wing, and the sad strangeness of those dreams in their foretelling. There was a race to come called Men, whom the Elves must protect and guide until they were ready to possess the Light that was to be denied to her own people. She did not know the name they would take for themselves when they had risen up, but she knew they were to come and where to find them, for the Elves' duty if the Darkness could be slain was guardianship.

Meanwhile, the Elves would retain only the small magics of seeing and hearing the Brightfolk, homely abilities to keep tea hot and pots from over-boiling, a woodswise understanding of the paths of the weather and the seasons. The only Mages among them would be the Dragonmages, handing their Dragonbonds off to their successors with their own deathspell, and inevitably that would sometimes fail, and sometimes fail again, until Tannatarie and her Twelve were gone, and Magery was gone from the world.

For a while.

Until the rise of Men.

"Will it be worth it?" Vieliessar said aloud. She sat at the High Table, the seat at her tuathal hand empty to symbolize her Consort to Come.

"One can never know whether a course of action is worth the losses it required," Thurion said. "Especially when one is at the start of it." He sat at her deosil side tonight, displaced by her ghostly future Bondmate. "It is true that our losses have been horrific, but we are here. If we have not mastered the Endarkened, at least the endless battle against the Otherfolk is ended, and the Landbond are free. No mother will ever again have to abandon a child in the woodlands to die because she cannot feed it."

"It has always been about freedom for you, hasn't it?" Vieliessar said to Thurion.

"To the Landbond, freedom and survival are much the same thing," he answered. "We have survived."

"And we can hope your wedding won't be as much of a disaster as your Enthroning was," Helecanth added from behind Vieliessar's chair.

"Simple enough," Vieliessar retorted. "It shall be delayed until none of us cares about it, *I* shall not wear a dress, and there shall be no ritual or ceremony whatsoever."

Her friends and listeners laughed—as she had meant them to—and Vieliessar snapped her fingers to set the fire alight (old habits were hard to break) and watched as flames hissed upward into the falling snow.

"Mama, I must be first," Adalieriel said gravely, and Vieliessar came down from the High Table to stand in front of her daughter. She placed her hand on Adalieriel's head and listened.

No. Nothing. She breathed out a long sigh of relief.

"I am sorry, my daughter. You do not go to the Sanctuary this year." The words came automatically, even though there was no longer a Sanctuary to send Liri to. Vieliessar handed Liri the silver ribbon and the packet of sweetmeats that every child here would receive, and hugged her.

Calan was too young to test—though what that had really meant, before the fall of the Hundred Houses, was that the Sanctuary didn't want to have to foster children much younger than ten or twelve. She gave Calan a sweetmeat anyway, then turned to welcome the next child.

A change in the wind blew a gust of cold air into the cave and Vieliessar shivered. *I suppose I have grown soft living in a Flower Forest all these sennights.* Then a vast wave of bitter cold swept across the High Table.

Vieliessar could hear cries of fear from the children. This was a burning, biting, deadly cold—and growing colder by the minute.

"Flee!" Vieliessar cried. "Warhunt—to me! We are attacked!" She Called her sword to her and wished for armor. But her armor was metal and wouldn't do. Then she turned and ran in the direction of the cold.

"Githachi! Summon the Silver Swords!" Helecanth cried, and followed her.

⊰◈⊱

The warm air of the Flower Forest was turned to fog by the cold. It made the air smell winter-sharp, with an odd undertone like metal, or rotting meat.

Here in the center of the meadow, it was night-dark, for even the risen moon did not give enough light. Vieliessar sprayed globes of Silverlight from her fingers, turning the meadow bright as day. She fought to keep her teeth from chattering in the cold.

She'd been joined by a taille of Warhunters and the komen who had heard her call, Helecanth, Rithdeliel, and Gelduin among them. All they had to navigate by was the worsening cold. It enveloped them, making throats and lungs burn. It became so hard to breathe that the lack of air made Vieliessar dizzy.

Then the cold was so fierce that a sphere of crystal-clear air appeared in the middle of the fog. And she saw it.

"What is that?" Rithdeliel demanded.

"Another monster," Iardalaith answered, sounding both edgy and bored. "See if it can talk."

"After it's dead, I will ask it," Helecanth said grimly.

It was as if one of the riverine eels had grown to monster size. It was nearly as long as the tall pines of the Flower Forest were tall. Its pale hide was fleshy like soft tallow and covered with a grey slime. There were no legs or tail Vieliessar could see. Its head was round and snoutless, and its mouth small, lips pursed in a profane kiss, but the rest of its face was covered with dozens of eyes, large and bulging and wet and black.

The smell of it was much stronger up close. It made her nose and throat burn with every breath. Even the touch of its gaze seemed chilling.

Behind it was a blackened track of frost-killed vegetation. Everything near it had withered, even the low-lying branches of the trees. Any water had been frozen solid—shallow streams, pools of rain, even raindrops gathered on twigs and branches. It moved across the forest floor with the sort of humping motion a kitterpillan might make, and was heading directly toward the fire.

Vieliessar could sense her people arrayed around her, waiting for her signal to attack. She ran in front of it, ignoring Helecanth's and Iardalaith's cries. It reared up, half its length off the ground. Its underside was covered with deep ridges, like sucking mouths, which must be how it moved itself forward.

Vieliessar Cast Fire.

There was a high horrible keening sound, and a nauseating stench of burning slime. The creature tried to rear up even further, but simply fell sideways.

Unharmed.

"Let me save you!" Tannatarie cried, and Vieliessar shook her head wordlessly.

The coldwyrm righted itself and thrashed after her. In its wake came fog, confusing the eye with its eddies. Iardalaith stepped into its way and it seemed to hesitate between the two of them, its tiny mouth working.

Then its mouth opened, exposing needle-shaped silvery fangs, and it lunged toward Iardalaith.

This was like the game against the monsters all of them had fought before. Now Vieliessar made herself the bait and the creature turned. Everything around it turned black with cold and died.

As we will if it touches us.

They'd lured it out into the Round Meadow now. Rithdeliel rushed forward, flourishing his sword. He struck at its side and his blow landed fairly, but the slit he opened was sealed over again with icy slime and with his next strike his sword shattered.

Vieliessar tossed him her sword. She doubted a sword would slay this thing, but they had to try. Gelduin's mace was having better effect—meaning only that it wasn't shattering.

Tannatarie landed in the Round Meadow. She reared back and hesitated, wings fanning, seeming almost to wince from the cold.

"Get out of there!" Elderin cried from above. The coldwyrm's head swung toward Tannatarie, and its jaws dropped open. Its breath stank and was killing cold. The white Dragon tried to leap away, but she was slowed by the cold and almost seemed to stumble.

"Here, wyrm! If you want fire, have some more!" Iardalaith cast Fire at puissance strength. It wreathed the head of the ice wyrm, lighting it in a weird multicolor corona and turning the silverlight to freakish shades of purple and gold.

Its eyes popped like overripe fruit, and black ichor trickled down its face like tears.

"Over here, you disgusting thing!" Isilla yelled. The creature's blinded head whipped around to focus on Isilla, moaning and wailing in a way that made everyone want to hold their ears, and reared back above their heads again.

It was blind now, but Vieliessar was willing to bet its eyes would regenerate if given time, for it clearly belonged to the Endarkened. It flung itself forward as Isilla dodged, and swung its head from side to side like a questing serpent. It was turning away from the fire toward the forest now, turning toward the Dragon's Gate and the settlement.

We have to stop it. I think we can kill it if we can just make it stop moving.

Vieliessar cast Snow.

Weather spells were the trickiest of all to manage, for they meant moving large volumes of air around to make the effects happen, and to do that without something unforeseen happening elsewhere required skill. But the Flower Forest was filled with raindrops from the melted snow, and there was actual snow falling upon them in the meadow. In addition, she knew she could steal some snow from the Uradabhur without harm.

Heavy snow began falling on the coldwyrm. It sizzled like hot grease when it touched the creature's skin, melted, and refroze.

Iardalaith and Isilla understood what she was doing at once and added their efforts, and soon the coldwyrm was mewing plaintively as it struggled forward under a deep and increasing shell of ice. The Lightless had formed a semicircle of protection behind the Lightborn, but they were helpless against this creature and they knew it.

"Tannatarie! Elderin! Drop something on it!" Vieliessar said.

Elderin was already aloft. Tannatarie galloped across the Round Meadow, flinging herself into the sky. Vieliessar could hear her calling to the other Dragons. "Come, my little loves! We will crush the nasty wyrm under sticks and stones!"

Sorgane was the first to find something. An oak. He pulled the dead tree out of the earth and carried it to the coldwyrm, dropping it across its back. It slid across the ice and snow that encrusted the wyrm, but it showed the idea was sound.

The coldwyrm wriggled free. The ice made a tinkling sound as the wyrm shed it, but by that time Tannatarie and Elderin were back, one with another tree, one with a stone. Telleval darted behind them to scoop up the first now-frozen log and drop it on the coldwyrm again.

Having found their rhythm and their strategy, the defenders and the Dragons worked to stop the creature: stop it moving, stop it attacking, stop it spitting freezing poison.

They knew they had won when the temperature began to rise, but a vast swath of the Flower Forest around the Round Meadow had been burnt black by cold.

The moment it was dead, the combatants fled into the Flower Forest, anxiously scanning the sky for the red-winged Endarkened or their monstrous minions. After a few moments, the Lightborn relaxed. If the Endarkened were out there, they were far away.

"Is everyone all right?" Thurion asked wearily.

"If 'alive' counts," Isilla said. "What was that thing?"

"Something new," Tangisen said bitterly. "Something 'exciting' and 'fun.'"

"We have *got* to find the Endarkened's weak point or we will be fighting them until the end of time. We have got to be able to *do* that," Iardalaith said.

Vieliessar looked out over the cave and then around them at the space in the woods where the feasting tables had been. Everything was neat and orderly, with no dropped belongings or overturned chairs. "At least we have learned to flee gracefully and in good order. Come. Perhaps we won't be attacked next Midwinter," she said wearily.

"If we live that long," Isilla said.

No one laughed.

⊰⧈⊱

For some time after the coldwyrm attack Vieliessar was far too busy convincing her people not to simply bolt into the West on the heels of this latest attack to think of anything else.

"It was not one of the Endarkened. Master Cegusara, consider. It was a monster, true, and a mystery, but it is dead and all is well."

The Master of Scouts regarded Vieliessar doubtfully. "We are beset by salamander flutterbyes and blighting eels, by voracious beetles and loathy wyrms. And now by this Great Wyrm. What next?"

"I do not know. But I do know that running from it is not the answer. Nor, I must remind you, is the West ours by right or seizin any longer, for the treaty may yet stand. We cannot flee into it—"

"Because *you threw it away*!" Lady Munariel (who styled herself determinedly "of House Inglethendragir") said.

"Do you challenge me?" Vieliessar asked softly. "For I am King until I die. And I say it is better and safer to remain here."

"Is death the price of speaking truth to you?" Munariel returned. "Because I labored nine years in the mills of a mad Lightborn who proclaimed himself 'Lord,' and truckle I shall no longer."

"If I may interrupt?" Tannatarie said, lowering her head far enough to make each of the women step back. "Rimanet is missing and should not be. I ask you: is her Bonded with her?"

From the look on Vieliessar's face, she had no idea.

"Niviel is barely Raneriliet's age," Lady Munariel said. "I will get him and the other children to search. They will think of places we will not if she is hiding."

"Let it be so," Vieliessar said. "I thank you for your wise counsel." Munariel moved away. Vieliessar put a hand on Tannatarie's muzzle.

::*Your timing, as always, was excellent*::

::*Niviel's is not*:: Tannatarie replied.

⚜

The Dragons, and the Dragonbonded, searched for Niviel and Rimanet until the end of Cold Moon, and never found a trace of either one.

CHAPTER THIRTY-NINE

SWORD MOON IN THE ELEVENTH YEAR OF THE HIGH KING'S REIGN: THE ANVIL OF NECESSITY

There is no life without war.

—Arilcarion War-Maker, *Of the Sword Road*

Since Midwinter there had been no more unpleasant discoveries in Nomaitemil Flower Forest, and the Uradabhur was flowering. If the springtide brought more monsters, well, her people were used to fighting monsters.

And now the snow was melting and Vieliessar could embark upon the plan she'd decided to follow on the day of Leutric's death.

⁂

The Medhartha Range cut the northern end of Daroldan off from the mountain ranges beyond. It looked as if someone had taken the top edge of the mountains and simply squeezed them into points, and much of it (since the battle of the Western Reach) was simply a sheer cliff falling down to the sea. The rocks were unstable; once Tannatarie had landed on a perch that looked solid only to find it sheer off under her weight, taking more of the mountainside with it and battering much of the scree below into sand.

After that, Tannatarie had given the mountains a wide berth.

Vieliessar had been here a moonturn, blazing her trail through the Forest Izalbama and then climbing the mountain face until she slipped back, climbing until she reached a dead end, or night fell, or another obstacle presented itself, but always climbing. She had come—so she thought—with nothing more than the minimum supplies to live rough in the springtide Flower Forest, but when she pulled the saddle off of Tannatarie's back, Pouncewarm jumped to her shoulder.

"I told you to stay home!" she cried in exasperation.

"I, I, I, go everywhere," the Palugh sang. "Up to the sky and down to the sea, who dares that path? Me!"

"It's bad taste to answer your own riddles," Vieliessar muttered. But there was no point in trying to send the Palugh—or any Palugh, actually—away if he'd decided to follow her here.

She'd come this far west because the surviving Gryphons supposedly roosted here, where the safety of the Flower Forest was but a few heartbeats away, but neither she nor Tannatarie (and probably not Pouncewarm) had seen a Gryphon since they had arrived here. (Vieliessar suspected that had been the Gryphons' intention.)

With all you know of me, you think I will simply go away in disappointment? How little you know of me, Winged Ones.

And if she must climb all the way to the very top of the highest surviving peak a hundred times to speak with them, then that was what she would do.

She had done nothing of what Runacar had advised. She did not come to the Gryphons as Empress of the Nine Races. She had not spent a year in politics and diplomacy. And she would not leave until she had what she'd come for.

As she had done every day since the first day, Vieliessar woke from where she slept with Pouncewarm beneath Tannatarie's sheltering wing, rose and stretched and made tea, then resumed her assault upon the mountain.

She could have Lifted herself to the top. Tannatarie could have flown with her to the top. It seemed important to do it this way. Without Magery. With nothing but need.

Each morning she left the Flower Forest and climbed to where the Flower Forest turned to the Forest Izalbama and the forest turned to boulders and scree with Pouncewarm bounding along beside her. Then she began to climb. The rocks were sharp and dusty under her boots, and though at first she could walk upright on the slope, soon enough she must crouch, using both hands and feet to feel her way up the increasingly steep incline.

The first time Pouncewarm had leapt to her back because the slope proved challenging she had barely kept from screaming in pain. It was only the Palugh's penitential expression—and the fact he'd followed her order to return to the camp—that saved him from becoming a fur hearth rug.

After that, he followed her along the incline until that was impossible. After that, she would see him in various places ahead peering down at her. But each day she failed to reach the top.

Tannatarie hadn't seen any Gryphons during their initial overflight of the Medharthas. She suspected neither of them was meant to see any Gryphons. That they were meant to give up and go back to Ceoprentrei and let Darkness take them fingerswidth by fingerswidth until all of them were dead.

I have never in the whole of my life done things the easy way. I am not going to begin now.

She leaned back gingerly to try to see the route ahead, then continued. The first rock she set her foot on broke off; she stuck the fingers of both hands into cracks in the rock face and clung, scrabbling with both feet. Eventually she found purchase again.

She could probably cast Shield in time if she fell. If she was hurt beyond her capacity to heal herself, Tannatarie could carry her back to Ceoprentrei and the Lightborn Healers.

If a Gryphon attacked her, she was helpless.

Her muscles trembled with effort. She forced her body another step up the rock face.

"I'm not going anywhere!" she shouted into the wind. "I am Vieliessar Farcarinon, High King of the Elves, Empress of the Brightfolk, and the Otherfolk, and the Folk of the Clear Waters, she who will go down into death defending them, and I will be heard!"

There had been the icewyrm at Midwinter, and as soon as the weather began to warm, new horrors. Hideous red wasps, longer than a thumb. An animal like a cross between a mouse and a weasel that ate everything in its path; it had devoured half the Uradabhur—including pearl beetles—before the Lightborn had come up with a countermeasure. Ice tigers and snow lions, seeming homely and familiar in comparison to creatures of the Endarkened, but starving for meat and not caring where they got it.

They could not go on playing this monstrous game of xaique against the enemy. Sooner or later they would lose. And Vieliessar didn't even know why they were fighting. Runacar had hinted that the Gryphons did. Or at least knew how to end it.

She reached a place in her climb just below a parapet where she hoped to snatch a few moments rest.

::*Look out::* Tannatarie warned.

There was a flash of light above her as her line of vision was blocked.

Caerthalien had been in the center of the Western Reaches, nowhere a Gryphon would be found. *Lannarien's Book of Living Things* told Vieliessar their habitat was the far Grand Windsward, but the Endarkened had driven them westward until they nested in the mountains that rose up above the Forest Izalbama.

Other than Tannatarie, the Gryphon was the largest living thing she had ever seen. Its shoulders were hunched and its wings spread wide; she could hear the grating of its lion-claws and eagle-talons on the rock and imagine the lashing of its tail. Its feathers rattled like the lake reeds in the wind. The Gryphon's neck feathers were ruffled out like a mane, and the blue of its underside made twining shapes as it turned its head to focus one great golden eye on her. The sun glittered off its wingfeathers as if they were metal.

"Here you are," it said. Its beak was half-open, its black tongue curling as it spoke. Its voice was raw and scratchy, and seemed to come from deep in its throat instead of from its mouth.

"Here I am," Vieliessar agreed. Her shoulders began to ache, and she was aware of how very vulnerable she was. It would be a long fall, and Tannatarie might not be able to reach her in time.

"If I hail you as king of everything, will you go away?" the Gryphon asked. "We are still counting our dead."

"So are we," Vieliessar answered evenly. "And we can both count until there are no more to count. Or you can help me."

There was a scraping noise as the Gryphon let her hindquarters slide down to the ledge. She folded her wings neatly, hiding their blue underside. The tufted tip of her tail lashed fretfully.

She reached out one large taloned foreclaw and held it before Vieliessar's face. "Take hold, Child of Stars. You are about to fall."

Gripping the Gryphon's claw, Vieliessar looked back the way she had come and immediately regretted it, for the ground seemed much farther away than she had thought. Tannatarie, looking up at her worriedly from the ground, seemed smaller than Pouncewarm, a figure that could be covered with one hand.

"Thank you," Vieliessar said, trying to find somewhere to put her feet. "I didn't want to fall."

"I suppose it wouldn't hurt you really," the Gryphon suggested. "My name is Marosia, and I already know yours. Did you have a destination, Child of Stars?"

"I must speak to whoever made the Gryphons' treaty with Leutric the Great Bull."

"Leutric is dead," Marosia said. "And the treaty is void. Why should it matter now?"

"Nevertheless," Vieliessar said. "This is what I have come to ask for. I will return every day until you—or someone else—grants my petition."

"You call yourself High King but come to beg favors? Very well then. Come with me."

Holding on to Marosia's talon, Vieliessar allowed herself to be lifted onto the outcropping. Marosia clung to its side. "Get on my back," the Gryphon said tersely. "Don't bend my feathers. And don't fall off."

As soon as Vieliessar was settled, Marosia dove off the edge of the outcropping. Her rapid wingbeats made a clapping sound, and the wind whistled through her feathers.

It was a very different experience from riding Tannatarie. Vieliessar could only use balance and her thigh muscles to hold herself in place, and if Marosia wished, she could simply dash Vieliessar on the rocks below—where they would see which of the winged ones could reach her faster.

To Vieliessar's surprise, their path took them around the peak she'd been climbing. Instead of another peak beyond, there was a wide meadow, as if from some long-vanished *tehukohiakhazarishtial*, surrounded by a jagged wall. The meadow was filled with soil and green grass, clearly cultivated by the Gryphons themselves.

::*I can't see you!::* Tannatarie's voice was frantic.

::*I'm all right::* Vieliessar answered soothingly. ::*Stay where you are::*

::*If they hurt you, I'll eat the lot of them::* the Dragon vowed wrathfully.

Marosia landed and sat down meaningfully. Vieliessar slid from her back and got to her feet, turning slowly in a circle. Pouncewarm followed, springing to the grass and walking in wide outward spirals around Marosia, his fluffy tail curved in a reaping hook.

There were Gryphons perched all along the rim of the crater, some singly, some in clusters. They reminded her irresistibly of crows. There were not many, but enough to make Vieliessar feel . . .

Endangered? Threatened? Fearful?

No. Rune had said they were pacifists. They weren't going to hurt her. But she wasn't going to be able to get them to do what she wanted without . . .

Force?

She sighed.

"The Endarkened have been hammering at the gates of Ceoprentrei for moonturns now. Since Imrathalion. They don't come themselves, but it is taking all our spellcraft to keep their creatures out of the Flower Forest. If they overrun it, we must come west, no matter what promises we made to Leutric."

"Leutric is dead," Marosia observed dispassionately.

"And his promises—our promises—our *treaty*—died with him. I have been told this. And I say this should not be so. A promise should pass from generation to generation like a farmstead, or a sword. I will hold Leutric's treaty and pass it to my children, and their children, that the Nine Races will always stand to help one another."

"And who are you to say this?"

"I am greatdaughter to Pelashia Celenthodiel," Vieliessar said simply. "I am your kin."

All the time she had been speaking, the Gryphons had been coming closer in hops and glides. Now they formed a semicircle around Vieliessar and Pouncewarm.

"Daughter of Pelashia?" one of them asked mockingly. "Where is your horn, O Star-Crowned?"

"Do not ask questions to which you know the answer—and I am told the Gryphons know all," Vieliessar answered.

"Not enough to make you give up and go away," Marosia said. "Very well." She opened her beak wide and emitted a long whistle ending in a click. "The treaty is once again in force, in all its provisions, and you are Empress of the Nine Races. Satisfied?"

"Not until you have told me how to kill Endarkened," Vieliessar said stubbornly. "Even the power of my Dragons cannot make them mortal, and what is immortal cannot be slain."

"But Mosirinde told you the answer to that question long ago," said a Gryphon who had not spoken before. "Have you forgotten?"

There was a roaring in Vieliessar's ears, and the ground seemed to shift beneath her feet. An answer!

She took a deep breath.

"I was taught nothing of such a tale," Vieliessar said honestly. "All I know is that the Otherfolk call her 'Truefriend,' and there is no scroll left by her hand."

"—Plenty of them."

"—Maybe not in Elves' libraries."

"—Elves burn books."

"—Elves forget. We don't."

All the Gryphons seemed to be talking at once now. Their voices sounded like the cawing of a murder of crows, and it made Vieliessar's ears hurt. "*Tell* me," she begged, raising her voice to be heard. "*Teach me!*" It was too much to hope that any of Mosirinde's writings remained in the Library of Arevethmonion—if Hamphuliadiel had known about them, he would have destroyed them as he had so many other scrolls.

And the Library was buried, anyway.

Silence. A silence so deep Vieliessar could hear the wind blowing over the rocks.

"Is that what you have come to us for? Knowledge?" Marosia said. She made that whistle-click sound again. "Not everyone who asks receives, O Empress and Queen."

"Do you understand that the Endarkened will kill you?" Vieliessar said in a dangerously level voice.

"Do you understand that they already have?" Marosia answered acidly. "We are all that is left. One Ascension, and the scraps of a few more. Who can we dance with so there will be chicks in the spring? There is no one else."

Vieliessar mentally cursed Lannarien and his *Book of Living Things* from back to front and front to back again. He'd never made any note about this aspect of Gryphons. Perhaps he hadn't known.

"I know you have no cause to wish us well, but surely you wish to save the other races? The Hippogriffs? The Bearwards? The Dragons?"

"*You* solve their problems, Empress of the Nine Races."

"If I am Empress of the Nine Races, you are bound—by *treaty*—to help," Vieliessar said through gritted teeth.

The effect of her statement was electrifying. Various Gryphons mantled their wings, or spread them, or made short bounding hops toward her. Feathers were ruffled. Discussions in the click-whistle language that Vieliessar couldn't follow took place.

"What are they saying?" Vieliessar whispered, kneeling down beside Pouncewarm.

"O greatest of warriors next to I, you trap them in a snare and now they seek to escape. But they cannot! Clever Pouncewarm, Brave Pouncewarm, to advise you."

"If you have any other advice, let me know," Vieliessar said, stroking his head.

The Gryphons seemed to have come to a decision. One she had not noticed before stepped forward. The feathers around his eyes and beak were white with age, and the blue of his neck and breast were faded.

She got to her feet to face him and waited until he spoke.

"I am Selkaw, oldest among us. If you will fly with us, we will teach you what you have come to learn."

❧❦❧

At the end of her life, flying with the Ascensions would still lie bright and vivid in Vieliessar's mind. Tannatarie flew stately and slow as the Gryphons, brightly blue on belly and underwing, golden bronze above, flew around her.

The Gryphons were talking, but it was not a conversation Vieliessar was privileged to join. The shattered remains of the Ascensions flew their patterns as if their missing members were present. They'd known she was coming long before she arrived, of course. Known she was coming, and what she would ask for.

The question was: Would they give it?

❧❦❧

There was a great flurry of wings as the Gryphons suddenly abandoned their patterns and flew straight up. Tannatarie followed as Vieliessar clung to the saddle, marshaling spells in her head against a fall. The world below was small; too tiny to be accurate, for its horizon tricked her with its seeming curve.

And then the Gryphons turned, wings folded, and fell.

The air was full of a chorus of whistling as the air fought through their feathers. Their claws were spread, their talons outthrust, ready to strike and kill invisible prey.

::*What do we do?*:: Tannatarie asked.

"We land," Vieliessar said.

❧❦❧

Tannatarie followed the last of the Gryphons to the ground. Her landing made the ground shake, and the snap of her wings was a sharp crack! Vieliessar looked up at the Gryphons perched on the outcroppings all around them.

"I claim your fealty, and with it your succor and help in disaster: not only mine, but the rest of the Nine Races', as you must come to us in time of need. As it was in Leutric's time, it is in mine, and for always."

"It seems a lot for a little," a Gryphon said.

"It is nothing for everything," Vieliessar answered. "But most of all I want the wisdom of your long lives added to mine. If you must go your ways, so be it. But I would have the answer to my question first."

CHAPTER FORTY

SWORD MOON TO FIRE MOON IN THE ELEVENTH YEAR OF THE HIGH KING'S REIGN: THE SHADOW OF THE BEGINNING

To want the victory is not enough. One must know what will happen if one gains it.

—Arilcarion War-Maker, *Of the Sword Road*

Vieliessar returned to Nomaitemil and told no one anything of what the Gryphons had told her. It was not the whole of the answer, anyway, as the desire to win is not the whole of the war. She must plan how to get there.

And who among her beloveds must die.

Meanwhile the life of the outside world went on. With the melting of the ice-gate across Ceoprentrei, traffic increased along the Sanctuary Road, but instead of Woodwose leaving Ceoprentrei, more came to live there. Of course her own people began to look more and more like Woodwose every day as they became a part of the forest, with their spangles and tatters and ability to vanish into invisibility without any magic at all.

Both Woodwose and Sanctuary Lightborn found partners among the Dragons, as did a few more of the Warhunt. Five to the Warhunt, seven to the rest, all of whom must be taught the battle magic. Or magic itself. (The Warhunt was running out of explanations as to why Hamphuliadiel had withheld so many spells from his Sanctuary Lightborn.)

Woodwose were not alone in coming to settle in Alpine Nomaitemil: Brownies and Fauns, Bearwards and Centaurs, all came bringing with them the news of (and arguing about) whether the treaty was void or binding. For whatever reason, they came, and to each of them Vieliessar posed the question: What if the treaty stood? What if it would stand forever, no matter who lived or who died? What then?

No one was ready to give her an answer, but the Centaurs cleared more space in front of the Eastern Gate and built a *town,* chopping down trees and using oxen to drag the large stones out of the way. They marked fields out with lines of smaller stones, and built hay-barns and cow barns and every other kind of barn. The Palugh, naturally, were delighted, and even Pouncewarm left Vieliessar's side to hunt in the warm midnight darkness of barns for his squeaking prey.

And still the Otherfolk came.

The only ones of the Nine Races who did not come were the Minotaurs.

Or Runacar.

Vieliessar gathered up an expeditionary force, including Isilla, blue Telleval's Bonded, and Pendray, *pirozaduta* Oziana's Bonded, and set them to mapping all of vast Ceoprentrei, down to the last fingerwidth. On every clear day one could look down the valley and see Telleval and Oziana making circles in the sky, studying the ground below.

And then the real work of knitting a dozen people into one began.

The links already in place were strong: the Elves had gladly turned over the remains of their own livestock to the Centaurs in exchange for grain and meat to be delivered at Harvest time.

In this brave new world, gold had little value, nor silver, nor even elvensilver. Copper and bronze were priceless, and glass was beyond price, but iron was king of them all, and the Elves traded copper and bronze and iron the Lightborn pulled from the ground for other things they wanted, such as meat for their Dragons and themselves. They built bee-skeps in hope; they could search the forest for a Queen Bee, and if they could not find one, they would try to lure a queen if the Lightborn could figure out how to craft a spell for it, and then there would be honey as well. The Centaurs and the Bearwards had kept bees, but their hives had been lost in the duels of sorcery that had washed over them.

Vieliessar paid out a hundredweight in iron for a Centaur to take a message to Audalo's court and bring back an answer.

When Sword Moon came, summer came, and the orchards and vines, arbors and vineyards, bushes and trees were heavy with fruit. Nomaitemil remained virginal, a spring maiden wreathed in leaves and flowers. The plantings the Elves and the Otherfolk had brought with them ebbed and flourished like a slowly beating heart; swelling to fruitfulness and harvest and then dwindling into sleep again. In summer the Brightfolk came to Nomaitemil. Most of Vieliessar's folk could not see them at all, others could discern no sapient thing, only light. Once again Vieliessar must soothe her folk and teach them what she herself did not know.

Calan saw them better than Liri, but Andhel (as with all Woodwose) saw them best of all, and Vieliessar humbly extracted the Woodwose's promise to teach her children—and any others she could—the art of *seeing*.

Knowing what she intended, she knit the links of governance as tightly as she could. Calan was betrothed to Githachi, to wed at Frost Moon, though he would be treated as a child for many Wheelturns to come. He was her heir, with Thurion and Rithdeliel his regents, and she hoped that would be enough.

Adalieriel was not betrothed.

And each day Vieliessar took long pleasure flights that only she and Tannatarie knew were not.

And at last Vieliessar had everything she needed.

⇥⭤⇤

For the last time Vieliessar and Tannatarie made their lone flight eastward.

The Uradabhur was still mostly grass and bush; the widely spaced Flower Forests grew slowly, even with careful tending. A little distance further and they stepped through Door into the Arzhana, where reeds and moss lined the handspan streams. The keeps and manor houses stood empty.

There were no bones and the stones lay bare.

Door again, and the bright vastness of the Grand Windsward surrounded them. The Dragonmages had, all of them, poured the most Light into the Grand Windsward of any place save Ceoprentrei, until by rights it ought to glow, or hover in the air, or both. But it had grass, and Flower Forests in the old places, and nothing more.

Then Tannatarie swooped across Greythunder Glairyrill and beyond it lay the belt of low, rolling grass-covered hills that stood between the river and the cold grey waters of the east.

Vieliessar stopped her partner at the water's edge, looking eastward as if she could see her destination from where they stood.

"Are we going to dawdle around here all day?" Tannatarie asked.

"No," said Vieliessar with a sigh, "we're going to dawdle somewhere else." She lifted Tannatarie into the air and sent them through the fourth and last Door.

⊰⊱

There was no sign of the land they had left, only the grey and restless sea. Tannatarie circled until she found what they were seeking, stooped low, and landed. Her talons grated across stone as lifeless as if it had been scrubbed. The only marks upon it were the scratches made by her previous landings.

East of here were more rocks in the ocean. Some as large as all Jer-a-kalaliel, some so tiny Tannatarie could not land on them. As far as Vieliessar and her partner had dared to fly they were all the same: sterile, scoured, empty. There were mountains, but no rolling hills, for there was no soil to be found anywhere.

This was the east whose war her ancestors and the Otherfolks' ancestors had fled, but there was no artifact of that conflict. No tree, no stick of wood, no wrought-stone castels, nor even monuments. Perhaps their war had scoured them away. Perhaps it was the Endarkened.

Perhaps Jer-a-kalaliel would come to look like this if they could not stand against the Endarkened.

She had come so far east that day had faded into night. Beneath her feet the rock was dry. No hint of ocean spray reached it; that was for the edges of this place to endure, not its center, even so flat and far from land. The rock was the size of four Great Halls lashed together; its surface was relatively even. It would hold the folk Vieliessar needed it to hold so that she could do what must be done.

She had known that before she came. The rest was nerves, as before any other battle.

She mounted Tannatarie. This time she did not have to lift her; the great Dragon faced into the ocean's eternal winds and spread her wings wide. Soon they were airborne. And Vieliessar returned to Alpine Nomaitemil to begin to wait.

⇥Ⅱ⇤

She did not have long to wait, for Runacar reached the place she had chosen within a fortnight of her flight east.

"I told you that you would hear of me," she said in greeting.

"Hail, High King and Queen Empress," Runacar answered. "I don't know how much use the revival of the treaty will be, though." He looked around apprehensively for Tannatarie; Vieliessar pointed a finger at the sky. There, Runacar could see a wren-tiny speck circling in the sky above. The white Dragon.

"It doesn't matter. The treaty is useless, though it's nice to have. You told me that in the first place. So I went to the Gryphons directly. They told me what I must do to make the Endarkened mortal. Then we can kill them," she added helpfully. "Maybe they'll leave us alone then."

"The dead ones certainly will." She saw Runacar's chest heave as he took a deep steadying breath. "And if the Gryphons have known this answer all along—and known the Bones of the Earth would be useless—*why haven't they mentioned this to anyone?*"

"Because until I was born—and trained at the Sanctuary of the Star—and stood my vigil at the Shrine of the Star—it wasn't possible. And if there was someone who'd done all those things but hadn't spent the last ten years fleeing those red-winged monsters, they wouldn't do it."

"But you will."

"I will. To rid the world of the Endarkened, I will also rid it of the Starry Hunt as well. Great Power for Great Power. Equal sacrifices, on our part and theirs. But *we* are already mortal."

"It doesn't seem as if the Starry Hunt would do something like that just for the asking. Or come at your bidding, for that matter."

"They will come. *He* will come. The Child of the Prophecy is the true leader of the Hunt. I always have been. The Huntlord told me at my vigil that I had come to end the Hunt. I was too young to understand it then."

"And now you are old and wise." Runacar could clearly not decide whether he was making a joke or not. "Well enough. What business is this of mine?"

"You will bear witness," Vieliessar answered. "And when the treaty stands again, all of its provisions stand again, and you and I will wed."

Runacar got to his feet. "You can't mean that. Or want that."

"I must wed my Bondmate," Vieliessar said with grim emphasis. "But I will give you no children. I have my own to place on the throne."

"I hold myself completely unconsoled," Runacar said bitterly. "And have you considered, lady wife, that despite your best intentions our marriage might produce more than scandal?"

"Not if I kill you in our nuptial bed," she said. "I have a theory to prove."

"A theory?" Runacar said.

That the Dragonbond was enough to save her life when the Soulbond was severed.

"A theory," Vieliessar agreed. "Also, you are responsible for the deaths of everyone in my family, so yours will be a lawful murder, and I am *really* tired of *ruling*." It wasn't what she meant to say, but somehow she was always blurting out uncomfortable truths to Runacar.

"You are an *idiot*," Runacar said. "If we live, we will all remember your name forever. And you want to *quit*?"

"I'm *tired*," Vieliessar said. "I want to stop."

"There's no stopping short of death," Runacar said simply. "No matter how many people you kill. Though I suppose I must come as representative of the Otherfolk. Or do you mean me to provide the horses for the sacrifice?"

"This spell will require a greater sacrifice," Vieliessar said. "All must bleed, though they will not die. One—blood of my blood—must die."

Runacar stared at her for a long moment, and all she could sense through the Soulbond was churning emotion held in check by iron discipline. She remembered again what it was so easy for her to forget, that here was a War Prince of Caerthalien, raised from the cradle to be a master of war.

"There are times when I actually forget you are a monster of infamy," he said conversationally. "You mean Liri."

Vieliessar did not even pretend he had guessed wrongly. "You began this. Your family slew mine and I was sent to the Sanctuary of the Star. Now I can end the eternal war—at least part of it. And I will."

"Then why not your own life?" Runacar asked.

"The terms of the spell are clear. One of my blood—not me—must die. *And there aren't that many to choose from.*"

Runacar strode over to his horse and leaned his forehead against the leather of the saddle. "We both know Adalieriel is not your child. Pick someone else. Her mother—whoever that is. Whose are they anyway? Some Landbond's?"

"Children of a high knight of Farcarinon and her noble chosen consort. Be happy."

"Why summon me here to tell me this? If the treaty is once more in force, you and I must wed. Rather I would marry Adalieriel—or no one."

"I summoned you to ask you to bear witness," Vieliessar said quietly. "Pouncewarm will come, of course, and I think Andhel as well. The Otherfolk must be represented. And you will understand the need for this act better than they."

"Never. I'll sheathe my blade in your guts first—I'm sure I can survive long enough to see you taken by the Hunt."

"I'm sure you can, only—who will hold your people and mine together without war if both of us are gone? It is among the reasons I choose another to die in my place. Is not peace worth a sacrifice of its own?"

"Not Liri," Runacar said. "Not her."

"Oh my darling," Vieliessar said. She might have been talking to Tannatarie, so gentle and anguished was her tone. "I am sorry, but in this war children die. Rimanet was among the first to be Bonded—by Niviel Lightsister, too young ever to have left the Sanctuary were it peacetime. And at Midwinter Niviel and Rimanet vanished, and no one has ever been able to say where they went. We all looked, Rune. There was nothing to find."

"And this is supposed to console me? I'm to become an accomplice because *everyone does it*?"

"A witness. So it will never happen again."

CHAPTER FORTY-ONE

THUNDER MOON IN THE ELEVENTH YEAR OF THE HIGH KING'S REIGN: BLOOD SINGS DEEP

If you would sacrifice your life in battle, think what effect it will have. Then think again.

—Runacar Battlemaster, *A History of the Scouring of the West*

The sky was summer bright and summer blue. The rock beneath the feet of the assembled company was warm, but the warmth in the air was leeched away by the constant briny wind that blew with the sound of snapping battle flags. The Dragons that had come—Tannatarie, Elderin, and Telleval—stood some distance away from the Elves, almost as if they were judging them.

::*And I am, my love*:: Tannatarie said sadly. ::*It is not too late to choose another course!*::

::*Show me one that will work*:: Vieliessar answered stonily. ::*No? Then hold your peace until this is done*::

Aloud she said, "I thank you all for coming without knowing the reason for coming. Now I shall explain. I have brought you here to cast a spell which the Gryphons disclosed to me. It will render the Endarkened killable."

"Everyone knows the Elves kill horses for magic," Andhel said dismissively. "But I don't see any horses here."

"This spell requires a greater sacrifice," Vieliessar said.

Three days after Vieliessar had spoken to Runacar, she had gathered the rest of her witnesses—she must have them, for good or ill—and returned to the Sanctuary of the Star to give Runacar the chance to come or stay behind.

She'd dared not bring him to Ceoprentrei. It wasn't safe for him.

Runacar looked thunderous, and as if he might speak out at any moment, but said nothing, merely coming to stand at Andhel's side. Andhel regarded him curiously, but when he made no acknowledgment of her, she ignored him. Iardalaith, Isilla, and Thurion all looked wary. Pouncewarm sat at Vieliessar's feet. Helecanth, as always, looked stoic, and Adalieriel's eyes gleamed with excitement at being allowed to come on this great adventure. Deornoth, the Minotaur member of Audalo's court, was the third of the Otherfolk witnesses.

"Here is Door," Vieliessar said. "Let us pass through it."

A moment later all of them stood on the large flat expanse of isolated land that Vieliessar had visited so many times before. They had left Ceoprentrei at dawn; a footstep later it was late morning. The effect was disorienting.

Pouncewarm jumped up into Vieliessar's arms. "Do you never listen to wise counsel, small one? You could have stayed behind," she asked. The Palugh simply purred.

"So this is how you mean to do it," Runacar said. "Trapping us all here until we comply."

"No," Vieliessar said. "I am too weary to cast Door again. Someone else will have to cast it for our return. Telleval and Elderin already know everything Tannatarie knows. And you have three other Dragonmages."

"So are you going to sacrifice one of the Dragons for this big spell of yours?" Andhel asked. "And what will it do, anyway? The spell."

"It will make the Endarkened mortal," Vieliessar answered steadily. "And the sacrifice it requires is great."

"But it isn't you," Runacar snarled. "It's never you. You can wade through blood all the way to your breastplate and it doesn't touch you— you just go on and on, unmarked, like gleaming elvensilver."

"It's one of us," Adalieriel said, then: "It's me, isn't it, Mama? I'm the sacrifice."

Runacar started forward. Helecanth put out a hand to stop him. He looked at her in surprise. Her face was expressionless.

Vieliessar knelt down before Adalieriel. "As we sacrifice to the Hunt for victory before a battle, we must sacrifice now—but only the one who will go consenting. If the others don't agree to bleed, and you don't agree to be the sacrifice, then I must start again."

"Let's kill the King now," Iardalaith said chattily to Isilla. "It's two Dragons against one."

Vieliessar ignored him. She took Liri's hands in hers. "Adalieriel, will you serve me in this?"

Runacar took two steps forward, reaching for his sword. "She isn't your daughter! You'll kill her and it won't work!"

"Mama?" Adalieriel said.

"The blood of sacrifice is the food of the Starry Hunt," Vieliessar said, ignoring Runacar. "This time we want Them to grant us a very great boon, so a very great sacrifice is needed."

"Me," Liri said.

"Only if you say yes, my darling. It must be with your whole heart. If that cannot be, I shall choose elsewhere."

"I understand, Mama. It's almost like going into battle, isn't it? And winning. And *they* can't get me?"

"No, darling, never."

Now Thurion was helping Helecanth to hold Runacar back. "Bleed and beg, War Prince, as so many of us did," he whispered in Runacar's ear.

Now Vieliessar drew from her armor a blade that was as sharp and brilliant as glass; a metal so bright it seemed almost liquid. She cut a diagonal slice first across her own left forearm, then Liri's. Rising, she turned toward Helecanth, who had turned Runacar over to Thurion to remove her gauntlet to bare her skin. Vieliessar cut swiftly. The blood from her own wound was whipped by the wind and spattered against Helecanth's armor. Vieliessar turned to Iardalaith. "You are oathbound in this," she reminded him, and he held out his own arm.

Then a turn to the tuathal, where Runacar stood, waiting, in Thurion's and Andhel's arms. "Will you consent?" Vieliessar asked him gently.

"I will not," Runacar said fiercely. "And I will see you ride at Their deosil hand by sunset."

"You better than any man living will understand my reasons. I beg you, lord husband, consent to this."

He dropped his chin to his chest and stood silent and unconsenting. She left him for Thurion. Thurion's marking was easily accomplished, for he wore Lightborn robes.

By now the rising tide of foulness could be felt by the four Lightborn. "Something's coming," said Isilla, holding out her arm.

Deornoth stepped back out of the circle of Elves. Pouncewarm jumped into his arms to get a better view.

"I know," Vieliessar said. She returned to her starting place. Helecanth knelt before Adalieriel. She had removed her cloak to protect the shivering child from the cold sea wind. Adalieriel looked up at both of them trustingly.

"My King, you will not have her." It was Helecanth who spoke. "If her blood will call Them, then twice over will mine: You know I am sister to Nataranweiya, who was your mother. Let mine be the sacrifice."

Vieliessar nodded, numb with shock. Adalieriel ran to her and clung, then after a moment turned and ran to Helecanth.

"I will say goodbye," Adalieriel said gravely. "And I will find you when I die."

Helecanth dipped her fingers in the blood welling from her arm and marked Liri's forehead. "I will find you when you die and we will ride together forever, my own."

Vieliessar drew Liri back from Helecanth. Helecanth knelt and opened her placket and fauld, for she—like Iardalaith, Runacar, and Vieliessar—was wearing full plate armor. Then she held out her hand for the knife and thrust it in and up through her half-laced aketon. By death-reflex her body jerked the weapon free, and dark blood pulsed from the wound.

Then the body fell to its side and sprawled, lifeless.

"Ah, Vielle, could you have found no other way?" Thurion whispered. He knelt over Helecanth's body, closing her eyes and straightening her limbs.

An electrical tension even the Lightless could sense now filled the air.

Thurion got to his feet with a huffed-out groan. "They're coming, I think."

"They are," Vieliessar agreed. "This battle will be fast, or we will lose it. Adalieriel, go to Tannatarie. She will give you what protection she may."

Helecanth's cape trailing, the child ran toward the Dragon, who raised a wing to shelter her. The sky turned a sickly coppery shade, and the wind dropped. Runacar snatched up the blade of sacrifice and slashed his forearm. "Consent! And I hate magic!" he shouted into the malevolent lull.

And then everything changed.

He was never afterward able to describe the battle, except in flickers. Here, the presence of *He Who Is*, a vast and horrific specter covering half the sky, unseen but imagined as if from a Storysinger's telling. There, the Hunt, following eagerly and with avarice, and for the first time Runacar understood why of all the Nine Races, it was the Elves who were called upon to make this sacrifice. The other races all loved the Powers that watched over them, but the Elves feared the Hunt.

Runacar wondered if the Endarkened feared *He Who Is*.

There were living creatures in the air. Not Endarkened, but the enemy nevertheless. Blood red monsters with leathery wings and long beaklike mouths full of teeth. They dove at Vieliessar and the others, ignoring the Dragons as if they did not recognize them as a threat. Even so, it was better than the sight of the Hunt. The sky turned from yellow to black, and strange and terrible stars filled the sky. A numbing wind whipped up out of the stillness, and Runacar searched desperately for a target he could focus on so he would not have to look at the Hunt.

And a new figure was standing on the battlefield. His hair hung to his waist, ornately braided in designs no one could read. His armor was the same shining black as the alien sky, and covered with stars.

He searched all their faces, as if seeking someone. At last his gaze fell on Vieliessar.

"But did you not love us?" the Huntsman asked her. "Did we not do everything for you?"

"You gave us centuries of war," Vieliessar said gently. "But we don't want that anymore."

The Huntsman threw back his head and roared in anguish.

And then the two Powers clashed.

Lightless light met scorching cold, and Runacar heard the horns of the Hunt give tongue. Behind that sound came a terrible shriek, and despite his self-promises, Runacar looked up.

The Hunt was led by the Huntsman, and behind him followed all the members of the Hunt since the beginning of Time, a rade that vanished into the distance.

But at the Huntsman's tuathal side flew a Dragon, its body as red as blood, and its rider no more than a child.

The two Powers clashed. The people on the ground tried to avoid seeing anything of that battle while defending themselves against the corporeal beings *He Who Is* had carried in his wake.

Then a high, shrill—*mortal*—scream pierced the air, and Liri was in the grasp of *He Who Is*. The gate between the worlds opened once more—opened by *He Who Is*. Before it had time to close, the Hunt swarmed after him.

"*Liri!*" Thurion screamed.

But as the Hunt continued to gallop into the rent in the sky, something flew the other way. The Dragon. Now it shone whiter than Tannatarie and glowed like moonlight, and it held Adalieriel in its claws. It swooped low enough to drop her safely, then soared skyward to join the Hunt once more.

The fissure closed.

The darkness dissipated.

The sky turned blue and the winds turned warm.

"And now the Hunt will harry the Endarkened Great Power until the end of time," Runacar said. "And we won't have any gods anymore."

"We didn't make good use of them when we had them," Iardalaith said. "Perhaps we're better off.'"

"Perhaps," Vieliessar said wearily. "Let's go home."

CHAPTER FORTY-TWO

THUNDER MOON IN THE ELEVENTH YEAR OF THE HIGH KING'S REIGN: THE FOREST WIDE WILL BE YOUR BRIDE

What you seek determines who you must be to go searching for it. Who you are determines how you will go. The tale of that seeker begins years before the first step.

—harwing Lightbrother, The Craft of the Swordmaster

It was Isilla and Telleval who opened Door for their return, for Vieliessar—if not Tannatarie—was drained by the combination of the first casting and the battle that followed it. Vieliessar was nearly staggering with weariness when she placed Liri before her on Tannatarie's saddle, grateful that the journey would be quick.

The child was stricken and silent, with tears streaming down her face. Her skin and her clothes were spattered with wind-driven drops of blood from the dedications the others had made. *All must bleed, but I would not have brought her with us if I knew she would see what she has seen and live,* Vieliessar thought. *Better she die before it began.* She could sense Runacar's roiling anger and . . . grief? through the Soulbond, but that link was not enough to tell her who had angered him and who he grieved for.

Thurion climbed up behind Isilla, and Runacar and Andhel stood close beside Tannatarie. Iardalaith placed Helecanth's body on Elderin's saddle. "All honor to her," he said quietly. "She deserves a hero's pyre."

A thing she will not get, Vieliessar thought sadly. Over the moonturns of their flight westward it had become Elven custom to suspend the bodies of their dead among the trees that sheltered them, to give something back to the Flower Forests that sheltered them so selflessly.

One . . . Two . . . Three steps and they were back beside the Shrine in

Arevethmonion. Even this early in Thunder the weather was summer hot, and to move beneath the canopy of the Flower Forest was a balm to the senses. There, Elderin knelt so that Thurion could claim his sorrowful burden.

"That was fun, of course," Iardalaith said, but this time his bravado didn't sound truly genuine. "What now?"

"We go on fighting," Vieliessar said wearily. "We don't know how many Endarkened there are or how discouraged they'll be by this."

"I don't care if they're discouraged so long as they're dead," Isilla snarled. "Won't they be in for a surprise the next time they attack us? Let's go tell the council that the spell seems to have worked. We can . . . we can say Helecanth died in the fighting."

"They never knew the price the Gryphons told me we would have to pay for this," Vieliessar said. "I will not speak of it unless I must, but should they think a blood sacrifice was not fulfilled as expediently by my aunt as by my daughter?"

As she spoke she glanced up through the forest canopy. There were Gryphons circling in the sky, blue and gold against the lighter blue of the sky.

"Is there anyone here who does not know the truth?" Runacar said roughly. "Here, give her to me." He slipped Adalieriel down from Tannatarie's saddle and cradled her in his arms. Slowly her tears turned to silent sobs.

"No one at all, thank you for reminding us," Iardalaith said. "And I'll thank you not to bring it up again. Which reminds me, somebody put a Peacebond on Caerthalien before we take him back to Nomaitemil or the council will forget they aren't supposed to murder him."

"Thank you," Runacar said, though he didn't sound so much ironic as weary.

"There will be no need of a Peacebond, nor is righteous killing murder," a familiar voice said from the ruins of the Sanctuary.

⊣⊨⊢

Early that morning, Vieliessar had called her council together to tell them (most of) what she had learned from the Gryphons and what she planned. She had told them then that any discussion they might wish to have could await her return.

They had taken her at her word.

There were perhaps three tailles of armed men: heavy infantry, pike-men, and archers. Of the council and other highborn, Sierdalant was here, and Rithdeliel of Farcarinon. Annobeunna Keindostibaent (to Vieliessar's surprise, as she could not imagine any argument they two would be on the same side of) was present, and Aradreleg Lightsister was not.

War Prince Shanilya Thadan of the Arzhana stood a little behind Rithdeliel's shoulder, her face bland and faintly smiling.

"What are you—" Vieliessar began.

"*Eeeeeeeowwwwwwww!*" Pouncewarm cried. "Nasty Warlord! Wicked Warlord! I, great warrior, I defend pretty Rune! I!" The Palugh bounded out from behind Vieliessar's party into the midst of the waiting meisne. Rithdeliel kicked at him as he ran by; Pouncewarm evaded the kick effortlessly. He leaped into the air, kicking off from Shanilya Tha-dan's chest hard enough to make the War Prince stagger, then bounded back to Iardalaith's shoulder in a nerve-wracking squeal of claws on ar-mor, and settled down to purr.

"I hate you, cat," Iardalaith muttered. Pouncewarm purred louder.

"We have much to tell you," Vieliessar said, ignoring Pouncewarm for the moment. "But we would prefer to refresh ourselves first. Nor is this a place we have the right to invest. Let us go to Nomaitemil and summon the full council to hear us."

"The council need not be summoned now. Nor will it be, save to ac-knowledge its new king," Rithdeliel said. "We have tolerated your mad-ness and your filth for long enough. No more."

His words were enough of a shock to make Vieliessar aware of how exhausted she was. She and Isilla were too drained by casting Door over such a long distance, and Iardalaith had long been an uncertain ally.

"By Sword and Star, I remember you as a general with more wit than this," Runacar said, astonished. "She has done what she has said she would do. She has made the Endarkened mortal. They can be beaten now. Is this the moment to depose her?"

"When better?" Rithdeliel asked. "I do not even intend to immure her for a decade of Wheelturns in a lightless dungeon as your father, Caerthalien, did to me. She may live as one of the common Lightborn if she chooses."

"May I?" Vieliessar asked dangerously. "Rithdeliel, you have been my friend, my brother, my teacher. What can you want that I would not freely give you?"

"I have told you again and again that you must drive the animals out of Ceoprentrei. But you will not. And their numbers will increase until it is they who drive us into Great Sea Ocean—and who knows what obscenities they will commit before that day? For this act you may rule no longer."

"Elves," Andhel said. "Always making speeches. What's nastier—to be a Gryphon, or to roast and eat one?"

"Andhel," Vieliessar said quietly, to hush her. "We cannot drive the Otherfolk anywhere, because that will break the treaty I swore with Leutric and with Audalo after him. And to seal it, I shall marry Runacarendalur Caerthalien, now Rune Battlemaster. He is my Bondmate as much as Tannatarie is."

"Then we will have to see which ones of you survive its severing." Rithdeliel stepped forward, his hand on the hilt of his sword.

"You are an idiot," Runacar announced. With one swift pivot, he placed Adalieriel in Andhel's arms. "Run," he suggested. "And now, idiot Warlord, I challenge you." Runacar slammed down his visor and closed the lappets of his helm.

A Wild of Wulvers appeared out of the forest to dive into the midst of Rithdeliel's meisne. "Fight! Fight! Fight!" they yelped joyously, before breaking into howls of glee. The meisne, oddly unwilling to hurt creatures whom they had fought beside, tried to shoo the Wulvers away, with little success.

Vieliessar could see Centaurs and Minotaurs coming to the edge of the clearing, and could sense more Otherfolk gathering in the forest behind her. But numbers didn't matter, nor by what metric one side outnumbered the other. What mattered was that Elvenkind was once more going to war with itself.

Suddenly she felt strong arms circle her from behind and lift her off her feet; she began to struggle until a voice growled in her ear: "Quiet, girl. We're on your side."

A Bearward.

Just as at Imrathalion, she was passed hand to hand by the largest of the Otherfolk: Bearwards and Minotaurs. When the last of the Bearwards had deposited her in front of what had once been the Astromancer's Tower, she turned and saw Runacar being carried to her side, with Pouncewarm bounding along beside the Minotaur.

Once he'd been released, Runacar staggered over to her. "What's going on?" he asked.

"I think the more important question right now is: Do you know how to ride a Gryphon?" Vieliessar answered.

When Runacar looked up, he could see two Gryphons circling to land.

⊰⊱

They dismounted from the Gryphons at the top of the Astromancer's Tower. Pouncewarm stropped the back of Runacar's legs, making him stagger, and he clutched at Vieliessar's arm for support.

"Do we jump off?" Runacar asked. On the ground below, he could see that the tower was completely surrounded by Otherfolk and Elves—and Woodwose too, he supposed. You couldn't really tell them apart anymore.

"No," Vieliessar answered. "We marry. Here and now."

Pouncewarm, Cloudfoot, and Shadowdance arrived, bringing with them the necessary things: a filled winecup, a Vilya fruit, and a Vilya flower. They stood on their hind legs, reaching up toward the two Elves with their burdens. Runacar handed Vieliessar the Vilya flower and she handed him the Vilya fruit, and all the world seemed to breathe a sigh of relief. They were irrevocably married.

"We're going to rule with the consent of the ruled," Vieliessar said, and began to laugh in mixed exhaustion and giddiness. "They've chosen us."

"Yes," Tannatarie the White said. "Before, even in your king-domain, there have been those who ruled and those who submitted. That time is past. Now we all will choose. Nor will you always get your own way because you think it's a good idea, my own darling."

Whatever she meant to say in return was drowned, even in her own ears, by the sound of the cheering.

THUNDER MOON IN THE ELEVENTH YEAR OF THE HIGH KING'S REIGN: LIKE A DEVICE OF FROST AND SILVER

War is a dance. But so are many other things. Be creative.

—Mosirinde Truefriend

The Otherfolk must have been planning for this day for some time, for what had once been the Astromancer's scrying chamber had been made over into quite a comfortable bedchamber.

There'd been a celebration after the wedding, naturally. And Vieliessar had forborne to take any vengeance on her enemies. "For that day is done, and besides, yours was a singularly inept uprising. This is my mercy, and mark it well, for I do not show it often."

Runacar felt no different than he had before taking the Vilya. Vieliessar said she had marked and sealed them, as Lightborn were taught to do. He remembered the cool touch of her fingers on his forehead, the way she'd inspected him gravely. "Please love my children," she'd said, very quietly, "for your own will supplant them."

"I swear to," he'd said in a low voice. Whatever the future would hold began here, with love. These children would never know the violence that had scarred his life and, he suspected, Vieliessar's.

He walked through the revelers until he reached the edge of them, then walked onward. He could not know that what he sought was here, but he hoped.

"Hello, Runacar, my love," Melisha said.

He fell to his knees beside her and buried his face in the fur of her neck. "I came to say goodbye," he said, his voice muffled.

"Not goodbye," Melisha said. "Not even for a little while. You will send your firstborn to me when they are old enough, and I will teach them as Pelashia taught Mosirinde. What we have had will change, it is true. But it will not end."

Runacar choked back all the useless words he wanted to say. *I love you,* he thought. *I love you. I will love you forever.*

Melisha stepped back, tossing her head. "Go, beloved. Go and find your bride."

⚜

He awoke, and found himself staring out the window of what had once been the Astromancer's chamber—and was now theirs. The moon was framed by the open shutters, palely pink in the night sky.

Vieliessar—*wife!* his mind supplied, each time he thought her name—was not in their bed. A number of firmly banished (at the start of the night) Otherfolk were here, including Pouncewarm, who had taken possession of Vieliessar's pillow, and three Wulvers who were lying immovably across Runacar's legs. *I suppose Pouncewarm let the Wulvers in,* he thought muzzily.

He struggled upright with the Wulvers muttering protests and trying to hold their places. Now he could see that Vieliessar was across the room at the desk (whose desk it had been before tonight, Runacar did not know), making notes and diagrams on a large roll of vellum.

"What are you making?" he asked.

"Battle plans," Vieliessar answered.

Runacar struggled further upright. "But the Endarkened aren't ever coming back."

"Oh, they are," Vieliessar said. "Someday. And when they do, we'll be ready."

She turned and regarded her husband. And when they fought—the Light, the Nine Races, Elvenkind, every beast and flower, every cloud and stream, the very stars themselves—they would fight as one people with one purpose.

"We will have a fight we can win."

"Someday is not today," Runacar said. "Come back to bed, wife."

And Vieliessar laughed, and set down her stylus, and did.

ABOUT THE AUTHORS

MERCEDES LACKEY is the author of the bestselling Valdemar series, the Diana Tregarde novels, Tales of the Five Hundred Kingdoms, and many other books, including *Trio of Sorcery, Phoenix and Ashes, Sacred Ground, The Firebird, The Fairy Godmother,* and *Alta.* She is also the coauthor, with Andre Norton, of the Halfblood Chronicles, including *Elvenborn.* Lackey was born in Chicago and graduated from Purdue University. She has worked as an artist's model, a computer programmer, and for American Airlines, and has written lyrics and recorded more than fifty songs. She lives in Oklahoma.

JAMES MALLORY is the author of the Merlin trilogy (*Merlin: The Old Magic; Merlin: The King's Wizard;* and *Merlin: The End of Magic*). He lives in Oregon.

Together, Lackey and Mallory are the bestselling coauthors of the Obsidian Trilogy (*The Outstretched Shadow, To Light a Candle,* and the *New York Times* bestseller *When Darkness Falls*), the Enduring Flame trilogy (*The Phoenix Unchained, The Phoenix Endangered,* and *The Phoenix Transformed*), and the Dragon Prophecy trilogy (*Crown of Vengeance, Blade of Empire,* and *Deliverance of Dragons*).

Visit Mercedes Lackey at:
mercedeslackey.com
facebook.com/MercedesLackey
Twitter @ mercedeslackey
Goodreads: Mercedes Lackey

Visit James Mallory at:
merlinscribe.dreamwidth.org
Goodreads: James Mallory